EVERYMAN, I will go with thee,

and be thy guide,

In thy most need to go by thy side

SAMUEL RICHARDSON

Born at Derby in 1689, the son of a joiner.
Came to London at seventeen, and entered
the printing trade, eventually purchasing
the moiety of the patent of King's Printer.
Died in London in 1761.

SAMUEL RICHARDSON

Clarissa

OR, THE HISTORY OF A YOUNG LADY

IN FOUR VOLUMES · VOLUME THREE

Introduction by

JOHN BUTT, M.A., B.LITT., F.B.A.

*Regius Professor of Rhetoric and English Literature
in the University of Edinburgh*

DENT: LONDON
EVERYMAN'S LIBRARY
DUTTON: NEW YORK

NO. *884*

SBN: 460 00884 6

THE HISTORY OF CLARISSA HARLOWE

Letter I—Mr. Lovelace to John Belford, Esq.

A LETTER is put into my hands by Wilson himself.—Such a letter!

A letter from Miss Howe to her cruel friend! I made no scruple to open it.

It is a miracle that I fell not into fits at the reading of it; and at the thought of what *might* have been the consequence had it come into the hands of *this Clarissa Harlowe*. Let my justly excited rage excuse my irreverence.

Collins, though not his day, brought it this afternoon to Wilson's with a particular desire that it might be sent with all speed to Miss Beaumont's lodgings, and given, if possible, into her own hands. He had before been here (at Mrs. Sinclair's) with intent to deliver it to the lady with his own hand; but was told [*too truly told!*] that she was abroad; but that they would give her anything he should leave for her the moment she returned. But he cared not to trust them with his business, and went away to Wilson's (as I find by the description of him at both places) and there left the letter, but not till he had a second time called here and found her not come in.

The letter [which I shall enclose, for it is too long to transcribe] will account to thee for *Collins's* coming hither.

O this devilish Miss Howe! Something must be resolved upon and done with that little fury!

Thou wilt see the margin of this cursed letter crowded with indices [❋]. I put them to mark the places which call for vengeance upon the vixen writer, or which require animadversion. Return thou it to me the moment thou hast perused it.

Read it here, and avoid trembling for me if thou canst.

To Miss Lætitia Beaumont

Wednesday, June 7.

MY DEAREST FRIEND,—You will perhaps think that I have been too long silent. But I had begun two letters at different times since my last, and written a great deal each time, and

I

with spirit enough I assure you, incensed as I was against the
ⅹabominable wretch you are with, particularly on reading yours
of the twenty-first of the past month.[1]

ⅹ   The *first* I intended to keep open till I could give you some
account of my proceedings with Mrs. Townsend.   It was some
days before I saw her; and this intervenient space giving me
time to reperuse what I had written, I thought it proper to lay
that aside and to write in a style a little less fervent, for you
ⅹwould have blamed me, I know, for the freedom of some of my
ⅹexpressions [*execrations*, if you please].   And when I had gone
a good way in the *second*, the change in your prospects, on his
communicating to you Miss Montague's letter, and his better
behaviour, occasioning a change in your mind, I laid that aside
also.   And in this uncertainty thought I would wait to see the
issue of affairs between you before I wrote again, believing all
would soon be decided one way or other.

I had still, perhaps, held this resolution [as every appearance,
according to your letters, was more and more promising], had
not the two passed days furnished me with intelligence which
it highly imports you to know.

But I must stop here and take a little walk to try and keep
down that just indignation which rises to my pen when I am
about to relate to you what I must communicate.

I am not my own mistress enough—then my mother,
always up and down, and watching as if I were writing to a
fellow.   But I will try if I can contain myself in tolerable
bounds.

The women of the house where you are—O my dear—the
women of the house—but you never thought highly of them,
so it cannot be very surprising—nor would you have *stayed so*
ⅹ*long with them, had not the notion of removing to one of your own,*
made you less uneasy, and less curious about their characters
ⅹand behaviour.   Yet I could *now* wish that you had been less
reserved among them—but I tease you.   In short, my dear,
ⅹyou are certainly in a devilish house! Be assured that the
woman is one of the vilest of women—nor does she go to you
by her right name.—Very true! Her name is *not* Sinclair, nor
is the street she lives in, Dover Street.   Did you never go out
by yourself and discharge the coach or chair, and return by
ⅹanother coach or chair? If you did [yet I don't remember that
you ever wrote to me that you did], you would never have

found your way to the vile house, either by the woman's name, *Sinclair*, or by the street's name mentioned by that Doleman in his letter about the lodgings.[1]

The wretch might indeed have held out these false lights a little more excusably had the house been an honest house, and had his end only been to prevent mischief from your brother. But this contrivance was antecedent, as I think, to your brother's project; so that no excuse can be made for his intentions at the *time*—the man, whatever he may *now* intend, ✻was certainly then, even *then*, a villain in his heart!

✻   I am excessively concerned that I should be prevailed upon, between *your* over-niceness, on one hand, and my *mother's* positiveness, on the other, to be satisfied without knowing how to direct to you at your lodgings. I think, too, that the proposal that I should be put off to a *third-hand* knowledge, or rather veiled in a *first-hand* ignorance, came from him—and that it was only acquiesced in by you, as it was by me,[2] upon needless and weak considerations—because, truly, I might have it to say, if challenged, *that I knew not where to send to you*! I am ashamed of myself! Had this been at *first* excusable, it could not be a good reason for going on in the folly, when you had no liking to the house, and when he began to play tricks and ✻delay with you. What! I was to mistrust myself, was I? I was to allow it to be thought that I could not keep my own secret? But the house *to be taken at this time, and at that* ✻*time*, led us both on—like fools, like tame fools in a string. ✻Upon my life, my dear, this man is a vile, a contemptible villain —I must speak out! How has he laughed in his sleeve at us both, I warrant, for I can't tell how long!

And yet who could have thought that a man of fortune, and some *reputation* [this Doleman, I mean; not your wretch, to be sure!], formerly a rake indeed [I inquired after him, long ago; and so was the easier satisfied], but married to a woman of family—having had a palsy-blow—and, one would ✻think, a penitent, should recommend such a house [why, my dear, he could not *inquire* of it, but must find it to be bad]

---

[1] See vol. ii, pp. 108 and 113.
[2] See vol. ii, pp. 173 and 178.   Where the reader will observe, that the proposal came from herself; which, as it was also mentioned by Mr. Lovelace (vol. ii, p. 199), she may be presumed to have forgotten. So that Clarissa had a double inducement for acquiescing with the proposed method of carrying on the correspondence between Miss Howe and herself by Wilson's conveyance, and by the name of Lætitia Beaumont.

to such a man as Lovelace, to bring his future, nay, his *then*
supposed, bride to?

❋ I write, perhaps, with too much violence to be clear. But
I cannot help it.   Yet I lay down my pen and take it up every
ten minutes, in order to write with some temper—my mother,
too, in and out.   What need I (she asks me) lock myself in, if
I am only reading past correspondences?—for that is my
❋pretence when she comes poking in with her face sharpened
to an edge, as I may say, by a curiosity that gives her more
❋pain than pleasure.   The Lord forgive me, but I believe I
shall huff her next time she comes in.

Do *you* forgive me too, my dear.   My mother *ought*, because
she says I am my father's girl, and because I am sure I am *hers*.
I don't know what to do—I don't know what to write next—I
have so much to write, yet have so little patience, and so
little opportunity.

But I will tell you how I came by my intelligence.   *That* being
❋a *fact* and requiring the less attention, I will try to account
to you for *that*.

Thus then it came about: "Miss Lardner (whom you have
seen at her Cousin Biddulph's) saw you at St. James's Church
on Sunday was fortnight.   She kept you in her eye during the
whole time, but could not once obtain the notice of yours, though
she curtsied to you twice.   She thought to pay her compliments to you when the service was over, for she doubted not
❋but you were married; and for an odd reason—*Because you
came to church by yourself*.   Every eye (as usual, wherever you
are, she said) was upon you; and this seeming to give you
hurry, and you being nearer the door than she, you slid out
before she could get to you.   But she ordered her servant to
follow you till you were housed.   This servant saw you step
into a chair which waited for you, and you ordered the men
to carry you to the place where they took you up.

"The next day Miss Lardner sent the same servant, out of
mere curiosity, to make private inquiry whether Mr. Lovelace
were, or were not, with you there.   And this inquiry brought
out, from *different* people, that the house was suspected to be
one of those genteel wicked houses which receive and accommodate *fashionable people* of both sexes.

"Miss Lardner, confounded at this strange intelligence,
made further inquiry, enjoining secrecy to the servant she had
sent, as well as to the gentleman whom she employed; who had

it confirmed from a rakish friend who knew the house, and told him that there were two houses; the one *in which all decent appearances were preserved, and guests rarely admitted*: the other, the receptacle of those who were absolutely engaged, and broken to the vile yoke."

※ Say, my dear creature, say, shall I not execrate the wretch? But words are weak. What can I say that will suitably express my abhorrence of such a villain as he must have been, when he meditated to carry a Clarissa to such a place?

"Miss Lardner kept this to herself some days, not knowing what to do; for she loves you, and admires you of all women. At last she revealed it, but in confidence, to Miss Biddulph by letter. Miss Biddulph, in like confidence, being afraid it would distract *me* were I to know it, communicated it to Miss Lloyd; and so, like a whispered scandal, it passed through several canals; and then it came to me. Which was not till last Monday."

I thought I should have fainted upon the surprising communication. But rage taking place, it blew away the sudden illness. I besought Miss Lloyd to re-enjoin secrecy to every one. I told her that I would not for the world that my ※mother, or any of your family, should know it. And I instantly caused a trusty friend to make what inquiries he could about Tomlinson.

※ I had thoughts to have done it before I had this intelligence; but not imagining it to be needful, and little thinking that you could be in such a house, and as you were pleased with your ※changed prospects, I forbore. And the rather forbore, as the matter is so laid, that Mrs. Hodges is supposed to know nothing of the projected treaty of accommodation; but, on the contrary, that it was designed to be a secret to her, and to everybody but immediate parties, and it was Mrs. Hodges that I had proposed to sound by a *second* hand.

※ Now, my dear, it is certain, without applying to that too much favoured housekeeper, that there is not such a man within ten miles of your uncle. Very true! One *Tomkins* there is, about four miles off, but he is a day-labourer; and one *Thompson*, about five miles distant the other way, but he is a parish schoolmaster, poor, and about seventy.

※ A man, though but of eight hundred pounds a year, cannot come from one county to settle in another but everybody in both must know it and talk of it.

※ Mrs. Hodges may yet be sounded at a distance, if you will.

Your uncle is an old man. Old men imagine themselves
under obligation to their paramours, if younger than them-
＊selves, and seldom keep anything from their knowledge. But
if we suppose him to make a secret of the designed treaty, it is
impossible, *before* that treaty was thought of, but she must
have seen him, at least have *heard* your uncle speak praisefully
of a man he is said to be so intimate with, let him have been
ever so little a while in those parts.

＊   Yet, methinks, the story is so plausible; Tomlinson, as you
describe him, is so good a man, and so much of a gentleman;
the end to be answered by his being an impostor, so much
＊*more than necessary* if Lovelace has villainy in his head; and
＊as you are in such a house—your wretch's behaviour to him
was so petulant and lordly; and Tomlinson's answer so full
＊of spirit and circumstance; and then what he communicated to
you of Mr. Hickman's application to your uncle, and of Mrs.
Norton's to your mother [some of which particulars, I am
＊satisfied, his vile agent Joseph Leman could not reveal to his
viler employer]; his pressing on the marriage-day, in the name
＊of your uncle, which it could not answer any *wicked* purpose
for him to do; and what he writes of your uncle's proposal, to
have it thought that you were married from the time that you
have lived in one house together; and that to be made to
agree with the time of Mr. Hickman's visit to your uncle; the
＊insisting on a trusty person's being present at the ceremony, at
＊that uncle's nomination—*These things make me willing to try
for a tolerable construction to be made of all*; though I am so much
puzzled by what occurs on both sides of the question, that I
＊cannot but abhor the devilish wretch, whose inventions and
contrivances are for ever employing an inquisitive head, as
＊mine is, without affording the means of absolute detection.

But this is what I am ready to conjecture, that Tomlinson,
specious as he is, is a machine of Lovelace; and that he is
＊employed for some end, which has not yet been answered.
This is certain, that not only Tomlinson, but Mennell, who, I
think, attended you more than once at this vile house, must
know it to *be* a vile house.

What can you then think of Tomlinson's declaring himself
in *favour* of it, upon inquiry?

Lovelace too must know it to be so; if not before he brought
you to it, soon after.

＊   Perhaps the *company he found there* may be the most
probable way of accounting for his bearing with the house,

and for his strange suspensions of marriage, when it was in his power to call such an angel of a woman his.

❋ O my dear, the man is a villain! the greatest of villains, in every light! I am convinced that he is. And this Doleman must be another of his implements!

❋ There are so many wretches who think *that* to be no sin, which is one of the greatest and the most ungrateful of all sins, to ruin young creatures of our sex who place their confidence in them; that the wonder is less than the shame, that people of figure, of *appearance* at least, are found to promote the horrid purposes of profligates of fortune and interest!

❋ But can I think [you will ask with indignant astonishment] that Lovelace can have designs upon your honour?

❋ That such designs he *has had,* if he *still* hold them not, I can have no doubt, now that I know the house he has brought you to, to be a vile one. This is a clue that has led me to account for all his behaviour to you ever since you have been in his hands.

Allow me a brief retrospection of it all.

❋ We both know that pride, revenge, and a delight to tread in unbeaten paths, are principal ingredients in the character of this finished libertine.

❋ He hates all your family, yourself excepted; and I have several times thought that I have seen him stung and mortified ❋ that love has obliged him to kneel at your footstool, because you are a *Harlowe.* Yet is this wretch a savage in love. Love that humanizes the fiercest spirits has not been able to ❋ subdue his. His *pride,* and the credit which a few *plausible* ❋ qualities, sprinkled among his *odious ones,* have given him, have secured him too good a reception from our eye-judging, our undistinguishing, our self-flattering, our too-confiding sex, to make assiduity and obsequiousness, and a conquest of his unruly passions, any part of his study.

❋ He has some reason for his animosity to *all* the men, and to *one* woman of your family. He has always shown you, and ❋ his own family too, that he prefers his pride to his interest. He is a declared marriage-hater; a notorious intriguer; full of his inventions, and glorying in them. He never could draw you into declarations of love; nor till your *wise* relations persecuted you as they did, to receive his addresses as a lover. ❋ He knew that you professedly disliked him for his immoralities; he could not therefore justly blame you for the coldness and indifference of your behaviour to him.

✳ The prevention of mischief was your first main view in the correspondence he drew you into. He ought not, then, to have wondered that you declared your preference of the *single life* to *any* matrimonial engagement. He knew that this was *always* your preference, and *that* before he tricked you away ✳so artfully. What was his conduct to you afterwards, that you should of a sudden change it?

Thus was your whole behaviour regular, consistent, and dutiful to those to whom by birth you owed duty; and neither prudish, coquettish, nor tyrannical to him.

✳ He had *agreed* to go on with you upon those your own terms, and to rely only on *his own merits* and *future reformation* for your favour.

✳ It was plain to me, indeed, to whom you communicated all that *you knew* of your own heart, though not all of it that *I found out*, that love had pretty early gained footing in it. And this you yourself would have discovered sooner than you ✳did, had not his alarming, his unpolite, his rough conduct, kept it under.

✳ I knew by experience that love is a fire that is not to be played with without burning one's fingers; I knew it to be a dangerous thing for two single persons of different sexes to ✳enter into familiarity and correspondence with each other; since, as to the latter, must not a person be capable of premeditated art who can sit down to write, and not write from the heart?—And a woman to write her heart to a man practised in deceit, or even to a man of some character, what advanta does it give him over her?

✳ As this man's vanity had made him imagine that no woman could be proof against love, when his address was honourable, no wonder that he struggled, like a lion held in toils, against a passion that he thought not returned. And how could you, *at first*, show a return in love to so fierce a spirit, and who had seduced you away by vile artifices, but to the approval of those artifices?

✳ Hence, perhaps, it is not difficult to believe that it became possible for such a wretch as this to give way to his old prejudices against marriage, and to that revenge which had always been a first passion with him.

This is the only way, I think, to account for his horrid views in bringing you to a vile house.

And now may not all the rest be naturally accounted for? His delays—his teasing ways—his bringing you to bear with his lodging in the same house—his making you pass to the people of it as his wife; *though restrictively so*, yet with hope, no doubt (vilest of villains as he is!), to take you at advantage—his bringing you into the company of his libertine companions—the attempt of imposing upon you that Miss Partington for a bedfellow, very probably his own invention for the worst of purposes—his terrifying you at many different times—his obtruding himself upon you when you went out to church, no doubt to prevent your finding out what the people of the house were—the advantages he made of your brother's foolish project with Singleton.

See, my dear, how naturally all this follows from the discovery made by Miss Lardner. See how the monster, whom I thought, and so often called, a *fool*, comes out to have been all the time one of the greatest villains in the world!

But if this be so, what [it would be asked by an indifferent person] has hitherto saved you? Glorious creature! What, morally speaking, but your watchfulness! What but that, and the majesty of your virtue; *the native dignity*, which, in a situation so very difficult (friendless, destitute, passing for a wife, cast into the company of creatures accustomed to betray and ruin innocent hearts), has hitherto enabled you to battle, overawe, and confound such a dangerous libertine as this; so habitually remorseless, as you have observed him to be; so very various in his temper; so inventive; so seconded, so supported, so instigated, too probably, as he has been!—That *native dignity*, that *heroism* I will call it, which has, on all proper occasions, exerted itself in its *full* lustre, unmingled with that charming obligingness and condescending sweetness, which is evermore the *softener* of that dignity, when your mind is free and unapprehensive!

Let me stop to admire and to bless my beloved friend, who, unhappily for herself, at an age so tender, unacquainted as she was with the world, and with the vile arts of libertines, having been called upon to sustain the hardest and most shocking trials, from persecuting relations on one hand, and from a villainous lover on the other, has been enabled to give such an illustrious example of fortitude and prudence as never woman gave before her; and who, as I have heretofore observed,[1] has made a far greater figure in adversity than she possibly could have made, had all her shining qualities been exerted in their full force and power, by the continuance of

[1] See vol. ii, p. 282.

that prosperous run of fortune which attended her for eighteen
years of life out of nineteen.

❋   But now, my dear, do I apprehend that you are in greater
danger than ever yet you have been in; if you are not married
in a week; and yet stay in this abominable house. For
were you out of it, I own I should not be much afraid for you.
    These are my thoughts, on the most deliberate consideration:
❋"That he is now convinced that he has not been able to draw
you off your guard; that therefore, if he can obtain no new
advantage over you as he goes along, he is resolved to do you
all the *poor justice* that it is in the power of such a wretch as
he to do you. He is the rather induced to this, as he sees
that all his own family have warmly engaged themselves in
❋your cause; and that it is his *highest interest* to be just to you.
Then the horrid wretch loves you (as well he may) above all
women. I have no doubt of this; with *such* a love as such a
❋wretch is capable of; with *such* a love as Herod loved his
Mariamne. He is now therefore, very probably, at last, in
earnest."
    I took time for inquiries of different natures, as I knew by
the train you are in, that whatever his designs are, they
❋cannot ripen either for good or evil till something shall result
from this new device of his about Tomlinson and your uncle.
    Device I have no doubt that it is, whatever this dark, this
impenetrable spirit intends by it.
❋   And yet I find it to be true that Counsellor Williams (whom
Mr. Hickman knows to be a man of eminence in his profession)
❋has actually as good as finished the settlements; that two
drafts of them have been made; one avowedly to be sent to
one Captain Tomlinson, as the clerk says:—and I find that a
licence has actually been more than once endeavoured to be
obtained! and that difficulties have hitherto been made,
❋equally to Lovelace's vexation and disappointment. My
mother's proctor, who is very intimate with the proctor applied
to by the wretch, has come at this information in confidence;
and hints that, as Mr. Lovelace is a man of high fortunes,
these difficulties will probably be got over.
    But here follow the causes of my apprehension of your
danger; which I should not have had a thought of (since
❋nothing *very* vile has yet been attempted) but on finding
what a house you are in, and, on that discovery, laying together
and ruminating on past occurrences.

"You are obliged, from the present favourable appearances,
to give him your company whenever he requests it. You are
under a necessity of forgetting, or seeming to forget, past
disobligations; and to receive his addresses as those of a
betrothed lover. You will incur the censure of prudery and
affectation, even perhaps in your own apprehension, if you keep
him at that distance which has hitherto been your security.
His sudden (and as suddenly recovered) illness has given him
an opportunity to find out that you love him. [*Alas, my dear,
I knew you loved him!*] He is, as you relate, every hour more
and more an encroacher upon it. He has seemed to change
his nature, and is all love and gentleness. The wolf has put
on the sheep's clothing; yet more than once has shown his
teeth and his hardly sheathed claws. The instance you have
given of his freedom with your person,[1] which you could not
but resent; and yet, as matters are circumstanced between you,
could not but pass over, when Tomlinson's letter called you into
his company,[2] show the advantage he has now over you; and also,
that if he can obtain greater, he will. And for this very reason
(as I apprehend) it is, that Tomlinson is introduced; that is to
say, to give you the greater security, and to be a mediator, if
mortal offence be given you, by any villainous attempt. The
day seems not now to be so much in your power as it ought to
be, since that now partly depends on your uncle, whose
presence, at your own motion, he has wished on the occasion.
A wish, were all real, very unlikely, I think, to be granted."

And thus situated, should he offer greater freedoms, must
you not forgive him?

I fear nothing (as I know who has said) that devil carnate
or incarnate can fairly do against a virtue so established.[3]
But surprises, my dear, in such a house as that you are in, and
in such circumstances as I have mentioned, I greatly fear! The
man, one who has already triumphed over persons worthy of
his alliance.

What then have you to do but to fly this house, this infernal
house! O that your heart would let you fly the *man*!

If you should be disposed so to do, Mrs. Townsend shall be
ready at your command. But if you meet with no impediments, no new causes of doubt, I think your reputation in the

---

[1] She means the freedom Mr. Lovelace took with her before the fire-plot.
See vol. ii, pp. 475-6. When Miss Howe wrote this letter she could not
know of that.
[2] See vol. ii, pp. 477-80.
[3] See Mrs. Norton's letter, vol. ii, p. 207.

eye of the world, though not your happiness, is concerned, that
※you should be his.   And yet I cannot bear that these libertines
should be rewarded for their villainy with the best of the sex,
when the worst of it are too good for them.

But if you meet with the least ground for suspicion; if he
would detain you at the odious house, or wish you to stay,
※now you know what the people are; fly *him*, whatever your
prospects are, as well as *them*.

In one of your next airings, if you have no other way,
※refuse to return with him.   Name *me* for your intelligencer,
that you are in a bad house; and if you think you cannot now
break with him, seem rather to believe that he may not know
※it to be so; and that I do not believe he does; and yet this
belief in us both must appear to be very gross.

But suppose you desire to go out of town for the air, this
sultry weather, and insist upon it?   You may plead your
health for so doing.   He dare not resist such a plea.   Your
※brother's foolish scheme, I am told, is certainly given up; so
you need not be afraid on that account.

If you do not fly the house upon reading of this, or some way
or other get out of it, I shall judge of his power over you, by the
little you will have over either him or yourself.

※   One of my informants has made slight inquiries concerning
Mrs. Fretchville.   Did he ever name to you the street or
square she lived in?—I don't remember that you, in any of
※yours, mentioned the place of her abode to me.   Strange, very
strange, this, I think!   No such person or house can be found,
near any of the new streets or squares, where the lights I had
from your letters led me to imagine her house might be.   Ask
※him what street the house is in, if he has not told you; and
let me know.   If he make a difficulty of that circumstance, it
※will amount to a detection.   And yet I think you have enough
without this.

I shall send this long letter by Collins, who changes his day
to oblige me; and that he may try (now I know where you are)
to get it into your own hands.   If he cannot, he will leave it at
Wilson's.   As none of our letters by that conveyance have
miscarried when you have been in more *apparently* disagreeable
situations than you are in at present, I hope that this will go
safe, if Collins should be obliged to leave it there.

※   I wrote a short letter to you in my first agitations.   It
contained not above twenty lines, all full of fright, alarm, and
execration.   But being afraid that my vehemence would too

much affect you, I thought it better to wait a little, as well for the reasons already hinted at, as to be able to give you as many particulars as I could, and my thoughts upon all. And now, I think, taking to your aid other circumstances, as they *have* offered, or *may* offer, you will be sufficiently armed to resist all his machinations, be they what they will.

✻ One word more. Command me up, if I can be of the least service or pleasure to you. I value not fame; I value not censure; nor even life itself, I verily think, as I do your honour and your friendship—for is not your honour my honour? And is not your friendship the pride of my life?

May Heaven preserve you, my dearest creature, in honour and safety, is the prayer, the hourly prayer, of

Your ever faithful and affectionate

ANNA HOWE.

Thursday Morn. 5. I have written all night.

To Miss Howe

MY DEAREST CREATURE,—How you have shocked, confounded, surprised, astonished me, by your dreadful communication! My *heart is too weak* to bear up against such a stroke as this!— When all hope was with me! When my prospects were so much mended! But can there be such villainy in men as in this vile principal, and equally vile agent?

I am really ill—very ill. Grief and surprise, and *now* I will say despair, have overcome me! All, all, you have laid down as conjecture, appears to *me now* to be *more* than conjecture!

O that your mother would have the goodness to permit me the presence of the only comforter that my afflicted, my half-broken heart, could be raised by! But I charge you, think not of coming up without her indulgent permission. I am too ill at present, my dear, to think of combating with this dreadful man; and of flying from this horrid house!—*My bad writing will show you this.* But my illness will be my present security, should he indeed have meditated villainy. Forgive, O forgive me, my dearest friend, the trouble I have given you! All must soon— but why add I grief to grief, and trouble to trouble? But I charge you, my beloved creature, not to think of coming up without your mother's leave, to the truly desolate and broken-spirited

CLARISSA HARLOWE.

Well, Jack! And what thinkest thou of this last letter? Miss Howe values not either *fame* or *censure*; and thinkest thou that this letter will not bring the little fury up, though she could procure no other conveyance than her higgler's panniers, one for herself, the other for her maid? She knows where to come now. Many a little villain have I punished for knowing more than I would have her know; and that by adding to her knowledge and experience. What thinkest thou, Belford, if, by getting hither this virago, and giving *cause* for a lamentable letter from her to the fair fugitive, I should be able to recover *her*? Would she not visit that friend in *her* distress, thinkest thou, whose intended visit to her in *hers* brought her into the condition from which she herself had so perfidiously escaped?

Let me enjoy the thought!

Shall I send this letter? Thou seest I have left room, if I fail in the exact imitation of so charming a hand, to avoid too strict a scrutiny. Do they not both deserve it of me? Seest thou not how the raving girl threatens her mother? Ought she not to be punished? And can I be a worse devil, or villain, or monster, than she calls me in the long letter I enclose (and has called me in her former letters), were I to punish them both as my vengeance urges me to punish them? And when I have executed that my vengeance, how charmingly satisfied may they both go down into the country and keep house together, and have a much better reason than their pride could give them, for living the single life they have both seemed so fond of?

I will set about transcribing it this moment, I think. I can resolve afterwards. Yet what has poor Hickman done to deserve this of me? But gloriously would it punish the mother (as well as daughter) for all her sordid avarice; and for her undutifulness to honest Mr. Howe, whose heart she actually broke. I am on tiptoe, Jack, to enter upon this project. Is not one country as good to me as another, if I should be obliged to take another tour upon it?

But I will not venture. Hickman is a good man, they tell me. I love a good man. I hope one of these days to be a good man myself. Besides, I have heard within this week something of this honest fellow that shows he has a soul; when I thought, if he had one, that it lay a little of the deepest to emerge to notice, except on very extraordinary occasions; and that then it presently sunk again into its *cellula adiposa*. The man is a *plump man*. Didst ever see him, Jack?

But the principal reason that withholds me (for 'tis a tempting project!) is, for fear of being utterly blown up, if I should not be quick enough with my letter, or if Miss Howe should deliberate on setting out, or try her mother's consent first; in which time a letter from my frighted beauty might reach her; for I have no doubt, wherever she has refuged, but her first work was to write to her vixen friend. I will therefore go on patiently, and take my revenge upon the little fury at my leisure.

But, in spite of my compassion for Hickman, whose better character is sometimes my envy, and who is one of those mortals that bring clumsiness into credit with the *mothers*, to the disgrace of us clever fellows, and often to our disappointment, with the *daughters*; and who has been very busy in assisting these double-armed beauties against me; I swear by all the *dii majores*, as well as *minores*, that I will have Miss Howe, if I cannot have her more exalted friend! And then, if there be as much flaming love between these girls as they pretend, what will my charmer profit by her escape?

And now that I shall permit Miss Howe to reign a little longer, let me ask thee, if thou hast not, in the enclosed letter, a fresh instance that a great many of my difficulties with her sister-toast are owing to this flighty girl! 'Tis true that here was naturally a confounded sharp wintry air; and if a little cold water was thrown into the path, no wonder that it was instantly frozen; and that a poor honest traveller found it next to impossible to keep his way; one foot sliding back as fast as the other advanced, to the endangering of his limbs or neck. But yet I think it impossible that she should have baffled me as she has done (novice as she is, and never before from under her parents' wings) had she not been armed by a virago, who was formerly very near showing that she could better advise than practise. But this, I believe, I have said more than once before.

I am loath to reproach *myself*, now the cruel creature has escaped me; for what would that do but add to my torment? Since evils self-caused, and avoidable, admit not of palliation or comfort. And yet, if *thou* tellest me that all *her* strength was owing to *my* weakness, and that I have been a cursed coward in this whole affair; why then, Jack, I may blush, and be vexed; but, by my soul, I cannot contradict thee.

But this, Belford, I hope—that if I can turn the poison of the enclosed letter into wholesome ailment; that is to say, if I can make use of it to my advantage; I shall have *thy* free consent to do it.

I am always careful to open covers cautiously, and to preserve seals entire. I will draw out from this cursed letter an alphabet. Nor was Nick Rowe ever half so diligent to learn Spanish, at the Quixote recommendation of a certain peer, as I will be to gain a mastery of this vixen's hand.

Letter II—Miss Clarissa Harlowe to Miss Howe

Thursday Evening, June 8.

AFTER my last, so full of other hopes, the contents of this will surprise you. O my dearest friend, the man has at last proved himself to be a villain!

It was with the utmost difficulty last night that I preserved myself from the vilest dishonour. He extorted from me a promise of forgiveness, and that I would see him next day as if nothing had happened; but if it were possible to escape from a wretch, who, as I have too much reason to believe, formed a plot to fire the house, to frighten me, almost naked, into his arms, how could I see him next day?

I have escaped—Heaven be praised that I have!—And have now no other concern than that I fly from the only hope that could have made such an husband tolerable to me; the reconciliation with my friends, so agreeably undertaken by my uncle.

All my present hope is to find some reputable family, or person of my own sex, who is obliged to go beyond sea, or who lives abroad; I care not whither; but if I might choose, in some one of our American colonies—never to be heard of more by my relations, whom I have so grievously offended.

Nor let your generous heart be moved at what I write. If I can escape the dreadfullest part of my father's malediction (for the temporary part is already in a manner fulfilled, which makes me tremble in apprehension of the other), I shall think the wreck of my worldly fortunes a happy composition.

Neither is there need of the renewal of your so often tendered goodness to me; for I have with me rings and other valuables, that were sent me with my clothes, which will turn into money to answer all I can want, till Providence shall be pleased to put me into some way to help myself, if, for my further punishment, my life is to be lengthened beyond my wishes.

Impute not this scheme, my beloved friend, either to dejection on one hand, or to that romantic turn on the other, which we have supposed generally to obtain with our sex, from fifteen to twenty-two; for, be pleased to consider my unhappy situation, in the light in which it really must appear to every considerate person who knows it. In the first place, the man, who has had the assurance to think me, and to endeavour to make me, his *property*, will hunt me from place to place and search after me as a 'stray; and he knows he may do so with impunity, for whom have I to protect me from him?

Then as to my estate, the envied estate, which has been the original cause of all my misfortunes, it shall never be mine upon litigated terms. What is there in being enabled to boast that I am worth more than I *can use*, or *wish to use*? And if my power is circumscribed, I shall not have that to answer for, which I should have, if I did not use it as I ought; which very few do. I shall have no husband, of whose interest I ought to be so regardful, as to prevent me doing *more* than justice to others, that I may not do *less* to him. If therefore my father will be pleased (as I shall presume, in proper time, to propose to him) to pay two annuities out of it, one to my dear Mrs. Norton, which may make her easy for the remainder of her life, as she is now growing into years; the other of fifty pounds *per annum*, to the same good woman, for the use of *my poor*, as I have had the vanity to call a certain set of people, concerning whom she knows all my mind; that so as few as possible may suffer by the consequences of my error; God bless them, and give them heart's ease and content, with the rest!

Other reasons for my taking the step I have hinted at, are these:

This wicked man knows I have no friend in the world but you; your neighbourhood therefore would be the first he would seek for me in, were you to think it possible for me to be concealed in it; and in this case you might be subjected to inconveniences greater even than those which you have already sustained on my account.

From my Cousin Morden, were he to come, I could not hope protection; since by his letter to me it is evident that my brother has engaged him in his party; nor would I, by any means, subject so worthy a man to danger; as might be the case, from the violence of this ungovernable spirit.

These things considered, what better method can I take than to go abroad to some one of the English colonies, where nobody but yourself shall know anything of me; nor you, let me tell you, presently, nor till I am fixed, and (if it please God) in a course of living tolerably to my mind. For it is no small part of my concern, that my indiscretions have laid so heavy a tax upon you, my dear friend, to whom once I hoped to give more pleasure than pain.

I am at present at one Mrs. Moore's at Hampstead. My heart misgave me at coming to this village, because I had been here with him more than once; but the coach hither was so ready a conveniency that I knew not what to do better. Then I shall stay here no longer than till I can receive your answer to this; in which you will be pleased to let me know if I cannot be hid, according to your former contrivance [happy, had I given into it at the time!], by Mrs. Townsend's assistance, till the heat of the search be over. The Deptford road, I imagine, will be the right direction to hear of a passage and to get safely aboard.

Oh, why was the great fiend of all unchained, and permitted to assume so specious a form, and yet allowed to conceal his feet and his talons, till with the one he was ready to trample upon my honour, and to strike the other into my heart!—And what had I done that he should be let loose particularly upon me!

Forgive me this murmuring question, the effect of my impatience, my *guilty* impatience, I doubt; for, as I have escaped with my honour, and nothing but my worldly prospects, and my pride, my ambition, and my vanity have suffered in this wreck of my hopefuller fortunes, may I not still be more happy than I deserve to be? And is it not in my own power still, by the divine favour, to secure the great stake of all? And who knows but that this very path into which my inconsideration has thrown me, strewed as it is with briers and thorns which tear in pieces my gaudier trappings, may not be the right path to lead me into the great road to my future happiness; which might have been endangered by evil communication?

And after all, are there not still more deserving persons than I, who never failed in any capital point of duty, that have been more humbled than myself; and some too, by the errors of parents and relations, by the tricks and baseness of guardians and trustees, and in which their own rashness or folly had no part?

I will then endeavour to make the best of my present lot. And join with me, my best, my only friend, in praying that my punishment may end here; and that my present afflictions may be sanctified to me.

This letter will enable you to account for a line or two, which I sent to Wilson's to be carried to you, only for a feint to get his servant out of the way. He seemed to be left, as I thought, for a spy upon me. But he returning too soon, I was forced to write a few lines for him to carry to his master, to a tavern near Doctors' Commons, with the same view; and this happily answered my end.

I wrote early in the morning a bitter letter to the wretch, which I left for him obvious enough; and I suppose he has it by this time. I kept no copy of it. I shall recollect the contents, and give you the particulars of all, at more leisure.

I am sure you will approve of my escape—the rather, as the people of the house must be very vile; for they, and that Dorcas too, did hear me (I know they did) cry out for help; if the fire had been other than a villainous plot (although in the morning, to blind them, I pretended to think it otherwise) they would have been alarmed as much as I; and have run in, hearing me scream, to *comfort me*, supposing my terror was the fire; to *relieve me*, supposing it were anything else. But the vile Dorcas went away as soon as she saw the wretch throw his arms about me!—Bless me, my dear, I had only my slippers and an under-petticoat on. I was frighted out of my bed by her cries of fire; and that I should be burnt to ashes in a moment —and she to go away, and never to return, nor anybody else! And yet I heard women's voices in the next room; indeed I did. —An evident contrivance of them all:—God be praised, I am out of their house!

My terror is not yet over; I can hardly think myself safe; every well-dressed man I see from my windows, whether on horseback or on foot, I think to be him.

I know you will expedite an answer. A man and horse will be procured me to-morrow early, to carry this. To be sure, you cannot return an answer by the same man, because you must see Mrs. Townsend first; nevertheless, I shall wait with impatience till you *can*; having no friend but you to apply to; and being such a stranger to this part of the world, that I know not which way to turn myself; whither to go; nor what to do.— What a dreadful hand have I made of it!

Mrs. Moore, at whose house I am, is a widow and of good character; and of this, one of her neighbours, of whom I bought a handkerchief, purposely to make inquiry before I would venture, informed me.

I will not set my foot out of doors till I have your direction; and I am the more secure, having dropped words to the people of the house where the coach set me down, as if I expected a chariot to meet me in my way to Hendon, a village a little distance from this. And when I left their house, I walked backward and forward upon the hill; at first, not knowing what to do; and afterwards, to be certain that I was not watched before I ventured to inquire after a lodging.

You will direct for me, my dear, by the name of Mrs. Harriot Lucas.

Had I not made my escape when I did, I was resolved to attempt it again and again. He was gone to the Commons for a licence, as he wrote me word; for I refused to see him, notwithstanding the promise he extorted from me.

How hard, how next to impossible, my dear, to avoid many *lesser* deviations, when we are betrayed into a *capital* one!

For fear I should not get away at my first effort, I had apprised him that I would not set eye upon him under a week, in order to gain myself time for it in different ways; and were I so to have been watched as to have made it necessary, I would, after such an instance of the connivance of the women of the house, have run out into the street and thrown myself into the next house I could have entered, or claimed protection from the first person I had met. *Women to desert the cause of a poor creature of their own sex in such a situation, what must they be?* Then, such poor guilty sort of figures did they make in the morning after he was gone out—so earnest to get me upstairs, and to convince me, by the scorched window-boards and burnt curtains and valance, that the fire was real—that (although I seemed to believe all they would have me believe) I was more and more resolved to get out of their house at all adventures.

When I began, I thought to write but a few lines. But be my subject what it will, I know not how to conclude when I write to *you*. It was *always* so; it is not therefore owing peculiarly to that most interesting and unhappy situation, which you will allow, however, to engross at present the whole mind of

Your unhappy, but ever affectionate
CLARISSA HARLOWE.

Letter III—Mr. Lovelace to John Belford, Esq.

Friday Morning, past Two o'clock.

Io Triumphe! Io Clarissa, sing!—Once more, what a happy man thy friend!—A silly dear novice, to be heard to tell the coachman whither to carry her!—And to go to *Hampstead*, of all the villages about London!—The place where we had been together more than once!

Methinks I am sorry she managed no better! I shall find the

recovery of her too easy a task, I fear! Had she but known
how much difficulty enhances the value of anything with me,
and had she had the least notion of obliging me by it, she would
never have stopped short at *Hampstead*, surely.

Well, but after all this exultation, thou wilt ask, "If I have
already got back my charmer?" I have not; but knowing
where she is, is almost the same thing as having her in my
power. And it delights me to think how she will start and
tremble when I first pop upon her! How she will look with
conscious guilt, that will more than wipe off my guilt of
Wednesday night, when she sees her injured lover, and
acknowledged husband, from whom, the greatest of felonies, she
would have stolen herself.

But thou wilt be impatient to know how I came by my lights.
Read the enclosed here, and remember the instructions which
from time to time, as I have told thee, I have given my fellow,
in apprehension of such an elopement; and that will tell thee all,
and what I may reasonably expect from the rascal's diligence
and management, if he wishes ever to see my face again.

I received it about half an hour ago, just as I was going to lie
down in my clothes; and it has made me so much alive, that,
midnight as it is, I have sent for a Blunt's chariot to attend
me here by day-peep, with *my usual coachman,* if possible; and
knowing not else what to do with myself, I sat down, and in the
joy of my heart have not only written thus far, but have
concluded upon the measures I shall take when admitted to her
presence; for well am I aware of the difficulties I shall have to
contend with from her perverseness.

Honnored Sur,—This is to sertifie your Honner, as how I am
heer at Hamestet, wher I have found out my lady to be in
logins at one Mrs. Moore's, near upon Hamestet Hethe. And
I have so ordered matters, that her ladiship cannot stur but I
must have notice of her goins and comins. As I knowed I
dursted not look into your Honner's fase, if I had not found out
my lady, thoff she was gone off the premis's in a quarter of an
hour, as a man may say; so I knowed you would be glad at
heart to know I had found her out; and so I send thiss Petur
Partrick, who is to have five shillins, it being now near twelve
of the clock at nite; for he would not stur without a hearty
drinck too besides; and I was willing all shulde be snug likeways
at the logins before I sent.

I have munny of youre Honner's; but I thought as how if the

man was payed by me beforend, he mought play trix; so left that to your Honner.

My lady knows nothing of my being hereaway. But I thoute it best not to leve the plase, because she has tacken the logins but for a fue nites.

If your Honner come to the Upper Flax, I will be in site all the day about the tapp-house or the Hethe; I have borroued an other cote, instead of your Honner's liferie, and a blacke wigg; soe cannot be knoen by my lady, iff as howe she shuld see me; and have made as if I had the toothe-ake, so with my hancriffe at my mothe, the teth which your Honner was pleased to bett out with your Honner's fyste, and my dam'd wide mothe, as your Honner notifys it to be, cannot be knoen to be mine.

The tow inner letters I had from my lady, before she went off the prems's. One was to be left at Mr. Wilson's for Miss Howe. The next was to be for your Honner. But I knowed you was not at the plase directed; and being afear'd of what fell out, so I kept them for your Honner, and so could not give um to you, until I seed you. Miss How's I only made belief to her ladiship as I carred it, and sed as how there was nothing left for hur, as shee wished to knoe; so here they be bothe.

I am, may it plese your Honner,
Your Honner's most dutiful,
and, wonce more, happy sarvant,
WM. SUMMERS.

The two *inner* letters, as Will calls them, 'tis plain, were wrote for no other purpose, but to send him out of the way with them, and one of them to amuse me. That directed to Miss Howe is only this:

Thursday, June 8.

I WRITE this, my dear Miss Howe, only for a feint, and to see if it will go current. I shall write at large very soon, if not miserably prevented!!!

CL. H.

Now, Jack, will not *her feints* justify *mine*? Does she not invade my province, thinkest thou? And is it not now fairly come to *Who shall most deceive and cheat the other?* So, I thank my stars, we are upon a par at last, as to this point, which is a great ease to my conscience, thou must believe. And if what

Hudibras tells us is true, the dear fugitive has also abundance of pleasure to come.

> Doubtless the pleasure is as great
> In being cheated, as to cheat.
> As lookers-on find most delight,
> Who least perceive the juggler's sleight;
> And still the less they understand,
> The more admire the sleight of hand.

This is my dear juggler's letter to me; the other *inner* letter sent by Will.

Thursday, June 8.

MR. LOVELACE,—Do not give me cause to dread your return.   If you would not that I should hate you for ever, send me half a line by the bearer, to assure me that you will not attempt to see me for a week to come.   I cannot look you in the face without equal confusion and indignation.   The obliging me in this is but a poor atonement for your last night's vile behaviour.

You may pass this time in a journey to Lord M.'s; and I cannot doubt, if the ladies of your family are as favourable to me as you have assured me they are, but that you will have interest enough to prevail with one of them to oblige me with her company.   After your baseness of last night, you will not wonder that I insist upon this proof of your future honour.

If Captain Tomlinson comes meantime, I can hear what he has to say, and send you an account of it.

But in less than a week, if you see me, it must be owing to a fresh act of violence, of which you know not the consequence.

Send me the requested line, if ever you expect to have the forgiveness confirmed, the promise of which you extorted from

The unhappy

CL. H.

Now, Belford, what canst thou say in behalf of this sweet rogue of a lady?   What *canst* thou say for her?   'Tis apparent that she was fully determined upon an elopement when she wrote it; and thus would she make me of party against myself, by drawing me in to give her a week's time to complete it; and, more wicked still, send me upon a fool's errand to bring up one of my cousins.—When we came, to have the satisfaction of finding her gone off, and me exposed for ever!   What punishment can be bad enough for such a little villain of a lady!

But mind, moreover, how plausibly she accounts by this billet (supposing she should not find an opportunity of eloping before I returned) for the resolution of not seeing me for a week; and for the bread and butter expedient!—So childish, as we thought it!

The chariot is not come; and if it were, it is yet too soon for everything but my impatience. And as I have already taken all my measures, and can think of nothing but my triumph, I will resume her violent letter, in order to strengthen my resolutions against her. I was *before* in too gloomy a way to proceed with it; but now the subject is all alive to me, and my gayer fancy, like the sunbeams, will irradiate it, and turn the solemn deep green into a brighter verdure.

When I have called upon my charmer to explain some parts of her letter, and to atone for others, I will send it, or a copy of it, to thee.

Suffice it at present to tell thee, in the first place, that *she is determined never to be my wife.* To be sure, there ought to be no compulsion in so material a case. Compulsion was her parents' fault, which I have censured so severely, that I shall hardly be guilty of the same. I am therefore glad I know her mind as to this essential point.

I have *ruined* her, she says!—Now that's a fib, take it in her own way—if I had, she would not perhaps have run away from me.

She is *thrown upon the wide world!*—Now I own that Hampstead Heath affords very pretty and very *extensive* prospects; but 'tis not the *wide world* neither; and suppose *that* to be her grievance, I hope soon to restore her to a *narrower.*

I am the *enemy of her soul, as well as of her honour!*—Confoundedly severe! Nevertheless, another fib! For I love her soul very well; but think no more of it in this case than of my own.

She is to be *thrown upon strangers!*—And is not that her own fault? Much against my will, I am sure!

She is cast from a state of *independency* into one *of obligation.* She never was in a state of *independency*; nor is it fit a woman should, of any age, or in any state of life. And as to the state of obligation, there is no such thing as living without being beholden to somebody. Mutual obligation is the very essence and soul of the social and commercial life. Why should *she* be exempt from it? I am sure the person she raves at desires not such an exemption—has been long *dependent* upon her, and would rejoice to owe *further obligations* to her than he can boast of hitherto.

She talks of her *father's curse*; but have I not repaid him for it a hundred-fold in the same coin? But why must the faults of other people be laid at my door? Have I not enow of my own?

But the grey-eyed dawn begins to peep.—Let me sum up all.

In short, then, the dear creature's letter is a collection of invectives not very new to *me*; though the occasion for them, no doubt, is new to *her*. A little sprinkling of the romantic and contradictory runs through it. She loves and she hates; she encourages me to pursue her, by telling me I safely may; and yet she begs I will not. She apprehends poverty and want, yet resolves to give away her estate; to gratify whom? Why, in short, those who have been the cause of her misfortunes. And finally, though she resolves never to be mine, yet she has some regrets at leaving me, because of the opening prospects of a reconciliation with her friends.

But never did morning dawn so tardily as this! Neither is the chariot yet come.

A gentleman to speak with me, Dorcas? Who can want me thus early?

Captain Tomlinson, sayest thou! Surely he must have travelled all night! Early riser as I am, how could he think to find me up *thus* early?

Let but the chariot come, and he shall accompany me in it to the bottom of the hill (though he return to town on foot; for the captain is all obliging goodness), that I may hear all he has to say, and tell him all my mind, and lose no time.

Well, now am I satisfied that this rebellious flight will turn to my advantage, as all crushed rebellions do to the advantage of a sovereign in possession.

Dear captain, I rejoice to see you—just in the nick of time. See! See!

> The rosy-finger'd morn appears,
> And from her mantle shakes her tears;
> The sun arising, mortals cheers,
> And drives the rising mists away,
> In promise of a glorious day.

Excuse me, sir, that I salute you from my favourite bard. He that rises with the lark will sing with the lark. Strange news since I saw you, captain! Poor mistaken lady! But you have too much goodness, I know, to reveal to her Uncle Harlowe the errors of this capricious beauty. It will all turn out for the best. You must accompany me part of the way. I know the delight you take in composing differences. But 'tis the task of the prudent to heal the breaches made by the rashness and folly of the imprudent.

And now [all around me so still and so silent], the rattling of the chariot-wheels at a street's distance do I hear! And to this angel of a woman I fly!

Reward, O god of love [the cause is thy own]; reward thou, as it deserves, my suffering perseverance!—Succeed my endeavours to bring back to thy obedience this charming fugitive! Make her acknowledge her rashness; repent her insults; implore my forgiveness; beg to be reinstated in my favour, and that I will bury in oblivion the remembrance of her heinous offence against thee, and against me, thy faithful votary.

The chariot at the door! I come! I come!
I attend you, good captain——
Indeed, sir——
Pray, sir—civility is not ceremony.

And now, dressed like a bridegroom, my heart elated beyond that of the most desiring one (attended by a footman whom my beloved never saw), I am already at Hampstead!

Letter IV—Mr. Lovelace to John Belford, Esq.

Upper Flask, Hampstead, Friday morn. 7 o'clock (June 9).

I AM now here, and here have been this hour and half. What an industrious spirit have I! Nobody can say that I eat the bread of idleness. I take true pains for all the pleasure I enjoy. I cannot but admire myself strangely; for certainly, with this active soul, I should have made a very great figure in whatever station I had filled. But had I been a prince!—To be sure I should have made a most *noble* prince! I should have led up a military dance equal to that of the great Macedonian. I should have added kingdom to kingdom, and despoiled all my neighbour sovereigns, in order to have obtained the name of *Robert the Great*. And I would have gone to war with the Great Turk, and the Persian, and Mogul, for their seraglios;

for not one of those Eastern monarchs should have had a pretty woman to bless himself with till I had done with her.

And now I have so much leisure upon my hands, that, after having informed myself of all necessary particulars, I am set to my shorthand writing in order to keep up with time as well as I can; for the subject is now become worthy of me; and it is yet too soon, I doubt, to pay my compliments to my charmer, after all her fatigues for two or three days past. And, moreover, I have abundance of matters preparative to my future proceedings to recount, in order to connect and render all intelligible.

I parted with the captain at the foot of the hill, trebly instructed; that is to say, as to the *fact*, to the *probable*, and to the *possible*. If my beloved and I can meet and make up without the mediation of this worthy gentleman, it will be so much the better. As little foreign aid as possible in my amorous conflicts has always been a rule with me; though here I have been obliged to call in so much. And who knows but it may be the better for the lady the less she makes necessary? I cannot bear that she should sit so indifferent to me as to be in earnest to part with me for ever upon so *slight*, or even upon *any* occasion. *If I find she is*—but no more threatenings till she is in my power—thou knowest what I have vowed.

All Will's account, from the lady's flight to his finding her again, all the accounts of the people of the house, the coachman's information to Will, and so forth, collected together, stand thus.

"The Hampstead coach, when the dear fugitive came to it, had but two passengers in it. But she made the fellow go off directly, paying for the vacant places.

"The two passengers directing the coachman to set them down at the Upper Flask, she bid him set her down there also.

"They took leave of her [very respectfully no doubt], and she went into the house and asked if she could not have a dish of tea, and a room to herself for half an hour.

"They showed her up to the very room where I am now. She sat at the very table I now write upon; and, I believe, the chair I sit in was hers." O Belford, if thou knowest what love is, thou wilt be able to account for these *minutiæ*.

"She seemed spiritless and fatigued. The gentlewoman herself chose to attend so genteel and lovely a guest. She asked her if she would have bread and butter to her tea?

"No. She could not eat.

"They had very good biscuits.

"As she pleased.

III—B ⁸⁸⁴

"The gentlewoman stepped out for some; and returning on a sudden, she observed the sweet fugitive endeavouring to restrain a violent burst of grief which she had given way to in that little interval.

"However, when the tea came, she made the landlady sit down with her, and asked her abundance of questions about the villages and roads in that neighbourhood.

"The gentlewoman took notice to her, *that she seemed to be troubled in mind*.

"Tender spirits, she replied, could not part with *dear* friends without concern."

She meant *me*, no doubt.

"She made no inquiry about a lodging, though by the sequel, thou'lt observe, that she seemed to intend to go no farther that night than Hampstead. But after she had drank two dishes, and put a biscuit in her pocket [sweet soul, to serve for her supper perhaps], she laid down half a crown; and refusing change, sighing, took leave, saying she would proceed towards Hendon, the distance to which had been one of her questions.

"They offered to send to know if a Hampstead coach were not to go to Hendon that evening.

"No matter, she said—perhaps she might meet the chariot."

Another of her *feints*, I suppose; for how, or with whom, could anything of this sort have been concerted since yesterday morning?

"She had, as the people took notice to one another, something so uncommonly noble in her air, and in her person and behaviour, that they were sure she was of quality. And having no servant with her of either sex, her eyes [her fine eyes, the gentlewoman called them, stranger as she was, and a woman!] being swelled and red, they were sure there was an elopement in the case, either from parents or guardians; for they supposed her too young and too maidenly to be a married lady; and were she married, no husband would let such a fine young creature be unattended and alone; nor give her cause for so much grief as seemed to be settled in her countenance. Then, at times, she seemed to be so bewildered, they said, that they were afraid she had it in her head to make away with herself.

"All these things put together, excited their curiosity; and they engaged a *peery* servant, as they called a footman who was drinking with Kit the hostler at the tap-house, to watch all her motions. This fellow reported the following particulars, as they were re-reported to me.

"She indeed went towards Hendon, passing by the sign of the Castle on the Heath; then, stopping, looked about her, and down into the valley before her. Then, turning her face towards London, she seemed, by the motion of her handkerchief to her eyes, to weep; repenting [who knows?] the rash step she had taken, and wishing herself back again."

Better for her, if she do, Jack, once more I say! Woe be to the girl who could think of marrying me, yet be able to run away from me, and renounce me for ever!

"Then, continuing on a few paces, she stopped again; and, as if disliking her road, again seeming to weep, directed her course back towards Hampstead."

I am glad she wept so much, because no heart bursts (be the occasion for the sorrow what it will) which has that kindly relief. Hence I hardly ever am moved at the sight of these pellucid fugitives in a fine woman. How often, in the past twelve hours, have I wished that I could cry most confoundedly!

"She then saw a coach-and-four driving towards her empty. She crossed the path she was in, as if to meet it; and seemed to intend to speak to the coachman, had he stopped or spoke first. He as earnestly looked at *her*. Every one did so who passed her (so the man who dogged her was the less suspected)."—Happy rogue of a coachman, hadst thou known whose notice thou didst engage, and whom thou mightest have obliged! It was the divine Clarissa Harlowe at whom thou gazedst!—Mine own Clarissa Harlowe!—But it was well for me that thou wert as undistinguishing as the beasts thou drovest; otherwise, what a wild-goose chase had I been led?

"The lady as well as the coachman, in short, seemed to want resolution; the horses kept on [the fellow's head and eyes, no doubt, turned behind him], and the distance soon lengthened beyond recall. With a wistful eye she looked after him; sighed and wept again; as the servant who then slyly passed her observed.

"By this time she had reached the houses. She looked up at every one as she passed; now and then breathing upon her bared hand, and applying it to her swelled eyes, to abate the redness and dry the tears. At last, seeing a bill up for letting lodgings, she walked backwards and forwards half a dozen times, as if unable to determine what to do. And then went further into the town; and there the fellow, being spoken to by one of his familiars, lost her for a few minutes; but he soon saw her come out of a linen-drapery shop, attended with a servant-maid, having, as he believed, bought some little matters, and, as it proved, got that maidservant to go with her to the house she is now at.[1]

"The fellow, after waiting about an hour, and not seeing her come out, returned, concluding that she had taken lodgings there."

And here, supposing my narrative of the dramatic kind, ends Act the first.   And now begins

ACT II

SCENE.—*Hampstead Heath, continued.*

Enter my Rascal.

WILL, having got at all these particulars, by exchanging others as frankly against them, which I had formerly prepared him with both verbally and in writing; I found the people already of my party, and full of good wishes for my success, repeating to me all they told him.

But he had first acquainted me with the accounts he had given them of his lady and me.   It is necessary that I give thee the particulars of his tale—and I have a little time upon my hands; for the maid of the house, who had been out of an errand, tells us that she saw Mrs. Moore [with whom must be my first business] go into the house of a young gentleman, within a few doors of her, who has a maiden sister, Miss Rawlins by name, *so notified* for prudence, that none of her acquaintance undertake anything of consequence without consulting her.

Meanwhile my honest coachman is walking about Miss Rawlins's door, in order to bring me notice of Mrs. Moore's return to her own house.   I hope her gossip's tale will be as soon told as mine.   Which take as follows:

Will told them, before I came, "That his lady was but lately married to one of the finest gentlemen in the world.   But that, he being very gay and lively, she was *mortal* jealous of him; and in a fit of that sort, had eloped from him.   For although she loved him dearly, and he doted upon her (as well he might, since, as they had seen, she was the finest creature *that ever the sun shone upon*), yet she was apt to be very wilful and sullen, if he might take the liberty to say so—but truth was truth;—and if she could not have her own way in everything, would be for leaving him.   That she had three or four times played his master such tricks; but with all the virtue and innocence in the world; running away to an intimate friend of hers, who, though a young lady of honour, was but too indulgent to her in this her *only* failing; for which reason his master had brought her to London lodgings; their usual residence being in the country; and that, on his refusing to satisfy her about a lady he had been seen with in St. James's Park, she had, for the first time since she came to town, served his master thus; whom he had left half-distracted on that account."

And truly well he might, poor gentleman! cried the honest folks, pitying me before they saw me.

"He told them how he came by his intelligence of her; and made himself such an interest with them, that they helped him to a change of clothes for himself; and the landlord, at his request, privately inquired if the lady actually remained at Mrs. Moore's, and for how long she had taken the lodgings; which he found only to be for a week certain; but she had said that she believed she should hardly stay so long. And then it was that he wrote his letter, and sent it by honest Peter Partrick, as thou hast heard."

When I came, my person and dress having answered Will's description, the people were ready to worship me. I now and then sighed, now and then put on a lighter air; which, however, I designed should show more of vexation ill-disguised, than of real cheerfulness; and they told Will it was a thousand pities so fine a lady should have such *skittish tricks*; adding, that she might expose herself to great dangers by them, for that there were rakes everywhere [*Lovelaces in every corner, Jack*!], and many about that town, who would leave nothing unattempted to get into her company; and although they might not prevail upon her, yet might they nevertheless hurt her reputation, and, in time, estrange the affections of so fine a gentleman from her.

Good sensible people, these!—Hey, Jack!

Here, landlord; one word with you. My servant, I find, has acquainted you with the reason of my coming this way. An unhappy affair, landlord! A very unhappy affair! But never was there a more virtuous woman.

So, sir, she seems to be. A thousand pities her ladyship has such ways—and to so good-humoured a gentleman as you seem to be, sir.

Mother-spoilt, landlord! Mother-spoilt!—that's the thing! But [sighing] I must make the best of it. What I want *you* to do for me, is to lend me a great-coat. I care not what it is. If my spouse should see me at a distance, she would make it very difficult for me to get at her speech. A great-coat with a cape, if you have one. I must come upon her before she is aware.

I am afraid, sir, I have none fit for such a gentleman as you.

Oh, anything will do!—the worse the better.

Exit Landlord. Re-enter with two great-coats.

Ay, landlord, this will be best; for I can button the cape over the lower part of my face. Don't I look devilishly down and concerned, landlord?

I never saw a gentleman with a better-natured look. 'Tis pity you should have such trials, sir.

I must be very unhappy, no doubt of it, landlord. And yet I am a little pleased, you must needs think, that I have found her out before any great inconvenience has arisen to her. However, if I cannot break her of these freaks, she 'll break my heart; for I do love her with all her failings.

The good woman, who was within hearing of all this, pitied me much.

Pray, your honour, said she, if I may be so bold, was madam ever a mamma?

No!—and I sighed. We have been but a little while married; and as I may say to *you*, it is her own fault that she is not in that way. [Not a word of a lie in this, Jack.] But to tell you truth, madam, she may be compared to the dog in the manger——

I understand you, sir [simpering]. She is but young, sir. I have heard of one or two such skittish young ladies in my time, sir. But when madam is in that way, I dare say, as she loves you (and it would be strange if she did not!), all this will be over, and she may make the best of wives.

That 's all my hope.

She is as fine a lady as I ever beheld. I hope, sir, you won't be too severe. She 'll get over all these freaks, if once she be a mamma, I warrant.

I can't be severe to her; she knows that. The moment I see her, all resentment is over with me, if she give me but one kind look.

All this time I was adjusting my horseman's coat, and Will was putting in the ties of my wig,[1] and buttoning the cape over my chin.

I asked the gentlewoman for a little powder. She brought me a powder-box, and I lightly shook the puff over my hat, and flapped one side of it, though the lace looked a little too gay for

[1] The fashionable wigs at that time.

my covering; and slouching it over my eyes, Shall I be known, think you, madam?

Your honour is so expert, sir! I wish, if I may be so bold, your lady has not some *cause* to be jealous. But it will be impossible, if you keep your laced clothes covered, that anybody should know you in that dress to be the same gentleman— except they find you out by your clocked stockings.

Well observed. Can't you, landlord, lend or sell me a pair of stockings that will draw over these? I can cut off the feet, if they won't go into my shoes.

He could let me have a pair of coarse, but clean, stirrup-stockings, if I pleased.

The best in the world for the purpose.

He fetched them. Will drew them on; and my legs then made a good gouty appearance.

The good woman, smiling, wished me success; and so did the landlord. And as thou knowest that I am not a bad mimic, I took a cane, which I borrowed of the landlord, and stooped in the shoulders to a quarter of a foot of less height, and stumped away cross to the bowling-green, to practise a little the hobbling gait of a gouty man. The landlady whispered her husband, as Will tells me, He's a good one, I warrant him— I dare say the fault lies not all of one side. While mine host replied, that I was so lively and so good-natured a gentleman, that he did not know who could be angry with me, do what I would. A sensible fellow! I wish my charmer were of the same opinion.

And now I am going to try if I can't agree with goody Moore for lodgings and other conveniences for my sick wife.

"Wife, Lovelace!" methinks thou interrogatest.

Yes, *wife*; for who knows what cautions the dear fugitive may have given in apprehension of me?

"But has goody Moore any other lodgings to let?"

Yes, yes; I have taken care of that; and find that she has just such conveniences as I want. And I know that my wife will like them. For, although married, I can do everything I please; and that's a bold word, you know. But had she only a garret to let, I would have liked it; and been a poor author afraid of arrests, and made that my place of refuge; yet would have made shift to pay beforehand for what I had. I can suit myself to any condition, that's my comfort.

The widow Moore returned! say you?—Down, down, flutterer!

This impertinent heart is more troublesome to me than my conscience, I think. I shall be obliged to hoarsen my voice, and roughen my character, to keep up with its puppily dancings.

But let me see, shall I be angry or pleased when I am admitted to my beloved's presence?

Angry, to be sure. Has she not broken her word with me? At a time too when I was meditating to do her grateful justice? And is not breach of word a dreadful crime in good folks? I have ever been for forming my judgment of the nature of things and actions, not so much from what they are in themselves, as from the characters of the actors. Thus it would be as odd a thing in such as we to *keep* our words with a woman, as it would be wicked in her to *break* hers to us.

Seest thou not that this unseasonable gravity is admitted to quell the palpitations of this unmanageable heart? But still it will go on with its boundings. I 'll try as I ride in my chariot to *tranquillize*.

"Ride, Bob! so little a way?"

Yes, ride, Jack; for am I not lame? And will it not look well to have a lodger who keeps his chariot? What widow, what servant, asks questions of a man with an equipage?

My coachman, as well as my other servant, is under Will's tuition.

Never was there such a hideous rascal as he has made himself. The devil only and his *other* master can know him. They both have set their marks upon him. As to my honour's mark, it will never be out of *his damned wide mothe*, as he calls it. For the dog will be hanged before he can lose the rest of his teeth by age.

I am gone.

Letter V—Mr. Lovelace to John Belford, Esq.

Hampstead, Friday Night, June 9.

Now, Belford, for the narrative of narratives. I will continue it as I have opportunity; and that so dexterously, that if I break off twenty times, thou shalt not discern where I piece my thread.

Although grievously afficted with the gout, I alighted out of my chariot (leaning very hard on my cane with one hand, and on my new servant's shoulder with the other) the same instant almost that he had knocked at the door, that I might be sure of admission into the house.

I took care to button my great-coat about me, and to cover with it even the pommel of my sword, it being a little too gay

for my years. I knew not what occasion I might have for my
sword. I stooped forward; blinked with my eyes to conceal
their lustre [no vanity in saying that, Jack!]; my chin wrapped
up for the toothache; my slouched, laced hat, and so much of
my wig as was visible, giving me, all together, the appearance
of an antiquated beau.

My wife, I resolved beforehand, should have a complication
of disorders.

The maid came to the door. I asked for her mistress. She
showed me into one of the parlours; and I sat down with a
gouty Oh!

Enter Goody Moore

Your servant, madam—but you must excuse me; I cannot
well stand. I find by the bill at the door, that you have lodgings
to let [mumbling my words as if, like my man Will, I had lost
some of my fore-teeth]; be pleased to inform me what they are;
for I like your situation—and I will tell you my family—I have
a wife, a good old woman—older than myself, by the way, a
pretty deal. She is in a bad state of health, and is advised into
the Hampstead air. She will have two maidservants and a
footman. The coach or chariot (I shall not have them up both
together) we can put up anywhere, and the coachman will be
with his horses.

When, sir, shall you want to come in?

I will take them from this very day; and if convenient, will
bring my wife in the afternoon.

Perhaps, sir, you would board, as well as lodge?

That as you please. It will save me the trouble of bringing
my cook, if we do. And I suppose you have servants who know
how to dress a couple of dishes. My wife must eat plain food,
and I don't love kickshaws.

We have a single lady, who will be gone in two or three days.
She has one of the best apartments; that will then be at liberty.

You have one or two good ones meantime, I presume, madam,
just to receive my wife; for we have lost time. These damned
physicians—excuse me, madam, I am not used to curse; but it
is owing to the love I have for my wife—they have kept her in
hand till they are ashamed to take more fees, and now advise
her to the air. I wish we had sent her hither at first. But we
must now make the best of it.

Excuse me, madam (for she looked hard at me), that I am
muffled up thus in this warm weather. I am but too sensible

that I have left my chamber sooner than I ought, and perhaps shall have a return of my gout for it. I came out thus muffled up with a dreadful pain in my jaws; an ague in them, I believe. But my poor dear will not be satisfied with anybody's care but mine. And, as I have told you, we have lost time.

You shall see what accommodations I have, if you please, sir. But I doubt you are too lame to walk up stairs.

I can make shift to hobble up now I have rested a little. I'll just look upon the apartment my wife is to have. Anything may do for the servants; and as you seem to be a good sort of gentlewoman, I shan't stand for a price, and will pay well besides for the trouble I shall give.

She led the way; and I, helping myself by the banisters, made shift to get up with less fatigue than I expected from ankles so weak. But oh! Jack, what was Sixtus the Vth's artful depression of his natural powers to mine, when, as the half-dead Montalto, he gaped for the pretendedly unsought pontificate, and the moment he was chosen, leapt upon the prancing beast, which it was thought by the amazed conclave he was not able to mount without help of chairs and men? Never was there a more joyous heart and lighter heels than mine joined together; yet both denied their functions; the one fluttering in secret, ready to burst its bars for relief-ful expression, the others obliged to an hobbling motion; when, unrestrained, they would, in their master's imagination, have mounted him to the lunar world without the help of a ladder.

There were three rooms on a floor; two of them handsome; and the third, she said, still handsomer; but the lady was in it.

I saw, I saw she was! for as I hobbled up, crying out upon my weak ankles, in the hoarse mumbling voice I had assumed, I beheld a little piece of her as she just cast an eye (with the door ajar, as they call it) to observe who was coming up; and seeing such an old clumsy fellow, great-coated in weather so warm, slouched and muffled up, she withdrew, shutting the door without any emotion. But it was not so with me; for thou canst not imagine how my heart danced to my mouth at the very glimpse of her, so that I was afraid the thump, thump, thumping villain, which had so lately thumped as much to no purpose, would have choked me.

I liked the lodgings well; and the more as she said the third room was still handsomer. I must sit down, madam [and chose the darkest part of the room]. Won't you take a seat yourself? No price shall part us—but I will leave the terms to

you and my wife, if you please; and also whether for board or
not. Only please to take this for earnest, putting a guinea into
her hand.—And one thing I will say; my poor wife loves money;
but is not an ill-natured woman. She was a great fortune to
me; but, as the real estate goes away at her death, I would fain
preserve her for that reason, as well as for the love I bear her as
an honest man. But if she make too close a bargain with you,
tell *me*; and unknown to *her*, I will make it up. This is my
constant way; she loves to have her pen'orths; and I would
not have her vexed or made uneasy on any account.

She said I was a very considerate gentleman; and upon the
condition I had mentioned, she was content to leave the terms
to my lady.

But, madam, cannot a body just peep into the other apartment, that I may be more particular to my wife in the furniture
of it?

The lady desires to be private, sir—but—and was going to
ask her leave.

I caught hold of her hand. However, stay, stay, madam;
it mayn't be proper, if the lady loves to be private. Don't let
me intrude upon the lady——

No intrusion, sir, I dare say; the lady is good-humoured.
She will be so kind as to step down into the parlour, I dare say.
As she stays so little a while, I am sure she will not wish to stand
in my way.

No, madam, that's true, if she be good-humoured, as you say,
—Has she been with you long, madam?

She came but yesterday, sir——

I believe I just now saw the glimpse of her. She seems to be
an elderly lady.

No, sir; you're mistaken. She's a young lady; and one of
the handsomest I ever saw.

Not so, I beg her pardon! Not but that I should have liked
her the better, were she to stay longer, if she had been elderly.
I have a strange taste, madam, you'll say, but I really, for my
wife's sake, love every elderly woman. Indeed I ever thought
age was to be reverenced, which made me (taking the fortune
into the scale too, *that* I own) make my addresses to my present
dear.

Very good of you, sir, to respect age; we all hope to live to
be old.

Right, madam. But you say the lady is beautiful. Now
you must know, that though I choose to converse with the

elderly, yet I love to see a beautiful young woman, just as I love to see fine flowers in a garden. There's no casting an eye upon her, is there, without her notice? For in this dress, and thus muffled up about my jaws, I should not care to be seen any more than she, let her love privacy as much as she will.

I will go ask if I may show a gentleman the apartment, sir; and as you are a married gentleman, and not *over*-young, she'll perhaps make the less scruple.

Then, like me, she loves elderly folks best perhaps. But it may be she has suffered by young ones?

I fancy she has, sir, or is afraid she shall. She desired to be very private; and if by description inquired after, to be denied.

Thou art true woman, goody Moore, thought I!

Good lack! Good lack! What may be her story then, I pray?

She is pretty reserved in her story; but to tell you my thoughts, I believe *love* is in the case; she is always in tears, and does not much care for company.

Nay, madam, it becomes not me to dive into ladies' secrets; I want not to pry into other people's affairs. But, pray, how does she employ herself?—Yet she came but yesterday; so you can't tell.

Writing continually, sir.

These women, Jack, when you ask them questions by way of information, don't care to be ignorant of anything.

Nay, excuse me, madam, I am very far from being an inquisitive man. But if her case be difficult, and not merely *love*, as she is a friend of yours, I would give her my advice.

Then you are a lawyer, sir——

Why, indeed, madam, I was some time at the Bar; but I have long left practice; yet am much consulted by my friends in difficult points. In a pauper case I frequently *give* money; but never *take* any from the richest.

You are a very good gentleman, then, sir.

Ay, madam, we cannot live always here; and we ought to do what good we can—but I hate to appear officious. If the lady stay any time, and think fit, upon better acquaintance, to let me into her case, it may be a happy day for her, if I find it a just one; for, you must know, that when I was at the Bar, I never was such a sad fellow as to undertake, for the sake of a paltry fee, to make white black, and black white; for what would that have been but to endeavour to establish iniquity by quirks, while I robbed the innocent?

You are an excellent gentleman, sir: I wish [and then she

sighed] I had had the happiness to know there was such a lawyer in the world; and to have been acquainted with him.

Come, come, Mrs. Moore, I think your name is, it may not be too late—when you and I are better acquainted, I may help *you* perhaps. But mention nothing of this to the lady; for, as I said, I hate to appear officious.

This prohibition I knew, if goody Moore answered the specimen she had given of her womanhood, would make her take the first opportunity to tell, were it to be necessary to my purpose that she should.

I appeared, upon the whole, so indifferent about seeing the room, or the lady, that the good woman was the more eager I should see both. And the rather, as I, to stimulate her, declared that there was more required in my eye to merit the character of a handsome woman than most people thought necessary; and that I had never seen six truly lovely women in my life.

To be brief, she went in; and after a little while came out again. The lady, sir, is retired to her closet. So you may go in and look at the room.

Then how my heart began again to play its pug's tricks!

I hobbled in, and stumped about, and liked it very much; and was sure my wife would. I begged excuse for sitting down, and asked, Who was the minister of the place? If he were a good preacher? Who preached at the chapel? And if *he* were a good preacher, and good *liver* too, madam—I must inquire after *that*: for I love, I must needs say, that the clergy should practise what they preach.

Very right, sir; but that is not so often the case as were to be wished.

More's the pity, madam. But I have a great veneration for the clergy in general. It is more a satire upon human nature, than upon the cloth, if we suppose those who have the *best* opportunities to be good, less perfect than other people. For my part, I don't love *professional* any more than *national* reflections.—But I keep the lady in her closet. My gout makes me rude.

Then up from my seat stumped I. What do you call these window-curtains, madam?

Stuff-damask, sir.

It looks mighty well, truly. I like it better than silk. It is warmer to be sure, and much fitter for lodgings in the country; especially for people in years. The bed is in a pretty taste.

It is neat and clean, sir: that's all we pretend to.

Ay, mighty well—very well—a silk camlet, I think—very well, truly!—I am sure my wife will like it. But we would not turn the lady out of her lodging for the world. The other two apartments will do for us at the present.

Then stumping towards the closet, over the door of which hung a picture—What picture is that?—Oh! I see: a St. Cecilia!

A common print, sir——

Pretty well, pretty well! It is after an Italian master. I would not for the world turn the lady out of her apartment. We can make shift with the other two, repeated I, louder still: but yet mumblingly hoarse; for I had as great regard to uniformity in accent, as to my words.

O Belford! to be so near my angel, think what a painful constraint I was under!

I was resolved to fetch her out, if possible: and pretending to be going—You can't agree as to any *time*, Mrs. Moore, when we can have this third room, can you?—Not that [whispered I, loud enough to be heard in the next room; not that] I would incommode the lady: but I would tell my wife *when*-abouts—and women, you know, Mrs. Moore, love to have everything before them of this nature.

Mrs. Moore, says my charmer [and never did her voice sound so harmonious to me. Oh! how my heart bounded again! It even talked to me, in a manner; for I thought I *heard*, as well as felt, its unruly flutters; and every vein about me seemed a pulse; Mrs. Moore], you may acquaint the gentleman that I shall stay here only for two or three days at most, till I receive an answer to a letter I have written into the country; and rather than be your hindrance, I will take up with any apartment a pair of stairs higher.

Not for the world! Not for the world, young lady! cried I. My wife, well as I love her, should lie in a garret, rather than put such a considerate lady, as you seem to be, to the least inconveniency.

She opened not the door yet; and I said, But since you have so much goodness, madam, if I could but just look into the closet as I stand, I could tell my wife whether it is large enough to hold a cabinet she much values, and will have with her wherever she goes.

Then my charmer opened the door, and blazed upon me, as it were, in a flood of light, like what one might imagine would strike a man, who, born blind, had by some propitious power been blessed with his sight, all at once, in a meridian sun.

Upon my soul, I never was so strangely affected before. I had much ado to forbear discovering myself that instant: but hesitatingly, and in great disorder, I said, looking into the closet and around it, There is room, I see, for my wife's cabinet; and it has many jewels in it of high price; but, upon my soul [for I could not forbear swearing, like a puppy: habit is a cursed thing, Jack—], nothing so valuable as the lady I see, can be brought into it.

She started, and looked at me with terror. The truth of the compliment, as far as I know, had taken dissimulation from my accent.

I saw it was impossible to conceal myself longer from her, any more than (from the violent impulses of my passion) to forbear manifesting myself. I unbuttoned therefore my cape, I pulled off my flapped, slouched hat; I threw open my great-coat, and, like the devil in Milton [an odd comparison though!]

> I started up in my own form divine,
> Touch'd by the beam of her celestial eye,
> More potent than Ithuriel's spear!—

Now, Belford, for a similitude—now for a likeness to illustrate the surprising scene, and the effect it had upon my charmer, and the gentlewoman!—But nothing *was* like it, or equal to it   The plain fact can only describe it, and set it off—thus then take it.

She no sooner saw who it was, than she gave three violent screams; and, before I could catch her in my arms (as I was about to do the moment I discovered myself), down she sunk at my feet, in a fit; which made me curse my indiscretion for so suddenly, and with so much emotion, revealing myself.

The gentlewoman, seeing so strange an alteration in my person and features, and voice, and dress, cried out, Murder, help! murder, help! by turns, for half a dozen times running. This alarmed the house, and up ran two servant-maids, and *my* servant after them. I cried out for water and hartshorn, and every one flew a different way, one of the maids as fast down as she came up; while the gentlewoman ran out of one room into another, and by turns up and down the apartment we were in, without meaning or end, wringing her foolish hands, and not knowing what she did.

Up then came running a gentleman and his sister, fetched, and brought in by the maid who had run down; and who having let in a cursed crabbed old wretch, hobbling with his gout, and mumbling with his hoarse broken-toothed voice, was metamorphosed all at once into a lively gay young fellow, with a clear accent, and all his teeth; and she would have it, that I was neither more nor less than the devil, and could not keep her eye from my foot; expecting, no doubt, every minute to see it discover itself to be cloven.

For my part, I was so intent upon restoring my angel, that I regarded nobody else. And at last, she slowly recovering motion, with bitter sighs and sobs (only the whites of her eyes however appearing for some moments), I called upon her in the tenderest accent, as I kneeled by her, my arm supporting her head; My angel! My charmer! My Clarissa! Look upon me, my dearest life! I am not angry with you! I will forgive you, my best beloved!

The gentleman and his sister knew not what to make of all this: and the less, when my fair one, recovering her sight, snatched another look at me; and then again groaned, and fainted away.

I threw up the closet sash for air, and then left her to the care of the young gentlewoman, the same notable Miss Rawlins, whom I had heard of at the Flask; and to that of Mrs. Moore; who by this time had recovered herself; and then retiring to one corner of the room, I made my servant pull off my gouty stockings, brush my hat, and loop it up into the usual smart cock.

I then stepped to the closet to Mr. Rawlins, whom, in the general confusion, I had not much minded before. Sir, said I, you have an uncommon scene before you. The lady is my wife, and no gentleman's presence is necessary here but my own.

I beg pardon, sir; *if* the lady be your wife, I have no business here. *But*, sir, by her concern at seeing you——

Pray, sir, none of your *ifs* and *buts*, I beseech you: nor *your* concern about the *lady's* concern. You are a very unqualified judge in this cause; and I beg of you, sir, to oblige me with your absence. The women only are proper to be present on this occasion, added I; and I think myself obliged to them for their care and kind assistance.

'Tis well he made not another word: for I found my choler begin to rise. I could not bear that the finest neck, and arms, and foot, in the world, should be exposed to the eyes of any man living but mine.

I withdrew once more from the closet, finding her beginning to recover, lest the sight of me too soon should throw her back again.

The first words she said, looking round her with great emotion,

were, Oh! hide me, hide me! Is he gone? Oh! hide me! Is
he gone?

Sir, said Miss Rawlins, coming to me with an air both peremptory and assured, this is some surprising case. The lady cannot
bear the sight of you. What you have done is best known to
yourself. But another such fit will probably be her last. It
would be but kind therefore for you to retire.

It behoved me to have so notable a person of my party; and
the rather as I had disobliged her impertinent brother.

The dear creature, said I, may *well* be concerned to see me.
If *you*, madam, had a husband who loved you as I love her, you
would not, I am confident, fly from him, and expose yourself to
hazards, as she does whenever she has not all her way—and yet
with a mind not capable of intentional evil—but mother-spoilt!
This is her fault, and all her fault: and the more inexcusable it is,
as I am the man of her choice, and have reason to think she loves
me above all the men in the world.

Here, Jack, was a story to support to the lady; face to face too![1]

[1] And here, Belford, lest thou, through inattention, shouldst be surprised
at my assurance, let me remind thee (and that, thus, by way of marginal
observation, that I may not break in upon my narrative) that this my
intrepidity was but a consequence of the measures I had previously
concerted (as I have from time to time acquainted thee) in apprehension
of such an event as has fallen out. For had not the dear creature already
passed for my wife, before no less than four worthy gentlemen of family
and fortune? [See vol. ii, p. 219]   And before Mrs. Sinclair, and her house-
hold, and Miss Partington? — And had she not agreed to her uncle's
expedient, that she *should* pass for such, from the time of Mr. Hickman's
application to that uncle [See vol. ii, p. 479]; and that the worthy
Captain Tomlinson should be allowed to propagate that belief; as he
had actually reported it to two families (*they possibly to more*); purposely
that it might come to the ears of James Harlowe; and serve for a foundation
for Uncle John to build his reconciliation scheme upon? [See vol. ii, p. 480.]
And canst thou think that nothing was meant by all this contrivance?
And that I am not still *further* prepared to support my story?

Indeed, I little thought, at the time that I formed these precautionary
schemes, that she would ever have been able, *if willing*, to get out of my
hands. All that I hoped I should have occasion to have recourse to them
for, was only in case I should have the courage to make the grand attempt,
and should succeed in it, to bring the dear creature [and *this out of tenderness to her*; for what attention did I ever yet pay to the grief, the execrations,
the tears of a woman I had triumphed over?] to bear me in her sight; to
expostulate with me; to be pacified by my pleas, and by my own future
hopes, founded upon the reconciliatory project, upon my reiterated vows,
and upon the captain's assurances—since, in that case, to forgive me, to
have gone on with me *for a week*, would have been to forgive me, to have
gone on with me *for ever*. And then had my eligible life of honour taken
place; her trials would all have been then over; and she would have known
nothing but gratitude, love, and joy, to the end of one of our lives. For
never would I, never could I, have abandoned such an admirable creature
as this. Thou knowest, I never was a sordid villain to any of her inferiors
—her *inferiors*, I may say—for who is not her inferior?

You *speak* like a gentleman; you *look* like a gentleman, said Miss Rawlins. But, sir, this is a strange case; the lady seems to dread the sight of you.

No wonder, madam; taking her a little on one side nearer to Mrs. Moore. I have three times already forgiven the dear creature.—But this *jealousy*! There is a spice of *that* in it—and of *frenzy* too [whispered I, that it might have the face of a secret, and of consequence the more engage their attention]—but our story is too long——

I then made a motion to go to my beloved. But they desired that I would walk into the next room; and they would endeavour to prevail upon her to lie down.

I begged that they would not suffer her to talk; for that she was accustomed to fits, and when in this way, would talk of anything that came uppermost: and the more she was suffered to run on, the worse she was; and if not kept quiet, would fall into ravings; which might possibly hold her a week.

They promised to keep her quiet; and I withdrew into the next room; ordering every one down but Mrs. Moore and Miss Rawlins.

She was full of exclamations. Unhappy creature! miserable! ruined! and undone! she called herself; wrung her hands, and begged they would assist her to escape from the terrible evils she should otherwise be made to suffer.

They preached patience and quietness to her; and would have had her to lie down; but she refused; sinking, however, into an easy chair; for she trembled so, she could not stand.

By this time I hoped that she was enough recovered to bear a presence that it behoved me to make her bear; and fearing she would throw out something in her exclamations that would still more disconcert me, I went into the room again.

Oh! there he is! said she, and threw her apron over her face. I cannot see him!—I cannot look upon him! Begone, begone! touch me not!

For I took her struggling hand, beseeching her to be pacified; and assuring her that I would make all up with her upon her own terms and wishes.

Base man! said the violent lady, I have no wishes, but never to behold you more! Why must I be thus pursued and haunted? Have you not made me miserable enough already? Despoiled of all succour and help, and of every friend, I am contented to be poor, low, and miserable, so I may be free from your persecutions.

Miss Rawlins stared at me [a confident slut this Miss Rawlins,

thought I]: so did Mrs. Moore. I told you so! whisperingly said
I, turning to the women; shaking my head with a face of great
concern and pity; and then to my charmer, My dear creature,
how you rave! You will not easily recover from the effects of
this violence. Have patience, my love. Be pacified; and we
will coolly talk this matter over: for you expose yourself, as well
as me: these ladies will certainly think you have fallen among
robbers, and that I am the chief of them.

So you are! so you are! stamping, her face still covered [*she
thought of Wednesday night, no doubt*]; and sighing as if her heart
were breaking, she put her hand to her forehead—I shall be
quite distracted!

I will not, my dearest love, uncover your face. You shall *not*
look upon me, since I am so odious to you. But this is a violence
I never thought you capable of.

And I would have pressed her hand, as I held it, with my lips;
but she drew it from me with indignation.

Unhand me, sir, said she. I will not be touched by you.
Leave me to my fate. What right, what title, have you to
persecute me thus?

What right, what title, my dear!—But this is not a time—I
have a letter from Captain Tomlinson—here it is—offering it to
her——

I will receive nothing from your hands—tell me not of Captain
Tomlinson—tell me not of anybody—you have no *right* to
invade me thus—once more leave me to my fate—have you
not made me miserable enough?

I touched a delicate string, on purpose to set her in such a
passion before the women, as might confirm the intimation I
had given of a frenzical disorder.

What a turn is here! Lately so happy! Nothing wanting
but a reconciliation between you and your friends! That
reconciliation in such a happy train—shall so *slight*, so *accidental*
an occasion be suffered to overturn all our happiness?

She started up with a trembling impatience, her apron falling
from her indignant face. Now, said she, that thou *darest* to call
the occasion *slight* and *accidental*, and that I am happily out of
thy vile hands, and out of a house I have reason to believe *as*
vile, traitor and wretch that thou art, I will venture to cast an
eye upon thee—and oh, that it were in my power, in mercy to my
sex, to look thee first into shame and remorse, and then into
death!

This violent tragedy speech, and the high manner in which

she uttered it, had its desired effect. I looked upon the women, and upon her, by turns, with a pitying eye; and they shook their wise heads and besought *me* to retire, and *her* to lie down to compose herself.

This hurricane, like other hurricanes, was presently allayed by a shower. She threw herself once more into her armed chair, and begged pardon of the women for her passionate excess; but not of me: yet I was in hopes, that when compliments were stirring, I should have come in for a share.

Indeed, ladies, said I [with assurance enough, thou'lt say], this violence is not natural to my beloved's temper—misapprehension——

Misapprehension, wretch! And want I excuses from thee!

By what a scorn was every lovely feature agitated!

Then turning her face from me, I have not patience, O thou guileful betrayer, to look upon thee! Begone, begone! With a face so unblushing, how darest thou my presence?

I thought then that the character of a husband obliged me to be angry.

You may one day, madam, repent this treatment—by my soul you may. You know I have not deserved it of you—you *know* I have not.

Do I know you have not? Wretch! Do I know——

You do, madam—and never did man of my figure and consideration [I thought it was proper to throw that in] meet with such treatment.

She lifted up her hands: indignation kept her silent.

But all is of a piece with the charge you bring against me of *despoiling you of all succour and help*, of making you *poor* and *low*, and with other unprecedented language. I will only say, before these two gentlewomen, that since it *must* be so, and since your former esteem for me is turned into so riveted an aversion, I will soon, *very* soon, make you entirely easy. I *will* be gone—I *will* leave you to *your own fate*, as you call it; and may that be happy! Only, that I may not appear to be a spoiler, a robber indeed, let me know whither I shall send your apparel, and everything that belongs to you, and I will send it.

Send it to this place; and assure me that you will never molest me more; never more come near me; and that is all I ask of you.

I *will* do so, madam, said I, with a dejected air. But did I ever think I should be so indifferent to you? However, you must permit me to insist on your reading this letter; and on your seeing Captain Tomlinson, and hearing what he has to say from your uncle. He will be here by and by.

Don't trifle with me, said she, in an imperious tone. Do as you offer. I will not receive any letter from your hands. If I see Captain Tomlinson, it shall be on his *own* account; not on *yours*. You tell me you will send me my apparel: if you would have me believe anything you say, let this be the test of your sincerity. Leave me *now*, and send my things.

The women stared. They did nothing but stare; and appeared to be more and more at a loss what to make of the matter between us.

I pretended to be going from her in a pet: but when I had got to the door, I turned back; and, as if I had recollected myself, One word more, my dearest creature! Charming even in your anger! O my fond soul! said I, turning half round, and pulling out my handkerchief.

I believe, Jack, my eyes did glisten a little. I have no doubt but they did. The women pitied me. Honest souls! They showed that they had each of them a handkerchief as well as I. So, hast thou not observed (to give a familiar illustration) every man in a company of a dozen, or more, obligingly pull out his watch, when some one has asked what 's o'clock? As each man of a like number, if one talks of his beard, will fall to stroking his chin with his four fingers and thumb.

One word only, madam, repeated I (as soon as my voice had recovered its tone): I have represented to Captain Tomlinson in the most favourable light the cause of our present misunderstanding. You know what your uncle insists upon; and which you have acquiesced with. The letter in my hand [and again I offered it to her] will acquaint you with what you have to apprehend from your brother's active malice.

She was going to speak in a high accent, putting the letter from her, with an open palm—Nay, hear me out, madam—The captain, you know, has reported our *marriage* to two different persons. It is come to your brother's ears. My own relations have also heard of it. Letters were brought me from town this morning, from Lady Betty Lawrance and Miss Montague. Here they are. [I pulled them out of my pocket, and offered them to her, with that of the captain; but she held back her still open palm, that she might not receive them.] Reflect, madam, I beseech you, reflect upon the fatal consequences which this your high resentment may be attended with.

Ever since I knew you, said she, I have been in a wilderness of doubt and error. I bless God that I am out of your hands. I will transact for myself what relates to myself. I dismiss all your solicitude for me. Am I not my own mistress! Have you any title——

The women stared. [The devil stare ye, thought I! Can ye do nothing but stare?] It was high time to stop her here.

I raised my voice to drown hers. You used, my dearest creature, to have a tender and apprehensive heart—you never had so much reason for such a one as now.

Let me judge for myself, upon what I shall *see*, not upon what I shall *hear*. Do you think I shall ever——

I dreaded her going on. I *must* be heard, madam, raising my voice still higher. You must let me read one paragraph or two of this letter to you, if you will not read it yourself——

Begone from me, man! Begone from me with thy letters! What pretence hast thou for tormenting me thus? What right—what title——

Dearest creature, what questions you ask! Questions that you can as well answer yourself——

I *can*, I *will*—and *thus* I answer them——

Still louder raised I my voice. She was overborne. Sweet soul! It would be hard, thought I [and yet I was very angry with her], if such a spirit as thine cannot be brought to yield to such a one as mine!

I lowered my voice on her silence. All gentle, all *entreative*, my accent: my head bowed; one hand held out; the other on my honest heart: For Heaven's sake, my dearest creature, resolve to see Captain Tomlinson with temper. He would have come along with me: but I was willing to try to soften your mind first on this fatal misapprehension; and this for the sake of your own wishes: for what is it otherwise to me whether your friends are or are not reconciled to us? *Do I want any favour from them?* For your own mind's sake, therefore, frustrate not Captain Tomlinson's negotiation. That worthy gentleman will be here in the afternoon. Lady Betty will be in town, with my Cousin Montague, in a day or two. They will be your visitors. I beseech you do not carry this misunderstanding so far, as that Lord M. and Lady Betty and Lady Sarah may know it. [*How considerable this made me look to the women!*] Lady Betty will not let you rest till you consent to accompany her to her own seat, and to that lady may you safely entrust your cause.

Again, upon my pausing a moment, she was going to break out. I liked not the turn of her countenance, nor the tone of her

voice—"And thinkest thou, base wretch," were the words she
did utter. I again raised my voice and drowned hers. *Base
wretch*, madam! You know that I have not deserved the violent
names you have called me. Words so opprobrious! from a
mind so gentle! But this treatment is from *you*, madam!—From
you, whom I love more than my own soul. By that soul, I swear
that I do. [The women looked upon each other. They seemed
pleased with my ardour. Women, whether wives, maids, or
widows, love ardours. Even Miss Howe, thou knowest, speaks
up for ardours.[1]] Nevertheless, I must say that you have
carried matters too far for the occasion. I see you hate me——

She was just going to speak—If we are to *separate for ever*,
in a strong and solemn voice, proceeded I, this island shall not
long be troubled with me. Meantime, only be pleased to give
these letters a perusal, and consider what is to be said to your
uncle's friend; and what he is to say to your uncle. Anything
will I come into (renounce me if you will) that shall make for
your peace, and for the reconciliation *your heart was so lately
set upon*. But I humbly conceive that it is necessary that you
should come into better temper with me, were it but to give a
favourable appearance to what *has passed*, and weight to any
future application to your friends, in whatever way you shall
think proper to make it.

I then put the letters into her lap, and retired into the next
apartment with a low bow and a very solemn air.

I was soon followed by the two women. Mrs. Moore withdrew
to give the fair perverse time to read them: Miss Rawlins for the
same reason; and because she was sent for home.

The widow besought her speedy return. I joined in the same
request; and she was ready enough to promise to oblige us.

I excused myself to Mrs. Moore for the disguise I had appeared
in at first, and for the story I had invented. I told her that I held
myself obliged to satisfy her for the whole floor we were upon; and
for an upper room for my servant; and that for a month certain.

She made many scruples, and begged she might not be urged
on this head, till she had consulted Miss Rawlins.

I consented; but told her that she had taken my earnest; and
I hoped there was no room for dispute.

Just then Miss Rawlins returned, with an air of eager curiosity;
and having been told what had passed between Mrs. Moore and
me, she gave herself airs of office immediately: which I humoured,
plainly perceiving that if I had *her* with me, I had the other.

[1] See vol. ii, pp. 292, 317.

She wished, if there were time for it, and if it were not quite impertinent in her to desire it, that I would give Mrs. Moore and her a brief history of an affair, which, as she said, bore the face of novelty, mystery, and surprise: for sometimes it looked to her as if we were married; at other times, that point appeared doubtful; and yet the lady did not absolutely deny it; but upon the whole, thought herself highly injured.

I said that ours was a very particular case: that were I to acquaint them with it, some part of it would hardly appear credible. But, however, as they seemed to be persons of discretion, I would give them a brief account of the whole; and this in so plain and sincere a manner, that it should clear up to their satisfaction everything that had passed, or might hereafter pass between us.

They sat down by me, and threw every feature of their faces into attention. I was resolved to go as near the truth as possible, lest anything should drop from my spouse to impeach my veracity; and yet keep in view what passed at the Flask.

It is necessary, although thou knowest my whole story, and a good deal of my views, that thou shouldst be apprised of the substance of what I told them.

"I gave them, in as concise a manner as I was able, the history of our families, fortunes, alliances, antipathies; her brother's and mine particularly. I averred the truth of our private marriage." The captain's letter, which I will enclose, will give thee my reasons for that: and besides, the women might have proposed a parson to me by way of compromise. "I told them the condition my spouse had made me swear to; and which she held me to, in order, I said, to induce me the sooner to be reconciled to her relations."

"I owned that this restraint made me sometimes ready to fly out." And Mrs. Moore was so good as to declare, that *she did not much wonder at it.*

Thou art a very good sort of a woman, Mrs. Moore, thought I.

As Miss Howe has actually detected our mother; and might possibly find some way still to acquaint her friend with her discoveries; I thought it proper to prepossess them in favour of Mrs. Sinclair and her two nieces.

I said, "They were gentlewomen born; that they had not bad hearts; that indeed my spouse did not love them; they having once jointly taken the liberty to blame her for her over-niceness with regard to me. People, I said, even *good* people, who knew themselves to be guilty of a fault they had no inclination to mend, were too often least patient, when told of it; as they could less bear than others to be thought indifferently of."

Too often the case, they owned.

"Mrs. Sinclair's house was a very handsome house, and fit to receive the first quality. [True enough, Jack!] Mrs. Sinclair was a woman very easy in her circumstances: a widow-gentlewoman —as *you*, Mrs. Moore, are. Lets lodgings—as *you*, Mrs. Moore, do. Once had better prospects—as *you*, Mrs. Moore, may have had: the relict of Colonel Sinclair;—you, Mrs. Moore, might know Colonel Sinclair—he had lodgings at Hampstead."

She had heard of the name.

Oh, he was related to the best families in Scotland: and his widow is not to be reflected upon because she lets lodgings, you know, Mrs. Moore; you know, Miss Rawlins."

Very true, and very true; and they must needs say, it did not look quite so pretty, in such a lady as my spouse, to be so censorious.

A foundation here, thought I, to procure these women's help to get back the fugitive, or their connivance at least at my doing so; as well as for anticipating any future information from Miss Howe.

I gave them a character of that virago: and intimated "that for a head to contrive mischief, and a heart to execute it, she had hardly her equal in her sex."

To *this* Miss Howe it was, Mrs. Moore said, she supposed, that my spouse was so desirous to dispatch a man and horse, by day-dawn, with a letter she wrote before she went to bed last night; proposing to stay no longer than till she had received an answer to it.

The very same, said I. I *knew* she would have immediate recourse to her. I should have been but too happy, could I have prevented such a letter from passing, or so to have managed as to have it given into Mrs. Howe's hands, instead of her daughter's. Women who had lived some time in the world knew *better* than to encourage such skittish pranks in young wives.

Let me just stop to tell thee, while it is in my head, that I have since given Will his cue to find out where the man lives who is gone with the fair fugitive's letter; and, if possible, to see him on his return, before he sees her.

I told the women, "I despaired that it would ever be better with us while Miss Howe had so strange an ascendancy over my spouse, and remained herself *unmarried*; and until the reconciliation with her friends could be effected; or a *still* happier event.

as I should think it, who am the last male of my family; and which my foolish vow, and her rigour, had hitherto——"

Here I stopped, and looked modest, turning my diamond ring round my finger: while goody Moore looked mighty significant, calling it a very particular case; and the maiden fanned away, and primmed and pursed, to show that what I said needed no further explanation.

"I told them the occasion of our present difference: I avowed the reality of the fire: but owned that I would have made no scruple of breaking the unnatural oath she had bound me in (having an husband's right on my side), when she was so accidentally frightened into my arms: and I blamed myself excessively that I did not; since she thought fit to carry her resentment so high, and had the injustice to suppose the fire to be a contrivance of mine."

Nay, for that matter, Mrs. Moore said—as we were *married*, and *madam* was so *odd*—every gentleman *would not*—and there stopped Mrs. Moore.

"To suppose I should have recourse to such a *poor* contrivance, said I, when I saw the dear creature *every hour*." Was not this a bold put, Jack?

A most extraordinary case, truly! cried the maiden; fanning, yet coming in with her *Well-buts*; and her sifting *Pray, sir's!* and her restraining *Enough, sir's!*—flying *from* the question *to* the question; her seat now and then uneasy, for fear my *want of delicacy* should hurt her abundant *modesty*; and yet it was difficult to satisfy her *super*-abundant *curiosity*.

"My beloved's jealousy [and jealousy of itself, to female minds, accounts for a thousand unaccountablenesses], and the imputation of her half-frenzy, brought upon her by her father's wicked curse, and by the previous persecutions she had undergone from all her family, were what I dwelt upon, in order to provide against what might happen."

In short, "I owned against myself most of the offences which I did not doubt but she would charge me with in their hearing: and as every cause has a black and a white side, I gave the worst parts of our story the gentlest turn. And when I had done, acquainted them with some of the contents of that letter of Captain Tomlinson which I had left with the lady. I concluded with cautioning them to be guarded against the inquiries of James Harlowe, and of Captain Singleton, or of any sailor-looking men."

This thou wilt see from the letter itself was necessary to be done. Here therefore thou mayest read it. And a charming letter to my purpose wilt thou find it to be, if thou givest the least attention to its contents.

To Robert Lovelace, Esq.

Wedn. June 7.

DEAR SIR,—Although I am obliged to be in town to-morrow, or next day at farthest, yet I would not dispense with writing to you, by *one of my servants* (whom I send up before me upon a particular occasion), in order to advertise you, *that it is probable you will hear from some of your own relations on your [supposed[1]] nuptials.* One of the persons (Mr. Lilburne by name) to whom I hinted my belief of your marriage, happens to be acquainted with Mr. Spurrier, Lady Betty Lawrance's steward; and (not being under any restriction) mentioned it *to* Mr. Spurrier, and he to Lady Betty, as a thing certain; and this (though I have not the honour *to be personally known to her ladyship*) brought on an inquiry from her ladyship to me by her gentleman; who coming to me in company with Mr. Lilburne, I had no way but to confirm the report. And I understand that Lady Betty takes it amiss that she was not acquainted with so desirable a piece of news from yourself.

Her ladyship, it seems, has *business that calls her to town* [and you will possibly choose to put her right. If you do, it will, I presume, *be in confidence*; that nothing may transpire from your *own* family to contradict what I have given out].

[I have ever been of opinion, *that truth ought to be strictly adhered to on all occasions*: and am concerned that I have (though with so good a view) departed from my old maxim. But my dear friend Mr. John Harlowe would have it so. Yet I never knew a departure of this kind a *single* departure. But, to make the best of it now, allow me, sir, once more to beg the lady, as soon as possible, to authenticate the report given out.] When both you and the lady join in the acknowledgment of your marriage, it will be impertinent in any one to be inquisitive as to the *day or week*. [And if as privately celebrated as you intend (while the gentlewomen with whom you lodge are properly instructed, as you say they are, and who actually believe you were married long ago), who shall be able to give a contradiction to my report?]

And yet it is very probable that minute inquiries will be made;

---

[1] What is between hooks [ ] thou mayest suppose, Jack, I sunk upon the women, in the account I gave them of the contents of this letter.

and this is what renders precaution necessary. For Mr. James Harlowe will not believe that you are married; and is sure, he says, that you both lived together when Mr. Hickman's application was made to Mr. John Harlowe: and if you lived together *any* time unmarried, he infers from *your* character, Mr. Lovelace, that it is not probable that you would ever marry. And he leaves it to his two uncles to decide, if you even *should be married*, whether there be not room to believe that his sister was *first dishonoured*; and if so, to judge of the title she will have to their favour, or to the forgiveness of any of her family. I believe, sir, this part of my letter had best be kept from the lady.

Young Mr. Harlowe is *resolved to find this out*, and *to come at his sister's speech likewise*; and for that purpose sets out *to-morrow*, as I am well informed, *with a large attendance armed*; and *Mr. Solmes is to be of the party*. And what makes him the more earnest to find it out, is this: Mr. John Harlowe has told the whole family that he will alter and new-settle his will. Mr. Antony Harlowe is resolved to do the same by his; for, it seems, he has now given over all thoughts of changing his condition; *having lately been disappointed in a view he had of that sort with Mrs. Howe*. These two brothers generally *act in concert*; and Mr. James Harlowe dreads (and let me tell you, that he has reason for it, on *my* Mr. Harlowe's account) that his younger sister will be, at last, more benefited than he wishes for, by the alteration intended. He has already been endeavouring to sound his Uncle Harlowe on this subject; and wanted to know whether any *new application* had been made to him on his sister's part. Mr. Harlowe avoided a direct answer, and expressed his wishes for a general reconciliation, and his hopes that his niece were married. This offended the furious young man, and he reminded his uncle of engagements they had all entered into at his sister's going away, *not to be reconciled but by general consent*.

Mr. John Harlowe complains to me often of the uncon-trollableness of his nephew; and says, that now that the young man has not anybody of whose superior sense he stands in awe, he observes not decency in his behaviour to any of them. And this makes *my* Mr. Harlowe still more desirous than ever of bringing his younger niece into favour again. I will not say all I might of this young man's extraordinary rapaciousness: but one would think *that these grasping men expect to live for ever*!

"I took the liberty but within these two hours to propose to set on foot (and offered my cover) to a correspondence between *my friend and his daughter-niece*, as he still sometimes fondly calls her. She was mistress of so much prudence, I said, that I was sure she could better direct everything to its desirable end than anybody else could. But he said he did not think himself entirely at liberty to take such a step *at present*; and that it was best that he should have it in his power to say, occasionally, that he had not any correspondence *with* her, or letter *from* her.

"You will see, sir, from all this, the necessity of keeping our treaty an *absolute secret*; and if the lady has mentioned it to her *worthy friend* Miss Howe, I hope it is in confidence."

[And now, sir, a few lines in answer to yours of Monday last.]

[Mr. Harlowe was very well pleased with your readiness to come into his proposal. But as to what you *both* desire, that he will be present at the ceremony, he said that his nephew watched all his steps so narrowly, that he thought it was not practicable (if he were inclinable) to oblige you: but that he consented, with all his heart, that I should be the person whom he had stipulated should be privately present at the ceremony on his part.]

[However, I think, I have an *expedient* for this, if your lady *continues* to be very desirous of her uncle's presence (except he should be more determined than his answer to me seemed to import); of which I shall acquaint you, and perhaps of what he says to it, *when I have the pleasure to see you in town*. But, indeed, I think you have *no time to lose*. Mr. Harlowe is impatient to hear that you are actually one; and I hope I may carry him down word, when I leave you next, that *I saw* the ceremony performed.]

[If any obstacle arises from the lady (from *you* it cannot), I shall be tempted *to think a little hardly of her punctilio*.]

Mr. Harlowe hopes, sir, that you will rather take pains to *avoid*, than to *meet*, this violent young man. He had the better opinion of you, let me tell you, sir, from the account I gave him of your moderation and politeness; neither of which are qualities with his nephew. *But we have all of us something to amend.*

You cannot imagine how dearly my friend still loves this excellent niece of his. I will give you an instance of it, which affected me a good deal: "If once more, said he (the last time but one we were together), I can but see this sweet child gracing the upper end of my table, as mistress of my house, in my *allotted month*; all the rest of the family present but as her guests; for so I formerly *would* have it; and had her *mother's consent for it* "—There he stopped; for he was forced to turn his reverend

face from me.   Tears ran down his cheeks.   Fain would he have
hid them: but he could not—"Yet—yet, said he—how—how—"
(poor gentleman, he perfectly sobbed)—"how shall I be able to
bear the first meeting!"

I bless God I am *no hard-hearted man*, Mr. Lovelace: my eyes
showed to my worthy friend that he had no reason to be
ashamed of his humanity before me.

I will put an end to this long epistle.   Be pleased to make my
compliments acceptable to the most excellent of women; as well
as believe me to be, dear sir,

Your faithful friend, and humble servant,

ANTONY TOMLINSON.

During the conversation between me and the women, I had
planted myself at the farther end of the apartment we were in,
over against the door, which was open; and opposite to the
lady's chamber door, which was shut.   I spoke so low that it
was impossible for her, at that distance, to hear what we said;
and in this situation I could see if her door opened.

I told the women that what I had mentioned to my spouse of
Lady Betty's coming to town with her Niece Montague, and of
their intention to visit my beloved, whom they had never seen,
nor she them, was real; and that I expected news of their arrival
every hour.   I then showed them copies of the other two letters
which I had left with *her*; the one from Lady Betty, the other
from my Cousin Montague.   And here thou mayest read them
if thou wilt.

Eternally reproaching, eternally upbraiding me, are my
impertinent relations.   But they are fond of occasions to find
fault with me.   Their love, their love, Jack, and their dependence on my known good humour, are their inducements.

To Robert Lovelace, Esq.

Wedn. Morn. June 7.

DEAR NEPHEW,—I understand that at length all our wishes
are answered in your happy marriage.   But I think we might as
well have heard of it directly from you, as from the roundabout
way by which we have been made acquainted with it.   Methinks, sir, the *power* and the *will* we have to oblige you, should
not expose us the more to your slights and negligence.   My
brother had set his heart upon giving to you the wife we have
all so long wished you to have.   But if you were actually married

at the time you made him that request (*supposing, perhaps, that his gout would not let him attend you*), it is but like *you*.[1] If your lady had *her* reasons to wish it to be private while the differences between her family and self continue, you might nevertheless have communicated it to us with *that* restriction; and we should have forborne the public manifestations of our joy, upon an event we have so long desired.

The distant way we have come to know it, is by my steward; who is acquainted with a friend of Captain Tomlinson, to whom that gentleman revealed it: and he, it seems, had it from yourself and lady, with such circumstances as leave it not to be doubted.

I am, indeed, very much disobliged with you: so is Lady Sarah. But I shall have a very speedy opportunity to tell you so in person; being obliged to go to town on my old Chancery affair. My Cousin Leeson, who is, it seems, removed to Albemarle Street, has notice of it. I shall be at *her* house, where I bespeak your attendance on Sunday night. I have written to my Cousin Charlotte for either her, or her sister, to meet me at Reading, and accompany me to town. I shall stay but a few days; my business being matter of form only. On my return I shall pop upon Lord M. at M. Hall, to see in what way his last fit has left him.

Meantime, having told you my mind on your negligence, I cannot help congratulating you both upon the occasion. Your fair lady particularly, upon her entrance into a family which is prepared to admire and love her.

My principal intention of writing to you (dispensing with the necessary punctilio) is that you may acquaint my dear new niece that I will not be denied the honour of her company down with me into Oxfordshire. I understand that your proposed house and equipages cannot be soon ready. She shall be with me till they are. I insist upon it. This shall make all up. My house shall be her own. My servants and equipages hers.

Lady Sarah, who has not been out of her own house for months, will oblige me with her company for a week, in honour of a niece so dearly beloved, as I am sure she will be of us all.

Being but in lodgings in town, neither you nor your lady can require much preparation.

Some time on Monday I hope to attend the dear young lady, to make her my compliments; and to receive *her* apology for *your* negligence: which, and her going down with me, as I said

---

[1] I gave Mrs. Moore and Miss Rawlins room to think this reproach *just*, Jack.

before, shall be full satisfaction. Meantime, God bless *her* for her courage [tell her I say so]: and bless you *both* in each other; and that will be happiness to us all—particularly to

Your truly affectionate aunt,

ELIZ. LAWRANCE.

To Robert Lovelace, Esq.

DEAR COUSIN,—At last, as we understand, there is some hope of you. Now does my good lord run over his bead-roll of proverbs; of *black oxen, wild oats, long lanes*, and so forth.

Now, cousin, say I, is your time come; and you will be no longer, I hope, an infidel either to the power or excellence of the sex you have pretended hitherto so much to undervalue; nor a ridiculer or scoffer at an institution which all sober people reverence, and all rakes, sooner or later, are brought to reverence, or to wish they had.

I want to see how you become your silken fetters: whether the charming yoke fits light upon your shoulders. If with such a sweet yoke-fellow it does not, my lord, and my sister, as well as I, think that you will deserve a closer tie about your neck.

His lordship is very much displeased that you have not written him word of the day, the hour, the manner, and everything. But I ask him, how he can *already* expect any mark of deference or politeness from you? He must stay, I tell him, till that sign of reformation, among others, appear from the influence and example of your lady: but that, if ever you will be good for anything, it will be quickly seen. And, oh, cousin, what a vast, vast journey have you to take from the dreary land of libertinism, through the bright province of reformation, into the serene kingdom of happiness!—You had need to lose no time. You have many a weary step to tread, before you can overtake those travellers who set out for it from a less remote quarter. But you have a charming pole-star to guide you; that 's your advantage. I wish you joy of it: and as I have never yet expected any highly complaisant thing from you, *I make no scruple to begin first*; but it is purely, I must tell you, in respect to my new cousin; whose accession into our family we most heartily congratulate and rejoice in.

I have a letter from Lady Betty. She commands either my attendance or my sister's at Reading, to proceed with her to town, to Cousin Leeson's. She puts Lord M. in hopes that she shall certainly bring down with her our lovely new relation; for

she says she will not be denied. His lordship is the willinger
to let *me* be the person, as I am in a manner wild to see her; my
sister having two years ago had that honour at Sir Robert
Biddulph's. So get ready to accompany us in our return;
except your lady has objections strong enough to satisfy us all.
Lady Sarah longs to see her; and says this accession to the
family will supply to it the loss of her beloved daughter.

I shall soon, I hope, pay my compliments to the dear lady in
person: so have nothing to add, but that I am

Your old mad playfellow and cousin,

CHARLOTTE MONTAGUE.

The women having read the copies of these two letters, I
thought that I might then threaten and swagger. "But very
little heart have I, said I, to encourage such a visit from Lady
Betty and Miss Montague to my spouse. For after all, I am
tired out with her strange ways. She is not what she was, and
(as I told her in your hearing, ladies) I will leave this plaguy
island, though the place of my birth, and though the stake I
have in it is very considerable, and go and reside in France or
Italy, and never think of myself as a married man, *nor live
like one.*"

O dear! said one.

That would be a sad thing! said the other.

Nay, madam (turning to Mrs. Moore)—Indeed, madam (to
Miss Rawlins), I am quite desperate. I can no longer bear such
usage. I have had the good fortune to be favoured by the
smiles of very fine ladies, though I say it [and I looked modest],
both abroad and at home. [*Thou knowest this to be true, Jack.*]
With regard to my spouse here, I had but one hope left (for as
to the reconciliation with her friends, I scorn them all too much
to value that, but for her sake); and that was, that if it pleased
God to bless us with children, she might entirely recover her
usual serenity; and we might then be happy. But the reconciliation her heart was so much set upon is now, as I hinted
before, entirely hopeless—made so by this rash step of hers, and
by the rasher temper she is in: since (as you will believe) her
brother and sister, when they come to know it, will make a fine
handle of it against us both; affecting, as they do at present, to
disbelieve our marriage—and the dear creature herself too ready
to countenance such a disbelief—as nothing *more than the
ceremony—as nothing more—hem!—as nothing more than the
ceremony——*

Here, as thou wilt perceive, I was bashful; for Miss Rawlins, by her preparatory primness, put me in mind that it was *proper to be so.*

I turned half round; then facing the fan-player, and the matron: You *yourselves*, ladies, knew not what to believe till *now*, that I have told you our story: and I do assure you, that I shall not give myself the same trouble to convince people I hate: people from whom I neither expect nor desire any favour; and who are determined *not* to be convinced. And what, pray, must be the issue, when her uncle's friend comes, although he seems to be a *truly worthy man*? Is it not natural for him to say, "To what purpose, Mr. Lovelace, should I endeavour to bring about a reconciliation between Mrs. Lovelace and her friends, by means of her elder uncle, when a good understanding is wanting between yourselves?" A fair inference, Mrs. Moore! A fair inference, Miss Rawlins! And here is the unhappiness— till she is reconciled to them, this cursed oath, in her notion, is binding.

The women seemed moved; for I spoke with great earnestness, though low—and, besides, they love to have their sex, and its favours, appear of importance to us. They shook their deep heads at each other and looked sorrowful: and this moved my tender heart too.

'Tis an unheard-of case, ladies—had she not preferred me to all mankind—There I stopped—and that, resumed I, feeling for my handkerchief, is what staggered Captain Tomlinson when he heard of her flight; who, the last time he saw us together, saw the most affectionate couple on earth!—the most affectionate couple on earth!—in the accent grievous, repeated I.

Out then I pulled my handkerchief, and putting it to my eyes, arose and walked to the window. It makes me weaker than a woman! Did I not love her as never man loved *his wife*! [I have no doubt but I do, Jack].

There again I stopped; and resuming: Charming creature as you see she is, I wish I had never beheld her face!—Excuse me, ladies; traversing the room. And having rubbed my eyes till I supposed them red, I turned to the women; and, pulling out my letter-case, I will show you one letter—here it is—read it, Miss Rawlins, if you please—it will confirm to you how much all my family are prepared to admire her. I am freely treated in it; so I am in the two others: but after what I have told you, nothing need be a secret to you two.

She took it with an air of eager curiosity, and looked at

the seal, ostentatiously coroneted; and at the superscription, reading out, *To Robert Lovelace, Esq.*—Ay, madam—Ay, Miss—that's my name [giving myself an air, though I had told them before], I am not ashamed of it. My wife's maiden name—*unmarried* name, I should rather say—fool that I am!—and I rubbed my cheek for vexation [fool enough in conscience, Jack!] —was Harlowe—Clarissa Harlowe—you heard me call her *my Clarissa.*

I did, but thought it to be a feigned or love-name, said Miss Rawlins.

I wonder what is Miss Rawlins's love-name, Jack. Most of the fair romancers have in their early womanhood chosen love-names. No parson ever gave more *real* names, than I have given *fictitious* ones. And to very good purpose: many a sweet dear has answered me a letter for the sake of owning a name which her godmother never gave her.

No—it was her real name, I said.

I bid her read out the whole letter. If the spelling be not exact, Miss Rawlins, said I, you will excuse it; the writer is a lord. But, perhaps, I may not show it to my spouse; for if those I have left with her have no effect upon her, neither will this: and I shall not care to expose my Lord M. to her scorn. Indeed I begin to be quite careless of consequences.

Miss Rawlins, who could not but be pleased with this mark of my confidence, looked as if she pitied me.

And here thou mayest read the letter, No. III.

To Robert Lovelace, Esq.

M. Hall, Wedn. June 7.

COUSIN LOVELACE,—I think you might have found time to let us know of your nuptials being actually solemnized. I might have expected this piece of civility from you. But perhaps the ceremony was performed at the very time that you asked me to be your lady's father—but I shall be angry if I proceed in my guesses—and *little said is soon amended.*

But I can tell you that Lady Betty Lawrance, whatever Lady Sarah does, will not so soon forgive you as I have done. *Women resent slights longer than men.* You that know so much of the sex (I speak it not, however, to your praise) might have known *that.* But never was you before acquainted with a lady of such an amiable character. I hope there will be but one soul between you. I have before now said, that I will disinherit you and settle all I can upon her, if you prove not a good husband to her.

May this marriage be crowned with a great many fine boys (I desire no girls) to build up again a family so ancient! The first boy shall take my surname by Act of Parliament. That is in my will.

Lady Betty and Niece Charlotte will be in town about business *before you know where you are*. They long to pay their compliments to your fair bride. I suppose you will hardly be at the Lawn when they get to town: because Greme informs me you have sent no orders there for your lady's accommodation.

Pritchard has all things in readiness for signing. I will take no advantage of your slights. Indeed I am too much used to them—more praise to my patience than to your complaisance, however.

One reason for Lady Betty's going up, as I may tell you *under the rose*, is to buy some suitable presents for Lady Sarah and all of us to make on this agreeable occasion.

We would have blazed it away, could we have had timely notice, and thought it would have been agreeable to all round. The *like occasions don't happen every day*.

My most affectionate compliments and congratulations to my new niece, conclude me, for the present, in violent pains, that with all your heroicalness would make you mad,

Your truly affectionate uncle,

M.

This letter clenched the nail. Not but that, Miss Rawlins said, she saw I had been a wild gentleman; and, truly, she thought so the moment she beheld me.

They began to intercede for my spouse (so nicely had I turned the tables); and that I would not go abroad, and disappoint a reconciliation so much wished for on one side, and such desirable prospects on the other in my own family.

Who knows, thought I to myself, but more may come of this plot than I had even promised myself? What a happy man shall I be, if these women can be brought to join to carry my marriage into consummation!

Ladies, you are exceedingly good to us both. I should have some hopes, if my unhappily-nice spouse could be brought to dispense with the unnatural oath she has laid me under. You see what my case is. Do you think I may not insist upon her absolving me from this abominable oath? Will you be so good as to give your advice, that one apartment may serve for a man and his wife at the hour of retirement?—Modestly put, Belford! —And let me here observe, that few rakes would find a language so decent as to engage modest women to talk with him in, upon such subjects.

They both simpered and looked upon one another.

These subjects always make women simper, at least. No *need* but of the most delicate hints to *them*. A man who is gross in a woman's company, ought to be knocked down with a club: for, like so many musical instruments, touch but a single wire, and the dear souls are sensible all over.

To be sure, Miss Rawlins learnedly said, playing with her fan, a casuist would give it that the matrimonial vow ought to supersede any other obligation.

Mrs. Moore, for her part, was of opinion that, if the lady owned herself to be a wife, she ought to behave *like* one.

Whatever be my luck, thought I, with this *all-eyed* fair one, any other woman in the world, from fifteen to five-and-twenty, would be mine upon my own terms before the morning.

And now that I may be at hand to take all advantages, I will endeavour, said I to myself, to make sure of good quarters.

I am your lodger, Mrs. Moore, in virtue of the earnest I have given you for these apartments, and for any one you can spare above for my servants: indeed for *all* you have to spare—for who knows what my spouse's brother may attempt? I will pay you your own demand; and that for a month or two certain (board included), as I shall or shall not be your hindrance. Take *that* as a pledge; or in part of payment—offering her a thirty pound bank-note.

She declined taking it; desiring she might consult the lady first; adding, that she doubted not my honour; and that she would not let her apartments to any other person, whom she knew not something of, while I and the lady were here.

The Lady! The Lady! from both the women's mouths continually (which still implied a doubt in their hearts): and not *Your spouse*, and *Your lady, sir*.

I never met with such women, thought I:—so thoroughly convinced but this moment, yet already doubting—I am afraid I have a couple of sceptics to deal with.

I knew no reason, I said, for my wife to object to my lodging in the same house with her here, any more than in town at Mrs. Sinclair's. But were she to make such objection, I would not quit possession; since it was not unlikely that the same freakish disorder which brought her to Hampstead, might carry her absolutely out of my knowledge.

They both seemed embarrassed; and looked upon one another; yet with such an air as if they thought there was reason in what I said. And I declared myself her boarder, as well as lodger; and dinner-time approaching, was not denied to be the former.

Letter VI—Mr. Lovelace to John Belford, Esq.

I THOUGHT it was now high time to turn my whole mind to my beloved; who had had full leisure to weigh the contents of the letters I had left with her.

I therefore requested Mrs. Moore to step in, and desire to know whether she would be pleased to admit me to attend her in her apartment, on occasion of the letters I had left with her; or whether she would favour me with her company in the dining-room?

Mrs. Moore desired Miss Rawlins to accompany her in to the lady. They tapped at her door, and were both admitted.

I cannot but stop here for one minute to remark, though against myself, upon that security which innocence gives, that nevertheless had better have in it a greater mixture of the serpent with the dove. For here, heedless of all I could say behind her back, because she was satisfied with her own worthiness, she permitted me to go on with my own story, without interruption, to persons as great strangers to her as to me; and who, as strangers to *both*, might be supposed to lean to the side most injured: and that, as I managed it, was to mine. A dear silly soul, thought I at the time, to depend upon the goodness of her own heart, when the heart cannot be seen into but by its actions; and she, to appearance, a runaway, an eloper, from a tender, a most indulgent husband! To neglect to cultivate the opinions of individuals, when the whole world is governed by appearance!

Yet, what can be expected of an angel under twenty? She has a world of knowledge; knowledge *speculative*, as I may say; but no *experience*! How should she? Knowledge by theory only is a vague uncertain light: a will-o'-the-wisp, which as often misleads the doubting mind as puts it right.

There are many things in the world, could a moralizer say, that would afford inexpressible pleasure to a reflecting mind, were it not for the mixture they come to us with. To be graver

still; I have seen parents [perhaps my own did so] who delighted
in those very qualities in their children while young, the natural
consequences of which (too much indulged and encouraged) made
them, as they grew up, the plague of their hearts.—To bring
this home to my present purpose, I must tell thee that I adore
this charming creature for her vigilant prudence; but yet I
would not, methinks, wish her, by virtue of that prudence,
which is, however, necessary to carry her above the *devices* of
all the rest of the world, to be too wise for *mine*.

My revenge, my *sworn* revenge, is nevertheless (adore her as I
will) uppermost in my heart. Miss Howe says, that my love is
an *Herodian* love[1]: by my soul, that girl's a witch! I am half-
sorry to say, *that I find a pleasure in playing the tyrant over what
I love*. Call it an ungenerous pleasure, if thou wilt: softer hearts
than mine know it. The women to a woman know it, and *show*
it too, whenever they are trusted with power. And why should
it be thought strange, that I, who love them so dearly, and
study them so much, should catch the infection of them?

Letter VII—*Mr. Lovelace to John Belford, Esq.*

I will now give thee the substance of the dialogue that passed
between the two women and the lady.

Wonder not that a perverse wife makes a listening husband.
The event, however, as thou wilt find, justified the old observation, *That listeners seldom hear good of themselves*. Conscious of
their own demerits, if I may guess by myself [there's ingenuousness, Jack!], and fearful of censure, they seldom find
themselves disappointed. There is something of sense, after all,
in these proverbs, in these phrases, in this *wisdom of nations*.

Mrs. Moore was to be the messenger; but Miss Rawlins began
the dialogue.

Your spouse, madam—[Devil!—Only to fish for a negative
or affirmative declaration.]

Cl. My *spouse*, madam——

Miss R. Mr. Lovelace, madam, avers that you are married
to him; and begs admittance, or your company in the dining-
room, to talk upon the subject of the letters he left with you.

Cl. He is a poor wicked wretch. Let me beg of you, madam,
to favour me with your company as often as possible while he is
hereabouts, and I remain here.

[1] See p. 10.

Miss R. I shall with pleasure attend you, madam. But, methinks, I could wish you would *see* the gentleman, and hear what he has to say on the subject of the letters.

Cl. My case is a hard, a very hard one—I am quite bewildered! —I know not what to do! I have not a friend in the world that can or will help me! Yet had none *but* friends till I knew *that man*!

Miss R. The gentleman neither looks nor talks like a bad man. —Not a *very* bad man; as men go.

As men go! Poor Miss Rawlins, thought I!—And dost thou know, *how men go*?

Cl. O madam, you know him not! He can put on the appearance of an angel of light; but has a black, a very black heart!

Poor I!

Miss R. I could not have thought it, truly! But men are very deceitful nowadays.

Nowadays!—A fool!—Have not her history books told her that they were always so?

Mrs. Moore [sighing]. I have found it so, I am sure, to my cost!

Who knows but in her time, poor goody Moore may have met with a Lovelace, or a Belford, or some such vile fellow? My little harum-scarum beauty knows not what strange histories every woman living, who has had the least independence of will, could tell her, were such to be as communicative as she is. But here 's the thing; I have given her cause enough of offence; but not enough to make her hold her tongue.

Cl. As to the letters he has left with me, I know not what to say to *them*: but am resolved never to have anything to say to *him*.

Miss R. If, madam, I may be allowed to say so, I think you carry matters very far.

Cl. Has he been making a bad cause a good one with you, madam? That he can do with those who know him not. Indeed I heard him talking, though not what he said, and am indifferent about it. But what account does he give of himself?

I was pleased to hear this. To arrest, to stop her passion, thought I, in the height of its career, is a charming presage.

Then the busy Miss Rawlins fished on, to find out from her either a *confirmation* or *disavowal* of my story. Was Lord M. my uncle? Did I court her at first with the allowance of her friends, her brother excepted? Had I a rencounter with that brother? Was she so persecuted in favour of a very disagreeable man, one Solmes, as to induce her to throw herself into my protection?

None of these were denied. All the objections she *could* have made were stifled, or kept in, by the consideration (as she mentioned) that she should stay there but a little while; and that her story was too long. But Miss Rawlins would not be thus easily answered.

Miss R. He says, madam, that he could not prevail for marriage, till he had consented, under a solemn oath, to separate beds, while your family remained unreconciled.

Cl. Oh, the wretch! What can be still in his head, to endeavour to pass these stories upon strangers?

So no direct denial, thought I! Admirable! All will do by and by!

Miss R. He has owned that an accidental fire had frightened you very much on Wednesday night, and that—and that—and that — an accidental fire had frightened you — very much frightened you—last Wednesday night!

Then, after a short pause: In short, he owned that he had taken some innocent liberties, which might have led to a breach of the oath you had imposed upon him: and that this was the cause of your displeasure.

I would have been glad to see how my charmer then looked. To be sure she was at a loss in her own mind to justify herself for resenting so highly an offence so trifling. She hesitated—did not presently speak—when she did, she wished that she, Miss Rawlins, might never meet with any man who would take such innocent liberties with *her*.

Miss Rawlins pushed further.

Your case, to be sure, madam, is very particular. But if the hope of a reconciliation with your own friends is made more distant by your leaving him, give me leave to say, that 'tis pity —'tis pity—[I suppose the maiden then primmed, fanned, and blushed;—'tis pity] the oath cannot be dispensed with; especially as he owns he has not been so strict a liver.

I could have gone in and kissed the girl.

Cl. You have heard *his* story. Mine, as I told you before, is too long, and too melancholy; my disorder on seeing the wretch is too great; and my time here is too short, for me to enter upon it. And if he has any end to serve by his own vindication, in which I shall not be a *personal* sufferer, let him make himself appear as white as an angel; with all my heart.

III—*C 884

My love for her, and the excellent character I gave her, were then pleaded.

Cl. Specious seducer! Only tell me if I cannot get away from him by some back way?

How my heart then went *pit-a-pat!* to speak in the female dialect.

Cl. Let me look out. [I heard the sash lifted up.] Whither does that path lead to? Is there no possibility of getting to a coach? Surely he must deal with some fiend, or how could he have found me out? Cannot I steal to some neighbouring house, where I may be concealed till I can get quite away? You are good people! I have not been always among such! Oh, help me, help me, ladies [with a voice of impatience], or I am ruined!

Then pausing: Is that the way to Hendon? [pointing, I suppose]. Is Hendon a private place? The Hampstead coach, I am told, will carry passengers thither.

Mrs. Moore. I have an honest friend at Mill Hill [devil fetch her! thought I]; where, if such be your determination, madam, and if you think yourself in danger, you may be safe, I believe.

Cl. Any-whither, if I can but escape from *this man*! Whither does that path lead to, out yonder? What is that town on the right hand called?

Mrs. M. Highgate, madam.

Miss R. On the side of the heath is a little village called North End. A kinswoman of mine lives there. But her house is small. I am not sure she could accommodate such a lady.

Devil take *her* too! thought I. I imagined that I had made myself a better interest in these women. But the whole sex love plotting—and plotters too, Jack.

Cl. A barn, an outhouse, a garret, will be a palace to me, if it will but afford me a refuge from *this man*!

Her senses, thought I, are much livelier than *mine*. What a devil have I done, that she should be so *very* implacable! I told thee, Belford, all I did: was there anything in it so *very* much amiss! Such prospects of family reconciliation before her too! To be sure she is a very *sensible* lady!

She then espied my new servant walking under the window, and asked if he were not one of mine?

Will was on the look-out for old Grimes [so is the fellow called whom my beloved has dispatched to Miss Howe]. And being told that the man she saw *was* my servant; I see, said she, that there is no escaping, unless you, madam [to Miss Rawlins, I suppose], can befriend me till I can get farther. I have no doubt that that fellow is planted about the house to watch my steps. But the wicked wretch his master has no *right to control me*. He shall not hinder me from going whither I please. I will raise the town upon him, if he molests me. Dear ladies, is there no back door for me to get out at while you hold him in talk?

Miss R. Give me leave to ask you, madam, is there no room to hope for accommodation? Had you not better see him? He certainly loves you dearly: he is a fine gentleman: you may exasperate him and make matters more unhappy for yourself.

Cl. O Mrs. Moore, O Miss Rawlins! you know not the man! I wish not to see his face, nor to exchange another word with him as long as I live.

Mrs. Moore. I don't find, Miss Rawlins, that the gentleman has misrepresented anything. You see, madam [to my Clarissa], how respectful he is; not to come in till permitted. He certainly loves you dearly. Pray, madam, let him talk to you as he wishes to do, on the subject of the letters.

Very kind of Mrs. Moore. Mrs. Moore, thought I, is a very good woman. I did not curse her then.

Miss Rawlins said something; but so low, that I could not hear what it was. Thus it was answered.

Cl. I am greatly distressed! I know not what to do! But, Mrs. Moore, be so good as to give his letters to him—here they are. Be pleased to tell him that I wish him and Lady Betty and Miss Montague a happy meeting. He never can want excuses to them for what has happened, any more than pretences to those he would delude. Tell him that he has ruined me in the opinion of my own friends. I am for that reason the less solicitous how I appear to his.

Mrs. Moore then came to me; and I, being afraid that something would pass meantime between the other two, which I should not like, took the letters and entered the room, and found them retired into the closet; my beloved whispering with an air of earnestness to Miss Rawlins, who was all attention.

Her back was towards me; and Miss Rawlins, by pulling her sleeve, giving intimation of my being there—Can I have no retirement uninvaded, sir? said she, with indignation, as if she were interrupted in some talk her heart was in. What business have you here, or with me? You have your letters; have you not?

Lovel. I have, my dear; and let me beg of you to consider what you are about. I every moment expect Captain Tomlinson here. Upon my soul, I do. He has promised to keep from your uncle what has happened: but what will he think if he find you hold in this strange humour?

Cl. I will endeavour, sir, to have patience with you for a moment or two, while I ask you a few questions before this lady, and before Mrs. Moore [who just then came in], both of whom you have prejudiced in your favour by your specious stories:—Will you say, sir, that we are married together? Lay your hand upon your heart, and answer me, am I your wedded wife?

I am gone too far, thought I, to give up for such a push as this, home one as it is.

My dearest soul! how can you put such a question? Is it either for *your* honour or *my own*, that it should be doubted? Surely, surely, madam, you cannot have attended to the contents of Captain Tomlinson's letter.

She complained often of want of spirits throughout our whole contention, and of weakness of person and mind, from the fits she had been thrown into: but little reason had *she* for this complaint, as I thought, who was able to hold me to it, as she did. I own that I was excessively concerned for her several times.

You and I! *Vilest of men——*

My name is Lovelace, madam——

Therefore it is that I call you the *vilest of men.* [Was this pardonable, Jack?]. *You* and *I* know the truth, the *whole* truth. I want not to clear up my reputation with these gentlewomen: that is already lost with every one I had most reason to value: but let me have this *new* specimen of what you are capable of— say, wretch (say, Lovelace, if thou hadst rather), art thou really and truly my wedded husband? Say! answer without hesitation.

She trembled with impatient indignation; but had a wildness in her manner, which I took some advantage of, in order to parry this cursed thrust. And a cursed thrust it was; since, had I positively averred it, she never would have believed anything I said: and had I owned that I was not married, I had destroyed my own plot, as well with the women as with her; and could have no pretence for pursuing her, or hindering her from going whithersoever she pleased. Not that I was ashamed to aver it, had it been consistent with policy. I would not have thee think me such a milksop neither.

Lovel. My dearest love, how wildly you talk! What would you *have* me answer? Is it necessary that I *should* answer? May I not re-appeal this to your own breast, as well as to Captain

Tomlinson's treaty and letter? You know yourself how matters stand between us.—And Captain Tomlinson——

Cl. O wretch! Is this an answer to my question? Say, are we married, or are we not?

Lovel. What *makes a marriage*, we all know. If it be the union of two hearts [there was a turn, Jack!], to my utmost grief, I must say we are *not*; since now I see you hate me. If it be the completion of marriage, to my confusion and regret, I must own we are *not*. But, my dear, will you be pleased to consider what answer half a dozen people whence you came could give to your question? And do not now, in *the disorder of your mind*, and in the height of passion, bring into question before these gentle-women a point you have acknowledged before those who know us better.

I would have whispered her about the treaty with her uncle, and about the contents of the captain's letter; but, retreating and with a rejecting hand, Keep thy distance, *man*, cried the dear insolent—to thy own heart I appeal, since thou evadest me thus pitifully! I own no marriage with thee!—Bear witness, ladies, I do not. And cease to torment me, cease to follow me. Surely, surely, faulty as I have been, I have not deserved to be *thus* persecuted! I resume, therefore, my former language: you have no right to pursue me: you *know* you have not: begone, then; and leave me to make the best of my hard lot. O my dear cruel father! said she, in a violent fit of grief [falling upon her knees, and clasping her uplifted hands together], thy heavy curse is completed upon thy devoted daughter! I am *punished*, dread-fully punished, *by the very wretch in whom I had placed my wicked confidence!*

By my soul, Belford, the little witch with her words, but more by her manner, moved *me!* Wonder not then, that her action, her grief, her tears, set the women into the like compassionate manifestations.

Had I not a cursed task of it?

The two women withdrew to the farther end of the room, and whispered—A strange case! There is no frenzy here—I just heard said.

The charming creature threw her handkerchief over her head and neck, continuing kneeling, her back towards me, and her face hid upon a chair, and repeatedly sobbed with grief and passion.

I took this opportunity to step to the women, to keep them steady.

You see, ladies [whispering], what an unhappy man I am! You see what a spirit this dear creature has! All, all owing to her implacable relations, and to her father's curse. A curse upon them all; they have turned the head of the most charming woman in the world!

Ah! sir, sir, replied Miss Rawlins, whatever be the fault of her relations, all is not as it should be between you and her. 'Tis plain she does not think herself married: 'tis *plain* she does not: and if you have any value for the poor lady, and would not totally deprive her of her senses, you had better withdraw, and leave to time and cooler consideration the event in your favour.

She will compel me to this at last, I fear, Miss Rawlins; I *fear* she will; and then we are both undone: for I cannot live without her; she knows it too well: and she has not a friend who will look upon her: this also she knows. Our marriage, when her uncle's friend comes, will be proved incontestably. But I am ashamed to think I have given her room to believe it no marriage: that's what she harps upon!

Well, 'tis a strange case, a very strange one, said Miss Rawlins; and was going to say further, when the angry beauty, coming towards the door, said, Mrs. Moore, I beg a word with you. And they both stepped into the dining-room.

I saw her, just before, put a parcel into her pocket, and followed them out, for fear she should slip away; and stepping to the stairs, that she *might not go by me*, Will, cried I, aloud [though I knew he was not near]. Pray, child, to a maid who answered, call either of my servants to me.

She then came up to me with a wrathful countenance: Do you call your servant, sir, to hinder me, between you, from going whither I please?

Don't, my dearest life, misinterpret everything I do. Can you think me so mean and so unworthy as to employ a servant to constrain you? I call him to send to the public-houses, or inns in this town, to inquire after Captain Tomlinson, who may have alighted at some one of them, and be now, perhaps, needlessly adjusting his dress; and I would have him come, were he to be without clothes, God forgive me! for I am stabbed to the heart by your cruelty.

Answer was returned that neither of my servants was in the way.

Not in the way, said I! Whither can the dogs be gone?

O sir! with a scornful air; not far, I'll warrant. One of them was under the window just now; according to order, I suppose, to watch my steps. But I will do what I please and go whither I please; and that to your face.

God forbid that I should hinder you in anything that you may do with safety to yourself!

Now I verily believe that her design was to slip out in pursuance of the closet-whispering between her and Miss Rawlins; perhaps to Miss Rawlins's house.

She then stepped back to Mrs. Moore and gave her something, which proved to be a diamond ring, and desired her (not whisperingly, but with an air of defiance to me) that that might be a pledge for her till she defrayed her demands; which she should soon find means to do; having no more money about her than she might have occasion for before she came to an acquaintance's.

Mrs. Moore would have declined taking it; but she would not be denied; and then, wiping her eyes, she put on her gloves. Nobody has a right to stop me, said she! I *will* go! Whom should I be afraid of? Her very question, charming creature! testifying her fear.

I beg pardon, madam [turning to Mrs. Moore, and curtsying], for the trouble I have given you. I beg pardon, madam, to Miss Rawlins [curtsying likewise to her]. You may both hear of me in a happier hour, if such a one fall to my lot—and God bless you both!—struggling with her tears till she sobbed—and away was tripping.

I stepped to the door: I put it to; and setting my back against it, took her struggling hand.—My dearest life! My angel! said I, why will you thus distress me? Is this the forgiveness which you so solemnly promised?

Unhand me, sir! You have no business with me! You have no right over me! You *know* you have not.

But whither, whither, my dearest love, would you go? Think you not that I will follow you, were it to the world's end? Whither would you go?

Well do you ask me, whither I would go, who have been the occasion that I have not a friend left! But God, who knows my innocence and my upright intentions, will not wholly abandon me when I am out of your power; but while in it, I cannot expect a gleam of the Divine grace or favour to reach me.

How severe is this! How shockingly severe! Out of *your* presence, my angry fair one! I can neither hope for the one nor the other. As my Cousin Montague, in the letter you have read, observes, you are my pole-star and my guide; and if ever I am to be happy, either here or hereafter, it must be in and by you.

She would then have opened the door. But I respectfully opposing her, Begone, man! Begone, Mr. Lovelace, said she: stop not my way. If you would not that I should attempt the window, give me passage by the door; for, once more, you have *no right to detain me.*

Your resentments, my dearest life, I will own to be well grounded. I will acknowledge that I have been all in fault. On my knee [and down I dropped] I ask your pardon. And can you refuse to ratify your own *promise?* Look forward to the happy prospect before us. See you not my Lord M. and Lady Sarah longing to bless *you,* for blessing me, and their whole family? Can you take no pleasure in the promised visit of Lady Betty and my Cousin Montague? And in the protection *they* offer you, if you are dissatisfied with *mine?* Have you no wish to see your uncle's friend? Stay only till Captain Tomlinson comes. Receive from him the news of your uncle's compliance with the wishes of both.

She seemed altogether distressed; was ready to sink; and forced to lean against the wainscot as I kneeled at her feet. A stream of tears at last burst from her less indignant eyes. Good Heaven, said she, lifting up her lovely face, and clasped hands, what is at last to be my destiny! Deliver me from this dangerous man; and direct me! I know not what I do; what I can do; nor what I ought to do!

The women, as I had owned our marriage to be but half completed, heard nothing in this whole scene to contradict (not flagrantly to contradict) what I had asserted: they believed they saw in her returning temper and staggered resolution, a love for me, which her indignation had before suppressed; and they joined to persuade her to tarry till the captain came, and to hear his proposals; representing the dangers to which she would be exposed; the fatigues she might endure; a lady of her appearance, unguarded, unprotected. On the other hand, they dwelt upon my declared contrition, and on my promises; for the performance of which they offered to be bound. So much had my kneeling humility affected them.

Women, Jack, tacitly acknowlege the inferiority of their sex, in the pride they take to behold a kneeling lover at their feet.

She turned from me and threw herself into a chair.

I arose, and approached her with reverence. My dearest creature, said I—and was proceeding—but with a face glowing with conscious dignity, she interrupted me — Ungenerous, ungrateful Lovelace! You know not the value of the heart you have insulted! Nor can you conceive how much my soul despises your meanness. But meanness must ever be the portion of the man who can act vilely!

The women, believing we were likely to be on better terms, retired. The dear perverse opposed their going; but they saw I was desirous of their absence. And when they had withdrawn, I once more threw myself at her feet, and acknowledged my offences; implored her forgiveness for this one time, and promised exactest circumspection for the future.

It was impossible for her, she said, to keep her *memory* and *forgive* me. What hadst thou *seen* in the conduct of Clarissa Harlowe, that should encourage such an insult upon her, as thou didst dare to make? How meanly must thou think of *her*, that *thou* couldst presume to be so guilty, and expect *her* to be so weak as to forgive thee?

I besought her to let me read over to her Captain Tomlinson's letter. I was sure it was impossible she could have given it the requisite attention.

I *have* given it the requisite attention, said she; and the other letters, too. So that what I say is upon deliberation. And what have I to fear from my brother and sister? They can but *complete* the ruin of my fortunes with my father and uncles. Let them, and welcome. You, sir, I thank you, have lowered my fortunes; but I bless God that my mind is not sunk with my fortunes. It is, on the contrary, raised above fortune, and above you; and for half a word they shall have the estate they have envied me for, and an acquittal from me of all expectations from my family that may make them uneasy.

I lifted up my hands and eyes in silent admiration of her.

My brother, sir, may think me ruined. To the praise of *your* character, he may think it impossible to be with *you* and be innocent. You have but too well justified their harshest censures by every part of your conduct. But now that I have escaped from you, and that I am out of the reach of your mysterious devices, I will wrap myself up in mine own innocence [and then the passionate beauty folded her arms about herself], and leave to time, and to my future circumspection, the re-establishment of my character. Leave me then, sir, pursue me not!——

Good Heaven! interrupting her—and all this, for what? Had I *not* yielded to your entreaties (forgive me, madam), you could not have carried farther your resentments.

Wretch! Was it not crime enough to give *occasion* for those *entreaties*? Wouldst thou make a merit to me, that thou didst not utterly ruin *her* whom thou oughtest to have protected? Begone, man! turning from me, her face crimsoned over with passion. See me no more! I cannot bear thee in my sight!

Dearest, dearest creature!

If I forgive thee, Lovelace—and there she stopped. To endeavour, proceeded she, to endeavour, by *premeditation*, by *low contrivance*, by *cries of Fire!*—to terrify a poor creature who had consented to take a wretched chance with thee for life!

For Heaven's sake—offering to take her repulsing hand as she was flying from me towards the closet.

What hast thou to do, to plead the sake of Heaven in thy favour, O darkest of human minds!

Then turning *from me*, wiping her eyes, and again turning *towards me*, but her sweet face half aside, What difficulties hast thou involved me in! *Thou that hadst a plain path before thee,* after thou hadst betrayed me into thy power. At once my mind takes in the whole of thy crooked behaviour; and if thou thinkest of Clarissa Harlowe as her proud heart tells her thou oughtest to think of her, thou wilt seek thy fortunes elsewhere. How often hast thou provoked me to tell thee that my soul is above thee?

For Heaven's sake, madam, for a soul's sake, which it is in your power to save from perdition, forgive me the past offence. I am the greatest villain on earth, if it was a premeditated one. Yet I presume not to excuse myself. On your mercy I throw myself. I will not offer any plea, but that of penitence. See but Captain Tomlinson. See but Lady Betty and my cousin; let *them* plead for me; let *them* be guarantees for my honour.

If Captain Tomlinson come while I stay here, I may see *him*. But as for *you*, sir——

Dearest creature! let me beg of you not to aggravate my offence to the captain when he comes. Let me beg of you——

What askest thou? Is it not that I shall be a party against myself? That I shall palliate——

Do not charge me, madam, interrupted I, with villainous premeditation! Do not give such a construction to my offence as may weaken your uncle's opinion—as may strengthen your brother's——

She flung from me to the farther end of the room [*she could go no farther*]; and just then Mrs. Moore came up, and told her

that dinner was ready; and that she had prevailed upon Miss
Rawlins to give her her company.

You must excuse me, Mrs. Moore, said she. Miss Rawlins I
hope also will—but I cannot eat—I cannot go down. As you
you, sir, I suppose you will think it right to depart hence; at least
till the gentleman comes whom you expect.

I respectfully withdrew into the next room, that Mrs. Moore
might acquaint her (I durst not myself) that I was her lodger and
boarder, as (whisperingly) I desired she would: and meeting Miss
Rawlins in the passage, Dearest Miss Rawlins, said I, stand my
friend: join with Mrs. Moore to pacify my spouse, if she has any
new flights upon my having taken lodgings, and intending to
board here. I hope she will have more generosity than to
think of hindering a gentlewoman from letting her lodgings.

I suppose Mrs. Moore (whom I left with my fair one) had
apprised her of this before Miss Rawlins went in; for I heard her
say, while I withheld Miss Rawlins—"No, indeed: he is much
mistaken—surely he does not think I will."

They both expostulated with her, as I could gather from bits
and scraps of what they said; for they spoke so low that I could
not hear any distinct sentence, but from the fair perverse, whose
anger made her louder. And to this purpose I heard her deliver
herself in answer to different parts of their talk to her: "Good
Mrs. Moore, dear Miss Rawlins, press me no further—I cannot
sit down at table with him!"

They said something, as I suppose in my behalf. "Oh, the
insinuating wretch! What defence have I against a man, who,
go where I will, can turn every one, even of the virtuous of my
sex, in his favour?"

After something else said, which I heard not distinctly,
"This is execrable cunning! Were you to know his wicked heart,
he is not without hope of engaging you two good persons to
second him in the vilest of his machinations."

How came it (thought I at the instant) by all this penetration? My devil surely does not play me booty. If I thought he
did, I would marry, and live honest, to be even with him.

I suppose then they urged the plea which I hinted to Miss
Rawlins at going in, that she would not be Mrs. Moore's
hindrance; for thus she expressed herself—"He will no doubt
pay you your own price. You need not question his liberality.
But one house cannot hold us. Why, if it would, did I fly from
him, to seek refuge among strangers?"

Then in answer to somewhat else they pleaded—"'Tis a

mistake, madam; I am *not* reconciled to him. I will believe nothing he says. Has he not given you a flagrant specimen of what a man he is, and of what he is capable, by the disguises you saw him in? My story is too long, and my stay here will be but short; or I could convince you that my resentments against him are but too well founded."

I suppose then that they pleaded for *her* leave for *my* dining with them: for she said; "I have nothing to say to that. It is your own house, Mrs. Moore. It is your own table. You may admit whom you please to it. Only leave me at my liberty to choose my company."

Then in answer, as I suppose, to their offer of sending her up a plate—"A bit of bread, if you please, and a glass of water: that 's all I can swallow at present. I am really very much discomposed. Saw you not how bad I was? Indignation only could have supported my spirits!"

"I have no objection to his dining with you, madam," added she, in reply, I suppose, to a further question of the same nature. "But I will not stay a night in the house where he lodges."

I presume Miss Rawlins had told her that she would not stay dinner, for she said, "Let me not deprive Mrs. Moore of your company, Miss Rawlins. You will not be displeased with his talk. He can have no design upon you."

Then I suppose they pleaded what I might say behind her back, to make my own story good. "I care not what he says, or what he thinks of *me*. Repentance and amendment are all the harm I wish him, whatever becomes of me!"

By her accent, she wept when she spoke these last words.

They came out both of them wiping their eyes; and would have persuaded me to relinquish the lodgings, and to depart till her uncle's friend came. But I knew better. I did not care to trust the devil, well as she and Miss Howe suppose me to be acquainted with him, for finding her out again, if once more she escaped me.

What I am most afraid of is, that she will throw herself among her own relations; and if she does, I am confident they will not be able to withstand her affecting eloquence. But yet, as thou'lt see, the captain's letter to me is admirably calculated to obviate my apprehensions on this score; particularly in that passage where it is said, that her uncle thinks not himself at liberty to correspond directly with her, or to receive applications from her, *but through Captain Tomlinson*, as is strongly implied.[1]

[1] See p. 55.

I must own (notwithstanding the revenge I have so solemnly vowed) that I would very fain have made for her a merit with myself *in her returning favour*, and have owed as little as possible to the mediation of Captain Tomlinson. My pride was concerned in this: and this was one of my reasons for not bringing him with me. Another was that if I were obliged to have recourse to his assistance, I should be better able (by visiting her without him) to direct him what to say or to do, as I should find out the turn of her humour.

I was, however, glad at my heart that Mrs. Moore came up so seasonably with notice that dinner was ready. The fair fugitive was all in all. She had the game in her own hands; and by giving me so good an excuse for withdrawing, I had time to strengthen myself; the captain had time to come; and the lady to cool. Shakespeare advises well:

> Oppose not Rage, while Rage is in its force;
> But give it way awhile, and let it waste.
> The rising deluge is not stopt with dams;
> Those it o'erbears, and drowns the hope of harvest.
> But, wisely manag'd, its divided strength
> Is sluic'd in channels, and securely drain'd:
> And when its force is spent, and unsupply'd,
> The residue with mounds may be restrain'd,
> And dry-shod we may pass the naked ford.

I went down with the women to dinner. Mrs. Moore sent her fair boarder up a plate; but she only ate a little bit of bread, and drank a glass of water. I doubted not but she would keep her word, when it was once gone out. Is she not an Harlowe? She seems to be inuring herself to hardships, which at the worst she can never know; since, though she should ultimately refuse to be obliged to me, or (to express myself more suitably to my own heart) to *oblige me*, every one who sees her must befriend her.

But let me ask thee, Belford, art thou not solicitous for me in relation to the contents of the letter which the angry beauty has written and dispatched away by man and horse; and for what may be Miss Howe's answer to it? Art thou not ready to inquire, whether it be not likely that Miss Howe, when she knows of her saucy friend's flight, will be concerned about her letter, which she must know could not be at Wilson's till after that flight; and so, probably, would fall into my hands?

All these things, as thou 'lt see in the sequel, are provided for with as much contrivance as human foresight can admit.

I have already told thee that Will is upon the look-out for old Grimes. Old Grimes is it seems a gossiping, sottish rascal; and if Will can but light of him, I 'll answer for the consequence: for has not Will been my servant upwards of seven years?

Letter VIII—Mr. Lovelace. [In continuation]

WE had at dinner, besides Miss Rawlins, a young widow-niece of Mrs. Moore, who is come to stay a month with her aunt—*Bevis* her name; very forward, very lively, and a great admirer of *me*, I assure you; hanging smirkingly upon all I said; and prepared to approve of every word before I spoke: and who, by the time we had half dined (by the help of what she had collected before), was as much acquainted with our story as either of the other two.

As it behoved me to prepare them in my favour against whatever might come from Miss Howe, I improved upon the hint I had thrown out above-stairs against that mischief-making lady. I represented her to be an arrogant creature, revengeful, artful, enterprising, and one who, had she been a man, would have sworn and cursed, and committed rapes, and played the devil, as far as I knew [*I have no doubt of it, Jack*]: but who, nevertheless, by advantage of a female education, and pride and insolence, I believed was *personally* virtuous.

Mrs. Bevis allowed that there was a *vast deal* in education— and in *pride* too, she said. While Miss Rawlins came with a prudish, God forbid that virtue should be owing to education only! However, I declared that Miss Howe was a subtle contriver of mischief; one who had always been *my* enemy: her motives I knew not: but despising the man whom her mother was desirous she should have, one Hickman; although I did not directly aver that she would rather have had me; yet they all immediately imagined that *that* was the ground of her animosity to me, and of her envy to my beloved; and it was a pity, they said, that so fine a young lady did not see through such a pretended friend.

And yet nobody (added I) has more reason than she to know by *experience* the force of a hatred founded in envy; as I hinted to *you* above, Mrs. Moore, and to *you*, Miss Rawlins, in the case of her sister Arabella.

I had compliments made to my person and talents on this occasion; which gave me a singular opportunity of displaying my modesty, by disclaiming the merit of them, with a *No, indeed!—I should be very vain, ladies, if I thought so.* While thus abasing myself, and exalting Miss Howe, I got their opinion both for modesty and generosity; and had all the graces which I disclaimed thrown in upon me besides.

In short, they even oppressed that modesty, which (to speak modestly of myself) their praises *created*, by disbelieving all I said against myself.

And, truly, I must needs say, they have almost persuaded even me myself, that Miss Howe is actually in love with me. I have often been willing to hope this. And who knows but she may? The captain and I have agreed that it shall be so insinuated *occasionally*. And what's thy opinion, Jack? She certainly hates Hickman: and girls who are *disengaged* seldom *hate*, though they may not *love*: and if she had rather have *another*, why not that *other* ME? For am I not a smart fellow, and a rake? And do not your sprightly ladies love your smart fellows, and your rakes? And where is the wonder, that the man who could engage the affections of Miss Harlowe, should engage those of a lady (with her[1] *alas's*) who would be honoured in being deemed her second?

Nor accuse thou me of SINGULAR vanity in this presumption, Belford. Wert thou to know the secret vanity that lurks in the hearts of those who *disguise* or *cloak it best*, thou wouldst find great reason to acquit, at least, to allow for, *me*: since it is generally the *conscious over-fulness of conceit* that makes the hypocrite most upon his guard to conceal it. Yet with these fellows, proudly humble as they are, it will break out sometimes in spite of their cloaks, though but in self-denying, compliment-begging self-degradation.

But now I have undervalued myself, in apologizing to thee on this occasion, let me use another argument in favour of my observation, that the ladies generally prefer a rake to a sober man; and of my presumption upon it, that Miss Howe is in love with me. It is this: Common fame says, that Hickman is a very virtuous, a very innocent fellow—a *male-virgin*, I warrant!— An odd dog I always thought him. Now women, Jack, like not novices. *Two maidenheads meeting together in wedlock, the first child must be a fool,* is their common aphorism. They are pleased with a love of the sex that is founded in the *knowledge of it*. Reason good; novices expect more than they can possibly find in the commerce with them. The man who knows them, yet has *ardours* for them, to borrow a word from Miss Howe,[2] though those ardours are generally owing more to the *devil*

---

[1] See p. 11 where Miss Howe says, *Alas, my dear, I knew you loved him!*
[2] See vol. ii, pp. 292, 317.

within him, than to the witch *without* him, is the man who makes them the highest and most grateful compliment. He knows *what to expect*, and *with what to be satisfied*.

Then the merit of a woman, in some cases, must be *ignorance*, whether *real* or *pretended*. The man, in *these* cases, must be an *adept*. Will it then be wondered at, that a woman prefers a libertine to a novice? While she expects in the one the confidence *she* wants, she considers the other and herself as two parallel lines; which, though they run side by side, can never meet.

Yet in this the sex is generally mistaken too; for these sheepish fellows are sly. I myself was modest once; and this, as I have elsewhere hinted to thee,[1] has better enabled me to judge of both sexes.

But to proceed with my narrative:

Having thus prepared every one against any letter that should come from Miss Howe, and against my beloved's messenger's return, I thought it proper to conclude that subject with a hint that my spouse could not bear to have anything said *that reflected upon Miss Howe*; and with a deep sigh, added, that I had been made very unhappy more than once by the ill-will of ladies whom I had never offended.

The widow Bevis believed that might very easily be.

These hints within doors, joined with others to Will both without and within [for I intend he shall fall in love with widow Moore's maid, and have saved one hundred pounds in my service, at least], will be great helps, as things may happen.

Letter IX—Mr. Lovelace. [In continuation]

WE had hardly dined, when my coachman, who kept a look-out for Captain Tomlinson, as Will did for old Grimes, conducted hither that worthy gentleman, attended by one servant, *both* on horseback. He alighted. I went out to meet him at the door.

Thou knowest his solemn appearance, and unblushing freedom; and yet canst not imagine what a dignity the rascal assumed, nor how respectful to him I was.

I led him into the parlour, and presented him to the women, and them to him. I thought it highly imported me (as they might still have some diffidences about our marriage, from my fair one's home-pushed questions on that head) to convince them entirely of the truth of all I had asserted. And how could I do this better, than by dialoguing a little with him before them?

[1] See vol. ii, p. 55.

Dear captain, I thought you long; for I have had a terrible conflict with my spouse.

Capt. I am sorry that I am later than my intention—my account with my banker [there's a dog, Jack!] took me up longer time to adjust than I had foreseen [all the time pulling down and stroking his ruffles]: for there was a small difference between us—only twenty pounds, indeed, which I had taken no account of.

The rascal has not seen twenty pounds of his own these ten years.

Then had we between us the characters of the Harlowe family: I railing against them all; the captain taking his dear friend Mr. John Harlowe's part; with a *Not so fast! Not so fast, young gentleman!* and the like free assumptions.

He accounted for *their* animosity by *my* defiances: no good family, having such a charming daughter, would care to be *defied,* instead of *courted*: he *must* speak his mind: never was a double-tongued man. He appealed to the ladies, if he were not right.

He got them of his side.

The correction I had given the brother, he told me, must have aggravated matters.

How valiant this made me look to the women! The sex love us mettled fellows at their hearts.

Be that as it would, I should never love any of the family but my spouse; and, wanting nothing from them, I would not, but for *her* sake, have gone so far as I *had* gone towards a reconciliation.

This was very good of me, Mrs. Moore said.

Very good indeed; Miss Rawlins.

Good! It is *more* than good; it is very generous, said the widow.

Capt. Why, so it is, I must needs say: for I am sensible that Mr. Lovelace has been rudely treated by them all—more rudely than it could have been imagined a man of his *quality* and *spirit* would have put up with. But then, sir [turning to me], I think you are amply rewarded in such a lady; and that you ought to forgive the father for the daughter's sake.

Mrs. Moore. Indeed so I think.

Miss R. So must every one think who has seen the lady.

Widow B. A fine lady, to be sure! But she has a violent spirit; and some very odd humours too, by what I have heard. The value of good husbands is not known till they are lost!

Her conscience then drew a sigh from her.

Lovel. Nobody must reflect upon my angel. An angel she is. Some little blemishes, indeed, as to her over-hasty spirit, and as to her unforgiving temper. But this she has from the Harlowes; instigated too by *that* Miss Howe. But her innumerable excellences are all her own.

Capt. Ay, talk of spirit, there 's a spirit, now you have named Miss Howe! [And so I led him to confirm all I had said of that vixen.] Yet she was to be pitied too; looking with meaning at me.

As I have already hinted, I had before agreed with him to impute secret love *occasionally* to Miss Howe, as the best means to invalidate all that might come from her in my disfavour.

Capt. Mr. Lovelace, but that I know your modesty, or *you* could give a reason——

Lovel. [looking down, and very modest]. I can't think so, captain—but let us call another cause.

Every woman present could look me in the face, so bashful was I.

Capt. Well, but as to our *present* situation—only it mayn't be proper—looking upon me, and round upon the women.

Lovel. O captain, you may say anything before this company —only, Andrew [to my new servant, who attended us at table], do you withdraw: this good girl [looking at the maidservant] will help us to all we want.

Away went Andrew: he wanted not his cue; and the maid seemed pleased at my honour's preference of her.

Capt. As to our *present* situation, I say, Mr. Lovelace—why, sir, we shall be all *untwisted*, let me tell you, if my friend Mr. John Harlowe were to know what *that* is. He would as much question the truth of your being married, as the rest of the family do.

Here the women perked up their ears; and were all silent attention.

Capt. I asked you before for particulars, Mr. Lovelace: but you *declined giving them.* Indeed it may not be *proper* for me to be acquainted with them. But I must own that it is past my comprehension that a wife can resent anything a husband can do (that is not a breach of the peace) so far as to think herself justified for *eloping* from him.

Lovel. Captain Tomlinson—sir—I do assure you, that I shall be offended—I shall be extremely concerned—if I hear that word *eloping* mentioned again.

Capt. Your nicety, and your love, sir, may make *you* take offence—-but it is my way to call everything by its proper name, let who will be offended.

Thou canst not imagine, Belford, how brave, and how independent, the rascal looked.

Capt. When, *young gentleman*, you shall think proper to give us particulars, we will find a word for this rash act in so admirable a lady, that shall please you better. You see, sir, that, being the representative of my dear friend Mr. John Harlowe, I speak as freely as I suppose *he* would do, if present. But you blush, sir—I beg your pardon, Mr. Lovelace: it becomes not a modest man to pry into those secrets which a modest man cannot reveal.

I did not blush, Jack; but denied not the compliment, and looked down: the women seemed delighted with my modesty: but the widow Bevis was more inclined to laugh at me than praise me for it.

Capt. Whatever be the cause of this step (I will not again, sir, call it *elopement*, since that harsh word wounds your tenderness), I cannot but express my surprise upon it, when I recollect the affectionate behaviour, which I was witness to between you, when I attended you last. *Over-love*, sir, I think you once mentioned—but *over-love* [smiling], give me leave to say, sir, is an odd cause of quarrel—few ladies——

Lovel. Dear captain! And I tried to blush.

The women also tried; and, being more used to it, succeeded better. Mrs. Bevis indeed has a red-hot countenance, and always blushes.

Miss R. It signifies nothing to mince the matter: but the lady above as good as denies her marriage. You *know*, sir, that she does; turning to me.

Capt. Denies her marriage! Heavens! how then have I imposed upon my dear friend Mr. John Harlowe!

Lovel. Poor dear! But let not her *veracity* be called in question. She would not be guilty of a wilful untruth for the world.

Then I had all their praises again.

Lovel. Dear creature!—she thinks she has reason for her denial. You know, Mrs. Moore; you know, Miss Rawlins; what I owned to you above, as to my vow.

I looked down, and, as once before, turned round my diamond ring.

Mrs. Moore looked awry; and with a leer at Miss Rawlins, as to her partner in the hinted-at reference.

Miss Rawlins looked down as well as I; her eyelids half-closed, as if mumbling a paternoster, meditating her snuff-box, the difference between her nose and chin lengthened by a close-shut mouth.

She put me in mind of the pious Mrs. Fetherstone at Oxford, whom I pointed out to thee once, among other grotesque figures, at St. Mary's Church, whither we went to take a view of her two sisters: her eyes shut, not daring to trust her heart with them open; and but just half rearing the lids, to see who the next comer was; and falling them again, when her curiosity was satisfied.

The widow Bevis gazed, as if on the hunt for a secret.

The captain looked archly, as if half in possession of one.

Mrs. Moore at last broke the bashful silence. Mrs. Lovelace's behaviour, she said, could be no otherwise so well accounted for, as by the ill offices of *that* Miss Howe; and by the severity of her relations; which might but too probably have affected her head a little at times: adding that it was very generous in me to give way to the storm when it was up, rather than to exasperate at such a time.

But let me tell you, sirs, said the widow Bevis, that is not what one husband in a thousand would have done.

I desired that *no part of this conversation might be hinted to my spouse*; and looked still more bashfully. Her great fault, I must own, was over-delicacy.

The captain leered round him; and said, he believed he could guess from the hints I had given him in town (of my *over-love*), and from what had now passed, that we had not consummated our marriage.

O Jack! how sheepishly then looked, or endeavoured to look, thy friend! how primly goody Moore! how affectedly Miss Rawlins!—while the honest widow Bevis gazed around her fearless; and though only simpering with her mouth, her eyes laughed outright, and seemed to challenge a laugh from every eye in the company.

He observed that I was a phœnix of a man, if so; and he could not but hope that all matters would be happily accommodated in a day or two; and that then he should have the pleasure to aver to her uncle, that he was present, as he might say, on our wedding-day.

The women seemed all to join in the same hope.

Ah, captain! Ah, ladies!—how happy should I be, if I could bring my dear spouse to be of the same mind!

It would be a very happy conclusion of a very knotty affair, said widow Bevis; and I see not why we may not make this very night a merry one.

The captain superciliously smiled at me. He saw plainly enough, he said, that we had been at *children's play* hitherto. A man of my character, who could give way to such a caprice as this, must have a prodigious value for his lady. But one thing he would venture to tell me; and that was this—that, however desirous young skittish ladies might be to have their way in this particular, it was a very bad setting-out for the man; as it gave his bride a very high proof of the power she had over him: and he would engage, that no woman, *thus* humoured, ever valued the man the more for it; but very much the contrary— and there were *reasons to be given why she should not.*

Well, well, captain, no more of this subject before the ladies. *One* feels [shrugging my shoulders in a bashful *try-to-blush* manner] that *one* is *so* ridiculous—I have been punished enough for my tender folly.

Miss Rawlins had taken her fan, and would needs hide her face behind it—I suppose because her blush was not quite ready.

Mrs. Moore hemmed, and looked down, and by that gave hers over.

While the jolly widow, laughing out, praised the captain as one of Hudibras's metaphysicians, repeating,

> He knew what's what, and that's as high
> As metaphysic wit can fly.

This made Miss Rawlins blush indeed:—Fie, fie, Mrs. Bevis! cried she, unwilling, I suppose, to be thought absolutely ignorant.

Upon the whole, I began to think that I had not made a bad exchange of our professing mother, for the unprofessing Mrs. Moore. And indeed the women and I, and my beloved too, all mean the same thing: we only differ about the manner of coming at the proposed end.

Letter X—Mr. Lovelace. [In continuation]

It was now high time to acquaint my spouse that Captain Tomlinson was come. And the rather, as the maid told us that the lady had asked her if such a gentleman [describing him] was not in the parlour?

Mrs. Moore went up, and requested, in my name, that she would give us audience.

But she returned, reporting my beloved's desire that Captain Tomlinson would excuse her for the present. She was very ill. Her spirits were too weak to enter into conversation with him; and she must lie down.

I was vexed, and at first extremely disconcerted. The captain was vexed too. And my concern, thou mayest believe, was the greater on *his account*.

She had been very much fatigued, I own. Her fits in the morning must have disordered her: and she had carried her resentment so high, that it was the less wonder she should find herself low, when her raised spirits had subsided. *Very* low, I may say; if sinkings are proportioned to risings; for she had been lifted up above the standard of a common mortal.

The captain, however, sent up in his own name, that if he could be admitted to drink one dish of tea with her, he should take it for a favour; and would go to town, and dispatch some necessary business, in order, if possible, to leave his morning free to attend her.

But she pleaded a violent headache; and Mrs. Moore confirmed the plea to be just.

I would have had the captain lodge there that night, as well in compliment to him, as introductory to my intention of entering myself upon my new-taken apartment: but his hours were of too much importance to him to stay the evening.

It was indeed very inconvenient for him, he said, to return in the morning; but he was willing to do all in his power to heal this breach, and that as well for the sakes of me and my lady, as for that of his dear friend Mr. John Harlowe; who must not know how far this misunderstanding had gone. He would therefore only drink one dish of tea with the ladies and me.

And accordingly, after he had done so, and I had had a little private conversation with him, he hurried away.

His fellow had given him, in the interim, a high character to Mrs. Moore's servants: and this reported by the widow Bevis (who, being no proud woman, is *hail fellow well met*, as the saying is, with all her aunt's servants) he was a *fine* gentleman, a *discreet* gentleman, a man of *sense* and *breeding*, with them all: and it was pity, that, with such great business upon his hands, he should be obliged to come again.

My life for yours, audibly whispered the widow Bevis, there is *humour* as well as *headache* in somebody's declining to see this worthy gentleman. Ah, Lord! how happy might some people be if they would!

No perfect happiness in this world, said I, very gravely, and with a sigh; for the widow must know that I heard her. If we have not *real* unhappiness, we can make it, even from the overflowings of our good fortune.

Very true, and, Very true, the two widows. A charming observation! Mrs. Bevis. Miss Rawlins smiled *her* assent to it; and I thought she called me in her heart, charming man! for she professes to be a great admirer of moral observations.

I had hardly taken leave of the captain, and sat down again with the women, when Will came; and calling me out, "Sir, sir," said he, grinning with a familiarity in his looks as if what he had to say entitled him to take liberties; "I have got the fellow down! I have got old Grimes—Hah, hah, hah, hah!—He is at the Lower Flask—almost in the condition of *David's sow*, and please your honour—[the dog himself not much better] here is his letter—from—from Miss Howe—Ha, ha, ha, ha!" laughed the varlet; holding it fast, as if to make conditions with me, and to excite my praises as well as my impatience.

I could have knocked him down; but he would have his *say* out—"Old Grimes knows not that I have the letter—I must get back to him before he misses it—I only made a pretence to go out for a few minutes—but—but"—and then the dog laughed again—"he *must* stay—old Grimes *must* stay—till I go back to pay the reckoning."

D—n the prater! Grinning rascal! The letter—the letter!

He gathered in his *wide mothe*, as he calls it, and gave me the letter; but with a *strut*, rather than a *bow*; and then sidled off like one of widow Sorlings's dunghill cocks, exulting after a great feat performed. And all the time that I was holding up the billet to the light, to try to get at its contents without breaking the seal [for, dispatched in a hurry, it had no cover], there stood he, laughing, shrugging, playing off his legs; now stroking his shining chin; now turning his hat upon his thumb—then leering in my face, flourishing with his head—O Christ! now and then cried the rascal——

What joy has this dog in mischief! More than I can have in the completion of my most favourite purposes! These fellows are ever happier than their masters.

I was once thinking to rumple up this billet till I had broken the seal. *Young* families [Miss Howe's is not an ancient one] love ostentatious sealings: and it might have been supposed to have been squeezed in pieces in old Grimes's breeches pocket. But I was glad to be *saved* the guilt as well as suspicion of having a hand in so dirty a trick; for thus much of the contents (enough for my purpose) I was enabled to scratch out in character without it; the folds depriving me only of a few connecting words; which I have supplied between hooks.

My Miss Harlowe, thou knowest, had *before* changed her name to *Miss* Lætitia Beaumont. Another *alias* to it, now, Jack; for this billet was directed to her by the name of *Mrs.* Harriot Lucas. I have learned her to be half a rogue, thou seest.

"I CONGRATULATE you, my dear, with all my heart and soul, upon [your escape] from the villain. [I long] for the particulars of all. [My mother] is out: but, expecting her return every minute, I dispatched [your] messenger instantly. [I will endeavour to come at] Mrs. Townsend without loss of time; and will write at large in a day or two, if in that time I can see her. [Meantime I] am excessively uneasy for a letter I sent you yesterday by Collins, [who must have left it at] Wilson's after you got away. [It is of very] great importance. [I hope the] villain has it not. I would not for the world [that he should.] Immediately send for it, if, by so doing, the place you are at [will not be] discovered. If he has it, let me know it by some way [out of] hand. If not, you need not send.

"Ever, ever yours,

"*June* 9.   A. H."

O Jack, what heart's-ease does this *interception* give me! I sent the rascal back with the letter to old Grimes, and charged him to drink no deeper. He owned that he was *half-seas over*, as he phrased it.

Dog! said I, are you not to court one of Mrs. Moore's maids to-night?

Cry your mercy, sir! I will be sober. I had forgot that. But old Grimes is plaguy tough—I thought I should never have got him down.

Away, villain! Let old Grimes come; and on horseback, too, to the door——

He shall, and please your honour, if I can get him on the saddle, and if he can sit——

And charge him not to have alighted, nor to have seen *any*body——

Enough, sir! familiarly nodding his head, to show he took me. And away went the villain—into the parlour, to the women, I. In a quarter of an hour came old Grimes on horseback, waving to his saddle-bow, now on this side, now on that; his head, at others, joining to that of his more sober beast.

It looked very well to the women, that I made no effort to speak to old Grimes (though I wished *before them*, that I knew the contents of what he brought); but, on the contrary, desired that they would instantly let my spouse know that her messenger was returned.

Down she flew, violently as she had the headache!

Oh, how I prayed for an opportunity to be revenged of her for the ungrateful trouble she had given to her uncle's friend!

She took the letter from old Grimes with her own hands, and retired to an inner parlour to read it.

She presently came out again to the fellow, who had much ado to sit his horse. Here is your money, friend. I thought you long. But what shall I do to get somebody to go to town immediately for me? I see *you* cannot.

Old Grimes took his money; let fall his hat in doffing it; had it given him; and rode away; his eyes isinglass, and set in his head, as I saw through the window; and in a manner speechless; all his language hiccoughs. My dog need not to have gone so deep with this *tough* old Grimes. But the rascal was in his kingdom with him.

The lady applied to Mrs. Moore: she mattered not the price. Could a man and horse be engaged for her? Only to go for a letter left for her, at one Mr. Wilson's in Pall Mall.

A poor neighbour was hired. A horse procured for him. He had his directions.

In vain did I endeavour to engage my beloved when she was below. Her headache, I suppose, returned. She, like the rest of her sex, can be ill or well when she pleases.

I see her drift, thought I: it is to have all her lights from Miss Howe before she resolves; and to take her measures accordingly.

Up she went, expressing great impatience about the letter she had sent for; and desired Mrs. Moore to let her know if I offered to send any of my servants to town—to get at the letter, I suppose, was her fear: but she might have been quite easy on that head; and yet perhaps would not, had she known that the worthy Captain Tomlinson (who will be in town before her messenger) will leave there the important letter: which I hope will help to pacify her, and to reconcile her to me.

O Jack! Jack! thinkest thou that I will take all this roguish pains, and be so often called villain, for nothing?

But yet, is it not taking pains to come at the finest creature in the world, not for a *transitory moment* only, but for one of our lives? The struggle only, Whether I am to have her in *my own way*, or in *hers*?

But now I know thou wilt be frightened out of thy wits for me. What, Lovelace! wouldst thou let her have a letter that will inevitably blow thee up; and blow up the mother, and all her nymphs!—yet not intend to reform, not intend to marry?

Patience, puppy! Canst thou not trust thy master?

Letter XI—Mr. Lovelace. [*In continuation*]

I WENT up to my new-taken apartment, and fell to writing in character, as usual. I thought I had made good my quarters. But the cruel creature, understanding that I intended to take up my lodgings there, declared with so much violence against it, that I was obliged to submit, and to accept of another lodging, about twelve doors off, which Mrs. Moore recommended. And all the advantage I could obtain was, that Will, unknown to my spouse, and for fear of a freak, should lie in the house.

Mrs. Moore, indeed, was unwilling to disoblige *either* of us. But Miss Rawlins was of opinion that nothing more ought to be allowed me: and yet Mrs. Moore owned that the refusal was a strange piece of tyranny to a husband, if I *were* a husband.

I had a good mind to make Miss Rawlins smart for it. Come and see Miss Rawlins, Jack. If thou likest her, I 'll get her for thee with a *wet finger*, as the saying is!

The widow Bevis indeed stickled hard for me [an innocent or injured man will have friends everywhere]. She said that to *bear much* with some wives, was to be obliged to bear more: and I reflected, with a sigh, *that tame spirits must always be imposed upon.* And then, in my heart, I renewed my vows of revenge upon this haughty and perverse beauty.

The second fellow came back from town about nine o'clock, with Miss Howe's letter of Wednesday last. "Collins, *it seems*, when he left it, had desired that it might be safely and speedily delivered into Miss Lætitia Beaumont's own hands. But Wilson, understanding that neither she nor I were in town [*he could not know of our difference, thou must think*], resolved to take care of it till our return, in order to give it into one of our own hands; and now delivered it to her messenger."

This was told *her*. Wilson, I doubt not, is in her favour upon it.

She took the letter with great eagerness, opened it in a hurry [I am glad she did: yet, I believe, all was right] before Mrs. Moore and Mrs. Bevis [Miss Rawlins was gone home]; and said, She would not for the world that I should have had that letter, for the sake of her dear friend the writer; who had written to her very uneasily about it.

Her *dear friend*! repeated Mrs. Bevis, when she told me this: such mischief-makers are always deemed *dear friends* till they are found out!

The widow says that I am the finest gentleman she ever beheld.

I have found a warm kiss now and then very kindly taken.

I might be a very wicked fellow, Jack, if I were to do all the mischief in my power. But I am evermore for quitting a too easy prey to *reptile rakes*. What but difficulty (though the lady is an angel) engages me to so much perseverance here? And *here, conquer or die,* is now the determination!

I have just now parted with this honest widow. She called upon me at my new lodgings. I told her that I saw I must be further obliged to her in the course of this difficult affair. She must allow me to make her a handsome present when all was happily over. But I desired that she would take no notice of what should pass between us, *not even to her aunt*; for that she, as I saw, was in the power of Miss Rawlins: and Miss Rawlins, being a maiden gentlewoman, knew not the *right* and the *fit* in matrimonial matters, as she, my dear widow, did.

Very true: how *should* she? said Mrs. Bevis, proud of knowing —nothing! But, for her part, she desired no present. It was enough if she could contribute to reconcile man and wife, and disappoint mischief-makers. She doubted not, that such an envious creature as Miss Howe was glad that Mrs. Lovelace had eloped—jealousy and love *was* Old Nick!

See, Belford, how charmingly things work between me and my new acquaintance the widow! Who knows but that she may, after a little further intimacy (though I am banished the house on nights), contrive a midnight visit for me to my spouse, when all is still and fast asleep?

Where can a woman be safe, who has once entered the lists with a contriving and intrepid lover?

But as to this *letter*, methinks thou sayest, of Miss Howe?

I knew thou wouldst be uneasy for me: but did not I tell thee that I had provided for everything? That I always took care to keep seals entire, and to preserve covers?[1] Was it not easy then, thinkest thou, to contrive a shorter letter out of a longer; and to copy the very words?

I can tell thee, it was so well ordered, that, not being suspected to have been in my hands, it was not easy to find me out. Had it been my beloved's hand, there would have been no imitating it for such a length. Her delicate and even mind is seen in the very cut of her letters. Miss Howe's hand is no bad one; but is not so equal and regular. That little devil's natural impatience hurrying on her fingers, gave, I suppose, from the beginning, her handwriting, as well as the rest of her, its fits and starts, and those peculiarities, which, like strong muscular lines in a face, neither the pen, nor the pencil, can miss.

Hast thou a mind to see what it was I *permitted* Miss Howe to write to her lovely friend? Why then, read it here, as extracted from hers of Wednesday last, with a few additions of my own. The additions underscored.

MY DEAREST FRIEND,—You will perhaps think that I have been too long silent. But I had begun two letters at different times since my last, and written a great deal each time; and with spirit enough, I assure you; incensed as I was against the abominable wretch you are with, particularly on reading yours of the twenty-first of the past month.

The FIRST I intended to keep open till I could give you some account of my proceedings with Mrs. Townsend. It was some days before I saw her: and this intervenient space giving me time to reperuse what I had written, I thought it proper to lay that aside, and to write in a style a little less fervent; for you would have blamed me, I knew, for the freedom of some of my expressions [execrations, if you please]. And when I had gone a good way in the SECOND, the change in your prospects, on his communicating to you Miss Montague's letter, and his better behaviour, occasioning a change in your mind, I laid that aside also: and in this uncertainty thought I would wait to see the issue of affairs between you before I wrote again; believing that all would soon be decided one way or other.

Here I was forced to break off. I am *too little* my own mistress. My mother[2] is always up and down; and watching as if I were writing to a fellow. What need I [she asks me] lock myself in,[3] if I am only reading past correspondences? For that is my pretence, when she comes poking in with her face sharpened to an edge, as I may say, by a curiosity that gives her more pain than pleasure. The Lord forgive me; but I believe I shall huff her next time she comes in.

Do you forgive me too, my dear. My mother ought; because she says I am my father's girl; and because I am sure I am hers.

Upon my life, my dear, I am sometimes of opinion that this vile man was capable of meaning you dishonour. When I look back upon his past conduct, I cannot help thinking so. What a villain, if so! But now I hope, and verily believe, that he has laid aside such thoughts. My reasons for both opinions I will give you.

For the first; to wit, that he had it once in his head to take you at advantage if he could; I consider[1] that pride, revenge, and a delight to tread in unbeaten paths, are principal ingredients in the character of this finished libertine. He hates all your family, yourself excepted—yet is a savage in love. His pride, and the credit which a few plausible qualities, sprinkled among his odious ones, have given him, have secured him too good a reception from our eye-judging, our undistinguishing, our self-flattering, our too-confiding sex, to make assiduity and obsequiousness, and a conquest of his unruly passions, any part of his study.

He has some reason for his animosity to all the men, and to one woman, of your family. He has always shown you, and his own family too, that he prefers his pride to his interest. He is a declared marriage-hater; a notorious intriguer; full of his inventions, and glorying in them. As his vanity had made him imagine that no woman could be proof against his love, no wonder that he struggled like a lion held in toils,[2] against a passion that he thought not returned.[3] Hence, perhaps, it is not difficult to believe that it became possible for such a wretch as this to give way to his old prejudices against marriage; and to that revenge *which* had always been a first passion with him.[4]

And hence may we account for his delays; his teasing ways; his bringing you to bear with his lodging in the same house; his making you pass to the people of it as his wife; his bringing you into the company of his libertine companions; the attempt of imposing upon you that Miss Partington for a bedfellow, etc.

My reasons for the contrary opinion; to wit, that he is now resolved to do you all the justice in his power to do you; are these: That he sees that all his own family[5] have warmly engaged

---

[1] See p 7.   [2] See p. 8.   [3] Ibid.   [4] Ibid.   [5] See p. 210.

themselves in your cause: that the horrid wretch loves you; with such a love, *however*, as Herod loved his Mariamne: that, on inquiry, I find it to be true that Counsellor Williams (whom Mr. Hickman knows to be a man of eminence in his profession) has actually as good as finished the settlements: that two drafts of them have been made; one avowedly to be sent to *this very* Captain Tomlinson: and I find that a licence has actually been more than once endeavoured to be obtained, and that difficulties have hitherto been made, equally to Lovelace's vexation and disappointment. My mother's proctor, who is very intimate with the proctor applied to by the wretch, has come at this information in confidence; and hints, that as Mr. Lovelace is a man of high fortunes, these difficulties will probably be got over.

I had once resolved to make strict inquiry about Tomlinson; and still, if you will, your uncle's favourite housekeeper may be sounded, at distance.

I know that the matter is so laid,[1] that Mrs. Hodges is supposed to know nothing of the treaty set on foot by means of Captain Tomlinson. But your uncle is an old man;[2] and old men imagine themselves to be under obligation to their paramours, if younger than themselves, and seldom keep anything from their knowledge. Yet, methinks, there can be no need; since Tomlinson, as you describe him, is so good a man, and so much of a gentleman; the end to be answered by his being an impostor so much more than necessary, if Lovelace has villainy in his head. And thus what he communicated to you of Mr. Hickman's application to your uncle, and of Mrs. Norton's to your mother (some of which particulars I am satisfied his vile agent Joseph Leman could not reveal to his viler employer); his pushing on the marriage-day, in the name of your uncle; which it could not answer any wicked purpose for him to do; and what he writes of your uncle's proposal, to have it thought that you were married from the time that you had lived in one house together; and that to be made to agree with the time of Mr. Hickman's visit to your uncle; the insisting on a trusty person's being present at the ceremony, at that uncle's nomination— these things make me *assured that he now at last means honourably.*

But if any unexpected delays should happen on his side, acquaint me, my dear, with the very street where Mrs. Sinclair lives; and where Mrs. Fretchville's house is situated (which I cannot find that you have ever mentioned in your former letters—which is a little

XI]   CLARISSA HARLOWE   97

odd); and I will make strict inquiries of them, and of Tomlinson too; and I will (if your heart will let you take my advice) soon procure you a refuge from him with Mrs. Townsend.

But why do I now, when you seem to be in so good a train, puzzle and perplex you with my retrospections? And yet they may be of use to you, if any delay happen on his part.

But that I think cannot well be. What you have therefore now to do, is so to behave to this proud-spirited wretch, as may banish from his mind all remembrance of past disobligations,[1] and to receive his addresses as those of a betrothed lover. You will incur the censure of prudery and affectation, if you keep him at that distance which you have hitherto *kept him at.* His sudden (and as suddenly recovered) illness has given him an opportunity to find out that you love him. [Alas, my dear, I knew you loved him!] He has seemed to change his nature, and is all love and gentleness. *And no more quarrels now, I beseech you.*

I am very angry with him, nevertheless, for the freedoms which he took with your person;[2] *and I think some guard is necessary, as he is certainly an encroacher. But indeed all men are so; and you are such a charming creature, and have kept him at such a distance! But no more of this subject. Only, my dear, be not over-nice, now you are so near the state. You see what difficulties you laid yourself under,* when Tomlinson's letter called you again into *the wretch's* company.

If you meet with no impediments, no new causes of doubt,[3] your reputation in the eye of the world is concerned, that you should be his, *and, as your uncle rightly judges, be thought to have been his before now.* And yet, *let me tell you,* I can *hardly* bear *to think* that these libertines should be rewarded for their villainy with the best of the sex, when the worst of it are too good for them.

I shall send this long letter by Collins,[4] who changes his day to oblige me. As none of our letters by Wilson's conveyance have miscarried, when you have been in more apparently disagreeable situations than you are in at present, I *have no doubt* that this will go safe.

Miss Lardner[5] (whom you have seen at her cousin Biddulph's) saw you at St. James's Church on Sunday was fortnight. She kept you in her eye during the whole time; but could not once obtain the notice of yours, though she curtsied to you twice. She thought to pay her compliments to you when the service

---

[1] See p. 11.   [2] See vol. ii, pp. 475–6.   [3] See p. 11.
[4] See p. 12.   [5] See p. 4.

was over; for she doubted not but you were married—and for an odd reason—because you came to church by yourself. Every eye, as usual, wherever you are, she said, was upon you; and this seeming to give you hurry, and you being nearer the door than she, you slid out before she could go to you. But she ordered her servant to follow you till you were housed. This servant saw you step into a chair which waited for you; and you ordered the men to carry you to the place where they took you up. She *describes the house* as a very genteel house, and fit to receive people of fashion: *and what makes me mention this, is, that perhaps you will have a visit from her; or message, at least.*

So that you have Mr. Doleman's testimony to the credit of the house and the people you are with; and he is a man of fortune, and some reputation; formerly a rake indeed; but married to a woman of family; and, having had a palsy-blow, one would think, a penitent.[1] You have *also Mr. Mennell's at least passive testimony; Mr.* Tomlinson's; *and now, lastly, Miss Lardner's; so that there will be the less need for inquiry: but you know my busy and inquisitive temper, as well as my affection for you, and my concern for your honour. But all doubt will soon be lost in certainty.*

Nevertheless I must add, that I would have you command me up, if I can be of the least service or pleasure to you.[2] I value not fame; I value not censure; nor even life itself, I verily think, as I do your honour, and your friendship. For is not your honour my honour? And is not your friendship the pride of my life?

May Heaven preserve you, my dearest creature, in honour and safety, is the prayer, the hourly prayer, of

Your ever faithful and affectionate

ANNA HOWE.

Thursday Morn. 5.

I have written all night. *Excuse indifferent writing. My crow-quills are worn to the stumps, and I must get a new supply.*

These ladies always write with crow-quills, Jack.

If thou art capable of taking in all my *providences*, in this letter, thou wilt admire my sagacity and contrivance almost as much as I do myself. Thou seest that Miss Lardner, Mrs. Sinclair, Tomlinson, Mrs. Fretchville, Mennell, are all mentioned in it. My first liberties with her person also. [Modesty, modesty, Belford, I doubt, is more confined to time, place, and

[1] See p. 3.   [2] See p. 13.

occasion, even by the most delicate minds, than those minds would have it believed to be.] And why all these taken notice of by me from the genuine letter, but for fear some future letter from the vixen should escape my hands, in which she might refer to these names? And if none of them were to have been found in this that is to pass for hers, I might be routed *horse and foot*, as Lord M. would phrase it in a like case.

Devilish hard (and yet I may thank myself) to be put to all this plague and trouble! And for *what*, dost thou ask? O Jack, for a triumph of more value to me *beforehand* than an imperial crown! Don't ask me the value of it a *month hence*. But what indeed is an imperial crown itself, when a man is used to it?

Miss Howe might well be anxious about the letter she wrote. Her sweet friend, from what I have let pass of hers, has reason to rejoice in the thought that it fell not into my hands.

And now must all my contrivances be set at work, to intercept the expected letter from Miss Howe; which is, as I suppose, to direct her to a place of safety, and out of my knowledge. Mrs. Townsend is, no doubt, in this case, to smuggle her off. I hope the *villain*, as I am so frequently called between these two girls, will be able to manage this point.

But what, perhaps, thou askest, if the lady should take it into her head, by the connivance of Miss Rawlins, to quit this house privately in the night?

I have thought of this, Jack. Does not Will lie in the house? And is not the widow Bevis my fast friend?

Letter XII—*Mr. Lovelace to John Belford, Esq.*

Saturday, 6 o'clock, June 10.

THE lady gave Will's sweetheart a letter last night to be carried to the post-house as this morning, directed for Miss Howe, under cover to Hickman. I dare say neither cover nor letter will be seen to have been opened. The contents but eight lines—to own—"The receipt of her double-dated letter in safety; and referring to a longer letter which she intends to write, when she shall have a quieter heart and less trembling fingers. But mentions something to have happened [my detecting her, she means] which has given her very great flutters, confusions, and apprehensions: but which she will await the issue of [some hopes for me hence, Jack!] before she gives her fresh perturbation or concern on her account. She tells her how impatient she shall be for her next," etc.

III—*D 884

Now, Belford, I thought it would be but kind in me to save Miss Howe's concern on these alarming hints; since the curiosity of such a spirit must have been prodigiously excited by them. Having therefore so good a copy to imitate, I wrote; and, taking out that of my beloved, put under the same cover the following short billet; inscriptive and conclusive parts of it in her own words.

Hampstead, Tuesday Evening.

MY EVER DEAR MISS HOWE,—A few lines only, till calmer spirits and quieter fingers be granted me, and till I can get over the shock which your intelligence has given me—to acquaint you— that your kind long letter of Wednesday, and, as I may say, of Thursday morning, is come safe to my hands. On receipt of yours by my messenger to you, I sent for it from Wilson's. There, thank Heaven! it lay. May that Heaven reward you for all your past, and for all your *intended* goodness to

Your for ever obliged
CL. HARLOWE.

I took great pains in writing this. It cannot, I hope, be suspected. Her hand is so *very* delicate. Yet hers is written less beautifully than she usually writes: and I hope Miss Howe will allow somewhat for *hurry of spirits*, and *unsteady fingers*.

My consideration for Miss Howe's *ease of mind* extended still farther than to the instance I have mentioned.

That this billet might be with her as soon as possible (and before it could have reached Hickman by the post) I dispatched it away by a servant of Mowbray's. Miss Howe, had there been any failure or delay, might, as thou wilt think, have communicated her anxieties to her fugitive friend; and she *to me*, perhaps in a way I should not have been pleased with.

Once more wilt thou wonderingly question—All this pains for a single girl?

Yes, Jack! But is not this girl a CLARISSA? And who knows but kind fortune, as a reward for my perseverance, may toss me in her charming friend? Less likely things have come to pass, Belford. And to be sure I shall have her, if I resolve upon it.

Letter XIII—Mr. Lovelace to John Belford, Esq.

Eight o'clock, Sat. Morn. June 10.

I AM come back from Mrs. Moore's, whither I went in order to attend my charmer's commands. But no admittance—a very bad night.

Doubtless she must be as much concerned that she has carried her resentments so very far, as I have reason to be that I made such a poor use of the opportunity I had on Wednesday night.

But now, Jack, for a brief review of my present situation; and a slight hint or two of my precautions.

I have seen the women this morning, and find them half right, half doubting.

Miss Rawlins's brother tells her that she *lives* at Mrs. Moore's. Mrs. Moore can do nothing without Miss Rawlins.

People who keep lodgings at public places expect to get by every one who comes into their purlieus. Though not permitted to lodge there myself, I have engaged all the rooms she has to spare, to the very garrets; and *that*, as I have told thee before, for a month certain, and at her own price, board included; my spouse's and all: but she must not at present know it. So I hope I have Mrs. Moore fast *by the interest*.

This, devil-like, is suiting temptations to inclinations.

I have always observed, and, I believe, I have hinted as much formerly,[1] that all dealers, though but for pins, may be taken in by customers for pins, sooner than by a direct bribe of ten times the value; especially if pretenders to conscience: for the offer of a bribe would not only give room for suspicion; but would startle and alarm their scrupulousness; while a high price paid for what you buy, is but submitting to be cheated in the method the person makes a profession to get by. Have I not said that human nature is a rogue?[2] And do not I know that it is?

To give a higher instance, how many proud senators in the year 1720 were induced, by presents or subscriptions of South Sea stock, to contribute to a scheme big with national ruin; who yet would have spurned the man who should have presumed to offer them even twice the sum certain that they had a chance to gain by the stock? But to return to my *review*, and to my *precautions*.

Miss Rawlins fluctuates as she hears the lady's story, or as

---

[1] See vol. ii, p. 96.　　　　　　　[2] Ibid. pp. 102, 276.

she hears mine. Somewhat of an infidel, I doubt, is this Miss Rawlins. I have not yet considered *her* foible. The next time I see her, I will take particular notice of all the moles and freckles in her mind: and then *infer* and *apply*.

The widow Bevis, as I have told thee, is all my own.

My man Will lies in the house. My other new fellow attends upon *me*; and cannot therefore be quite stupid.

Already is Will over head and ears in love with one of Mrs. Moore's maids. He was struck with her the moment he set his eyes upon her. A raw country wench too. But all women, from the countess to the cook-maid, are put into high good humour with themselves when a man is taken with them at first sight. Be they ever so *plain* [no woman can be *ugly*, Jack!] they 'll find twenty good reasons, besides the great one (*for sake's sake*), by the help of the glass without (and perhaps in spite of it) and conceit within, to justify the honest fellow's *caption*.

"The rogue has saved £150 in my service"—more by 50 than I bid him save. No doubt he thinks he *might* have done so; though I believe not worth a groat. "The best of masters I—passionate, indeed: but soon appeased."

The wench is extremely kind to him already. The other maid is also very civil to him. He has a husband for *her* in his eye. She cannot but say that Mr. Andrew, my *other* servant [the girl is for fixing the *person*], is a very well-spoken civil young man.

"We common folks have our joys, and please your honour, says honest Joseph Leman, like as our betters have."[1] And true says honest Joseph—did I prefer ease to difficulty, I should envy these low-born sinners some of their joys.

But if Will had *not* made amorous pretensions to the wenches, we all know that servants, united in one *common compare-note cause*, are intimate the moment they see one another—great genealogists too; they know immediately the whole kin and kin's kin of each other, though dispersed over the three kingdoms, as well as the genealogies and kin's kin of those whom they serve.

But my precautions end not here.

O Jack, with such an invention, what occasion had I to carry my beloved to Mrs. Sinclair's?

My spouse may have *further* occasion for the messengers whom she dispatched, one to Miss Howe, the other to Wilson's.

[1] See vol. ii, p. 146

With one of these Will is already well acquainted, as thou hast heard—to mingle liquor is to mingle souls with these fellows; with the other messenger he will soon be acquainted, if he be not *already*.

The captain's servant has *his* uses and instructions assigned him. I have hinted at some of them already.[1] *He* also serves a most humane and considerate master. I love to make everybody respected to my power.

The post, general and penny, will be strictly watched likewise. Miss Howe's Collins is remembered to be described. Miss Howe's and Hickman's liveries also.

James Harlowe and Singleton are warned against. I am to be acquainted with any inquiry that shall happen to be made after my spouse, whether by her married or maiden name, before *she* shall be told of it—and this that I may have it in my power to *prevent mischief*.

I have ordered Mowbray and Tourville (and Belton, if his health permit) to take their quarters at Hampstead for a week, with their fellows to attend them. I spare thee for the present, because of thy private concerns. But hold thyself in cheerful readiness, however, as a mark of thy *allegiance*.

As to my spouse herself, has she not reason to be pleased with me for having permitted her to receive Miss Howe's letter from Wilson's? A plain case, either that I am no deep plotter, or that I have no further views than to make my peace with her for an offence so slight and so *accidental*.

Miss Howe says, though prefaced with an *alas!* that her charming friend loves me: she must therefore yearn after this reconciliation—prospects so fair—if she used me with less rigour, and more politeness; if she showed me any *compassion*; seemed inclinable to spare me, and to make the most favourable constructions; I cannot but say that it would be impossible not to show *her* some. But to be insulted and defied by a rebel in one's power, what prince can bear that?

But I return to the scene of action. I must keep the women steady. I had no opportunity to talk to my worthy Mrs. Bevis in private.

Tomlinson, a dog, not come yet!

_____
[1] See p. 88.

Letter XIV—Mr. Lovelace to John Belford, Esq.

From my Apartments at Mrs. Moore's.

MISS RAWLINS at her brother's; Mrs. Moore engaged in house-hold matters; widow Bevis dressing; I have nothing to do but write. This cursed Tomlinson not yet arrived! Nothing to be done without him.

I think he shall complain in pretty high language of the treatment he met with yesterday. "What are our affairs to him? He can have no view but to serve us. Cruel, to send back to town, *un-audienced,* unseen, a man of his business and importance. He never stirs a foot, but something of consequence depends upon his movements. A confounded thing to trifle thus humorsomely with such a gentleman's movements! These women think that all the business of the world must stand still for their *figaries* [a good female word, Jack!]: the greatest triflers in the creation, to fancy themselves the most important beings in it—*marry come up!* as I have heard goody Sorlings say to her servants, when she has rated at them, with mingled anger and disdain."

After all, methinks I want these *tostications* [thou seest how women, and women's words, fill my mind] to be over, *happily* over, that I may sit down quietly and reflect upon the dangers I have passed through, and the troubles I have undergone. I have a *reflecting* mind, as thou knowest; but the very word *reflecting* implies *all got over.*

What briers and thorns does the wretch rush into (a scratched face and tattered garments the unavoidable consequence) who will needs be for striking out a new path through overgrown underwood; quitting *that* beaten out for him by those who have travelled the same road before him!

A visit from the widow Bevis, in my own apartment. She tells me that my spouse had thoughts last night, after I was gone to my lodgings, of removing from Mrs. Moore's.

I almost wish she had attempted to do so.

Miss Rawlins, it seems, who was applied to upon it, dissuaded her from it.

Mrs. Moore also, though she did not own that Will lay in the house (or rather sat up in it, courting), set before her the difficulties, which, in her opinion, she would have to get clear off, without my knowledge; assuring her, that she could be nowhere

more safe than with her, till she had fixed whither to go.   And
the lady herself recollected that if she went, she might miss the
expected letter from her dear friend Miss Howe; which, as she
owned, was to direct her future steps.

She must also surely have some curiosity to know what her
uncle's friend had to say to her from her uncle, contemptuously
as she yesterday treated a man of his importance.   Nor could
she, I should think, be absolutely determined to put herself out
of the way of receiving the visits of two of the principal ladies
of my family, and to break entirely with me in the face of them
all.   Besides, whither could she have gone?   Moreover, Miss
Howe's letter coming (after her elopement) so safely to her
hands, must surely put her into a more confiding temper with
me, and with every one else, though she would not immediately
own it.

But these good folks have so *little* charity!   Are such *severe*
censurers!   Yet who is *absolutely perfect*?   It were to be wished,
however, that *they* would be so modest as to doubt themselves
sometimes: then would they allow for others, as others (excellent
as they imagine themselves to be) must for them.

Saturday, One o'clock.

Tomlinson at last is come.   Forced to ride five miles about
(though I shall impute his delay to great and important business)
to avoid the sight of two or three impertinent rascals, who, little
thinking whose affairs he was employed in, wanted to obtrude
themselves upon him.   I think I will make this fellow easy,
if he behave to my liking in this affair.

I sent up the moment he came.

She desired to be excused receiving his visit till four this
afternoon.

Intolerable!   No consideration!   None at all in this sex, when
their cursed humours are in the way!   Pay-day, pay-*hour*,
rather, will come!   Oh, that it were to be the next!

The captain is in a pet.   Who can blame him?   Even the
women think a man of his consequence, and generously coming
to serve *us*, hardly used.   Would to Heaven she had attempted
to get off last night: the women not my enemies, who knows but
the husband's exerted authority might have met with such
connivance, as might have concluded either in carrying her
back to her former lodgings, or in consummation at Mrs.
Moore's, in spite of exclamations, fits, and the rest of the
female obsecrations?

My beloved has not appeared to anybody this day, except to Mrs. Moore. Is, it seems, extremely low: unfit for the interesting conversation that is to be held in the afternoon. Longs to hear from her dear friend Miss Howe—yet cannot expect a letter for a day or two. Has a bad opinion of all mankind. No wonder! Excellent creature as she is! with such a *father*, such *uncles*, such a *brother*, as she has!

How does she look?

Better than could be expected from yesterday's fatigue, and last night's ill rest.

These tender doves know not, till put to it, what they can bear; especially when engaged in love affairs; and their attention wholly engrossed. But the sex love busy scenes. Still-life is their aversion. A woman will *create* a storm, rather than be without one. So as they can preside in the whirlwind, and direct it, they are happy. But my beloved's misfortune is, that she must live in tumults; yet neither raise them herself, nor be able to control them.

Letter XV—Mr. Lovelace to John Belford, Esq.

Sat. Night, June 10.

What will be the issue of all my plots and contrivances, devil take me if I am able to divine. But I will not, as Lord M. would say, *forestall my own market.*

At four, the appointed hour, I sent up to desire admittance in the captain's name and my own.

She would wait upon the *captain* presently [not upon *me*!]; and in the parlour, if it were not engaged.

The dining-room being *mine*, perhaps that was the reason of her naming the parlour—mighty nice again, if so! No good sign for me, thought I, this stiff punctilio.

In the parlour, with me and the captain, were Mrs. Moore, Miss Rawlins, and Mrs. Bevis.

The women said they would withdraw when the lady came down.

Lovel. Not except she chooses you should, ladies. People who are so much above-board as I am, need not make secrets of any of their affairs. Besides, you three ladies are now acquainted with all our concerns.

Capt. I have some things to say to your lady, that perhaps she would not herself choose that anybody should hear; not even *you*, Mr. Lovelace, as you and her family are not upon such a good foot of understanding as were to be wished.

Lovel. Well, well, captain, I must submit. Give us a sign to withdraw; and we will withdraw.

It was better that the exclusion of the women should come from him, than from me.

Capt. I will bow, and wave my hand, thus—when I wish to be alone with the lady. Her uncle dotes upon her. I hope, Mr. Lovelace, you will not make a reconciliation more difficult, for the earnestness which my dear friend shows to bring it to bear: but indeed I must tell you, *as I told you more than once before*, that I am afraid you have made lighter of the occasion of this misunderstanding to me, than it ought to have been made.

Lovel. I hope, Captain Tomlinson, you do not question my veracity!

Capt. I beg your pardon, Mr. Lovelace—but those things which we men may think lightly of, may not be light to a woman of delicacy. And then, if you *have* bound yourself by a vow, you ought——

Miss Rawlins bridling, her lips closed (but her mouth stretched to a smile of approbation, the longer for not buttoning), tacitly showed herself pleased with the captain for his delicacy.

Mrs. Moore *could* speak—*Very true*, however, was all she said, with a motion of her head that expressed the bow-approbatory.

For my part, said the jolly widow, staring with eyes as big as eggs, I know what I know—but man and wife *are* man and wife; or they are *not* man and wife. I have no notion of standing upon such niceties.

But here she comes! cried one, hearing her chamber door open. Here she comes! another, hearing it shut after her—and down dropped the angel among us.

We all stood up, bowing and curtsying; and could not help it. For she entered with such an air as commanded all our reverence. Yet the captain looked plaguy grave.

Cl. Pray keep your seats, ladies. Pray do not go [for they made offers to withdraw; yet Miss Rawlins would have burst, had she been suffered to retire]. Before this time you have heard all my story, I make no doubt—pray keep your seats—at least all Mr. Lovelace's.

A very saucy and whimsical beginning, thought I.

Captain Tomlinson, your servant, addressing herself to him with inimitable dignity. I hope you did not take amiss my declining your visit yesterday. I was really incapable of talking upon any subject that required attention.

Capt. I am glad I see you better now, madam. I hope I do.

Cl. Indeed I am not well. I would not have excused myself from attending you some hours ago, but in hopes I should have been better. I beg your pardon, sir, for the trouble I have given you; and shall the rather expect it, as *this day will*, I hope, *conclude it all*.

Thus set! thus determined! thought I—yet to have *slept* upon it! But, as what she said was capable of a good, as well as a bad construction, I would not put an unfavourable one upon it.

Lovel. The captain was sorry, my dear, he did not offer his attendance the moment he arrived yesterday. He was afraid that you took it amiss that he did not.

Cl. Perhaps I thought that my *uncle's* friend might have wished to see me as soon as he came [how we stared!]—But, sir [to me], it might be *convenient to you* to detain him.

The devil, thought I! So there really was resentment, as well as headache, as my good friend Mrs. Bevis observed, in her refusing to see the honest gentleman.

Capt. You *would* detain me, Mr. Lovelace—I was for paying my respects to the lady the moment I came——

Cl. Well, sir [interrupting him], to waive this; for I would not be thought captious—if you have not suffered inconvenience, in being obliged to come again, I shall be easy.

Capt. [half-disconcerted]. A *little* inconvenience, I can't say but I have suffered. I have, indeed, too many affairs upon my hands. But the desire I have to serve you and Mr. Lovelace, as well as to oblige my dear friend your Uncle Harlowe, make great inconveniences but small ones.

Cl. You are very obliging, sir. Here is a great alteration since you parted with us last.

Capt. A great one indeed, madam! I was very much surprised at it, on Thursday evening, when Mr. Lovelace conducted me to your lodgings, where we hoped to find you.

Cl. Have you anything to say to me, sir, from my uncle himself, that requires my *private* ear? Don't go, ladies [for the women stood up, and offered to withdraw]. If Mr. Lovelace stays, I am sure *you* may.

I frowned. I bit my lip. I looked at the women; and shook my head.

Capt. I have nothing to offer but what Mr. Lovelace is a

party to, and may hear, except one private word or two, which may be postponed to the last.

Cl. Pray, ladies, keep your seats. Things are altered, sir, since I saw you. You can mention nothing that relates to *me* now, to which *that gentleman* can be a party.

Capt. You surprise me, madam! I am sorry to hear this! Sorry for your *uncle's* sake! Sorry for your sake! Sorry for Mr. *Lovelace's* sake! And yet I am sure he must have given greater occasion than he has mentioned to me, or——

Lovel. Indeed, captain, indeed, ladies, I have told you great part of my story! And what I told you of my offence was the truth:—what I concealed of my story was only what I apprehended would, if known, cause this dear creature to be thought more censorious than charitable.

Cl. Well, well, sir, say what you please. Make me as black as you please. Make yourself as white as you can. I am not now in your power: that consideration will comfort me for all.

Capt. God forbid that I should offer to plead in behalf of a crime that a woman of virtue and honour cannot forgive. But surely, surely, madam, this is going too far.

Cl. Do not blame me, Captain Tomlinson. I have a good opinion of you, as my *uncle's* friend. But if you are Mr. *Lovelace's* friend, that is another thing; for my interests and Mr. Lovelace's must now be for ever separated.

Capt. One word with you, madam, if you please—offering to retire.

Cl. You may say all that you please to say before these gentlewomen. Mr. Lovelace may have secrets. I have none. You seem to think me faulty: I should be glad that all the world knew my heart. Let my enemies sit in judgment upon my actions: fairly scanned, I fear not the result. Let them even ask me my most secret thoughts, and, whether they make for me, or against me, I will reveal them.

Capt. Noble lady! who can say as you say?

The women held up their hands and eyes; each as if she had said, Not I.

No disorder here, said Miss Rawlins! But (judging by her own heart) a confounded deal of improbability, I believe she thought.

Finely *said*, to be sure, said the widow Bevis, shrugging her shoulders.

Mrs. Moore sighed.

Jack Belford, thought I, knows all mine: and in this I am more ingenuous than any of the three, and a fit match for this paragon.

Cl. How Mr. Lovelace has found me out here, I cannot tell. But such mean devices, such artful, such worse than Waltham disguises put on, to obtrude himself into my company; such bold, such shocking untruths——

Capt. The favour of but one word, madam, in private——

Cl. In order to support a right which he has not over me! O sir!—O Captain Tomlinson!—I think I have reason to say that the man (there he stands!) is capable of any vileness!

The women looked upon one another, and upon me, by turns, to see how I bore it. I had such dartings in my head at the instant, that I thought I should have gone distracted. My brain seemed on fire. What would I have given to have had her alone with me! I traversed the room; my clenched fist to my forehead. Oh, that I had anybody here, thought I, that Hercules-like, when flaming in the tortures of Deianira's poisoned shirt, I could tear in pieces!

Capt. Dear lady! see you not how the poor gentleman—Lord, how have I imposed upon your uncle, at this rate! How happy did I tell him, I saw you! How happy I was sure you would be in each other!

Cl. O sir, you don't know how many premeditated offences I *had forgiven* when I saw you last, before I could appear to you what I hoped then I might for the future be! But now you may tell my uncle, if you please, that I cannot hope for his mediation. Tell him that my guilt, in giving this man an opportunity to spirit me away from my *tried*, my *experienced*, my *natural* friends (harshly as they treated me), stares me every day more and more in the face; and still the more, as my fate seems to be drawing to a crisis, according to the malediction of my offended father!

And then she burst into tears, which even affected that dog, who, brought to abet me, was himself all *Belforded* over.

The women, so used to cry without grief, as they are to laugh without reason, by mere force of example [confound their promptitudes!], must needs pull out *their* handkerchiefs. The less wonder, however, as I myself, between confusion, surprise, and concern, could hardly stand it.

What's a tender heart good for? Who can be happy that has a *feeling* heart? And yet thou 'lt say, that he who has it not, must be a tiger, and no man.

Capt. Let me beg the favour of one word with you, madam, in private; and that on my *own* account.

The women hereupon offered to retire. She insisted that if *they* went, *I* should not stay.

Capt. Sir, bowing to me, shall I beg——

I hope, thought I, that I may trust this solemn dog, instructed as he is. She does not doubt him. I 'll stay out no longer than to give her time to spend her first fire.

I then passively withdrew, with the women—but with such a bow to my goddess, that it won for me every heart but that I wanted *most* to win; for the haughty maid bent not her knee in return.

The conversation between the captain and the lady, when we were retired, was to the following effect:—They both talked loud enough for me to hear them—the lady from anger, the captain with design; and thou mayst be sure there was no listener but myself. What I was imperfect in was supplied afterwards; for I had my vellum-leaved book to note all down. If she had known this, perhaps she would have been more sparing of her invectives—and but *perhaps* neither.

He told her, that as her brother was absolutely resolved to see her; and as he himself, in compliance with her uncle's expedient, had reported her marriage; and as that report had reached the ears of Lord M., Lady Betty, and the rest of my relations; and as he had been obliged, in consequence of his *first* report, to vouch it; and as her brother might find out where she was, and apply to the women here, for a confirmation or refutation of the marriage; he had thought himself obliged to countenance the report before the women: that this had embarrassed him not a little, as he would not for the world that she should have cause to think him capable of prevarication, contrivance, or double-dealing; and that this made him desirous of a private conversation with her.

It was true, she said, she *had* given her consent to such an expedient, believing it was her *uncle's*; and little thinking that it would lead to so many errors. Yet she might have known that one error is frequently the parent of many. Mr. Lovelace had made her sensible of the truth of that observation, on more occasions than one; and it was an observation that he, the captain, had made, in one of the letters that was shown her yesterday.[1]

He hoped that she had no mistrust of *him*: that she had no

[1] See p. 53.

doubts of *his honour*. If, madam, you suspect me—if you think me capable—what a man—the Lord be merciful to me!—what a man must you think me!

I hope, sir, there cannot be a man in the world who could deserve to be suspected in such a case as this. I do *not* suspect you. If it were possible there could be *one* such man, I am sure, Captain Tomlinson, a father of children, a man in years, of sense and experience, cannot be that man.

He told me, that just then he thought he felt a sudden flash from her eye, an *eye-beam* as he called it, dart through his shivering reins; and he could not help trembling.

The dog's conscience, Jack! Nothing else! I have felt half a dozen such flashes, such eye-beams, in as many different conversations with this soul-piercing beauty.

Her uncle, she must own, was not accustomed to think of such expedients: but she had reconciled this to herself, as the case was unhappily uncommon; and by the regard he had for her honour.

This set the puppy's heart at ease, and gave him more courage.

She asked him if he thought Lady Betty and Miss Montague intended her a visit?

He had no doubt but they did.

And does he imagine, said she, that I could be brought to countenance to them the report you have given out?

[*I had hoped to bring her to this, Jack, or she had not seen their letters.* But I had told the captain that I believed I must give up this expectation.]

No. He believed that I had not such a thought. He was pretty sure that I intended, when I saw *them*, to tell them (as in confidence) the naked truth.

He then told her that her uncle had already made some steps towards a general reconciliation. The moment, madam, that he knows you are really married, he will enter into conference with your *father* upon it; having actually expressed to your *mother* his desire to be reconciled to you.

And what, sir, said my mother? What said my *dear* mother?

With great emotion she asked this question; holding out her sweet face, as the captain described her, with the most earnest attention, as if she would shorten the way which his words were to have to her heart.

Your mother, madam, burst into tears upon it: and your uncle was so penetrated by *her* tenderness, that he could not

proceed with the subject.   But he intends to enter upon it with
her in form, as soon as he hears that the ceremony is over.

By the tone of her voice she wept.   The dear creature, thought
I, begins to relent! And I grudged the dog his eloquence.   I
could hardly bear the thought that any man breathing should
have the power which I had lost, of persuading this high-souled
woman, though in my own favour.   And, wouldst thou think it?
this reflection gave me more uneasiness at the moment, than I
felt from her reproaches, violent as they were; or than I had
pleasure in her supposed relenting.   For there is beauty in
everything she says and does: beauty in her passion: beauty in
her tears! Had the captain been a young fellow, and of rank and
fortune, *his* throat would have been in danger; and I should
have thought very hardly of *her*.

O Captain Tomlinson, said she, you know not what I have
suffered by this man's strange ways.   He had, as I was not
ashamed to tell him yesterday, a *plain path before him*.   He at
first betrayed me into his power: but when I *was* in it—There
she stopped.   Then resuming—O sir, you know not what a
strange man he has been! An unpolite, a rough-mannered
man! In disgrace of his birth, and education, and knowledge,
an unpolite man! And so acting, as if his worldly and personal
advantages set him above those graces which distinguish a
gentleman.

The first woman that ever said or that ever thought so of me,
that 's my comfort, thought I! But this (spoken to her *uncle's
friend* behind my back) helps to heap up thy already too full
measure, dearest! It is down in my vellum book.

Cl. When I look back on his whole behaviour to a poor young
creature (for I am but a *very* young creature!), I cannot acquit
him either of great folly, or of deep design.   And, last Wednesday—There she stopped; and I suppose turned away her
face.

I wonder she was not ashamed to hint at what she thought
so shameful; and that to a *man*, and *alone* with him.

Capt. Far be it from me, madam, to offer to enter too closely
into so tender a subject.   Mr. Lovelace owns that you have
reason to be displeased with him.   But he so solemnly clears
himself to me of *premeditated* offence——

Cl. He cannot clear himself, Mr. Tomlinson.   The people of
the house must be very vile, as well as he.   I am convinced, that
there was a wicked confederacy—but no more upon such a
subject.

Capt. Only one word more, madam. He tells me that you promised to pardon him. He tells me——

He knew, interrupted she, that he deserved not pardon, or he had not extorted that promise from me. Nor had I given it to him, but to shield myself from the vilest outrage——

Capt. I could wish, madam, inexcusable as his behaviour has been, since he has *something* to plead in the reliance he made upon your *promise,* that, for the sake of appearances to the world, and to avoid the mischiefs that may follow if you absolutely break with him, you could prevail upon your naturally generous mind to lay an obligation upon him by your forgiveness.

She was silent.

Capt. Your father and mother, madam, deplore a daughter lost to them, whom your generosity to Mr. Lovelace may restore: do not put it to the possible chance that they may have cause to deplore a double loss; the losing of a *son,* as well as a *daughter,* who, by his own violence, which you may perhaps prevent, may be for ever lost to them, and to the whole family.

She paused. She wept. She owned that she felt the force of this argument.

I will be the making of this fellow, thought I!

Capt. Permit me, madam, to tell you that I do not think it would be difficult to prevail upon your uncle, if you insist upon it, to come up privately to town, and to give you with his own hand to Mr. Lovelace—except, indeed, your present misunderstanding were to come to his ears. Besides, madam, your brother, it is likely, may at this very time be in town; and he is resolved to find you out——

Cl. Why, sir, should I be so much afraid of my *brother*? My brother has injured *me,* not I *him.* Will my brother offer to me what Mr. Lovelace has offered? Wicked, ungrateful man! to insult a friendless, unprotected creature, made friendless by himself! I cannot, cannot think of him in the light I once thought of him. What, sir, to put myself into the power of a wretch, who has acted by me with so much vile premeditation? Who shall pity, who shall excuse me, if I do, were I to suffer ever so much from him? No, sir. Let Mr. Lovelace leave me —let my brother find me. I am not such a poor creature as to be afraid to face the brother who has injured me.

Capt. Were you and your brother to meet only to confer together, to expostulate, to clear up difficulties, it were another thing. But what, madam, can you think will be the issue of an interview (Mr. Solmes with him) when he finds you *unmarried,* and resolved never to have Mr. Lovelace; supposing Mr. Lovelace were *not* to interfere; which cannot be imagined?

Cl. Well, sir, I can only say I am a very unhappy creature! I must resign to the will of Providence, and be patient under evils, which *that* will not permit me to shun. But I have taken my measures. Mr. Lovelace can never make *me* happy, nor I *him.* I wait here only for a letter from Miss Howe. That must determine me——

Determine you as to Mr. Lovelace, madam? interrupted the captain.

Cl. I am already determined as to him.

Capt. If it be not in his favour, I have done. I cannot use stronger arguments than I have used, and it would be impertinent to repeat them. If you cannot forgive his offence, I am sure it must have been much greater than he has owned to me. If you are absolutely determined, be pleased to let me know what I shall say to your uncle? You was pleased to tell me, *that this day would put an end to what you called my trouble*: I should not have thought it any, could I have been an humble means of reconciling persons of worth and honour to each other.

Here I entered with a solemn air.

Lovel. Captain Tomlinson, I have heard a great part of what has passed between you and this unforgiving (however otherwise excellent) lady. I am cut to the heart to find the dear creature so determined. I could not have believed it possible, with such prospects, that I had so little a share in her esteem. Nevertheless I must do myself justice with regard to the offence I was so unhappy as to give, since I find you are ready to think it much greater than it really was.

Cl. I hear not, sir, your recapitulations. I am, and ought to be, the sole judge of insults offered to my person. I enter not into discussion with you, nor hear you on the shocking subject. And was going.

I put myself between her and the door. You *may* hear all I have to say, madam. My *fault* is not of such a nature, but that you *may.* I will be a just accuser of myself; and will not wound your ears.

I then protested that the fire was a real fire [so it was]. I disclaimed [less truly indeed] premeditation. I owned that I was hurried on by the violence of a youthful passion, and by a sudden impulse, which few other persons, in the like situation, would have been able to check: that I withdrew, at her command and entreaty, on the promise of *pardon,* without having offered the least indecency, or any freedom that would not have been forgiven by persons of delicacy, surprised in an attitude so charming—her terror, on the alarm of fire, calling for a soothing behaviour and personal tenderness, she being ready to fall into fits: my hoped-for happy day so near, that I might be presumed to be looked upon as a betrothed lover. And that this excuse might be pleaded *even for the women of the house*, that they, thinking us actually married, might suppose themselves to be the less concerned to interfere on so tender an occasion. [There, Jack, was a bold insinuation in behalf of the women!]

High indignation filled her disdainful eye, eye-beam after eye-beam flashing at me. Every feature of her sweet face had soul in it. Yet she spoke not. Perhaps, Jack, she had a thought, that this *plea for the women* accounted for my contrivance to have her pass to them as married, when I *first carried her thither*.

Capt. Indeed, sir, I must say that you did not well to add to the apprehensions of a lady so much terrified before.

The dear creature offered to go by me. I set my back against the door, and besought her to stay a few moments. I had not said thus much, my dearest creature, but for *your* sake, as well as for *my own*, that Captain Tomlinson should not think I had been viler than I was. Nor will I say one word more on the subject, after I have appealed to your own heart, whether it was not necessary that I should *say so much*; and to the captain, whether otherwise he would not have gone away with a much worse opinion of me, if he had judged of my offence by the violence of your resentment.

Capt. Indeed I *should*. I *own* I should. And I am very glad, Mr. Lovelace, that you are able to defend yourself thus far.

Cl. That cause must be well tried, where the offender takes his seat upon the same bench with the judge. I submit not mine to me—nor, give me leave to say, to you, Captain Tomlinson, though I am willing to have a good opinion of you. Had not the man been assured that he had influenced you in his favour, he would not have brought you up to Hampstead.

Capt. That I am *influenced*, as you call it, madam, is for the sake of your uncle, and for your own sake, more (I will say to Mr. Lovelace's face) than for his. What can I have in view, but peace and reconciliation? I have, from the *first*, blamed, and I now, *again*, blame Mr. Lovelace, for adding distress to distress, and terror to terror; the lady, as you acknowledge, sir [*looking valiantly*], ready *before* to fall into fits.

Lovel. Let me own to you, Captain Tomlinson, that I have been a very faulty, a very foolish man; and, if this dear creature *ever* honoured me with her love, an *ungrateful* one. But I have had too much reason to doubt it. And this is now a flagrant proof that she never had the value for me which my proud heart wished for; that, with such prospects before us; a day so near; settlements approved and drawn; her uncle mediating a general reconciliation, which, for *her* sake, not *my own*, I was desirous to give in to; she can, for an offence so *really* slight, on an occasion so *truly* accidental, renounce me for ever; and, with me, all hopes of that reconciliation in the way her uncle had put it in, and she had acquiesced with; and risk all consequences, *fatal ones* as they may too possibly be. By my soul, Captain Tomlinson, the dear creature must have hated me all the time she was intending to honour me with her hand. And now she must resolve to abandon me, as far as I know, with a preference in her heart of the most odious of men—in favour of *that Solmes*, who, as you tell me, accompanies her brother: and with what hopes, with what view, accompanies him? How can I bear to think of this?

Cl. It is fit, sir, that you should judge of my regard for you by your own conscious demerits. Yet you know, or you would not have dared to behave to me as sometimes you did, that you had *more of it* than you deserved.

She walked from us; and then returning, Captain Tomlinson, said she, I will own to you, that I was not *capable* of resolving to give my *hand*, and—*nothing but my hand*. Have I not given a flagrant proof of this to the once most indulgent of parents? which has brought me into a distress which this man has heightened, when he ought, in gratitude and honour, to have endeavoured to render it supportable. I had even a *bias*, sir, in his favour, I scruple not to own it. Long (much too long!) bore I with his unaccountable ways, attributing his errors to *unmeaning gaiety*, and to a want of knowing what *true delicacy*, and *true generosity*, required from a heart susceptible of grateful impressions to one involved by his means in unhappy circumstances. It is now *wickedness* in him (a wickedness which discredits all his *professions*) to say, that his last cruel and ungrateful insult was not a *premeditated* one. But what need I say more of this insult, when it was of such a nature, that it has changed that bias in his favour, and made me choose to forego all the inviting prospects he talks of, and to run all hazards, to free myself from his power?

O my dearest creature! how happy for us both, had I been able to *discover that bias*, as you condescend to call it, through such reserves as man never encountered with!

He *did* discover it, Captain Tomlinson. He brought me, *more than once, to own it*; the more needlessly brought me to own it, as I dare say his own *vanity* gave him *no cause to doubt it*; and as I had no other motive in not being *forward* to own it, than my too just apprehensions of his *want of generosity*. In a word, Captain Tomlinson (and now that I am determined upon my measures, I the less scruple to say it), I should have despised myself, had I found myself capable of affectation or tyranny to the man I intended to marry. I have always blamed the dearest friend I have in the world for a fault of this nature. In a word——

Lovel. And had my angel really and indeed the favour for me she is pleased to own? Dearest creature, forgive me. Restore me to your good opinion. Surely I have not sinned beyond forgiveness. You say that I extorted from you the promise you made me. But I could not have presumed to make that promise the condition of my obedience, had I not thought there *was room to expect* forgiveness. Permit, I beseech you, the prospects to take place that were opening so agreeably before us. I will go to town, and bring the licence. All difficulties to the obtaining of it are surmounted. Captain Tomlinson shall be witness to the deeds. He will be present at the ceremony on the part of your uncle. Indeed he gave me hope that your uncle himself——

Capt. I *did*, Mr. Lovelace: and I will tell you my grounds for the hope I gave. I proposed to my dear friend (your uncle, madam) that he should give out, that he would take a turn with me to my little farm-house, as I call it, near Northampton, for a week or so. Poor gentleman! he has of late been very little abroad! Too visibly indeed declining! Change of air, it might be given out, was good for him. But I see, madam, that this is too *tender* a subject——

The dear creature wept. She knew how to apply as meant the captain's hint to the *occasion* of her uncle's declining state of health.

Capt. We might indeed, I told him, set out in that road, but turn short to town in *my* chariot; and he might see the ceremony performed with his own eyes, and be the desired father, as well as the beloved uncle.

She turned from us, and wiped her eyes.

Capt. And, really, there seem now to be but two objections to this; as Mr. Harlowe discouraged not the proposal—The one, the unhappy misunderstanding between you; which I would not by any means he should know; since then he might be apt to give weight to Mr. James Harlowe's unjust surmises. The other, that it would necessarily occasion some delay to the ceremony; which certainly may be performed in a day or two— if——

And then he reverently bowed to my goddess. Charming fellow! But often did I curse my stars for making me so much obliged to his adroitness.

She was going to speak; but, not liking the turn of her countenance (although, as I thought, its severity and indignation seemed a little abated), I said, and had like to have blown myself up by it—One expedient I have just thought of——

Cl. None of your *expedients*, Mr. Lovelace! I abhor your *expedients*, your *inventions*—I have had too many of them.

Lovel. See, Captain Tomlinson! — See, sir! — Oh, how we expose ourselves to you! Little did you think, I dare say, that we have lived in such a continued misunderstanding together! But you will make the best of it all. We may yet be happy. Oh, that I could have been assured that this dear creature loved *me* with the hundredth part of the love I have for *her*! Our diffidences have been mutual. I presume to say that she has too much punctilio: I am afraid that I have too little. Hence our difficulties. But I have a heart, Captain Tomlinson, a heart that bids me hope for her love, because it is resolved to deserve it as much as man *can* deserve it.

Capt. I am indeed surprised at what I have seen and heard. I defend not Mr. Lovelace, madam, in the offence he has given you—as a father of daughters myself, I *cannot* defend him; though his fault seems to be lighter than I had apprehended— but in my conscience, madam, I think you carry your resentment too high.

Cl. Too high, sir! Too high to the man that might have been happy if he would! Too high to the man that has held *my soul in suspense* an hundred times, since (by artifice and deceit) he obtained a power over me! Say, Lovelace, thyself say, art thou not the *very* Lovelace, who by insulting *me*, hast wronged thy *own hopes*? The wretch that appeared in vile disguises, personating an old lame creature, seeking for lodgings for thy sick wife? Telling the gentlewomen here stories all of thine own invention; and asserting to them an husband's right over

me, which thou hast not?—And is it [turning to the captain]
to be expected that I should give credit to the protestations
of *such a man*?

Lovel. Treat me, dearest creature, as you please, I will
bear it: and yet your scorn and your violence have fixed
daggers in my heart. But was it possible, without those disguises, to come at your speech? And could I lose you, if study,
if invention, would put it in my power to arrest your anger, and
give me hope to engage you to confirm to me the *promised
pardon?* The address I made to you before the women, as if the
marriage ceremony had passed, was in consequence of what your
uncle *had advised*, and what *you had acquiesced with*; and the
rather made, as your brother, and Singleton, and Solmes, were
resolved to find out whether what was reported of your marriage
were true or not, that they might take their measures accordingly; and in hopes to prevent that mischief, which I have been
too studious to prevent, since this tameness has but invited
insolence from your brother and his confederates.

Cl. O thou strange wretch, how thou talkest!—But, Captain
Tomlinson, give me leave to say, that, were I inclined to enter
farther upon this subject, I would appeal to Miss Rawlins's
judgment (whom else have I to appeal to?). She seems to be a
person of prudence and honour; but not to any *man's* judgment, whether I carry my resentment beyond fit bounds,
when I resolve——

Capt. Forgive, madam, the interruption—but I think there
can be no reason for this. You ought, as you said, to be the
sole judge of indignities offered you. The gentlewomen here
are strangers to you. You will perhaps stay but a little while
among them. If you lay the state of your case before any of
them, and your brother come to inquire of them, your uncle's
intended mediation will be discovered, and rendered abortive—
I shall appear in a light that I never appeared in, in my life—for
these women may not think themselves obliged to keep the
secret.

Charming fellow!

Cl. Oh, what difficulties has one fatal step involved me in!
But there is no necessity for such an appeal to anybody. I
am resolved on my measures.

Capt. Absolutely resolved, madam?

Cl. I am.

Capt. What shall I say to your Uncle Harlowe, madam?
Poor gentleman! how will he be surprised!—You see, Mr.

Lovelace—you see, sir [turning to me with a flourishing hand], but you may *thank yourself*—and admirably stalked he from us.

True, by my soul, thought I. I traversed the room, and bit my unpersuasive lips, now upper, now under, for vexation.

He made a profound reverence to her—and went to the window, where lay his hat and whip; and, taking them up, opened the door. Child, said he, to somebody he saw, pray order my servant to bring my horse to the door——

Lovel. You won't go, sir—I hope you won't! I am the unhappiest man in the world! You won't go—yet, alas! But you won't go, sir! There may be yet hopes that Lady Betty may have some weight——

Capt. Dear Mr. Lovelace! and may not my worthy friend, an affectionate uncle, hope for *some* influence upon his *daughter-niece*?—But I beg pardon—a letter will always find me disposed to serve the lady, and that as well for her sake, as for the sake of my dear friend.

She had thrown herself into a chair; her eyes cast down: she was motionless, as in a profound study.

The captain bowed to her again: but met with no return to his bow. *Mr. Lovelace,* said he (with an air of equality and independence), *I am yours.*

Still the dear unaccountable sat as immovable as a statue; stirring neither hand, foot, head, nor eye—I never before saw any one in so profound a reverie, in so waking a dream.

He passed by her to go out at the door she sat near, though the passage by the other door was his direct way; and bowed again. She moved not. I will not disturb the lady in her meditations, sir. Adieu, Mr. Lovelace. *No farther, I beseech you.*

She started, sighing. Are you going, sir?

Capt. I am, madam. I could have been glad to do you service: but I see it is not in my power.

She stood up, holding out one hand, with inimitable dignity and sweetness. I am sorry you are going, sir! I can't help it. I have no friend to advise with. Mr. Lovelace has the art (or good fortune, perhaps I should call it) to make himself many. Well, sir, if you will go, I can't help it.

Capt. I will *not* go, madam; his eyes twinkling. [Again seized with a fit of humanity!] I will *not* go, if my longer stay can do you either service or pleasure. What, sir (turning to me), what, Mr. Lovelace, was your expedient? Perhaps something may be offered, madam——

She sighed, and was silent.

REVENGE, *invoked I to myself, keep thy throne in my heart. If the usurper* LOVE *once more drive thee from it, thou wilt never regain possession!*

Lovel. What I had thought of, what I had intended to propose [and I sighed], was this: That the dear creature, if she will not forgive me, as she promised, will suspend the displeasure she has conceived against me, till Lady Betty arrives. That lady may be the mediatrix between us. This dear creature may put herself into *her* protection, and accompany her down to her seat in Oxfordshire. It is one of her ladyship's purposes to prevail on her supposed new niece to go down with her. It may pass to every one but to Lady Betty, and to you, Captain Tomlinson, and to your friend Mr. Harlowe (as he desires), that we have been some time married: and her being with my relations, will amount to a proof to James Harlowe that we *are*; and our nuptials may be privately, and at this beloved creature's pleasure, solemnized; and your report, captain, authenticated.

Capt. Upon my honour, madam, clapping his hand upon his breast, a charming expedient! This will answer every end.

She mused—she was greatly perplexed—at last, God direct me! said she: I know not what to do. A young unfriended creature, whom have I to advise with? Let me retire, if I *can* retire.

She withdrew with slow and trembling feet, and went up to her chamber.

For Heaven's sake, said the penetrated varlet [his hands lifted up]; for Heaven's sake, take compassion upon this admirable woman! I cannot proceed—I cannot proceed—she deserves all things——

Softly!—damn the fellow!—the women are coming in.

He sobbed up his grief—turned about—hemmed up a more *manly* accent. Wipe thy cursed eyes. He did. The sunshine took place on one cheek, and spread slowly to the other, and the fellow had his whole face again.

The women all three came in, led by that ever-curious Miss Rawlins. I told them that the lady was gone up to consider everything: that we had hopes of her. And such a representation we made of all that had passed, as brought either tacit or declared blame upon the fair perverse for hardness of heart and over-delicacy.

The widow Bevis, in particular, put out one lip, tossed up her head, wrinkled her forehead, and made such motions with her now lifted-up, now cast-down eyes, as showed that she thought there was a great deal of perverseness and affectation in the lady. Now and then she changed her censuring looks to looks of pity of me, but (as she said) she loved not to aggravate! A poor business, *God help 's*! shrugging up her shoulders, to make such a rout about! And then her eyes laughed heartily. Indulgence was a good thing! Love was a good thing! But too much was too much!

Miss Rawlins, however, declared, after she had called the widow Bevis, with a prudish simper, a *comical gentlewoman*! that there must be something in our story which she could not fathom; and went from us into a corner, and sat down, seemingly vexed that she could not.

Letter XVI—Mr. Lovelace. [*In continuation*]

THE lady stayed longer above than we wished; and I hoping that (lady-like) she only waited for an *invitation* to return to us, desired the widow Bevis, in the captain's name (who wanted to go to town), to request the favour of her company.

I cared not to send up either Miss Rawlins or Mrs. Moore on the errand, lest my beloved should be in a *communicative disposition*; especially as she had hinted at an appeal to Miss Rawlins; who, besides, has such an unbounded curiosity.

Mrs. Bevis presently returned with an answer (winking and pinking at me) that the lady would follow her down. Miss Rawlins could not but offer to retire, as the others did. Her eyes, however, intimated that she had rather stay. But they not being answered as she seemed to wish, she went with the rest, but with slower feet; and had hardly left the parlour, when the lady entered it by the other door; a melancholy dignity in her person and air.

She sat down. Pray, Mr. Tomlinson, be seated.

He took his chair over against her. I stood behind hers, that I might give him *agreed upon* signals, should there be occasion for them.

As thus: A wink of the left eye was to signify, *Push that point, captain.*

A wink of the right, and a nod, was to indicate *approbation* of what he had said.

My forefinger held up, and biting my lip, *Get off of that as fast as possible.*

A right forward nod, and a frown, *Swear to it, captain*.

My whole spread hand, *To take care not to say too much on that particular subject*.

A scowling brow, and a positive nod, was to bid him *rise in his temper*.

And these motions I could make, even those with my hand, without holding up my arm, or moving my wrist, had the women been there; as, when the motions were agreed upon, I knew not but they would.

She hemmed—I was going to speak, to spare her supposed confusion: but this lady never wants presence of mind, when presence of mind is necessary either to her honour, or to that conscious dignity which distinguishes her from all the women I ever knew.

I have been considering, said she, as well as I was able, of everything that has passed; and of all that has been said; and of my unhappy situation. I mean no ill; I wish no ill, to any creature living, Mr. Tomlinson. I have always delighted to draw favourable rather than unfavourable conclusions; sometimes, as it has proved, for very bad hearts. Censoriousness, whatever faults I have, is not *naturally* my fault. But, circumstanced as I am; treated as I have been, unworthily treated, by a man who is full of contrivances, and glories in them——

Lovel. My dearest life! But I will not interrupt you.

Cl. Thus treated, it becomes me to doubt—it concerns my honour to doubt, to fear, to apprehend—*your* intervention, sir, is so seasonable, so kind, for *this man*—my uncle's expedient, the first of the kind he ever, I believe, thought of; a plain, honest, good-minded man, as he is, not affecting such expedients —your report in conformity to it the consequences of that report; the alarm taken by my brother; his rash resolution upon it— the alarm taken by Lady Betty, and the rest of Mr. Lovelace's relations—the *sudden* letters written to him upon it, which, with yours, he showed me—all ceremony, among persons *born observers of ceremony*, and entitled to value themselves upon *their distinction*, dispensed with—all these things have happened *so* quick, and some of them *so* seasonable——

Lovel. Lady Betty, you see, madam, in her letter, dispenses with punctilio, avowedly in compliment to you. Charlotte, in hers, professes to do the same for the same reason. Good Heaven! that the respect intended you by my relations, who, in every other case, are really punctilious, should be thus construed! They were glad, madam, to have an opportunity to compliment you at my expense. Every one of my family takes delight in railing me. But their joy on the supposed occasion——

Cl. Do I doubt, sir, that you have not something to say for anything you think fit to do? I am speaking to Captain Tomlinson, sir. I wish you would be pleased to withdraw—at least to come from behind my chair.

And she looked at the captain, observing, no doubt, that his eyes seemed to take lessons from mine.

A fair match, by Jupiter!

The captain was disconcerted. The dog had not had such a blush upon his face for ten years before. I bit my lip for vexation: walked about the room; but nevertheless took my post again; and blinked with my eyes to the captain, as a caution for him to take more care of *his*: and then scowling with my brows, and giving the nod positive, I as good as said, *Resent that, captain.*

Capt. I hope, madam, you have no suspicion that I am capable——

Cl. Be not displeased with me, Captain Tomlinson. I have told you that I am not of a suspicious temper. Excuse me for the sake of my sincerity. There is not, I will be bold to say, a sincerer heart in the world than hers before you.

She took out her handkerchief, and put it to her eyes.

I was going at the instant, after her example, to vouch for the honesty of *my* heart; but my conscience *Mennelled* upon me; and would not suffer the meditated vow to pass my lips. A devilish thing, thought I, for a man to be so little himself, when he has most occasion for himself!

The villain Tomlinson looked at me with a rueful face, as if he begged leave to cry for company. It might have been as well, if he *had* cried. A feeling heart, or the tokens of it given by a sensible eye, are very reputable things, when kept in countenance by the occasion.

And here let me fairly own to thee, that twenty times in this trying conversation I said to myself, that could I have thought that I should have all this trouble, and incurred all this guilt, I would have been honest at first. But why, Jack, is this dear creature so lovely, yet so invincible? Ever heardst thou before, that the sweets of May blossomed in December?

Capt. Be pleased—be pleased, madam—if you have doubts of my honour——

A whining varlet! He should have been quite angry. For

what gave I him the nod positive? He should have stalked again to the window, as for his whip and hat.

Cl. I am only making such observations as my youth, my inexperience, and my present unhappy circumstances, suggest to me. A worthy heart (such, I hope, is Captain Tomlinson's) need not fear an examination—need not fear being looked into. Whatever doubts *that* man, who has been the *cause of my errors*, and, as my severe father imprecated, *the punisher of the errors he has caused*, might have had of me, or of my honour, I would have forgiven him for them, if he had fairly proposed them to me: for some doubts perhaps *such a man* might have of the future conduct of a creature whom he could induce to correspond with him against *parental prohibition*, and against the *lights which her own judgment threw in upon her*: and if he had propounded them to me like a man and a gentleman, I would have been glad of the opportunity given me to clear my intentions, and to have shown myself entitled to his good opinion—and I hope *you*, sir——

Capt. I am ready to hear all your doubts, madam, and to clear them up——

Cl. I will only put it, sir, to your conscience and honour——

The dog sat uneasy: he shuffled with his feet: her eye was upon him: he was therefore, after the rebuff he had met with, afraid to look at me for my motions; and now turned his eyes towards me, then from me, as if he would *unlook* his own looks.

Cl. That all is true that you have written, and that you have told me.

I gave him a right forward nod, and a frown—as much as to say, *Swear to it, captain.* But the varlet did not round it off as I would have had him. However, he averred that it was.

He had hoped, he said, that the circumstances with which his commission was attended, and what he had communicated to her, *which he could not know but from his dear friend her uncle*, might have shielded him even from the *shadow* of suspicion. But I am contented, said he, stammering, to be thought—to be thought—what—what you please to think me—till, till, you are satisfied——

A whore's bird!

Cl. The circumstances you refer to, I must own, *ought* to shield you, sir, from suspicion; but the man before you is a man that would make an angel suspected, should that angel plead for him.

I came forward—traversed the room—was indeed in a bloody

passion.—I have no patience, madam! And again I bit my unpersuasive lips.

Cl. No man ought to be impatient at imputations he is not ashamed to deserve. An innocent man *will not* be outrageous upon such imputations. A guilty man *ought not.* [Most excellently would this charming creature cap sentences with Lord M.!] But I am not now trying you, sir, [to me] on the foot of your *merits.* I am only sorry that I am constrained to put questions to this *worthier* gentleman [*worthier* gentleman, Jack!] which perhaps I ought not to put, so far as they regard *himself.* And I hope, Captain Tomlinson, that you, who know not Mr. Lovelace so well as, to my unhappiness, I do, and who have children of your own, will excuse a poor young creature, who is deprived of all worthy protection, and who has been insulted and endangered by the most *designing man in the world,* and perhaps *by a confederacy of his creatures.*

There she stopped; and stood up, and looked at me; fear, nevertheless, apparently mingled with her anger. And so it ought. I was glad, however, of this poor sign of love. No one fears whom they value not.

Women's tongues were licensed, I was going to say; but my conscience would not let me call her a *woman*; nor use to her so vulgar a phrase. I could only rave by my motions; lift up my eyes, spread my hands, rub my face, pull my wig, and look like a fool. Indeed, I had a great mind to run mad. Had I been alone with her, I would; and she should have taken the consequences.

The captain interposed in my behalf; gently, however, and as a man not quite sure that he was himself acquitted. Some of the pleas we had both insisted on, he again enforced—and, speaking low—Poor gentleman! said he, who can but pity him! Indeed, madam, it is easy to see, with all his failings, the power you have over him!

Cl. I have no pleasure, sir, in distressing any one—not even *him,* who has so much distressed *me.* But, sir, when I THINK, and when I see him before me, I cannot command my temper! Indeed, indeed, Captain Tomlinson, Mr. Lovelace has not acted by me either as a grateful, a generous, or a *prudent* man! He knows not, as I told him yesterday, the value of the heart he has insulted!

There the angel stopped; her handkerchief at her eyes.

O Belford, Belford! that she should so greatly excel, as to make me, at times, a villain in my own eyes!

I besought her pardon. I promised that it should be the study of my whole life to deserve it. My faults, I said, *whatever* they had been, were rather faults in her *apprehension* than in *fact*. I besought her to give way to the expedient I had hit upon—I repeated it. The captain enforced it, for her uncle's sake. I once more, for the sake of the general reconciliation; for the sake of all my family; for the sake of preventing future mischief.

She wept—she seemed staggered in her resolution—she turned from me. I mentioned the letter of Lord M. I besought her to resign to Lady Betty's mediation all our differences, if she would not forgive me *before* she saw her.

She turned towards me—she was going to speak; but her heart was full—and again she turned away her face—then, half turning it to me, her handkerchief at her eyes—And do you *really* and *indeed* expect Lady Betty and Miss Montague? And do you—again she stopped.

I answered in a solemn manner.

She turned from me her whole face, and paused, and seemed to consider. But, in a passionate accent, again turning towards me [Oh, how difficult, Jack, for a Harlowe spirit to forgive!]: Let her ladyship come, if she pleases, said she—I cannot, cannot wish to *see* her; and if I did see her, and she were to plead for you, I cannot wish to *hear* her! The more I *think*, the less can I forgive an attempt, that I am convinced was intended to *destroy* me. [A plaguy strong word for the occasion, supposing she was right!] What has my conduct been, that an insult of *such* a nature should be offered to me, as it would be a *weakness* to forgive? I am sunk in my own eyes! And how can I receive a visit that must depress me more?

The captain urged her in my favour with greater earnestness than before. We both even clamoured, as I may say, for mercy and forgiveness. [Didst thou never hear the good folks talk of taking Heaven by storm?] Contrition repeatedly avowed —a total reformation promised—the happy expedient again urged.

Cl. I have taken my measures. I have gone too far to recede, or to *wish* to recede. My mind is prepared for adversity. That I have not *deserved* the evils I have met with, is my consolation! I have written to Miss Howe what my intentions are. My heart is not *with* you—it is *against* you, Mr. Lovelace. I had not written to you as I did in the letter I left behind me, had I not resolved, whatever became of me, to renounce you for ever.

I was full of hope now. Severe as her expressions were, I saw she was afraid that I should think of what she had written. And indeed, her letter is violence itself. *Angry people, Jack, should never write while their passion holds.*

Lovel. The severity you have shown me, madam, whether by pen or by speech, shall never have place in my remembrance, but for your *honour*. In the light you have taken things, all is deserved, and but the natural result of virtuous resentment; and I adore you, even for the pangs you have given me.

She was silent. She had employment enough with her handkerchief at her eyes.

Lovel. You lament, sometimes, that you have no friends of your own sex to consult with. Miss Rawlins, I must confess, is too inquisitive to be confided in. [I liked not, thou mayest think, her appeal to Miss Rawlins.] She *may* mean well. But I never in my life knew a person who was fond of prying into the secrets of others, that was fit to be trusted. The curiosity of such is governed by pride, which is not gratified but by whispering about a secret till it becomes public, in order to show either their consequence or their sagacity. It is so in every case. What man or woman, who is *covetous* of *power* or of *wealth*, is covetous of either for the sake of making a right use of it? But in the ladies of my family you *may* confide. It is their ambition to think of you as one of themselves. Renew but your consent to pass *to the world*, for the sake of your uncle's expedient, and for the prevention of mischief, as a lady some time married. Lady Betty may be acquainted with the naked truth; and you may (*as she hopes you will*) accompany her to her seat; and, if it *must* be so, consider me as in a state of penitence or probation, to be accepted or rejected, as I may appear to deserve.

The captain again clapped his hand on his breast, and declared upon his honour, that this was a proposal that, were the case that of his own daughter, and she were not resolved upon *immediate* marriage (which yet he thought by far the more eligible choice), he should be very much concerned were she to refuse it.

Cl. Were I with Mr. Lovelace's relations, and to pass as his wife to the world, I could not have any choice. And how could he be then in a state of probation? O Mr. Tomlinson, you are too much his *friend* to see into his drift.

Capt. His friend, madam, as I said before, as I am *yours* and your *uncle's*, for the sake of a general reconciliation, which must begin with a better understanding between yourselves.

Lovel. Only, my dearest life, resolve to attend the arrival and visit of Lady Betty: and permit her to arbitrate between us.

Capt. There can be no harm in *that*, madam. You can suffer no inconvenience from *that*. If Mr. Lovelace's offence be such that a woman of Lady Betty's character judges it to be unpardonable, why then——

Cl. [interrupting; and to me] If I am not invaded by you, sir—if I am (as I ought to be) my own mistress, I think to stay here, in this *honest house* [and then had I an *eye-beam*, as the captain calls it, flashed at me], till I receive a letter from Miss Howe. That, I hope, will be in a day or two. If in that time the ladies come whom you expect, and if they are desirous to see the creature whom you have made unhappy, I shall know whether I can or cannot receive their visit.

She turned short to the door, and retiring, went upstairs to her chamber.

O sir, said the captain, as soon as she was gone, what an angel of a woman is this! I *have been*, and I *am*, a very wicked man. But if anything should happen amiss to this admirable lady, through my means, I shall have more cause for self-reproach than for all the bad actions of my life put together.

And his eyes glistened.

Nothing can happen amiss, thou sorrowful dog! What *can* happen amiss? Are we to form our opinion of things by the romantic notions of a girl who supposes *that* to be the greatest which is the slightest of evils? Have I not told thee our whole story? Has she not broken her promise? Did I not generously spare her, when in my power? I was decent, though I had her at such advantage. Greater liberties have I taken with girls of a common character at a common romping-bout, and all has been laughed off, and handkerchief and head-clothes adjusted, and petticoats shaken to rights, in my presence. Never man, in the like circumstances, and resolved as I was resolved, goaded on as I was goaded on, as well by her own sex as by the impulses of a violent passion, was ever so decent. Yet what mercy does she show me?

Now, Jack, this pitiful dog was such another unfortunate one as thyself—his arguments serving to confirm me in the very purpose he brought them to prevail upon me to give up. Had he left me to myself, to the tenderness of my own nature, moved as I was when the lady withdrew; and had he sat down, and made odious faces, and said nothing; it is very possible that I should have taken the chair over against him which she had quitted; and have cried and blubbered with him for half an hour together. But the varlet to *argue* with me! To pretend to *convince* a man, who knows in his heart that he is doing a wrong thing! He must needs think that this would put me upon trying what I could say for myself; and when the excited compunction can be carried from the *heart* to the *lips*, it must evaporate in words.

Thou perhaps, in this place, wouldst have urged the same pleas that he urged. What I answered to him therefore may do for thee, and spare *thee* the trouble of writing, and *me* of reading, a good deal of nonsense.

Capt. You was pleased to tell me, sir, that you only proposed *to try her virtue*; and that you believed you should actually marry her.

Lovel. So I shall, and cannot help it. I have no doubt but I shall. And as to *trying* her, is she not now in the height of her trial? Have I not reason to think that she is coming about? Is she not now yielding up her resentment for an attempt which she thinks she ought *not* to forgive? And if she do, may she not forgive the *last attempt*? Can she, in a word, resent *that* more than she does *this*? Women often, for their own sakes, will keep the *last secret*; but will ostentatiously din the ears of gods and men with their clamours upon a successless offer. It was my folly, my weakness, that I gave her not more cause for this her unsparing violence!

Capt. O sir, you never will be able to subdue this lady without force.

Lovel. Well, then, puppy, must I not endeavour to find a proper time and place——

Capt. Forgive me, sir! But can you think of force to such a fine creature?

Lovel. Force, indeed, I abhor the thought of; and for what, thinkest thou, have I taken all the pains I have taken, and engaged so many persons in my cause, but to avoid the necessity of *violent* compulsion? But yet, imaginest thou that I expect *direct consent* from such a lover of forms as this lady is known to be? Let me tell thee, McDonald, that thy master Belford has urged on thy side of the question all that thou canst urge. Must I have every sorry fellow's conscience to pacify, as well as my own? By my soul, Patrick, she has a friend *here* [clapping my hand on my breast] that pleads for her with greater and more irresistible eloquence than all the men in the world can plead for her. And had she *not escaped me*? And yet how have I answered my first design of trying her,[1] and in *her* the virtue of the most virtuous of the sex? Perseverance, man! Perseverance! What, wouldst thou have me decline a trial that may make for the honour of a sex we all so dearly love?

Then, sir, you have no thoughts—no thoughts—[looking still more sorrowfully] of marrying this wonderful lady?

Yes, yes, Patrick, but I have. But let me, first, to gratify *my* pride, bring down *hers*. Let me see that she loves me well enough to forgive me for my *own* sake. Has she not heretofore lamented that she stayed not in her father's house, though the consequence must have been, if she *had*, that she would have been the wife of the odious Solmes? If now she be brought to consent to be mine, seest thou not that the *reconciliation* with her *detested relations* is the *inducement*, as it *always* was, and not *love* of *me*? Neither her virtue nor her love can be established but upon full trial; the *last* trial—but if her resistance and resentment be such as hitherto I have reason to expect they will be, and if I find in that resentment less of hatred of *me* than of the *fact*, then shall she be mine in her own way. Then, hateful as is the *life of shackles* to me, will I *marry her*.

Well, sir, I can only say that I am dough in your hands, to be moulded into what shape you please. But if, as I said before——

None of thy *saids-before*, Patrick. I remember all thou saidst—and I know all thou canst *further* say. Thou art only, Pontius Pilate - like, washing thine own hands (don't I know thee?) that thou mayst have something to silence thy conscience with by loading me. But we have gone too far to recede. Are not all our engines in readiness? Dry up thy sorrowful eyes. Let unconcern and heart's ease once more take possession of thy solemn features. Thou hast hitherto performed extremely well. Shame not thy *past* by thy *future* behaviour; and a rich reward awaits thee. If thou *art* dough, *be* dough; and I slapped him on the shoulder. Resume but thy former shape, and I 'll be answerable for the event.

He bowed assent and compliance: went to the glass; and began to untwist and unsadden his features: pulled his wig right, as if that, as well as his head and heart, had been discomposed by his compunction; and once more became old Lucifer's and mine.

But didst thou think, Jack, that there was so much—what

[1] See vol. ii, p. 35 *et seq.*

shall I call it—in this Tomlinson? Didst thou imagine that such a fellow as that had bowels? That nature, so long dead and buried in him, as to all humane effects, should thus revive and exert itself? Yet why do I ask this question of thee, who, to my equal surprise, hast shown, on the same occasion, the like compassionate sensibilities?

As to Tomlinson, it looks as if poverty had made him the wicked fellow *he* is; as plenty and wantonness have made us what *we* are. *Necessity*, after all, is the test of principle. But what is there in this dull word, or thing, called HONESTY, that even I, who cannot in my present views be served by it, cannot help thinking even the accidental emanations of it amiable in Tomlinson, though demonstrated in a *female case*; and judging *better of him* for being capable of such?

Letter XVII—Mr. Lovelace to John Belford, Esq.

THIS debate between the captain and me was hardly over, when the three women, led by Miss Rawlins, entered, hoping no intrusion—but very desirous, the maiden said, to know if we were likely to accommodate.

O yes, I hope so. You know, ladies, that your sex must, in these cases, preserve their forms. They must be courted to comply with their own happiness. A lucky expedient we have hit upon. The uncle has his doubts of our marriage. He cannot believe, nor will anybody, that it is possible that a man so much in love, the lady so desirable——

They all took the hint. It was a very extraordinary case, the two widows allowed. Women, Jack, [as I believe I have observed[1] elsewhere], have a high opinion of what they can do for us. Miss Rawlins desired, if I pleased, to let them know the expedient; and looked as if there was no need to proceed in the rest of my speech.

I begged that they would not let the lady know I had told them what this expedient was; and they should hear it.

They promised.

It was this: That to oblige and satisfy Mr. Harlowe, the ceremony was to be *again performed*. He was to be *privately present*, and to give his niece to me with his own hands. And she was retired to consider of it.

Thou seest, Jack, that I have provided an excuse, to save my veracity to the women here, in case I should incline to marriage,

[1] See p. 60.

and she should choose to have Miss Rawlins's assistance at the ceremony. Nor doubted I to bring my fair one to save my credit on this occasion, if I could get her to consent to be mine.

A charming expedient! cried the widow. They were all three ready to clap their hands for joy upon it. Women love to be married twice at least, Jack; though not indeed to the *same man*; and all blessed the reconciliatory scheme, and the proposer of it; and, supposing it came from the captain, they looked at him with pleasure, while his face shone with the applause implied. He should think himself very happy, if he could bring about a general reconciliation; and he flourished with his head like my man Will, on his victory over old Grimes; bridling by turns, like Miss Rawlins in the height of a prudish fit.

But now it was time for the captain to think of returning to town, having a great deal of business to dispatch before morning: nor was he certain that he should again be able to attend us at Hampstead before he went home.

And yet, as everything was drawing towards a crisis, I did not intend that he should leave Hampstead this night.

A message to the above effect was carried up, at my desire, by Mrs. Moore; with the captain's compliments, and to know if she had any commands for him to her uncle?

But I hinted to the women, that it would be proper for them to withdraw, if the lady did come down; lest she should not care to be so free before *them* on a proposal so particular, as she would be to *us*, who had offered it to her consideration.

Mrs. Moore brought down word that the lady was following her. They all three withdrew; and she entered at one door, as they went out at the other.

The captain accosted her, repeating the contents of the message sent up; and desired that she would give him her commands in relation to the report he was to make to her Uncle Harlowe.

I know not what to say, sir, nor what I would have *you* to say, to my uncle. Perhaps you may have business in town— perhaps you need not see my uncle, till I have heard from Miss Howe; till after Lady Betty—I don't know what to say.

I implored the return of that value which she had so generously acknowledged once to have had for me. I presumed, I said, to flatter myself that Lady Betty, in her own person, and in the name of all my family, would be able, on my promised reformation and contrition, to prevail in my favour; especially as our prospects in other respects with regard to the general reconciliation wished for were so happy. But let me owe to *your own generosity*, my dearest creature, said I, rather than to the mediation of *any person on earth*, the forgiveness I am an humble suitor for. How much more agreeable to *yourself*, O best beloved of my soul, must it be, as well as *obliging to me*, that your first personal knowledge of my relations, and theirs of you (for they will not be denied attending you), should not be begun in recriminations and appeals! As Lady Betty will be here so soon, it will not perhaps be possible for you to receive her visit with a brow absolutely serene. But, dearest, dearest creature, I beseech you, let the misunderstanding pass as a slight one— as a misunderstanding cleared up. Appeals give pride and superiority to the persons appealed to, and are apt to lessen the appellant, not only in their eye, but in her own. Exalt not into judges those who are prepared to take lessons and instructions from you. The individuals of my family are as proud as I am said to be. But they will cheerfully resign to your superiority— you will be the first woman of the family in every one's eyes.

This might have done with any other woman in the world but *this*; and yet she is the only woman in the world of whom it may with truth be said. But thus, angrily, did she disclaim the compliment.

Yes, indeed! [and there she stopped a moment, her sweet bosom heaving with a noble disdain]. Cheated out of myself from the very first! A fugitive from my own family! Renounced by my relations! Insulted by you! Laying humble claim to the protection of yours! Is not this the light in which I must appear, not only to the ladies of your family, but to all the world? Think you, sir, that in these circumstances, or even had I been in the *happiest*, that I could be affected by this plea of undeserved superiority? You are a stranger to the mind of Clarissa Harlowe, if you think her capable of so poor and so *undue* a pride!

She went from us to the farther end of the room.

The captain was again affected—Excellent creature! I called her; and, reverently approaching her, urged further the plea I had last made.

It is but lately, said I, that the opinions of my relations have been more than indifferent to me, whether good or bad; and it is for *your* sake, more than for *my own*, that I now wish to stand well with my whole family. The principal motive of Lady Betty's coming up, is to purchase presents for the whole family to make on the happy occasion.

This consideration, turning to the captain, with so noble-minded a dear creature, I know, can have no weight; only as it will show their value and respect. But what a damp would their worthy hearts receive, were they to find their admired new niece, as they now think her, not only *not* their niece, but capable of renouncing me for ever! They love me. They *all* love me. I have been guilty of carelessness and levity to them, indeed; but of carelessness and levity only; and *that* owing to a pride that has set me above meanness, though it has not done everything for me.

My whole family will be guarantees for my good behaviour to this dear creature, their niece, their daughter, their cousin, their friend, their chosen companion and directress, all in one. Upon my soul, captain, we *may*, we *must* be happy.

But, dearest, dearest creature, let me on my knees [and down I dropped, her face all the time turned half from me, as she stood at the window, her handkerchief often at her eyes], on my knees let me plead your *promised* forgiveness; and let us not appear to them, on their visit, thus unhappy with each other. Lady Betty, the next hour that she sees you, will write her opinion of you, and of the likelihood of our future happiness, to Lady Sarah her sister, a weak-spirited woman, who now hopes to supply to herself, in my bride, the lost daughter she still mourns for!

The captain then joined in, and re-urged her uncle's hopes and expectations; and his resolution effectually to set about the general reconciliation; the mischief that might be prevented; and the certainty that there was that her uncle might be prevailed upon to give her to me with his own hand, if she made it her choice to wait for his coming up. But, for his own part, he humbly advised, and fervently pressed her, to make the very next day, or Monday at farthest, my happy day.

Permit me, dearest lady, said he, and I could kneel to you myself [bending his knee], though I have no interest in my earnestness, but the pleasure I should have to be able to serve you all, to beseech you to give me an opportunity to assure your uncle that I myself saw with my own eyes the happy knot tied! All misunderstandings, all doubts, all diffidences, will then be at an end.

And what, madam, rejoined I, still kneeling, can there be in your new measures, be they what they will, that can so happily, so *reputably*, I will presume to say, for all around, obviate the present difficulties?

Miss Howe herself, if she love you, and if she love your fame, madam, urged the captain, his knee still bent, must congratulate you on such a happy conclusion.

Then turning her face, she saw the captain half kneeling— O sir! O Captain Tomlinson! Why this *undue* condescension? extending her hand to his elbow, to raise him. I cannot bear this! Then casting her eye on me, Rise, Mr. Lovelace, kneel not to the poor creature whom you have insulted! How cruel the occasion for it! And how mean the submission!

Not mean to such an angel! Nor can I rise, but to be forgiven!

The captain then re-urged once more the day. He was amazed, he said, if she ever valued me——

O Captain Tomlinson, interrupted she, how much are you the friend of this man! *If I had never valued him, he never would have had it in his power to insult me*; nor could I, if I had never regarded him, have *taken to heart as I do*, the insult (execrable as it was) so undeservedly, so ungratefully given—but let him retire—for a moment let him retire.

I was more than half afraid to trust the captain by himself with her. He gave me a sign that I might depend upon him. And then I took out of my pocket his letter to me, and Lady Betty's, and Miss Montague's, and Lord M.'s letters (which last she had not then seen); and giving them to him, Procure for me, in the first place, Mr. Tomlinson, a reperusal of these three letters; and of *this* from Lord M. And I beseech you, my dearest life, give them due consideration: and let me on my return find the happy effects of that consideration.

I then withdrew; with slow feet, however, and a misgiving heart.

The captain insisted upon this reperusal previously to what she had to say to him, as he tells me. She complied, but with some difficulty; as if she was *afraid* of being *softened in my favour*.

She lamented her unhappy situation; destitute of friends, and not knowing whither to go, or what to do. She asked questions, *sifting* questions, about her uncle, about her family, and after what he knew of Mr. Hickman's fruitless application in her favour.

He was well prepared in this particular; for I had shown him the letters and extracts of letters of Miss Howe, which I had so happily come at.[1] Might she be assured, she asked him, that her brother, with Singleton, and Solmes, were actually in quest of her?

He averred that they were.

She asked, If he thought I had hopes of prevailing on her to go back to town?

[1] See vol. ii, p. 364 *et seq.*

He was sure I had not.

Was he really of opinion that Lady Betty would pay her a visit?

He had no doubt of it.

But, sir; but, Captain Tomlinson [impatiently turning from him, and again to him], I know not what to do—but were I *your* daughter, sir—were *you* my own father—Alas, sir, I have neither father nor mother!

He turned from her, and wiped his eyes.

O sir! you have humanity! [She wept too.] There are some men in the world, thank Heaven, that *can* be moved. O sir, I have met with hard-hearted men—in my own family too—or I could not have been so unhappy as I am—but I make everybody unhappy!

His eyes no doubt ran over.

Dearest madam! Heavenly lady! Who can—who can—hesitated and blubbered the dog, as he owned. And indeed I heard some part of what passed, though *they both* talked lower than I wished; for, from the nature of *their* conversation, there was no room for altitudes.

THEM, and BOTH, and THEY! How it goes against me to include this angel of a creature, and any man on earth but myself, in *one* word!

Capt. Who can forbear being affected? But, madam, you *can* be no other man's.

Cl. Nor would I be. But he is so sunk with me! To fire the house! An artifice so vile!—contrived for the worst of purposes! Would you have a daughter of yours—But what would I say? Yet you see, that I have nobody in whom I can confide! Mr. Lovelace is a vindictive man! He could not love the creature whom he could insult as he has insulted me!

She paused. And then resuming—In short, I never, never can forgive *him*, nor he *me*. Do you think, sir, I would have gone so far as I have gone, if I had intended ever to draw with him in one yoke? I left behind me *such* a letter——

You know, madam, he has acknowledged the justice of your resentment——

O sir, he can acknowledge, and he can retract, fifty times a day. But do not think I am trifling with myself and you, and want to be *persuaded* to forgive him, and to be *his*. There is not a creature of my sex, who would have been *more explicit*, and *more frank*, than I would have been, from the moment I *intended* to be his, had I had a heart like *my own* to deal with.

I was always *above reserve*, sir, I will presume to say, where I had no cause of doubt. Mr. Lovelace's conduct has made me appear, perhaps, *over-nice*, when my heart wanted to be *encouraged* and *assured*; and when, if it had been so, my whole behaviour would have been governed by it.

She stopped, her handkerchief at her eyes.

I inquired after the minutest part of her behaviour, as well as after her words. I love, thou knowest, to trace human nature, and more particularly female nature, through its most secret recesses.

The pitiful fellow was lost in silent admiration of her. And thus the noble creature proceeded.

It is the fate in unequal unions, that tolerable creatures, through them, frequently incur censure, when, more happily yoked, they might be entitled to praise. And shall I not shun a union with a man that might lead into errors a creature who flatters herself that she is blest with an inclination to be good; and who wishes to make every one happy with whom she has any connection, even to her very servants?

She paused, taking a turn about the room—the fellow, devil fetch him, a mummy all the time: then proceeded:

Formerly, indeed, I hoped to be an humble means of reforming him. But, when I have *no such hope*, is it right [you are a serious man, sir] to make a venture that shall endanger *my own morals*?

Still silent was the varlet. If my advocate had nothing to say for me, what hope of carrying my cause?

And now, sir, what is the result of all? It is this: That you will endeavour, if you have that influence over him which a man of your sense and experience ought to have, to prevail upon him, and that for *his own* sake, as well as for *mine*, to leave me free to pursue my own destiny. And of this you may assure him, that I never will be any other man's.

Impossible, madam! I know that Mr. Lovelace would not hear mew ith patience on such a topic. And I do assure you that I have *some spirit*, and should not care to take an indignity from him, or from any man living.

She paused, then resuming—And think you, sir, that my uncle will refuse to receive a letter from me? [*How averse, Jack, to concede a tittle in my favour!*]

I knew, madam, as matters are circumstanced, that he would not *answer* it. If you please I will carry one down from you.

And will he not pursue his intentions in *my* favour, nor be himself reconciled to me, except I am married?

From what your brother gives out, and affects to believe, on Mr. Lovelace's living with you in the same——

No more, sir—I am an unhappy creature!

He then re-urged that it would be in her power instantly, or on the morrow, to put an end to all her difficulties.

How can that *be*? said she: The licence *still* to be obtained? The settlements *still* to be signed? Miss Howe's answer to my last *unreceived*? And shall I, sir, be in such a HURRY, as if I thought my *honour in danger if I delayed*? Yet *marry* the man from whom only it *can* be endangered! Unhappy, thrice unhappy Clarissa Harlowe! In how many difficulties has one rash step involved thee? And she turned from him and wept.

The varlet, by way of comfort, wept too: yet her tears, as he might have observed, were tears that indicated rather a *yielding* than a *perverse* temper.

There is a sort of stone, thou knowest, so soft in the quarry, that it may in a manner be cut with a knife; but if the opportunity be not taken, and it is exposed to the air for any time, it will become as hard as marble, and then with difficulty it yields to the chisel.[1] So this lady, not taken at the moment, after a turn or two across the room, gained more resolution; and then she declared, as she had done once before, that she would wait the issue of Miss Howe's answer to the letter she had sent her from hence, and take her measures accordingly—leaving it to him, meantime, to make what report he thought fit to her uncle—the kindest that *truth* could bear, she doubted not from Captain Tomlinson: and she should be glad of a few lines from him, to hear what *that* was.

She wished him a good journey. She complained of her head; and was about to withdraw: but I stepped round to the door next the stairs, as if I had but just come in from the garden (which, as I entered, I called a very pretty one), and took her reluctant hand, as she was going out: My dearest life, you are not going?—What hopes, captain? Have you not some hopes to give me of pardon and reconciliation?

She said she would not be detained. But I would not let her go till she had promised to return, when the captain had reported to me what her resolution was.

And when he had, I sent up and claimed her promise; and she came down again, and repeated (as what she was determined

[1] The nature of the Bath stone, in particular.

upon) that she would wait for Miss Howe's answer to the letter she had written to her, and take her measures according to its contents.

I expostulated with her upon it, in the most submissive and earnest manner. She made it necessary for me to repeat many of the pleas I had before urged. The captain seconded me with equal earnestness. At last, each fell down on his knees before her.

She was distressed. I was afraid at one time she would have fainted. Yet neither of us would rise without some concessions. I pleaded my own sake; the captain, his dear friend her uncle's; and *both* repleaded the prevention of future mischief; and the peace and happiness of the two families.

She owned herself unequal to the conflict. She sighed. She sobbed. She wept. She wrung her hands.

I was perfectly eloquent in my vows and protestations. Her tearful eyes were cast down upon me; a glow upon each charming cheek; a visible anguish in every lovely feature. At last, her trembling knees seeming to fail her, she dropped into the next chair; her charming face, as if seeking for a hiding-place (which a mother's bosom would have best supplied), sinking upon her own shoulder.

I forgot at the instant all my vows of revenge. I threw myself at her feet as she sat; and, snatching her hand, pressed it with my lips. I besought Heaven to forgive my past offences, and prosper my future hopes, as I designed honourably and justly by the charmer of my heart, if once more she would restore me to her favour. And I thought I felt drops of scalding water [could they be tears?] trickle down upon my cheeks; while my cheeks, glowing like fire, seemed to scorch up the unwelcome strangers.

I then arose, not doubting of an *implied* pardon in this silent distress. I raised the captain. I whispered him, By my soul, man, I am in earnest. Now talk of reconciliation, of her uncle, of the licence, of settlements—and raising my voice, If now at last, Captain Tomlinson, my angel will give me leave to call so great a blessing mine, it will be impossible that you should say too much to her uncle in praise of my gratitude, my affection, and fidelity to his charming niece; and he may begin as soon as he pleases, his kind schemes for effecting the desirable reconciliation! Nor shall he prescribe any terms to me that I will not comply with.

The captain blessed me with his eyes and hands. Thank God! whispered he. We approached the lady together.

Capt. What hinders, dearest madam, what now hinders, but that Lady Betty Lawrance, when she comes, may be acquainted with the truth of everything? And that then she may assist privately at your nuptials? I will stay till they are celebrated; and then shall I go down with the happy tidings to my dear Mr. Harlowe. And all will, all must, soon be happy.

I must have an answer from Miss Howe, replied the still trembling fair one. I cannot change my new measures but with her advice. I will forfeit all my hopes of happiness in this world, rather than forfeit her good opinion, and that she should think me giddy, unsteady, or precipitate. All I will further say on the present subject is this, that, when I have her answer to what I *have* written, I will write to her the whole state of the matter, as I shall then be enabled to do.

Lovel. Then must I despair for ever! O Captain Tomlinson, Miss Howe hates me! Miss Howe——

Capt. Not so, perhaps—when Miss Howe knows your concern for having offended, she will never advise, that, with such prospects of general reconciliation, the hopes of so many considerable persons in both families should be frustrated. Some little time, as this excellent lady has foreseen and hinted, will necessarily be taken up in actually procuring the licence, and in perusing and signing the settlements. In that time Miss Howe's answer may be received; and Lady Betty may arrive; and she, no doubt, will have weight to dissipate the lady's doubts, and to accelerate the day. It shall be my part, meantime, to make Mr. Harlowe easy. All I fear from delay is from Mr. James Harlowe's quarter; and therefore all must be conducted with prudence and privacy; as your uncle, madam, has proposed.

She was silent. I rejoiced in her silence. The dear creature, thought I, has actually forgiven me in her heart! But why will she not lay me under obligation to her, by the generosity of an explicit declaration? And yet, as that would not accelerate anything, while the licence is not in my hands, she is the less to be blamed (if I do her justice) for taking more time to *descend*.

I proposed, as on the morrow night, to go to town; and doubted not to bring the licence up with me on Monday morning. Would she be pleased to assure me that she would not depart from Mrs. Moore's?

She should stay at Mrs. Moore's till she had an answer from Miss Howe.

I told her that I hoped I might have her *tacit* consent, at least, to the obtaining of the licence.

I saw by the turn of her countenance that I should not have asked this question. She was so far from *tacitly* consenting, that she declared to the contrary.

As I never intended, I said, to ask her to enter again into a house, with the people of which she was so much offended, would she be pleased to give orders for her clothes to be brought up hither? Or should Dorcas attend her for any of her commands on that head?

She desired not ever more to see anybody belonging to that house. She might perhaps get Mrs. Moore or Mrs. Bevis to go thither for her, and take her keys with them.

I doubted not, I said, that Lady Betty would arrive by that time. I hoped she had no objection to my bringing that lady and my Cousin Montague up with me?

She was silent.

To be sure, Mr. Lovelace, said the captain, the lady can have no objection to this.

She was still silent. So silence in this case was assent.

Would she be pleased to write to Miss Howe?

Sir! Sir! peevishly interrupting. No more questions; no prescribing to me. You will do as you think fit. So will I, as I please. I own no obligation to you. Captain Tomlinson, your servant. Recommend me to my Uncle Harlowe's favour: and was going.

I took her reluctant hand, and besought her only to promise to meet me early in the morning.

To what purpose meet you? Have you more to say than has been said? I have had enough of vows and protestations, Mr. Lovelace. To what purpose should I meet you to-morrow morning?

I repeated my request, and that in the most fervent manner, naming six in the morning.

"You know that I am always stirring before that hour, at this season of the year," was the half-expressed consent.

She then again recommended herself to her uncle's favour; and withdrew.

And thus, Belford, has she *mended her markets*, as Lord M. would say, and I worsted mine. Miss Howe's next letter is now the hinge on which the fate of both must turn. I shall be absolutely ruined and undone, if I cannot intercept it.

Letter XVIII—Mr. Lovelace to John Belford, Esq.

Sat. Midnight.

No rest, says a text that I once heard preached upon, *to the wicked*—and I cannot close my eyes (yet wanted only to compound for half an hour in an elbow-chair)—so must scribble on.

I parted with the captain after another strong debate with him in relation to what is to be the fate of this lady. As the fellow has an excellent head, and would have made an eminent figure in any station of life, had not his early days been tainted with a deep crime, and he detected in it; and as he had the right side of the argument; I had a good deal of difficulty with him; and at last brought myself to promise, that if I could prevail upon her generously to forgive me, and to reinstate me in her favour, I would make it my whole endeavour to get off of my contrivances, as happily as I could (only that Lady Betty and Charlotte *must come*); and then, substituting him for her uncle's proxy, take shame to myself, and marry.

But, if I should, Jack (with the strongest antipathy to the state that ever man had), what a figure shall I make in rakish annals? And can I have taken all these pains for nothing? Or for a wife only, that, however excellent [and *any* woman, do I think, I could make good, because I could make any woman *fear* as well as *love* me], might have been obtained without the plague I have been at, and much more reputably than with it? And hast thou not seen, that this haughty woman [forgive me that I call her *haughty*! and a *woman*! Yet is she not haughty?] knows not how to forgive with graciousness? Indeed has not at all forgiven me? But holds my soul in a *suspense* which has been so grievous to her own.

At this silent moment, I think, that if I were to pursue my former scheme, and resolve to try whether I cannot make a greater fault serve as a sponge to wipe out the less; and then be forgiven for that; I can justify myself to *myself*; and that, as the fair invincible would say, is all in all.

As it is my intention, in all my reflections, to avoid repeating at least dwelling upon, what I have before written to thee though the state of the case may not have varied; so I would have thee to reconsider the *old* reasonings (particularly those contained in my answer to thy last[1] expostulatory nonsense).

[1] See vol. ii, pp. 490 *et seq.*

and add the *new*, as they fall from my pen; and then I shall think myself invincible;—at least, as arguing rake to rake.

I take the gaining of this lady to be essential to my happiness: and is it not natural for *all men* to aim at obtaining whatever they think will make them happy, be the object more or less considerable in the eyes of others?

As to the manner of endeavouring to obtain her, by falsification of oaths, vows, and the like—do not the poets of two thousand years and upwards tell us that Jupiter laughs at the perjuries of lovers? And let me add to what I have heretofore mentioned on that head, a question or two.

Do not the mothers, the aunts, the grandmothers, the governesses of the pretty innocents, always, from their very cradles to riper years, preach to them the deceitfulness of men? That they are not to regard their oaths, vows, promises? What a parcel of fibbers would all these reverend matrons be, if there were not now and then a pretty credulous rogue taken in for a justification of their preachments, and to serve as a beacon lighted up for the benefit of the rest?

Do we not then see that an honest prowling fellow is a necessary evil on many accounts? Do we not see that it is highly requisite that a sweet girl should be now and then drawn aside by him? And the more eminent the girl, in the graces of person, mind, and fortune, is not the example likely to be the more efficacious?

If these *postulata* be granted me, who, I pray, can equal my charmer in all these? Who therefore so fit for an example to the rest of the sex? At worst, I am entirely within my worthy friend Mandeville's assertion, *That private vices are public benefits.*

Well then, if this sweet creature must *fall*, as it is called, for the benefit of all the pretty fools of the sex, she *must*; and there's an end of the matter. And what would there have been in it of uncommon or rare, had I not been so long about it? And so I dismiss all further argumentation and debate upon the question: and I impose upon thee, when thou writest to me, an eternal silence on this head.

Wafered on, as an after-written introduction to the paragraphs which follow, marked with turned commas [thus, "]:

LORD, Jack, what shall I do now! How one evil brings on another! Dreadful news to tell thee! While I was meditating a simple robbery, here have I (in my own defence indeed) been guilty of murder! A bloody murder! So I believe it will prove. At her last gasp! Poor impertinent opposer! Eternally resisting! Eternally contradicting! There she lies, weltering in her blood! Her death's wound have I given her! But she was a thief, an impostor, as well as a tormentor. She had stolen my pen. While I was sullenly meditating, doubting, as to my future measures, she stole it; and thus she wrote with it, in a hand exactly like my own; and would have faced me down that it was really my own handwriting.

"But let me reflect, before it be too late. On the manifold perfections of this ever-admirable creature let me reflect. The hand yet is only held up. The blow is not struck. Miss Howe's next letter may blow thee up. In policy thou shouldst be now at least honest. Thou canst not live without her. Thou wouldst rather marry her than lose her absolutely. Thou mayst undoubtedly prevail upon her, inflexible as she seems to be, for marriage. But if now she find thee a villain, thou mayst never more engage her attention, and she perhaps will refuse and abhor thee.

"Yet already have I not gone too far? Like a repentant thief, afraid of his gang, and obliged to go on, in fear of hanging till he comes to be hanged, I am afraid of the gang of my cursed contrivances.

"As I hope to live, I am sorry (at the present writing) that I have been such a foolish plotter, as to put it, as I fear I have done, out of my *own power* to be honest. I hate compulsion in all forms; and cannot bear, even to be *compelled* to be the wretch my choice has made me! So now, Belford, as thou hast said, I am a machine at last, and no free agent.

"Upon my soul, Jack, it is a very foolish thing for a man of spirit to have brought himself to such a height of iniquity, that he must proceed, and cannot help himself; and yet to be next to certain that his very victory will undo him.

"Why was such a woman as this thrown in my way, whose very fall will be her glory, and perhaps not only my shame, but my destruction?

"What a happiness must that man know, who moves regularly to some laudable end, and has nothing to reproach himself with in his progress to it! When, by honest means, he attains this end, how great and unmixed must be his enjoyments! What a happy man, in this particular case, had I been, had it been given me to *be* only what I wished to *appear* to be!"

Thus far had my *conscience* written with my pen; and see

what a recreant she had made me! I seized her by the throat—
There!—*There*, said I, thou vile impertinent! Take *that*, and *that*!
How often have I given thee warning! And now, I hope, thou
intruding varletess, have I done thy business!

Puling and low-voiced, rearing up thy detested head, in
vain implorest thou *my* mercy, who, in *thy* day, hast showed me
so little! Take *that*, for a rising blow! And now will *thy* pain,
and *my* pain from *thee*, soon be over. Lie there! Welter on!
Had I not given thee thy death's wound, thou wouldst have
robbed me of all my joys. Thou couldst not have mended me,
'tis plain. Thou couldst only have thrown me into despair.
Didst thou not see that I had gone too far to recede? Welter
on, once more I bid thee! Gasp on! *That* thy last gasp, surely!
How hard diest thou!

ADIEU! Unhappy man! ADIEU!

'Tis kind in thee, however, to bid me *Adieu*!

Adieu, Adieu, Adieu, to thee, O thou inflexible, and, till now,
unconquerable bosom intruder. Adieu to thee for ever!

Letter XIX—*Mr. Lovelace to John Belford, Esq.*

Sunday Morn. (*June* 11) 4 *o'clock.*

A FEW words to the verbal information thou sentest me last
night concerning thy poor old man; and then I rise from my
seat, shake myself, refresh, new-dress, and so to my charmer,
whom, notwithstanding her reserves, I hope to prevail upon to
walk out with me on the heath this warm and fine morning.

The birds must have awakened her before now. They are in
full song. She always gloried in accustoming herself to behold
the sun rise; one of God's natural wonders, as once she called it.

Her window salutes the east. The valleys must be gilded by
his rays, by the time I am with her; for already have they made
the uplands smile, and the face of nature cheerful.

How unsuitable wilt thou find this gay preface to a subject
so gloomy as that I am now turning to!

I am glad to hear thy tedious expectations are at last answered.

Thy servant tells me that thou art plaguily grieved at the
old fellow's departure.

I can't say but thou mayst *look* as if thou wert; harassed as
thou hast been for a number of days and nights with a close
attendance upon a dying man, beholding his drawing-on hour—
pretending, for decency's sake, to whine over his excruciating

pangs; to be in the way to answer a thousand impertinent inquiries after the health of a man thou wishedst to die—to pray by him—for so once thou wrotest to me!—to read by him—To be forced to join in consultation with a crew of solemn and parading doctors, and their officious zanies the apothecaries, joined with the butcherly tribe of scarificators; all combined to carry on the physical farce, and to cut out thongs both from his flesh and his estate—to have the superadded apprehension of dividing thy interest in what he shall leave with a crew of eager-hoping, never-to-be-satisfied relations, legatees, and the devil knows who, of private gratifiers of passions laudable and illaud-able—in these circumstances, I wonder not that thou lookest before servants (as little grieved at heart as thyself, and who are gaping after legacies, as thou after *heirship*) as if thou indeed wert grieved; and as if the most wry-faced woe had befallen thee.

Then, as I have often thought, the reflection that must naturally arise from such mortifying objects, as the death of one with whom we have been familiar, must afford, when we are obliged to attend it in its slow approaches, and in its face-twisting pangs, that it will one day be our own case, goes a great way to credit the appearance of grief.

And this it is that, seriously reflected upon, may temporarily give a fine air of sincerity to the wailings of lively widows, heart-exulting heirs, and residuary legatees of all denominations; since, by keeping down the inward joy, those interesting reflections must sadden the aspect, and add an appearance of real concern to the assumed sables.

Well, but, now thou art come to the reward of all thy watchings, anxieties, and close attendances, tell me what it is; tell me if it compensate thy trouble, and answer thy hope?

As to myself, thou seest, by the gravity of my style, how the subject has helped to mortify me. But the necessity I am under of committing either speedy matrimony, or a rape, has saddened over my gayer prospects, and, more than the case itself, contributed to make me sympathize with thy present joyful sorrow.

Adieu, Jack. I must be soon out of my pain; and my Clarissa shall be soon out of hers—for so does the arduousness of the case require.

Letter XX—Mr. Lovelace to John Belford, Esq.

Sunday Morning.

I HAVE had the honour of my charmer's company for two complete hours. We met before six in Mrs. Moore's garden. A walk on the heath refused me.

The sedateness of her aspect, and her kind compliance in this meeting, gave me hopes. And all that either the captain or I had urged yesterday to obtain a full and free pardon, that re-urged I; and I told her, besides, that Captain Tomlinson was gone down with hopes to prevail upon her Uncle Harlowe to come up in person, in order to present to me the greatest blessing that man ever received.

But the utmost I could obtain was, that she would take no resolution in my favour till she received Miss Howe's next letter.

I will not repeat the arguments I used: but I will give thee the substance of what she said in answer to them.

She had considered of everything, she told me. My whole conduct was before her. The house I carried her to must be a vile house. The people early showed what they were capable of, in the earnest attempt made to fasten Miss Partington upon her; as she doubted not, with my approbation. [Surely, thought I, she has not received a duplicate of Miss Howe's letter of detection!] They heard her cries. My insult was undoubtedly premeditated. By my whole recollected behaviour to her, previous to it, it must be so. I had the vilest of views, no question. And my treatment of her put it out of all doubt.

Soul all over, Belford! She seems sensible of liberties that my passion made me insensible of having taken; or she could not so deeply resent.

She besought me to give over all thoughts of her. Sometimes, she said, she thought herself cruelly treated by her nearest and dearest relations: at *such* times, a spirit of repining, and even of resentment, took place; and the reconciliation, at other times so desirable, was not then so much the favourite wish of her heart, as was the scheme she had formerly planned—of taking her good Norton for her directress and guide, and living upon her own estate in the manner her grandfather had intended she should live.

This scheme she doubted not that her Cousin Morden, who was one of her trustees for that estate, would enable her (and that, as she hoped, without litigation) to pursue. And if he can, and does, what, sir, let me ask you, said she, have I seen in your conduct that should make me prefer to it a union of interests, where there is such a disunion in minds?

So thou seest, Jack, there is *reason*, as well as *resentment*, in the preference she makes against me! Thou seest that she presumes to think that she can be happy *without* me; and that she must be unhappy *with* me!

I had besought her, in the conclusion of my re-urged arguments, to write to Miss Howe before Miss Howe's answer could come, in order to lay before her the present state of things; and if she *would* defer to her judgment, to let her have an opportunity to give it, on the full knowledge of the case——

So I would, Mr. Lovelace, was the answer, if I were in doubt myself, which I would prefer; marriage, or the scheme I have mentioned. You cannot think, sir, but the latter must be my choice. I wish to part with you with temper—don't put me upon repeating——

Part with me, madam! interrupted I—I cannot bear those words! But let me beseech you, however, to write to Miss Howe. I hope, if Miss Howe is not my enemy——

She is not the enemy of your *person*, sir; as you would be convinced, if you *saw her last letter to me*.[1] But were she not an enemy to your *actions*, she would not be *my* friend, nor the friend of *virtue*. Why will you provoke from me, Mr. Lovelace, the harshness of expression, which, however deserved by you, I am unwilling just now to use: having suffered enough in the two past days from my own vehemence?

I bit my lip for vexation. I was silent.

Miss Howe, proceeded she, knows the full state of matters already, sir. The answer I expect from her respects *myself*, not *you*. Her heart is too warm in the cause of friendship, to leave me in suspense one moment longer than is necessary, as to what I want to know. Nor does her answer depend absolutely upon herself. She must see a person first; and that person perhaps must see others.

The cursed smuggler-woman, Jack! Miss Howe's Townsend, I doubt not! Plot, contrivance, intrigue, stratagem! Underground moles these women—but let the earth cover me! let me be a mole too, thought I, if they carry their point!—and if this lady escape me now!

She frankly owned that she had once thought of embarking

---

[1] The lady innocently means Mr. Lovelace's forged one. See p. 94 of this volume.

out of all our ways for some one of our American colonies; but now that she had been *compelled* to see me (which had been her greatest dread, and which she would have given her life to avoid), she thought she might be happiest in the resumption of her former favourite scheme, if Miss Howe could find her a reputable and private asylum, till her Cousin Morden could come. But if he came not soon, and if she had a difficulty to get to a place of refuge, whether from her brother or from *anybody else* [meaning me, I suppose], she might yet perhaps go abroad: for, to say the truth, she could not think of returning to her father's house; since her brother's rage, her sister's upbraidings, her father's anger, her mother's still more affecting sorrowings, and her own consciousness under them all, would be insupportable to her.

O Jack! I am sick to death, I pine, I die for Miss Howe's next letter! I would bind, gag, strip, rob, and do anything but murder, to intercept it.

But, determined as she seems to be, it was evident to me, nevertheless, that she has still some tenderness for me.

She often wept as she talked, and much oftener sighed. She looked at me twice with an eye of *undoubted* gentleness, and three times with an eye *tending* to compassion and softness: but its benign rays were as often *snatched* back, as I may say, and her face averted, as if her sweet eyes were not to be trusted, and could not stand against my eager eyes; seeking, as they did, for a lost heart in hers, and endeavouring to penetrate to her very soul.

More than once I took her hand. She struggled not *much* against the freedom. I pressed it once with my lips. She was not *very* angry. A frown indeed; but a frown that had more distress in it than indignation.

How came the dear soul (clothed as it is with such a silken vesture) by all its steadiness?[1] Was it necessary that the active gloom of such a tyrant of a *father* should commix with such a passive sweetness of a will-less *mother*, to produce a constancy, an equanimity, a steadiness, in the *daughter*, which never woman before could boast of? If so, she is more obliged to that despotic father than I could have imagined a creature to be, who gave distinction to every one related to her beyond what the crown itself can confer.

[1] See vol. i, pp. 38, 39, 63, 93, 94 for what she herself says on that steadiness which Mr. Lovelace, though a *deserved* sufferer by it, cannot help admiring.

I hoped, I said, that she would admit of the intended visit, which I had so often mentioned, of the two ladies.

She was *here*. She had seen *me*. She could not help herself at present. She ever had the highest regard for the ladies of my family, because of their worthy characters. There she turned away her sweet face, and vanquished a half-risen sigh.

I kneeled to her then. It was upon a verdant cushion; for we were upon the grasswalk. I caught her hand. I besought her with an earnestness that called up, as I could feel, my heart to my eyes, to make me, by her forgiveness and example, more worthy of them, and of her own kind and generous wishes. By my soul, madam, said I, you stab me with your goodness, your undeserved goodness! and I cannot bear it!

Why, why, thought I, as I did several times in this conversation, will she not *generously* forgive me? Why will she make it necessary for me to bring Lady Betty and my cousin to my assistance? Can the fortress expect the same advantageous capitulation, which yields not to the summons of a resistless conqueror, as if it gave not the trouble of bringing up and raising its heavy artillery against it?

What *sensibilities*, said the divine creature, withdrawing her hand, must thou have suppressed! What a dreadful, what a judicial hardness of heart must thine be; who canst be capable of such emotions as sometimes thou hast shown; and of such sentiments as sometimes have flowed from thy lips; yet canst have so far overcome them all, as to be able to act as thou hast acted, and that from settled purpose and premeditation; and this, as it is *said*, throughout the whole of thy life, from infancy to this time!

I told her that I had hoped, from the generous concern she had expressed for me, when I was so suddenly and dangerously taken ill——[the ipecacuanha experiment, Jack!]

She interrupted me. Well have you rewarded me for the concern you speak of! However, I will frankly own, now that I am determined to think no more of you, that you might (unsatisfied as I nevertheless was with you) have made an interest——

She paused. I besought her to proceed.

Do you suppose, sir, and turned away her sweet face as we walked—Do you suppose that I had not thought of laying down a plan to govern myself by, when I found myself so unhappily over-reached, and cheated, as I may say, out of myself? When I found that I could not *be*, and *do*, what I wished *to be*, and *to do*, do you imagine that I had not cast about what was the *next* proper course to take? And do you believe that this *next* course has not cost me some pain to be obliged to——

There again she stopped.

But let us break off discourse, resumed she. The subject grows too—she sighed—Let us break off discourse—I will go in —I will prepare for church—[The devil! thought I.] Well, as I *can* appear in these everyday worn clothes—looking upon herself—I will go to church.

She then turned from me to go into the house.

Bless me, my beloved creature, bless me with the continuance of this affecting conversation. Remorse has seized my heart! I have been excessively wrong. Give me further cause to curse my heedless folly, by the continuance of this calm, but soul-penetrating conversation.

No, no, Mr. Lovelace. I have said too much. Impatience begins to break in upon me. If you can excuse me to the ladies, it will be better for my mind's sake, and for your credit's sake, that I do not see them. Call me to *them* over-nice, petulant, prudish; what you please, call me to them. Nobody but Miss Howe, to whom, next to the Almighty, and my own mother, I wish to stand acquitted of wilful error, shall know the whole of what has passed. Be happy, as you may! *Deserve* to be happy, and happy you will be, in your own reflection at least, were you to be ever so unhappy in other respects. For myself, if I shall be enabled, on due reflection, to look back upon my own conduct, without the great reproach of having wilfully, and against the light of my own judgment, erred, I shall be more happy than if I had all that the world accounts desirable.

The noble creature proceeded; for I could not speak.

This self-acquittal, when spirits are lent me to dispel the darkness which at present too often overclouds my mind, will, I hope, make me superior to all the calamities that can befall me.

Her whole person was informed by her sentiments. She seemed to be taller than before. How the God within her exalted her, not only above me, but above herself!

Divine creature! (as I *thought* her) I *called* her. I acknowledged the superiority of her mind; and was proceeding—but she interrupted me. All human excellence, said she, is comparative only. My mind, I believe, is indeed superior to yours, debased as yours is by evil habits: but I had not known it to be so, if you had not *taken pains* to convince me of the inferiority of yours.

How great, how sublimely great, this creature! By my soul, I cannot forgive her for her virtues! There is no bearing the consciousness of the infinite inferiority she charged me with. But why will she break from me, when good resolutions are taking place? The red-hot iron she refuses to strike—Oh, why will she suffer the yielding wax to harden?

We had gone but a few paces towards the house, when we were met by the impertinent women, with notice that breakfast was ready. I could only, with uplifted hands, beseech her to give me hope of a renewed conversation after breakfast.

No; she would go to church.

And into the house she went, and upstairs directly. Nor would she oblige me with her company at the tea-table.

I offered by Mrs. Moore to quit both the table and the parlour, rather than she should exclude herself, or deprive the two widows of the favour of her company.

That was not all the matter, she told Mrs. Moore. She had been struggling to keep down her temper. It had cost her some pains to do it. She was desirous to compose herself, in hopes to receive benefit by the divine worship she was going to join in.

Mrs. Moore hoped for her presence at dinner.

She had rather be excused. Yet, if she could obtain the frame of mind she hoped for, she might not be averse to show that she had got above those sensibilities, which gave consideration to a man who deserved not to be to her what he had been.

This said, no doubt, to let Mrs. Moore know that the garden-conversation had not been a reconciling one.

Mrs. Moore seemed to wonder that we were not upon a better foot of understanding, after so long a conference; and the more, as she believed that the lady had given in to the proposal for the repetition of the ceremony, which I had told them was insisted upon by her Uncle Harlowe. But I accounted for this, by telling both widows that she was resolved to keep on the reserve till she heard from Captain Tomlinson, whether her uncle would be present in person at the solemnity, or would name that worthy gentleman for his proxy.

Again I enjoined strict secrecy, as to this particular; which was promised by the widows, as well for themselves, as for Miss Rawlins; of whose taciturnity they gave me such an account, as showed me that she was *secret-keeper-general* to all the women of fashion at Hampstead.

The Lord, Jack! What a world of mischief, at this rate, must

Miss Rawlins know! What a Pandora's box must her bosom be! Yet, had I nothing that was more worthy of my attention to regard, I would engage to open it, and make my uses of the discovery.

And now, Belford, thou perceivest that all my reliance is upon the mediation of Lady Betty and Miss Montague; and upon the hope of intercepting Miss Howe's next letter.

Letter XXI—Mr. Lovelace to John Belford, Esq.

THE fair inexorable is actually gone to church, with Mrs. Moore and Mrs. Bevis. But Will closely attends her motions; and I am in the way to receive any occasional intelligence from him.

She did not *choose* [a mighty word with the sex! as if they were *always* to have their own wills!] that I should wait upon her. I did not much press it, that she might not apprehend that I thought I had reason to doubt her voluntary return.

I once had it in my head to have found the widow Bevis other employment. And I believe she would have been as well pleased with my company as to go to church; for she seemed irresolute when I told her that two out of a family were enough to go to church for one day. But having her things on (as the women call everything), and her Aunt Moore expecting her company, she thought it best to go—*Lest it should look oddly, you know*, whispered she, to one who was above regarding how it looked.

So here am I in my dining-room; and have nothing to do but write, till they return.

And what will be my subject, thinkest thou? Why, the old beaten one, to be sure; self-debate—through temporary remorse: for the blow being not struck, her guardian angel is redoubling his efforts to save her.

If it be not *that* [and yet what power should *her* guardian angel have over *me*?], I don't know what it is that gives a check to my revenge, whenever I meditate treason against so sovereign a virtue. Conscience is dead and gone, as I told thee; so it cannot be that. A young conscience growing up, like the phœnix, from the ashes of the old one, it cannot be, surely. But if it were, it would be hard, if I could not overlay a young conscience.

Well then, it must be LOVE, I fancy. LOVE itself, inspiring love of an object so adorable—some little attention possibly paid too to thy whining arguments in her favour.

Let LOVE then be allowed to be the moving principle; and the rather, as LOVE naturally makes the lover loath to disoblige the object of its flame; and knowing that an offence of the *meditated* kind will be a mortal offence to her, cannot bear that I should think of giving it.

Let LOVE and me talk together a little on this subject—be it a *young conscience*, or *love*, or *thyself*, Jack, thou seest that I am for giving every whiffler audience. But *this* must be the last debate on this subject; for is not her fate in a manner at its crisis? And must not my next step be an irretrievable one, tend it which way it will?

.   .   .   .

And now the debate is over.

A thousand charming things (for LOVE is gentler than CONSCIENCE) has this little urchin suggested in her favour.

He pretended to know both our hearts: and he would have it, that though my love was a prodigious strong and potent love; and though it has the merit of many months' faithful service to plead, and has had infinite difficulties to struggle with; yet that it is not THE RIGHT SORT OF LOVE.

Right sort of love! A puppy! But, with due regard to your deityship, said I, what merit has she with YOU, that *you* should be of her party? Is *hers*, I pray you, a *right sort of love*? Is it *love* at all? She don't *pretend* that it is. She owns not your sovereignty. What a d—l moves *you*, to plead thus earnestly for a rebel who despises your power?

And then he came with his *ifs* and *ands*—and it would *have been*, and *still*, as he believed, would be, love, and a love of the exalted kind, if I would encourage it by the *right sort of love* he talked of: and, in justification of his opinion, pleaded her own confessions, as well those of yesterday as of this morning: and even went so far back as to my ipecacuanha illness.

I never talked so familiarly with his godship before: thou mayest think, therefore, that his dialect sounded oddly in my ears. And then he told me how often I had thrown cold water upon the most charming flame that ever warmed a lady's bosom, while yet but young and rising.

I required a definition of this *right sort* of love. He tried at it: but made a sorry hand of it: nor could I, for the soul of me, be convinced that what he meant to extol was LOVE.

Upon the whole, we had a notable controversy upon this subject, in which he insisted upon the *unprecedented merit* of the lady. Nevertheless I got the better of him; for he was struck absolutely dumb, when (waiving her present perverseness, which yet was a sufficient answer to all his pleas) I asserted, and offered to prove it, by a thousand instances *impromptu,* that love was not governed by *merit,* nor could be under the dominion of *prudence,* or any other *reasoning power*: and that if the lady were capable of love, it was of such a sort of love *as he had nothing to do with,* and which never before reigned in a female heart.

I asked him what he thought of her flight from me, at a time when I was more than half overcome by the *right sort of love* he talked of? And then I showed him the letter she wrote, and left behind her for me, with an intention, no doubt, absolutely to break my heart, or to provoke me to hang, drown, or shoot myself; to say nothing of a multitude of declarations from her, defying his power, and imputing all that looked like love in her behaviour to me, to the persecution and rejection of her friends; which made her think of me but as a last resort.

LOVE then gave her up. The letter, he said, deserved neither pardon nor excuse. He did not think he had been pleading for such a *declared* rebel. And as to the rest, he should be a betrayer of the rights of his own sovereignty, if what I had alleged were true, and he were still to plead for her.

I swore to the truth of all. And *truly* I swore: which perhaps I do not always do.

And now what thinkest thou must become of the lady, whom LOVE itself gives up, and CONSCIENCE cannot plead for?

Letter XXII—Mr. Lovelace to John Belford, Esq.

Sunday Afternoon.

O BELFORD! what a hair's-breadth escape have I had! Such an one, that I tremble between terror and joy at the thoughts of what *might* have happened, and did not.

What a perverse girl is this, to contend with her fate; yet has reason to think that her very stars fight against her! I am the luckiest of men! But my breath almost fails me, when I reflect upon what a slender thread my destiny hung.

But not to keep thee in suspense; I have, within this half-hour, obtained possession of the expected letter from Miss Howe —and by *such* an accident! But here, with the former, I dispatch this; thy messenger waiting.

Letter XXIII—Mr. Lovelace. [In continuation]

THUS it was—My charmer accompanied Mrs. Moore again to church this afternoon. I had been very earnest, in the first place, to obtain her company at dinner: but in vain. According to what she had said to Mrs. Moore,[1] I was *too considerable* to her to be allowed that favour. In the *next* place, I besought her to favour me, after dinner, with another garden walk. But she *would* again go to church. And what reason have I to rejoice that she did!

My worthy friend Mrs. Bevis thought one sermon a day, *well* observed, enough; so stayed at home to bear me company.

The lady and Mrs. Moore had not been gone a quarter of an hour, when a young country-fellow on horseback came to the door, and inquired for Mrs. *Harriot Lucas.* The widow and I (undetermined how we were to entertain each other) were in the parlour next the door; and hearing the fellow's inquiry, O my dear Mrs. Bevis, said I, I am undone, undone for ever, if you don't help me out! Since here, in all probability, is a messenger from that implacable Miss Howe with a letter; which if delivered to Mrs. Lovelace, may undo all we have been doing.

What, said she, would you have me do?

Call the maid in this moment, that I may give her her lesson; and if it be as I imagine, I 'll tell you what you shall do.

Widow. Margaret! Margaret! come in this minute.

Lovel. What answer, Mrs. Margaret, did you give the man, upon his asking for Mrs. *Harriot Lucas?*

Peggy. I only asked, what was his business, and who he came from? (for, sir, your honour's servant had told me how things stood): and I came at your call, madam, before he answered me.

Lovel. Well, child, if ever you wish to be happy in wedlock yourself, and would have people disappointed, who want to make mischief between you and your husband, get out of him his message, or letter, if he has one, and bring it to me, and say nothing to Mrs. Lovelace, when she comes in; and here is a guinea for you.

Peggy. I will do all I can to serve your honour's worship for nothing [nevertheless, with a ready hand, taking the guinea]: for Mr. William tells me what a good gentleman you be.

Away went Peggy to the fellow at the door.

Peggy. What is your business, friend, with Mrs. *Harry Lucas?*

[1] See p. 154.

Fellow. I must speak to her her own self.

Lovel. My *dearest* widow, do you personate Mrs. Lovelace—
for Heaven's sake do you personate Mrs. Lovelace!

Widow. *I* personate Mrs. Lovelace, sir! How can I do that?
She is fair: I am brown. She is slender: I am plump——

Lovel. No matter, no matter. The fellow may be a new-
come servant: he is not in livery, I see. He may not know her
person. You can but be bloated, and in a dropsy.

Widow. Dropsical people look not so fresh and ruddy as I
do——

Lovel. True—but the clown may not know that. 'Tis but
for a present deception.

Peggy, Peggy, called I, in a female tone, softly at the door.
Madam, answered Peggy; and came up to me to the parlour door.

Lovel. Tell him the lady is ill; and has lain down upon the
couch. And get his business from him, whatever you do.

Away went Peggy.

Lovel. Now, my dear widow, lie along on the settee, and
put your handkerchief over your face, that, if he *will* speak to
you himself, he may not see your eyes and your hair. So—
that's right. I'll step into the closet by you.

I did so.

Peggy [returning]. He won't deliver his business to me. He
will speak to Mrs. Harry Lucas her own self.

Lovel. [holding the door in my hand]. Tell him that this is
Mrs. Harriot Lucas; and let him come in. Whisper him (if he
doubts) that she is bloated, dropsical, and not the woman she was.

Away went Margery.

Lovel. And now, my dear widow, let me see what a charming Mrs. Lovelace you'll make! Ask if he comes from Miss
Howe. Ask if he live with her. Ask how she does. Call her,
at every word, your dear Miss Howe. Offer him money—take
this half-guinea for him—complain of your head, to have a
pretence to hold it down; and cover your forehead and eyes
with your hand, where your handkerchief hides not your face.
—That's right—and dismiss the rascal [here he comes] as soon
as you can.

In came the fellow, bowing and scraping, his hat poked out
before him with both his hands.

Fellow. I am sorry, madam, an't please you, to find you
be'n't well.

Widow. What is your business with me, friend?

Fellow. You are Mrs. Harriot Lucas, I suppose, madam?

Widow. Yes. Do you come from Miss Howe?

Fellow. I do, madam.

Widow. Dost thou know my right name, friend?

Fellow. I can give a shrewd guess. But that is none of my business.

Widow. What *is* thy business? I hope Miss Howe is well?

Fellow. Yes, madam; pure well, I thank God. I wish you were so too.

Widow. I am too full of grief to be well.

Fellow. So belike I have *hard* say.

Widow. My head aches so dreadfully, I cannot hold it up. I must beg of you to let me know your business?

Fellow. Nay, and that be all, my business is soon known. It is but to give this letter into your own *partiklar* hands— here it is.

Widow [taking it]. From my dear friend Miss Howe?—Ah, my head!

Fellow. Yes, madam: but I am sorry you are so bad.

Widow. Do you live with Miss Howe?

Fellow. No, madam: I am one of her tenant's sons. Her lady mother must not know as how I came of this errand. But the letter, I suppose, will tell you all.

Widow. How shall I satisfy you for this kind trouble?

Fellow. Nohow at all. What I do is for love of Miss Howe She will satisfy me more than enough. But, mayhap, you can send no answer, you are so ill.

Widow. Was you ordered to wait for an answer?

Fellow. No. I cannot say as that I was. But I was bidden to observe how you looked, and how you was; and if you did write a line or so, to take care of it, and give it only to our young landlady in secret.

Widow. You see I look strangely Not so well as I used to do.

Fellow. Nay, I don't know that I ever saw you but once before; and that was at a stile, where I met you and my young landlady; but knew better than to stare a gentlewoman in the face; especially at a stile.

Widow. Will you eat, or drink, friend?

Fellow. A cup of small ale, I don't care if I do.

Widow. Margaret, take the young man down, and treat him with what the house affords.

Fellow. Your servant, madam. But I stayed to eat as I came along, just upon the heath yonder, or else, to say the truth, I had been here sooner. [*Thank my stars, thought I, thou didst.*] A piece of powdered beef was upon the table, at the sign of the Castle, where I stopped to inquire for this house: and so, though I only intended to wet my whistle, I could not help eating. So shall only taste of your ale; for the beef was woundily corned.

Prating dog! Pox on thee! thought I.

He withdrew, bowing and scraping.

Margaret, whispered I, in a female voice [whipping out of the closet, and holding the parlour door in my hand], get him out of the house as fast as you can, lest they come from church, and catch him here.

Peggy. Never fear, sir.

The fellow went down, and, it seems, drank a large draught of ale; and Margaret finding him very talkative, told him, she begged his pardon; but she had a sweetheart just come from sea, whom she was forced to hide in the pantry; so was sure he would excuse her from staying with him.

Ay, ay, to be sure, the clown said: *for if he could not make sport, he would spoil none.* But he whispered her, that one Squire Lovelace was a *damnation rogue,* if the truth might be told.

For what? said Margaret. And could have given him, she told the widow (who related to me all this), a good dowse of the chaps.

For kissing all the women he came near.

At the same time, the dog wrapped himself round Margery, and gave her a smack, that, she told Mrs. Bevis afterwards, she might have heard into the parlour.

Such, Jack, is human nature: thus does it operate in all degrees; and so does the clown, as well as his betters, practise what he censures; and censure what he practises! Yet this sly dog knew not but the wench had a sweetheart locked up in the pantry! If the truth were known, some of the ruddy-faced dairy wenches might perhaps call him a *damnation rogue,* as justly as their betters of the same sex might Squire Lovelace.

The fellow told the maid, that, by what he discerned of the young lady's face, it looked very *rosy* to what he took it to be; and he thought her a good deal fatter, as she lay, and not so tall.

All women are born to intrigue, Jack; and practise it more or less, as fathers, guardians, governesses, from dear experience, can tell; and in love affairs are naturally expert, and quicker in their wits by half than men. This ready, though raw, wench gave an instance of this, and improved on the dropsical hint I had given her. The lady's seeming plumpness was owing to a dropsical disorder, and to the round posture she lay in.—*Very likely, truly*. Her appearing to him to be shorter, he might have observed, was owing to her drawing her feet up, from pain, and because the couch was too short, she supposed.—*Adso, he did not think of that.* Her rosy colour was owing to her grief and headache.—*Ay, that might very well be.* But he was highly pleased that he had given the letter into Mrs. Harriot's own hand, as he should tell Miss Howe.

He desired once more to see the lady at his going away, and would not be denied. The widow therefore sat up, with her handkerchief over her face, leaning her head against the wainscot.

He asked if she had any *particular* message.

No: she was so ill she could not write; which was a great grief to her.

Should he call next day? for he was going to London, now he was so near; and should stay at a cousin's that night, who lived in a street called Fetter Lane.

No: she would write as soon as able, and send by the post.

Well, then, if she had nothing to send by him, mayhap he might stay in town a day or two; for he had never seen the Lions in the Tower, nor Bedlam, nor the tombs; and he would make a holiday or two, as he had leave to do, if she had no business or message that required his posting down next day.

She had not.

She offered him the half-guinea I had given her for him; but he refused it, with great professions of disinterestedness, and love, as he called it, to Miss Howe; to serve whom, he would ride to the world's end, or *even* to Jericho.

And so the shocking rascal went away: and glad at my heart was I when he was gone; for I feared nothing so much as that he would have stayed till they came from church.

Thus, Jack, got I my *heart's ease*, the letter of Miss Howe; and through such a train of accidents, as makes me say, that the lady's stars fight against her. But yet I must attribute a good deal to my own precaution, in having taken right measures: for had I not secured the widow by my stories, and the maid by my servant, all would have signified nothing. And so heartily were they secured, the one by a single guinea, the other by half a dozen warm kisses, and the aversion they both had to such wicked creatures as delighted in making mischief between man and wife, that they promised that neither Mrs. Moore, Miss Rawlins, Mrs. Lovelace, nor anybody living, till a week at least were past, and till I gave leave, should know anything of the matter.

The widow rejoiced that I had got the mischief-maker's letter. I excused myself to her, and instantly withdrew with it; and, after I had read it, fell to my shorthand, to acquaint thee with my good luck: and they not returning so soon as church was done (stepping, as it proved, in to Miss Rawlins's, and tarrying there a while, to bring that busy girl with them to drink tea), I wrote thus far to thee, that thou mightest, when thou camest to this place, rejoice with me upon the occasion.

They are all three just come in.

I hasten to them.

Letter XXIV—Mr. Lovelace to John Belford, Esq.

I HAVE begun another letter to thee, in continuation of my narrative: but I believe I shall send thee this before I shall finish that.   By the enclosed thou wilt see, that neither of the correspondents deserve mercy from me: and I am resolved to make the ending with one, the beginning with the other.

If thou sayest that the provocations I have given to *one* of them will justify *her* freedoms; I answer, so they *will*, to any other person but myself.   But he that is capable of giving those provocations, and has the power to punish those who abuse him *for* giving them, *will* show his resentment; and the more remorselessly, perhaps, as he has *deserved* the freedoms.

If thou sayest, it is, however, wrong to do so; I reply, that it is nevertheless human nature:—and wouldst thou not have me be a *man*, Jack?

Here read the letter, if thou wilt.   But thou art not my friend, if thou offerest to plead for either of the saucy creatures, after thou *hast* read it.

To Mrs. Harriot Lucas, at Mrs. Moore's, at Hampstead

AFTER the discoveries I had made of the villainous machinations of the *most abandoned of men*, particularized in my long letter of Wednesday last,[1] you will believe, my dearest friend, that my surprise upon perusing yours of Thursday evening from Hampstead [1] was not so great as my indignation.   Had the *villain* attempted to fire a city instead of a house, I should not have

[1] See Letter i of this volume.   [2] See Letter ii, ibid.

wondered at it. All that I am amazed at is, that he (whose
boast, as I am told, it is, *that no woman shall keep him out of her
bedchamber, when he has made a resolution to be in it*) did not
discover *his foot* before. And it is as strange to me, that, having
got you at such a shocking advantage, and in such a horrid
house, you could, at the time, *escape dishonour*, and afterwards
get from such a set of *infernals*.

I gave you, in my long letter of Wednesday and Thursday last,
reasons why you ought to mistrust that specious Tomlinson.
That man, my dear, must be a solemn villain. *May lightning
from Heaven blast the wretch who has set him, and the rest of his*
REMORSELESS GANG, *at work, to endeavour to destroy the most
consummate virtue!* Heaven be praised! you have escaped from
all their snares, and *now are out of danger*. So I will not trouble
you at present with the particulars that I have further collected
relating to this abominable imposture.

For the same reason, I forbear to communicate to you some
new stories of the *abhorred wretch himself*, which have come to my
ears. One, in particular, of so *shocking* a nature! Indeed, my
dear, the man's a devil.

The whole story of Mrs. Fretchville, and her house, I have no
doubt to *pronounce*, likewise, an absolute fiction. *Fellow!
How my soul spurns the villain!*

Your thought of going abroad, and your reasons for so doing,
most sensibly affect me. But, be comforted, my dear; I hope
you will not be under a necessity of quitting your native country.
Were I sure that that must be the cruel case, I would abandon
all my own better prospects, and soon be with you. And I
would accompany you whithersoever you went, and share
fortunes with you: for it is impossible that I should be happy,
if I knew that you were exposed not only to the perils of the
sea, but to the attempts of other vile men; your personal graces
attracting every eye, and exposing you to those hourly dangers,
which others, less distinguished by the gifts of nature, might
avoid. All that I know that beauty (so greatly coveted, and
so greatly admired) is good for.

Oh, my dear, were I ever to marry, and to be the mother of a
CLARISSA [*Clarissa* must be the name, if promisingly lovely],
how often would my heart ache for the dear creature, as she
grew up, when I reflected that a prudence and discretion unexampled in woman, had not, in *you*, been a sufficient protection
to that beauty which had drawn after it as many admirers as
beholders! How little should I regret the attacks of that *cruel*

distemper, as it is called, which frequently makes the greatest ravages in the finest faces!

Sat. Afternoon.

I have just parted with Mrs. Townsend.[1] I thought you had once seen her with me: but she says she never had the honour to be personally known to you. She has a *manlike spirit*. She knows the world. And her two brothers being in town, she is sure she can engage *them* in so good a cause, and (if there should be occasion) *both their ships' crews*, in your service.

Give your consent, my dear; and the *horrid villain* shall be repaid with *broken bones, at least,* for all his vileness!

The misfortune is, Mrs. Townsend cannot be with you till *Thursday next, or Wednesday at soonest*. Are you sure you can be safe where you are till then? I think you are too near London; and perhaps you had better be *in it*. If you remove, let me, the very moment, know *whither*.

How my heart is torn, to think of the necessity so dear a creature is driven to, of hiding herself! *Devilish fellow!* He must have been sportive and wanton in his inventions. Yet that cruel, that savage sportiveness has saved you from the sudden violence which he has had recourse to in the violation of others, of names and families not contemptible. For such the *villain* always gloried to spread his snares.

The *vileness* of this *specious monster* has done more than any other consideration could do, to bring Mr. Hickman into credit with me. Mr. Hickman alone knows (from me) of your flight, and the reason of it. Had I not given him the reason, he might have thought *still worse* of the vile attempt. I communicated it to him by showing him your letter from Hampstead. When he had read it [*and he trembled and reddened,* as he read] he threw himself at my feet, and besought me to permit him to attend you, and to give you the protection of his house. The good-natured man had tears in his eyes, and was repeatedly earnest on this subject; proposing to take his chariot and four, or a set, and in person, in the face of all the world, give himself the glory of protecting such an oppressed innocent.

I could not but be pleased with him. And I let him know that I was. I hardly expected so much spirit from him. But a man's passiveness to a beloved object of our sex may not, perhaps, argue want of courage on proper occasions.

I thought I ought, in return, to have some consideration for his safety, as such an open step would draw upon him the

[1] For the account of Mrs. Townsend, etc., see vol. ii, pp. 346–7.

vengeance of the most *villainous enterpriser* in the world, who has always a *gang of fellows*, such as himself, at his call, ready to support one another in the vilest outrages. But yet, as Mr. Hickman might have strengthened his hands by legal recourses, I should not have stood upon it, had I not known your delicacy, [since such a step must have made a great noise, and given occasion for scandal, as if some advantage had been gained over you], and were there not the greatest probablity that all might be more silently, and more effectually, managed by Mrs. Townsend's means.

Mrs. Townsend will in person attend you—she *hopes*, on Wednesday. Her brothers, and some of their people, will scatteringly, and as if they knew nothing of you [so we have contrived], see you safe not only to London, but to her house at Deptford.

She has a kinswoman, who will take your commands there, if she herself be obliged to leave you. And there you may stay, till the wretch's fury on losing you, and his search, are over.

He will very soon, 'tis likely, enter upon some *new villainy*, which may engross him: and it may be given out that you are gone to lay claim to the protection of your Cousin Morden at Florence.

Possibly, if he can be made to believe it, he will go over in hopes to find you there.

After a while, I can procure you a lodging in one of our neighbouring villages; where I may have the happiness to be your daily visitor. And if this Hickman be not silly and apish, and if my mother do not do unaccountable things, I may the sooner think of marrying, that I may, without control, receive and entertain the darling of my heart.

Many, very many, happy days do I hope we shall yet see together: and as this is *my* hope, I expect that it will be *your* consolation.

As to your estate, since you are resolved not to litigate for it, we will be patient, either till Colonel Morden arrives, or till shame compels some people to be just.

Upon the whole, I cannot but think your prospects *now* much happier than they could have been, had you been actually married to such a man as this. I must, therefore, congratulate you upon your escape, not only from a *horrid libertine*, but from *so vile a husband*, as he *must* have made to any woman; but more especially to a person of your virtue and delicacy.

You hate him, heartily hate him, I hope, my dear—I am *sure* you do. It would be strange, if so much purity of life and manners were not to abhor what is so repugnant to itself.

In your letter before me, you mention one written to me for a *feint*.[1] I have not received any such. Depend upon it, therefore, that he must have it. And if he has, it is a wonder that he did not likewise get my long one of the 7th. Heaven be praised that he did not; *and that it came safe to your hands*!

I send this by a young fellow, whose father is one of our tenants, with command to deliver it to no other hands but yours. He is to return directly, if you give him any letter. If not, he will proceed to London upon his own pleasures. He is a simple fellow; but very honest. So you may say anything to him. If you write not by him, I desire a line or two, as soon as possible.

My mother knows nothing of *his* going to you. Nor yet of your abandoning the *fellow*! Forgive me! But he is not *entitled* to good manners.

I shall long to hear how you and Mrs. Townsend order matters I wish she could have been with you sooner. But I have lost no time in engaging her, as you will suppose. I refer to *her*, what I have further to say and advise. So shall conclude with my prayers, that Heaven will direct and protect my dearest creature, and make your future days happy!

ANNA HOWE.

And now, Jack, I will suppose, that thou hast read this cursed letter. Allow me to make a few observations upon some of its contents.

It is strange to Miss Howe, that having got her friend at such a shocking advantage, etc.] And it is strange to me, too. If ever I have such another opportunity given me, the cause of both our wonder, I believe, will cease.

So thou seest Tomlinson is further detected. No such person as Mrs. Fretchville. *May lightning from Heaven*—O Lord, O Lord, O Lord! What a horrid vixen is this! My *gang*, my *remorseless gang*, too, is brought in—and thou wilt plead for these girls again: wilt thou? *Heaven be praised*, she says, that her friend is out of danger—Miss Howe should be sure of *that*: and that she herself is safe. But for this termagant (as I have often said) I must surely have made a better hand of it.

New stories of me, Jack! What can they be? I have not found that my generosity to my Rosebud ever did me *due* credit

<hr />

[1] See Letters ii, iii of this volume.

with this pair of friends. Very hard, Belford, that credits cannot be set against debits, and a balance struck in a rake's favour, as well as in that of every *common* man! But he from whom no good is expected, is not allowed the merit of the good he does.

I ought to have been a little more attentive to *character* than I have been. For, notwithstanding that the measures of right and wrong are said to be so manifest, let me tell thee that *character* biases and runs away with all mankind. Let a man or woman once establish themselves in the world's opinion, and all that either of them do will be sanctified. Nay, in the very courts of justice, does not *character* acquit or condemn as often as facts, and sometimes even in spite of facts? Yet [impolitic that I have been, and am!] to be so careless of mine! And now, I doubt, it is irretrievable. But to leave moralizing.

Thou, Jack, knowest almost all my enterprises worth remembering. Can this particular story, which this girl hints at, be that of Lucy Villars? Or can she have heard of my intrigue with the pretty gipsy, who met me in Norwood, and of the trap I caught her cruel husband in [a fellow as gloomy and tyrannical as old Harlowe], when he pursued a wife, who would not have deserved ill of *him*, if he had deserved well of *her*? But he was not quite drowned. The man is alive at this day: and Miss Howe mentions the story as a *very* shocking one. Besides, both these are a twelvemonth old, or more.

But evil fame and scandal are always *new*. When the offender has forgot a vile fact, it is often told to one and to another, who, having never heard of it before, trumpet it about as a novelty to others. But well said the honest corregidor at Madrid [a saying with which I enriched Lord M.'s collection], *Good actions are remembered but for a day: bad ones for many years after the life of the guilty*. Such is the relish that the world has for scandal. In other words, such is the desire which every one has to exculpate himself by blackening his neighbour. You and I, Belford, have been very kind to the world, in furnishing it with many opportunities to gratify its devil.

Miss Howe will abandon her own better prospects, and share fortunes with her, were she to go abroad.] Charming romancer! I must set about this girl, Jack. I have always had hopes of a woman whose passions carry her into such altitudes! Had I attacked Miss Howe first, her passions (inflamed and guided, as I could have managed them) would have brought her to my lure in a fortnight.

XXIV]   CLARISSA HARLOWE   169

But thinkest thou [and yet I think thou dost] that there is anything in these high flights among the sex? Verily, Jack, these vehement friendships are nothing but chaff and stubble, liable to be blown away by the very wind that raises them. Apes! mere apes of *us*! they think the word *friendship* has a pretty sound with it; and it is much talked of; a fashionable word: and so, truly, a single woman, who thinks she has a soul, and knows that she wants something, would be thought to have found a fellow soul for it in her own sex. But I repeat, that the word is a *mere* word, the thing a *mere* name with them; a cork-bottomed shuttlecock, which they are fond of striking to and fro, to make one another glow in the frosty weather of a single state; but which, when a *man* comes in between the pretended *inseparables*, is given up, like their music, and other maidenly amusements; which, nevertheless, may be necessary to keep the pretty rogues out of more active mischief. They then, in short, having caught the *fish*, lay aside the *net*.[1]

Thou hast a mind, perhaps, to make an exception for these two ladies. With all my heart. My Clarissa has, if *woman* has, a soul capable of friendship. Her flame is bright and steady. But Miss Howe's, were it not kept up by her mother's opposition, is too vehement to endure. How often have I known opposition not only cement friendship, but create love? I doubt not but poor Hickman would fare the better with this vixen, if her mother were as heartily against him, as she is for him.

Thus much indeed, as to these two ladies, I will grant thee; that the active spirit of the one, and the meek disposition of the other, may make their friendship more durable than it would otherwise be; for this is certain, that in every friendship, whether male or female, there must be a man and a woman spirit (that is to say, one of them a *forbearing* one) to make it permanent.

But this I pronounce, as a truth which all experience confirms; that friendship between women never holds to the sacrifice of capital gratifications, or to the endangering of life, limb, or estate, as it often does in our nobler sex.

Well, but next comes an indictment against poor *beauty*! What has beauty done, that *Miss Howe* should be offended at it? Miss Howe, Jack, is a charming girl. *She* has no reason to

---

[1] He alludes here to the story of a pope, who (once a poor fisherman), through every preferment he rose to, even to that of the cardinalate, hung up in view of all his guests his net, as a token of humility. But, when he arrived at the pontificate, he took it down, saying, that there was no need of the net, when he had caught the fish.

quarrel with beauty! Didst ever see her? Too much fire and
spirit in her eye, indeed, for a girl! But that's no fault with a
man, that can lower that fire and spirit at pleasure; and I know
I am the man that can.

A sweet auburn beauty, is Miss Howe. A first beauty among
beauties, when her sweeter friend [with such an assemblage of
serene gracefulness, of natural elegance, of native sweetness,
yet conscious, though not arrogant dignity, every feature
glowing with intelligence] is not in company.

The difference between the two, when together, I have sometimes delighted to *read*, in the address of a stranger entering
into the presence of both, when standing side by side. There
never was an instance on such an occasion where the stranger
paid not his first devoirs to my Clarissa.

A respectful solemn awe sat upon every feature of the ad-
dresser's face. His eye seemed to ask leave to approach her;
and lower than common, whether man or woman, was the bow
or curtsy. And although this awe was immediately diminished
by her condescending sweetness, yet went it not so entirely off,
but that you might see the reverence remain, as if the person
saw more of the goddess than of the woman in her.

But the moment the same stranger turns to Miss Howe
(though proud and saucy, and erect and bridling, she), you will
observe by the turn of his countenance, and the air of his
address, a kind of equality assumed. He appears to have
discovered the woman in her, charming as that woman is. He
smiles. He seems to expect repartee and smartness, and is
never disappointed. But then visibly he prepares himself to
give as well as *take*. He dares, after he has been a while in her
company, to dispute a point with her—every point yielded up
to the other, though no assuming or dogmatical air compels it.

In short, with Miss Howe a bold man sees [no doubt but Sir
George Colmar did] that he and she may either very soon be
familiar together [I mean with innocence], or he may so far incur
her displeasure, as to be forbidden her presence for ever.

For my own part, when I was first introduced to this lady,
which was by my goddess when she herself was a visitor at Mrs.
Howe's, I had not been half an hour with her, but I even
hungered and thirsted after a romping bout with the lively rogue;
and in the second or third visit, was more deterred by the
delicacy of her friend, than by what I apprehended from her
own. This charming creature's presence, thought I, awes us
both. And I wished her absence, though any other woman

were present, that I might try the difference in Miss Howe's behaviour before her friend's face, or behind her back.

Delicate women *make* delicate women, as well as decent men. With all Miss Howe's fire and spirit, it was easy to see, by her very eye, that she watched for lessons, and feared reproof, from the penetrating eye of her milder-dispositioned friend[1]: and yet it was as easy to observe, in the candour and sweet manners of the other, that the fear which Miss Howe stood in of her, was more owing to her own generous apprehension that she fell short of her excellences, than to Miss Harlowe's consciousness of excellence over *her*. I have often, since I came at Miss Howe's letters, revolved this just and fine praise contained in one of them[2]: "Every one saw that the preference they gave *you* to *themselves*, exalted you not into any visible triumph over them; for you had always something to say, on every point you carried, that raised the yielding heart, and left every one pleased and satisfied with themselves, though they carried not off the palm."

As I propose, in my more advanced life, to endeavour to atone for my youthful freedoms with individuals of the sex, by giving cautions and instructions to the whole, I have made a memorandum to enlarge upon this doctrine; to wit, That it is full as necessary to direct daughters in the choice of their female companions, as it is to guard them against the designs of men.

I say not this, however, to the disparagement of Miss Howe. She has from *pride*, what her friend has from *principle*. [The Lord help the sex, if they had not pride!] But yet I am confident that Miss Howe is indebted to the conversation and correspondence of Miss Harlowe for her highest improvements. But, both these ladies out of the question, I make no scruple to aver [and I, Jack, should know something of the matter] that there have been more girls ruined, at least *prepared* for ruin, by their own sex (taking in servants, as well as companions) than *directly* by the attempts and delusions of men.

But it is time enough, when I am old and joyless, to enlarge upon this topic.

As to the comparison between the two ladies, I will expatiate more on that subject (for I like it) when I have *had them both*—which this letter of the vixen girl's, I hope thou wilt allow, warrants me to try for.

[1] Miss Howe, in vol. ii, p. 43, says, *That she was always more afraid of Clarissa than of her mother*; and ibid. p. 132, *That she fears her almost as much as she loves her*; and in many other places in her letters verifies this observation of Lovelace.

[2] See vol. ii, p. 281.

I return to the consideration of a few more of its contents, to justify my vengeances so nearly now in view.

As to Mrs. Townsend; her manlike spirit; her two brothers; and their ships' crews—I say nothing but this to the insolent threatening—Let 'em come!—

But as to her sordid menace—To *repay the horrid villain*, as she calls me, *for all my vileness* by BROKEN BONES! Broken bones, Belford! Who can bear this porterly threatening! Broken bones, Jack! Damn the little vulgar—Give me a name for her—but I banish all *furious* resentment. If I get these two girls into my power, Heaven forbid that I should be a second Phalaris, who turned his bull upon the artist! No bones of theirs will I break! They shall come off with me upon much lighter terms!

But these fellows are smugglers, it seems. And am not I a smuggler too? I am; and have not the least doubt, but I shall have secured my goods before Thursday, or Wednesday either.

But did I want a plot, what a charming new one does this letter of Miss Howe strike me out! I am almost sorry that I have fixed upon one. For here, how easy would it be for me to assemble a crew of swabbers, and to create a Mrs. Townsend (whose person, thou seest, my beloved knows not) to come on Tuesday, at Miss Howe's repeated solicitations, in order to carry my beloved to a warehouse of my own providing?

This, however, is my triumphant hope, that at the very time that these ragamuffins will be at Hampstead (looking for us), my dear Miss Harlowe and I [so the Fates, I imagine, have ordained] shall be fast asleep in each other's arms in town. Lie still, villain, till the time comes. My heart, Jack! my heart! It is always thumping away on the remotest prospects of this nature.

But it seems that *the vileness of this specious monster* [meaning me, Jack!] has brought Hickman into credit with her. So I have done *some* good! But to whom, I cannot tell: for this poor fellow, should I permit him to have this termagant, will be punished, as many times we all are, by the enjoyment of his own wishes. Nor can she be happy, as I take it, with him, were he to govern himself by her will, and have none of his own; since never was there a directing wife who knew where to stop: power makes such a one wanton—she despises the man she can govern. Like Alexander, who wept that he had no more worlds to conquer, she will be looking out for new exercises for her power, till she grow uneasy to herself, a discredit to her husband, and a plague to all about her.

But this honest fellow, it seems, with *tears in his eyes*, and with *humble prostration*, besought the vixen to *permit* him to set out in his *chariot and four*, in order to *give himself the glory of protecting such an oppressed innocent, in the face of the whole world*. Nay, he *reddened*, it seems; and *trembled* too! as he read the fair complainant's letter. How *valiant* is all this! Women love *brave* men; and no wonder that his *tears*, his *trembling*, and his *prostration*, gave him high reputation with the *meek* Miss Howe.

But dost think, Jack, that I in the like case (and equally affected with the distress) should have acted thus? Dost think that I should not first have rescued the lady, and then, if needful, have asked excuse for it, the lady in my hand? Wouldst not *thou* have done thus, as well as I?

But 'tis best as it is. Honest Hickman may now sleep in a whole skin. And yet that is more perhaps than he would have done (the lady's deliverance *unattempted*), had I come at this *requested permission* of his any other way than by a letter that it must not be known I have intercepted.

Miss Howe thinks I may be diverted from pursuing my charmer, by some new-started *villainy*. *Villainy* is a word that she is extremely fond of. But I can tell her, that it is impossible I should, till the end of this *villainy* be obtained. Difficulty is a *stimulus* with such a spirit as mine. I thought Miss Howe knew me better. Were she to offer herself, person for person, in the romancing zeal of her friendship, to save her friend, it should not do, while the dear creature is on this side the moon.

She thanks Heaven that her friend has received her letter of the 7th. We are all glad of it. She ought to thank me too. But I will not at present claim her thanks.

But when she rejoices that the letter went safe, does she not, in effect, call out for vengeance, and *expect* it? All in good time, Miss Howe. *When settest thou out for the Isle of Wight, love?*

I will close at this time with desiring thee to make a *list* of the virulent terms with which the enclosed letter abounds: and then, if thou supposest that I have made such another, and have added to it all the flowers of the same blow, in the former letters of the same saucy creature, and those in that of Miss Harlowe which she left for me on her elopement, thou wilt certainly think that I have provocations sufficient to justify me in all I shall do to either.

Return the enclosed the moment thou hast perused it.

Letter XXV—Mr. Lovelace to John Belford, Esq.

Sunday Night—Monday Morning.

I WENT down with revenge in my *heart*, the contents of Miss Howe's letter almost engrossing me, the moment that Miss Harlowe and Mrs. Moore (accompanied by Miss Rawlins) came in: but in my countenance all the gentle, the placid, the serene, that the glass could teach; and in my behaviour all the polite, that such an *unpolite* creature, as she has often told me I am, could put on.

Miss Rawlins was sent for home almost as soon as she came in, to entertain an unexpected visitor; to her great regret, as well as to the disappointment of my fair one, as I could perceive from the looks of both: for they had agreed, it seems, if I went to town, as I said I intended to do, to take a walk upon the heath; at least in Mrs. Moore's garden; and who knows what might have been the issue, had the spirit of curiosity in the one met with the spirit of communication in the other?

Miss Rawlins promised to return, if possible: but sent to excuse herself; her visitor intending to stay with her all night.

I rejoiced in my heart, at her message; and, after much supplication, obtained the favour of my beloved's company for another walk in the garden, having, as I told her, abundance of things to say, to propose, and to be informed of, in order ultimately to govern myself in my future steps.

She had vouchsafed, I should have told thee, with eyes turned from me, and in a *half-aside* attitude, to sip two dishes of tea in my company—Dear soul! How anger *unpolishes* the most polite! for I never saw Miss Harlowe behave so awkwardly. I imagined she knew not how to be awkward.

When we were in the garden, I poured my whole soul into her attentive ear; and besought her returning favour.

She told me that she had formed her scheme for her future life: that, vile as the treatment was which she had received from me, that was not all the reason she had for rejecting my suit: but that, on the maturest deliberation, she was convinced that she could neither be happy with me, nor make me happy; and she enjoined me, for both our sakes, to think no more of her.

The captain, I told her, was rid down post, in a manner, to forward my wishes with her uncle. Lady Betty and Miss Montague were undoubtedly arrived in town by this time. I would set out early in the morning to attend them. They

adored her. They longed to see her. They *would* see her.
They would not be denied her company into Oxfordshire.
Whither could she better go, to be free from her brother's
insults? Whither, to be absolutely made unapprehensive of
anybody else? Might I have any hopes of her returning favour
if Miss Howe could be prevailed upon to intercede for me?

Miss Howe prevailed upon to intercede for you! repeated she,
with a scornful bridle, but a very pretty one. And there she
stopped.

I *repeated* the concern it would be to me to be under a necessity
of mentioning the misunderstanding to Lady Betty and my
cousin, as a misunderstanding still to be made up; and as if I
were of very *little* consequence to a dear creature who was of
so *much* to me; urging that these circumstances would extremely
lower me, not only in my own opinion, but in that of my
relations.

But still she referred to Miss Howe's next letter; and all the
concession I could bring her in this whole conference, was, that
she would wait the arrival and visit of the two ladies, if they
came in a day or two, or before she received the expected letter
from Miss Howe.

Thank Heaven for this! thought I. And now may I go to
town with hopes at my return to find thee, dearest, where I
shall leave thee.

But yet, as she may find reasons to change her mind in my
absence, I shall not entirely trust to this. My fellow, therefore,
who is in the house, and who, by Mrs. Bevis's kind intelligence,
will know every step she can take, shall have Andrew and a horse
ready, to give me immediate notice of her motions; and moreover, go whither she will, he shall be one of her retinue, though
unknown to herself, if possible.

This was all I could make of the fair inexorable. Should I
be glad of it, or sorry for it?

Glad, I believe: and yet my pride is confoundedly abated to
think that I had so little hold in the affections of this daughter
of the Harlowes.

Don't tell me that virtue and principle are her guides on this
occasion! 'Tis *pride*, a greater pride than my own, that governs
her. Love, she has none, thou seest; nor ever had; at least not
in a superior degree. Love, that deserves the name, never was
under the dominion of *prudence*, or of any *reasoning* power.
She cannot bear to be thought a *woman*, I warrant! And if, in
the last attempt, I find her *not* one, what will she be the worse for

the trial? No one is to blame for suffering an evil he cannot shun or avoid.

Were a general to be overpowered, and robbed by a highwayman, would he be less fit for the command of an army on that account? If indeed the general, pretending great valour, and having boasted that he never would be robbed, were to make but faint resistance when he was brought to the test, and to yield his purse when he was master of his own sword, then indeed will the highwayman who robs him be thought the braver man.

But from these last conferences am I furnished with one argument in defence of my favourite purpose, which I never yet pleaded.

O Jack! what a difficulty must a man be allowed to have, to conquer a predominant passion, be it what it will, when the gratifying of it is in his *power*, however wrong he knows it to be to resolve to gratify it! Reflect upon this; and then wilt thou be able to account for, if not to excuse, a projected crime, which has *habit* to plead for it, in a breast as stormy as uncontrollable!

This that follows is my new argument—

Should she fail in the trial; should I succeed; and should she refuse to go on with me; and even resolve not to marry me (of which I can have no notion); and should she disdain to be obliged to me for the handsome provision I should be proud to make for her, even to the *half of my estate*; yet cannot she be altogether unhappy. Is she not entitled to an independent fortune? Will not Colonel Morden, as her trustee, put her in possession of it? And did she not in our former conference point out the *way of life*, that she always preferred to the *married life* —to wit, "To take her good Norton for her directress and guide, and to live upon her own estate in the manner her grandfather desired she should live?"[1]

It is moreover to be considered, that she cannot, according to her own notions, recover above *one half* of her fame, were we now to intermarry; so much does she think she has suffered by her going off with me. And will she not be always repining and mourning for the loss of the *other half*? And if she must live a life of such uneasiness and regret for *half*, may she not as well repine and mourn for the *whole*?

Nor, let me tell thee, will her own scheme of penitence, in this case, be half so perfect, if she do *not* fall, as if she *does*: for what a foolish penitent will she make, who has nothing to repent of?

[1] See Letter xx of this volume.

She piques herself, thou knowest, and makes it matter of reproach to me, that she went not off with me by her own consent; but was tricked out of herself.

Nor upbraid thou me upon the meditated breach of vows so repeatedly made. She will not, thou seest, *permit* me to fulfil them. And if she *would*, this I have to say, that at the time I made the most solemn of them, I was fully determined to keep them. But what prince thinks himself obliged any longer to observe the articles of treaties the most sacredly sworn to, than suits with his interest or inclination; although the consequence of the infraction must be, as he knows, the destruction of thousands?

Is not this then the result of all, that Miss Clarissa Harlowe, if it be not her own fault, may be as virtuous *after* she has lost her honour, as it is called, as she was *before*? She may be a more eminent example to her sex; and if she yield (a *little* yield) in the trial, may be a *completer penitent*. Nor can she, but by her own wilfulness, be reduced to *low fortunes*.

And thus may her *old* nurse and she; an *old* coachman; and a pair of *old* coach-horses; and two or three *old* maidservants, and perhaps a *very old* footman or two (for everything will be old and penitential about her), live very comfortably together; reading *old* sermons, and *old* prayer books; and relieving *old* men, and *old* women; and giving *old* lessons, and *old* warnings, upon new subjects, as well as *old* ones, to the young ladies of her neighbourhood; and so pass on to a good *old* age, doing a great deal of good both by precept and example in her generation.

And is a woman who can live thus prettily without *control*; who ever did prefer, and who *still* prefers, the *single* to the *married life*; and who will be enabled to do everything that the plan she had formed will direct her to do; to be said to be ruined, undone, and such sort of stuff? I have no patience with the pretty fools, who use those strong words, to describe a transitory evil; an evil which a mere church form makes none!

At this rate of romancing, how many *flourishing ruins* dost thou, as well as I, know? Let us but look about us, and we shall see some of the haughtiest and most *censorious* spirits among our acquaintance of that sex now passing for chaste wives, of whom strange stories might be told; and others, whose husbands' hearts have been made to ache for their gaieties, both before and after marriage; and yet know not half so much of them, as some of us honest fellows could tell them.

But, having thus satisfied myself in relation to the worst that

can happen to this *charming creature*; and that it will be her own
fault, if she be unhappy; I have not at all reflected upon what is
likely to be *my own lot*.

This has always been my notion, though Miss Howe grudges
us rakes the best of the sex, and says that the worst is too
good for us[1]; that the wife of a libertine ought to be pure,
spotless, uncontaminated. To what purpose has such a one
lived a free life, but to know the world, and to make his advantages of it? And, to be *very* serious, it would be a misfortune
to the public for two persons, heads of a family, to be both bad;
since between two such, a race of varlets might be propagated
(Lovelaces and Belfords, if thou wilt) who might do great
mischief in the world.

Thou seest at bottom that I am not an abandoned fellow;
and that there is a mixture of gravity in me. This, as I grow
older, may increase; and when my active capacity begins to
abate, I may sit down with the preacher, and resolve all my past
life into vanity and vexation of spirit.

This is certain, that I shall never find a woman so well suited
to my taste as Miss Clarissa Harlowe. I only wish that I may
have such a lady as her to comfort and adorn my setting sun.
I have often thought it very unhappy for us both, that so
excellent a creature sprang up a little too late for my *setting-out*,
and a little too early in my *progress*, before I can think of
returning. And yet, as I have picked up the sweet traveller
in my way, I cannot help wishing that she would bear me
company in the *rest* of my journey, although she were to step
out of her own path to oblige me. And then, perhaps, we could
put up in the *evening* at the same *inn*; and be very happy in
each other's conversation; recounting the difficulties and
dangers we had passed in our way to it.

I imagine that thou wilt be apt to suspect that some passages
in this letter were written in town. Why, Jack, I cannot but
say that the Westminster air is a little grosser than that at
Hampstead; and the conversation of Mrs. Sinclair, and the
nymphs, less innocent than Mrs. Moore's and Miss Rawlins's.
And I think in my heart that I can say and write those things
at one place, which I cannot at the other; nor indeed anywhere else.

I came to town about seven this morning. All necessary
directions and precautions remembered to be given.

I besought the favour of an audience before I set out. I was

[1] See Letter i of this volume.

desirous to see which of her lovely faces she was pleased to put on, after another night had passed. But she was resolved, I found, to leave our quarrel open. She would not give me an opportunity so much as to entreat her again to close it, before the arrival of Lady Betty and my cousin.

I had notice from my proctor, by a few lines brought by man and horse, just before I set out, that all difficulties had been for two days past surmounted; and that I might have the licence for fetching.

I sent up the letter to my beloved, by Mrs. Bevis, with a repeated request for admittance to her presence upon it: but neither did this stand me in stead. I suppose she thought it would be allowing of the consequences that were naturally to be expected to follow the obtaining of this instrument, if she had consented to see me on the contents of this letter, having refused me that honour before I sent it up to her. No surprising her. No advantage to be taken of her inattention to the nicest circumstances.

And now, Belford, I set out upon business.

Letter XXVI—Mr. Lovelace to John Belford, Esq.

Monday, June 12.

DIDST ever see a licence, Jack?

Edmund, by Divine permission, Lord Bishop of London, to our well-beloved in Christ, Robert Lovelace [Your servant, my good lord! What have I done to merit so much goodness, who never saw your lordship in my life?], *of the parish of St. Martin's in the Fields, bachelor, and Clarissa Harlowe, of the same parish, spinster, sendeth greeting. WHEREAS ye are, as is alleged, determined to enter into the holy state of Matrimony* [This is only alleged, thou observest], *by and with the consent of, etc. etc. etc., and are very desirous of obtaining your marriage to be solemnized in the face of the Church: We are willing that such your honest desires* [Honest desires, Jack!] *may more speedily have their due effect: and therefore, that ye may be able to procure such marriage to be freely and lawfully solemnized in the parish church of St. Martin's in the Fields, or St. Giles's in the Fields, in the county of Middlesex, by the Rector, Vicar, or Curate thereof, at any time of the year* [At ANY time of the year, Jack!] *without publication of banns: Provided, that by reason of any pre-contract* [I verily think that I have had three or four pre-contracts in my time; but the good girls have not claimed upon them of a long while], *consanguinity, affinity, or any other lawful cause whatsoever, there be no lawful impediment in this behalf; and that there be not at this time any action, suit, plaint, quarrel, or demand, moved or depending before any judge ecclesiastical or temporal, for or concerning any marriage contracted by or with either of you; and that the said marriage be openly solemnized in the church above mentioned, between the hours of eight and twelve in the forenoon; and without prejudice to the minister of the place where the said woman is a parishioner: We do hereby, for good causes* [It cost me—let me see, Jack—what did it cost me?], *give and grant our Licence, or Faculty, as well to you the parties contracting, as to the Rector, Vicar, or Curate of the said church, where the said marriage is intended to be solemnized, to solemnize the same, in manner and form above specified, according to the rites and ceremonies prescribed in the Book of Common Prayer in that behalf published by authority of Parliament. Provided always, that if hereafter any fraud shall appear to have been committed, at the time of granting this Licence, either by false suggestions, or concealment of the truth* [Now this, Belford, is a little hard upon us: for I cannot say that every one of our suggestions is literally true: so, in good conscience, I ought not to marry under this Licence], *the Licence shall be void to all intents and purposes, as if the same had not been granted. And in that case, we do inhibit all ministers whatsoever, if anything of the premises shall come to their knowledge, from proceeding to the celebration of the said marriage, without first consulting Us, or our Vicar-general. Given, etc.*

Then follow the registrar's name, and a large pendent seal, with these words round it: SEAL OF THE VICAR-GENERAL AND OFFICIAL-PRINCIPAL OF THE DIOCESE OF LONDON.

A good whimsical instrument, take it all together! But what, thinkest thou, are the arms to this matrimonial harbinger? Why, in the first place, *two crossed swords*—to show that marriage is a state of offence as well as defence: *three lions*—to denote that those who enter into the state ought to have a triple proportion of courage. And [couldst thou have imagined that these priestly fellows, in so solemn a case, would cut their jokes upon poor souls who come to have their *honest desires* put in a way to be gratified?] there are *three crooked horns*, smartly top-knotted with ribbons; which being the ladies' wear, seem to indicate that they may very probably adorn, as well as bestow, the bull's feather.

To describe it according to heraldry art, if I am not mistaken:

Gules, two swords, saltire-wise, or; second coat, a chevron sable between three bugle horns, OR [*so it ought to be*]: on a chief of the second, three lions rampant of the first—but the devil take them for their hieroglyphics, should I say, if I were determined in good earnest to marry

And determined to marry I would be, were it not for this consideration, that once married, and I am married for life.

That's the plague of it! Could a man do as the birds do, change every Valentine's Day [a *natural* appointment! for birds have not the *sense*, forsooth, to fetter themselves, as we wiseacre men take great and solemn pains to do], there would be nothing at all in it. And what a glorious time would the *lawyers* have, on the one hand, with their *noverint universi's*, and suits commenceable on restitution of goods and chattels; and the *parsons*, on the other, with their indulgences (renewable annually as *other* licences) to the *honest desires* of their clients?

Then, were a stated mulct, according to rank or fortune, to be paid on every change, towards the exigencies of the State [but none on *renewals* with the *old loves*, for the sake of encouraging constancy, especially among the *minores*], the change would be made sufficiently difficult, and the whole public would be the better for it; while those children, which the parents could not agree about maintaining, might be considered as the *children of the public*, and provided for like the children of the ancient Spartans; who were (as ours would in this case be) a nation of heroes. How, Jack, could I have improved upon Lycurgus's institutions, had I been a lawgiver?

Did I never show thee a scheme which I drew up on such a notion as this?—In which I demonstrated the *conveniences*, and obviated the *inconveniences*, of changing the present mode to this? I believe I never did.

I remember I proved, to a demonstration, that such a change would be a means of annihilating, absolutely annihilating, four or five very atrocious and capital sins. *Rapes*, vulgarly so called; adultery, and fornication; nor would *polygamy* be panted after. Frequently would it prevent *murders* and *duelling*: hardly any such thing as *jealousy* (the cause of shocking violences) would be heard of: and hypocrisy between man and wife be banished the bosoms of each. Nor, probably, would the reproach of *barrenness* rest, as now it too often does, where it is least deserved. Nor would there possibly be such a person as a barren woman.

Moreover, what a multitude of domestic quarrels would be

avoided, were such a scheme carried into execution? Since both sexes would bear with each other, in the view that they could help themselves in a few months.

And then what a charming subject for conversation would be the gallant and generous last partings between man and wife! Each, perhaps, a new mate in eye, and rejoicing secretly in the manumission, could *afford* to be complaisantly sorrowful in appearance. "He presented *her* with this jewel, it will be said by the reporter, for *example* sake: she *him* with that. How *he* wept! How *she* sobbed! How they looked after one another!" Yet, that's the jest of it, neither of them wishing to stand another twelvemonth's trial.

And if giddy fellows, or giddy girls, misbehave in a first marriage, whether from *noviceship*, having expected to find more in the matter than can be found; or from *perverseness* on *her* part, or *positiveness* on *his*, each being mistaken in the other [a mighty difference, Jack, in the same person, an *inmate*, or a *visitor*]; what a fine opportunity will each have, by this scheme, of recovering a lost character, and of setting all right in the next adventure?

And, O Jack! with what joy, with what rapture, would the *changelings* (or *changeables*, if thou like that word better) number the weeks, the days, the hours, as the annual obligation approached to its desirable period!

As for the spleen or vapours, no such malady would be known or heard of. The physical tribe would, indeed, be the sufferers, and the only sufferers; since fresh health and fresh spirits, the consequences of sweet blood and sweet humours (the mind and body continually pleased with each other), would perpetually flow in; and the joys of *expectation*, the highest of all our joys, would invigorate and keep all alive.

But that no body of men might suffer, the *physicians*, I thought, might turn *parsons*, as there would be a great demand for parsons. Besides, as they would be partakers in the general benefit, they must be sorry fellows indeed, if they preferred themselves to the public.

Every one would be married a dozen times at least. Both men and women would be careful of their characters, and polite in their behaviour, as well as delicate in their *persons*, and elegant in their *dress* [a great matter each of these, let me tell thee, to keep passion alive], either to induce a *renewal* with the *old love*, or to recommend themselves to a *new*. While the newspapers would be crowded with paragraphs; all the world their readers, as all the world would be concerned to see *who and who's together*—

"Yesterday, for instance, entered into the holy state of matrimony" [we should all speak reverently of matrimony then] "the Right Honourable Robert Earl Lovelace" [I shall be an earl by that time] "with Her Grace the Duchess Dowager of Fifty-manors; his lordship's one-and-thirtieth wife." I shall then be contented, perhaps, to take up, as it is called, with a widow. But she must not have had more than one husband neither. Thou knowest that I am nice in these particulars.

I know, Jack, that thou, for thy part, wilt approve of my scheme.

As Lord M. and I, between us, have three or four boroughs at command, I think I will get into Parliament, in order to bring in a Bill for this good purpose.

Neither will the Houses of Parliament, nor the Houses of Convocation, have reason to object to it. And all the courts, whether *spiritual* or *sensual*, *civil* or *uncivil*, will find their account in it when passed into a law.

By my soul, Jack, I should be apprehensive of a general insurrection, and that incited by the women, were such a Bill to be thrown out. For here is the excellency of the scheme: the women will have equal reason with the men to be pleased with it.

Dost think that *old prerogative Harlowe*, for example, must not, if such a law were in being, have pulled in his horns? So excellent a wife as he has, would never else have *renewed* with such a gloomy tyrant: who, as well as all other married tyrants, must have been upon good behaviour from year to year.

A termagant wife, if such a law were to pass, would be a phœnix.

The *churches* would be the only *market-places* for the fair sex; and *domestic excellence* the capital recommendation.

Nor would there be an *old maid* in Great Britain, and all its territories. For what an odd soul she must be, who could not have her *twelvemonth's trial*?

In short, a total alteration for the better, in the *morals* and *way of life* in both sexes, must, in a very few years, be the consequence of such a salutary law.

Who would have expected such a one from me? I wish the devil owe me not a spite for it.

Then would not the distinction be very pretty, Jack? as in flowers; such a gentleman, or such a lady, is an ANNUAL—such a one a PERENNIAL.

One difficulty, however, as I remember, occurred to me, upon the probability that a wife might be *enceinte*, as the lawyers call it. But thus I obviated it—

That no man should be allowed to marry another woman without his *then* wife's consent, till she were brought to bed, and he had defrayed all incident charges; and till it was agreed upon between them whether the child should be *his*, *hers*, or the *public's*. The women in this case to have what I call the *coercive option*: for I would not have it in the man's power to be a dog neither.

And indeed, I gave the turn of the scale in every part of my scheme in the women's favour: for dearly do I love the sweet rogues.

How infinitely more preferable this my scheme to the polygamy one of the old patriarchs; who had wives and concubines without number! I believe David and Solomon had their hundreds *at a time*. Had they not, Jack?

Let me add, that *annual Parliaments*, and *annual marriages*, are the projects next my heart. How could I expatiate upon the benefits that would arise from both!

Letter XXVII—Mr. Lovelace to John Belford, Esq.

WELL, but now my plots thicken; and my employment of writing to thee on this subject will soon come to a conclusion. For now, having got the licence; and Mrs. Townsend with her tars being to come to Hampstead next Wednesday or Thursday; and another letter possibly or message from Miss Howe, to inquire how Miss Harlowe does, upon the rustic's report of her ill health, and to express her wonder that she has not heard from her in answer to hers on her escape; I must soon blow up the lady, or be blown up myself. And so I am preparing, with Lady Betty and my Cousin Montague, to wait upon my beloved with a coach and four, or a set; for Lady Betty will not stir out with a pair for the world; though but for two or three miles. And this is a well-known part of her character.

But as to the arms and crest upon the coach and trappings?

Dost thou not know that a Blunt's must supply her, while her own is new-lining and repairing? An opportunity she is willing to take now she is in town. Nothing of this kind can be done to her mind in the country. Liveries nearly Lady Betty's.

Thou hast seen Lady Betty Lawrance several times, hast thou not, Belford?

No, never in my life

But thou hast—and lain with her too; or fame does thee more credit than thou deservest. Why, Jack, knowest thou not Lady Betty's other name?

Other name! Has she two?

She has. And what thinkest thou of Lady Bab. Wallis?

Oh, the devil!

Now thou hast it. Lady Barbara, thou knowest, lifted up in circumstances, and by pride, never appears or produces herself, but on occasions special, to pass to men of quality or price, for a duchess, or countess, at least. She has always been admired for a grandeur in her air that few women of quality can come up to: and never was supposed to be other than what she passed for; though often and often a paramour for lords.

And who, thinkest thou, is my Cousin Montague?

Nay, how should I know?

How indeed! Why, my little Johanetta Golding, a lively, yet modest-looking girl, is my Cousin Montague.

There, Belford, is an aunt! There's a cousin! Both have wit at will. Both are accustomed to ape quality. Both are genteelly descended. Mistresses of themselves; and well educated —yet past pity. True *Spartan* dames; ashamed of nothing but *detection*—always, therefore, upon their guard against that. And in their own conceit, when assuming top parts, the very quality they ape.

And how dost think I dress them out? I 'll tell thee.

Lady Betty in a rich gold tissue, adorned with jewels of high price.

My Cousin Montague in a pale pink, standing on end with silver flowers of her own working. Charlotte, as well as my beloved, is admirable at her needle. Not quite so richly jewelled out as Lady Betty; but ear-rings and solitaire very valuable, and infinitely becoming.

Johanetta, thou knowest, has a good complexion, a fine neck, and ears remarkably fine. So has Charlotte. She is nearly of Charlotte's stature too.

Laces both, the richest that could be procured.

Thou canst not imagine what a sum the loan of the jewels cost me; though but for three days.

This sweet girl will half ruin me. But seest thou not by this time that her reign is short? It must be so. And Mrs. Sinclair has already prepared everything for her reception once more.

.   .   .   .   .   .

Here come the ladies—attended by Susan Morrison, a tenant-farmer's daughter, as Lady Betty's woman; with her hands before her, and thoroughly instructed.

How dress advantages women! especially those who have naturally a genteel air and turn, and have had education!

Hadst thou seen how they paraded it—cousin, and cousin, and nephew, at every word; Lady Betty bridling and looking *haughtily condescending*: Charlotte galanting her fan, and swimming over the floor without touching it.

How I long to see my niece-elect! cries one—for they are told that we are not married; and are pleased that I have not put the slight upon them that they had apprehended from me.

How I long to see my dear cousin that is to be, the other!

Your la'ship, and your la'ship, and an awkward curtsy at every address, prim Susan Morrison.

Top your parts, ye villains! You know how nicely I distinguish. There will be no passion in *this case* to blind the judgment, and to help on meditated delusion, as when you engage with titled sinners. My charmer is as cool and as distinguishing, though not quite so learned in her own sex, as I am. Your commonly assumed dignity won't do for me now. Airs of superiority, as if *born* to rank. But no over-do! Doubting nothing. Let not your faces arraign your hearts.

Easy and unaffected! Your very dresses will give you pride enough.

A little *graver*, Lady Betty. More significance, less bridling in your dignity.

That 's the air! Charmingly hit——Again——You have it.

Devil take you! Less arrogance. You are got into airs of *young quality*. Be less sensible of your new condition. People born to dignity command respect without needing to require it.

Now for *your* part, Cousin Charlotte!

Pretty well. But a little too frolickly that air—yet have I prepared my beloved to expect in you both great vivacity and quality-freedom.

Curse those eyes! Those glancings will never do. A downcast bashful turn, if you can command it. Look upon me. Suppose me now to be my beloved.

Devil take that leer! Too *significantly* arch! Once I knew you the girl I would now have you to be.

Sprightly, but not confident, Cousin Charlotte! Be sure forget not to look down, or aside, when looked at. When eyes meet eyes, be yours the retreating ones. Your face will bear examination.

O Lord! O Lord! that so young a creature can so soon forget the innocent appearance she first charmed by; and which I thought born with you all! Five years to ruin what twenty had been building up! How natural the latter lesson! How difficult to regain the former!

A stranger, as I hope to be saved, to the principal arts of your sex! Once more, what a devil has your heart to do in your eyes?

Have I not told you that my beloved is a great observer of the eyes? She once quoted upon me a text,[1] which showed me how she came by her knowledge. Dorcas's were found guilty of treason the first moment she saw her.

Once more, suppose *me* to be my charmer. Now you are to encounter my *examining* eye, and my *doubting* heart——

That's my dear!

Study that air in the pier-glass!

Charming! Perfectly right!

Your honours, now, devils!

Pretty well, Cousin Charlotte, for a young country lady! Till form yields to familiarity, you *may* curtsy low. You must not be supposed to have forgot your boarding-school airs.

But too low, too low, Lady Betty, for your years and your quality. The common fault of your sex will be your danger: aiming to be young too long! The devil's in you all, when you judge of yourselves by your wishes, and by your vanity! Fifty, in that case, is never more than fifteen.

Graceful ease, conscious dignity, like that of my charmer, oh, how hard to hit!

Both together now.

Charming! That's the air, Lady Betty! That's the cue, Cousin Charlotte, suited to the character of each! But, once more, be sure to have a guard upon your eyes.

Never fear, nephew!

Never fear, cousin.

A dram of Barbados each——

And now we are gone.

---

[1] Ecclus. xxvi: *The whoredom of a woman may be known in her haughty looks and eyelids. Watch over an impudent eye, and marvel not if it trespass against thee.*

Letter XXVIII—Mr. Lovelace to John Belford, Esq.

At Mrs. Sinclair's, Monday Afternoon.

ALL's right, as heart can wish! In spite of all objection—in spite of a reluctance next to fainting—in spite of all foresight, vigilance, suspicion—once more is the charmer of my soul in her old lodgings!

Now throbs away every pulse! Now thump, thump, thumps my bounding heart for something!

But I have not time for the particulars of our management.

My beloved is now directing some of her clothes to be packed up—never more to enter this house! Nor ever more will she, I dare say, when once again out of it!

Yet not so much as a condition of forgiveness! The Harlowe-spirited fair one will not *deserve* my mercy! She will wait for Miss Howe's next letter; and then, if she find a *difficulty in her new schemes* [thank her for nothing], will—will what? Why even *then* will take time to consider whether I am to be forgiven, or for ever rejected. An indifference that revives in my heart the remembrance of a thousand of the like nature. And yet Lady Betty and Miss Montague [*a man would be tempted to think, Jack, that they wish her to provoke my vengeance*] declare that I ought to be satisfied with such a proud suspension!

They are entirely attached to her. Whatever she says, *is*, *must be*, Gospel! They are guarantees for her return to Hampstead this night. They are to go back with her. A supper bespoken by Lady Betty at Mrs. Moore's. All the vacant apartments there, by my permission (for I had engaged them for a month certain), to be filled with them and their attendants, for a week at least, or till they can prevail upon the dear perverse, as they hope they shall, to restore me to her favour, and to accompany Lady Betty to Oxfordshire.

The dear creature has thus far condescended that she will write to Miss Howe and acquaint her with the present situation of things.

If she write, I shall see what she writes. But I believe she will have other employment soon.

Lady Betty is sure, she tells her, that she shall prevail upon her to forgive me; though she dares say that I deserve not forgiveness. Lady Betty is too delicate to inquire strictly into the nature of my offence. But it must be an offence against *herself*, against *Miss Montague*, against the *virtuous of the whole sex*, or it could not be so highly resented. Yet she will not leave her till she forgive me, and till she see our nuptials privately celebrated. Meantime, as she approves of her *uncle's expedient*, she will address her as *already my wife before strangers*.

Stedman, her solicitor, may attend her for orders, in relation to her Chancery affair, at Hampstead. Not one hour they *can* be favoured with, will they lose from the company and conversation of so dear, so charming a new relation.

Hard then if she had not obliged them with her company, in their coach and four, to and from their Cousin Leeson's, who longed (as they themselves had done) to see a lady so justly celebrated.

"How will Lord M. be raptured when he sees her, and can salute her as his niece!

"How will Lady Sarah bless herself! She will now think her loss of the dear daughter she mourns for happily supplied!"

Miss Montague dwells upon every word that falls from her lips. She perfectly adores her new cousin: "For her cousin she *must* be. And her cousin will she call her! She answers for equal admiration in her sister Patty.

"Ay, cry I (whispering loud enough for her to hear), how will my cousin Patty's dove's eyes glisten and run over, on the very first interview! So gracious, so noble, so unaffected a dear creature!"

"What a happy family," chorus we all, "will ours be!"

These and such-like congratulatory admirations every hour repeated: her modesty hurt by the ecstatic praises:—"Her graces are too natural to herself for her to be proud of them: but she must be content to be punished for excellences that cast a shade upon the *most* excellent!"

In short, we are here, as at Hampstead, all joy and rapture: all of us, except my beloved; in whose sweet face [her almost fainting reluctance to re-enter these doors not overcome] reigns a kind of anxious serenity! But how will even that be changed in a few hours!

Methinks I begin to pity the half-apprehensive beauty! But avaunt, thou unseasonably-intruding pity! Thou hast more than once already well-nigh undone me! And, adieu, reflection! Begone, consideration! and commiseration! I dismiss ye all, for at least a week to come! Be remembered her broken word! Her flight, when my fond soul was meditating mercy to her! Be remembered her treatment of me in her letter on her escape to Hampstead! Her Hampstead virulence! What is it she ought not to expect from an unchained Beelzebub, and a plotting villain?

Be her preference of the single life to *me* also remembered! That she despises me! That she even refuses to be my WIFE! A proud Lovelace to be denied a *wife*! To be more proudly rejected by a daughter of the *Harlowes*! The ladies of my own family [she thinks them the ladies of my family] supplicating in vain for her returning favour to their despised kinsman, and taking laws from her still prouder punctilio.

Be the execrations of her vixen friend likewise remembered, poured out upon me from *her* representations, and thereby made her *own* execrations!

Be remembered still more particularly the Townsend plot, set on foot between them, and now, in a day or two, ready to break out; and the *sordid threatenings* thrown out against me by that little fury.

Is not *this* the crisis for which I have been long waiting? Shall Tomlinson, shall these women, be engaged; shall so many engines be set at work, at an immense expense, with infinite contrivance; and all to no purpose?

Is not *this* the hour of her trial—and in *her*, of the trial of the virtue of her whole sex, so long premeditated, so long threatened? Whether her frost be frost indeed? Whether her virtue be principle? Whether, if *once subdued, she will not be always subdued*? And will she not want the very crown of her glory, the proof of her till now all-surpassing excellence, if I stopped short of the ultimate trial?

Now is the end of purposes long overawed, often suspended, at hand. And need I to throw the sins of her cursed family into the too weighty scale?

Abhorred be force!—be the thoughts of force! There's no triumph over the will in force! This I know I have said.[1] But would I not have avoided it, if I could? Have I not tried every other method? And have I any other recourse left me? Can she resent the *last outrage* more than she has resented a *fainter effort*? And if her resentments run ever so high, cannot I repair by matrimony? She will not refuse me, I know, Jack; the haughty beauty will not refuse me, when her pride of being corporally inviolate is brought down; when she can tell no tales, but when (be her resistance what it will) even her own sex will suspect a yielding in resistance; and when that modesty, which may fill her bosom with resentment, will lock up her speech.

[1] See vol. ii, p. 398.

But how know I, that I have not made my own difficulties?
Is she not a woman? What redress lies for a perpetrated evil?
Must she not *live*? Her piety will secure her life. And will not
time be my friend? What, in a word, will be her behaviour
afterwards? She cannot fly me! She must forgive me—and
as I have often said, *once forgiven, will be for ever forgiven.*

Why then should this enervating pity unsteel my foolish heart?

It shall not. All these things will I remember; and think of
nothing else, in order to keep up a resolution, which the women
about me will have it I shall be still unable to hold.

I'll teach the dear charming creature to emulate me in
contrivance! I'll teach her to weave webs and plots against her
conqueror! I'll show her, that in her smuggling schemes she is
but a spider compared to me, and that she has all this time been
spinning only a cobweb!

.   .   .   .   .   .

What shall we do now! We are immersed in the depth of
grief and apprehension! How ill do women bear disappointment!
Set upon going to Hampstead, and upon quitting for ever a
house she re-entered with infinite reluctance; what things she
intended to take with her ready packed up; herself on tiptoe
to be gone; and I prepared to attend her thither; she begins to be
afraid that she shall not go this night; and in grief and despair
has flung herself into her old apartment; locked herself in; and
through the keyhole Dorcas sees her on her knees—praying, I
suppose, for a safe deliverance.

And from what? And wherefore these agonizing apprehensions?

Why, here, this unkind Lady Betty, *with* the dear creature's
knowledge, though to her concern, and this mad-headed Cousin
Montague *without* it, while she was employed in directing her
package, have hurried away in the coach to their own lodgings
[only, indeed, to put up some night-clothes, and so forth, in
order to attend their sweet cousin to Hampstead]; and, no less
to my surprise than hers, are not yet returned.

I have sent to know the meaning of it.

In a great hurry of spirits, she would have had me to go
myself. Hardly any pacifying her! The girl, God bless her! is
wild with her own idle apprehensions! What is she afraid of?

I curse them both for their delay. My tardy villain, how he
stays! Devil fetch them! Let them send their coach, and we'll
go without them. In her hearing I bid the fellow tell them so.

Perhaps he stays to bring the coach, if anything happens to hinder the ladies from attending my beloved this night.

.　　.　　.　　.　　.　　.

Devil take them, again say I! They *promised* too they would not stay, because it was but two nights ago that a chariot was robbed at the foot of Hampstead Hill; which alarmed my fair one when told of it!

Oh! here's Lady Betty's servant with a billet.

> *To Robert Lovelace, Esq.*　　　*Monday Night.*
>
> EXCUSE us, dear nephew, I beseech you, to my dearest kinswoman. One night cannot break squares. For here Miss Montague has been taken violently ill with three fainting fits, one after another. The hurry of her joy, I believe, to find your dear lady so much surpass all expectation [never did family-love, you know, reign so strong as among us], and the too eager desire she had to attend her, have occasioned it: for she has but weak spirits, poor girl! well as she looks.
>
> If she be better, we will certainly go with you to-morrow morning, after we have breakfasted with *her*, at your lodgings. But, whether she be, or not, I will do myself the pleasure to attend your lady to Hampstead: and will be with you for that purpose about nine in the morning. With due compliments to your most worthily beloved, I am
>
> Yours affectionately,
>
> ELIZAB. LAWRANCE.

Faith and troth, Jack, I know not what to do with myself: for here, just now having sent in the above note by Dorcas, out came my beloved with it in her hand: in a fit of frenzy! True, by my soul!

She had indeed complained of *her head* all the evening.

Dorcas ran to me, out of breath, to tell me that her lady was coming in some strange way: but she followed her so quick, that the frighted wench had not time to say in what way.

It seems, when she read the billet—Now indeed, said she, am I a lost creature! O the poor Clarissa Harlowe!

She tore off her head-clothes; inquired where I was: and in she came, her shining tresses flowing about her neck; her ruffles torn, and hanging in tatters about her snowy hands; with her arms spread out, as if starting from their orbits. Down sunk she at my feet, as soon as she approached me; her charming bosom heaving to her uplifted face; and

clasping her arms about my knees, Dear Lovelace, said she, if
ever—if ever—if ever—and, unable to speak another word,
quitting her clasping hold, down prostrate on the floor sunk she,
neither in a fit nor out of one.

I was quite astonished. All my purposes suspended for a few
moments, I knew neither what to say, nor what to do. But,
recollecting myself, Am I *again*, thought I, in a way to be overcome, and made a fool of! If I now recede, I am gone for ever.

I raised her: but down she sunk, as if quite disjointed; her
limbs failing her—yet not in a fit neither. I never heard of or
saw such a dear unaccountable: almost lifeless, and speechless
too for a few moments. What must her apprehensions be at
that moment! And for what? A high-notioned dear soul!
Pretty ignorance! thought I.

Never having met with so sincere, so unquestionable a re-
pugnance, I was staggered—I was confounded. Yet how should
I know that it would be so till I tried? And how, having proceeded thus far, could I stop, were I *not* to have had the women
to goad me on, and to make light of circumstances, which they
pretended to be better judges of than I?

I lifted her, however, into a chair; and in words of disordered
passion, told her, all her fears were needless: wondered at them:
begged of her to be pacified: besought her reliance on my faith
and honour: and revowed all my old vows, and poured forth
new ones.

At last, with a heart-breaking sob, I see, I see, Mr. Lovelace,
in broken sentences she spoke, I see, I see—that at last—at last
—I am ruined! Ruined, if *your* pity—let me implore your pity!
And down on her bosom, like a half-broken-stalked lily, top-
heavy with the overcharging dews of the morning, sunk her
head, with a sigh that went to my heart.

All I could think of to reassure her, when a little recovered,
I said.

Why did I not send for their coach, as I had intimated? It
might return in the morning for the ladies.

I had actually done so, I told her, on seeing her strange
uneasiness. But it was then gone to fetch a doctor for Miss
Montague, lest his chariot should not be so ready.

Ah! Lovelace! said she, with a doubting face; anguish in
her imploring eye.

Lady Betty would think it very strange, I told her, if she were
to know it was so disagreeable to her to stay one night for *her*
company in a house where she had passed *so many*!

She called me names upon this. She had called me names before. I was patient.

Let her go to Lady Betty's lodgings, then; *directly* go; if the person I called Lady Betty was really Lady Betty.

IF, my dear! Good Heaven! What a villain does that IF show you believe me to be!

I cannot help it. I beseech you once more, let me go to Mrs. Leeson's, if *that* IF ought not to be said.

Then assuming a more resolute spirit—I will go! I will inquire my way! I will go by myself! And would have rushed by me.

I folded my arms about her to detain her; pleading the bad way I heard poor Charlotte was in; and what a farther concern her impatience, if she went, would give to poor Charlotte.

She would believe nothing I said, unless I would instantly order a coach (since she was not to have Lady Betty's, nor was permitted to go to Mrs. Leeson's), and let her go in it to Hampstead, late as it was; and all alone; so much the better: for in the house of *people* of whom Lady Betty, upon inquiry, had heard a bad character [*dropped foolishly this, by my prating new relation, in order to do credit to herself, by depreciating others*]; everything, and every face, looking with so much meaning vileness, as well as *my own* [*thou art still too sensible, thought I, my charmer!*], she was resolved not to stay another night.

Dreading what might happen as to her intellects, and being very apprehensive that she might possibly go through a great deal before morning (though more violent she could not well be with the worst she dreaded), I humoured her, and ordered Will to endeavour to get a coach directly, to carry us to Hampstead; I cared not at what price.

Robbers, with whom I would have terrified her, she feared not—*I* was all her fear, I found; and this house her terror: for I saw plainly that she now believed that Lady Betty and Miss Montague were both impostors.

But her mistrust is a little of the latest to do her service!

And, O Jack, the rage of love, the rage of revenge, is upon me! By turns they tear me! The progress already made—the women's instigations—the power I shall have to try her to the utmost, and still to marry her, if she be not to be brought to cohabitation—let me perish, Belford, if she escape me now!

   .   .   .   .   .

Will is not yet come back. Near eleven.

   .   .   .   .   .

Will is this moment returned. No coach to be got, either *for love or money.*

Once more she urges—To Mrs. Leeson's let me go, Lovelace! Good Lovelace, let me go to Mrs. Leeson's! What is Miss Montague's illness to my terror?—For the Almighty's sake, Mr. Lovelace!—her hands clasped.

O my angel! What a wildness is this! Do you know, do you see, my dearest life, what appearances your causeless apprehensions have given you? Do you know it is past eleven o'clock?

Twelve, one, two, three, four—any hour—I care not. If you mean me honourably, let me go out of this hated house!

Thou'lt observe, Belford, that though this was written afterwards, yet (as in other places) I write it as it was spoken and happened, as if I had retired to put down every sentence as spoken. I know thou likest this lively *present-tense* manner, as it is one of my peculiars.

Just as she had repeated the last words, *If you mean me honourably, let me go out of this hated house,* in came Mrs. Sinclair, in a great ferment. And what, pray, madam, has *this house* done to you? Mr. Lovelace, you have known me some time; and, if I have not the niceness of this lady, I hope I do not deserve to be treated thus!

She set her huge arms akembo: *Hoh!* madam, let me tell you, I am amazed at your freedoms with my character! And, Mr. Lovelace [holding up, and violently shaking, her head], if you are a gentleman, and a man of honour——

Having never before seen anything but obsequiousness in this woman, little as she liked her, she was frighted at her masculine air, and fierce look—God help me! cried she—what will become of me now! Then, turning her head hither and thither, in a wild kind of amaze, Whom have I for a protector! What will become of me now!

I will be your protector, my dearest love! But indeed you are uncharitably severe upon poor Mrs. Sinclair! Indeed you are! She is a gentlewoman born, and the relict of a man of honour; and though left in such circumstances as oblige her to let lodgings, yet would she scorn to be guilty of a wilful baseness.

I hope so—it may be so—I may be mistaken—but—but there is no crime, I presume, no treason, to say I don't like her house.

The old dragon straddled up to her, with her arms kemboed again, her eyebrows erect, like the bristles upon a hog's back, and, scowling over her shortened nose, more than half hid her ferret eyes. Her mouth was distorted. She pouted out her blubber-lips, as if to bellows up wind and sputter into her horse-nostrils; and her chin was curdled, and more than usually prominent with passion.

With two *hoh-madams* she accosted the frighted fair one; who, terrified, caught hold of my sleeve.

I feared she would fall into fits; and, with a look of indignation, told Mrs. Sinclair that these apartments were mine; and I could not imagine what she meant, either by listening to what passed between me and my spouse, or to come in uninvited; and still more I wondered at her giving herself these strange liberties.

I may be to blame, Jack, for suffering this wretch to give herself these airs; but her coming in was without my orders.

The old beldam, throwing herself into a chair, fell a blubbering and exclaiming. And the pacifying of her, and endeavouring to reconcile the lady to her, took up till near one o'clock.

And thus, between terror, and the late hour, and what followed, she was diverted from the thoughts of getting out of the house to Mrs. Leeson's, or anywhere else.

Letter XXIX—*Mr. Lovelace to John Belford, Esq.*

Tuesday Morn., June 13.

AND now, Belford, I can go no farther. The affair is over. Clarissa lives. And I am

Your humble servant,
R. LOVELACE.

The whole of this black transaction is given by the injured lady to Miss Howe, in her subsequent letters, dated Thursday, July 6. See pp. 350 *et. seq.*

Letter XXX—*Mr. Belford to Robert Lovelace, Esq.*

Watford, Wedn., June 14.

O THOU savage-hearted monster! What work hast thou made in *one guilty hour*, for a *whole age* of repentance!

I am inexpressibly concerned at the fate of this matchless lady! She could not have fallen into the hands of any other man breathing, and suffered as she has done with thee.

I had written a great part of another long letter, to try to soften thy flinty heart in her favour; for I thought it but too likely that thou shouldst succeed in getting her back again to the accursed woman's. But I find it would have been too late, had I finished it, and sent it away. Yet cannot I forbear writing, to urge thee to make the *only* amends thou now canst make her, by a proper use of the licence thou hast obtained.

Poor, poor lady! It is a pain to me that I ever saw her. Such an adorer of virtue to be sacrificed to the vilest of her sex; and thou their implement in the devil's hands, for a purpose so base, so ungenerous, so inhumane! Pride thyself, O cruellest of men, in this reflection; and that thy triumph over a woman, who for thy sake was abandoned of every friend she had in the world, was effected, not by advantages taken of her weakness and credulity; but by the blackest artifice; after a long course of studied deceits had been tried to no purpose.

I can tell thee, it is well either for thee or for me, that I am not the brother of the lady. Had I been her brother, her violation must have been followed by the blood of one of us.

Excuse me, Lovelace; and let not the lady fare the worse for my concern for her. And yet I have but one *other* motive to ask thy excuse; and that is, because I owe to thy own communicative pen the knowledge I have of thy barbarous villainy; since thou mightest, if thou wouldst, have passed it upon me for a common seduction.

Clarissa lives, thou sayest. That she does is my wonder; and these words show that thou thyself (though thou couldst, nevertheless, proceed) hardly expectedst she would have survived the outrage. What must have been the poor lady's distress (watchful as she had been over her honour) when dreadful certainty took place of cruel apprehension! And yet a man may guess what it must have been, by that which thou paintest, when she suspected herself tricked, deserted, and betrayed, by the pretended ladies.

That thou couldst behold her frenzy on this occasion, and her half-speechless, half-fainting prostration at thy feet, and yet retain thy evil purposes, will hardly be thought credible, even by those who know *thee*, if they have seen *her*.

Poor, poor lady! With such noble qualities as would have adorned the most exalted married life, to fall into the hands of the *only* man in the world who could have treated her as thou hast treated her! And to let loose the old dragon, as thou properly callest her, upon the before-affrighted innocent, what a barbarity was *that*! What a *poor* piece of barbarity! in order to obtain by terror what thou despairedst to gain by love, though supported by stratagems the most insidious!

O Lovelace! Lovelace! *had I doubted it before, I should now be convinced that there must be a* WORLD AFTER THIS, *to do justice to injured merit, and to punish barbarous perfidy!* Could the divine SOCRATES, and the divine CLARISSA, otherwise have suffered?

But let me, if possible, for one moment, try to forget this villainous outrage on the most excellent of women.

I have business here which will hold me yet a few days; and then perhaps I shall quit this house for ever.

I have had a solemn and tedious time of it. I should never have known that I had half the respect I really find I had for the old gentleman, had I not so closely, at his earnest desire, attended him, and been a witness of the tortures he underwent.

This melancholy occasion may possibly have contributed to humanize me: but surely I never could have been so remorseless a caitiff as *thou* hast been, to a woman of *half* this lady's excellence.

But prithee, dear Lovelace, if thou 'rt a man, and not a devil, resolve, out of hand, to repair thy sin of ingratitude, by conferring upon thyself the highest honour thou *canst* receive, in making her lawfully thine.

But if thou canst not prevail upon thyself to do her this justice, I think I should not scruple a tilt with thee [an everlasting rupture *at least* must follow] if thou sacrificest her to the accursed woman.

Thou art desirous to know what advantage I reap by my uncle's demise. I do not certainly know; for I have not been so greedily solicitous on this subject as some of the kindred have been, who ought to have shown more decency, as I have told them, and suffered the corpse to have been cold before they had begun their hungry inquiries. But, by what I gathered from the poor man's talk to me, who oftener than I wished touched upon the subject, I deem it will be upwards of £5,000 in cash, and in the funds, after all legacies paid, besides the real estate, which is a clear £1,000 a year.

I wish from my heart thou wert a money lover! Were the estate to be of double the value, thou shouldst have it every shilling; only upon one condition [for my circumstances before were as easy as I wish them to be while I am single]—that thou wouldst permit me the honour of being this fatherless lady's *father*, as it is called, at the altar.

Think of this, my dear Lovelace: be honest: and let me present thee with the brightest jewel that man ever possessed; and then, body and soul, wilt thou bind to thee for ever thy

BELFORD.

Letter XXXI—Mr. Lovelace to John Belford, Esq.

Thursday, June 15.

LET me alone, you great dog, you!—Let me alone! have I heard a lesser boy, his coward arms held over his head and face, say to a bigger, who was pommelling him, for having run away with his apple, his orange, or his gingerbread.

So say I to thee, on occasion of thy severity to thy poor friend, who, as thou ownest, has furnished thee (ungenerous as thou art!) with the weapons thou brandishest so fearfully against him. And to what purpose, when the mischief is done? when, of consequence, the affair is irretrievable? and when a CLARISSA could not move me?

Well, but after all, I must own that there is something very singular in this lady's case: and, at times, I cannot help regretting that I ever attempted her; since not *one power either of body or soul* could be moved in my favour; and since, to use the expression of the philosopher, on a much graver occasion, there is no difference to be found between the skull of King Philip and that of another man.

But people's extravagant notions of things alter not *facts*, Belford: and, when all's done, Miss Clarissa Harlowe has but run the fate of a thousand others of her sex—only that they did not set such a romantic value upon what they call their *honour*; that's all.

And yet I will allow thee this—That if a person sets a high value upon anything, be it ever such a trifle in itself, or in the eye of others, the robbing of that person of it is *not* a trifle to *him*. Take the matter in this light, I own I have done wrong, great wrong, to this admirable creature.

But have I not known twenty and twenty of the sex, who have seemed to carry their notions of virtue high; yet, when brought to the test, have abated of their severity? And how should we be convinced that *any* of them are proof, till they are tried?

A thousand times have I said that I never yet met with such a woman as this. If I *had*, I hardly ever should have attempted Miss Clarissa Harlowe. Hitherto she is all angel: and was not that the point which at setting out I proposed to try?[1] And was not *cohabitation* ever my darling view? And am I not now, at last, in the high road to it? It is true that I have nothing to

[1] See vol. ii, p. 42.

boast of as to her will. *The very contrary.* But now are we
come to the test, whether she cannot be brought to make the
best of an irreparable evil. If she exclaim [she has reason to
exclaim, and I will sit down with patience by the hour together
to hear her exclamations, till she is tired of them], she will then
descend to expostulation perhaps: expostulation will give me
hope: expostulation will show that she hates me not. And if
she hate me not, she will forgive: and if she *now* forgive, then
will all be over; and she will be mine upon my own terms: and
it shall then be the whole study of my future life to make her
happy.

So, Belford, thou seest that I have journeyed on to this stage
[indeed, through infinite mazes, and as infinite remorses] with one
determined point in view from the first. To thy urgent supplication then, that I will do her grateful justice by marriage, let
me answer in Matt Prior's two lines on his hoped-for auditor-
ship; as put into the mouths of his St. John and Harley;

> ——Let that be done, which Matt doth say.
> YEA, quoth the Earl—BUT NOT TO-DAY.

Thou seest, Jack, that I make no resolutions, however, against
doing her, one time or other, the wished-for justice, even were I
to succeed in my principal view, *cohabitation.* And of this I do
assure thee, that, if I ever marry, it must, it shall be Miss
Clarissa Harlowe. Nor is her honour at all impaired with *me*,
by what she has *so far* suffered: but the contrary. She must only
take care, that, if she be at last brought to forgive me, she show
me that her Lovelace is the only man on earth whom she could
have forgiven on the like occasion.

But, ah, Jack! what, in the meantime, shall I do with this
admirable creature? At present [I am loath to say it—but, at
present] she is quite stupefied.

I had rather, methinks, she should have retained all her active
powers, though I had suffered by her nails and her teeth, than
that she should be sunk into such a state of absolute—insensibility (shall I call it?) as she has been in ever since Tuesday
morning. Yet, as she begins a little to revive, and now and then
to call names, and to exclaim, I dread almost to engage with the
anguish of a spirit that owes its extraordinary agitations to a
niceness that has no example either in ancient or modern story.
For, after all, what is there in her case that should *stupefy* such
a glowing, such a *blooming* charmer? Excess of grief, excess of
terror, has made a person's hair stand on end, and even (as we

have read) changed the colour of it. But that it should so stupefy, as to make a person, at times, insensible to those imaginary wrongs which would raise others *from* stupefaction, is very surprising!

But I will leave this subject, lest it should make me too grave.

I was yesterday at Hampstead, and discharged all obligations there, with no small applause. I told them that the lady was now as happy as myself: and that is no great untruth; for I am not altogether so, when I allow myself to *think*.

Mrs. Townsend, with her tars, had not been then there. I told them what I would have them say to her, if she came.

Well, but, after all [how many *after all's* have I?] I could be very grave, were I to give way to it. The devil take me for a fool! What's the matter with me, I wonder! I must breathe a fresher air for a few days.

But what shall I do with this admirable creature the while? Hang me, if I know! For, if I stir, the venomous spider of this habitation will want to set upon the charming fly, whose silken wings are already so entangled in my enormous web, that she cannot move hand or foot: for so much has grief stupefied her, that she is at present as destitute of will as she always seemed to be of desire. I must not therefore think of leaving her yet for two days together.

Letter XXXII—*Mr. Lovelace to John Belford, Esq.*

I HAVE just now had a specimen of what the resentment of this dear creature will be when quite recovered: an affecting one! For, entering her apartment after Dorcas; and endeavouring to soothe and pacify her disordered mind; in the midst of my blandishments, she held up to Heaven, in a speechless agony, the innocent licence (which she has in her own power); as the poor distressed Catalans held up their English treaty, on an occasion that keeps the worst of my actions in countenance.

She seemed about to call down vengeance upon me; when, happily, the leaden god, in pity to her trembling Lovelace, waved over her half-drowned eyes his somniferous wand, and laid asleep the fair exclaimer, before she could go half through her intended imprecation.

Thou wilt guess, by what I have written, that some *little* art has been made use of: but it was with a *generous* design (if thou 'lt allow me the word on such an occasion) in order to lessen the too quick sense she was likely to have of what she was to suffer. A contrivance I never had occasion for before, and had not thought of now, if Mrs. Sinclair had not proposed it to me: to whom I left the management of it: and I have done nothing but curse her ever since, lest the quantity should have for ever damped her charming intellects.

Hence my concern—for I think the poor lady ought not to have been so treated. *Poor lady*, did I say? What have I to do with thy creeping style? But have not I the worst of it; since her insensibility has made me but a thief to my own joys?

I did not intend to tell thee of this little *innocent* trick; for such I designed it to be; but that I hate disingenuousness: to thee, especially: and as I cannot help writing in a more serious vein than usual, thou wouldst perhaps, had I not hinted the true cause, have imagined that I was sorry for the fact itself: and this would have given *thee* a good deal of trouble in scribbling dull persuasives to repair by matrimony; and *me*, in reading thy crude nonsense. Besides, one day or other, thou mightest, had I not confessed it, have heard of it in an aggravated manner; and I know thou hast such an high opinion of this lady's virtue, that thou wouldst be disappointed, if thou hadst reason to think that she was subdued by *her own* consent, or any the *least* yielding in her will. And so is she beholden to me, in some measure, that, at the expense of *my* honour, she may so justly form a plea which will entirely salve *hers*.

And now is the whole secret out.

Thou wilt say I am a horrid fellow! As the lady does, that I am the *unchained Beelzebub*, and a *plotting villain*: and as this is what you both said beforehand, and nothing worse *can* be said, I desire, if thou wouldst not have me quite serious with thee, and that I should think thou meanest more by thy tilting hint than I am willing to believe thou dost, that thou wilt forbear thy invectives: for is not the thing done? Can it be helped? And must I not now try to make the best of it? And the rather do I enjoin thee this, and inviolable secrecy; because I begin to think that my punishment will be greater than the fault, were it to be only from my own reflection.

Letter XXXIII—Mr. Lovelace to John Belford, Esq.

Friday, June 16.

I AM sorry to hear of thy misfortune; but hope thou wilt not long lie by it. Thy servant tells me what a narrow escape thou hadst with thy neck. I wish it may not be ominous: but I think thou seemest not to be in so enterprising a way as formerly; and yet, merry or sad, thou seest a rake's neck is always in danger, if not from the hangman, from his own horse. But 'tis a vicious toad, it seems; and I think thou shouldst never venture upon his back again; for 'tis a plaguy thing for rider and horse both to be vicious.

Thy fellow tells me thou desirest me to continue to write to thee in order to *divert* thy chagrin on thy forced confinement: but how can I think it in my *power* to divert, when my subject is not pleasing to myself?

Csæer never knew what it was to be *hipped*, I will call it, till he came to be what Pompey was; that is to say, till he arrived at the height of his ambition: nor did thy Lovelace know what it was to be gloomy, till he had completed his wishes upon the most charming creature in the world.

And yet why say I *completed*? when the *will*, the *consent*, is wanting—and I have still views before me of obtaining that?

Yet I could almost join with thee in the wish, which thou sendest me up by thy servant, unfriendly as it is, that I had had thy misfortune before Monday night last: for here the poor lady has run into a contrary extreme to that I told thee of in my last: for now is she as much too lively, as before she was too stupid; and, abating that she has pretty frequent lucid intervals, would be deemed raving mad, and I should be obliged to confine her.

I am most confoundedly disturbed about it: for I begin to fear that her intellects are irreparably hurt.

Who the devil could have expected such strange effects from a cause so common and so slight?

But these high-souled and high-sensed girls, who had set up for shining lights and examples to the rest of the sex, are with such difficulty brought down to the common standard, that a wise man, who prefers his peace of mind to his glory in subduing one of that exalted class, would have nothing to say to them.

I do all in my power to quiet her spirits, when I force myself into her presence.

I go on, begging pardon one minute; and vowing truth and honour another.

I would at first have persuaded her, and offered to call witness to the truth of it, that we were actually married. Though the licence was in her hands, I thought the assertion might go down in her disorder; and charming consequences I hoped would follow. But this would not do.

I therefore gave up that hope: and now I declare to her, that it is my resolution to marry her, the moment her Uncle Harlowe informs me that he will grace the ceremony with his presence.

But she believes nothing I say; nor (whether in her senses, or not) bears me with patience in her sight.

I pity her with all my soul; and I curse myself, when she is in her wailing fits, and when I apprehend that intellects, so charming, are for ever damped. But more I curse these women, who put me upon such an expedient! Lord! Lord! what a hand have I made of it! *And all for what?*

Last night, for the first time since Monday last, she got to her pen and ink: but she pursues her writing with such eagerness and hurry, as show too evidently her discomposure.

I hope, however, that this employment will help to calm her spirits.

.   .   .   .   .

Just now Dorcas tells me that what she writes she tears, and throws the paper in fragments under the table, either as not knowing what she does, or disliking it: then gets up, wrings her hands, weeps, and shifts her seat all round the room: then returns to her table, sits down, and writes again.

.   .   .   .   .

One odd letter, as I may call it, Dorcas has this moment given me from her. *Carry this,* said she, *to the vilest of men.* Dorcas, a toad, brought it, without any further direction, to *me.* I sat down, intending (though 'tis pretty long) to give thee a copy of it: but, for my life, I cannot; 'tis so extravagant. And the original is too much an original to let it go out of my hands.

But some of the scraps and fragments, as either torn through, or flung aside, I will copy, for the novelty of the thing, and to show thee how her mind works now she is in this whimsical way. Yet I know I am still furnishing thee with new weapons against myself. But spare thy comments. My own reflections render them needless. Dorcas thinks her lady will ask for them: so wishes to have them to lay again under her table.

By the first thou 'lt guess that I have told her that Miss Howe is very ill, and can't write; that she may account the better for not having received the letter designed for her.

Paper I. *(Torn in two pieces.)*

MY DEAREST MISS HOWE,—O what dreadful, dreadful things have I to tell you! But yet I cannot tell you neither. But say, are you really ill, as a vile, vile creature informs me you are?

But he never yet told me truth, and I hope has not in this: and yet, if it were not true, surely I should have heard from you before now! But what have I to do to upbraid? You may well be tired of me! And if you are, I can forgive you; for I am tired of myself: and all my own relations were tired of me long before you were.

How good you have always been to me, mine own dear Anna Howe! But how I ramble!

I sat down to say a great deal—my heart was full—I did not know what to say first—and thought, and grief, and confusion, and (O my poor head!) I cannot tell what—and thought, and grief, and confusion, came crowding so thick upon me; *one* would be first, *another* would be first, *all would* be first; so I can write nothing at all. Only that, whatever they have done to me, I cannot tell; but I am no longer what I was in any one thing. In any one thing did I say? Yes, but I am; for I am still, and I ever will be,

Your true——

Plague on it! I can write no more of this eloquent nonsense myself; which rather shows a raised, than a quenched, imagination: but Dorcas shall transcribe the others in separate papers, as written by the whimsical charmer: and some time hence, when all is over, and I can better bear to read them, I may ask thee for a sight of them. Preserve them, therefore; for we often look back with pleasure even upon the heaviest griefs, when the cause of them is removed.

Paper II. *(Scratched through, and thrown under the table.)*

—And can you, my dear honoured papa, resolve for ever to reprobate your poor child? But I am sure you would not, if you knew what she has suffered since her unhappy—And will nobody plead for your poor suffering girl? No one good body? Why, then, dearest sir, let it be an act of your own innate goodness, which I have so much experienced, and so much abused. I don't presume to think you should receive me—no, indeed! My name is—I don't know what my name is! I never dare to wish to come into your family again! But your heavy curse, my papa—yes, I *will* call you papa, and help yourself as you can —for you are my own dear papa, whether you will or not—and though I am an unworthy child—yet I *am* your child——

Paper III

A lady took a great fancy to a young lion, or a bear, I forget which—but a bear, or a tiger, I believe it was. It was made her a present of when a whelp. She fed it with her own hand: she nursed up the wicked cub with great tenderness; and would play with it without fear or apprehension of danger: and it was obedient to all her commands: and its tameness, as she used to boast, increased with its growth; so that, like a lapdog, it would follow her all over the house. But mind what followed: at last, somehow, neglecting to satisfy its hungry maw, or having otherwise disobliged it on some occasion, it resumed its nature; and on a sudden fell upon her, and tore her in pieces. And who was most to blame, I pray? The brute, or the lady? The lady, surely! For what *she* did was *out* of nature, *out* of character, at least: what it did was *in* its own nature.

Paper IV

How art thou now humbled in the dust, thou proud Clarissa Harlowe! Thou that never steppedst out of thy father's house but to be admired! Who wert wont to turn thine eye, sparkling with healthful life, and self-assurance, to different objects at once as thou passedst, as if (for so thy penetrating sister used to say) to plume thyself upon the expected applauses of all that beheld thee! Thou that usedst to go to rest satisfied with the adulations paid thee in the past day, and couldst put off everything but thy vanity!

Paper V

Rejoice not now, my Bella, my sister, my friend; but pity the humbled creature, whose foolish heart you used to say you beheld through the thin veil of humility which covered it.

I must have been so! My fall had not else been permitted.

You penetrated my proud heart with the jealousy of an elder sister's searching eye.

You knew me better than I knew myself.

Hence your upbraidings and your chidings, when I began to totter.

But forgive now those vain triumphs of my heart.

I thought, poor proud wretch that I was, that what you said was owing to your envy.

I thought I could acquit my intention of any such vanity.

I was too secure in the knowledge I thought I had of my own heart.

My supposed advantages became a snare to me.

And what now is the end of all?

Paper VI

What now is become of the prospects of a happy life, which once I thought opening before me? Who now shall assist in the solemn preparations? Who now shall provide the nuptial ornaments, which soften and divert the apprehensions of the fearful virgin? No court now to be paid to my smiles! No encouraging compliments to inspire thee with hope of laying a mind not unworthy of thee under obligation! No elevation now for conscious merit, and applauded purity, to look down from on a prostrate adorer, and an admiring world, and up to pleased and rejoicing parents and relations!

Paper VII

Thou pernicious caterpillar, that preyest upon the fair leaf of virgin fame, and poisonest those leaves which thou canst not devour!

Thou fell blight, thou eastern blast, thou overspreading mildew, that destroyest the early promises of the shining year! that mockest the laborious toil, and blastest the joyful hopes, of the painful husbandman!

Thou fretting moth, that corruptest the fairest garment!

Thou eating canker-worm, that preyest upon the opening bud, and turnest the damask rose into livid yellowness!

If, as religion teaches us, God will judge us, in a great measure, by our benevolent or evil actions to one another—O wretch!

bethink thee, in time bethink thee, how great must be thy condemnation!

Paper VIII

At first, I saw something in your air and person that displeased me not. Your birth and fortunes were no small advantages to you. You acted not ignobly by my passionate brother. Everybody said you were brave: everybody said you were generous. A *brave* man, I thought, could not be a *base* man: a *generous* man could not, I believed, be *ungenerous*, where he acknowledged *obligation*. Thus prepossessed, all the rest that my soul loved and wished for in your reformation, I hoped! I knew not, but by report, any flagrant instances of your vileness. You seemed frank as well as generous: frankness and generosity ever attracted me: whoever kept up those appearances, I judged of their hearts by my own; and whatever qualities *I wished* to find in them, I was *ready* to find; and, *when* found, I believed them to be natives of the soil.

My fortunes, my rank, my character, I thought a further security. I was in none of those respects unworthy of being the niece of Lord M. and of his two noble sisters. Your vows, your imprecations—But, oh! you have barbarously and basely conspired against that honour, which you ought to have protected: and now you have made me—what is it of vile that you have *not* made me?

Yet, God knows my heart, I had no culpable inclinations! I honoured virtue! I hated vice! But I knew not that you were vice itself!

Paper IX

Had the happiness of any the poorest outcast in the world, whom I had never seen, never known, never before heard of, lain as much in *my* power as my happiness did in *yours*, my benevolent heart would have made me fly to the succour of such a poor distressed—with what pleasure would I have raised the dejected head, and comforted the desponding heart! But who now shall pity the poor wretch, who has increased, instead of diminished, the number of the miserable!

Paper X

LEAD me, where my own thoughts themselves may lose me;
Where I may doze out what I 've left of Life,
Forget myself, and that day 's guilt!——
Cruel Remembrance!—how shall I appease thee?

—Oh! you have done an act
That blots the face and blush of modesty;
    Takes off the rose
From the fair forehead of an innocent Love,
And makes a blister there!—

    Then down I laid my head,
Down on cold earth, and for a while was dead;
And my freed Soul to a strange Somewhere fled!
    Ah! sottish Soul! said I,
When back to its cage again I saw it fly,
    Fool! to resume her broken chain,
  And row the galley here again!
    Fool! to that Body to return,
Where it condemn'd and destin'd is to *mourn*.

O my Miss Howe! if thou hast friendship, help me,
And speak the words of peace to my divided Soul,
    That wars within me,
And raises ev'ry sense to my confusion.
    I 'm tott'ring on the brink
Of peace; and thou art all the hold I 've left!
Assist me—in the pangs of my affliction!

When Honour 's lost, 'tis a relief to die:
Death 's but a sure retreat from infamy.

        Then farewell, Youth,
          And all the joys that dwell
        With Youth and Life!
          And Life itself, farewell!

        For Life can never be sincerely blest.
        Heav'n punishes the *Bad*, and proves the *Best*.

[right margin, vertical:] Death only can be dreadful to the Bad: To Innocence 'tis like a bugbear dress'd To frighten children. Pull but off the mask, And he 'll appear a friend.

[vertical:] I could a Tale unfold— Would harrow up thy soul!—

[lower left, vertical:] By swift misfortunes How am I pursu'd! Which on each other Are, like waves, renew'd!

After all, Belford, I have just skimmed over these tran-
scriptions of Dorcas; and I see there are method and good sense

in some of them, wild as others of them are; and that her memory, which serves her so well for these poetical flights, is far from being impaired. And this gives me hope that she will soon recover her charming intellects—though I shall be the sufferer by their restoration, I make no doubt.

But, in the letter she wrote to me, there are yet greater extravagances; and though I said it was too affecting to give thee a copy of it, yet, after I have let thee see the loose papers enclosed, I think I may throw in a transcript of that. Dorcas therefore shall here transcribe it. *I* cannot. The reading of it affected me ten times more than the severest reproaches of a regular mind could do.

To Mr. *Lovelace*

I NEVER intended to write another line to you. I would not see you, if I could help it. O that I never had!

But tell me of a truth, is Miss Howe really and truly ill? Very ill? And is not her illness poison? And don't *you* know who gave it her?

What you, or Mrs. Sinclair, or somebody (I cannot tell who) have done to my poor head, you best know: but I shall never be what I was. My head is gone. I have wept away all my brain, I believe; for I can weep no more. Indeed I have had my full share; so it is no matter.

But, good now, Lovelace, don't set Mrs. Sinclair upon me again. I never did her any harm. She *so* affrights me, when I see her! Ever since—when was it? I cannot tell. *You* can, I suppose. She may be a good woman, as far as I know. She was the wife of a man of honour—very likely—though forced to let lodgings for her livelihood. Poor gentlewoman! Let her know I pity her: but don't let her come near me again—pray don't!

Yet she may be a very good woman——

What would I say! I forget what I was going to say.

O Lovelace, you are Satan himself; or he helps you out in everything; and that's as bad!

But have you really and truly sold yourself to him? And for how long? What duration is your reign to have?

Poor man! The contract *will* be out; and then what will be your fate!

O Lovelace! if you could be sorry for yourself, I would be sorry too—but when all my doors are fast, and nothing but the keyhole open, and the key of late put into that, to be where you are, in a manner without opening any of them—O wretched, wretched Clarissa Harlowe!

For I never will be Lovelace—let my uncle take it as he pleases.

Well, but now I remember what I was going to say. It is for *your* good—not *mine*—for nothing can do me good now! O thou villainous man! thou hated Lovelace!

But Mrs. Sinclair may be a good woman. If you love me—but that you don't—but don't let her bluster up with her worse than mannish airs to me again! Oh, she is a frightful woman! If she *be* a woman! She needed not to put on that *fearful mask* to scare me out of my poor wits. But don't tell her what I say—I have no hatred to her—it is only fright, and foolish fear, that 's all. She may not *be* a bad woman—but neither are all *men*, any more than all *women*, alike. God forbid they should be like you!

Alas! you have killed my head among you—I don't say who did it! God forgive you all! But had it not been better to have put me out of all your ways at once? You might safely have done it! For nobody would require me at your hands—no, not a soul—except, indeed, Miss Howe would have said, when she should see you, What, Lovelace, have you done with Clarissa Harlowe? And then you could have given any slight gay answer—Sent her beyond sea; or, She has run away from me, as she did from her parents. And this would have been easily credited; for you know, Lovelace, she that could run away from *them*, might very well run away from *you*.

But this is nothing to what I wanted to say. Now I have it!

I have lost it again—This foolish wench comes teasing me. For what purpose should I eat? For what end should I wish to live? I tell thee, Dorcas, I will neither eat nor drink. I cannot be worse than I am.

I will do as you 'd have me—good Dorcas, look not upon me so fiercely—but thou canst not look so bad as I have seen somebody look.

Mr. Lovelace, now that I remember what I took pen in hand to say, let me hurry off my thoughts, lest I lose them again. Here I am sensible—and yet I am hardly sensible neither—but I know my head is not as it should be, for all that—therefore, let me propose one thing to you: it is for *your* good—not *mine*: and this is it:

I must needs be both a trouble and an expense to you. And here my Uncle Harlowe, when he knows how I am, will never wish any man to have me: no, not even *you*, who have been the occasion of it—barbarous and ungrateful! A less complicated villainy cost a Tarquin—but I forget what I would say again——

Then *this* is it—I never shall be myself again: I have been a very wicked creature—a vain, proud, poor creature—full of secret pride—which I carried off under an humble guise, and deceived everybody—my sister says so—and now I am punished. So let me be carried out of this house, and out of your sight; and let me be put into that Bedlam privately, which once I saw: but it was a sad sight to me then! Little as I thought what I should come to *myself*! That is all I would say: this is all I have to wish for—then I shall be out of all your ways; and I shall be taken care of; and bread and water, without your tormentings, will be dainties; and my straw bed the easiest I have lain in—for—I cannot tell how long!

My clothes will sell for what will keep me there, perhaps, as long as I shall live. But, Lovelace, *dear* Lovelace, I will call you; for you have cost me enough, I 'm sure!—don't let me be made a show of, for my *family's* sake; nay, for your *own sake*, don't do that. For when I know all I have suffered, which yet I do not, and no matter if I never do—I may be apt to rave against you by name, and tell of all your baseness to a poor humbled creature, that once was as proud as anybody—but of what I can't tell—except of mine own folly and vanity—but let that pass—since I am punished enough for it——

So, suppose, instead of Bedlam, it were a private madhouse, where nobody comes! That will be better a great deal.

But, another thing, Lovelace: don't let them use me cruelly when I am there—*you* have used me cruelly enough, you know! Don't let *them* use me cruelly; for I will be very tractable; and do as anybody would have me do—except what you would have me do—for that I never will. Another thing, Lovelace: don't let this *good* woman; I was going to say *vile* woman; but don't tell her that—because she won't let you send me to this happy refuge, perhaps, if she were to know it——

Another thing, Lovelace: and let me have pen, and ink, and paper, allowed me—it will be all my amusement—but they need not send to anybody I shall write to, what I write, because it will but trouble them: and somebody may do you a mischief, may be—I wish not that anybody do anybody a mischief upon my account.

You tell me that Lady Betty Lawrance, and your Cousin Montague, were here to take leave of me; but that I was asleep, and could not be waked. So you told me at first I was married, you know; and that you were my husband. Ah! Lovelace! look to what you say. But let not them (for they will sport with my misery), let not *that* Lady Betty, let not *that* Miss Montague, whatever the *real* ones may do; nor Mrs. Sinclair neither, nor any of her lodgers, nor her nieces, come to see me in my place—*real* ones, I say; for, Lovelace, I shall find out all your villainies in time—indeed I shall—so put me there as soon as you can—it is for *your* good—then all will pass for ravings that I can say, as, I doubt not, many poor creatures' exclamations do pass, though there may be too much truth in them for all that—and you know *I began to be mad at Hampstead*—so you said. Ah! villainous man! what have you not to answer for!

.   .   .   .   .   .

A little interval seems to be lent me. I had begun to look over what I have written. It is not fit for any one to see, so far as I have been able to reperuse it: but my head will not hold, I doubt, to go through it all. If, therefore, I have not already mentioned my earnest desire, let me tell you, it is *this*: that I be sent out of this abominable house without delay, and locked up in some private madhouse about this town; for such it seems there are; never more to be seen, or to be produced to anybody, except in your own vindication, if you should be charged with the murder of my person; a much lighter crime than that of my honour, which the greatest villain on earth has robbed me of. And deny me not this my last request, I beseech you; and one other, and that is, never to let me see you more! This surely may be granted to

The miserably abused

CLARISSA HARLOWE.

I will not hear thy heavy preachments, Belford, upon this affecting letter. So, not a word of that sort! The paper, thou 'lt see, is blistered with the tears even of the hardened transcriber; which has made her ink run here and there.

Mrs. Sinclair is a true heroine, and, I think, shames us all. And she is a *woman* too! Thou 'lt say, the best things corrupted become the worst. But this is certain, that whatever the sex set their hearts upon, they make thorough work of it. And hence it is, that a mischief which would end in simple robbery among men rogues, becomes murder, if a woman be in it.

I know thou wilt blame me for having had recourse to *art*.

But do not physicians prescribe opiates in acute cases, where the violence of the disorder would be apt to throw the patient into a fever of delirium? I aver that my motive for this expedient was *mercy*; nor could it be anything else. For a rape, thou knowest, to us rakes, is far from being an undesirable thing. Nothing but the law stands in our way, upon that account; and the opinion of what a modest woman will suffer rather than become a *viva voce* accuser, lessens much an honest fellow's apprehensions on that score. Then, if these *somnivolencies* [I hate the word *opiates* on this occasion] have turned her head, that is an effect they frequently have upon some constitutions; and in this case was rather the fault of the dose, than the design of the giver.

But is not wine itself an opiate in degree? How many women have been taken advantage of by wine, and other still more intoxicating viands? Let me tell thee, Jack, that the *experience* of many of the *passive* sex, and the *consciences* of many more of the *active*, appealed to, will testify that thy Lovelace is not the worst of villains. Nor would I have *thee* put me upon clearing myself by comparisons.

If she escape a settled delirium when my plots unravel, I think it is all I ought to be concerned about. What, therefore, I desire of thee is, that if two constructions may be made of my actions, thou wilt afford me the most favourable. For this, not only friendship, but my own ingenuousness, which has furnished thee with the knowledge of the facts against which thou art so ready to inveigh, require of thee.

.   .   .   .   .   .

Will is just returned from an errand to Hampstead; and acquaints me that Mrs. Townsend was yesterday at Mrs. Moore's, accompanied by three or four rough fellows; a greater number (as supposed) at a distance. She was strangely surprised at the news that my spouse and I are entirely reconciled; and that two fine ladies, my relations, came to visit her, and went to town with her: where she is very happy with me. *She* was sure we were not married, she said, unless it was while we were at Hampstead: and *they* were sure the ceremony was not performed there. But that the lady *is* happy and easy, is unquestionable: and a fling was thrown out by Mrs. Moore and Mrs. Bevis at *mischief-makers*, as they knew Mrs. Townsend to be acquainted with Miss Howe.

Now, since my fair one can neither receive, nor send away

letters, I am pretty easy as to this Mrs. Townsend and her employer. And I fancy Miss Howe will be puzzled to know what to think of the matter, and afraid of sending by Wilson's conveyance; and perhaps suppose that her friend slights her; or has changed her mind in my favour, and is ashamed to own it; as she has not had an answer to what she wrote; and will believe that the rustic delivered her last letter into her own hand.

Meantime, I have a little project come into my head, of a *new* kind—just for amusement-sake, that 's all: variety has irresistible charms. I cannot live without intrigue. My charmer has no passions; that is to say, none of the passions that I want her to have. She engages all my reverence. I am at present more inclined to regret what I have done, than to proceed to new offences: and shall regret it till I see how she takes it when recovered.

Shall I tell thee my project? 'Tis not a high one. 'Tis this: to get hither Mrs. Moore, Miss Rawlins, and my widow Bevis; for they are desirous to make a visit to my spouse, now we are so happy together. And, if I can order it right, Belton, Mowbray, Tourville, and I, will show them a little more of the ways of this wicked town than they at present know. Why should they be *acquainted* with a man of my character and not be the *better* and *wiser* for it? I would have everybody rail against rakes with *judgment* and *knowledge*, if they *will* rail. Two of these women gave me a great deal of trouble: and the third, I am confident, will forgive a merry evening.

Thou wilt be curious to know what the *persons* of these women are, to whom I intend so much distinction. I think I have not heretofore mentioned anything characteristic of their persons.

Mrs. *Moore* is a widow of about thirty-eight; a little mortified by misfortunes; but those are often the merriest folks, when warmed. She has good features still; and is what they call much of a gentlewoman, and very neat in her person and dress. She has given over, I believe, all thoughts of our sex: but when the dying embers are raked up about the half-consumed stump, there will be fuel enough left, I dare say, to blaze out, and give a comfortable warmth to a half-starved bystander.

Mrs. *Bevis* is comely; that is to say, plump; a lover of mirth, and one whom no grief ever dwelt with, I dare say, for a week together: about twenty-five years of age: Mowbray will have very little difficulty with her, I believe; for one cannot do everything one's self. And yet sometimes women of this free cast, when it comes to the point, answer not the promises their cheerful forwardness gives a man who has a view upon them.

Miss *Rawlins* is an agreeable young lady enough; but not beautiful. She has sense, and would be thought *to know the world*, as it is called; but, for her knowledge, is more indebted to *theory* than *experience*. A mere whipped-syllabub knowledge this, Jack, that always fails the person who trusts to it, when it should hold to do her service. For such young ladies have so much dependence upon their own understanding and wariness, are so much above the cautions that the less opinionative may be benefited by, that their presumption is generally their over-throw, when attempted by a man of experience, who knows how to flatter their vanity, and to magnify their wisdom, in order to take advantage of their folly. But, for Miss Rawlins, if I can add *experience* to her *theory*, what an accomplished person will she be! And how much will she be obliged to me; and not only *she*, but all those who may be the better for the *precepts* she thinks herself already so well qualified to give! Dearly, Jack, do I love to engage with these *precept-givers* and *example-setters*.

Now, Belford, although there is nothing striking in any of these characters; yet may we, at a pinch, make a good frolicky half-day with them, if, after we have softened their wax at table by encouraging viands, we can set our women and them into dancing: dancing, which all women love, and all men should therefore promote, for *both* their sakes.

And thus, when Tourville sings, Belton fiddles, Mowbray makes rough love, and I smooth; and thou, Jack, wilt be by that time well enough to join in the chorus; the devil's in 't if we don't mould them into what shape we please—our own women, by their laughing freedoms, encouraging them to break through all their customary reserves: for women to women, thou knowest, are great darers and incentives; not one of them loving to be outdone or outdared, when their hearts are thoroughly warmed.

I know, at first, the difficulty will be the *accidental* absence of my dear Mrs. Lovelace, to whom principally they will design their visit: but if we can exhilarate them, they won't then wish to see her; and I can form twenty accidents and excuses, from one hour to another, for her absence, till each shall have a subject to take up all her thoughts.

I am really sick at heart for a frolic, and have no doubt but this will be an agreeable one. These women already think me a wild fellow; *nor do they like me the less for it*, as I can perceive;

and I shall take care that they shall be treated with so much freedom before one another's faces, that in policy they shall keep each other's counsel. And won't this be doing a kind thing by them? since it will knit an indissoluble band of union and friendship between three women who are neighbours, and at present have only *common* obligations to one another: for thou wantest not to be told, that secrets of love, and secrets of this nature, are generally the strongest cement of female friendships.

But, after all, if my beloved should be happily restored to her intellects, we may have scenes arise between us that will be sufficiently busy to employ all the faculties of thy friend, without looking out for new occasions. Already, as I have often observed, has she been the means of saving scores of her sex; yet without her own knowledge.

Saturday Night.

By Dorcas's account of her lady's behaviour, the dear creature seems to be recovering. I shall give the earliest notice of this to the worthy Captain Tomlinson, that he may apprise Uncle John of it. I must be properly enabled, from that quarter, to pacify her, or, at least, to rebate her first violence.

Letter XXXIV—Mr. Lovelace to John Belford, Esq.

Sunday Afternoon, 6 o'clock (June 18).

I WENT out early this morning, and returned not till just now; when I was informed that my beloved, in my absence, had taken it into her head to attempt to get away.

She tripped down, with a parcel tied up in a handkerchief, her hood on; and was actually in the entry, when Mrs. Sinclair saw her.

Pray, madam, whipping between her and the street door, be pleased to let me know whither you are going?

Who has a right to control me? was the word.

I have, madam, by order of your spouse: and, kemboing her arms, as she owned, I desire you will be pleased to walk up again.

She would have spoken; but could not: and bursting into tears, turned back, and went up to her chamber: and Dorcas was taken to task for suffering her to be in the passage before she was seen.

This shows, as we hoped last night, that she is recovering her charming intellects.

Dorcas says she was visible to her but once before, the whole day; and then seemed very solemn and sedate.

I will endeavour to see her. It must be in her own chamber, I suppose; for she will hardly meet me in the dining-room. What advantage will the confidence of our sex give me over the modesty of hers, if she be recovered! *I*, the most confident of men: *she*, the most delicate of women. Sweet soul! methinks I have her before me: her face averted: speech lost in sighs—abashed—conscious—what a triumphant aspect will this give me, when I gaze in her downcast countenance!

This moment Dorcas tells me she believes she is coming to find me out. She asked her after me: and Dorcas left her, drying her red-swollen eyes at her glass [no design of moving me by her tears!]; sighing too sensibly for my courage. But to what purpose have I gone thus far, if I pursue not my principal end? Niceness must be a little abated. She knows the worst. That she cannot fly me; that she must see me; and that I can look her into a sweet confusion; are circumstances greatly in my favour. What can she do but rave and exclaim? I am used to raving and exclaiming—but, if recovered, I shall see how she behaves upon this our first sensible interview after what she has suffered.

Here she comes!

Letter XXXV—*Mr. Lovelace to John Belford, Esq.*

Sunday Night.

NEVER blame me for giving way to have art used with this admirable creature. All the princes of the air, or beneath it, joining with me, could never have subdued her while she had her senses.

I will not anticipate—only to tell thee that I am too much awakened by her to think of sleep, were I to go to bed; and so shall have nothing to do, but to write an account of our odd conversation, while it is so strong upon my mind that I can think of nothing else.

She was dressed in a white damask night-gown, with less negligence than for some days past. I was sitting with my pen in my fingers; and stood up when I first saw her, with great complaisance, as if the day were still her own. And so indeed it is.

She entered with such dignity in her manner, as struck me

with great awe, and prepared me for the poor figure I made in the subsequent conversation. A poor figure indeed! But I will do her justice.

She came up with quick steps, pretty close to me; a white handkerchief in her hand; her eyes neither fierce nor mild, but very earnest; and a fixed sedateness in her whole aspect, which seemed to be the effect of deep contemplation: and thus she accosted me, with an air and action that I never saw equalled.

You see before you, sir, the wretch whose preference of you to all your sex you have rewarded—as it indeed *deserved* to be rewarded. My father's dreadful curse has already operated upon me in the very letter of it, as to this life; and it seems to me too evident that it will not be your fault that it is not entirely completed in the loss of my soul, as well as of my honour—which you, villainous man! have robbed me of, with a baseness so unnatural, so inhuman, that, it seems, you, even *you*, had not the heart to attempt it, till my senses were made the previous sacrifice.

Here I made an hesitating effort to speak, laying down my pen: but she proceeded: Hear me out, guilty wretch! abandoned man! *Man*, did I say? Yet what name else can I? since the mortal worryings of the fiercest beast would have been more natural, and infinitely more welcome, than what you have acted by me; and that with a premeditation and contrivance worthy only of that single heart which now, *base* as well as ungrateful as thou art, seems to quake within thee. And well mayest thou quake; well mayest thou tremble, and falter, and hesitate, as thou dost, when thou reflectest upon what I have suffered for thy sake, and upon the returns thou hast made me!

By my soul, Belford, my whole frame was shaken: for not only her looks and her action, but her voice, so solemn, was inexpressibly affecting: and then my cursed guilt, and her innocence, and merit, and rank, and superiority of talents, all stared me at that instant in the face so formidably, that my present account, to which she unexpectedly called me, seemed, as I then thought, to resemble that general one to which we are told we shall be summoned, when our conscience shall be our accuser.

But she had had time to collect all the powers of her eloquence. The whole day probably in her intellects. And then I was the more disappointed, as I had thought I could have gazed the dear creature into confusion: but it is plain that the sense she has of her wrongs sets this matchless woman *above all lesser, all weaker* considerations.

My dear—my love—I—I—I never—no never—lips trembling, limbs quaking, voice inward, hesitating, broken—never surely did miscreant look so *like* a miscreant! While thus she proceeded, waving her snowy hand, with all the graces of moving oratory.

I have no pride in the confusion visible in thy whole person. I have been all the day praying for a composure, if I could not escape from this vile house, that should once more enable me to look up to my destroyer with the consciousness of an innocent sufferer. Thou seest me, since my wrongs are beyond the power of *words to express*, thou seest me, *calm enough* to wish, that thou mayest continue harassed by the workings of thy own conscience, till effectual repentance take hold of thee, that so thou mayest not forfeit all title to *that* mercy which thou hast not shown to the poor creature now before thee, who had so well deserved to meet with a faithful friend, where she met with the worst of enemies.

But tell me (for no doubt thou hast *some* scheme to pursue), tell me, since I am a prisoner, as I find, in the vilest of houses, and have not a friend to protect or save me, what thou intendest shall become of the remnant of a life not worth the keeping? Tell me, if yet there are more evils reserved for me; and whether thou hast entered into a compact with the grand deceiver, in the person of his horrid agent in this house; and if the ruin of my soul, that my father's curse may be fulfilled, is to complete the triumphs of so vile a confederacy? Answer me! Say, if thou hast courage to speak out to her whom thou hast ruined, tell me what *further* I am to suffer from thy barbarity?

She stopped here; and, sighing, turned her sweet face from me, drying up with her handkerchief those tears which she endeavoured to restrain; and, when she could not, to conceal from my sight.

As I told thee, I had prepared myself for high passions, raving, flying, tearing execration: these transient violences, the workings of sudden grief, and shame, and vengeance, would have set us upon a par with each other, and quitted scores. These have I been accustomed to; and, as nothing violent is lasting, with these I could have wished to encounter. But such a majestic composure—seeking me—whom yet, it is plain, by her attempt to get away, she would have avoided seeing—no Lucretia-like vengeance upon herself in her thought—yet swallowed up, her whole mind swallowed up, as I may say, by a grief so heavy, as, in her own words, to be beyond the power of

speech to express—and to be able, discomposed as she was to the
very morning, to put such a home question to me, as if she had
penetrated my future view—how could I avoid looking like a
fool, and answering, as before, in broken sentences, and confusion?

What—what-a—what has been done—I, I, I—cannot but say
—must own—must confess—hem—hem——is not right—is not
what should have been—but-a—but—but—I am truly—truly
—sorry for it—upon my soul I am—and—and—will do all—
do everything—do what—whatever is incumbent upon me—all
that you—that you—that you shall require, to make you
amends!

O Belford! Belford! whose the triumph now! HERS, or MINE?

Amends! O thou truly despicable wretch! Then, lifting up
her eyes—Good Heaven! who shall pity the creature who could
fall by so base a mind! Yet—and then she looked indignantly
upon me—yet, I hate thee not (base and low-souled as thou art!)
half so much as I hate myself, that I saw thee not sooner in thy
proper colours! That I hoped either morality, gratitude, or
humanity, from a libertine, who, to *be* a libertine, must have got
over and defied all moral sanctions.[1]

She then called upon her Cousin Morden's name, as if he had
warned her against a man of free principles; and walked towards
the window; her handkerchief at her eyes: but, turning short
towards me, with an air of mingled scorn and majesty [*what, at
the moment, would I have given never to have injured her!*], What
amends hast *thou* to propose! What amends can such a one as
thou make to a person of spirit, or common sense, for the evils
thou hast so inhumanly made me suffer?

As soon, madam—as soon—as—as soon as your uncle—or—
not waiting——

Thou wouldst tell me, I suppose—I know what thou wouldst
tell me—but thinkest thou that *marriage will satisfy for a guilt
like thine*? Destitute as thou hast made me both of friends and
fortune, I too much despise the wretch *who could rob himself
of his wife's virtue,* to endure the thoughts of thee in the light
thou seemest to hope I will accept thee in!

I hesitated an interruption: but my meaning died away
upon my trembling lips. I could only pronounce the word
marriage—and thus she proceeded:

Let me therefore know whether I am to be controlled in the
future disposal of myself? Whether, in a country of liberty, as

---

[1] *Her Cousin Morden's words to her in his letter from Florence.* *See* vol. ii,
p. 260.

this, where the *sovereign* of it must be guilty of *your* wickedness; and where *you* neither durst have attempted it, had I one friend or relation to look upon me; I am to be kept here a prisoner, to sustain fresh injuries? Whether, in a word, you intend to hinder me from going whither my destiny shall lead me?

After a pause; for I was still silent:

Can you not answer me this plain question? I quit all claim, all expectation, upon you — what right have you to detain me here?

I could not speak. What could I say to such a question?

O wretch! wringing her uplifted hands, had I not been robbed of my senses, and that in the *basest* manner—you best know how —had I been able to account for myself, and your proceedings, or to have known but how the days passed; a whole week should not have gone over my head, as I find it has done, before I had told you, what I now tell you, *That the man who has been the villain to me you have been, shall never make me his wife.* I will write to my uncle, to lay aside his kind intentions in my favour —all my prospects are shut in—I give myself up for a lost creature as to this world—hinder me not from entering upon a life of severe penitence, for corresponding, after prohibition, with a wretch who has too well justified all their warnings and inveteracy; and for throwing myself into the power of your vile artifices. Let me try to secure the only hope I have left. This is all the amends I ask of you. I repeat, therefore, Am I *now* at liberty to dispose of myself as I please?

Now comes the fool, the miscreant again, hesitating his broken answer: My dearest love, I am confounded, quite confounded, at the thought of what—of what has been done; and at the thought of—to whom. I see, I see, there is no withstanding your eloquence! Such irresistible proofs of the love of virtue *for its own sake*—did I never hear of, nor meet with, in all my reading. And if you can forgive a repentant villain, who thus on his knees implores your forgiveness [then down I dropped, absolutely in earnest in all I said], I vow by all that's sacred and just (and may a thunderbolt strike me dead at your feet, if I am not sincere!) that I will by marriage, before to-morrow noon, without waiting for your uncle, or anybody, do you all the justice I now *can* do you. And you shall ever after control and direct me as you please, till you have made me more worthy of your angelic purity than now I am: nor will I presume so much as to touch your garment, till I have the honour to call so great a blessing lawfully mine.

O thou guileful betrayer! There is a just God, whom thou invokest: yet the thunderbolt descends not; and thou livest to imprecate and deceive!

My dearest life! rising; for I hoped she was relenting——

Hadst thou not sinned beyond the *possibility of forgiveness*, interrupted she; and this had been the first time that thus thou solemnly promisest and invokest the vengeance thou hast as often defied; the desperateness of my condition might have induced me to think of taking a wretched chance with a man so profligate. But, *after what I have suffered by thee*, it would be *criminal* in me to wish to bind my soul in covenant to a man so nearly allied to perdition.

Good God! how uncharitable! I offer not to defend—would to Heaven that I could recall—*so nearly allied to perdition*, madam!—so *profligate* a man, madam!

O how short is expression of *thy* crimes, and of *my* sufferings! Such premeditation in thy baseness! To prostitute the characters of persons of honour of thy own family—and all to delude a poor creature, whom thou oughtest—but why talk I to thee? Be thy crimes upon thy head! Once more I ask thee, Am I, or am I not, at my own liberty *now*?

I offered to speak in defence of the women, declaring that they really were the very persons——

Presume not, interrupted she, base as thou art, to say one word in thine own vindication on this head. I have been contemplating their behaviour, their conversation, their over-ready acquiescences to my declarations in thy disfavour; their free, yet affectedly reserved light manners: and now, that the sad event has opened my eyes, and I have compared facts and passages together, in the little interval that has been lent me, I wonder I could not distinguish the behaviour of the unmatron-like jilt whom thou broughtest to betray me, from the worthy lady whom thou hast the honour to call thy aunt: and that I could not detect the superficial creature whom thou passedst upon me for the virtuous Miss Montague.

Amazing uncharitableness in a lady so good herself! That the high spirits those ladies were in to see *you*, should subject them to such censures! I do most solemnly vow, madam——

That they were, interrupting me, *verily* and *indeed* Lady Betty Lawrance and thy Cousin Montague! O wretch! I see by thy solemn averment [*I had not yet averred it*] what credit ought to be given to all the rest. Had I no other proof——

Interrupting her, I besought her patient ear. "I had found

myself, *I told her*, almost *avowedly* despised and hated. I had no hope of gaining her love, or her confidence. The letter she had left behind her, on her removal to Hampstead, sufficiently convinced me that she was entirely under Miss Howe's influence, and waited but the return of a letter from her to enter upon measures that would deprive me of her for ever: Miss Howe had *ever* been my enemy: more so *then*, no doubt, from the contents of the letter she had written to her on her first coming to Hampstead: that I dared not to stand the event of such a letter; and was glad of an opportunity, by Lady Betty's and my cousin's means (though they knew not my motive), to get her back to town; far, at the *time*, from *intending* the outrage which my despair, and her want of confidence in me, put me so vilely upon——"

I would have proceeded; and particularly would have said something of Captain Tomlinson and her uncle; but she would not hear me further. And indeed it was with visible indignation, and not without several angry interruptions, that she heard me say so much.

Would I dare, she asked me, to offer at a palliation of my baseness? The two women, she was convinced, were impostors. She knew not but Captain Tomlinson, and Mr. Mennell, were so too. But, whether *they* were so or not, *I* was. And she insisted upon being at her own disposal for the remainder of her short life—for indeed she abhorred me in every light; and more particularly in that in which I offered myself to her acceptance.

And, saying this, she flung from me; leaving me absolutely shocked and confounded at her part of a conversation, which she began with such uncommon, however severe composure, and concluded with so much sincere and unaffected indignation.

And now, Jack, I must address one serious paragraph *particularly* to thee.

I have not yet touched upon cohabitation—her uncle's mediation she does not absolutely discredit, as I had the pleasure to find by one hint in this conversation—yet she suspects my future views, and has doubts about Mennell and Tomlinson.

I *do* say, if she come *fairly* at her *lights*, at her *clues*, or what shall I call them? her penetration is *wonderful*.

But if she do *not* come at them fairly, *then* is her incredulity, *then* is her antipathy to me evidently accounted for.

I will speak out—Thou couldst not, surely, play me booty, Jack? Surely thou couldst not let thy weak pity for *her* lead thee to an unpardonable breach of trust to thy *friend*, who has been so unreserved in his communications to thee?

I cannot believe thee capable of such a baseness. Satisfy me, however, upon this head. I must make a cursed figure in her eye, vowing and protesting, as I shall not scruple occasionally to vow and protest, if all the time she has had unquestionable informations of my perfidy. I know thou as little fearest me, as I do thee, in any point of manhood; and wilt scorn to deny it, if thou *hast* done it, when thus home pressed.

And here I have a good mind to stop, and write no farther, till I have thy answer.

And so I will.

Monday morn. past three.

Letter XXXVI—Mr. Lovelace to John Belford, Esq.

Monday Morn. 5 *o'clock* (*June* 19).

I *must* write on. Nothing else can divert me: and I think thou canst not have been a dog to me.

I would fain have closed my eyes: but sleep flies me. Well says *Horace*, as translated by *Cowley*:

> The halcyon *Sleep* will never build his nest
>   In any stormy breast.
> 'Tis not enough, that he does find
>   *Clouds* and *Darkness* in the mind:
> *Darkness* but half his work will do.
> 'Tis not enough: He must find *Quiet* too.

Now indeed do I from my heart wish that I had never known this lady. But who would have thought there had been such a woman in the world? Of all the sex I have hitherto known, or heard, or read of, it was *once subdued, and always subdued*. The *first* struggle was generally the *last*; or, at least, the subsequent struggles were so much fainter and fainter, that a man would rather have them, than be without them. But how know I yet——

.   .   .   .   .   .

It is now near six. The sun, for two hours past, has been illuminating everything about me: for that impartial orb shines upon mother Sinclair's house, as well as upon any other: but nothing within me can it illuminate.

At day-dawn I looked through the keyhole of my beloved's door. She had declared she would not put off her clothes any more in this house. There I beheld her in a sweet slumber, which I hope will prove refreshing to her disturbed senses; sitting in her elbow-chair, her apron over her head; her head supported by one sweet hand, the other hand hanging down upon her side, in a sleepy lifelessness; half of one pretty foot only visible.

See the difference in our cases, thought I! She, the charming injured, can sweetly sleep, while the varlet injurer cannot close his eyes; and has been trying to no purpose the whole night to divert his melancholy, and to fly from himself!

As every vice generally brings on its own punishment, even in *this* life, if anything were to tempt me to doubt of *future* punishment, it would be, that there can hardly be a greater than that which I at this instant experience in my own remorse.

I hope it will go off. If not, well will the dear creature be avenged; for I shall be the most miserable of men.

Six o'clock.

Just now Dorcas tells me that her lady is preparing openly, and without disguise, to be gone. Very probable. The humour she flew away from me in last night has given me expectation of such an enterprise.

Now, Jack, to be thus hated and despised! And if I *have* sinned beyond forgiveness——

.   .   .   .   .   .

But she has sent me a message by Dorcas, that she will meet me in the dining-room; and desires [odd enough!] that the wench may be present at the conversation that shall pass between us. This message gives me hope.

Nine o'clock.

Confounded art, cunning villainy! By my soul, she had like to have slipped through my fingers. She meant nothing by her message but to get Dorcas out of the way, and a clear coast. Is a fancied distress sufficient to justify this lady for dispensing with her principles? Does she not show me that she can wilfully deceive, as well as I?

Had she been in the fore-house, and no passage to go through to get at the street door, she had certainly been gone. But her haste betrayed her: for Sally Martin happening to be in the fore-parlour, and hearing a swifter motion than usual, and a rustling of silks, as if from somebody in a hurry, looked out; and seeing who it was, stepped between her and the door, and set her back against it.

You must not go, madam. Indeed you must not.

By what right? And how dare you? And such-like imperious airs the dear creature gave herself. While Sally called out for her aunt; and half a dozen voices joined instantly in the cry, for me to hasten down, to hasten down in a moment.

I was gravely instructing Dorcas abovestairs, and wondering what would be the subject of the conversation to which the wench was to be a witness, when these outcries reached my ears. And down I flew. And there was the charming creature, the sweet deceiver, panting for breath, her back against the partition, a parcel in her hand [women make no excursions without their parcels], Sally, Polly (but Polly obligingly pleading for her), the mother, Mabel, and Peter (the footman of the house) about her; all, however, keeping their distance; the mother and Sally between her and the door—in her soft rage the dear soul repeating, I *will* go! Nobody has a right—I *will* go! If you kill me, women, I won't go up again!

As soon as she saw me, she stepped a pace or two towards me; Mr. Lovelace, I *will* go! said she. Do you authorize these women—What right have they, or *you* either, to stop me?

Is this, my dear, preparative to the conversation you led me to expect in the dining-room? And do you think I can part with you thus? Do you think I will?

And am I, sir, to be thus beset! Surrounded thus? What have these women to do with me?

I desired them to leave us, all but Dorcas, who was down as soon as I. I then thought it right to assume an air of resolution, having found my tameness so greatly triumphed over. And now, my dear, said I (urging her reluctant feet), be pleased to walk into the fore-parlour. Hence, since you will not go upstairs, here we may *hold our parley*; and Dorcas *be witness to it*. And now, madam, seating her, and sticking my hands in my sides, your pleasure!

Insolent villain! said the furious lady. And, rising, ran to the window, and threw up the sash [she knew not, I suppose, that there were iron rails before the windows]. And, when she found she could not get out into the street, clasping her uplifted hands together, having dropped her parcel—For the love of God, good honest man! For the love of God, mistress (to two passersby), a poor, poor creature, said she, ruined——

I clasped her in my arms, people beginning to gather about
III—*H 884

the window: and then she cried out, Murder! Help! Help! and carried her up to the dining-room, in spite of her little plotting heart (as I may now call it), although she violently struggled, catching hold of the banisters here and there, as she could. I would have seated her there; but she sunk down half-motionless, pale as ashes. And a violent burst of tears happily relieved her.

Dorcas wept over her. The wench was actually moved for her!

Violent hysterics succeeded. I left her to Mabel, Dorcas, and Polly; the latter the most supportable to her of the sisterhood.

This attempt, so resolutely made, alarmed me not a little.

Mrs. Sinclair and her nymphs are much more concerned; because of the reputation of their house, as they call it, having received some insults (broken windows threatened) to make them produce the young creature who cried out.

While the mobbish inquisitors were in the height of their office, the women came running up to me, to know what they should do; a constable being actually fetched.

Get the constable into the parlour, said I, with three or four of the forwardest of the mob, and produce one of the nymphs, onion-eyed, in a moment, with disordered head-dress and handkerchief, and let her own herself the person: the occasion, a female skirmish; but satisfied with the justice done her. Then give a dram or two to each fellow, and all will be well.

Eleven o'clock.

All done as I advised; and all *is* well.

Mrs. Sinclair wishes she never had seen the face of so skittish a lady; and she and Sally are extremely pressing with me, to leave the perverse beauty to their *breaking,* as they call it, for four or five days. But I cursed them into silence; only ordering double precaution for the future.

Polly, though she consoled the dear perverse one all she could, when *with her,* insists upon it *to me,* that nothing but terror will procure me tolerable usage.

Dorcas was challenged by the women upon her tears. She owned them real. Said she was ashamed of herself; but could not help it. So sincere, so *unyielding* a grief, in so *sweet* a lady!

The women laughed at her: but I bid her make no apologies for her tears, nor mind their laughing. I was glad to see them *so ready.* Good use might be made of such strangers. In short, I would have her indulge them often, and try if it were not possible to gain her lady's confidence by her concern for her.

She said that her lady *did* take kind notice of them to her; and was glad to see such tokens of humanity in her.

Well then, said I, your *part*, whether anything come of it or not, is to be *tender-hearted*. It can do no harm, if no good. But take care you are not *too suddenly*, or *too officiously* compassionate.

So Dorcas will be a humane, good sort of creature, I believe, very quickly with her lady. And as it becomes women to be so, and as my beloved is willing to think highly of her own sex; it will the more readily pass with her.

I thought to have had one trial (having gone so far) for *cohabitation*. But what hope can there be of succeeding? She is invincible! *Against all my notions, against all my conceptions* (thinking of her as a woman, and in the very bloom of her charms), *she is absolutely invincible*. My whole view, at the present, is to do her legal justice, if I can but once more get her out of her altitudes.

The *consent* of such a woman must make her ever new, ever charming. But, astonishing! Can the want of a church ceremony make such a difference!

She *owes* me her consent; for hitherto I have had nothing to boast of. All, of my side, has been *deep remorse, anguish of mind*, and *love increased* rather *than abated*.

How her proud rejection stings me! And yet I hope still to get her to listen to my stories of the family reconciliation, and of her uncle and Captain Tomlinson. And as she has given me a pretence to detain her against her will, she *must* see me, whether in temper or not—she cannot help it. And if love will not do, terror, as the women advise, must be tried.

A nice part, after all, has my beloved to act. If she forgive me easily, I resume perhaps my projects: if she carry her rejection into violence, that violence may make me desperate, and occasion fresh violence—she ought, since she thinks she has found the women out, to consider *where she is*.

I am confoundedly out of conceit with myself. If I give up my contrivances, my joy in stratagem, and plot, and invention, I shall be but a common man: such another dull heavy creature as thyself. Yet what does even my success in my machinations bring me, but disgrace, repentance, regret? But I am overmatched, egregiously overmatched, by this woman. What to do with her, or without her, I know not.

Letter XXXVII—Mr. Lovelace to John Belford, Esq.

I HAVE this moment intelligence from Simon Parsons, one of Lord M.'s stewards, that his lordship is very ill. Simon, who is my obsequious servant, in virtue of my presumptive heirship, gives me a hint in his letter that my presence at M. Hall will not be amiss. So I must accelerate, whatever be the course I shall be allowed or compelled to take.

No bad prospects for this charming creature, if the old peer would be so kind as to surrender; and many a summons has his gout given him. A good £8,000 a year, perhaps the title reversionary, or a still higher, would help me up with her.

Proudly as this lady pretends to be above all pride, grandeur will have its charms with her; for grandeur always makes a man's face shine in a woman's eye. I have a pretty good, because a clear, estate, as it is: but what a noble variety of mischief will £8,000 a year enable a man to do?

Perhaps thou 'lt say, I do *already* all that comes into my head: but that's a mistake—not one half, I will assure thee. And even *good folks*, as I have heard, love to have the *power* of doing mischief, whether they make *use of it*, or *not*. The late Queen Anne, who was a very good woman, was always fond of *prerogative*. And her ministers, in her name, in more instances than one, made a *ministerial* use of this her foible.

. . . .

But now, at last, am I to be admitted to the presence of my angry fair one: after three denials, nevertheless; and a *peremptory* from me, by Dorcas, that I must see her in her chamber, if I cannot see her in the dining-room.

Dorcas, however, tells me that she says, if she were at her own liberty, she would never see me more; and that she has been asking after the characters and conditions of the neighbours. I suppose, now she has found her voice, to call out for help from them, if there were any to hear her.

She will have it now, it seems, that I had the wickedness, from the very beginning, to contrive for her ruin, a house so convenient for dreadful mischief.

Dorcas begs of her to be pacified—entreats her to see me with patience—tells her that I am one of the most determined of men, as she has heard say—that gentleness may do with me; but that nothing else will, she believes. And what, as her ladyship (as she always styles her) is *married*, if I *had* broke my oath, or *intended* to break it!

She hinted plain enough to the honest wench, that she was *not* married. But Dorcas would not understand her.

This shows that she is resolved to keep no measures. And now is to be a trial of skill, whether she shall or not.

Dorcas has hinted to her my lord's illness, as a piece of intelligence that dropped in conversation from me.

But here I stop. My beloved, pursuant to my peremptory message, is just gone up into the dining-room.

Letter XXXVIII—Mr. Lovelace to John Belford, Esq.

Monday Afternoon.

PITY me, Jack, for pity's sake; since, if thou dost not, nobody else will: and yet never was there a man of my genius and lively temper that wanted it more. We are apt to attribute to the devil everything that happens to us which we would not *have* happen: but here, being (as perhaps thou 'lt say) the devil myself, my plagues arise from an angel. I suppose all mankind is to be plagued by its *contrary*.

She began with me like a true woman [*she* in the fault, *I* to be blamed] the moment I entered the dining-room: not the least apology, not the least excuse, for the uproar she had made, and the trouble she had given me.

I come, said she, into thy detested presence, because I cannot help it. But why am I to be imprisoned here? Although to no purpose, I cannot help——

Dearest madam, interrupted I, give not way to so much violence. You must know that your detention is entirely owing to the desire I have to make you all the amends that is in my power to make you. And this, as well for *your* sake as *my own*. Surely there is still *one* way left to repair the wrongs you have suffered——

Canst thou blot out the past week? *Several* weeks past, I should say; ever since I have been with thee? Canst thou call back time? If thou canst——

Surely, madam, again interrupting her, if I may be permitted to call you *legally* mine, I might have but anticip——

Wretch, that thou art! Say not another word upon this subject. When thou vowedst, when thou promisedst at Hampstead, I had begun to think that I must be thine. If I had consented, at the request of those I thought thy relations, this would have been a principal inducement, that I could then have brought thee, what was *most* wanted, an unsullied honour in dowry, to a wretch destitute of all honour; and could have met the gratulations of a family to which thy life has been one continued disgrace, with a consciousness of *deserving* their gratulations. But thinkest thou that I will give a harlot niece to thy honourable uncle, and to thy *real* aunts; and a cousin to thy cousins from a brothel? For such, in my opinion, is this detested house! Then, lifting up her clasped hands, "Great and good God of Heaven," said she, "give me patience to support myself under the weight of those afflictions, which Thou, for wise and good ends, though at present impenetrable by me, hast permitted!"

Then, turning towards me, who knew neither what to say *to* her, nor *for* myself, I renounce thee for ever, Lovelace! Abhorred of my soul! for ever I renounce thee! Seek thy fortunes where-soever thou wilt! Only now, that thou hast already ruined me——

Ruined you, madam—the world need not—I knew not what to say.

Ruined me in my *own* eyes; and that is the same to me as if *all the world* knew it. Hinder me not from going whither my mysterious destiny shall lead me.

Why hesitate you, sir? What right have you to stop me, as you lately did; and to bring me up by force, my hands and arms bruised with your violence? What right have you to detain me here?

I am cut to the heart, madam, with invectives so violent. I am but too sensible of the wrong I have done you, or I could not *bear* your reproaches. The man who perpetrates a villainy, and resolves to go on with it, shows not the compunction I show. Yet, if you think yourself in my power, I would caution you, madam, not to make me desperate. For you *shall* be mine, or my life shall be the forfeit! Nor is life worth having without you!

Be *thine*! I be *thine*! said the passionate beauty. Oh, how lovely in her violence!

Yes, madam, be *mine*! I repeat, you *shall* be mine! My very crime is your glory. My love, my admiration of you is increased by what has passed: *and so it ought.* I am willing, madam, to court your returning favour: but let me tell you, were the house beset by a thousand armed men, resolved to take you from me, they should not effect their purpose while I had life.

I never, never will be yours! said she, clasping her hands together, and lifting up her eyes. I never will be yours!

We may yet see many happy years, madam. All your friends may be reconciled to you. The treaty for that purpose is in greater forwardness than you imagine. You know *better* than to think the *worse* of yourself for suffering what you *could not help*. Enjoin but the terms I can make my peace with you upon, and I will instantly comply.

Never, never, repeated she, will I be yours!

Only forgive me, my dearest life, this *one* time! A virtue so invincible! What further view *can* I have against you? Have I attempted any further outrage? If you will be mine, your injuries will be injuries done to myself. You have too well guessed at the unnatural arts that have been used. But can a greater testimony be given of your virtue? And now I have only to hope, that although I cannot make you *complete* amends, yet that you will permit me to make you *all* the amends that can possibly be made.

Hear me out, I beseech you, madam; for she was going to speak with an aspect unpacifiedly angry: the God, whom you serve, requires but repentance and amendment: imitate *Him*, my dearest love, and bless me with the *means* of reforming a course of life that begins to be hateful to me. *That* was *once* your favourite point. Resume it, dearest creature: in charity to a soul, as well as body, which once, as I flattered myself, was *more* than indifferent to you, resume it. And let to-morrow's sun witness to our espousals.

I cannot judge thee, said she; but the God to whom thou so boldly referrest can; and assure thyself *He* will. But, if compunction has *really* taken hold of thee; if *indeed* thou art touched for thy ungrateful baseness, and meanest anything by pleading the holy example thou recommendest to my imitation; in this thy pretended repentant moment, let me sift thee thoroughly; and by thy answer I shall judge of the sincerity of thy pretended declarations.

Tell me, then, is there any reality in the treaty thou hast pretended to be on foot between my uncle and Captain Tomlinson, and thyself? Say, and hesitate not, is there any truth in that story? But, remember, if there be *not*, and thou avowest that there *is*, what further condemnation attends thy averment, if it be as solemn as I require it to be!

That was a cursed thrust. What could I say? Surely this merciless lady is resolved to damn me, thought I; and yet accuses me of a design against her soul! But was I not obliged to proceed as I had begun?

In short, I solemnly averred that there was! How one crime, as the good folks say, brings on another!

I added that the captain had been in town, and would have waited on her, had not she been indisposed: that he went down much afflicted, as well on her account, as on that of her uncle; though I had not acquainted him either with the nature of her disorder, or the ever to be regretted occasion of it; having told him that it was a violent fever: that he had twice since, by her uncle's desire, sent up to inquire after her health: and that I had already dispatched a man and horse with a letter, to acquaint him (and her uncle through him) with her recovery; making it my earnest request, that he would renew his application to her uncle for the favour of his presence at the private celebration of our nuptials; and that I expected an answer, if not this night, as to-morrow.

Let me ask thee next, said she (thou knowest the opinion I have of the women thou broughtest to me at Hampstead; and who have seduced me hither to my ruin; Let me ask thee) if, *really* and *truly*, they were Lady Betty Lawrance and thy Cousin Montague? What sayest thou—hesitate not—what sayest thou to this question?

Astonishing, my dear, that you should suspect them! But, knowing your strange opinion of them, what can I say to be believed?

And is *this* the answer thou returnest me? Dost thou *thus* evade my question? But let me know, for I am trying thy sincerity now, and shall judge of thy new professions by thy answer to this question; Let me know, I repeat, whether those women be *really* Lady Betty Lawrance and thy Cousin Montague?

Let me, my dearest love, be enabled to-morrow to call you lawfully mine, and we will set out the next day, if you please, to Berkshire, to my Lord M.'s, where they both are at this time; and you shall convince yourself by your own eyes, and by your own ears; which you will believe sooner than all I can say or swear.

Now, Belford, I had really some apprehension of treachery from thee; which made me so miserably evade; for else, I could *as* safely have sworn to the truth of this, as to that of the former: but she pressing me still for a categorical answer, I ventured plumb; and swore to it [*lover's oaths, Jack*] that they were really and truly Lady Betty Lawrance and my Cousin Montague.

She lifted up her hands and eyes—What can I think!—What *can* I think!

You *think* me a devil, madam; a very devil! or you could not, after you have put these questions to me, seem to doubt the truth of answers so solemnly sworn to.

And if I do think thee so, have I not cause? Is there another man in the world (I hope, for the sake of human nature, there is not) who could act by any poor friendless creature as thou hast acted by *me*, whom thou hast *made* friendless—and who, before I knew thee, had for a friend every one who knew me?

I told you, madam, *before*, that Lady Betty and my cousin were actually here, in order to take leave of you, before they set out for Berkshire: but the effects of my ungrateful crime (such, with shame and remorse, I own it to be) were the reason you could not see them. Nor could I be fond that they should see *you*: since they never would have forgiven me, had they known what had passed—and what reason had I to expect your silence on the subject, had you been recovered?

It signifies nothing now, that the cause of their appearance has been answered in my ruin, *who* or *what* they are: but, if thou averred thus solemnly to two falsehoods, what a wretch do I see before me!

I thought she had now reason to be satisfied; and I begged her to allow me to talk to her of to-morrow, as of the happiest day of my life. We have the licence, madam—and you *must* excuse me, that I cannot let you go hence till I have tried every way I *can* try to obtain your forgiveness.

And am I then (with a kind of frantic wildness) to be detained a prisoner in this horrid house? Am I, sir? Take care! Take care! holding up her hand, menacing, how you make me desperate! If I fall, though by my own hand, inquisition will be made for my blood: and be not out in thy plot, Lovelace, if it *should* be so—make *sure* work, I charge thee: dig a hole deep enough to cram in and conceal this unhappy body: for, depend upon it, that some of those who will not stir to protect me living, will move heaven and earth to avenge me dead!

A horrid dear creature! By my soul, she made me shudder! She had need indeed to talk of *her* unhappiness in falling into the hands of the only *man* in the world who could have used her as I have used her. She is the only *woman* in the world who could have shocked and disturbed me as she has done. So we are upon a foot in *that* respect. And I think I have the *worst* of it by much: since very little has been my joy; very much my trouble; and *her* punishment, as she calls it, is *over*: but when *mine* will, or what it *may be*, who can tell?

Here, only recapitulating (think, then, how I must be affected at the time), I was forced to leave off, and sing a song to myself. I aimed at a lively air; but I croaked rather than sung, and fell into the old dismal thirtieth of January strain. I hemmed up for a sprightlier note; but it would not do: and at last I ended, like a malefactor, in a dead psalm melody.

Heigh-ho! I gape like an unfledged kite in its nest, wanting to swallow a chicken, bobbed at its mouth by its marauding dam! What a-devil ails me! I can neither think nor write!

Lie down, pen, for a moment!

Letter XXXIX—*Mr. Lovelace to John Belford, Esq.*

THERE is certainly a good deal in the observation, *That it costs a man ten times more pains to be wicked, than it would cost him to be good.* What a confounded number of contrivances have I had recourse to, in order to carry my point with this charming creature; and, after all, how have I puzzled myself by it; and yet am near tumbling into the pit which it was the end of all my plots to shun! What a happy man had I been with such an excellence, could I have brought my mind to marry when I first prevailed upon her to quit her father's house! But *then*, as I have often reflected, how had I *known*, that a but blossoming beauty, who could carry on a private correspondence, and run such risks with a notorious wild fellow, was not prompted by inclination, which one day might give such a free liver as myself as much pain to reflect upon as, at the time, it gave me pleasure? Thou rememberest the host's tale in Ariosto. And *thy* experience, as well as *mine*, can furnish out twenty *Fiamettas* in proof of the imbecility of the sex.

But to proceed with my narrative.

The dear creature resumed the topic her heart was so firmly fixed upon; and insisted upon quitting the *odious house*, and that in very high terms.

I urged her to meet me the next day at the altar in either of the two churches mentioned in the licence. And I besought her, whatever were her resolution, to let me debate this matter calmly with her.

If, she said, I would have her give what I desired the least moment's consideration, I must not hinder her from being her

XXXIX] CLARISSA HARLOWE 237

own mistress. To what purpose did I ask her *consent*, if she had not a power over either her own person or actions?

Will you give me your honour, madam, if I consent to your quitting a house so disagreeable to you?

My honour, sir! said the dear creature—alas! And turned weeping from me with inimitable grace, as if she had said, Alas! You have robbed me of my honour!

I hoped then that her angry passions were subsiding; but I was mistaken: for, urging her warmly for the day; and that for the sake of our mutual honour, and the honour of both our families; in this high-flown and high-souled strain she answered me:

And canst thou, Lovelace, be so *mean*—as to wish to make a wife of the creature thou hast insulted, dishonoured, and abused, as thou hast me? Was it necessary to humble me down to the low level of thy baseness, before I could be a wife meet for thee? Thou hadst a father, who was a man of honour: a mother, who deserved a better son. Thou hast an uncle, who is no dishonour to the peerage of a kingdom, whose peers are more respectable than the nobility of any other country. Thou hast other relations also, who may be *thy* boast, though thou canst not be *theirs*—and canst thou not imagine that thou hearest them calling upon thee; the dead from their monuments; the living from their laudable pride; not to dishonour thy ancient and splendid house, by entering into wedlock with a creature whom thou hast levelled with the dirt of the street, and classed with the vilest of her sex?

I extolled her greatness of soul, and her virtue. I execrated myself for my guilt: and told her, how grateful to the *manes* of my ancestors, as well as to the wishes of the living, the honour I supplicated for would be.

But still she insisted upon being a free agent; of seeing herself in other lodgings before she would give what I urged the *least* consideration. Nor would she promise me favour even then, or to permit my visits. How then, as I asked her, could I comply, without resolving to lose her for ever?

She put her hand to her forehead often as she talked; and at last, pleading disorder in her head, retired; neither of us satisfied with the other. But *she* ten times more dissatisfied with me, than I with her.

Dorcas seems to be coming into favour with her——
What now! What now!

Monday Night.

How determined is this lady! Again had she like to have escaped us! What a fixed resentment! She only, I find, assumed a little calm, in order to quiet suspicion. She was got down, and actually had unbolted the street door, before I could get to her, alarmed as I was by Mrs. Sinclair's cookmaid, who was the only one that saw her fly through the passage: yet lightning was not quicker than I.

Again I brought her back to the dining-room, with infinite reluctance on her part. And before her face, ordered a servant to be placed constantly at the bottom of the stairs for the future.

She seemed even choked with grief and disappointment.

Dorcas was exceedingly assiduous about her; and confidently gave it as her own opinion, that the dear lady should be permitted to go to another lodging, since *this* was so disagreeable to her: were she to be killed for saying so, she would say it. And was *good* Dorcas for this afterwards.

But for some time the dear creature was all passion and violence.

I see, I see, said she, when I had brought her up, what I am to expect from your new professions, O vilest of men!

Have I offered to you, my beloved creature, anything that can justify this impatience after a more hopeful calm?

She wrung her hands. She disordered her head-dress. She tore her ruffles. She was in a perfect frenzy.

I dreaded her returning malady: but entreaty rather exasperating, I affected an angry air. I bid her expect the worst she had to fear—and was menacing on, in hopes to intimidate her, when dropping down at my feet,

'Twill be a mercy, said she, the highest act of mercy you can do, to kill me outright upon this spot—this happy spot, as I will, in my last moments, call it! Then, baring, with a still more frantic violence, part of her enchanting neck, Here, here, said the soul-harrowing beauty, let thy pointed mercy enter! And I will thank thee, and forgive thee for all the dreadful past! With my latest gasp will I forgive and thank thee! Or help *me* to the means, and I will myself put out of thy way so miserable a wretch! And bless thee for those means!

Why all this extravagant passion? Why all these exclamations? Have I offered any new injury to you, my dearest life? What a frenzy is this! Am I not ready to make you all the reparation that I *can* make you? Had I not reason to hope——

No, no, no, no—half a dozen times, as fast as she could speak.

Had I not reason to hope that you were meditating upon the means of making me happy, and yourself not miserable, rather than upon a flight so causeless and so precipitate?

No, no, no, no, as before, shaking her head with wild impatience, as resolved not to attend to what I said.

My resolutions are so honourable, if you will permit them to take effect, that I need not be solicitous whither you go, if you will but permit my visits, and receive my vows. And God is my witness that I bring you not back from the door with any view to your dishonour, but the contrary: and this moment I will send for a minister to put an end to all your doubts and fears.

Say this, and say a thousand times more, and bind every word with a solemn appeal to that God whom thou art accustomed to invoke to the truth of the vilest falsehoods, and all will still be short of what thou *hast* vowed and promised to me. And, were *not* my heart to abhor thee, and to rise against thee, for thy *perjuries*, as it *does*, I would not, I tell thee once more, I would not, bind my soul in covenant with such a man, for a thousand worlds!

Compose yourself, however, madam; for *your own sake,* compose yourself. Permit me to raise you up; *abhorred* as I am of your soul!

Nay, if I must not touch you; for she wildly slapped my hands; but with such a sweet passionate air, her bosom heaving and throbbing as she looked up to me, that although I was most sincerely enraged, I could with transport have pressed her to mine.

If I must not touch you, I will not. But depend upon it [and I assumed the sternest air I could assume, to try what *that* would do], depend upon it, madam, that this is not the way to avoid the evils you dread. Let me do what I will, I cannot be used worse! Dorcas, be gone!

She arose, Dorcas being about to withdraw; and wildly caught hold of her arm: O Dorcas! If thou art of mine own sex, leave me not, I charge thee! Then quitting Dorcas, down she threw herself upon her knees, in the furthermost corner of the room, clasping a chair with her face laid upon the bottom of it! O where can I be safe? Where, where can I be safe, from this man of violence?

This gave Dorcas an opportunity to confirm herself in her lady's confidence: the wench threw herself at my feet, while I seemed in violent wrath; and, embracing my knees, Kill me, sir, kill me, sir, if you please! I must throw myself in your way, to save my lady. I beg your pardon, sir—but you must be set on! God forgive the mischief-makers! But your own heart, if left to itself, would not permit these things! Spare, however, sir! spare my lady, I beseech you! bustling on her knees about me, as if I were intending to approach her lady, had I not been restrained by her.

This, humoured by me, Begone, devil! Officious devil, begone! startled the dear creature; who, snatching up hastily her head from the chair, and as hastily popping it down again in terror, hit her nose, I suppose, against the edge of the chair; and it gushed out with blood, running in a stream down her bosom; she herself too much affrighted to heed it!

Never was mortal man in such terror and agitation as I; for I instantly concluded that she had stabbed herself with some concealed instrument.

I ran to her in a wild agony, for Dorcas was frighted out of all her mock interposition.

What have you done! O what have you done! Look up to me, my dearest life! Sweet injured innocence, look up to me! What have you done! Long will I not survive you! And I was upon the point of drawing my sword to dispatch myself, when I discovered [what an unmanly blockhead does this charming creature make me at her pleasure!] that all I apprehended was but a bloody nose, which, as far as I know (for it could not be stopped in a quarter of an hour), may have saved her head and her intellects.

But I see by this scene, that the sweet creature is but a pretty coward at bottom; and that I can terrify her out of her virulence against me, whenever I put on a sternness and anger: but then, as a qualifier to the advantage this gives me over her, I find myself to be a coward too, which I had not before suspected, since I was capable of being so easily terrified by the apprehensions of her offering violence to herself.

Letter XL—Mr. Lovelace to John Belford, Esq.

BUT, with all this dear creature's resentment against me, I cannot, for my heart, think but she will get all over, and consent to enter the pale with me. Were she even to die to-morrow, and to know she should, would not a woman of her sense, of her punctilio, and in her situation, and of so proud a family, rather die married, than otherwise? No doubt but she would; although she were to hate the man ever so heartily. If so, there is now but one man in the world whom she can have—and that is *me*.

Now I talk [*familiar writing* is but *talking*, Jack] thus glibly of entering the pale, thou wilt be ready to question me, I know, as to my intentions on this head.

As much of my heart, as I know of it myself, will I tell thee. When I am *from* her, I cannot still help hesitating about marriage; and I even frequently resolve against it, and determine to press my favourite scheme for cohabitation. But when I am *with* her, I am ready to say, to swear, and to do, whatever I think will be most acceptable to her: and were a parson at hand, I should plunge at once, no doubt of it, into the state.

I have frequently thought, in *common* cases, that it is happy for many giddy fellows [there are giddy fellows, as well as giddy girls, Jack; and perhaps *those* are as often drawn in as *these*] that ceremony and parade are necessary to the irrevocable solemnity; and that there is generally time for a man to recollect himself in the space between the heated over-night and the cooler next morning; or I know not who could escape the sweet gipsies, whose fascinating powers are so much aided by our own raised imaginations.

A wife at any time, I used to say. I had ever confidence and vanity enough to think that no woman breathing could deny her hand when I held out mine. I am confoundedly mortified to find that this lady is able to hold me at bay, and to refuse all my *honest* vows.

What force [allow me a serious reflection, Jack: it *will* be put down! What force] have evil habits upon the human mind! When we enter upon a devious course, we think we shall have it in our power when we will to return to the right path. But it is not so, I plainly see: for who can acknowledge with more justice this dear creature's merits, and his own errors, than I? Whose regret, at times, can be deeper than mine, for the injuries I have done her? Whose resolutions to repair those injuries stronger? Yet how transitory is my penitence! How am I hurried away! Canst thou tell by what? O devil of youth, and devil of intrigue, how do ye mislead me! How often do we end in occasions for the deepest remorse, what we begin in wantonness!

At the present writing, however, the turn of the scale is in behalf of matrimony—for I despair of carrying with her my favourite point.

The lady tells Dorcas that her heart is broken; and that she shall live but a little while. I think nothing of that, if we marry.

In the first place, she knows not what a mind unapprehensive will do for her, in a state to which all the sex look forward with high satisfaction. How often have the whole sacred conclave been thus deceived in their choice of a Pope; not considering that the new dignity is of itself sufficient to give new life. A few months' heart's ease will give my charmer a quite different notion of things: and I dare say, as I have heretofore said,[1] once married, and I am married for life.

I will allow that her pride, in *one* sense, has suffered abasement: but her triumph is the greater in every other. And while I can think that all her trials are but additions to her honour, and that I have laid the foundations of her glory in my own shame, can I be called cruel, if I am *not* affected with her grief as some men would be?

And for what should her heart be broken? Her will is unviolated:—at *present*, however, her will is unviolated. The destroying of good habits, and the introducing of bad, to the corrupting of the whole heart, is the violation. That her will is not to be corrupted, that her mind is not to be debased, she has hitherto unquestionably proved. And if she give cause for further trials, and hold fast her integrity, what *ideas* will she have to dwell upon, that will be able to corrupt her morals? What *vestigia*, what *remembrances*, but such as will inspire abhorrence to the attempter?

What nonsense, then, to suppose that such a mere *notional violation* as she has suffered, should be able to cut asunder the strings of life?

Her religion, married, or not married, will set her above making such a trifling accident, such an *involuntary* suffering, fatal to her.

Such considerations as these they are that support me against all apprehensions of bugbear consequences: and I would have them have weight with thee; who art such a doughty advocate for her. And yet I allow thee this; that she really makes too much of it: takes it too much to heart. To be sure she ought to have forgot it by this time, except the charming, charming consequence happen, that still I am in hopes will happen, were I to proceed no further. And, if she apprehend this herself, then has the dear over-nice soul some reason for taking it so much to heart: and yet would not, I think, refuse to legitimate.

O Jack! had I an imperial diadem, I swear to thee that I would give it up, even to my *enemy*, to have one charming boy

[1] See p. 181.

by this lady. And should she *escape me*, and no such effect
follow, my revenge on her family, and, in *such* a case, on herself,
would be incomplete, and I should reproach myself as long
as I lived.

Were I to be sure that this foundation is laid [and why may
I not hope it is?], I should not doubt to have her still (should she
withstand her day of grace) on my own conditions: nor should I,
if it were so, question that *revived* affection in *her*, which a woman
seldom fails to have for the father of her first child, whether
born in wedlock, or out of it.

And prithee, Jack, see in this *aspiration*, let me call it, a
distinction in my favour from other rakes; who almost to a man
follow their inclinations without troubling themselves about
consequences. In imitation, as one would think, of the strutting
villain of a bird, which from feathered lady to feathered lady
pursues his imperial pleasures, leaving it to his sleek paramours
to hatch the genial product in holes and corners of their own
finding out.

Letter XLI—Mr. Lovelace to John Belford, Esq.

Tuesday Morning, June 20.

WELL, Jack, now are we upon another foot together. This dear
creature will not *let me be good*. She is now authorizing all my
plots by her own example.

Thou must be partial in the highest degree, if now thou
blamest me for resuming my former schemes, since in that case
I shall but follow her clue. No forced construction of her
actions do I make on this occasion in order to justify a bad
cause or a worse intention. A little pretence, indeed, served the
wolf when he had a mind to quarrel with the lamb; but this is not
now my case.

For here [wouldst thou have thought it?] taking advantage of
Dorcas's compassionate temper, and of some warm expressions
which the tender-hearted wench let fall against the cruelty of
men; and wishing to have it in her power to serve her; has she
given her the following note, signed by her maiden name: for
she has thought fit, in positive and plain words, to own to the
pitying Dorcas that she is not married.

Monday, June 19. . . .

*I the underwritten do hereby promise, that, on my coming into
possession of my own estate, I will provide for Dorcas Martindale*

in a gentlewoman-like manner, in my own house: or, if I do not soon obtain that possession, or should first die, I do hereby bind myself, my executors, and administrators, to pay to her, or her order, during the term of her natural life, the sum of five pounds on each of the four usual quarterly days in the year; that is to say, twenty pounds by the year; on condition that she faithfully assist me in my escape from an illegal confinement, under which I now labour. The first quarterly payment to commence and be payable at the end of three months immediately following the day of my deliverance. And I do also promise to give her, as a testimony of my honour in the rest, a diamond ring, which I have showed her. Witness my hand, this nineteenth day of June, in the year above written.

CLARISSA HARLOWE.

Now, Jack, what terms wouldst thou have me to keep with such a sweet corruptress? Seest thou not how she hates me? Seest thou not, however, that she must disgrace herself in the eye of the world, if she actually should escape? That she must be subjected to infinite distress and hazard? For whom has she to receive and protect her? Yet to determine to risk all these evils: and furthermore to stoop to artifice, to be guilty of the reigning vice of the times, of bribery and corruption! O Jack, Jack! *say* not, *write* not, another word in her favour!

Thou hast blamed me for bringing her to this house: but had I carried her to any other in England, where there would have been one servant or inmate capable either of *compassion* or *corruption*, what must have been the consequence?

But seest thou not, however, that, in this flimsy contrivance, the dear implacable, like a drowning man, catches at a straw to save herself! A straw shall she find to be the refuge she has resorted to.

Letter XLII—Mr. Lovelace to John Belford, Esq.

Tuesday Morning, 10 o'clock.

VERY ill—exceeding ill—as Dorcas tells me, in order to avoid seeing me—and yet the dear soul may be so in her *mind*. But is not that equivocation? Some one passion predominating, in every human breast, breaks through principle, and controls us all. Mine is *love* and *revenge* taking turns. Hers is *hatred*. But this is my consolation, that *hatred appeased is love begun*; or *love renewed* I may rather say, if love ever had footing here.

But *reflectioning* apart, thou seest, Jack, that her plot is beginning to work. To-morrow it is to break out.

I have been abroad, to set on foot a plot of circumvention.
All fair now, Belford!

I insisted upon visiting my indisposed fair one. Dorcas made
officious excuses for her. I cursed the wench in her hearing for
her impertinence; and stamped, and made a clutter; which was
improved into an apprehension to the lady that I would have
flung her faithful confidante from the top of the stairs to the
bottom.

He is a violent wretch! But, Dorcas [*dear* Dorcas now it is],
thou shalt have a friend in me to the last day of my life.

And what now, Jack, dost think the name of her *good angel* is?
Why *Dorcas Martindale*, christian and super (no more Wykes)
as in the promissory note in my former—and the dear creature
has bound her to her by the *most solemn* obligations, *besides* the
tie of interest.

Whither, madam, do you design to go when you get out of
this house?

I will throw myself into the first open house I can find; and
beg protection till I can get a coach, or a lodging in some
honest family.

What will you do for clothes, madam? I doubt you 'll not be
able to take any away with you, but what you 'll have on.

Oh, no matter for clothes, if I can but get out of this house.

What will you do for money, madam? I have heard his
honour express his concern, that he could not prevail upon you
to be obliged to him, though he apprehended that you must be
short of money.

Oh, I have rings, and other valuables. Indeed I have but four
guineas, and two of them I found lately wrapped up in a bit of
lace, designed for a charitable use: but now, alas! charity
begins at home! But I have one dear friend left, if she be living,
as I hope in God she is! to whom I can be obliged if I want. O
Dorcas! I must ere now have heard from her, if I had had
fair play.

Well, madam, yours is a hard lot. I pity you at my heart!

Thank you, Dorcas! I am unhappy that I did not think
before, that I might have confided in thy pity, and in thy sex!

I pitied you, madam, often and often: but you were always,
as I thought, diffident of me. And then I doubted not but you
were married; and I thought his honour was unkindly used by
you. So that I thought it my duty to wish well to his honour,
rather than to what I thought to be your humours, madam.
Would to Heaven that I had known before that you were not

married! Such a lady! Such a fortune! To be so sadly betrayed!

Ah, Dorcas! I was basely drawn in! My youth—my ignorance of the world—and I have some things to reproach myself with, when I look back.

Lord, madam, what deceitful creatures are these men! Neither oaths, nor vows—I am sure, I am sure [and then with her apron she gave her eyes half a dozen hearty rubs] I may curse the time I came into this house!

Here was accounting for her bold eyes! And was it not better for *Dorcas* to give up a house which her lady could not think worse of than she did, in order to gain the reputation of sincerity, than by offering to vindicate it, to make her proffered services suspected?

Poor Dorcas! Bless me! how little do we who have lived all our time in the country, know of this wicked town!

Had I *been able to write*, cried the veteran wench, I should certainly have given some other near relations I have in Wales a little *inkling* of matters; and they would have saved me from—from—from——

Her sobs were enough. The apprehensions of women on such subjects are ever aforehand with speech.

And then, sobbing on, she lifted her apron to her face again. She showed me how.

Poor Dorcas! Again wiping her own charming eyes.

All love, all compassion, is this dear creature to every one in affliction but me.

And would not an aunt protect her kinswoman? Abominable wretch!

I can't—I can't—I can't—say, my aunt was privy to it. She gave me good advice. She knew not for a great while that I was—that I was—that I was—ugh! ugh! ugh!—

No more, no more, good Dorcas—What a world do we live in! What a house am I in! But come, don't weep (though she herself could not forbear): my being betrayed into it, though to my own ruin, may be a happy event for thee: and if I live, it shall.

I thank you, my good lady, blubbering. I am sorry, very sorry, you have had so hard a lot. But it may be the saving of my soul, if I can get to your ladyship's house. Had I but known that your ladyship was not married, I would have eat my own flesh, before—before—before——

Dorcas sobbed and wept. The lady sighed and wept also.

But now, Jack, for a serious reflection upon the premises.

How will the good folks account for it, that Satan has such

faithful instruments, and that the bond of wickedness is a stronger bond than the ties of virtue; as if it were the nature of the human mind to be villainous? For here, had *Dorcas* been *good,* and been tempted as she was tempted to anything *evil,* I make no doubt but she would have yielded to the temptation.

And cannot our fraternity in a hundred instances give proof of the like predominance of vice over virtue? And that we have risked more to serve and promote the interests of the former, than ever a good man did to serve a good man or a good cause? For have we not been prodigal of life and fortune? Have we not defied the civil magistrate upon occasion? And have we not attempted rescues, and dared all things, only to extricate a pounded profligate?

Whence, Jack, can this be?

Oh! I have it, I believe. The vicious are as bad as they can be; and do the devil's work without looking after; while he is continually spreading snares for the others; and, like a skilful angler, suiting his baits to the fish he angles for.

Nor let even *honest* people, *so called,* blame poor Dorcas for her fidelity in a bad cause. For does not the *general,* who implicitly serves an ambitious prince in his unjust designs upon his neighbours, or upon his own oppressed subjects; and even the *lawyer,* who, for the sake of a paltry fee, undertakes to whiten a black cause, and to defend it against one he knows to be good, do the very same thing as Dorcas? And are they not both every whit as culpable? Yet the one shall be dubbed a hero, the other called an admirable fellow, and be contended for by every client, and his double-paced abilities shall carry him through all the high preferments of the law with reputation and applause.

Well, but what shall be done, since the lady is so much determined on removing? Is there no way to oblige her, and yet to make the very act subservient to my own views? I fancy such a way may be found out.

I will study for it.

Suppose I suffer her to make an escape? Her heart is in it. If she effect it, the triumph she will have over me upon it will be a counterbalance for all she has suffered.

I will oblige her if I can.

Letter XLIII—Mr. Lovelace to John Belford, Esq.

TIRED with a succession of fatiguing days and sleepless nights, and with contemplating the precarious situation I stand in with my beloved, I fell into a profound reverie; which brought on sleep; and that produced a dream; a fortunate dream; which, as I imagine, will afford my working mind the means to effect the obliging double purpose my heart is now once more set upon.

What, as I have contemplated, is the enjoyment of the finest woman in the world, to the contrivance, the bustle, the surprises, and at last the happy conclusion of a well-laid plot? The charming *roundabouts*, to come the *nearest way home*; the doubts; the apprehensions; the heartachings, the meditated triumphs— these are the joys that make the blessing dear. For all the rest, what is it? What but to find an angel in imagination dwindled down to a woman in fact? But to my dream:

Methought it was about nine on Wednesday morning that a chariot, with a dowager's arms upon the doors, and in it a grave matronly lady [not unlike Mother H. in the face; but in her heart O how unlike!], stopped at a grocer's shop about ten doors on the other side of the way, in order to buy some groceries: and me-thought Dorcas, having been out to see if the coast were clear for her lady's flight, and if a coach were to be got near the place, espied this chariot with the dowager's arms, and this matronly lady: and what, methought, did Dorcas, that subtle traitress, do, but whip up to the old matronly lady, and, lifting up her voice, say, Good my lady, permit me one word with your ladyship!

What thou hast to say to me, say on, quoth the old lady; the grocer retiring, and standing aloof, to give Dorcas leave to speak; who, methought, in words like these, accosted the lady.

"You seem, madam, to be a very good lady; and here, in this neighbourhood, at a house of no high repute, is an innocent lady of rank and fortune, beautiful as a May morning, and youthful as a rosebud, and full as sweet and lovely; who has been tricked thither by a wicked gentleman, practised in the ways of the town; and this very night will she be ruined, if she get not out of his hands. Now, O lady! if you will extend your compassionate goodness to this fair young lady, in whom, the moment you behold her, you will see cause to believe all I say; and let her have a place in your chariot, and remain in your protection for one day only, till she can send a man and horse to her rich and powerful friends; you may save from ruin a lady who has no equal for virtue as well as beauty."

Methought the old lady, moved with Dorcas's story, answered and said, "Hasten, O damsel, who in a happy moment art come to put it in my power to serve the innocent and the virtuous, which it has always been my delight to do: hasten to this young lady, and bid her hie hither to me with all speed; and tell her that my chariot shall be her asylum: and if I find all that thou sayest true, my house shall be her sanctuary, and I will protect her from all her oppressors."

Hereupon, methought, this traitress Dorcas hied back to the lady, and made report of what she had done. And, methought, the lady highly approved of Dorcas's proceeding, and blessed her for her good thought.

And I lifted up mine eyes, and behold the lady issued out of the house, and without looking back, ran to the chariot with the dowager's coat upon it, and was received by the matronly lady with open arms, and "Welcome, welcome, welcome, fair young lady, who so well answers the description of the faithful damsel: and I will carry you instantly to my house, where you shall meet with all the good usage your heart can wish for, till you can apprise your rich and powerful friends of your past dangers, and present escape."

"Thank you, thank you, thank you, thank you, worthy, thrice worthy lady, who afford so kindly your protection to a most unhappy young creature, who has been basely seduced and betrayed, and brought to the very brink of destruction."

Methought, then, the matronly lady, who had by the time the young lady came to her, bought and paid for the goods she wanted, ordered her coachman to drive home with all speed; who stopped not till he had arrived in a certain street not far from Lincoln's Inn Fields, where the matronly lady lived in a sumptuous dwelling, replete with damsels who wrought curiously in muslins, cambrics, and fine linen, and in every good work that industrious damsels love to be employed about, except the loom and the spinning-wheel.

And methought, all the way the young lady and the old lady rode, and after they came in, till dinner was ready, the young lady filled up the time with the dismal account of her wrongs and her sufferings, the like of which was never heard by mortal ear; and this in so moving a manner, that the good old lady did nothing but weep, and sigh, and sob, and inveigh against the arts of wicked men, and against that abominable Squire

Lovelace, who was a *plotting villain,* methought she said; and, more than that, an *unchained Beelzebub.*

Methought I was in a dreadful agony, when I found the lady had escaped; and in my wrath had like to have slain Dorcas, and our mother, and every one I met. But, by some quick transition, and strange metamorphosis, which dreams do not usually account for, methought, all of a sudden, this matronly lady was turned into the famous Mother H. herself; and, being an old acquaintance of Mother Sinclair, was prevailed upon to assist in my plot upon the young lady.

Then, methought, followed a strange scene; for, Mother H. longing to hear more of the young lady's story, and night being come, besought her to accept of a place in her own bed, in order to have all the talk to themselves. For, methought, two young nieces of hers had broken in upon them in the middle of the dismal tale.

Accordingly, going early to bed, and the sad story being resumed, with as great earnestness on one side, as attention on the other, before the young lady had gone far in it, Mother H. methought, was taken with a fit of the colic; and her tortures increasing, was obliged to rise to get a cordial she used to find specific in this disorder, to which she was unhappily subject.

Having thus risen, and stepped to her closet, methought she let fall the wax taper in her return; and then [O metamorphosis still stranger than the former! What unaccountable things are dreams!] coming to bed again in the dark, the young lady, to her infinite astonishment, grief, and surprise, found Mother H. turned into a young person of the other sex: and although Lovelace was the *abhorred of her soul,* yet, fearing it was some *other* person, it was matter of some consolation to her, when she found it was no other than himself, and that she had been still the bedfellow of but *one* and the *same* man.

A strange promiscuous huddle of adventures followed; scenes perpetually shifting; now nothing heard from the lady but sighs, groans, exclamations, faintings, dyings—from the gentleman but vows, promises, protestations, *disclaimers of purposes pursued,* and all the gentle and ungentle pressures of the lover's warfare.

Then, as quick as thought (for dreams, thou knowest, confine not themselves to the rules of the drama) ensued recoveries, lyings-in, christenings, the smiling boy, amply, even in *her own* opinion, rewarding the suffering mother.

Then the grandfather's estate yielded up, possession taken of it: living very happily upon it: her beloved Norton her companion; Miss Howe her visitor; and (admirable! thrice admirable!) enabled to *compare notes* with her; a charming girl, by the same father, to her friend's charming boy; who, as they grow up, in order to consolidate their mammas' friendships (for neither have dreams regard to *consanguinity*), intermarry; change names by Act of Parliament, to enjoy my estate—and I know not what of the like incongruous stuff.

I awoke, as thou mayest believe, in great disorder, and rejoiced to find my charmer in the next room, and Dorcas honest.

Now thou wilt say this was a very odd dream. And yet (for I am a strange dreamer) it is not altogether improbable that something like it may happen; as the pretty simpleton has the weakness to confide in Dorcas, whom till now she disliked.

But I forgot to tell thee one part of my dream; and that was that the next morning the lady gave way to such transports of grief and resentment, that she was with difficulty diverted from making an attempt upon her own life. But, however, at last was prevailed upon to resolve to live, and to make the best of the matter: a letter, methought, from Captain Tomlinson helping to pacify her, written to apprise me that her Uncle Harlowe would certainly be at Kentish Town on Wednesday night June 28, the following day (the 29th) being his birthday; and he doubly desirous on that account that our nuptials should be then privately solemnized in his presence.

But *is* Thursday the 29th her uncle's anniversary, methinks thou askest? It is; or else the day of celebration should have been earlier still. Three weeks ago I heard her say it was; and I have down the birthday of every one of her family, and the wedding-day of her father and mother. The minutest circumstances are often of great service in matters of the least importance.

And what sayest thou now to my dream?

Who says, that, sleeping and waking, I have not fine helps from some *body*, some *spirit* rather, as thou 'lt be apt to say? But no wonder that a Beelzebub has his devilkins to attend his call.

I can have no manner of doubt of succeeding in Mother H.'s part of the scheme; for will the lady (who resolves to throw herself into the *first house she can enter,* or to bespeak the protection of the *first person she meets*; and who thinks there can be no danger *out* of this house, equal to what she apprehends from me *in* it) scruple to accept of the chariot of a dowager, accidentally offering? And the lady's protection engaged by her faithful Dorcas, so highly bribed to promote her escape? And then Mrs. H. has the air and appearance of a venerable matron, and is not such a forbidding devil as Mrs. Sinclair.

The pretty simpleton knows nothing of the world; nor that people who have money never want assistants in their views, be they what they will. How else could the princes of the earth be so implicitly served as they are, *change they hands ever so often*, and be their purposes *ever so wicked*?

If I can but get her to *go on* with me till Wednesday next week, we shall be settled together pretty quietly by that time. And indeed, if she has any gratitude, and has in her the least of her sex's foibles, she must think I deserve her favour by the pains she has cost me. For dearly do they all love that men should take pains about them and for them.

And here, for the present, I will lay down my pen, and congratulate myself upon my happy invention (since her obstinacy puts me once more upon exercising it)—but with this resolution, I think, that, if the present contrivance fail me, I will exert all the faculties of my mind, all my talents, to procure for myself a legal right to her favour, and that in defiance of all my antipathies to the married state; and of the suggestions of the great devil out of the house, and of his secret agents in it. Since, if *now* she is not to be prevailed upon, or drawn in, it will be in vain to attempt her further.

Letter XLIV—Mr. Lovelace to John Belford, Esq.

Tuesday Night, June 20.

No admittance yet to my charmer! She is very ill—in a violent fever, Dorcas thinks. Yet will have no advice.

Dorcas tells her how much I am concerned at it.

But again let me ask, Does this lady do right to make herself ill, when she is *not* ill? For my own part, libertine as people think me, when I had *occasion* to be sick, I took a dose of ipecacuanha, that I might not be guilty of a falsehood; and most heartily sick was I; as she, who then pitied me, full well knew. But here to pretend to be very ill, only to get an opportunity to run away, in order to avoid forgiving a man who has offended her, how unchristian! If good folks allow themselves in these breaches of a known duty, and in these presumptuous contrivances to deceive, who, Belford, shall blame us?

I have a strange notion that the matronly lady will be certainly at the grocer's shop at the hour of nine to-morrow morning: for Dorcas heard me tell Mrs. Sinclair that I shall go out at eight precisely; and then she is to try for a coach: and if the dowager's chariot should happen to be there, how lucky will it be for my charmer! How strangely will my dream be made out!

.   .   .   .   .   .

I have just received a letter from Captain Tomlinson. Is it not wonderful? For that was part of my dream.

I shall always have a prodigious regard to dreams henceforward. I know not but I may write a book upon that subject; for my own experience will furnish out a great part of it. *Glanville of Witches*, and *Baxter's History of Spirits and Apparitions*, and the *Royal Pedant's Demonology*, will be nothing at all to *Lovelace's Reveries*.

The letter is just what I dreamed it to be. I am only concerned that Uncle John's anniversary did not happen three or four days sooner; for should any *new* misfortune befall my charmer, she may not be able to support her spirits so long as till Thursday in the next week. Yet it will give me the more time for new expedients should my present contrivance fail; which I cannot, however, suppose.

To Robert Lovelace, Esq.

Monday, June 19.

DEAR SIR,—I can now return you joy, for the joy you have given me, as well as my dear friend Mr. Harlowe, in the news of his beloved niece's happy recovery; for he is determined to comply with *her* wishes and *yours*, and to give her to you with his own hand.

As the ceremony has been necessarily delayed by reason of her illness, and as Mr. Harlowe's birthday is on Thursday the 29th of this instant June, when he enters into the seventy-fourth year of his age; and as time may be wanted to complete the dear lady's recovery; he is very desirous that the marriage shall be solemnized upon it; that he may afterwards have double joy on that day to the end of his life.

For this purpose he intends to set out privately, so as to be at Kentish Town on Wednesday se'nnight in the evening.

All the family used, he says, to meet to celebrate it with him; but as they are at present in too unhappy a situation for that, he will give out, that, not being able to bear the day at home, he has resolved to be absent for two or three days.

He will set out on horseback, attended only with one trusty servant, for the greater privacy. He will be at the most creditable-looking public-house there, expecting you both next morning, if he hear nothing from me to prevent him. And he will go to town with you after the ceremony is performed, in the coach he supposes you will come in.

He is very desirous that I should be present on the occasion. But *this* I have promised him, at his request, that I will be up before the day, in order to see the settlements executed, and everything properly prepared.

He is very glad that you have the licence ready.

He speaks very kindly of you, Mr. Lovelace; and says that if any of the family stand out after he has seen the ceremony performed, he will separate from them, and unite himself to his dear niece and her interests.

I owned to you, when in town last, that I took slight notice to my dear friend of the misunderstanding between you and his niece; and that I did this for fear the lady should have shown any little discontent in his presence, had I been able to prevail upon him to go up in person, as then was doubtful. But I hope nothing of that discontent remains now.

My absence, when your messenger came, must excuse me for not writing by him.

Be pleased to make my most respectful compliments acceptable to the admirable lady, and believe me to be

Your most faithful and obedient servant,
ANTONY TOMLINSON.

This letter I sealed, and broke open. It was brought, thou mayst suppose, by a particular messenger; the seal such a one as the writer need not be ashamed of. I took care to inquire after the captain's health, in my beloved's hearing; and it is now ready to be produced, as a pacifier, according as she shall *take on*, or *resent*, if the two metamorphoses happen pursuant to my wonderful dream; as, having great faith in dreams, I dare say they will. I think it will not be amiss in changing my clothes, to have this letter of the worthy captain lie in my beloved's way.

Letter XLV—Mr. Lovelace to John Belford, Esq.

Wedn. Noon, June 21.

WHAT shall I say now!—I who but a few hours ago had such faith in dreams, and had proposed out of hand to begin my treatise of *dreams sleeping* and *dreams waking*, and was pleasing myself with the dialoguings between the old matronly lady and the young lady; and with the two metamorphoses (absolutely assured that everything would happen as my dream chalked it out), shall nevermore depend upon those flying follies, those illusions of a fancy depraved, and run mad.

Thus confoundedly have matters happened.

I went out at eight o'clock in high good humour with myself, in order to give the sought-for opportunity to the plotting mistress and corrupted maid; only ordering Will to keep a good look-out for fear his lady should mistrust my plot, or mistake a hackney-coach for the dowager lady's chariot. But first I sent to know how she did; and received for answer, Very ill: had a very bad night: which latter was but too probable: since this *I* know, that people who have plots in their heads as seldom *have* as *deserve* good ones.

I desired a physician might be called in; but was refused.

I took a walk in St. James's Park, congratulating myself all the way on my rare inventions: then, impatient, I took coach, with one of the windows *quite* up, the other *almost* up, playing at bo-peep at every chariot I saw pass in my way to Lincoln's Inn Fields: and when arrived there I sent the coachman to desire any one of Mother H.'s family to come to me to the coach-side, not doubting but I should have intelligence of my fair fugitive there; it being then half an hour after ten.

A servant came, who gave me to understand that the matronly lady was just returned by herself in the chariot.

Frighted out of my wits, I alighted, and heard from the mother's own mouth that Dorcas had engaged her to protect the lady; but came to tell her afterwards that she had changed her mind, and would not quit the house.

Quite astonished, not knowing what might have happened, I ordered the coachman to lash away to our mother's.

Arriving here in an instant, the first word I asked was, if the lady was safe?

Mr. Lovelace gives here a very circumstantial relation of all that passed between the lady and Dorcas. But as he could only guess at her motives for refusing to go off, when Dorcas told her that she had engaged for her the protection of the dowager lady, it is thought proper to omit his relation, and to supply it by some memoranda *of the lady's. But it is first necessary to account for the occasion on which those* memoranda *were made.*

The reader may remember, that in the letter written to Miss Howe on her escape to Hampstead,[1] *she promises to give her the particulars of her flight at leisure.*

She had indeed thoughts of continuing her account of everything that had passed between her and Mr. Lovelace since her last narrative letter. But the uncertainty she was in from that time, with the execrable treatment she met with on her being deluded back again ; followed by a week's delirium ; had hitherto hindered her from prosecuting her intention. But, nevertheless, having it still in her view to perform her promise as soon as she had opportunity, she made minutes of everything as it passed, in order to help her memory: "which, *as she observes in one place,* she could less trust to since her late disorders than before."

In these minutes, or book of memoranda, *she observes,* "That having apprehensions that Dorcas might be a traitress, she would have got away while she was gone out to see for a coach; and actually slid downstairs with that intent. But that, seeing Mrs. Sinclair in the entry [*whom Dorcas had planted there while she went out*], she speeded up again, unseen."

She then went up to the dining-room, and saw the letter of Captain Tomlinson : on which she observes in her memorandum-book as follows.

"How am I puzzled now! He might leave this letter on purpose: none of the other papers left with it being of any consequence: what is the alternative? To stay, and be the wife of the vilest of men—how my heart resists that! To attempt to get off, and fail, ruin inevitable! Dorcas *may* betray me! I doubt she is *still* his implement! At his going out, he whispered her, as I saw, unobserved—in a very familiar manner too. Never fear, sir, with a curtsy.

In her agreeing to connive at my escape, she provided not for her own safety, if I got away: yet had reason, in that case, to expect his vengeance. And wants not forethought. To have taken her *with me,* was to be in the power of her intelligence, if a faithless creature. Let me, however, though I part not with my caution, keep my charity! Can there be any woman so vile to woman? Oh, yes! Mrs. Sinclair: her aunt. The Lord deliver

[1] See p. 19.

me! But, alas! I have put myself out of the course of His protection by the *natural* means—and am already ruined! A father's curse likewise against me! Having made vain all my friends' cautions and solicitudes, I must not hope for miracles in my favour!

"If I do escape, what may become of me, a poor, helpless, deserted creature! Helpless from sex!—from circumstances! Exposed to every danger! Lord protect me!

"His vile man not gone with him! Lurking hereabouts, no doubt, to watch my steps! I *will* not go away by the chariot, however."

.   .   .   .   .   .

"That this chariot should come so opportunely! So like his many *opportunelies*! That Dorcas should have the sudden thought! Should have the *courage* with the thought, to address a lady in behalf of an absolute stranger to that lady! That the lady should so readily consent! Yet the transaction between them to take up so much time, their distance in degree considered: for, arduous as the case was, and precious as the time, Dorcas was gone above half an hour! Yet the chariot was said to be ready at a grocer's not many doors off!

"Indeed, some elderly ladies are talkative: and there are, no doubt, *some* good people in the world——

"But that it should chance to be a widow lady, who could do what she pleased! That Dorcas should know her to be so by the lozenge! Persons in her station not usually so knowing, I believe, in heraldry.

"Yet some may! For servants are fond of deriving *collateral* honours and distinctions, as I may call them, from the quality, or people of rank, whom they serve.

"But his sly servant not gone with him! Then this letter of Tomlinson!——

"Although I am resolved never to have this wretch, yet, may I not *throw myself into my uncle's protection at Kentish Town or Highgate, if I cannot escape before ; and so get clear of him?* May not the evil I know, be less than what I may fall into, if I can avoid further villainy? Further villainy he has not yet threatened; freely and justly as I have treated him! I will not go, I think. At least, unless I can send this fellow out of the way." [1]

---

[1] She tried to do this; but was prevented by the fellow's pretending to put his ankle out, by a slip downstairs—*A trick*, says his contriving master, in his omitted relation, *I had learned him. on a like occasion, at Amiens.*

. . . . . .

"The fellow a villain! The wench, I doubt, a vile wench. At last concerned for her own safety. Plays off and on about a coach.

"All my hopes of getting off, at present, over! Unhappy creature! to what further evils art thou reserved! Oh, how my heart rises at the necessity I must still be under to see and converse with so very vile a man!"

Letter XLVI—Mr. Lovelace to John Belford, Esq.

Wednesday Afternoon.

DISAPPOINTED in her meditated escape; obliged, against her will, to meet me in the dining-room; and perhaps apprehensive of being upbraided for her art in feigning herself ill; I *expected* that the dear perverse would *begin* with me with spirit and indignation. But I was in hopes, from the gentleness of her natural disposition; from the consideration which I expected from her on her situation; from the contents of the letter of Captain Tomlinson, which Dorcas told me she had seen; and from the time she had had to cool and reflect since she last admitted me to her presence, that she would not have carried it so strongly through as she did.

As I entered the dining-room I congratulated her and myself upon her *sudden* recovery. And would have taken her hand, with an air of respectful tenderness: but she was resolved to begin where she left off.

She turned from me, drawing in her hand, with a repulsing and indignant aspect. I meet you once more, said she, because I cannot help it. What have you to say to me? Why am I to be thus detained against my will?

With the utmost solemnity of speech and behaviour I urged the ceremony. I saw I had nothing else for it. I had a letter in my pocket, I said [feeling for it, although I had not taken it from the table where I left it in the same room], the contents of which, if attended to, would make us both happy. I had been loath to show it to her before, because I hoped to prevail upon her to be mine *sooner* than the day mentioned in it.

I felt for it in all my pockets, watching her eye meantime, which I saw glance towards the table where it lay.

I was uneasy that I could not find it. At last, directed again by her sly eye, I spied it on the table at the further end of the room.

With joy I fetched it.   Be pleased to read that letter, madam;
with an air of satisfied assurance.

She took it, and cast her eye over it in such a careless way as
made it evident that she had read it before: and then unthank-
fully tossed it into the window-seat before her.

I urged her to bless me to-morrow, or Friday morning: at
least, that she would not render vain her uncle's journey, and
kind endeavours to bring about a reconciliation among us all.

Among us all! repeated she, with an air equally disdainful and
incredulous.   O Lovelace, thou art surely nearly allied to the
grand deceiver, in thy endeavour to suit temptations to inclinations!   But what honour, what faith, what veracity, were it
possible that I could enter into parley with thee on this subject
(which it is not), may I expect from such a man as thou hast
shown thyself to be?

I was touched to the quick.   A lady of your perfect character,
madam, who has feigned herself sick, on purpose to avoid seeing
the man who adored her, should not——

I know what thou wouldst say, interrupted she.   Twenty
and twenty low things, that my soul would have been above
being guilty of, and which I have despised myself for, have I
been brought into by the infection of thy company, and by the
necessity thou hast laid me under, of appearing mean.   But I
thank God, destitute as I am, that I am not, however, sunk so
low as to wish to be thine.

I, madam, as the injurer, *ought* to have patience.   It is for
the injured to reproach.   But your *uncle* is not in a plot against
you, it is to be hoped.   There are circumstances in the letter
you have cast your eyes over——

Again she interrupted me, Why, once more I ask you, am I
detained in this house?   Do I not see myself surrounded by
wretches, who, though they wear the habit of my sex, may yet,
as far as I know, lie in wait for my perdition?

She would be very loath, I said, that Mrs. Sinclair and her
nieces should be called up to vindicate themselves and their
house.

Would but they kill me, let them come, and welcome.   I will
bless the hand that will strike the blow!   Indeed I will.

'Tis idle, very idle, to talk of dying.   Mere young-lady talk,
when controlled by those they hate.   But let me beseech you,
dearest creature——

Beseech me nothing.   Let me not be detained thus against
my will!   Unhappy creature that I am, said she, in a kind of

frenzy, wringing her hands at the same time, and turning from me, her eyes lifted up! "Thy curse, O my cruel father, seems to be now in the height of its operation! My weakened mind is full of forebodings, that I am in the way of being a lost creature as to both worlds! Blessed, blessed God, said she, falling on her knees, save me, Oh, save me from myself, and from this man!"

I sunk down on my knees by her, excessively affected. Oh, that I could recall yesterday! Forgive me, my dearest creature, forgive what is past, as it cannot now but by one way be retrieved. Forgive me only on this condition—that my future faith and honour——

She interrupted me, rising, If you mean to beg of me never to seek to avenge myself by law, or by an appeal to my relations, to my Cousin Morden in particular, when he comes to England—

D—n the law, rising also [she started], and all those to whom you talk of appealing! I defy both the one and the other. All I beg is YOUR forgiveness; and that you will, on my unfeigned contrition, re-establish me in your favour——

Oh, no, no, no! lifting up her clasped hands, I never, never *will*, never, never *can* forgive you! And it is a punishment worse than death to me, that I am obliged to meet you, or to see you!

This is the last time, my dearest life, that you will ever see me in this posture, on this occasion: and again I kneeled to her. Let me hope that you will be mine next Thursday, your uncle's birthday, if not before. Would to Heaven I had never been a villain! Your indignation is not, cannot be, greater than my remorse. And I took hold of her gown; for she was going from me.

Be remorse thy portion! For thine own sake, be remorse thy portion! I never, never will forgive thee! I never, never will be thine! Let me retire! Why kneelest thou to the wretch whom thou hast so vilely humbled?

Say but, dearest creature, you will *consider*—say but you will take time to reflect upon what the honour of both our families requires of you. I will not rise. I will not permit you to withdraw [still holding her gown] till you tell me you will *consider*. Take this letter. Weigh well *your* situation, and *mine*. Say you will withdraw to *consider*; and then I will not presume to withhold you.

Compulsion shall do nothing with me. Though a slave, a prisoner, in circumstance, I am no slave in my will! Nothing will I promise thee. Withheld, compelled—nothing will I promise thee!

Noble creature! But not implacable, I hope! Promise me but to return in an hour!

Nothing will I promise thee!

Say but you will see me again this evening!

Oh, that I could say—that it were in my *power* to say—I never will see thee more! Would to Heaven I never were to see thee more!

Passionate beauty!—still holding her——

I speak, though with vehemence, the deliberate wish of my heart. Oh, that I could avoid *looking down* upon thee, mean groveller, and abject as insulting! Let me withdraw! My soul is in tumults! Let me withdraw!

I quitted my hold to clasp my hands together. Withdraw, O sovereign of my fate! Withdraw, if you *will* withdraw! My destiny is in your power! It depends upon your breath! Your scorn but augments my love! Your resentment is but too well founded! But, dearest creature, return, return, with a resolution to bless with pardon and peace your faithful adorer!

She flew from me. The angel, as soon as she found her wings, flew from me. I, the reptile kneeler, the despicable slave, no more the proud victor, arose; and, retiring, tried to comfort myself that, circumstanced as she is, destitute of friends and fortune; her uncle moreover, who is to reconcile all so soon (as, I thank my stars, she still believes), expected.

Oh, that she would forgive me! Would she but generously forgive me, and receive my vows at the altar, at the *instant* of her forgiving me, that I might not have time to relapse into my old prejudices! By my soul, Belford, this dear girl gives the lie to all our rakish maxims. There must be something more than a *name* in virtue! I now see that there is! *Once subdued, always subdued*—'tis an egregious falsehood! But oh, Jack, she never *was* subdued. What have I obtained but an increase of shame and confusion! While her glory has been established by her sufferings!

This one merit is, however, left me, that I have laid all her sex under obligation to me, by putting this noble creature to trials, which, so gloriously supported, have done honour to them all.

However—but no more will I add. What a force have evil habits! I will take an airing, and try to fly from myself. Do not thou upbraid me on my weak fits—on my contradictory purposes—on my irresolution—and all will be well.

Letter XLVII—Mr. Lovelace to John Belford, Esq.

Wednesday Night.

A MAN is just now arrived from M. Hall, who tells me that my lord is in a very dangerous way. The gout is in his stomach to an extreme degree, occasioned by drinking a great quantity of lemonade.

A man of £8,000 a year to prefer his appetite to his health! He deserves to die! But we have all of us our inordinate passions to gratify: and they generally bring their punishment along with them—so witnesses the nephew, as well as the uncle.

The fellow was sent up on other business; but stretched his orders a little, to make his court to a successor.

I am glad I was not at M. Hall at the time my lord took the grateful dose [it was certainly grateful to *him* at the time]. There are people in the world who would have had the wickedness to say that I had persuaded him to drink it.

The man says that his lordship was so bad when he came away that the family began to talk of sending for me in post-haste. As I know the old peer has a good deal of cash by him, of which he seldom keeps account, it behoves me to go down as soon as I can. But what shall I do with this dear creature the while? To-morrow over, I shall, perhaps, be able to answer my own question. I am afraid she will make me desperate.

For here have I sent to implore her company, and am denied with scorn.

.   .   .   .   .   .

I have been so happy as to receive, this moment, a third letter from my dear correspondent, Miss Howe. A little severe devil! It would have broken the heart of my beloved had it fallen into her hands. I will enclose a copy of it. Read it here.

Tuesday, June 20.

MY DEAREST MISS HARLOWE,—Again I venture to write to you (almost against inclination); and that by your former conveyance, little as I like it.

I know not how it is with you. It may be bad; and then it would be hard to upbraid you, for a silence you may not be able to help. But if not, what shall I say severe enough, that you have not answered either of my last letters? The first [1] of

[1] See p. 1 of this volume.

which [and I think it imported you too much to be silent upon it] you owned the receipt of. The other, which was delivered into your own hands,[1] was so pressing for the favour of a line from you, that I am amazed I could not be obliged—and still *more*, that I have not heard from you since.

The fellow made so strange a story of the condition he saw you in, and of your speech to him, that I know not what to conclude from it: only that he is a simple, blundering, and yet conceited fellow, who, aiming at description, and the rustic wonderful, gives an air of bumpkinly romance to all he tells. That this is his character, you will believe, when you are informed that he described you in grief excessive,[2] yet so improved in your person and features, and so *rosy*, that was his word, in your face, and so flush-coloured, and so plump in your arms, that one would conclude you were labouring under the operation of some malignant poison; and so much the rather, as he was introduced to you when you were upon a couch, from which you offered not to rise, or sit up.

Upon my word, Miss Harlowe, I am greatly distressed upon your account; for I must be so free as to say that, in your ready return with your deceiver, you have not at all answered my expectations, nor acted up to your own character: for Mrs. Townsend tells me, from the women at Hampstead, how cheerfully you put yourself into his hands again: yet, at the time, it was impossible you should be married!

Lord, my dear, what pity it is that you took so much pains to get from the man! But you know best! Sometimes I think it could not be *you* to whom the rustic delivered my letter. But it must too: yet it is strange I could not have one line by him:—not one:—and you so soon well enough to go with the wretch back again!

I am not sure that the letter I am now writing will come to your hands: so shall not say half that I have upon my mind to say. But if you think it *worth your while* to write to me, pray let me know what fine ladies, his relations, those were, who visited you at Hampstead, and carried you back again so joyfully to a place that I had so fully warned you. But I will say no more: at least till I *know* more: for I can do nothing but wonder, and stand amazed.

Notwithstanding all the man's baseness, 'tis plain there was more than a lurking love.—Good Heaven! But I have done! Yet I know not how to have done, neither! Yet I must—I *will*.

[1] See p. 163 of this volume.   [2] See Letter xxiii, ibid.

Only account to me, my dear, for what I cannot at all account for: and inform me whether you are really married, or not. And then I shall know whether there *must*, or must *not*, be a period shorter than that of one of our lives, to a friendship which has hitherto been the pride and boast of

Your
ANNA HOWE.

Dorcas tells me that she has just now had a *searching* conversation, as she calls it, with her lady. She is willing, she tells the wench, still to place a confidence in her. Dorcas hopes she has reassured her; but wishes me not to depend upon it. Yet Captain Tomlinson's letter must assuredly weigh with her. I sent it in just now by Dorcas, desiring her to reperuse it. And it was not returned me, as I feared it would be. And that's a good sign, I think.

I say *I think*, and *I think*; for this charming creature, entangled as I am in my own inventions, puzzles *me* ten thousand times more than I *her*.

Letter XLVIII—Mr. Lovelace to John Belford, Esq.

Thursday Noon, June 22.

LET me perish if I know what to make either of myself, or of this surprising creature—now calm, now tempestuous—but I know thou lovest not anticipation any more than I.

At my repeated requests, she met me at six this morning. She was ready dressed; for she has not had her clothes off ever since she declared that they never more should be off in this house. And charmingly she looked, with all the disadvantages of a three hours' violent stomach-ache (for Dorcas told me that she had been really ill), no rest, and eyes red, and swelled with weeping. Strange to me, that those charming fountains have not been long ago exhausted. But she is a woman. And I believe anatomists allow *that women have more weary heads than men*.

Well, my dearest creature, I hope you have now thoroughly considered of the contents of Captain Tomlinson's letter. But as we are thus early met, let me beseech you to make this my happy day.

She looked not favourably upon me. A cloud hung upon her brow at her entrance: but as she was going to answer me, a still greater solemnity took possession of her charming features.

Your air, and your countenance, my beloved creature, are not propitious to me. Let me beg of you, before you speak, to forbear all further recriminations: for already I have such a sense of my vileness to you, that I know not how to bear the reproaches of my own mind.

I have been endeavouring, said she, *since I am not permitted to avoid you,* to obtain a composure which I never more expected to see you in. How long I may enjoy it, I cannot tell. But I hope I shall be enabled to speak to you without that vehemence which I expressed yesterday, and could not help it.[1]

After a pause (for I was all attention) thus she proceeded:

It is easy for me, Mr. Lovelace, to see that further violences are intended me, if I comply not with your purposes; whatever they are, I will suppose them to be what you so solemnly profess they are. But I have told you, as solemnly, my mind, that I never *will*, that I never *can*, be yours; nor, if so, any man's upon earth. All vengeance, nevertheless, for the wrongs you have done me, I disclaim. I want but to slide into some obscure corner, to hide myself from you, and from every one who once loved me. The desire lately so near my heart, of a reconciliation with my friends, is much abated. They shall not receive me *now*, if they *would*. Sunk in mine own eyes, I now think myself unworthy of their favour. In the anguish of my soul, therefore, I conjure you, Lovelace [tears in her eyes], to leave me to my fate. In doing so, you will give me a pleasure the highest I now can know.

Whither, my dearest life——

No matter whither. I will leave to Providence, when I am out of this house, the direction of my future steps. I am sensible enough of my destitute condition. I know that I have not now a friend in the world. Even Miss Howe has given me up—or you are—but I would fain keep my temper! By your means I have lost them all—and you have been a barbarous enemy to me. You know you have.

She paused.

I could not speak.

The evils I have suffered, proceeded she [turning from me].

[1] The lady, in her minutes, says, "I fear Dorcas is a false one. May I not be able to prevail upon him to leave me at my liberty? Better to try than to trust to her. If I cannot prevail, but must meet him and my uncle, I hope I shall have fortitude enough to renounce him then. But I would fain avoid qualifying with the wretch, or to give him an expectation which I intend not to answer. If I am mistress of my own resolutions, my uncle himself shall not prevail with me to bind my soul in covenant with so vile a man."

however irreparable, are but *temporary* evils.   Leave me to my hopes of being enabled to obtain the Divine forgiveness for the offence I have been drawn in to give to my parents, and to virtue; that so I may avoid the evils that are *more than temporary*.   This is now all I have to wish for.   And what is it that I demand, that I have not a right to, and from which it is an illegal violence to withhold me?

It was impossible for me, I told her plainly, to comply.   I besought her to give me her hand as this very day.   I could not live without her.   I communicated to her my lord's illness, as a reason why I wished not to stay for her uncle's anniversary.   I besought her to bless me with her consent; and, after the ceremony was passed, to accompany me down to Berks.   And thus, my dearest life, said I, will you be freed from a house to which you have conceived so great an antipathy.

This, thou wilt own, was a princely offer.   And I was resolved to be as good as my word.   I thought I had killed my conscience, as I told thee, Belford, some time ago.   But conscience, I find, though it may be temporarily stifled, cannot die; and when it dare not speak aloud, will whisper.   And at this instant I thought I felt the revived varletess (on but a slight retrograde motion) writhing round my pericardium like a serpent; and in the action of a dying one (collecting all its force into its head), fix its plaguy fangs into my heart.

She hesitated, and looked down, as if irresolute.   And this set my heart up at my mouth.   And, believe me, I had instantly popped in upon me, in imagination, an old spectacled parson, with a white surplice thrown over a black habit [a fit emblem of the halcyon office, which, under a benign appearance, often introduces a life of storms and tempests], whining and snuffling through his nose the irrevocable ceremony.

I hope now, my dearest life, said I, snatching her hand, and pressing it to my lips, that your silence bodes me good.   Let me, my beloved creature, have but your *tacit* consent; and this moment I will step out and engage a minister—and then I promised how much my whole future life should be devoted to her commands, and that I would make her the best and tenderest of husbands.

At last, turning to me, I have told you my mind, Mr. Lovelace, said she.   Think you that I could thus solemnly—there she stopped—I am too much in your power, proceeded she; your prisoner, rather than a person free to choose for myself, or to say what I will *do* or *be*—but, as a testimony that you mean me well, let me instantly quit this house; and I will then give you such an answer in writing, as best befits my unhappy circumstances.

And imaginest thou, fairest, thought I, that this will go down with a Lovelace? Thou oughtest to have known that free-livers, like ministers of state, never part with a power put into their hands without an equivalent of twice the value.

I pleaded, that if we joined hands *this morning* (if not, *to-morrow*; if not, on *Thursday*, her uncle's birthday, and in his presence); and afterwards, as I had proposed, set out for Berks; we should, of course, quit this house; and, on our return to town, should have in readiness the house I was in treaty for.

She answered me not, but with tears and sighs: *fond of believing what I hoped*, I imputed her silence to the modesty of her sex. The dear creature (thought I), solemnly as she began with me, is ruminating, in a sweet suspense, how to put into fit words the gentle purposes of her condescending heart. But, looking in her averted face with a soothing gentleness, I plainly perceived that it was resentment, and not bashfulness, that was struggling in her bosom.[1]

At last she broke silence. I have no patience, said she, to find myself a slave, a prisoner, in a vile house. Tell me, sir, in so many words tell me, whether it be, or be not, your intention to permit me to quit it? To permit me the freedom which is my birthright as an English subject?

Will not the consequence of your departure hence be, that I shall lose you for ever, madam? And can I bear the thoughts of that?

She flung from me. My soul disdains to hold parley with thee, were her violent words—but I threw myself at her feet, and took hold of her reluctant hand, and began to imprecate, to vow, to promise—but thus the passionate beauty, interrupting me, went on:

I am sick of thee, MAN! One continued string of vows, oaths, and protestations, varied only by time and place, fills thy mouth! Why detainest thou me? My heart rises against thee, O thou *cruel implement of my brother's causeless vengeance*. All I beg of thee is, that thou wilt remit me the *future* part of my father's dreadful curse! The *temporary* part, base and ungrateful as thou art! thou hast completed!

---

[1] The lady, in her minutes, owns the difficulty she lay under to keep her temper in this conference. "But when I found," says she, "that all my entreaties were ineffectual, and that he was resolved to detain me, I could no longer withhold my impatience."

I was speechless! Well I might! Her *brother's* implement!
James Harlowe's implement! Zounds, Jack! what words were
these!

I let go her struggling hand. She took two or three turns
across the room, her whole haughty soul in her air. Then
approaching me, but in silence, turning from me, and again to
me, in a milder voice—I see thy confusion, Lovelace. Or is it
thy remorse? I have but one request to make thee—the request
so often repeated: that thou wilt this moment permit me to quit
this house. Adieu then, let me say, for *ever* adieu! And mayst
thou enjoy that happiness in this world, which thou hast robbed
me of; as thou hast of every friend I have in it!

And saying this, away she flung, leaving me in a confusion so
great, that I knew not what to think, say, or do.

But Dorcas soon roused me. Do you know, sir, running in
hastily, that my lady is gone downstairs!

No, sure! And down I flew, and found her once more at the
street door, contending with Polly Horton to get out.

She rushed by me into the fore parlour, and flew to the window,
and attempted once more to throw up the sash. Good people!
Good people! cried she.

I caught her in my arms and lifted her from the window. But
being afraid of hurting the charming creature (charming in her
very rage), she slid through my arms on the floor:—Let me die
here! Let me die here! were her words; remaining jointless and
immovable till Sally and Mrs. Sinclair hurried in.

She was visibly terrified at the sight of the old wretch; while I
(sincerely affected) appealed, Bear witness, Mrs. Sinclair! Bear
witness, Miss Martin! Miss Horton! Every one bear witness,
that I offer not violence to this beloved creature!

She then found her feet. O house [looking towards the
windows, and all round her, O house] contrived on purpose for
my ruin! said she—but let not that woman come into my
presence—nor that Miss Horton neither, who would not have
dared to control me, had she not been a base one!

Hoh, sir! Hoh, madam! vociferated the old dragon, her arms
kemboed, and flourishing with one foot to the extent of her
petticoats—What ado 's here about nothing! I never knew such
work in my life, between a chicken of a gentleman and a
tiger of a lady!

She was visibly affrighted: and upstairs she hastened. A bad
woman is certainly, Jack, more terrible to her own sex than even
a bad man.

I followed her up. She rushed by her own apartment into the dining-room: no terror can make her forget her punctilio.

To recite what passed there of invective, exclamations, threatenings, even of her own life, on one side; of expostulations, supplications, and sometimes menaces, on the other, would be too affecting; and, after my particularity in like scenes, these things may as well be imagined as expressed.

I will therefore only mention, that, at length, I extorted a concession from her. She had reason[1] to think it would have been worse for her on the spot, if she had not made it. It was, *That she would endeavour to make herself easy, till she saw what next Thursday, her uncle's birthday, would produce.* But oh, that it were not a sin, she passionately exclaimed on making this poor concession, to put an end to her own life, rather than yield to give me but *that* assurance!

This, however, shows me, that she is aware that the reluctantly given assurance may be fairly construed into a matrimonial expectation on my side. And if she will *now*, even *now*, look forward, I think, from my heart, that I will put on her livery, and wear it for life.

What a situation am I in, with all my cursed inventions? I am puzzled, confounded, and ashamed of myself, upon the whole. To take such pains to be a villain! But (for the *fiftieth* time) let me ask thee, Who would have thought that there had been such a woman in the world? Nevertheless, she had best take care that she carries not her obstinacy much further. She knows not what revenge for slighted love will make me do.

The busy scenes I have just passed through have given emotions to my heart which will not be quieted one while. My heart, I see (on reperusing what I have written), has communicated its tremors to my fingers; and in some places the characters are so indistinct and unformed, that thou 'lt hardly be able to make them out. But if one *half* of them only are intelligible, that will be enough to expose me to thy contempt, for the wretched hand I have made of my plots and contrivances. But surely, Jack, I have gained some ground by this promise.

---

[1] The lady mentions, in her memorandum-book, that she had no other way, as she apprehended, to save herself from instant dishonour, but by making this concession. Her only hope now, she says, if she cannot escape by Dorcas's connivance (whom, nevertheless, she suspects), is to find a way to engage the protection of her uncle, and even of the civil magistrate, on Thursday next, if necessary. "He shall see," says she, "tame and timid as he has thought me, what I dare to do to avoid so hated a compulsion, and a man capable of a baseness so premeditatedly vile and inhuman."

And now, one word to the assurances thou sendest me, that thou hast not betrayed my secrets in relation to this charming creature. Thou mightest have spared them, Belford. My suspicions held no longer than while I wrote about them.[1] For well I knew, when I allowed myself time to think, that thou hadst no *principles*, no *virtue*, to be misled by. A great deal of strong envy, and a little of weak pity, I knew to be thy motives. Thou couldst not provoke my anger, and my compassion thou ever hadst; and art now more especially entitled to it; because thou art a *pitiful* fellow.

All thy new expostulations in my beloved's behalf I will answer when I see thee.

Letter XLIX—Mr. Lovelace to John Belford, Esq.

Thursday Night.

CONFOUNDEDLY out of humour with this perverse woman! Nor wilt thou blame me, if thou art my friend. She regards the concession she made, as a concession extorted from her: and we are but just where we were before she made it.

With great difficulty I prevailed upon her to favour me with her company for one half-hour this evening. The necessity I was under to go down to M. Hall was the subject I wanted to talk upon.

I told her, that as she had been so good as to promise that she would endeavour to make herself easy till she saw the Thursday in next week over, I hoped that she would not scruple to oblige me with her word, that I should find her here at my return from M. Hall.

Indeed she would make me no such promise. Nothing of *this house* was mentioned to me, said she: you know it was not. And do you think that I would have given *my consent to my imprisonment in it?*

I was plaguily nettled, and disappointed too. If I go not down to M. Hall, madam, you'll have no scruple to stay here, I suppose, till Thursday is over?

If I cannot help myself, I must. But I insist upon being permitted to go out of this house whether *you* leave it or not.

Well, madam, then I will comply with your commands. And I will go out this very evening in quest of lodgings that you shall have no objection to.

[1] See pp. 224–5.

I will have no lodgings of your providing, sir—I will go to Mrs. Moore's at Hampstead.

Mrs. Moore's, madam? I have no objection to Mrs. Moore's. But will you give me your promise to admit me *there* to your presence?

As I do here—when I cannot help it.

Very well, madam. Will you be so good as to let me know what you intended by your promise to *make yourself easy*——

To *endeavour*, sir, to make myself easy—were the words—— *Till you saw what next Thursday would produce?*

Ask me no questions that may ensnare me. I am too sincere for the company I am in.

Let me ask you, madam, What meant you, when you said, "that, were it not a sin, you would die before you gave me that assurance?"

She was indignantly silent.

You thought, madam, you had given me room to hope your pardon by it?

When I think I ought to answer you with patience, I will speak.

Do you think yourself in my power, madam?

If I were not——And there she stopped.

Dearest creature, speak out—I beseech you, dearest creature, speak out.

She was silent; her charming face all in a glow.

Have you, madam, any reliance upon my honour?

Still silent.

You hate me, madam! You despise me more than you do the most odious of God's creatures!

You ought to despise *me*, if I did not.

You say, madam, you are in a *bad* house. You have *no reliance* upon my honour—you believe you *cannot avoid me*——

She arose. I beseech you, let me withdraw.

I snatched her hand, rising, and pressed it first to my lips, and then to my heart, in wild disorder. She might have felt the bounding mischief ready to burst its bars. You *shall* go—to your own apartment, if you please—but, by the great God of Heaven, I will accompany you thither!

She trembled. Pray, pray, Mr. Lovelace, don't terrify me so! Be seated, madam! I beseech you, be seated!

I will sit down——

Do then, madam—do then—all my soul in my eyes, and my heart's blood throbbing at my finger-ends.

I will, I will—you hurt me—pray, Mr. Lovelace, don't—don't

frighten me so—and down she sat, trembling; my hand still grasping hers.

I hung over her throbbing bosom, and putting my other arm round her waist—And you say you hate me, madam—and you say you despise me—and you say you promised me nothing——

Yes, yes, I *did* promise you—let me not be held down thus—you see I sat down when you bid me. Why [struggling] need you hold me down thus? I did promise *to endeavour to be easy till Thursday was over*! But you won't let me! How can I be easy? Pray, let me not be thus terrified.

And what, madam, *meant* you by your promise? Did you mean anything in my favour? You designed that I should, at the time, *think* you did. Did you mean anything in my favour, madam? Did you intend that I should *think* you did?

Let go my hand, sir—take away your arm from about me [struggling, yet trembling]. *Why do you gaze upon me so?*

Answer me, madam. Did you mean anything in my favour by your promise?

Let me not be thus constrained to answer.

Then pausing, and gaining more spirit, Let me go, said she: I am but a woman—but a *weak* woman—but my life is in my own power, though my person is not—I will not be thus constrained.

You shall not, madam, quitting her hand, bowing, but my heart at my mouth, and hoping farther provocation.

She arose, and was hurrying away.

I pursue you not, madam. I will try your generosity. Stop—return. This moment stop, return, if, madam, you would not make me desperate.

She stopped at the door; burst into tears. O Lovelace! How, how, have I deserved——

Be *pleased*, dearest angel, to return.

She came back—but with declared reluctance; and imputing her compliance to terror.

Terror, Jack, as I have heretofore found out, though I have so little benefited by the discovery, must be my resort, if she make it necessary. Nothing else will do with the inflexible charmer.

She seated herself over against me; extremely discomposed; but indignation had a visible predominance in her features.

I was going towards her, with a countenance intendedly changed to love and softness: Sweetest, dearest angel, were my words, in the tenderest accent: but, rising up, she insisted upon my being seated at a distance from her.

I obeyed—and begged her hand over the table, to my extended

hand; to see, as I said, if in anything she would oblige me—but nothing gentle, soft, or affectionate, would do.   She refused me her hand! Was she wise, Jack, to confirm to me that nothing but terror would do?

Let me only know, madam, if your promise to *endeavour* to wait with patience the event of next Thursday meant me favour?

Do you expect any voluntary favour from one to whom you give not a free choice?

Do you intend, madam, to honour me with your hand, in your uncle's presence, or do you not?

My heart and my hand shall never be separated.   Why, think you, did I stand in opposition to the will of my best, my natural friends?

I know what you mean, madam.   Am I then as hateful to you as the vile Solmes?

Ask me not such a question, Mr. Lovelace.

I *must* be answered.   Am I as hateful to you as the vile Solmes?

Why do you call Mr. Solmes vile?

Don't *you* think so, madam?

Why should I? Did Mr. Solmes ever do vilely by me?

Dearest creature! don't distract me by hateful comparisons! And perhaps by a more hateful preference.

Don't *you*, sir, put questions to me that you know I will answer truly, though my answer were ever so much to enrage you.

My heart, madam, my soul is all yours at present.   But you *must* give me hope, that your promise, in your own construction, binds you, no *new cause* to the contrary, to be mine on Thursday. How else can I leave you?

Let me go to Hampstead; and trust to my favour.

May I trust to it? Say, only, *may* I trust to it?

How will you trust to it, if you extort an answer to this question?

Say only, dearest creature, say only, *may* I trust to your favour, if you go to Hampstead?

How *dare* you, sir, if I *must* speak out, expect a promise of favour from me? What a mean creature must you think me, after your ungrateful baseness to me, were I to give you such a promise?

Then standing up, Thou hast made me, O vilest of men! [her hands clasped, and a face crimsoned over with indignation] an inmate of the vilest of houses—nevertheless, while I am in it,

I shall have a heart incapable of anything but abhorrence of *that* and of *thee*!

And round her looked the angel, and upon me, with fear in her sweet aspect of the consequence of her free declaration. But what a devil must I have been, I, who love bravery in a man, had I not been more struck with admiration of her fortitude at the instant, than stimulated by revenge?

Noblest of creatures! And do you think I can leave you, and my interest in such an excellence, precarious? No promise! No hope! If you make me not desperate, may lightning blast me, if I do you not all the justice it is in my power to do you!

If you have any intention to oblige me, leave me at my own liberty, and let me not be detained in this abominable house. To be constrained as I have been constrained! To be stopped by your vile agents! To be brought up by force, and to be bruised in my own defence against such illegal violence! I dare to die, Lovelace—and she who fears not death is not to be intimidated into a meanness unworthy of her heart and principles!

Wonderful creature! But why, madam, did you lead me to hope for something favourable for next Thursday? Once more, make me not desperate. With all your magnanimity, glorious creature! [I was more than half frantic, Belford] you *may*, you *may*—but do not, do not make me brutally threaten you! Do not, do not make me desperate!

My aspect, I believe, threatened still more than my words. I was rising—she arose. Mr. Lovelace, be pacified. You are even more dreadful than the Lovelace I have long dreaded—let me retire—I ask your *leave* to retire—you really frighten me—yet I give you no hope—from my heart I ab——

Say not, madam, you *abhor* me. You must, for your own sake, conceal your hatred—at least, not avow it. I seized her hand.

Let me retire—let me retire, said she, in a manner out of breath.

I will only say, madam, that I refer myself to your generosity. My heart is not to be trusted at this instant. As a mark of my submission to your will, you shall, *if you please*, withdraw. But I will not go to M. Hall—live or die my Lord M. I will not go to M. Hall—but will attend the effect of your promise. Remember, madam, you have promised *to endeavour to make yourself easy, till you see the event of next Thursday*. Next Thursday, remember, your uncle comes up to see us married—*that 's the event*. You think ill of your Lovelace—do not, madam, suffer your own morals to be degraded by the *infection*, as you called it, of his example.

Away flew the charmer with this half-permission—and no doubt thought that she had an escape—nor without reason.

I knew not for half an hour what to do with myself. Vexed at the heart, nevertheless (now she was from me, and when I reflected upon her hatred of me, and her defiances), that I suffered myself to be so overawed, checked, restrained.

And now I have written thus far (having, of course, recollected the whole of our conversation) I am more and more incensed against myself.

But I will go down to these women—and perhaps suffer myself to be laughed at by them.

Devil fetch them, they pretend to know their own sex. Sally was a woman well educated—Polly also—both have read—both have sense—of parentage not mean—once modest both—still they say had been modest, but for me—not entirely indelicate *now*; though too little nice for my *personal* intimacy, loath as they both are to have me think so—the old one, too, a woman of family, though thus (from bad inclination, as well as at first from low circumstances) miserably sunk:—and hence they all pretend to remember what *once* they were; and vouch for the inclinations and hypocrisy of the whole sex; and wish for nothing so ardently as that I will leave the perverse lady to their management, while I am gone to Berkshire; undertaking absolutely for her humility and passiveness on my return; and continually boasting of the many perverse creatures whom they have obliged to draw in their traces.

.   .   .   .   .   .

I am just come from these sorceresses.

I was forced to take the mother down; for she began with her Hoh, sirs! with me; and to catechize and upbraid me, with as much insolence as if I owed her money.

I made her fly the pit at last. Strange wishes wished we against each other, at her quitting it. What were they? I'll tell thee. She wished me married, and to be jealous of my wife; and my heir-apparent the child of another man. I was even with her with a vengeance. And yet thou wilt think that could not well be. As how? As how, Jack! Why I wished her conscience come to life! And I know by the gripes mine gives me every half-hour, that she would then have a cursed time of it.

Sally and Polly gave themselves high airs too. Their first

favours were thrown at me. [Women to boast of those favours which they were as willing to impart, first forms all the difficulty with them! as I to receive!] I was upbraided with ingratitude, *dastardice*, and all my difficulties with my angel charged upon myself, for want of following my blows; and for leaving the proud lady mistress of her own will, and nothing to *reproach herself with*. And all agreed that the arts used against her on a certain occasion had too high an operation for them or me to judge what her will *would have been* in the arduous trial. And then they blamed one another; as I cursed them all.

They concluded that I should certainly marry, and be *a lost man*. And Sally, on this occasion, with an affected and malicious laugh, snapped her fingers at me, and pointing two of each hand forkedly at me, bid me remember the lines I once showed her of my favourite *Jack* Dryden, as she always familiarly calls that celebrated poet:

> We women to new joys unseen may move:
> There are no prints left in the paths of Love.
> All goods besides by public marks are known:
> But those men most desire to keep, have none.

This infernal implement had the confidence further to hint, that when a wife, some other man would not find half the difficulty with my angel that I had found. Confidence indeed! But yet I must say, that this dear creature is the only woman in the world of whom I should not be jealous. And yet, if a man gives himself up to the company of these devils, they never let him rest till he either suspect or hate his wife.

But a word or two of other matters, if possible.

Methinks I long to know how causes go at M. Hall. I have another private intimation that the old peer is in the greatest danger.

I must go down. Yet what to do with this lady the mean-while! These cursed women are full of cruelty and enterprise. She will never be easy with them in my absence. They will have provocation and pretence therefore. But woe be to them, if——

Yet what will vengeance do, after an insult committed? The two nymphs will have jealous rage to goad them on—and what will withhold a jealous and already ruined woman?

To let her go elsewhere; that cannot be done. I am still resolved to be honest, if she 'll give me hope: if yet she 'll *let me* be honest—but I 'll see how she 'll be, after the contention she will certainly have between her resentment and the terror she had reason for from our last conversation. So let this subject rest till the morning. And to the old peer once more.

I shall have a good deal of trouble, I reckon, though no sordid man, to be decent on the expected occasion. Then how to act (I who am no hypocrite) in the days of condolement! What farces have I to go through; and to be a principal actor in them! I'll try to think of my own latter end; a grey beard, and a graceless heir; in order to make me serious.

Thou, Belford, knowest a good deal of this sort of grimace; and canst help a gay heart to a little of the dismal. But then every feature of thy face is cut out for it. My heart may be touched, perhaps, sooner than thine; for, believe me or not, I have a very tender one—but then, no man looking in my face, be the occasion for grief ever so great, will believe *that* heart to be deeply distressed.

All is placid, easy, serene, in my countenance. Sorrow cannot sit half an hour together upon it. Nay, I believe that Lord M.'s recovery, should it happen, would not affect me above a quarter of an hour. Only the new scenery (and the pleasure of aping an Heraclitus to the family, while I am a Democritus among my private friends) or I want nothing that the old peer can leave me. Wherefore then should grief sadden and distort such blithe, such jocund features as mine?

But as for thine, were there murder committed in the street, and thou wert but passing by, the murderer even in sight, the pursuers would quit *him*, and lay hold of *thee*: and thy very looks would hang, as well as apprehend, thee.

But one word to business, Jack. Whom dealest thou with for thy blacks? Wert thou well used? I shall want a plaguy parcel of them. For I intend to make every soul of the family mourn—*outside*, if not *in*.

Letter L—Mr. Lovelace to John Belford, Esq.

June 23, Friday Morning.

I WENT out early this morning, on a design that I know not yet whether I shall or shall not pursue; and on my return found Simon Parsons, my lord's Berkshire bailiff (just before arrived), waiting for me with a message in form, sent by all the family, to press me to go down, and that at my lord's particular desire; who wants to see me before he dies.

Simon has brought my lord's chariot and six [perhaps *my*

own by this time] to carry me down. I have ordered it to be in readiness by four to-morrow morning. The cattle shall smoke for the delay; and by the rest they 'll have in the interim, will be better able to bear it.

I am still resolved upon matrimony, if my fair perverse will accept of me. But, if she will not—why then I must give an uninterrupted hearing, not to my conscience, but to these women below.

Dorcas had acquainted her lady with Simon's arrival and errand. My beloved had desired to see him. But my coming in prevented his attendance on her, just as Dorcas was instructing him what questions he should *not* answer to, that might be asked of him.

I am to be admitted to her presence immediately, at my repeated request. Surely the acquisition in view will help me to make all up with her. She is just gone up to the dining-room.

.   .   .   .   .   .

Nothing will do, Jack! I can procure no favour from her, though she has obtained from me the point which she had set her heart upon.

I will give thee a brief account of what passed between us.

I first proposed instant marriage; and this in the most fervent manner: but was denied as fervently.

Would she be pleased to assure me that she would stay here only till Tuesday morning? I would but just go down and see how my lord was—to know whether he had anything particular to say, or enjoin me, while yet he was sensible, as he was very earnest to see me. Perhaps I might be up on Sunday. Concede in something! I beseech you, madam, show me some little consideration.

Why, Mr. Lovelace, must I be determined by your motions? Think you that I will voluntarily give a sanction to the imprisonment of my person? Of what importance to me ought to be your stay or your return?

Give a sanction to the imprisonment of your person! Do you think, madam, that I fear the law?

I might have spared this foolish question of defiance: but my pride would not let me. I thought she threatened me, Jack.

I *don't* think you fear the law, sir. You are too *brave* to have any regard either to moral or divine sanctions.

'Tis well, madam! But ask me anything I can do to oblige you, though in nothing will you oblige *me*.

Then I ask you, then I request of you, to let me go to Hampstead.

I paused—and at last: By my soul you shall. This very moment I will wait upon you, and see you fixed there, if you 'll promise me your hand on Thursday, in presence of your uncle.

I want not *you* to see me fixed—I will promise nothing.

Take care, madam, that you don't let me see that I can have no reliance upon your future favour.

I have been used to be threatened by you, sir; but I will accept of your company to Hampstead. I will be ready to go in a quarter of an hour. My clothes may be sent after me.

You know the condition, madam—next Thursday.

You dare not trust——

My infinite demerits tell me that I *ought* not. Nevertheless I *will* confide in your generosity. To-morrow morning (no *new cause* arising to give you reason to the contrary) as early as you please you may go to Hampstead.

This seemed to oblige her. But yet she looked with a face of doubt.

I will go down to the women, Belford. And having no better judges at hand, will hear what they say upon my critical situation with this proud beauty, who has so insolently rejected a Lovelace kneeling at her feet, though making an earnest tender of himself for a husband, in spite of all his prejudices to the state of shackles.

Letter LI—Mr. Lovelace to John Belford, Esq.

JUST come from the women.

"Have I gone so far, and am I afraid to go farther? Have I not already, as it is evident by her behaviour, sinned beyond forgiveness? A woman's tears used to be to me but as water sprinkled on a glowing fire, which gives it a fiercer and brighter blaze: what defence has this lady, but her tears and her eloquence? She was before taken at *no weak* advantage. She was *insensible* in her moments of trial. *Had* she been sensible, she *must* have been sensible. So they say. The methods taken with her have augmented her glory and her pride. She has now a tale to tell, that she *may* tell with honour to herself. No accomplice-inclination. She can look me into confusion, without being conscious of so much as a *thought* which she need to be ashamed of."

This, Jack, is the substance of the women's reasonings with me.

To which let me add that the dear creature now sees the necessity I am in to leave her. Detecting me is in her head. My contrivances are of such a nature, that I must appear to be the most odious of men if I am detected on this side matrimony. And yet I have promised, as thou seest, that she shall set out to Hampstead as soon as she pleases in the morning, and that without condition on her side.

Dost thou ask, what I meant by this promise?

No *new cause* arising, was the proviso on my side, thou 'lt remember. But there *will be* a new cause.

Suppose Dorcas should drop the promissory note given her by her lady? Servants, especially those who cannot read or write, are the most careless people in the world of written papers. Suppose I take it up?—at a time, too, that I was determined that the dear creature should be her own mistress? Will not this detection be a *new cause*? A cause that will carry with it against her the appearance of ingratitude?

That she designed it a *secret from me*, argues a *fear of detection*, and indirectly a *sense of guilt*. I wanted a pretence. Can I have a better? If I am in a violent passion upon the detection, is not passion a universally allowed extenuator of violence? Is not every man and woman obliged to excuse that fault in another, which at times they find attended with such ungovernable effects in themselves?

The mother and sisterhood, suppose, brought to sit in judgment upon the vile corrupted. The least benefit that must accrue from the accidental discovery, if not a pretence for *perpetration* [which, however, may be the case], an excuse for renewing my orders for her detention till my return from M. Hall [the fault her own]; and for keeping a stricter watch over her than before; with direction to send me any letters that may be written *by* her or *to* her. And when I return, the devil 's in it if I find not a way to make her choose lodgings for herself (since these are so hateful to her) that shall answer all my purposes; and yet I no more appear to direct her choice, than I did before in these.

Thou wilt curse me when thou comest to this place. I know thou wilt. But thinkest thou, that, after such a series of contrivance, I will lose this inimitable woman for want of a little more? A rake 's a rake, Jack! And what rake is withheld by *principle* from the perpetration of any evil his heart is set upon, and in which he thinks he can succeed? Besides, am I not in earnest as to marriage? Will not the generality of the world acquit me, if I *do* marry? And what is that injury which a *church rite* will at any time repair? Is not *the catastrophe of every story that ends in wedlock accounted happy*, be the difficulties in the progress to it ever so great?

But here, how am I engrossed by this lady, while poor Lord M., as Simon tells me, lies groaning in the most dreadful agonies! What must he suffer! Heaven relieve him! I have a too compassionate heart. And so would the dear creature have found, could I have thought that the worst of *her* sufferings is equal to the lightest of *his*. I mean as to fact; for, as to that part of hers which arises from extreme sensibility, I know nothing of that; and cannot, therefore, be answerable for it.

Letter LII—*Mr. Lovelace to John Belford, Esq.*

JUST come from my charmer. She will not suffer me to say half the obliging, the tender things, which my honest heart is ready to overflow with. A confounded situation that, when a man finds himself in humour to be eloquent, and pathetic at the same time, yet cannot engage the mistress of his fate to lend an ear to his fine speeches.

I can account now, how it comes about that lovers, when their mistresses are cruel, run into solitude, and disburthen their minds to *stocks* and *stones*: for am I not forced to make my complaints to *thee*?

She claimed the performance of my promise, the moment she saw me, of *permitting* her [haughtily she spoke the word] to go to Hampstead as soon as I was gone to Berks.

Most cheerfully I renewed it.

She desired me to give orders in her hearing.

I sent for Dorcas and Will. They came. Do you both take notice [but, perhaps, sir, I may take *you* with me] that your lady is to be obeyed in all her commands. She purposes to return to Hampstead as soon as I am gone. My dear, will you not have a servant to attend you?

I shall want no servant there.

Will you take Dorcas?

If I should want Dorcas, I can send for her.

Dorcas could not but say, she should be very proud——

Well, well, that may be at my return, if your lady permit. Shall I, my dear, call up Mrs. Sinclair, and give her orders to the same effect, in your hearing?

I desire not to see Mrs. Sinclair; nor any that belong to her.

As you please, madam.

And then (the servants being withdrawn) I urged her again for the assurance that she would meet me at the altar on Thursday next. But to no purpose. May she not thank herself for all that may follow?

One favour, however, I would not be denied; to be admitted to pass the evening with her.

All sweetness and obsequiousness will I be on this occasion. My whole soul shall be poured out to move her to forgive me. If she will not, and if the promissory note should fall in my way, my revenge will doubtless take total possession of me.

All the house in my interest, and every one in it not only engaging to intimidate and assist, as occasion shall offer, but staking all their experience upon my success, if it be not my own fault, what must be the consequence?

This, Jack, however, shall be her last trial; and if she behave as nobly *in* and *after* this *second* attempt [*all her senses about her*] as she has done after the *first*, she will come out an angel upon full proof, in spite of man, woman, and devil: then shall there be an end of all her sufferings. I will then renounce that vanquished devil, and reform. And if any vile machination start up, presuming to mislead me, I will sooner stab it in my heart as it rises, than give way to it.

A few hours will now decide all. But whatever be the event, I shall be too busy to write again, till I get to M. Hall.

Meantime I am in strange agitations. I must suppress them, if possible, before I venture into her presence. My heart bounces my bosom from the table. I will lay down my pen, and wholly resign to its impulses.

Letter LIII—Mr. Lovelace to John Belford, Esq.

Friday Night, or rather Sat. Morn. 1 o'clock.

I THOUGHT I should not have had either time or inclination to write another line before I got to M. Hall. But have the first; must find the last; since I can neither sleep, nor do anything but write, if I can do that. I am most *confoundedly* out of humour. The reason let it follow; if it will follow—no preparation for it from me.

I tried by gentleness and love to soften—what? Marble. A heart incapable either of love or gentleness. Her past injuries for ever in her head. Ready to receive a favour; the permission to go to Hampstead; but neither to deserve it, nor return any. So my scheme of the gentle kind was soon given over.

I then wanted her to provoke me: like a coward boy, who waits for the first blow before he can persuade himself to fight, I half challenged her to challenge or defy me: she seemed aware of her danger; and would not directly brave my resentment: but kept such a middle course, that I neither could find a pretence to offend, nor reason to hope: yet she believed my tale that her uncle would come to Kentish Town; and seemed not to apprehend that Tomlinson was an impostor.

She was very uneasy, upon the whole, in my company: wanted often to break from me: yet so held me to my promise of permitting her to go to Hampstead, that I knew not how to get off it; although it was impossible, in my precarious situation with her, to think of performing it.

In this situation; the women ready to assist; and if I proceeded not, as ready to ridicule me; what had I left me, but to pursue the concerted scheme, and to seek a pretence to quarrel with her, in order to revoke my promised permission, and to convince her that I would not be upbraided as the most brutal of ravishers for nothing?

I had agreed with the women, that if I could not find a pretence in her presence to begin my operations, the note should lie in my way, and I was to pick it up soon after her retiring from me. But I began to doubt at near ten o'clock (so earnest was she to leave me, suspecting my over-warm behaviour to her, and eager grasping of her hand two or three times, with eyestrings, as I felt, on the strain, while her eyes showed uneasiness and apprehension) that if she actually retired for the night, it might be a chance whether it would be easy to come at her again. Loath therefore to run such a risk, I stepped out at a little after ten, with intent to alter the preconcerted disposition a little; saying I would attend her again instantly. But as I returned, I met her at the door, intending to withdraw for the night. I could not persuade her to go back: nor had I presence of mind (so full of complaisancy as I was to her just before) to stay her by force: so she slid through my hands into her own apartment. I had nothing to do, therefore, but to let my former concert take place.

I should have premised (but care not for order of time, connexion, or anything else) that, between eight and nine in the evening, another servant of Lord M. on horseback came, to desire me to carry down with me Dr. S., the old peer having been

once (*in extremis*, as they judge he is now) relieved and reprieved
by him. I sent and engaged the doctor to accompany me
down; and am to call upon him by four this morning: or the
devil should have both my lord and the doctor, if I 'd stir till
I got all made up.

Poke thy damned nose forward into the event, if thou wilt—
curse me if thou shalt have it till its proper time and place;
and too soon then.

She had hardly got into her chamber, but I found a little
paper, as I was going into mine; which I took up; and, opening
it (for it was carefully pinned in another paper), what should it
be but a promissory note, given as a bribe, with a further promise
of a diamond ring, to induce Dorcas to favour her mistress's
escape?

How my temper changed in a moment! Ring, ring, ring,
ring I my bell, with a violence enough to break the string, and
as if the house were on fire.

Every devil frighted into active life: the whole house in an
uproar: up runs Will. Sir—sir—sir!—eyes goggling, mouth
distended. Bid the damned toad Dorcas come hither (as I
stood at the stair-head), in a horrible rage, and out of breath,
cried I.

In sight came the trembling devil—but standing aloof, from
the report made her by Will of the passion I was in, as well as
from what she heard.

Flash came out my sword immediately; for I had it ready on
—Cursed, confounded, villainous, bribery and corruption!

Up runs she to her lady's door, screaming out for safety and
protection.

Good your honour, interposed Will, for God's sake! O Lord,
O Lord!—receiving a good cuff.—

Take that, varlet, for saving the ungrateful *wretch* from my
vengeance!

Wretch ! I *intended* to say; but if it were some other word of
like ending, passion must be my excuse.

Up ran two or three of the sisterhood: What 's the matter!
What 's the matter!

The matter ! (for still my beloved opened not her door; on the
contrary, drew another bolt). This *abominable* Dorcas!—(Call
her aunt up! Let her see what a traitress she has placed
about me! And let her bring the toad to answer for herself)—
has taken a bribe, a provision for life, to betray her trust;
by that means to perpetuate a quarrel between a man and

his wife, and frustrate for ever all hopes of reconciliation between us!

Let me perish, Belford, if I have patience to proceed with the farce!

.   .   .   .   .   .

If I must resume, I must——

Up came the aunt puffing and blowing. As she hoped for mercy, *she* was not privy to it! She never knew such a plotting perverse lady in her life! Well might servants be at the pass they were, when such ladies as Mrs. Lovelace made no conscience of corrupting them. For *her* part, she desired no mercy for the wretch: no niece of hers, if she were not faithful to her trust! But what was the proof?

She was shown the paper——

But too evident! Cursed, cursed toad, devil, jade, passed from each mouth: and the vileness of the *corrupted*, and the unworthiness of the *corruptress*, were inveighed against.

Up we all went, passing the lady's door into the dining-room, to proceed to trial——

Stamp, stamp, stamp up, each on her heels; rave, rave, rave, every tongue——

Bring up the creature before us all, this instant——

And would she have got out of the house, say you?

These the noises and the speeches as we clattered by the door of the fair briberess.

Up was brought Dorcas (whimpering) between two, both bawling out: You must go—You shall go—'Tis fit you should answer for yourself—You are a discredit to all worthy servants —as they pulled and pushed her upstairs. She whining, I cannot see his honour—I cannot look so good and so generous a gentleman in the face. Oh, how shall I bear my aunt's ravings!

Come up, and be damned. Bring her forward, her imperial judge. What a plague, it is the *detection*, not the *crime*, that confounds you. You could be quiet enough for days together, as I see by the date, under the villainy. Tell me, ungrateful devil, tell me, who made the first advances?

Ay, disgrace to my family and blood, cried the old one, tell his honour—tell the truth! Who made the first advances?

Ay, cursed creature, cried Sally, who made the first advances?

I have betrayed one trust already! Oh, let me not betray another! My lady is a good lady! Oh, let not *her* suffer!

Tell all you know. Tell the whole truth, Dorcas, cried Polly

Horton. His honour loves his lady too well to make her suffer *much*; little as she requites his love!

Everybody sees that, cried Sally—too well, indeed, *for* his honour, I was going to say.

Till now, I thought she deserved my love. But to bribe a servant thus, who she supposed had orders to watch her steps, for fear of another elopement; and to impute that precaution to me as a crime! Yet I must love her. Ladies, forgive my weakness!——

Curse upon my grimaces!—if I have patience to repeat them! But thou shalt have it all. Thou canst not despise me more than I despise myself!

.   .   .   .   .   .

But suppose, sir, said Sally, you have my lady and the wench face to face? You see she cares not to confess.

Oh, my *carelessness*! cried Dorcas. Don't let my poor lady suffer! Indeed, if you all knew what I know, you would say her ladyship has been cruelly treated.

See, see, see, see!—repeatedly, every one at once. Only sorry for the *detection*, as your honour said—not for the *fault*.

Cursed creature, and devilish creature, from every mouth.

Your lady *won't*, she *dare* not come out to save you, cried Sally; though it is more his honour's mercy, than your desert, if he does not cut your vile throat this instant.

Say, repeated Polly, was it your lady that made the first advances, or was it you, you creature?

If the lady has so much honour, bawled the mother, excuse me, *so*—excuse me, sir [confound the old wretch! she had like to have said *son*!]—If the lady has so much honour, as we have supposed, she will appear to vindicate a poor servant, misled, as she has been, by such large promises! But I hope, sir, you will do them *both* justice: I *hope* you will! Good lack! Good lack! clapping her hands together, to grant her everything she could ask—to indulge her in her unworthy hatred to my poor innocent house!—to let her go to Hampstead, though your honour told us you could get no condescension from her; no, not the least! O sir, O sir, I hope—I hope—if your lady will not come out—I hope you will find a way to hear this cause in her presence. I value not my doors on such an occasion as this. Justice I ever loved. I desire you will come at the bottom of it in *clearance* to me. I'll be sworn I had no privity in this black corruption.

Just then, we heard the lady's door unbar, unlock, unbolt—
Now, sir!
Now, Mr. Lovelace!
Now, sir! from every encouraging mouth!
But, O Jack, Jack, Jack! I can write no more!

.　　.　　.　　.　　.　　.

If you must have it all, you must!

Now, Belford, see us all sitting in judgment, resolved to
punish the fair briberess—I, and the mother, the hitherto
dreaded mother, the nieces Sally, Polly, the traitress Dorcas,
and Mabel, a guard, as it were, over Dorcas, that she might not
run away, and hide herself: all predetermined, and of *necessity*
predetermined, from the journey I was going to take, and my
precarious situation with her—and hear her *unbolt, unlock,
unbar* the door; then, as it proved afterwards, put the key
into the lock on the outside, lock the door, and put it in her
pocket—Will, I knew, below, who would give me notice, if,
while we were all above, she should mistake her way, and go
downstairs, instead of coming into the dining-room: the street
doors also doubly secured, and every shutter to the windows
round the house fastened, that no noise or screaming should be
heard [such was the brutal preparation]—and then *hear* her
step towards us, and instantly *see* her enter among us, confiding
in her own innocence; and with a majesty in her person and
manner, that is *natural* to her; but which then shone out in all
its glory! Every tongue silent, every eye awed, every heart
quaking, mine, in a particular manner, sunk, throbless, and
twice below its usual region, to once at my throat—a shameful
recreant! She silent too, looking round her, first on me; then
on the mother, as no longer fearing her; then on Sally, Polly,
and the culprit Dorcas! Such the glorious power of innocence
exerted at that awful moment!

She would have spoken, but could not, looking down my
guilt into confusion. A mouse might have been heard passing
over the floor; her own light feet and rustling silks could not have
prevented it; for she seemed to tread air, and to be all soul.
She passed to the door, and back towards me, two or three
times, before speech could get the better of indignation; and
at last, after twice or thrice hemming, to recover her articulate
voice: "O thou contemptible and abandoned Lovelace, thinkest
thou that I see not through this poor villainous plot of thine,
and of these thy wicked accomplices?

"Thou, woman (looking at the mother), once my terror! always my dislike! but now my detestation! shouldst once more (for thine perhaps was the preparation) have provided for me intoxicating potions, to rob me of my senses——

"And then (*turning to me*), thou, wretch, mightest more securely have depended upon such a low contrivance as this!

"And ye, vile women, who perhaps have been the ruin, body and soul, of hundreds of innocents (you show me *how*, in full assembly), know that I am not married—ruined as I am, by your help, I bless God, I am *not* married to this miscreant. And I have friends that will demand my honour at your hands! And to whose authority I will apply; for none has this man over me. Look to it then, what further insults you offer me, or incite him to offer me. I am a person, though thus vilely betrayed, of rank and fortune I never will be his; and, to your utter ruin, will find friends to pursue you: and now I have this full proof of your detestable wickedness, and have heard your base incitements, will have no mercy upon you!"

They could not laugh at the poor figure I made. Lord! how every devil, conscience-shaken, trembled!

What a dejection must ever fall to the lot of guilt, were it given to innocence always thus to exert itself!

"And as for thee, thou vile Dorcas! Thou *double* deceiver! whining out thy pretended love for me! Begone, wretch! Nobody will hurt thee! Begone, I say! Thou hast too well acted thy part to be blamed by *any* here but myself—thou art safe: thy guilt is thy security in such a house as this! Thy shameful, thy poor part, thou hast as well acted as the low farce could give thee to act! As well as they each of them (thy superiors, though not thy betters), thou seest, can act theirs. Steal away into darkness! No inquiry after this will be made, whose the first advances, thine or mine."

And, as I hope to live, the wench, confoundedly frightened, slunk away; so did her sentinel Mabel; though I, endeavouring to rally, cried out for Dorcas to stay—but I believe the devil could not have stopped her, when an angel bid her begone.

Madam, said I, let me tell you; and was advancing towards her, with a fierce aspect, most cursedly vexed, and ashamed too.

But she turned to me; "Stop where thou art, O vilest and most abandoned of men! Stop where thou art! Nor, with that determined face, offer to touch me, if thou wouldst not that I should be a corpse at thy feet!"

To my astonishment, she held forth a penknife in her hand,

the point to her own bosom, grasping resolutely the whole handle, so that there was no offering to take it from her.

"I offer not mischief to anybody but myself. You, sir, and ye women, are safe from every violence of mine. The LAW shall be all my resource: the LAW," and she spoke the word with emphasis, that to such people carries natural terror with it, and now struck a panic into them.

No wonder, since those who will damn themselves to procure ease and plenty in this world, will tremble at everything that seems to threaten their methods of obtaining that ease and plenty.

"The LAW only shall be my refuge!"——

The infamous mother whispered me that it were better to *make terms* with this *strange* lady, and let her go.

Sally, notwithstanding all her impudent bravery at other times, said, *If* Mr. Lovelace had told *them* what was *not true* of her being his wife——

And Polly Horton, That she must *needs* say, the lady, if she were *not* my wife, had been very much injured; that was all.

That is not now a matter to be disputed, cried I: you and I know, madam.——

"We do, said she; and I thank God, I am *not* thine—*once more*, I thank God for it—I have no doubt of the further baseness that thou hadst intended me, by this vile and low trick: but I have my SENSES, Lovelace: and from my heart I despise thee, thou very poor Lovelace! How canst thou stand in my presence! Thou, that——"

Madam, madam, madam—these are insults not to be borne—and was approaching her.

She withdrew to the door, and set her back against it, holding the pointed knife to her heaving bosom; while the women held me, beseeching me not to provoke the violent lady—for their *house's* sake, and be cursed to them, they besought me—and all three hung upon me—while the truly heroic lady braved me at that distance:

"Approach me, Lovelace, with resentment, if thou wilt. I dare die. It is in defence of my honour. God will be merciful to my poor soul! I expect no mercy from thee! I have gained this distance, and two steps nearer me, and thou shalt see what I dare do!"

Leave me, women, to myself, and to my angel! They retired at a distance. O my beloved creature, how you terrify me! Holding out my arms, and kneeling on one knee—Not a step, not a step further, except to receive the death myself at that injured hand that threatens its own. I am a villain! the blackest of villains! Say you will sheathe your knife in the injurer's, not the injured's, heart; and then will I indeed approach you, but not else.

The mother twanged her damned nose; and Sally and Polly pulled out their handkerchiefs, and turned from us. They never in their lives, they told me afterwards, beheld such a scene.——

Innocence so triumphant: villainy so debased, they must mean!

Unawares to myself, I had moved onward to my angel. "And dost thou, dost thou, *still* disclaiming, *still* advancing, dost thou, dost thou, *still* insidiously move towards me?" [and her hand was extended]. "I dare—I dare—not rashly neither—my heart from *principle* abhors the act, which *thou* makest *necessary*! God, in Thy mercy! [lifting up her eyes and hands] God, in Thy mercy!"

I threw myself to the further end of the room. An ejaculation, a silent ejaculation, employing her thoughts that moment; Polly says the whites of her lovely eyes were only visible: and, in the instant that she extended her hand, *assuredly* to strike the fatal blow [how the very recital terrifies me!], she cast her eye towards me, and saw me at the utmost distance the room would allow, and heard my broken voice—my voice was utterly broken; nor knew I what I said, or whether to the purpose or not—and her charming cheeks, that were all in a glow before, turned pale, as if terrified at her own purpose; and lifting up her eyes—"Thank God!—Thank God! said the angel—delivered *for the present*; for the *present* delivered—from myself! Keep, sir, keep that distance" [looking down towards me, who was prostrate on the floor, my heart pierced as with a hundred daggers!]. "That distance has saved a life; to what reserved, the Almighty only knows!"

To *be* happy, madam; and to *make* happy! And oh, let me but hope for your favour for to-morrow—I will put off my journey till then—and may God——

Swear not, sir!—with an awful and piercing aspect. You have too, too often sworn! God's eye is upon us!—His more *immediate* eye; and looked wildly. But the women looked up to the ceiling, as if *afraid* of God's eye, and trembled. And well they might; and *I* too, who so very lately had each of us the devil in our hearts.

If not to-morrow, madam, say but next Thursday, your uncle's birthday; say but next Thursday!

"This I say, of this you may assure yourself, I never, never *will* be yours. And let me hope that I may be entitled to the performance of your promise, to be permitted to leave this *innocent* house, as one called it (but long have my ears been accustomed to such inversions of words), as soon as the day breaks."

Did my perdition depend upon it, that you cannot, madam, but upon terms. And I hope you will not terrify me—still dreading the accursed knife.

"Nothing less than an attempt upon my honour shall make me desperate. I have no view, but to defend my honour: with such a view only I entered into treaty with your infamous agent below The resolution you have seen, I trust, God will give me again, upon the same occasion. But for a *less*, I wish not for it. Only take notice, women, that I am no wife of *this man*: basely as he has used me, I am not his wife. He has no authority over me. If he go away by and by, and you act by his authority to detain me, look to it."

Then, taking one of the lights, she turned from us; and away she went, unmolested. Not a soul was *able* to molest her.

Mabel saw her, tremblingly, and in a hurry, take the key of her chamber door out of her pocket, and unlock it; and, as soon as she entered, heard her double lock, bar, and bolt it.

By her taking out her key, when she came out of her chamber to us, she no doubt suspected my design: which was, to have carried her in my arms thither, if she made such force necessary, after I had intimidated her; and to have been her companion for that night.

She was to have had several bedchamber women to assist to undress her upon occasion: but, from the moment she entered the dining-room with so much intrepidity, it was absolutely impossible to think of prosecuting my villainous designs against her.

.   .   .   .

This, this, Belford, was the hand I made of a contrivance from which I expected so much! And now am I ten times worse off than before.

Thou never sawest people in thy life look so like fools upon one another, as the mother, her partners, and I, did for a few minutes. And at last the two devilish nymphs broke out into insulting ridicule upon me; while the old wretch was concerned for her house, the reputation of her house. I cursed them all together; and, retiring to my chamber, locked myself in.

III—*K 884

And now it is time to set out: all I have gained, detection, disgrace, fresh guilt by repeated perjuries, and to be despised by her I *dote upon*; and, what is still worse to a proud heart, by *myself*.

Success, success in projects, is everything. What an admirable contriver did I think myself till now! Even for *this* scheme among the rest! But how pitifully foolish does it now appear to me! Scratch out, erase, never to be read, every part of my preceding letters where I have boastingly mentioned it. And never presume to rally me upon the cursed subject: for I cannot bear it.

But for the lady, by my soul I love her, I admire her, more than ever! I *must* have her. I *will* have her still—*with* honour, or *without*, as I have often vowed. My cursed fright at her accidental bloody nose, so lately, put her upon improving upon me thus. Had she threatened ME, I should soon have been master of *one* arm, and *in both*! But for so sincere a virtue to threaten *herself*, and not offer to intimidate *any other*, and with so much presence of mind, as to distinguish, in the very passionate intention, the necessity of the act, in defence of her *honour*, and so *fairly* to disavow *lesser* occasions; showed such a deliberation, such a choice, such a principle; and then keeping me so watchfully at a distance, that I could not seize her hand so soon as she could have given the fatal blow; how impossible not to be subdued by so *true* and so *discreet* a magnanimity!

But she is not *gone*. She shall not go. I will press her with letters for the Thursday. She shall yet be mine, legally mine. For, as to cohabitation, there is now no such thing to be thought of.

The captain shall give her away, as proxy for her uncle. My lord will die. My fortune will help my *will*, and set me above everything and everybody.

But here is the curse—she despises me, Jack! What man, as I have heretofore said, can bear to be despised, especially by his wife? O Lord! O Lord! What a hand, what a cursed hand, have I made of this plot! And here ends

The history of the lady and the penknife!!! The devil take the penknife!—It goes against me to say,

God bless the lady!

Near 5, *Sat. Morn.*

Letter LIV—Mr. Lovelace to Miss Clarissa Harlowe
[Superscribed to Mrs. Lovelace]

M. Hall, Sat. Night, June 24.

MY DEAREST LIFE,—If you do not impute to love, and to terror raised by love, the poor figure I made before you last night, you will not do me justice. I thought I would try to the very last moment, if, by complying with you in *everything*, I could prevail upon you to promise to be mine on Thursday next, since you refused me an earlier day. Could I have been so happy, you had not been hindered going to Hampstead, or wherever else you pleased. But when I could not prevail upon you to give me this assurance, what room had I (my demerit so great) to suppose that your going thither would not be to lose you for ever?

I will own to you, madam, that yesterday afternoon I picked up the paper dropped by Dorcas; who has confessed that she would have assisted you in getting away, if she had had an opportunity so to do; and undoubtedly dropped it by *accident*. And could I have prevailed upon you as to Thursday next, I would have made no use of it; secure as I should then have been in your word given, to be mine. But when I found you inflexible, I was resolved to try, if, by resenting Dorcas's treachery, I could not make *your* pardon of *me* the condition of *mine* to *her*: and if not, to make a handle of it to revoke my consent to your going away from Mrs. Sinclair's; since the consequence of that must have been so fatal to me.

So far, indeed, was my proceeding *low* and *artful*: and when I was challenged with it, as such, in so high and noble a manner, I could not avoid taking shame to myself upon it.

But you must permit me, madam, to hope that you will not punish me too heavily for so poor a contrivance, since no dishonour was meant you; and since, in the moment of its execution, you had as great an instance of my incapacity to defend a wrong, a low measure, and, at the same time, of your power over me, as mortal man could give—in a word, since you must have seen that I was absolutely under the control both of conscience and of love.

I will not offer to defend myself, for *wishing you to remain where you are*, till either you give me your word to meet me at the altar on Thursday; or till I have the honour of attending you, preparative to the solemnity which will make that day the happiest of my life.

I am but too sensible that this kind of treatment may appear to you with the face of an arbitrary and illegal imposition: but as the consequences, not only to *ourselves*, but to *both our families*, may be fatal, if you cannot be moved in my favour; let me beseech you to forgive this act of compulsion, on the score of the necessity you your dear self have laid me under to be guilty of it; and to permit the solemnity of next Thursday to include an act of oblivion of all past offences.

The orders I have given to the people of the house are: "That you shall be obeyed in every particular that is consistent with my expectations of finding you there on my return to town on Wednesday next: that Mrs. Sinclair, and her nieces, having incurred your just displeasure, shall not, without your orders, come into your presence: that neither shall Dorcas, till she has fully cleared her conduct to your satisfaction, be permitted to attend you: but Mabel, in her place; of whom you seemed some time ago to express some liking. Will I have left behind me to attend your commands. If he be either negligent or impertinent, *your* dismission shall be a dismission of him from my service for ever. But, as to letters which may be sent you, or any which you may have to send, I must humbly entreat that none such pass *from* or *to* you, for the few days that I shall be absent." But I do assure you, madam, that the seals of both sorts shall be sacred: and the letters, if such be sent, shall be given into your own hands the moment the ceremony is performed, or before, if you require it.

Meantime I will inquire, and send you word, how Miss Howe does; and to what, if I can be informed, her long silence is owing.

Dr. Perkins I found here, attending my lord, when I arrived with Dr. S. He acquaints me that your father, mother, uncles, and the still *less* worthy persons of your family, are well; and intend to be all at your Uncle Harlowe's next week; I presume, with intent to keep his anniversary. This can make no alteration, but a happy one, as to *persons*, on Thursday; because Mr. Tomlinson assured me, that, if anything fell out to hinder your uncle's coming up in person (which, however, he did not then expect), he would be satisfied if his friend the captain were proxy for him. I shall send a man and horse to-morrow to the captain, to be at greater certainty.

I send this by a special messenger, who will wait your pleasure in relation to the impatiently wished-for Thursday: which I humbly hope will be signified by a line.

My lord, though hardly sensible, and unmindful of everything but of your felicity, desires his most affectionate compliments to you. He has in readiness to present you a very valuable set of jewels; which he hopes will be acceptable, whether he lives to see you adorn them or not.

Lady Sarah and Lady Betty have also their tokens of respect ready to court your acceptance: but may Heaven incline you to give the opportunity of receiving their personal compliments, and those of my Cousins Montague, before the next week be out!

His lordship is exceeding ill. Dr. S. has no hopes of him. The only consolation I can have for the death of a relation who loves me so well, if he *do* die, must arise from the additional power it will put into my hands of showing how much I am,

My dearest life,
Your ever affectionate and faithful
LOVELACE.

Letter LV—Mr Lovelace to Miss Clarissa Harlowe
[Superscribed to Mrs. Lovelace]

M. Hall, Sunday Night, June 25.

MY DEAREST LOVE,—I cannot find words to express how much I am mortified at the return of my messenger without a line from you.

Thursday is so near, that I will send messenger after messenger every four hours, till I have a favourable answer; the one to meet the other, till its eve arrives, to know if I may venture to appear in your presence with the hope of having my wishes answered on that day.

Your love, madam, I neither expect, nor ask for; nor will, till my future behaviour gives you cause to think I deserve it. All I at present presume to wish, is to have it in my power to do you all the justice I can now do you and to your generosity will I leave it, to reward me, as I shall merit, with your affection.

At present, revolving my poor behaviour of Friday night before you, I think I should sooner choose to go to my last audit, unprepared for it as I am, than to appear in your presence, unless you give me some hope that I shall be received as your elected husband, rather than (however deserved) as a detested criminal.

Let me, therefore, propose an expedient, in order to spare my own confusion; and to spare you the necessity for that soul-harrowing recrimination, which I cannot stand, and which must be disagreeable to yourself—to name the church, and I will have everything in readiness; so that our next interview will be, in a manner, at the very altar; and then you will have the kind husband to forgive for the faults of the ungrateful lover. If your resentment be still too high to write more, let it only be in your own dear hand, these words, *St. Martin's Church, Thursday* —or these, *St. Giles's Church, Thursday*; nor will I insist upon any inscription or subscription, or so much as the initials of your name. This shall be all the favour I will expect, till the dear hand itself is given to mine, in presence of that Being whom I invoke as a witness of the inviolable faith and honour of

Your adoring,

LOVELACE.

Letter LVI—Mr. Lovelace to Miss Clarissa Harlowe
[*Superscribed to Mrs. Lovelace*]

M. Hall, Monday, June 26.

ONCE more, my dearest love, do I conjure you to send me the four requested words. There is no time to be lost. And I would not have next Thursday go over, without being entitled to call you mine, for the world; and that as well for your sake as my own. Hitherto all that has passed is between you and me only; but, after Thursday, if my wishes are unanswered, the whole will be before the world.

My lord is extremely ill, and endures not to have me out of his sight for one half-hour. But this shall not have the least weight with me if you be pleased to hold out the olive-branch to me in the four requested words.

I have the following intelligence from Captain Tomlinson:

"All your family are at your Uncle Harlowe's. Your uncle finds he cannot go up; and names Captain Tomlinson for his proxy. He proposes to keep all your family with him till the captain assures him that the ceremony is over.

"Already he has begun, with hope of success, to try to reconcile your mother to you."

My Lord M. but just now has told me how happy he should think himself to have an opportunity, before he dies, to salute you as his niece. I have put him in hopes that he shall see you; and have told him, that I will go to town on Wednesday, in

order to prevail upon you to accompany me down on Thursday
or Friday. I have ordered a set to be in readiness to carry me
up; and, were not my lord so very ill, my Cousin Montague tells
me she would offer *her* attendance on you. If you please,
therefore, we can set out for this place the moment the solemnity
is performed.

Do not, dearest creature, dissipate all these promising
appearances, and, by refusing to save your own and your
family's reputation in the eye of the world, use yourself worse
than the ungratefullest wretch on earth has used you. For, if
we are married, all the disgrace you imagine you have suffered
while a single lady, will be my own; and only known to ourselves.

Once more, then consider well the situation we are both in;
and remember, my dearest life, that Thursday will be soon here;
and that you have no time to lose.

In a letter sent by the messenger whom I dispatch with this,
I have desired that my friend, Mr. Belford, who is your very
great admirer, and who knows all the secrets of my heart, will
wait upon you, to know what I am to depend upon as to the
chosen day.

Surely, my dear, you never could, at any time, suffer half so
much from cruel suspense as I do.

If I have not an answer to this, either from your own goodness,
or through Mr. Belford's intercession, it will be too late for me
to set out: and Captain Tomlinson will be disappointed, who
goes to town on purpose to attend your pleasure.

One motive for the gentle restraint I have presumed to lay you
under, is to prevent the mischiefs that might ensue (as probably
to the *more* innocent, as to the *less*) were you to write to anybody
while your passions were so much raised and inflamed against me.
Having apprised you of my direction to the women in town on
this head, I wonder you should have endeavoured to send a
letter to Miss Howe, although in a cover directed to that young
lady's [1] servant; as you must think it would be likely to fall
into my hands.

The just sense of what I have deserved the contents *should be*,
leaves me no room to doubt what they *are*. Nevertheless, I
return it you enclosed, with the seal, as you will see, unbroken.

Relieve, I beseech you, dearest madam, by the four requested
words, or by Mr. Belford, the anxiety of

Your ever affectionate and obliged

LOVELACE.

[1] *The lady had made an attempt to send away a letter.*

Remember, there will not, there *cannot* be time for further writing, and for my coming up by Thursday, *your uncle's birthday.*

Letter LVII—Mr. Lovelace to John Belford, Esq.

Monday, June 26.

THOU wilt see the situation I am in with Miss Harlowe by the enclosed copies of three letters; to two of which I am so much scorned as not to have one word given me in answer; and of the third (now sent by the messenger who brings thee this) I am afraid as little notice will be taken—and if so, her day of grace is absolutely over.

One would imagine (so long used to constraint too as she has been) that she might have been satisfied with the triumph she had over us all on Friday night: a triumph that to this hour has sunk my pride and my vanity so much, that I almost hate the words *plot, contrivance, scheme*; and shall mistrust myself in future for every one that rises to my inventive head.

But seest thou not that I am under a necessity to continue her at Sinclair's, and to prohibit all her correspondences?

Now, Belford, as I really, in my present mood, think of nothing less than marrying her, if she let not Thursday slip; I would have thee attend her, in pursuance of the intimation I have given her in my letter of this date; and vow for me, swear for me, bind thy soul to her for my honour, and use what arguments thy friendly heart can suggest, in order to procure me an answer from her; which, as thou wilt see, she may give in four words only. And then I purpose to leave Lord M. (dangerously ill as he is) and meet her at her appointed church, in order to solemnize: if she will sign but *Cl. H.* to *thy* writing the four words, that shall do; for I would not come up to be made a fool of in the face of all my family and friends.

If she should let the day go off, I shall be desperate. I am entangled in my own devices, and cannot bear that she should detect me.

Oh, that I had been honest! What a devil are all my plots come to! What do they end in, but one grand plot upon myself, and a title to eternal infamy and disgrace! But, depending on thy friendly offices, I will say no more of this. Let her send me but one line! But *one* line! To treat me as *unworthy* of her notice; yet be altogether in my power—I cannot—I will not bear that.

My lord, as I said, is extremely ill. The doctors give him

over. He gives himself over. Those who would not have him die, are afraid he will die. But as to myself, I am doubtful: for these long and violent struggles between the constitution and the disease (though the latter has three physicians and an apothecary to help it forward, and all three, as to their prescriptions, of different opinions too) indicate a plaguy tough habit, and favour more of recovery than death: and the more so, as he has no sharp or acute mental organs to whet out his bodily ones, and to raise his fever above the symptomatic helpful one.

Thou wilt see in the enclosed what pains I am at to dispatch messengers; who are constantly on the road to meet each other, and one of them to link in the chain with a fourth, whose station is in London, and five miles onward, or till met. But, in truth, I have some other matters for them to perform at the same time, with my lord's banker and his lawyer; which will enable me, if his lordship is so good as to die this bout, to be an over-match for some of my other relations. I don't mean Charlotte and Patty; for they are noble girls; but others, who have been scratching and clawing underground like so many moles in my absence; and whose workings I have discovered since I have been down, by the little heaps of dirt they have thrown up.

A speedy account of thy commission, dear Jack! The letter travels all night.

Letter LVIII—Mr. Belford to Robert Lovelace, Esq.

London, June 27, Tuesday.

You must excuse me, Lovelace, from engaging in the office you would have me undertake, till I can be better assured you really intend honourably at last by this much injured lady.

I believe you know your friend Belford too well, to think he would be easy with you or with any man alive, who should seek to make him promise for him what he never intended to perform. And let me tell thee that I have not much confidence in the honour of a man, who by *imitation of hands* (I will only call it) has shown so little regard to the honour of his own relations.

Only that thou hast such jesuitical qualifyings, or I should think thee at last touched with remorse, and brought within view of being ashamed of thy cursed inventions by the ill success of thy last: which I heartily congratulate thee upon.

Oh, the divine lady! But I will not aggravate!

Nevertheless, when thou writest, that, in thy *present mood,* thou thinkest of marrying, and yet canst so *easily* change thy *mood*: when I know thy heart is against the state: that the four words thou courtest from the lady are as much to thy purpose, as if she wrote forty; since it will show she can forgive the highest injury that can be offered to woman; and when I recollect how easily thou canst find excuses to postpone; thou must be more explicit a good deal, as to thy real intentions, and future honour, than thou art; for I cannot trust to a temporary remorse; which is brought on by disappointment too, and not by principle; and the like of which thou hast so often got over.

If thou canst convince me time enough for the day, that thou meanest to do honourably by her, in *her own* sense of the word; or, if not time enough, wilt fix some other day (which thou oughtest to leave to her option, and not bind her down for the Thursday; and the rather, as thy pretence for so doing is founded on an absolute fiction); I will then most cheerfully undertake thy cause; by *person*, if she will admit me to her presence; if she will not, by *pen*. But, in this case, thou must allow me to be guarantee for thy faith. And, if so, as much as I value thee, and respect thy skill in all the qualifications of a gentleman, thou mayest depend upon it that I will act up to the character of a guarantee, with more honour than the princes of our day usually do—to their shame be it spoken.

Meantime, let me tell thee that my heart bleeds for the wrongs this angelic lady has received: and if thou dost *not* marry her, if she will *have* thee; and, when married, make her the best and tenderest of husbands; I would rather be a dog, a monkey, a bear, a viper, or a toad, than thee.

Command me with honour, and thou shalt find none readier to oblige thee than

Thy sincere friend,
JOHN BELFORD.

Letter LIX—Mr. Lovelace to John Belford, Esq.

M. Hall, June 27, Tuesday Night, near 12.

YOURS reached me this moment, by an extraordinary push in the messengers.

What a man of honour, thou, of a sudden!

And so, in the imaginary shape of a guarantee, thou threatenest me!

Had I *not* been in earnest as to the lady, I should not have offered to employ thee in the affair. But, let me say, that *hadst* thou undertaken the task, and I had afterwards thought fit to

change my mind, I should have contented myself to tell thee,
that that *was* my mind when thou engagedst for me, and to have
given thee the reasons for the change, and then left thee to thy
own direction: for never knew I what fear of man was—nor fear
of woman neither, till I became acquainted with Miss Clarissa
Harlowe; nay, what is *most* surprising, till I came to have her
in my power.

And so thou wilt not wait upon the charmer of my heart,
but upon terms and conditions! Let it alone, and be cursed; I
care not. But so much credit did I give to the value thou
expressedst for *her*, that I thought the office would have been as
acceptable to *thee*, as serviceable to me; for what was it, but to
endeavour to persuade her to consent to the reparation of her
own honour? For what have I done but disgraced myself, and
been a thief to my own joys? And if there be a union of hearts,
and an intention to solemnize, what is there wanting but the
foolish ceremony? And that I still offer. But if she will keep
back her hand; if she will make me hold out mine in vain, how
can I help it?

I write her one more letter, and if, after she has received that,
she keep silence, she must thank herself for what is to follow.

But, after all, my heart is wholly hers. I love her beyond
expression; and cannot help it. I hope, therefore, she will
receive this last tender as I wish. I hope she intends not, like
a true woman, to plague, and vex, and tease me, now she has
found her power. If she will take me to mercy now these
remorses are upon me (though I scorn to condition with *thee* for
my sincerity), all her trials, as I have heretofore declared, shall
be over; and she shall be as happy as I can make her: for,
ruminating upon all that has passed between us, from the first
hour of our acquaintance till the present, I must pronounce that
she is virtue itself, and, once more I say, has no equal.

As to what you hint, of leaving to her choice another day, do
you consider that it will be impossible that my contrivances
and stratagems should be much longer concealed? This makes
me press *that* day, though so near; and the more, as I have made
so much ado about her uncle's anniversary. If she send me the
four words, I will spare no fatigue to be in time, if not for the
canonical hour at church, for some other hour of the day in her
own apartment, or any other; for money will do everything:
and *that* I have never spared in this affair.

To show thee that I am not at enmity with thee, I enclose
the copies of two letters—one to her: it is the *fourth*, and must be

the *last* on the subject—the other to Captain Tomlinson; calculated, as thou wilt see, for him to show her

And now, Jack, interfere in this case or not, thou knowest the mind of

R LOVELACE.

Letter LX—Mr. Lovelace to Miss Clarissa Harlowe
[Superscribed to Mrs. Lovelace]

M. Hall, Wedn. Morn. One o'clock. June 28.

NOT one line, my dearest life, not one word, in answer to three letters I have written! The time is now so short, that this *must* be the last letter that can reach you on this side of the important hour that might make us legally one.

My friend Mr. Belford is apprehensive that he cannot wait upon you in time, by reason of some urgent affairs of his own.

I the less regret the disappointment, because I have procured a *more* acceptable person, as I hope, to attend you; Captain Tomlinson I mean: to whom I had applied for this purpose before I had Mr. Belford's answer.

I was the more solicitous to obtain this favour from him, because of the office he is to take upon him, as I humbly presume to hope, to-morrow. That office obliged him to be in town as this day: and I acquainted him with my unhappy situation with you; and desired that he would show me, on this occasion, that I had as much of his favour and friendship as your uncle had; since the whole treaty must be broken off, if he could not prevail upon you in my behalf.

He will dispatch the messenger directly; whom I propose to meet in person at Slough; either to proceed onward to London with a joyful heart, or to return back to M. Hall with a broken one.

I ought not (but cannot help it) to anticipate the pleasure Mr. Tomlinson proposes to himself, in acquainting you with the likelihood there is of your mother's seconding your uncle's views. For, it seems, he has privately communicated to her his laudable intentions· and *her* resolution depends, as well as *his*, upon what to-morrow will produce.

Disappoint not then, I beseech you, for a hundred persons' sakes, as well as for mine, *that* uncle and *that* mother, whose displeasure I have heard you so often deplore.

You may think it impossible for me to reach London by the

canonical hour. If it should, the ceremony may be performed in your own apartment, at any time in the day, or at night: so that Captain Tomlinson may have it to aver to your uncle, that it was performed on his anniversary.

Tell but the captain that you *forbid me not* to attend you: and that shall be sufficient for bringing to you, on the wings of love,

Your ever grateful and affectionate

LOVELACE.

Letter LXI—To Mr. Patrick M'Donald, at his lodgings, at Mr. Brown's, Peruke-maker, in St. Martin's Lane, Westminster

M. Hall, Wedn. Morning, Two o'clock.

DEAR M'DONALD,—The bearer of this has a letter to carry to the lady.[1] I have been at the trouble of writing a copy of it; which I enclose, that you may not mistake your cue.

You will judge of my reasons for antedating the enclosed sealed one,[2] directed to you by the name of Tomlinson; which you are to show the lady as in confidence. You will open it of course.

I doubt not your dexterity and management, dear M'Donald; nor your zeal; especially as the hope of cohabitation must now be given up. Impossible to be carried is that scheme. I might break her heart, but not incline her will. Am in earnest therefore to marry her, if she let not the day slip.

Improve upon the hint of her mother. That must touch her. But John Harlowe, *remember*, has *privately* engaged that lady— *privately*, I say; else (not to mention the reason for her Uncle Harlowe's former expedient), you know, she might find means to get a letter away to the one or the other, to know the truth; or to Miss Howe, to engage *her* to inquire into it: and if she should, the word *privately* will account for the uncle's and mother's denying it.

However, fail not, as from me, to charge our mother and her nymphs to redouble their vigilance both as to her person and letters. All 's upon a crisis now. But she must not be treated ill neither.

Thursday over, I shall know what to resolve upon.

If necessary, you must assume authority. The devil 's in 't, if such a girl as this shall awe a man of your years and experience. You are not in love with her as I am. Fly out, if she doubt your honour. Spirits *naturally* soft may be beat out of their play and

---

[1] See the preceding letter.　　　　[2] See the next letter.

borne down (though ever so much raised) by higher anger. All women are cowards at bottom: only violent where they *may*. I have often stormed a girl out of her mistrusts, and made her yield (before she knew where she was) to the point indignantly *mistrusted*; and that to make up with me, though I was the aggressor.

If this matter succeed as I 'd have it (or if *not*, and do not fail by your fault), I will take you off the necessity of pursuing your cursed smuggling; which otherwise may one day end fatally for you.

We are none of us perfect, M'Donald. This sweet lady makes me serious sometimes in spite of my heart. But as private vices are less blamable than public; and as I think *smuggling* (as it is called) a national evil; I have no doubt to pronounce you a much worse man than myself, and as such shall take pleasure in reforming you.

I send you enclosed ten guineas, as a small earnest of further favours. Hitherto you have been a very clever fellow.

As to clothes for Thursday, Monmouth Street will afford a ready supply. Clothes quite new would make your condition suspected. But you may defer that care till you see if she can be prevailed upon. Your riding-dress will do for the first visit. Nor let your boots be over clean. I have always told you the consequence of attending to the *minutiæ*, where art (or *imposture*, as the ill-mannered would call it) is designed—your linen rumpled and soily, when you wait upon her—easy terms these—just come to town—remember (as formerly) to loll, to throw out your legs, to stroke and grasp down your ruffles, as if of significance enough to be careless. What though the presence of a fine lady would require a different behaviour, are you not of years to dispense with politeness? You can have no design upon her, you know. You are a father yourself of daughters as old as she. Evermore is *parade* and *obsequiousness* suspectable: it must show either a foolish head, or a knavish heart. Assume airs of *consequence* therefore; and you will be treated as a *man* of consequence. I have often more than half ruined myself by my complaisance; and, being afraid of control, have brought control upon myself.

I think I have no more to say at present. I intend to be at Slough, or on the way to it, as by mine to the lady. Adieu, honest M'Donald.

R. L.

Letter LXII—To Captain Antony Tomlinson

[*Enclosed in the preceding; to be shown to the lady as in confidence*]

M. Hall, Tuesday Morn. June 27.

DEAR CAPTAIN TOMLINSON,—An unhappy misunderstanding having arisen between the dearest lady in the world and me (the particulars of which she perhaps may give you, but I will not, because I might be thought partial to myself); and she refusing to answer my most pressing and respectful letters; I am at a most perplexing uncertainty whether she will meet us or not next Thursday to solemnize.

My lord is so extremely ill, that if I thought she would not oblige me, I would defer going up to town for two or three days. He cares not to have me out of his sight: yet is impatient to salute my beloved as his niece before he dies. This I have promised to give him an opportunity to do; intending, if the dear creature will make me happy, to set out with her for this place directly from church.

With regret I speak it of the charmer of my soul; that irreconcilableness is her family fault. The less excusable indeed in *her*, as she herself suffers by it in so high a degree from her own relations.

Now, sir, as you *intended* to be in town some time before Thursday, if it be not too great an inconvenience to you, I could be glad you would go up as soon as possible, for my sake: and this I the more boldly request, as I presume that a man who has so many great affairs of his own in hand as you have, would be glad to be at a certainty himself as to the day.

You, sir, can so pathetically and justly set before her the unhappy consequences that will follow if the day be postponed, as well with regard to her uncle's disappointment, as to the part *you have assured me* her mother is willing to take in the wished-for reconciliation, that I have great hopes she will suffer herself to be prevailed upon. And a man and horse shall be in waiting to take your dispatches, and bring them to me.

But if you cannot prevail in my favour you will be pleased to satisfy your friend, Mr. John Harlowe, that it is not my fault that he is not obliged. I am, dear sir,

> Your extremely obliged
> And faithful servant,
> R. LOVELACE.

Letter LXIII—To Robert Lovelace, Esq.

Wedn. June 28, near 12 o'clock.

HONOURED SIR,—I received yours, as your servant desired me to acquaint you, *by ten this morning.* Horse and man were in a foam

I instantly equipped myself, as if come off from a journey, and posted away to the lady, intending to plead great affairs that I came not before, in order to favour your *antedate*; and likewise to be in a *hurry*, to have a pretence to *hurry her ladyship*, and to take no denial for her giving a *satisfactory* return to your messenger: but, upon my entering Mrs. Sinclair's house, I found all in the greatest consternation.

You must not, sir, be surprised. It is a trouble to me to be the relater of the bad news: but so it is—The lady is gone off. She was missed but half an hour before I came.

Her waiting-maid is run away, or hitherto is not to be found: so that they conclude it was by her connivance.

They had sent, before I came, to my honoured masters, Mr. Belton, Mr. Mowbray, and Mr. Belford. Mr. Tourville is out of town.

High words are passing between Madam Sinclair, and Madam Horton, and Madam Martin; as also with Dorcas. And your servant William threatens to hang or drown himself.

They have sent to know if they can hear of Mabel, the waiting-maid, at her mother's, who it seems lives in Chick Lane, West Smithfield; and to an uncle of hers also, who keeps an alehouse at Cowcross, hard by, and with whom she lived last.

Your messenger, having just changed his horse, is come back: so I will not detain him longer than to add, that I am, with great concern for this misfortune, and thanks for your seasonable favour and kind intentions towards me [I am sure this was not my fault],

Honoured sir,
Your most obliged, humble servant,
PATRICK M'DONALD.

Letter LXIV—Mr. Mowbray to Robert Lovelace, Esq.

Wednesday, 12 o'clock.

DEAR LOVELACE,—I have plaguy news to acquaint thee with. Miss Harlowe is gone off! Quite gone, by my soul! I have not time for particulars, your servant being gone off. But if I had, we are not yet come to the bottom of the matter. The ladies here are all blubbering like devils, accusing one another most confoundedly: whilst Belton and I damn them all together in thy name.

If thou shouldst hear that thy fellow Will is taken dead out of some horse-pond, and Dorcas cut down from her bed's tester from dangling in her own garters, be not surprised. Here's the devil to pay. Nobody serene but Jack Belford, who is taking minutes of examinations, accusations, and confessions, with the significant air of a Middlesex justice; and intends to write at large all particulars, I suppose.

I heartily condole with thee: so does Belton. But it may turn out for the best: for she is gone away with thy marks, I understand. A foolish little devil! Where will she mend herself? For nobody will look upon her. And they tell me that thou wouldst certainly have married her had she stayed. But I know thee better.

Dear Bobby, adieu. If Lord M. will die now, to comfort thee for this loss, what a *seasonable* exit would he make! Let's have a letter from thee. Prithee do. Thou canst write devil-like to Belford, who shows us nothing at all.

Thine heartily,

RD. MOWBRAY.

Letter LXV—Mr. Belford to Robert Lovelace, Esq.

Thursday, June 29.

THOU hast heard from M'Donald and Mowbray the news. Bad or good, I know not which thou 'lt deem it. I only wish I could have given thee joy upon the same account, before the unhappy lady was seduced from Hampstead: for then of what an ungrateful villainy hadst thou been spared the perpetration, which now thou hast to answer for!

I came to town purely to serve thee with her, expecting that thy next would satisfy me that I might endeavour it without dishonour: and at first when I found her gone, I half pitied thee; for now wilt thou be inevitably blown up: and in what an execrable light wilt thou appear to all the world! Poor Lovelace! Caught in thy own snares! Thy punishment is but beginning!

But to my narrative; for I suppose thou expectest all particulars from me, since Mowbray has informed thee that I have been collecting them.

"The noble exertion of spirit she had made on Friday night, had, it seems, greatly disordered her; insomuch that she was not visible till Saturday evening; when Mabel saw her; and she seemed to be very ill: but on Sunday morning, having dressed herself, as if designing to go to church, she ordered Mabel to get her a coach to the door.

"The wench told her she was to obey her in everything but the calling of a coach or chair, or in relation to letters.

"She sent for Will, and gave him the same command.

"He pleaded his master's orders to the contrary, and desired to be excused.

"Upon this, down she went herself, and would have gone out without observation: but finding the street door double locked, and the key not in the lock, she stepped into the street parlour, and would have thrown up the sash to call out to the people passing by, as they doubted not: but that, since her last attempt of the same nature, had been fastened down.

"Hereupon she resolutely stepped into Mrs. Sinclair's parlour in the back house; where were the old devil and her two partners; and demanded the key of the street door, or to have it opened for her.

"They were all surprised; but desired to be excused, and pleaded your orders.

"She asserted that you had no authority over her; and never should have any: that their present refusal was their own act and deed: she saw the intent of their back house, and the reason of putting her there: she pleaded her condition and fortune; and said they had no way to avoid utter ruin, but by opening their doors to her, or by murdering her, and burying her in their garden or cellar, too deep for detection: that already what had been done to her was punishable by death: and bid them at their peril detain her."

What a noble, what a right spirit has this charming creature, in cases that will justify an exertion of spirit!

"They answered that Mr. Lovelace could prove his marriage and would indemnify them.   And they all would have vindicated their behaviour on Friday night, and the reputation of their house: but refusing to hear them on that topic, she flung from them, threatening.

"She then went up half a dozen stairs in her way to her own apartment: but, as if she had bethought herself, down she stepped again, and proceeded towards the street parlour; saying, as she passed by the infamous Dorcas, I'll make myself protectors, though the windows suffer: but that wench, of her own head, on the lady's going out of that parlour to Mrs. Sinclair's, had locked the door, and taken out the key: so that finding herself disappointed, she burst into tears, and went menacing and sobbing upstairs again.

"She made no other attempt till the effectual one. Your letters and messages, they supposed, coming so fast upon one another (though she would not answer one of them), gave *her* some amusement, and an assurance to *them* that she would at last forgive you; and that then all would end as you wished.

"The women, in pursuance of your orders, offered not to obtrude themselves upon her; and Dorcas also kept out of her sight all the rest of Sunday; also on Monday and Tuesday. But by the lady's condescension (even to familiarity) to Mabel, they imagined that she must be working in her mind all that time to get away: they therefore redoubled their cautions to the wench: who told them so faithfully all that passed between her lady and her, that they had no doubt of her fidelity to her wicked trust.

"''Tis probable she might have been contriving something all this time; but saw no room for perfecting any scheme: the contrivance by which she effected her escape seems to me not to have been fallen upon till the very day: since it depended partly upon the *weather*, as it proved. But it is evident she hoped something from Mabel's simplicity, or gratitude, or compassion, by cultivating all the time her civility to her.

"Polly waited on her early on Wednesday morning; and met with a better reception than she had *reason* to expect. She complained however with warmth of her confinement. Polly said there would be a happy end to it (if it *were* a confinement) next day, she presumed. She absolutely declared to the contrary, in the way Polly meant it; and said, That Mr. Lovelace on his *return* [*which looked as if she intended to wait for it*], should have reason to repent the orders he had given, as *they all should* their observance of them: let him send twenty letters, she would not answer one, be the consequence what it would; nor give him hope of the least favour, while she was in that house. She had given Mrs. Sinclair and themselves fair warning, she said: no orders of another ought to make them detain a free person: but having made an open attempt to *go*, and been detained by them, she was the calmer, she told Polly; let *them* look to the consequence.

"But yet she spoke this with temper; and Polly gave it as her opinion (with apprehension for their own safety) that, having so good a handle to punish them all, she would not go away if she might. And what, inferred Polly, is the indemnity of a man who has committed the vilest of rapes on a person of condition; and must himself, if prosecuted for it, either fly or be hanged?

"Sinclair [so I will still call her], upon this representation of Polly, foresaw, she said, *the ruin of her poor house* in the issue of this *strange* business; and the infamous Sally and Dorcas bore their parts in the apprehension: and this put them upon thinking it advisable for the future, that the street door should generally in the daytime be only left upon a bolt-latch, as they called it, which anybody might open on the inside; and that the key should be kept in the door; that their numerous *comers* and *goers*, as they called their guests, should be able to give evidence *that she might have gone out if she would*: not forgetting, however, to renew their orders to Will, to Dorcas, to Mabel, and the rest, to redouble their vigilance on this occasion, to prevent her escape: none of them doubting, at the same time, that her love of a man so considerable in *their* eyes, and the prospect of what was to happen, as she had reason to believe, on Thursday, her uncle's birthday, would (though perhaps not till the *last hour*, for her *pride's sake*, was their word) engage her to change her temper.

"They believe that she discovered the key to be left in the door; for she was down more than once to walk in the little garden, and seemed to cast her eye each time to the street door.

"About eight yesterday morning, an hour after Polly had left her, she told Mabel she was sure she should not live long; and having a good many suits of apparel, which after her death would be of no use to anybody she valued, she would give her a brown lustring gown, which, with some alterations, to make it more suitable to her degree, would a great while serve her for a Sunday wear; for that she (Mabel) was the only person in that house of whom she could think without terror or antipathy.

"Mabel expressing her gratitude upon the occasion, the lady said she had nothing to employ herself about; and if she could get a workwoman directly, she would look over her things then, and give her what she intended for her.

"Her mistress's mantua-maker, the maid replied, lived but a little way off; and she doubted not that she could procure *her*, or one of her journey-women, to alter the gown out of hand.

"I will give you also, said she, a quilted coat, which will require but little alteration, if any; for you are much about my stature: but the gown I will give directions about, because the sleeves and the robings and facings must be altered for your wear, being, I believe, above your station: and try, said she, if you can get the workwoman, and we 'll advise about it. If she cannot come now, let her come in the afternoon; but I had rather now, because it will amuse me to give you a lift.

"Then stepping to the window, It rains, said she [and so it had done all the morning]: slip on the hood and short cloak I have seen you wear, and come to me when you are ready to go out, because you shall bring me in something that I want.

"Mabel equipped herself accordingly, and received her commands to buy her some trifles, and then left her; but, in her way out, stepped into the back parlour, where Dorcas was with Mrs. Sinclair, telling her where she was going, and on what account, bidding Dorcas look out till she came back. So faithful was the wench to the trust reposed in her, and so little had the lady's generosity wrought upon her.

"Mrs. Sinclair commended her; Dorcas envied her, and took her cue: and Mabel soon returned with the mantua-maker's journey-woman (she was resolved, she said, she would not come without her); and then Dorcas went off guard.

"The lady looked out the gown and petticoat, and before the workwoman caused Mabel to try it on; and, that it might fit the better, made the willing wench pull off her upper petticoat, and put on that she gave her. Then she bid them go into Mr. Lovelace's apartment, and contrive about it before the pier-glass there, and stay till she came to them, to give them her opinion.

"Mabel would have taken her own clothes, and hood, and short cloak with her: but her lady said, No matter; you may put them on again here, when we have considered about the alterations: there 's no occasion to litter the other room.

"They went; and instantly, as it is supposed, she slipped on Mabel's gown and petticoat over her own, which was white damask, and put on the wench's hood, short cloak, and ordinary apron, and down she went.

"Hearing somebody tripping along the passage, both Will and Dorcas whipped to the inner hall door, and saw her; but, taking her for Mabel, Are you going far, Mabel, cried Will?

"Without turning her face, or answering, she held out her hand, pointing to the stairs; which they construed as a caution for them to look out in her absence; and supposing she would not be long gone, as she had not in form repeated her caution to them, up went Will, tarrying at the stairs-head in expectation of the supposed Mabel's return.

"Mabel and the workwoman waited a good while, amusing themselves not disagreeably, the one with contriving in the way of her business, the other delighting herself with her fine gown and coat: but at last, wondering the lady did not come in to them, Mabel tiptoed it to her door, and tapping, and not being answered, stepped into the chamber.

"Will at that instant, from his station at the stairs-head, seeing Mabel in her *lady's* clothes; for he had been told of the present [gifts to servants fly from servant to servant in a minute], was very much surprised, having, as he thought, just seen her go out in *her own*; and stepping up, met her at the door. How the devil can this be? said he. Just now you went out in your own dress! How came you here in this? And how could you pass me unseen? But nevertheless, kissing her, said he would now brag he had kissed his lady, or one in her clothes.

"I am glad, Mr. William, cried Mabel, to see you here so diligently. But know you where my lady is?

"In my master's apartment, answered Will. Is she not? Was she not talking with you this moment?

"No, that's Mrs. Dolins's journey-woman.

"They both stood aghast, as they said; Will again recollecting he had seen Mabel, as he thought, go out in her own clothes. And while they were debating and wondering, up comes Dorcas with your fourth letter, just then brought for her lady; and seeing Mabel dressed out (whom she had likewise beheld a little before, as she supposed, in her common clothes) she joined in the wonder; till Mabel, re-entering the lady's apartment, missed her own clothes; and then suspecting what had happened, and letting the others into the ground of her suspicion, they all agreed that she had certainly escaped. And then followed such an uproar of mutual accusation, and *You should have done this*, and *You should have done that*, as alarmed the whole house; every apartment in both houses giving up its devil, to the number of fourteen or fifteen, including the mother and her partners.

"Will told them *his* story; and then ran out, as on the like occasion formerly, to make inquiry whether the lady was seen by any of the coachmen, chairmen, or porters, plying in that neighbourhood: while Dorcas cleared herself immediately, and that at the poor Mabel's expense, who made a figure as guilty as awkward, having on the suspected price of her treachery; which Dorcas, out of envy, was ready to tear from her back.

"Hereupon all the pack opened at the poor wench, while the

mother, foaming at the mouth, bellowed out her orders for seizing the suspected offender; who could neither be heard in her own defence, nor, *had* she been heard, would have been believed.

"That such a perfidious wretch should ever disgrace *her* house! was the mother's cry. *Good* people *might* be corrupted; but it was a fine thing if such a house as *hers* could not be faithfully served by cursed creatures who were hired knowing the business they were to be employed in, and who had no pretence to *principle*! Damn her! the wretch proceeded. She had no patience with her! Call the cook, and call the scullion!

"They were at hand.

"See that guilty *pyeball* devil, was her word (her lady's gown upon her back). But I'll punish her for a warning to all betrayers of their trust. Put on the great gridiron this moment (an oath or a curse at every word): make up a roaring fire. The cleaver bring me this instant—I'll cut her into quarters with my own hands; and carbonade and broil the traitress for a feast to all the dogs and cats in the neighbourhood; and eat the first slice of the toad myself, without salt or pepper.

"The poor Mabel, frightened out of her wits, expected every moment to be torn in pieces, having half a score open-clawed paws upon her all at once. She promised to confess all. But that all, when she had obtained a hearing, was nothing; for *nothing* had she to confess.

"Sally hereupon, with a *curse of mercy,* ordered her to retire; undertaking that she and Polly would examine her themselves, that they might be able to write all particulars to *his honour*; and then, if she could not clear herself, or, if guilty, give some account of the lady (who had been so *wicked* as to give them all this trouble), so as they might get her again, then the cleaver and gridiron might go to work with all her heart.

"The wench, glad of this reprieve, went upstairs; and while Sally was laying out the law, and prating away in her usual dictatorial manner, whipped on another gown, and sliding downstairs, escaped to her relations. And this flight, which was certainly more owing to *terror* than *guilt*, was, in the true Old Bailey construction, made a confirmation of the latter."

These are the particulars of Miss Harlowe's flight. Thou 'lt hardly think me too minute. How I long to triumph over thy impatience and fury on the occasion!

Let me beseech thee, my dear Lovelace, in thy next letter, to rave most gloriously! I shall be grievously disappointed if thou dost not.

Where, Lovelace, can the poor lady be gone? And who can describe the distress she must be in?

By thy former letters, it may be supposed that she can have very little money: nor, by the suddenness of her flight, more clothes than those she has on. And thou knowest who once said,[1] "Her parents will not receive her. Her uncles will not entertain her. Her Norton is in their direction, and cannot. Miss Howe dare not. She has not one friend or intimate in town; entirely a stranger to it." And, let me add, has been despoiled of her honour by the man for whom she made all these sacrifices; and who stood bound to her by a thousand oaths and vows, to be her husband, her protector, and friend!

How strong must be her resentment of the barbarous treatment she has received! How worthy of herself, that it has made her *hate* the man she once *loved*! And, rather than marry him, choose to expose her disgrace to the whole world; to forego the reconciliation with her friends which her heart was so set upon; and to hazard a thousand evils to which her youth and her sex may too probably expose an indigent and friendless beauty.

Rememberest thou not that home push upon thee, in one of the papers written in her delirium; of which, however, it savours not?

I will assure thee, that I have very often since most seriously reflected upon it: and as thy intended second outrage convinces me that it made no impression upon thee then, and perhaps thou hast never thought of it since, I will transcribe the sentence.

"If, as religion teaches us, God will judge us, in a great measure, by our benevolent or evil actions to one another. O wretch! bethink thee, in time bethink thee, how great must be thy condemnation!"[2]

And is this amiable doctrine the sum of religion? Upon my faith I believe it is. For to indulge a serious thought, since we are not atheists, except in *practice*, does God, the BEING of beings, want anything of us for HIMSELF? And does He not enjoin us works of mercy to one another, as the means to obtain *His* mercy? A sublime principle, and worthy of the SUPREME SUPERINTENDENT and FATHER of all things! But, if we *are* to be judged by this noble principle, what, *indeed*, must be *thy* condemnation on the score of this lady only! And what *mine*,

[1] See vol. ii, p. 275.   [2] See pp. 207–8 of this volume.

and what all our *confraternity's*, on the score of other women; though we are none of us half so bad as thou art, as well for want of inclination, I hope, as of opportunity!

I must add, that, as well for thy *own* sake, as for the *lady's*, I wish ye were yet to be married to each other. It is the only medium that can be hit upon to salve the honour of both. All that's past may yet be concealed from the world, and from her relations; and thou mayst make amends for all her sufferings, if thou resolvest to be a tender and kind husband to her.

And if this really be thy intention, I will accept, with pleasure, of a commission from thee that shall tend to promote so good an end, whenever she can be found; that is to say, if she will admit to her presence a man who professes friendship to thee. Nor can I give a greater demonstration, that I am

Thy sincere friend,
J. BELFORD.

P.S. Mabel's clothes were thrown into the passage this morning; nobody knows by whom.

Letter LXVI—Mr. Lovelace to John Belford, Esq.

Friday, June 30.

I AM ruined, undone, blown up, destroyed, and worse than annihilated, that's certain! But was not the news shocking enough, dost thou think, without thy throwing into the too weighty scale reproaches, which thou couldst have had no opportunity to make but for my own voluntary communications: at a time too when, as it falls out, I have another very sensible disappointment to struggle with?

I imagine, if there be such a thing as future punishment, it must be none of the smallest mortifications, that a *new* devil shall be punished by a worse *old one*. And, *take that!* And, *take that!* to have the old satyr cry to the screaming sufferer, laying on with a cat-o'-nine-tails, with a star of burning brass at the end of each: and, *for what! for what!* Why, if the truth might be fairly told, for not being so bad a devil as myself.

Thou art, surely, casuist good enough to know (what I have insisted upon [1] heretofore) that the sin of seducing a credulous and easy girl is as great as that of bringing to your lure an incredulous and watchful one.

However ungenerous an appearance what I am going to say may have from *my* pen, let me tell thee, that if such a woman as

[1] See vol. ii, pp. 252-3.

Miss Harlowe chose to enter into the matrimonial state [*I am resolved to disappoint thee in thy meditated triumph over my rage and despair I*], and, according to the old patriarchal system, to go on contributing to get sons and daughters, with no other view than to bring them up piously, and to be good and useful members of the commonwealth, what a devil had she to do, to let her fancy run a gadding after a rake? one whom she *knew* to be a rake?

Oh! but truly she hoped to have the merit of reclaiming him. She had formed pretty notions how charmingly it would look to have a penitent of her own making dangling at her side to church, through an applauding neighbourhood: and, as their family increased, marching with her thither, at the head of their boys and girls processionally as it were, boasting of the fruits of their *honest desires*, as my good lord bishop has it in his licence. And then, what a comely sight, all kneeling down together in one pew, according to eldership, as we have seen in effigy, a whole family upon some old monument, where the honest cavalier in armour is presented kneeling, with uplifted hands, and half a dozen jolter-headed, crop-eared boys behind him, ranged *gradatim* or step-fashion according to age and size, all in the same posture—facing his pious dame, with a ruff about her neck, and as many whey-faced girls all kneeling behind *her*: an altar between them, and an opened book upon it: over their heads semilunary rays darting from gilded clouds, surrounding an achievement-motto, IN COELO SALUS—or QUIES—perhaps, if they have happened to live the usual married life of brawl and contradiction.

It is certainly as much my misfortune to have fallen in with Miss Clarissa Harlowe, were I to have valued my reputation or ease, as it is that of Miss Harlowe to have been acquainted with me. And, after all, what have I done more than prosecute the maxims by which thou and I and every rake are governed, and which, before I knew this lady, we have pursued from pretty girl to pretty girl, as fast as we had set one down, taking another up; just as the fellows do with the flying coaches and flying horses at a country fair, with a *Who rides next! Who rides next!*

But here, in the present case, to carry on the volant metaphor (for I must either be merry, or mad), is a pretty little miss just come out of her hanging-sleeve coat, brought to buy a pretty little fairing; for the world, Jack, is but a great fair, thou knowest; and, to give thee serious reflection for serious, all its toys but tinselled hobby-horses, gilt gingerbread, squeaking trumpets, painted drums, and so forth.

Now behold this pretty little miss skimming from booth to booth, in a very pretty manner. One pretty little fellow called Wyerley perhaps; another jiggeting rascal called Biron, a third simpering varlet of the name of Symmes, and a more hideous villain than any of the rest, with a long bag under his arm, and parchment settlements tagged to his heels, ycleped Solmes; pursue her from raree-show to raree-show, shouldering upon one another at every turning, stopping when she stops, and set a spinning again when she moves. And thus dangled after, but still in the eye of her watchful guardians, traverses the pretty little miss through the whole fair, equally delighted and delighting: till at last, taken with the invitation of the *laced-hat orator*, and seeing several pretty little bib-wearers stuck together in the flying coaches, cutting safely the yielding air, in the one go-up the other go-down picture-of-the-world vehicle, and all with as little fear as wit, is tempted to ride next.

In then suppose she slyly pops, when *none of her friends are near her*: and if, after two or three ups and downs, her pretty head turns giddy, and she throws herself out of the coach when at its elevation, and so dashes out her pretty little brains, who can help it? And would you hang the poor fellow whose *professed trade* it was to set the pretty little creatures a flying?

'Tis true, this pretty little miss, being a *very* pretty little miss, being a *very much-admired* little miss, being a very *good* little miss, who always minded her book, and had passed through her sampler doctrine with high applause; had even stitched out in gaudy propriety of colours, an Abraham offering up Isaac, a Samson and the Philistines, and flowers, and knots, and trees, and the sun and the moon, and the seven stars, all hung up in frames with glasses before them, for the admiration of her future grandchildren: who likewise was entitled to a very pretty little estate: who was descended from a pretty little family upwards of one hundred years' gentility; which lived in a very pretty little manner, respected a very little on their own accounts, a great deal on hers:—

For such a pretty little miss as this to come to so great a misfortune, must be a very sad thing: but, tell me, would not the losing of any ordinary child, of any other less considerable family, of less shining or amiable qualities, have been as great and as heavy a loss to that family, as the losing this pretty little miss could be to hers?

To descend to a very low instance, and that only as to *personality*; hast thou any doubt, that thy strong-muscled bony face was as much admired by thy mother, as if it had been the face of a Lovelace, or any other handsome fellow? And had thy picture been drawn, would she have forgiven the painter, had he not expressed so exactly thy lineaments, as that every one should have discerned the likeness? The *handsome* likeness is all that is wished for. Ugliness made familiar to us, with the partiality natural to fond parents, will be beauty all the world over. Do thou apply.

.   .   .   .   .   .

But alas, Jack, all this is but a copy of my countenance, drawn to evade thy malice! Though it answer thy unfriendly purpose to own it, I cannot forbear to own it, that I am stung to the very soul with this unhappy—*accident*, must I call it? Have I nobody whose throat, either for carelessness or treachery, I ought to cut in order to pacify my vengeance?

When I reflect upon my *last* iniquitous intention, the *first* outrage so nobly resented, as well as, so far as she was able, so nobly *resisted*, I cannot but conclude that I was under the power of fascination from these accursed Circes; who, pretending to know their own sex, would have it that there is in every woman a yielding, or a weak-resisting moment to be met with: and that *yet*, and *yet*, and *yet*, I had not tried enough: but that, if neither love nor terror should enable me to hit that lucky moment, when, by help of their cursed arts, she was *once overcome*, she would be for *ever overcome*: appealing to all my experience, to all my knowledge of the sex, for a justification of their assertion.

My appealed-to experience, I own, was but too favourable to their argument: for dost thou think I could have held my purpose against such an angel as this, had I ever before met with one so much in earnest to defend her honour against the un-wearied artifices and perseverance of the man she loved? Why then were there not *more* examples of a virtue so immovable? Or why was this singular one to fall to my lot? Except indeed to *double my guilt*; and at the same time to convince all that should hear her story, *that there are angels as well as devils in the flesh?*

So much for confession; and for the sake of humouring my conscience; with a view likewise to disarm thy malice by acknowledgment: since no one shall say worse of me, than I will of myself on this occasion.

One thing I will nevertheless add, to show the sincerity of my contrition: 'Tis this, that if thou canst by any means find her out within these three days, or any time before she has discovered the stories relating to Captain Tomlinson and her uncle to be what they are; and if thou canst prevail upon her to consent; I will actually, in thy presence and his (he to represent her uncle), marry her.

I am still in hopes it may be so—she cannot be long concealed —I have already set all engines at work to find her out; and if I do, what *indifferent* persons [and no one of her *friends*, as thou observest, will look upon her] will care to embroil themselves with a man of my figure, fortune, and resolution? Show her this part then, or any other part, of this letter, at thy own discretion, if thou *canst* find her: for, after all, methinks I would be glad that this affair, which is bad enough in itself, should go off without worse personal consequences to anybody else; and yet it runs in my mind, I know not why, that sooner or later it will draw a few drops of blood after it; except she and I can make it up between ourselves. And this may be another reason why she should not carry her resentment too far—not that such an affair would give me much concern neither, were I to choose my man, or men; for I heartily hate all her family but herself; and ever shall.

.   .   .   .   .   .

Let me add, that the lady's plot to escape appears to me no extraordinary one. There was much more luck than probability that it should do: since, to make it succeed, it was necessary that Dorcas and Will, and Sinclair and her nymphs, should be all deceived, or off their guard. It belongs to me, when I see them, to give them my hearty thanks that they were; and that their selfish care to provide for their own future security, should induce them to leave their outward door upon their bolt-latch, and be cursed to them.

Mabel deserves a pitch-suit and a bonfire, rather than the lustring; and as her clothes are returned, let the lady's be put to her others, to be sent to her, when it can be told whither—but not till I give the word neither; for we must get the dear fugitive back again, if possible.

I suppose that my stupid villain, who knew not such a goddess-shaped lady with a mien so noble, from the awkward and bent-shouldered Mabel, has been at Hampstead to see after her. And yet I hardly think she would go thither. He ought to go through every street where bills for lodgings are up, to inquire after a new-comer. The houses of such as deal in women's matters, and tea, coffee, and such-like, are those to be inquired at for her. If some tidings be not quickly heard of her, I would not have either Dorcas, Will, or Mabel appear in my sight, whatever their superiors think fit to do.

This, though written in character, is a very long letter, considering it is not a narrative one, or a journal of proceedings, like most of my former; for such will unavoidably and naturally, as I may say, run into length. But I have so used myself to write a great deal of late, that I know not how to help it. Yet I must add to its length, in order to explain myself on a hint I gave at the beginning of it; which was, that I have another disappointment, besides this of Miss Harlowe's escape, to bemoan.

And what dost think it is? Why, the old peer, *pox* of his tough constitution (for that malady would have helped him on), has made shift by fire and brimstone, and the devil knows what, to force the gout to quit the counterscarp of his stomach, just as it had collected all its strength, in order to storm the citadel of his heart. In short they have, by the mere force of stink-pots, hand-grenades, and pop-guns, driven the slow-working pioneer quite out of the trunk into the extremities; and there it lies nibbling and gnawing upon his great toe; when I had hoped a fair end both of the distemper and the distempered.

But I, who could write to *thee* of laudanum, and the wet cloth, formerly, yet let £8,000 a year slip through my fingers, when I had entered upon it more than in imagination [for I had begun to ask the stewards questions, and to hear them talk of fines and renewals, and such sort of stuff], *deserve* to be mortified.

Thou canst not imagine how differently the servants, and even my cousins, look upon me since yesterday to what they did before. Neither the one nor the other bow or curtsy half so low. Nor am I a quarter so often *his honour*, and *your honour*, as I was within these few hours, with the former: and as to the latter—it is *Cousin Bobby* again, with the usual familiarity, instead of *sir*, and *sir*, and, *If you please, Mr. Lovelace*. And now they have the insolence to congratulate me on the recovery of the *best of uncles*; while I am forced to seem as much delighted as they, when, would it do me good, I could sit down and cry my eyes out.

I had bespoken my mourning in imagination, after the example of a certain foreign minister, who, before the death or even, last illness of Charles II as honest White Kennet tells us, had half exhausted Blackwell Hall of its sables—an indication, as the historian would insinuate, that the monarch was to be poisoned, and the ambassador in the secret—and yet, fool that I was, I could not take the hint. What a devil does a man read history for, if he cannot profit by the examples he finds in it?

But thus, Jack, is an observation of the old peer's verified, *that one misfortune seldom comes alone*: and so concludes

Thy doubly-mortified
LOVELACE.

Letter LXVII—Miss Clarissa Harlowe to Miss Howe
Wednesday Night, June 28.

O MY DEAREST MISS HOWE!—Once more have I escaped—but, alas! *I*, my *best self*, have *not* escaped! Oh, your poor Clarissa Harlowe! *You* also will hate me, I fear! Yet you won't, when you know all!

But no more of my self! my *lost* self. You that can rise in a morning to be blessed, and to bless; and go to rest delighted with your own reflections, and in your unbroken, unstarting slumbers, conversing with saints and angels, the former only more pure than yourself, as they have shaken off the encumbrance of body; YOU shall be my subject, as you have long, long been my only pleasure. And let me, at awful distance, revere my beloved Anna Howe, and in *her* reflect upon what her Clarissa Harlowe once was!

.   .   .   .

Forgive, Oh, forgive my rambling. My peace is destroyed. My intellects are touched. And what flighty nonsense must you read, if now you will vouchsafe to correspond with me, as formerly!

O my best, my dearest, my *only* friend! What a tale have I to unfold! But still upon *self*, this vile, this hated *self*! I will shake it off, if possible; and why should I not, since I think, except one wretch, I hate nothing so much? Self, then, be banished from *self* one moment (for I doubt it *will* for no longer), to inquire after a *dearer* object, my beloved Anna Howe!—whose mind, all robed in spotless white, charms and irradiates—but what would I say?——

.   .   .   .   .

And how, my dearest friend, after this rhapsody, which, on reperusal, I would not let go, but to show you what a distracted mind dictates to my trembling pen; *how do you?* You have been very ill, it seems. That you are *recovered*, my dear, let me hear. That your mother is well, pray let me hear, and hear quickly. This comfort surely is owing to me; for if life is no *worse* than chequer-work, I must now have a little white to come, having seen nothing but black, all unchequered dismal black, for a great, great while.

.   .   .   .   .   .

And what is all this wild incoherence for? It is only to beg to know how you have been, and how you now do, by a line directed for Mrs. Rachel Clark, at Mr. Smith's, a glove shop in King Street, Covent Garden; which (although my abode is a secret to everybody else) will reach the hands of—*your unhappy*—but that's not enough——

Your miserable

CLARISSA HARLOWE.

Letter LXVIII—Mrs. Howe to Miss Clarissa Harlowe
[Superscribed as directed in the preceding.]

Friday, June 30.

MISS CLARISSA HARLOWE,—You will wonder to receive a letter from me. I am sorry for the great distress you seem to be in. Such a hopeful young lady as you were! But see what comes of disobedience to parents!

For my part, although I pity you, yet I much more pity your poor father and mother. Such education as they gave you! such improvement as you made! and such delight as they took in you!—And all come to this!——

But pray, miss, don't make my Nancy guilty of your fault; which is that of disobedience. I have charged her over and over not to correspond with one who has made such a giddy step. It is not to her reputation, I am sure. You *knew* that I so charged her; yet you go on corresponding together, to my very great vexation; for she has been very perverse upon it more than once. *Evil communication*, miss—you know the rest.

Here, people cannot be unhappy by themselves, but they must involve their friends and acquaintance, whose discretion has kept them clear of their errors, into near as much unhappiness as if they had run into the like of their own heads! Thus my poor daughter is always in tears and grief. And she has postponed her own felicity, truly, because *you* are unhappy!

If people, who seek their own ruin, could be the only sufferers by their headstrong doings, it were something: but, O miss, miss, what have *you* to answer for, who have made as many grieved hearts as have known you? The whole sex is indeed wounded by you: for who but Miss Clarissa Harlowe was proposed by every father and mother for a pattern for their daughters?

I write a long letter, where I proposed to say but a few words; and those to forbid you writing to my Nancy: and this as well because of the false step you have made, as because it will grieve her poor heart, and do you no good. If you love her, therefore, write not to her. Your sad letter came into my hands, Nancy being abroad, and I shall not show it her: for there would be no comfort for her, if she saw it, nor for me whose delight she is—as you once was to your parents.

But you seem to be sensible enough of your errors now. So are all giddy girls, when it is too late: and what a crest-fallen figure then does their self-willed obstinacy and headstrongness compel them to make!

I may say too much: only as I think it proper to bear that testimony against your rashness which it behoves every careful parent to bear: and none more than

Your compassionating well-wisher,
ANNABELLA HOWE.

I send this by special messenger, who has business only so far as Barnet, because you shall have no need to write again; knowing how you love writing: and knowing, likewise, *that misfortune makes people plaintive.*

Letter LXIX—*Miss Clarissa Harlowe to Mrs. Hawe*

Saturday, July 1.

PERMIT me, madam, to trouble you with a few lines, were it only to thank you for your reproofs; which have, nevertheless, drawn fresh streams of blood from a bleeding heart.

My story is a dismal story. It has circumstances in it that would engage pity, and possibly a judgment not altogether unfavourable, were those circumstances known. But it is my business, and shall be *all* my business, to repent of my failings, and not endeavour to extenuate them.

Nor will I seek to distress your worthy mind. If *I cannot suffer alone,* I will make as few parties as I can in my sufferings. And indeed, I took up my pen with this resolution when I wrote the letter which has fallen into your hands. It was only to know,

III—*L 884

and that for a very particular reason, as well as for affection unbounded, if my dear Miss Howe, from whom I had not heard of a long time, were ill; as I had been told she was; and if so, how she now does. But my injuries being recent, and my distresses having been exceeding great, *self* would crowd into my letter. When distressed, the human mind is apt to turn itself to every one in whom it imagined or wished an interest, for pity and consolation. Or, to express myself better and more concisely, in your own words, *misfortune makes people plaintive*: and to whom, if not to a friend, can the afflicted complain?

Miss Howe being abroad when my letter came, I flatter myself that she is recovered. But it would be some satisfaction to me to be informed if she *has been ill*. Another line from *your* hand would be too great a favour: but, if you will be pleased to direct any servant to answer *yes*, or *no*, to that question, I will not be further troublesome.

Nevertheless, I must declare that my Miss Howe's friendship was all the comfort I had or expected to have in this world; and a line from her would have been a cordial to my fainting heart. Judge then, dearest madam, how reluctantly I must obey your prohibition—but yet I will endeavour to obey it; although I should have hoped, as well from the tenor of all that has passed between Miss Howe and me, as from *her* established virtue, that she could not be tainted by *evil communication*, had one or two letters been permitted. This, however, I ask not for, since I think I have nothing to do, but to beg of God (who, I hope, has not yet withdrawn His grace from me, although He is pleased to let loose His justice upon my faults) to give me a truly broken spirit, if it be not already broken enough, and then to take to His mercy

The unhappy
CLARISSA HARLOWE.

Two favours, good madam, I have to beg of you. The first that you will not let any of my relations know that you have heard from me. The other, that no living creature be apprised where I am to be heard of, or directed to. This is a point that concerns me more than I can express. In short, my preservation from further evils may depend upon it.

Letter LXX—Miss Clarissa Harlowe to Hannah Burton

Thursday, June 29.

MY GOOD HANNAH,—Strange things have happened to me since you were dismissed my service (so sorely against my will) and your pert fellow-servant set over me. But that must be all forgotten now.

How do you, my Hannah? Are you recovered of your illness? If you are, do you choose to come and be with me? Or *can* you conveniently?

I am a very unhappy creature, and, being among all strangers, should be glad to have *you* with me, of whose fidelity and love I have had so many acceptable instances.

Living or dying, I will endeavour to make it worth your while, my Hannah.

If you are recovered, as I hope, and if you have a good place, it may be they would bear with your absence, and suffer somebody in your room *for a month or so*: and, by that time, I hope to be provided for, and you may then return to your place.

Don't let any of my friends know of this my desire; whether you can come or not.

I am at Mr. Smith's, a hosier's and glove shop, in King Street, Covent Garden.

You must direct to me by the name of Rachel Clark.

Do, my good Hannah, come if you can, to your poor young mistress, who always valued you, and always will, whether you come or not.

I send this to your mother at St. Albans, not knowing where to direct to you. Return me a line, that I may know what to depend upon: and I shall see you have not forgotten the pretty hand you were taught, in happy days, by

Your true friend,

CLARISSA HARLOWE.

Letter LXXI—Hannah Burton.   [*In answer*]

Monday, July 3.

HONORED MADDAM,—I have not forgot to write, and never will forget anything you, my dear young lady, was so good as to larn me. I am very sorrowfull for your misfortens, my dearest young lady; so sorrowfull, I do not know what to do. Gladd at harte would I be to be able to come to you. But indeed I have not been able to stir out of my rome here at my mother's, ever since I was forsed to leave my plase with a roomatise, which has made me quite and clene helpless. I will pray for you night and day, my dearest, my kindest, my goodest young lady, who have been so badly used; and I am very sorry I cannot come to do you love and sarvice; which will ever be in the harte of mee to do, if it was in my power: who am,

Your most dewtifull sarvant to command,

HANNAH BURTON.

Letter LXXII—Miss Clarissa Harlowe to Mrs. Judith Norton
Thursday, June 29.

MY DEAR MRS. NORTON,—I address myself to you after a very long silence (which, however, was not owing either to want of love or duty), principally to desire you to satisfy me in two or three points, which it behoves me to know.

My father, and all the family, I am informed, are to be at my Uncle Harlowe's this day, as usual. Pray acquaint me, if they *have* been there? And if they were cheerful on the anniversary occasion? And also, if you have heard of any journey, or intended journey, of my brother, in company with Captain Singleton and Mr. Solmes.

Strange things have happened to me, my dear worthy and maternal friend—very strange things! Mr. Lovelace has proved a very barbarous and ungrateful man to me. But, God be praised, I have escaped from him. Being among absolute strangers (though I think worthy folks), I have written to Hannah Burton to come and be with me. If the good creature fall in your way, pray encourage her to come to me. I always intended to have her, she knows: but hoped to be in happier circumstances.

Say nothing to any of my friends that you have heard from me.

Pray, do you think my father would be prevailed upon, if I were to supplicate him by letter, to take off the heavy curse he laid upon me at my going from Harlowe Place? I can expect no other favour from him: but that being literally fulfilled as to my prospects in this life, I hope it will be thought to have operated far enough: and my heart is *so* weak!—it is *very* weak! But for my father's *own* sake—what *should* I say? Indeed, I hardly know how I *ought* to express myself on this sad subject! But it will give ease to my mind to be released from it.

I am afraid *my poor*, as I used to call the good creatures to whose necessities I was wont to administer by your faithful hands, have missed me of late. But now, alas! I am poor myself. It is not the least aggravation of my fault, nor of my regrets, that with such inclinations as God had given me I have put it out of my power to do the good I once pleased myself to think I was born to do. It is a sad thing, my dearest Mrs. Norton, to render useless to ourselves and the world, by our own rashness, the talents which Providence has entrusted to us, for the service of both.

But these reflections are now too late; and perhaps I ought to have kept them to myself. Let me, however, hope that you love me still. Pray let me hope that you do. And then, notwithstanding my misfortunes, which have made me seem ungrateful to the kind and truly maternal pains you have taken with me from my cradle, I shall have the happiness to think that there is *one* worthy person who hates not

The unfortunate

CLARISSA HARLOWE.

Pray remember me to my foster-brother. I hope he continues dutiful and good to you.

Be pleased to direct for Rachel Clark, at Mr. Smith's in King Street, Covent Garden. But keep the direction an absolute secret.

Letter LXXIII—Mrs. Norton. [In answer]

Saturday, July 1.

YOUR letter, my dearest young lady, cuts me to the heart! Why will you not let me know all your distresses! Yet you have said enough!

My son is very good to me. A few hours ago he was taken with a feverish disorder. But I hope it will go off happily, if his ardour for business will give him the recess from it which his good master is willing to allow him. He presents his duty to you, and shed tears at hearing your sad letter read.

You have been misinformed as to your family's being at your Uncle Harlowe's. They did not intend to be there. Nor was the day kept at all. Indeed, they have not stirred out, but to church (and that but three times), ever since the day you went away. Unhappy day for them, and for all who know you! To me, I am sure, most particularly so! My heart now bleeds more and more for you.

I have not heard a syllable of such a journey as you mention, of your brother, Captain Singleton, and Mr. Solmes. There has been some talk indeed of your brother's setting out for his northern estates: but I have not heard of it lately.

I am afraid no letter will be received from you. It grieves me to tell you so, my dearest young lady. No evil can have happened to you, which they do not *expect* to hear of; so great is their antipathy to the wicked man, and so bad is his character.

I cannot but think hardly of their unforgivingness: but there is no judging for others by one's self. Nevertheless I will add that, if you had had as gentle spirits to deal with as your own, or, I will be bold to say, as mine, these evils had never happened either to them or to you. I knew your virtue, and your love of virtue, from your very cradle; and I doubted not but *that*, with God's grace, would always be your guard. But you could never be driven; nor was there occasion to drive you—so generous, so noble, so discreet. But how does my love of your amiable qualities increase my affliction; as these recollections must do yours!

You are escaped, my dearest miss—happily, I hope—that is to say, with your honour—else how great must be your distress! Yet from your letter I dread the worst.

I am very seldom at Harlowe Place. The house is not the house it used to be, since you went from it. Then they are *so* relentless! And, as I cannot say harsh things of the beloved child of my *heart*, as well as *bosom*, they do not take it *amiss* that I stay away.

Your Hannah left her place ill some time ago; and, as she is still at her mother's at St. Albans, I am afraid she continues ill. If so, as you are among strangers, and I cannot encourage you at present to come into *these* parts, I shall think it my duty to attend you (let it be taken as it will) as soon as my Tommy's indisposition will permit; which I hope will be soon.

I have a little money by me. You say you *are poor yourself*. How grievous are those words from one entitled and accustomed to affluence! Will you be so good to command it, my beloved young lady? It is most of it your own bounty to me. And I should take a pride to restore it to its original owner.

Your poor bless you, and pray for you continually. I have so managed your last benevolence, and they have been so healthy, and have had such constant employ, that it has held out; and will hold out till the happier times return which I continually pray for.

Let me beg of you, my dearest young lady, to take to yourself all those aids which good persons, like you, draw from RELIGION in support of their calamities. Let your sufferings be what they will, I am sure you have been innocent in your intention. So do not despond. None are made to suffer above what they *can*, and therefore *ought* to bear.

We know not the methods of Providence, nor what wise ends it may have to serve in its seemingly severe dispensations to its poor creatures.

Few persons have greater reason to say this than myself. And since we are apt in calamities to draw more comfort from example than precept, you will permit me to remind you of my own lot: for who has had a greater share of afflictions than myself?

To say nothing of the loss of an excellent mother, at a time of life when motherly care is most wanted; the death of a dear father, who was an ornament to his cloth (and who had qualified me to be his scribe and amanuensis), just as he came within view of a preferment which would have made his family easy, threw me friendless into the wide world; threw me upon a very careless, and, which was much worse, a very unkind husband. Poor man! But he was spared long enough, thank God, in a tedious illness, to repent of his neglected opportunities, and his light principles; which I have always thought of with pleasure, although I was left the more destitute for his chargeable illness, and ready to be brought to bed, when he died, of my Tommy.

But this very circumstance, which I thought the unhappiest that I could have been left in (so short-sighted is human prudence!), became the happy means of recommending me to your mother, who, in regard to my character, and in compassion to my very destitute circumstances, permitted me, as I made a conscience of not parting with my poor boy, to nurse both you and him, born within a few days of each other. And I have never since wanted any of the humble blessings which God has made me contented with.

Nor have I known what a very great grief was, from the day of my poor husband's death, till the day that your parents told me how much they were determined that you should have Mr. Solmes; when I was apprised not only of your aversion to him, but how unworthy he was of you: for then I began to dread the consequences of forcing so generous a spirit; and, till then, I never feared Mr. Lovelace, attracting as was his person, and specious his manners and address. For I was sure you would never have him, if he gave you not good reason to be convinced

of his reformation; nor till your friends were as well satisfied in it
as yourself.   But that unhappy misunderstanding between your
brother and Mr. Lovelace, and their joining so violently to force
you upon Mr. Solmes, did all that mischief, which has cost you
and them so dear, and poor me all my peace!   Oh, what has not
this ungrateful, this doubly guilty man to answer for!

Nevertheless, you know not what God has in store for you yet!
But if you are to be punished all your days here, for example's
sake, in a case of such importance, for your one false step, be
pleased to consider that this life is but a state of probation; and
if you have your purification in it, you will be the more happy.
Nor doubt I that you will have the higher reward *hereafter* for
submitting to the will of Providence *here* with patience and
resignation.

You see, my dearest Miss Clary, that I make no scruple to call
the step you took a false one.   In *you* it was less excusable than
it would have been in any other young lady; not only because of
your superior talents, but because of the opposition between
your character and *his*: so that if you had been provoked to quit
your father's house, it needed not to have been with him.   Nor
needed I, indeed, but as an instance of my *impartial* love, to have
written this to you.[1]

After this, it will have an unkind, and perhaps at this time an
unseasonable appearance, to express my concern that you have
not before favoured me with a line.   Yet, if you can account to
yourself for your silence, I dare say I ought to be satisfied; for
I am sure you love me: as I both love and honour you, and ever
will, and the more for your misfortunes.

One consolation, methinks, I have, even when I am sorrowing
for your calamities; and that is, that I know not any young
person so qualified to shine the brighter for the trials she may be
exercised with: and yet it is a consolation that ends in adding
to my regrets for your afflictions, because you are blessed with a
mind so well able to bear prosperity, and to make everybody
round you the better for it.   *Woe unto him!* Oh, this wretched,
wretched man!   But I will forbear till I know more.

Ruminating on everything your melancholy letter suggests,
and apprehending, from the gentleness of your mind, the
amiableness of your person, and your youth, the further mis-

[1] Mrs. Norton, having only the family representation and invectives to
form her judgment upon, knew not that Clarissa had determined against
going off with Mr. Lovelace; nor how solicitous she had been to procure for
herself *any other* protection than his, when she apprehended that, if she
stayed she had no way to avoid being married to Mr. Solmes.

fortunes and inconveniences to which you may possibly be subjected, I cannot conclude without asking for your leave to attend you, and that in a very earnest manner.   And I beg of you not to deny me, on any consideration relating to *myself*, or even to the indisposition of my *other* beloved child; if I can be either of use or comfort to you.   Were it, my dearest young lady, but for two or three days, permit me to attend you, although my son's illness should increase, and compel me to come down again at the end of those two or three days.   I repeat my request likewise, that you will command from me the little sum remaining in my hands, of your bounty to your poor, as well as that dispensed to

Your ever affectionate and faithful servant,

JUDITH NORTON.

Letter LXXIV—Miss Cl. Harlowe to Lady Betty Lawrance

Thursday, June 29.

MADAM,—I hope you 'll excuse the freedom of this address, from one who has not the honour to be personally known to you, although you must have heard much of Clarissa Harlowe.   It is only to beg the favour of a line from your ladyship's hand (by the next post, if convenient) in answer to the following questions:

1. Whether you wrote a letter, dated, as I have a memorandum, Wednesday, June 7, congratulating your Nephew Lovelace on his supposed nuptials, as reported to you by Mr. Spurrier, your ladyship's steward, as from one Captain Tomlinson: and in it reproaching Mr. Lovelace as guilty of slight, etc., in not having acquainted your ladyship and the family with his marriage?

2. Whether your ladyship wrote to Miss Montague to meet you at Reading, in order to attend you to your Cousin Leeson's in Albemarle Street; on your being obliged to be in town on your *old Chancery affair*, I remember are the words? And whether you bespoke your nephew's attendance there on Sunday night the 11th?

3. Whether your ladyship and Miss Montague *did* come to town at that time?   And whether you went to Hampstead on Monday, in a hired coach and four, your own being repairing; and took from thence to town the young creature whom you visited there?

Your ladyship will probably guess that these questions are not asked for reasons favourable to your Nephew Lovelace.   But be the answer what it will, it can do *him* no hurt, nor *me* any good; only that I think I owe it to my former hopes (however deceived in them), and even to charity, that a person, of whom I was once willing to think better, should not prove so egregiously abandoned, as to be wanting, in *every* instance, to that veracity which is indispensable in the character of a gentleman.

Be pleased, madam, to direct to me (keeping the direction a secret for the present) to be left at the Belle Savage on Ludgate Hill, till called for.   I am

Your ladyship's most humble servant,
CLARISSA HARLOWE.

Letter LXXV—*Lady Betty Lawrance to Miss Cl. Harlowe*

Saturday, July 1.

DEAR MADAM,—I find that all is not as it should be between you and my Nephew Lovelace.   It will very much afflict me, and all his friends, if he has been guilty of any designed baseness to a lady of your character and merit.

We have been long in expectation of an opportunity to congratulate you and ourselves upon an event most earnestly wished for by us all; since all our hopes of *him* are built upon the power *you* have over him: for, if ever man adored a woman, he is that man, and you, madam, are that woman.

Miss Montague, in her last letter to me, in answer to one of mine, inquiring if she knew from him whether he could call you his, or was likely soon to have that honour, has these words: "I know not what to make of my Cousin Lovelace, as to the point your ladyship is so earnest about.   He sometimes says he is actually married to Miss Cl. Harlowe: at other times, that it is her own fault if he be not: he speaks of her not only with love, but with reverence: yet owns that there is a misunderstanding between them; but confesses that she is wholly faultless.   An angel, and not a woman, he says she is: and that no man living can be worthy of her."

This is what my Niece Montague writes.

God grant, my dearest young lady, that he may not have so heinously offended you that you *cannot* forgive him!   If you are not already married, and refuse to be his, I shall lose all hopes that he ever will marry, or be the man I wish him to be. So will Lord M.   So will Lady Sarah Sadleir.

I will now answer your questions: but, indeed, I hardly know what to write, for fear of widening still more the unhappy difference between you. But yet such a young lady must command everything from me. This then is my answer:

I wrote not any letter to him on or about the 7th of June.

Neither I nor my steward know such a man as Captain Tomlinson.

I wrote not to my niece to meet me at Reading, nor to accompany me to my Cousin Leeson's in town.

My Chancery affair, though, like most Chancery affairs, it be of long standing, is nevertheless now in so good a way that it cannot give me occasion to go to town.

Nor have I been in town these six months: nor at Hampstead for several years.

Neither shall I have any temptation to go to town, except to pay my congratulatory compliments to Mrs. Lovelace. On which occasion I should go with the greatest pleasure; and should hope for the favour of your accompanying me to Glenham Hall, for a month at least.

Be what will the reason of your inquiry, let me entreat you, my dear young lady, for Lord M.'s sake; for my sake; for this giddy man's sake, soul as well as body; and for all our family's sakes; not to suffer this answer to widen differences so far as to make you refuse him, if he already has not the honour of calling you his; as I am apprehensive he has not, by your signing by your family name.

And here let me offer to you my mediation to compose the difference between you, be it what it will. Your cause, my dear young lady, cannot be put into the hands of anybody living more devoted to your service, than into those of

Your sincere admirer, and humble servant,
ELIZ. LAWRANCE.

Letter LXXVI—Miss Clarissa Harlowe to Mrs. Hodges
Enfield, June 29.

MRS. HODGES,—I am under a kind of necessity to write to you, having no one among my relations to whom I dare write, or hope a line from, if I did. It is but to answer a question. It is this:

Whether you know such a man as Captain Tomlinson? And, if you do, whether he be very intimate with my Uncle Harlowe?

I will describe his person, lest, possibly, he should go by another name among you; although I know not why he should.

"He is a thin, tallish man, a little pock-fretten; of a sallowish complexion. Fifty years of age, or more. Of a good aspect when he looks up. He seems to be a serious man, and one who knows the world. He stoops a little in the shoulders. Is of Berkshire. His wife of Oxfordshire; and has several children. He removed lately into your parts from Northamptonshire."

I must desire you, Mrs. Hodges, that you will not let my uncle, nor any of my relations, know that I write to you.

You used to say that you would be glad to have it in your power to serve me. That, indeed, was in my prosperity. But I dare say you will not refuse me in a particular that will oblige me without hurting yourself.

I understand that my father, mother, and sister, and, I presume, my brother and my Uncle Antony, are to be at my Uncle Harlowe's this day. God preserve them all, and may they rejoice in many happy birthdays! You will write six words to me concerning their healths.

Direct, for a particular reason, to Mrs. Dorothy Salcomb, to be left till called for, at the Four Swans Inn, Bishopsgate Street.

You know my handwriting well enough, were not the contents of the letter sufficient to excuse my name, or any other subscription, than that of

YOUR FRIEND.

Letter LXXVII—Mrs. Hodges. [*In answer*]

Sat., July 1.

MADDAM,—I return you an anser, as you wish me to doe. Master is acquented with no sitch man. I am shure no sitch ever came to our house. And master sturs very little out. He has no harte to stur out. For why? Your obstincy makes um not care to see one another. Master's birthday never was kept soe before: for not a sole heere; and nothing but sikeing and sorrowin from master to think how it yused to bee.

I axed master, if soe bee he knoed sitch a man as one Captain Tomlinson? But sayed not whirfor I axed. He sed, No, not he.

Shure this is no trix nor forgary bruing against master by won Tomlinson. Won knoes not what cumpany you may have bin forsed to keep, sen you went away, you knoe, maddam. Exscuse me, maddam; but Lundon is a pestilent plase; and that Squire Luveless is a devil (for all he is sitch a like gentleman to look to) as I hev herd everyboddy say; and think as how you have found by thiss.

I truste, maddam, you wulde not let master cum to harme, if you knoed it, by anyboddy whoe may pretend to be acquented with him: but for fere, I querid with myself iff I shulde not tell him. Butt I was willin to show you, that I wulde plessure you in advarsity, if advarsity bee youre lott, as well as prosprity; for I am none of those as woulde doe otherwiss. Soe no more from

Your humble sarvant, to wish you well,
SARAH HODGES.

Letter LXXVIII—Miss Cl. Harlowe to Lady Betty Lawrance

Monday, July 3.

MADAM,—I cannot excuse myself from giving your ladyship this one trouble more; to thank you, as I most heartily do, for your kind letter.

I must own to you, madam, that the honour of being related to ladies as eminent for their virtue as for their descent, was at first no small inducement with me to lend an ear to Mr. Lovelace's address. And the rather, as I was determined, had it come to effect, to do everything in my power to deserve your favourable opinion.

I had another motive, which I knew would of itself give me merit with your whole family; a presumptuous one (a punishably presumptuous one, as it has proved), in the hope that I might be an humble means in the hand of Providence to reclaim a man who had, as I thought, good sense enough at bottom to be reclaimed; or at least gratitude enough to acknowledge the intended obligation, whether the generous hope were to succeed or not.

But I have been most egregiously mistaken in Mr. Lovelace; the only man, I persuade myself, pretending to be a gentleman, in whom I could have been so *much* mistaken: for while I was endeavouring to save a drowning wretch, I have been, not accidentally, but premeditatedly, and of set purpose, drawn in after him. And he has had the glory to add to the list of those he has ruined, a name that, I will be bold to say, would not have disparaged his own. And this, madam, by means that would shock humanity to be made acquainted with.

My whole end is served by your ladyship's answer to the

questions I took the liberty to put to you in writing. Nor have I a wish to make the unhappy man more odious to you than is necessary to excuse myself for absolutely declining your offered mediation.

When your ladyship shall be informed of the following particulars:

That after he had compulsatorily, as I may say, tricked me into the act of going off with him, he could carry me to one of the vilest houses, as it proved, in London:

That he could be guilty of a wicked attempt, in resentment of which I found means to escape from him to Hampstead:

That, after he had found me out there (I know not how), he could procure two women, dressed out richly, to personate your ladyship and Miss Montague; who, under pretence of engaging me to make a visit in town to your Cousin Leeson (promising to return with me that evening to Hampstead), betrayed me back again to the vile house: where, again made a prisoner, I was first robbed of my senses; and then of my honour. Why should I seek to conceal that disgrace from others which I cannot hide from myself?

When your ladyship shall know that, in the shocking progress to this ruin, wilful falsehoods, repeated forgeries (particularly of one letter from your ladyship, another from Miss Montague, and a third from Lord M.), and numberless perjuries, were not the least of his crimes:

You will judge that I can have no principles that will make me worthy of an alliance with ladies of yours and your noble sister's character, if I could not from my soul declare that such an alliance can never *now* take place.

I will not offer to clear myself entirely of blame: but, as to *him*, I have no fault to accuse myself of: my crime was the corresponding with him at first, when prohibited so to do by those who had a right to my obedience; made still more inexcusable by giving him a clandestine meeting, which put me into the power of his arts. And for this I am content to be punished: thankful that at last I have escaped from him; and have it in my power to reject so wicked a man for my husband: and glad if I may be a warning, since I cannot be an example: which once (very vain, and very conceited as I was) I proposed to myself to be.

All the ill I wish him is, that he may reform; and that I may be the last victim to his baseness. Perhaps this desirable wish may be obtained, when he shall see how his wickedness, his unmerited wickedness! to a poor creature, made friendless by his cruel arts, will end.

I conclude with my humble thanks to your ladyship for your favourable opinion of me; and with the assurance that I will be, while life is lent me,

Your ladyship's grateful and obliged servant,
CLARISSA HARLOWE.

Letter LXXIX—Miss Clarissa Harlowe to Mrs. Norton

Sunday Evening, July 2.

How kindly, my beloved Mrs. Norton, do you soothe the anguish of a bleeding heart! Surely you are mine own mother; and, by some unaccountable mistake, I must have been laid to a family that, having newly found out, or at least suspected, the imposture, cast me from their hearts, with the indignation that such a discovery will warrant.

Oh, that I had indeed been your own child, born to partake of your humble fortunes, an heiress only to that content in which you are so happy! Then should I have had a *truly* gentle spirit to have guided my ductile heart, which force and ungenerous usage sit so ill upon; and nothing of what has happened would have been.

But let me take heed that I enlarge not, by impatience, the breach already made in my duty by my rashness; since, had I not erred, my mother, at least, could never have been thought hard-hearted and unforgiving. Am I not then answerable, not only for my own faults, but for the consequences of them; which tend to depreciate and bring disgrace upon a maternal character never before called in question?

It is kind however in you to endeavour to extenuate the fault of one so greatly sensible of it: and could it be wiped off entirely, it would render me more worthy of the pains you have taken in my education: for it must add to your grief, as it does to my confusion, that, after such promising beginnings, I should have so behaved as to be a disgrace instead of a credit to you and my other friends.

But that I may not make you think me more guilty than I am, give me leave briefly to assure you, that when my story is known I shall be entitled to more compassion than blame, even on the score of going away with Mr. Lovelace.

As to all that happened afterwards, let me only say that although I must call myself a lost creature as to this world, yet have I this consolation left me, that I have not suffered either for want of circumspection, or through credulity or weakness. Not one moment was I off my guard, or unmindful of your early precepts. But (having been enabled to baffle many base contrivances) I was at last ruined by arts the most inhuman. But had I not been rejected by every friend, this low-hearted man had not dared, nor would have had opportunity, to treat me as he has treated me.

More I cannot, at this time, nor need I, say: and this I desire you to keep to yourself, lest resentments should be taken up when I am gone, that may spread the evil which I hope will end with me.

I have been misinformed, you say, as to my principal relations being at my Uncle Harlowe's. The day, you say, was not kept. Nor have my brother and Mr. Solmes—Astonishing! What complicated wickedness has this wretched man to answer for! Were I to tell you, you would hardly believe there could have been such a heart in man.

But one day you may know my whole story! At present I have neither inclination nor words. Oh, my bursting heart! Yet a happy, a wished relief! Were you present, my tears would supply the rest!

.   .   .   .   .

I resume my pen!

And so you fear no letter will be received from me. But DON'T *grieve to tell me so!* I expect everything bad. And such is my distress that had you not bid me hope for mercy from the Throne of Mercy, I should have been afraid that my father's dreadful curse would be completed with regard to both worlds.

For here, an additional misfortune! In a fit of frenzical heedlessness, I sent a letter to my beloved Miss Howe, without recollecting her private address; and it is fallen into her angry mother's hands: and so that dear friend perhaps has anew incurred displeasure on my account. And here too your worthy son is ill; and my poor Hannah, you think, cannot come to me. O my dear Mrs. Norton, *will* you, *can* you, censure *those* whose resentments against me Heaven seems to approve of? and will you acquit *her* whom *that* condemns?

Yet you bid me not despond. I will not, if I can help it. And, indeed, most seasonable consolation has your kind letter afforded me. Yet to God Almighty do I appeal, to avenge my wrongs, and vindicate my inno——

But hushed be my stormy passions! Have I not but this moment said that your letter gave me consolation! May *those* be forgiven who hinder my father from forgiving *me*! And this, as to *them*, shall be the harshest thing that shall drop from my pen.

But although your son should recover, I charge you, my dear Mrs. Norton, that you do not think of coming to me. I don't know still, but your mediation with my mother (although at present your interposition would be so little attended to) may be of use to procure me the revocation of that most dreadful part of my father's curse, which only remains to be fulfilled. The voice of nature must at last be heard in my favour, surely. It will only plead at first to my friends in the still conscious plaintiveness of a young and unhardened beggar! But it will grow more clamorous when *I* have the courage to be so, and shall demand, perhaps, the paternal protection from *further* ruin; and that forgiveness, which those will be little entitled to expect, for their own faults, who shall interpose to have it refused to me, for an *accidental*, not a *premeditated* error: and which, but for them, I had never fallen into.

But again impatiency, founded perhaps on self-partiality, that strange misleader! prevails.

Let me briefly say that it is necessary to my present and future hopes that you keep well with my family. And moreover, should you come, I may be traced out by that means by the most abandoned of men. Say not then that you think you ought to come up to me, *let it be taken as it will:*—for *my sake*, let me repeat (were my foster-brother recovered, as I hope he is), you must *not* come. Nor can I want your advice, while *I* can write, and *you* can answer me. And write I will as often as I stand in need of your counsel.

Then the people I am now with seem to be both honest and humane: and there is in the same house a widow lodger, of low fortunes, but of great merit—almost such another serious and good woman as the dear one to whom I am now writing; who has, as she says, given over all other thoughts of the world but such as shall assist her to leave it happily. How suitable to my own views! There seems to be a comfortable providence in *this* at least—so that at present there is nothing of exigence; nothing that can *require*, or even *excuse*, your coming, when so many better ends may be answered by your staying where you are. A time *may* come when I shall want your last and best assistance: and *then*, my dear Mrs. Norton—and *then* I will bespeak it, and embrace it with my whole heart—and *then* will it not be denied me by anybody.

You are very obliging in your offer of money. But although I was forced to leave my clothes behind me, yet I took several things of value with me, which will keep me from present want. You'll say I have made a miserable hand of it. So indeed I have—and, to look backwards, in a very little while too.

But what shall I do if my father cannot be prevailed upon to recall his malediction? O my dear Mrs. Norton, what a weight must a father's curse have upon a heart so apprehensive as mine! Did I think I should ever have a *father's curse* to deprecate? And yet, only that the temporary part of it is so terribly fulfilled, or I should be as earnest for its recall, for my *father's* sake, as for my own!

You must not be angry with me that I wrote not to you before. You are very right, and very kind, to say you are sure I love you. Indeed I do. And what a generosity [so like yourself!] is there in your praise, to attribute to me more than I merit, in order to raise an emulation in me to *deserve* your praises! You tell me what you expect from me in the calamities I am called upon to bear. May I behave answerably!

I *can* a little account *to myself* for my silence to you, my kind, my dear maternal friend! How equally sweetly and politely do you express yourself on this occasion! I was very desirous, for your sake, as well as for my own, that you should have it to say that we did not correspond: had they thought we did, every word you could have dropped in my favour would have been rejected; and my mother would have been forbid to see you, or to pay any regard to what you should say.

Then I had sometimes better and sometimes worse prospects before me. My worst would only have troubled you to know: my better made me frequently hope that, by the next post, or the next, and so on for weeks, I should have the best news to impart to you that *then* could happen; cold as the wretch had made my heart to *that best*. For how could I think to write to you, with a confession that I was not married, yet lived in the house (nor could I help it) with such a man? Who likewise had given it out to several, that we were actually married, although with restrictions that depended on the reconciliation with my friends? And to disguise the truth, or be guilty of a false-hood, either direct or equivocal, that was what you had never taught me.

But I might have written to you for advice, in my precarious situation, perhaps you will think. But, indeed, my dear Mrs. Norton, I was not lost for want of advice. And this will appear clear to you from what I have already hinted, were I to explain myself no further: for what need had the cruel spoiler to have had recourse to unprecedented arts—I will speak out plainer still (but you must not at present report it), to stupefying potions, and to the most brutal and outrageous force, had I been wanting in my duty?

A few words more upon this grievous subject:

When I reflect upon all that has happened to me, it is apparent that this generally supposed *thoughtless* seducer has acted by me upon a regular and preconcerted plan of villainy.

In order to set all his vile plots in motion, nothing was wanting, from the first, but to prevail upon me, either by force or fraud, to throw myself into his power: and when this was effected, nothing less than the intervention of the paternal authority (which I had not deserved to be exerted in my behalf) could have saved me from the effect of his deep machinations. Opposition from any other quarter would but too probably have precipitated his barbarous and ungrateful violence: and had *you* yourself been with me, I have reason *now* to think, that somehow or other you would have suffered in endeavouring to save me: for never was there, as now I see, a plan of wickedness more steadily and uniformly pursued than *his* has been, against an unhappy creature who merited better of *him*: but the Almighty has thought fit, according to the general course of His Providence, to make the fault bring on its own punishment: but surely not in consequence of my father's dreadful imprecation, "that I might be punished *here*" [O my mamma Norton, pray with me, if so, that *here* it stop!] "by the very wretch in whom I had placed my wicked confidence!"

I am sorry, for your sake, to leave off so heavily. Yet the rest must be brief.

Let me desire you to be secret in what I have communicated to you; at least till you have my consent to divulge it.

God preserve to you your more faultless child!

I will hope for His mercy, although I should not obtain that of any earthly person.

And I repeat my prohibition: you must not think of coming up to

Your ever dutiful

CL. HARLOWE.

The obliging person who left yours for me this day, promised to call to-morrow, to see if I should have anything to return.   I would not lose so good an opportunity.

Letter LXXX—Mrs. Norton to Miss Clarissa Harlowe

Monday Night, July 3.

OH, the barbarous villainy of this detestable man!

And is there a man in the world who could offer violence to so sweet a creature!

And are you sure you are now out of his reach?

You command me to keep secret the particulars of the vile treatment you have met with; or else, upon an unexpected visit which Miss Harlowe favoured me with, soon after I had received your melancholy letter, I should have been tempted to own I had heard from you, and to have communicated to her such parts of your two letters as would have demonstrated your penitence, and your earnestness to obtain the revocation of your father's malediction, as well as his protection from outrages that may still be offered to you. But then your sister would probably have expected a sight of the letters, and even to have been permitted to take them with her to the family.

Yet they *must* one day be acquainted with the sad story: and it is impossible but they must pity you, and forgive you, when they know your early penitence, and your unprecedented sufferings; and that you have fallen by the brutal force of a barbarous ravisher, and not by the vile arts of a seducing lover.

The wicked man gives it out at Lord M.'s, as Miss Harlowe tells me, that he is actually married to you: yet she believes it not; nor had I the heart to let her know the truth.

She put it close to me, whether I had not corresponded with you from the time of your going away? I could safely tell her (as I did) that I had not: but I said, that I was well informed that you took extremely to heart your father's imprecation; and that, if she would excuse me, I would say it would be a kind and sisterly part, if she would use her interest to get you discharged from it.

Among other severe things, she told me that my partial fondness for you made me very little consider the honour of the rest of the family: but, if I had not heard this from you, she supposed I was set on by Miss Howe.

She expressed herself with a good deal of bitterness against that young lady: who, it seems, everywhere, and to everybody (for you must think that your story is the subject of all conversations), rails against your family; treating them, as your sister says, with contempt and even with ridicule.

I am sorry such angry freedoms are taken, for two reasons; first, because such liberties never do any good. I have heard you own that Miss Howe has a satirical vein; but I should hope that a young lady of her sense, and right cast of mind, must know that the end of satire is not to exasperate, but amend; and should never be *personal*. If it *be*, as my good father used to say, it may make an impartial person suspect that the satirist has a natural spleen to gratify; which may be as great a fault in *him*, as any of those which he pretends to censure and expose in *others*.

Perhaps a hint of this from you will not be thrown away.

My second reason is, that these freedoms, from so warm a friend to you as Miss Howe is known to be, are most likely to be charged to your account.

My resentments are so strong against this vilest of men that I dare not touch upon the shocking particulars which you mention of his baseness. What defence, indeed, could there be against so determined a wretch, after you were in his power? I I will only repeat my earnest supplication to you, that, black as appearances are, you will not despair. Your calamities are exceeding great, but then you have talents proportioned to your trials. This everybody allows.

Suppose the worst, and that your family will not be moved in your favour, your Cousin Morden will soon arrive, as Miss Harlowe told me. If he should even be got over to their side, he will however see justice done you; and then may you live an exemplary life, making hundreds happy, and teaching young ladies to shun the snares in which you have been so dreadfully entangled.

As to the man you have lost, is a union with such a perjured heart as his, with such an admirable one as yours, to be wished for? A base, *low-hearted* wretch, as you justly call him, with all his pride of ancestry; and more an enemy to himself with regard to his present and future happiness than to you, in the barbarous and ungrateful wrongs he has done you: I need not, I am sure, exhort you to despise such a man as this; since not to be able to do so, would be a reflection upon a sex to which you have always been an honour.

Your moral character is untainted: the very nature of your sufferings, as you well observe, demonstrates *that*. Cheer up, therefore, your dear heart, and do not despair: for is it not GOD who governs the world, and permits some things, and directs others, as He pleases? And will He not reward *temporary sufferings*, innocently incurred, and piously supported, with *eternal felicity*? And what, my dear, is this poor needle's point of NOW to a *boundless* ETERNITY?

My heart, however, labours under a *double* affliction: for my poor boy is very, *very* bad—a violent fever—nor can it be brought to intermit—pray for *him*, my dearest miss—for his recovery, if God see fit. I hope God *will* see fit. If not (how can I bear to suppose that!), pray for *me*, that He will give me that patience and resignation which I have been wishing to you. I am, my dearest young lady,

Your ever affectionate
JUDITH NORTON.

Letter LXXXI—*Miss Cl. Harlowe to Mrs. Judith Norton*

Thursday, July 6.

I OUGHT not, especially at this time, to add to your afflictions—but yet I cannot help communicating to you (who now are my *only* soothing friend) a new trouble that has befallen me.

I had but one friend in the world, besides you; and she is utterly displeased with me[1]: it is grievous, but for one moment, to lie under a beloved person's censure; and this through imputations that affect one's honour and prudence. There are points so delicate, you know, my dear Mrs. Norton, that it is a degree of dishonour to have a vindication of one's self from them appear to be *necessary*. In the present case, my misfortune is, that I know not how to account, but by guess (so subtle have been the workings of the dark spirit I have been unhappily entangled by), for some of the facts that I am called upon to explain.

Miss Howe, in short, supposes she has found a flaw in my character. I have just now received her severe letter—but I shall answer it, perhaps, in better temper, if I first consider yours: for indeed my patience is almost at an end. And yet I ought to consider *that faithful are the wounds of a friend*. But so *many* things at once! O my dear Mrs. Norton, how shall so young a scholar in the school of affliction be able to bear such heavy and such various evils!

But to leave this subject for a while, and turn to your letter.

[1] See the next letter.

I am very sorry Miss Howe is so lively in her resentments on my account. I have always blamed her very freely for her liberties of this sort with my friends. I once had a good deal of influence over her kind heart, and she made all I said a law to her. But people in calamity have little weight in anything, or with anybody. Prosperity and independence are charming things on this account, that they give force to the counsels of a friendly heart; while it is thought insolence in the miserable to advise, or so much as to remonstrate.

Yet is Miss Howe an invaluable person: and is it to be expected that she should preserve the same regard for my judgment that she had before I forfeited all title to discretion? With what face can I take upon me to reproach a want of prudence in *her*? But if I can be so happy as to re-establish myself in her ever valued opinion, I shall endeavour to enforce upon her your just observations on this head.

You need not, you say, exhort me to despise such a man as him by whom I have suffered—indeed you need not: for I would choose the cruellest death rather than to be his. And yet, my dear Mrs. Norton, I will own to you, *that once I could have loved him—ungrateful man! had he permitted me to love him, I* once *could have loved him.* Yet he never deserved my love. And was not this a fault? But now, if I can but keep out of his hands, and obtain a last forgiveness, and that as well for the sake of my dear friends' future reflections, as for my own present comfort, it is all I wish for.

Reconciliation with my friends I do not expect; nor pardon from them; at least, till in extremity, and as a *viaticum.*

O my beloved Mrs. Norton, you cannot imagine what I have suffered! But indeed my heart is broken! I am sure I shall not live to take possession of that independence, which you think would enable me to atone in some measure for my past conduct.

While this is my opinion, you may believe I shall not be easy till I can obtain a last forgiveness.

I wish to be left to take my own course in endeavouring to procure this grace. Yet know I not, at present, what that course shall be.

I will write. But to *whom* is my doubt. Calamity has not yet given me the assurance to address myself to my FATHER. My UNCLES (well as they once loved me) are hard-hearted. They never had their masculine passions humanized by the tender name of FATHER. Of my BROTHER I have no hope. I have then but my MOTHER, and my SISTER, to whom I can apply.

"And may I not, my dearest mamma, be permitted to lift up my trembling eye to your all-cheering, and your once *more* than indulgent, your *fond* eye, in hopes of seasonable mercy to the poor sick heart that yet beats with life drawn from your own dearer heart? Especially when pardon only, and not restoration, is implored?"

Yet were I able to engage my mother's pity, would it not be a means to make *her* still more unhappy than I have already made her, by the opposition she would meet with, were she to try to give force to that pity?

To my SISTER then, I think, I will apply—yet how hard-hearted has my sister been! But I will not ask for protection; and yet I am in hourly dread that I shall want protection. All I will ask for at present (preparative to the last forgiveness I will implore) shall be only to be freed from the heavy curse that seems to have operated as far as it *can* operate as to *this* life. And surely it was passion, and not intention, that carried it so very far as to the *other*!

But why do I thus add to your distresses? It is not, my dear Mrs. Norton, that I have so *much* feeling for my *own* calamity that I have *none* for *yours*: since yours is indeed an addition to my own. But you have one consolation (a very great one) which I have not: that *your* afflictions, whether respecting your *more* or your *less* deserving child, rise not from any fault of your own.

But what can I do for you more than pray? Assure yourself, that in every supplication I put up for myself, I will, with equal fervour, remember both you and your son. For I am, and ever will be,

Your truly sympathizing and dutiful
CLARISSA HARLOWE.

Letter LXXXII—Miss Howe to Miss Clarissa Harlowe

[*Superscribed for Mrs. Rachel Clark, etc.*]

Wednesday, July 5.

MY DEAR CLARISSA,—I have at last heard from you from a quarter I little expected.

From my mother.

She had for some time seen me uneasy and grieving; and justly supposed it was about you. And this morning dropped a hint, which made me conjecture that she must have heard something of you more than I knew. And when she found that

this added to my uneasiness, she owned she had a letter in her
hands of yours, dated the 29th of June, directed for me.

You may guess that this occasioned a little warmth that
could not be wished for by either.

[It is surprising, my dear, *mighty* surprising! that, knowing
the prohibition I lay under of corresponding with you, you could
send a letter for me to our own house: since it must be fifty to
one that it would fall into my mother's hands, as you find
it did.]

In short, *she* resented that I should disobey her: *I* was as
much concerned that she should open and withhold from me *my*
letters: and at last she was pleased to compromise the matter
with me by giving up the letter, and permitting me to write to
you *once* or *twice*; she to see the contents of what I wrote. For,
besides the value she has for you, she could not but have a great
curiosity to know the occasion of so sad a situation as your
melancholy letter shows you to be in.

[But I shall get her to be satisfied with hearing me read what
I write; putting in between hooks, thus [ ], what I intend not to
read to her.]

Need I to remind you, Miss Clarissa Harlowe, of *three* letters I
wrote to you, to none of which I had any answer; except to the
first, and that a few lines only, promising a letter at large;
though you were well enough, the day after you received my
second, to go joyfully back again with him to the vile house?
But more of these by and by. I must hasten to take notice of
your letter of Wednesday last week; which you could *contrive*
should fall into my mother's hands.

Let me tell you that that letter has almost broken my heart.
Good God! what have you brought yourself to, Miss Clarissa
Harlowe? Could I have believed, that after you had escaped
from the miscreant (with such mighty pains and earnestness
escaped), and after such an attempt as he had made, you would
have been prevailed upon not only to forgive him, but (without
being married too) to return with him to that horrid house!—A
house I had given you such an account of!—Surprising! What
an intoxicating thing is *this love?* I *always* feared that you, even
you, were not proof against its *inconsistent* effects.

You your *best self* have not escaped! Indeed I see not how you
could expect to escape.

What a tale have you to unfold! You need not unfold it, my
dear: I would have engaged to prognosticate all that has
happened, had you but told me that you would once more have

put yourself into his power, after you had taken such pains to get out of it.

Your peace is destroyed! I wonder not at it: since now you must reproach yourself for a credulity so ill-placed.

Your intellect is touched! I am sure my heart bleeds for you: but, excuse me, my dear, I doubt your intellect was touched before you left Hampstead; or you would never have let him find you out there; or, when he did, suffer him to prevail upon you to return to the horrid brothel.

I tell you, I sent you *three letters*: the *first* of which, dated the 7th and 8th of June [1] (for it was written at twice), came safe to your hands, as you sent me word by a few lines dated the 9th: had it not, I should have doubted my own safety; since in it I gave you such an account of the abominable house, and threw such cautions in your way in relation to that Tomlinson, as the more surprised me that you could think of going back to it again, after you had escaped from it, and from Lovelace—O my dear! But nothing now will I ever wonder at!

The *second*, dated June 10 [2], was given into your own hand at Hampstead, on Sunday the 11th, as you was lying upon a couch, in a strange way, according to my messenger's account of you, bloated, and flush-coloured; I don't know how.

The *third* was dated the 20th of June.[3] Having not heard one word from you since the promising billet of the 9th, I own I did not spare you in it. I ventured it by the usual conveyance, by that Wilson's, having no other: so cannot be sure you received it. Indeed, I rather think you might not; because in yours, which fell into my mother's hands, you make no mention of it: and if you had had it, I believe it would have touched you too much to have been passed by unnoticed.

You have heard that I have been ill, you say. I had a cold, indeed; but it was so slight a one that it confined me not an hour. But I doubt not that strange things you have *heard*, and *been told*, to induce you to take the step you took. And, till you did take that step (the going back with this villain, I mean), I knew not a more pitiable case than yours: since everybody must have excused you before, who knew how you were used at home, and was acquainted with your prudence and vigilance. But, alas! my dear, we see that the *wisest people* are not to be depended upon, when *love*, like an *ignis fatuus*, holds up its misleading lights before their eyes.

[1] See pp. 1 et seq. of this volume.   [2] See pp 158 et seq., ibid.
[3] See pp. 262-4, ibid.

My mother tells me she sent you an answer, desiring you not to write to me, because it would grieve me. To be sure I *am* grieved; *exceedingly* grieved; and, *disappointed* too, you must permit me to say. For I had always thought that there never was such a woman, at your years, in the world.

But I remember once an argument you held, on occasion of a censure passed in company upon an excellent preacher, who was not a very excellent liver: *Preaching* and *practising,* you said, required quite different talents [1]: which, when united in the same person, made the man a saint; as *wit* and *judgment* going together constituted a genius.

You made it out, I remember, very prettily: but you never made it out, excuse me, my dear, more convincingly, than by that part of your late conduct which I complain of.

My love for you, and my concern for your honour, may possibly have made me a little of the severest: if you think so, place it to its proper account; to *that* love, and to *that* concern: which will but do justice to

Your afflicted and faithful

A. H.

P.S. My mother would not be satisfied without reading my letter herself; and that before I had fixed all my proposed hooks. She knows, by this means, and has excused, our former correspondence.

She indeed suspected it before: and so she very well might; knowing me, and knowing my love of you.

She has so much real concern for your misfortunes, that, thinking it will be a consolation to *you,* and that it will oblige *me,* she consents that you shall write to me the *particulars at large of your sad story*: but it is on condition that I show her all that has passed between us, relating to yourself and the vilest of men. I have the more cheerfully complied, as the communication cannot be to your disadvantage.

You may therefore write freely, and direct to our own house.

My mother promises to show me the copy of her letter to you, and your reply to it; which latter she has but just told me of. She already apologizes for the severity of hers: and thinks the sight of your reply will affect me too much. But having her promise, I will not dispense with it.

I doubt hers is severe enough. So I fear you will think mine: but you have taught me never to spare the *fault* for the *friend's*

[1] See vol. i, p. 245.

sake; and that a great error ought rather to be more inexcusable in the person we value, than in one we are indifferent to; because it is a reflection upon our choice of that person, and tends to a breach of the love of mind; and to expose us to the world for our partiality.   To the *love of mind*, I repeat; since it is impossible but the errors of the dearest friend must weaken our inward opinion of that friend; and thereby lay a foundation for future distance, and perhaps disgust.

God grant that you may be able to clear your conduct *after* you had escaped from Hampstead; as all *before* that time was noble, generous, and prudent: the man a devil, and you a saint! —Yet I hope you can; and therefore expect it from you.

I send by a particular hand.   He will call for your answer at your own appointment.

I am afraid this horrid wretch will trace out by the post offices where you are, if not careful.

To have *money*, and *will*, and *head*, to be a villain, is too much for the rest of the world, when they meet in one man.

Letter LXXXIII—*Miss Clarissa Harlowe to Miss Howe*

Thursday, July 6.

FEW young persons have been able to give more convincing proofs than myself, how little true happiness lies in the enjoyment of our own wishes.

To produce one instance only of the truth of this observation; what would I have given for weeks past for the favour of a letter from my dear Miss Howe, in whose friendship I placed all my remaining comfort?   Little did I think that the next letter she would honour me with, should be in such a style as should make me look more than once at the subscription, that I might be sure (the name not being written at length) that it was not signed by another A. H.   For surely, thought I, this is my sister Arabella's style: surely Miss Howe (blame me as she pleases in other points) could never repeat so *sharply* upon her friend, words written in the bitterness of spirit, and in the disorder of head; nor remind her, with asperity, and with mingled strokes of wit, of an argument held in the gaiety of a heart elated with prosperous fortunes (as mine then was), and very little apprehensive of the severe turn that argument would one day take against herself.

But what have *I*, sunk in my fortunes; my character forfeited; my honour lost [while *I* know it, I care not *who* knows it];

destitute of friends, and even of hope; what have *I* to do to show
a spirit of repining and expostulation to a dear friend, because
she is not *more* kind than a sister?

I find, by the rising bitterness which will mingle with the gall
in my ink, that I am not yet subdued enough to my condition:
and so, begging your pardon, that I should rather have formed
my expectations of favour from the indulgence you *used* to show
me, than from what I *now deserve* to have shown me, I will
endeavour to give a particular answer to your letter; although
it will take me up too much time to think of sending it by your
messenger to-morrow: he can put off his journey, he says, till
Saturday.   I will endeavour to have the whole narrative ready
for you by Saturday.

But how to defend myself in everything that has happened, I
cannot tell: since in some part of the time, in which my conduct
appears to have been censurable, I was not myself; and to this
hour know not all the methods taken to deceive and ruin me.

You tell me that in your first letter you gave me such an
account of the vile house I was in, and such cautions about that
Tomlinson, as make you wonder how I could think of going back.

Alas, my dear! I was tricked, most vilely tricked back, as you
shall hear in its place.

Without *knowing* the house was so very *vile* a house from your
intended information, I disliked the people too much, ever
voluntarily to have returned to it.   But had you really written
such cautions about Tomlinson, and the house, as you seem to
have *purposed* to do, they must, had they come in time, have
been of infinite service to me.   But not one word of either,
whatever was your *intention*, did you mention to me, in that
first of the *three* letters you so warmly TELL ME you *did* send me.
I will enclose it to convince you.[1]

But your account of your messenger's delivering to me your
second letter, and the description he gives of me, as *lying upon a
couch, in a strange way, bloated and flush-coloured, you don't know
how*, absolutely puzzles and confounds me.

Lord have mercy upon the poor Clarissa Harlowe! What can
this mean! *Who* was the messenger you sent? Was *he* one of
Lovelace's creatures too! Could nobody come near me but that
man's confederates, either *setting out so*, or *made so*? I know not
what to make of any one syllable of this! Indeed I don't.

Let me see.   You say this was *before* I went from Hampstead!

[1] The letter she encloses was Mr. Lovelace's forged one.   See pp. 94
et seq.

My intellects had not then been touched—nor had I ever been surprised by wine [strange if I had!]: how then could I be found in such a *strange way, bloated, and flush-coloured; you don't know how!* Yet what a vile, what a hateful figure has your messenger represented me to have made!

But indeed, I know nothing of ANY messenger from you.

Believing myself secure at Hampstead, I stayed longer there than I would have done, in hopes of the letter promised me in your short one of the 9th, brought me by my own messenger, in which you undertake to send for and engage Mrs. Townsend in my favour.[1]

I wondered I heard not from you: and was told you were sick; and, at another time, that your mother and you had had words on my account, and that you had refused to admit Mr. Hickman's visits upon it: so that I supposed, at one time, that you was not *able* to write; at another, that your mother's prohibition had its *due* force with you.   But now I have no doubt that the wicked man must have intercepted your letter; and I wish he found not means to *corrupt your messenger* to tell you so strange a story.

It was on Sunday, June 11, you say, that the man gave it me. I was at church twice that day with Mrs. Moore.   Mr. Lovelace was at her house the while, where he boarded, and wanted to have lodged; but I would not permit that, though I could not help the other.   In one of these spaces *it must be* that he had time to work upon the man.   You'll easily, my dear, find that out, by inquiring the time of his arrival at Mrs. Moore's, and other circumstances of the *strange way* he pretended to see me in, *on a couch*, and the rest.

Had anybody seen me afterwards, when I was betrayed back to the vile house, struggling under the operation of wicked potions, and robbed *indeed* of my intellects (for this, as you shall hear, was my dreadful case), I might then, perhaps, have appeared *bloated*, and *flush-coloured*, and *I know not how myself*.   But were you to see your poor Clarissa *now* (or even to have seen her at Hampstead *before* she suffered the vilest of all outrages), you would not think her *bloated*, or *flush-coloured*: indeed you would not.

In a word, it could not be *me* your messenger saw; nor (if anybody) who it was can I divine.

I will now, as *briefly* as the subject will permit, enter into the darker part of my sad story: and yet I must be somewhat circumstantial, that you may not think me capable of *reserve* or

[1] See p. 90.

palliation. The *latter* I am not conscious that I need.   I should be utterly inexcusable were I guilty of the *former* to you.   And yet, if you knew how my heart sinks under the thoughts of a recollection so painful, you would pity me.

As I shall not be able, perhaps, to conclude what I have to write in even two or three letters, I will begin a new one with my story; and send the whole of it together, although written at different periods, as I am able.

Allow me a little pause, my dear, at this place; and to subscribe myself

Your ever affectionate and obliged,
CLARISSA HARLOWE.

Letter LXXXIV—*Miss Clarissa Harlowe to Miss Howe*

Thursday Night.

HE had found me out at Hampstead: strangely found me out; for I am still at a loss to know by what means.

I was loath, in my billet of the 9th,[1] to tell you so, for fear of giving you apprehensions for me; and besides, I hoped then to have a shorter and happier issue to account to you for, through your assistance, than I met with.

She then gives a narrative of all that passed at Hampstead between herself, Mr. Lovelace, Captain Tomlinson, and the women there, to the same effect with that so amply given by Mr. Lovelace.

Mr. Lovelace, finding all he could say, and all Captain Tomlinson could urge, ineffectual, to prevail upon me to forgive an outrage so flagrantly premeditated, rested all his hopes on a visit which was to be paid me by Lady Betty Lawrance and Miss Montague.

In my uncertain situation, my prospects all so dark, I knew not to whom I might be obliged to have recourse in the last resort: and as those ladies had the best of characters, insomuch that I had reason to regret that I had not from the first thrown myself upon their protection (when I had forfeited *that* of my own friends), I thought I would not *shun* an interview with them, though I was too indifferent to their kinsman to *seek* it, as I doubted not that one end of their visit would be to reconcile me to him.

On Monday, the 12th of June, these pretended ladies came to

[1] See p. 100.

Hampstead; and I was presented to them, and they to me, by their kinsman.

They were richly dressed, and stuck out with jewels; the pretended Lady Betty's were particularly very fine.

They came in a coach and four, hired, as was confessed, while their own was repairing in town: a pretence made, I now perceive, that I should not guess at the imposture by the want of the real lady's arms upon it. Lady Betty was attended by her woman, whom she called Morrison; a modest country-looking person.

I had heard that Lady Betty was a fine woman, and that Miss Montague was a beautiful young lady, genteel, and graceful, and full of vivacity—such were these impostors; and having never seen either of them, I had not the least suspicion that they were not the ladies they personated; and being put a little out of countenance by the richness of their dresses, I could not help (fool that I was!) to apologize for my own.

The pretended Lady Betty then told me that her nephew had acquainted them with the situation of affairs between us. And although she could not but say that she was very glad that he had not put such a slight upon his lordship and them, as report had given them cause to apprehend (the reasons for which report, however, she much approved of); yet it had been matter of great concern to her, and to her Niece Montague, and would to the whole family, to find so great a misunderstanding subsisting between us, as, if not made up, might distance all their hopes.

She could easily tell who was in fault, she said. And gave him a look both of anger and disdain; asking him, how it was possible for him to give an offence of *such* a nature to so charming a lady [so she called me], as should occasion a resentment so strong?

He pretended to be awed into shame and silence.

My dearest niece, said she, and took my hand (I *must* call you niece, as well from love, as to humour your uncle's laudable expedient), permit me to be, not an advocate, but a mediatrix for him; and not for his sake, so much as for my own, my Charlotte's, and all our family's. The indignity he has offered to you, may be of too tender a nature to be inquired into. But as he declares that it was not a premeditated offence; whether, my dear [for I was going to rise upon it in my temper], it were or not; and as he declares his sorrow for it (and never did creature express a deeper sorrow for any offence than he); and as it is a reparable one; let *us*, for this one time, forgive him; and thereby lay an obligation upon this man of errors—let US, I say, my dear: for, sir [turning to him], an offence against such a peerless lady as this, must be an offence against *me*, against your *cousin* here, and against *all the virtuous* of our sex.

See, my dear, what a creature he had picked out! Could you have thought there was a woman in the world who could thus express herself, and yet be vile? But she had her principal instructions from him, and those written down too, as I have reason to think: for I have recollected since, that I once saw this Lady Betty (who often rose from her seat, and took a turn to the other end of the room with such emotion as if the joy of her heart would not let her sit still) take out a paper from her stays, and look into it, and put it there again. She might oftener, and I not observe it; for I little thought that there could be such impostors in the world.

I could not forbear paying great attention to what she said. I found my tears ready to start; I drew out my handkerchief, and was silent. I had not been so indulgently treated a great while by a person of character and distinction [such I thought her]; and durst not trust to the accent of my voice.

The pretended Miss Montague joined in on this occasion; and drawing her chair close to me, took my other hand, and besought me to forgive her cousin; and consent to rank myself as one of the principals of a family that had long, very long, coveted the honour of my alliance.

I am ashamed to repeat to you, my dear, now I know what wretches they are, the tender, the obliging, and the respectful things I said to them.

The wretch himself then came forward. He threw himself at my feet. How was I beset! The women grasping one my right hand, the other my left: the pretended Miss Montague pressing to her lips more than once the hand she held: the wicked man on his knees, imploring my forgiveness; and setting before me my happy and my unhappy prospects, as I should forgive or not forgive him. All that he thought would affect me in his former pleas, and those of Captain Tomlinson, he repeated. He vowed, he promised, he bespoke the pretended ladies to answer for him; and they engaged their honours in his behalf.

Indeed, my dear, I was distressed, perfectly distressed. I was sorry that I had given way to this visit. For I knew not how, in tenderness to relations (as I thought them) so worthy, to treat so freely as he deserved, a man nearly allied to them: so that my arguments, and my resolutions, were deprived of their greatest force.

I pleaded, however, my application to you. I expected every hour, I told them, an answer from you to a letter I had written, which would decide my future destiny.

They offered to apply to you themselves in person, in *their own behalf*, as they politely termed it. They besought me to write to you to hasten your answer.

I said I was sure that you would write the moment that the event of an application to be made to a third person enabled you to write. But as to the success of their requests in behalf of their kinsman, that depended not upon the expected answer; for *that*, I begged their pardon, was out of the question. I wished him well. I wished him happy. But I was convinced that I neither could make *him* so, nor he *me*.

Then! how the wretch promised! How he vowed! How he entreated! And how the women pleaded! And they engaged themselves, and the honour of their whole family, for his just, his kind, his tender behaviour to me.

In short, my dear, I was so hard set, that I was obliged to come to a more favourable compromise with them than I had intended. I would wait for your answer to my letter, I said: and if that made doubtful or difficult the change of measures I had resolved upon, and the scheme of life I had formed, I would then consider of the matter; and, if they would permit me, lay all before them, and take their advice upon it, in conjunction with yours, as if the one were my own aunt, and the other were my own cousin.

They shed tears upon this—of joy they called them—but since, I believe, to their credit, bad as they are, that they were tears of temporary remorse; for the pretended Miss Montague turned about, and, as I remember, said, There was no standing it.

But Mr. Lovelace was not so easily satisfied. He was fixed upon his villainous measures perhaps; and so might not be sorry to have a pretence against me. He bit his lip. He had been but too much used, he said, to such indifference, such coldness, in the very midst of his happiest prospects. I had on twenty occasions shown him, to his infinite regret, that any favour I was to confer upon him was to be the result of—there he stopped —and not of my choice.

This had like to have set all back again. I was exceedingly offended. But the pretended ladies interposed. The elder severely took him to task. He ought, she told him, to be

satisfied with what I had said.   She *desired* no other condition.
And what, sir, said she, with an air of authority, would you
commit errors, and expect to be *rewarded* for them?

They then engaged me in a more agreeable conversation.
The pretended lady declared, that she, Lord M. and Lady Sarah,
would directly and personally interest themselves to bring
about a general reconciliation between the two families, and
this either in open or private concert with my Uncle Harlowe,
as should be thought fit.   Animosities on one side had been
carried a great way, she said; and too little care had been shown
on the other to mollify or heal.   My father should see that they
could treat him as a brother and a friend; and my brother and
sister should be convinced that there was no room either for
the jealousy or envy they had conceived from motives too
unworthy to be avowed.

Could I help, my dear, being pleased with them?

Permit me here to break off.   The task grows too heavy, at
present, for the heart of

Your CLARISSA HARLOWE.

Letter LXXXV—Miss Clarissa Harlowe. [*In continuation*]

I WAS very ill, and obliged to lay down my pen.   I thought I
should have fainted.   But am better now; so will proceed.

The pretended ladies, the more we talked, the fonder seemed
to be of me.   And *the* Lady Betty had Mrs. Moore called up;
and asked her if she had accommodations for her niece and
self, her woman, and two menservants, for three or four days?

Mr. Lovelace answered for her that she had.

She would not ask her dear Niece Lovelace [*Permit me, my
dear*, whispered she, *this charming style before strangers !   I will
keep your uncle's secret*] whether she should be welcome or not
to be so near her.   But for the time she should stay in these
parts, she would come up every night.   What say *you,* Niece
Charlotte?

The pretended Charlotte answered, she should like to do so,
of all things.

The Lady Betty called her an obliging girl.   She liked the
place, she said.   Her Cousin Leeson would excuse her.   The
air, and my company, would do her good.   She never chose to
lie in the smoky town, if she could help it.   In short, my dear,
said she to me, I will stay till you hear from Miss Howe; and till
I have your consent to go with me to Glenham Hall.   Not one

moment will I be out of your company, when I can have it. Stedman, my solicitor, as the distance from town is so small, may attend me here for instructions. Niece Charlotte, one word with you, child.

They retired to the farther end of the room, and talked about their night-dresses.

The Miss Charlotte said, Morrison might be dispatched for them.

True, said the other; but I have some letters in my private box which I must have up. And you know, Charlotte, that I trust nobody with the keys of that.

Could not Morrison bring up that box?

No. She thought it safest where it was. She had heard of a robbery committed but two days ago at the foot of Hampstead Hill; and she should be ruined if she lost her box.

Well, then, it was but going to town to undress, and she would leave her jewels behind her, and return; and should be easier a great deal on all accounts.

For my part, I wondered they came up with them. But that was to be taken as a respect paid to me. And then they hinted at another visit of ceremony which they had thought to make, had they not found me so inexpressibly engaging.

They talked loud enough for me to hear them; on purpose, no doubt, though in affected whispers; and concluded with high praises of me.

I was not fool enough to believe, or to be puffed up with their encomiums; yet not suspecting them, I was not displeased at so favourable a beginning of acquaintance with ladies (whether I were to be related to them or not) of whom I had always heard honourable mention. And yet at the time, I thought, highly as they exalted *me*, that in some respects (though I hardly knew in what) they fell short of what I expected *them* to be.

The grand deluder was at the farther end of the room, another way; probably to give me an opportunity to hear these pre-concerted praises—looking into a book, which, had there not been a preconcert, would not have taken his attention for one moment. It was *Taylor's Holy Living and Dying*.

When the pretended ladies joined me, he approached me with it in his hand—A smart book, this, my dear! This old divine affects, I see, a mighty flowery style upon a very solemn subject. But it puts me in mind of an ordinary country funeral, where the young women, in honour of a defunct companion, especially if she were a virgin, or *passed for such*, make a flower-bed of her coffin.

And then, laying down the book, turning upon his heel, with one of his usual airs of gaiety, And are you determined, ladies, to take up your lodgings with my charming creature?

Indeed they were.

Never were there more cunning, more artful impostors, than these women. Practised creatures, to be sure: yet genteel; and they must have been well educated — once, perhaps, as much the delight of their parents, as I was of mine: and who knows by what arts ruined, body and mind! O my dear! how pregnant is this reflection!

But the *man*! Never was there a man so deep. Never so consummate a deceiver; except that detested Tomlinson; whose years and seriousness, joined with a solidity of sense and judgment that seemed uncommon, gave him, one would have thought, advantages in villainy the other had not time for. Hard, very hard, that I should fall into the knowledge of two such wretches; when two more such I hope are not to be met with in the world! Both so determined to carry on the most barbarous and perfidious projects against a poor young creature, who never did or wished harm to either.

Take the following slight account of these women's and of this man's behaviour to each other before me.

Mr. Lovelace carried himself to his pretended aunt with high respect, and paid a great deference to all she said. He permitted her to have all the advantage over him in the repartees and retorts that passed between them. I could, indeed, easily see that it *was* permitted, and that he forbore that *acumen*, that quickness, which he never spared showing to the pretended Miss Montague; and which a man of wit seldom knows how to spare showing, when an opportunity offers to display his wit.

The pretended Miss Montague was still more reverent in her behaviour to her pretended aunt. While the aunt kept up the dignity of the character she had assumed, rallying both of them with the air of a person who depends upon the superiority which years and fortune give over younger persons, who might have a view to be obliged to her, either in her life, or at her death.

The severity of her raillery, however, was turned upon Mr. Lovelace, on occasion of the character of the people who kept the lodgings, which, she said, I had thought myself so well warranted to leave privately.

This startled me. For having then no suspicion of the vile

Tomlinson, I concluded (and your letter of the 7th[1] favoured my conclusion) that if the house were notorious, either he, or Mr. Mennell, would have given me or him some hints of it; nor, although I liked not the people, did I observe anything in them very culpable, till the Wednesday night before, that they offered not to come to my assistance, although within hearing of my distress (as I am sure they were), and having as much reason as I to be frighted at the fire, had it been real.

I looked with indignation upon Mr. Lovelace at this hint.

He seemed abashed. I have not patience but to recollect the specious looks of this vile deceiver. But how was it possible that even that florid countenance of his should enable him to command a blush at his pleasure? For blush he did, more than once: and the blush, on this occasion, was a deep-dyed crimson, unstrained for, and natural, as I thought; but he is so much of the actor, that he seems able to enter into any character; and his muscles and features appear entirely under obedience to his wicked will.[2]

The pretended lady went on saying, she had taken upon herself to inquire after the people, on hearing that I had left the house in disgust; and though she heard not anything *much* amiss, yet she heard enough to make her wonder that he could carry his spouse, a person of so much delicacy, to a house, that, if it had not a *bad* fame, had not a *good* one.

You must think, my dear, that I liked the pretended Lady Betty the better for this. I suppose it was designed I should.

He was surprised, he said, that her ladyship should hear a bad character of the people. It was what he had never before heard that they deserved. It was easy, indeed, to see that they had not very great delicacy, though they were not indelicate. The nature of their livelihood, letting lodgings, and taking people to board (and yet he had understood that they were nice in these particulars), led them to aim at being free and obliging: and it was difficult, he said, for persons of cheerful dispositions so to behave as to avoid censure: openness of heart and countenance in the sex (more was the pity) too often

---

[1] His forged letter. See pp. 94 et seq.

[2] It is proper to observe that there was a more natural reason than this that the lady gives for Mr. Lovelace's blushing. It was a blush of indignation, as he owned afterwards to his friend Belford, in conversation; for the pretended Lady Betty had mistaken her cue in condemning the house, and he had much ado to recover the blunder, being obliged to follow her lead and vary from his first design, which was to have the people of the house spoken well of in order to induce her to return to it, were it but on pretence to direct her clothes to be carried to Hampstead.

subjected good people, whose fortunes did not set them above the world, to uncharitable censure.

He wished, however, that her ladyship would tell *what* she had heard: although now it signified but little, because he would never ask me to set foot within their doors again: and he begged she would not mince the matter.

Nay, no great matter, she said.   But she had been informed that there were more women-lodgers in the house than men: yet that their visitors were more men than women.   And this had been hinted to her (perhaps by ill-willers, she could not answer for that) in such a way, as if somewhat further were meant by it than was spoken.

This, he said, was the true innuendo way of characterizing used by detractors.   Everybody and everything had a black and a white side, of which well-willers and ill-willers may make their advantage.   He had observed that the front house was well let, and he believed more to the one sex than to the other; for he had seen, occasionally passing to and fro, several genteel modest-looking women; and who, it was very probable, were not so ill-beloved, but they might have visitors and relations of both sexes: but they were none of them anything to us, or we to them: we were not once in any of their companies: but in the genteelest and most retired house of the two, which we had in a manner to ourselves, with the use of a parlour to the street, to serve us for a servants' hall, or to receive common visitors, or our traders only, whom we admitted not upstairs.

He always loved to speak as he found.   No man in the world had suffered more from calumny than he himself had done.

Women, he owned, ought to be more scrupulous than men needed to be where they lodged.   Nevertheless, he wished that fact, rather than surmise, were to be the foundation of their judgments, especially when they spoke of one another.

He meant no reflection upon her ladyship's informants, or rather *surmisants* (as he might call them), be they who they would: nor did he think himself obliged to defend characters impeached, or not thought well of, by women of virtue and honour.   Neither were these people of importance enough to have so much said about them.

The pretended Lady Betty said, All who knew her would clear her of censoriousness: that it gave her some opinion, she must needs say, of the people, that he had continued there so long with me; that I had rather *negative* than *positive* reasons of dislike to them; and that so shrewd a man as she heard Captain Tomlinson was, had not objected to them.

I think, Niece Charlotte, proceeded she, as my nephew has not parted with these lodgings, you and I (for, as my dear Miss Harlowe dislikes the people, I would not ask *her* for her company) will take a dish of tea with my nephew there, before we go out of town, and then we shall see what sort of people they are. I have heard that Mrs. Sinclair is a mighty forbidding creature.

With all my heart, madam. In *your ladyship's* company I shall make no scruple of going any whither.

It was *ladyship* at every word; and as she seemed proud of her title, and of her dress too, I might have guessed that she was not used to *either*.

What say *you*, Cousin Lovelace? Lady Sarah, though a melancholy woman, is very inquisitive about all your affairs. I must acquaint her with every particular circumstance when I go down.

With all his heart. He would attend her whenever she pleased. She would see very handsome apartments, and very civil people.

The deuce is in them, said *the* Miss Montague, if they appear other to us.

They then fell into family talk; family happiness on my hoped-for accession into it. They mentioned Lord M.'s and Lady Sarah's great desire to see me. How many friends and admirers, with up-lift hands, I should have! [*O my dear, what a triumph must these creatures, and he, have over the poor devoted all the time!*] What a happy man he would be! They would not, *the* Lady Betty said, give themselves the mortification but to suppose that I should not be one of them!

Presents were hinted at. She resolved that I should go with her to Glenham Hall. She would not be refused, although she were to stay a week beyond her time for me.

She longed for the expected letter from you. I must write to hasten it, and to let Miss Howe know how everything stood since I wrote last. That might dispose me absolutely in *their* favour and in her nephew's; and then she hoped there would be no occasion for me to think of entering upon any new measures.

Indeed, my dear, I did at the time intend, if I heard not from you by morning, to dispatch a man and horse to you, with the particulars of *all*, that you might (if you thought proper) at

least put off Mrs. Townsend's coming up to another day.   But
I was miserably prevented.

She made me promise that I would write to you upon this
subject, whether I heard from you or not.   One of her servants
should ride post with my letter, and wait for Miss Howe's answer.

She then launched out in deserved praises of you, my dear.
How fond should she be of the honour of your acquaintance!

The pretended Miss Montague joined in with her, as well for
herself as for her sister.

Abominably well instructed were they both!

O my dear!   What risks may poor giddy girls run, when they
throw themselves out of the protection of their natural friends,
and into the wide world?

They then talked again of reconciliation and intimacy with
every one of my friends; with my mother particularly; and gave
the dear good lady the praises that every one gives her, who has
the happiness to know her.

Ah, my dear Miss Howe!   I had almost forgot my resentments against the pretended nephew!   So many agreeable
things said, made me think that, if you should advise it, and if
I could bring my mind to forgive the wretch for an outrage so
premeditatedly vile, and could forbear despising him for that
and his other ungrateful and wicked ways, I might not be unhappy in an alliance with such a family.   Yet, thought I at
the time, with what intermixtures does everything come to me
that has the appearance of good!   However, as my lucid hopes
made me see fewer faults in the behaviour of these pretended
ladies, than recollection and abhorrence have helped me since
to see, I began to reproach myself that I had not at first thrown
myself into their protection.

But amidst all these delightful prospects, I must not, said
the Lady Betty, forget that I am to go to town.

She then ordered her coach to be got to the door.   We will
all go to town together, said she, and return together.   Morrison
shall stay here, and see everything as I am used to have it, in
relation to my apartment, and my bed; for I am very particular
in some respects.   My Cousin Leeson's servants can do all I
want to be done with regard to my night-dresses, and the like.
And it will be a little airing for you, my dear, and a good opportunity for Mr. Lovelace to order what you want of your apparel
to be sent from your former lodgings to Mrs. Leeson's; and we
can bring it up with us from thence.

I had no intention to comply.   But as I did not imagine

that she would insist upon my going to town with them, I made no answer to that part of her speech.

I must here lay down my tired pen!

Recollection! Heart-affecting recollection! How it pains me!

Letter LXXXVI—Miss Clarissa Harlowe to Miss Howe

IN the midst of these agreeablenesses, the coach came to the door. The pretended Lady Betty besought me to give them my company to their Cousin Leeson's. I desired to be excused: yet suspected nothing. She would not be denied. How happy would a visit so condescending make her Cousin Leeson! Her Cousin Leeson was not unworthy of my acquaintance: and would take it for the greatest favour in the world.

I objected my dress. But the objection was not admitted. She bespoke a supper of Mrs. Moore to be ready at nine.

Mr. Lovelace, vile hypocrite, and wicked deceiver! seeing, as he said, my dislike to go, desired her ladyship not to insist upon it.

Fondness for my company was pleaded. She begged me to oblige her: made a motion to help me to my fan herself: and, in short, was so very urgent, that my feet complied against my speech and my mind: and being, in a manner, led to the coach by her, and made to step in first, she followed me; and her pretended niece, and the wretch, followed her: and away it drove.

Nothing but the height of affectionate complaisance passed all the way: over and over, what a joy would this unexpected visit give her Cousin Leeson! What a pleasure must it be to such a mind as mine to be able to give so much joy to everybody I came near!

The cruel, the savage seducer (as I have since recollected) was in rapture all the way; but yet such a sort of rapture as he took visible pains to check.

Hateful villain! How I abhor him! What mischief must be then in his plotting heart! What a devoted victim must I be in all their eyes!

Though not pleased, I was nevertheless just then thoughtless of danger; they endeavouring thus to lift me up above all apprehension of that, and above myself too.

But think, my dear, what a dreadful turn all had upon me, when, through several streets and ways I knew nothing of, the coach slackening its pace, came within sight of the dreadful house of the dreadfullest woman in the world, as she proved to me.

Lord be good unto me! cried the poor fool, looking out of the coach. Mr. Lovelace!—Madam! turning to the pretended Lady Betty—Madam! turning to the niece, my hands and eyes lifted up—Lord be good unto me!

What! What! What, my dear!

He pulled the string. What need to have come this way? said he. But since we are, I will but ask a question. My dearest life, *why* this apprehension?

The coachman stopped: *his* servant, who, with one of hers, was behind, alighted. Ask, said he, if I have any letters? Who knows, my dearest creature, turning to me, but we may already have one from the captain? We will not go out of the coach! Fear nothing—why so apprehensive? Oh! these fine spirits! cried the execrable insulter.

Dreadfully did my heart then misgive me: I was ready to faint. Why this terror, my life? You shall not stir out of the coach—but one question, now the fellow has drove us this way.

Your lady will faint, cried the execrable Lady Betty, turning to him. My dearest niece! (niece I *will* call you, taking my hand) we must alight, if you are so ill. Let us alight—only for a glass of water and hartshorn—indeed we must alight.

No, no, no—I am well—quite well. Won't the man drive on? I am well—quite well—indeed I am. *Man*, drive on, putting my head out of the coach. *Man*, drive on! though my voice was too low to be heard.

The coach stopped at the door. How I trembled!

Dorcas came to the door, on its stopping.

My dearest creature, said the vile man, gasping, as it were for breath, you shall *not* alight. Any letters for me, Dorcas?

There are two, sir. And here is a gentleman, Mr. Belton, sir, waits for your honour; and has done so above an hour.

I 'll just speak to him. Open the door. You shan't step out, my dear. A letter perhaps from the captain already! You shan't step out, my dear.

I sighed as if my heart would burst.

But we *must* step out, nephew: your lady will faint. Maid, a glass of hartshorn and water! My dear, you *must* step out. You will faint, child—we must cut your laces. [I believe my complexion was all manner of colours by turns]. Indeed, you must step out, my dear.

He knew, he said, I should be well, the moment the coach

drove from the door. I should *not* alight. By his soul, I should not.

Lord, Lord, nephew, Lord, Lord, cousin, both women in a breath, what ado you make about nothing! You *persuade* your lady to be afraid of alighting! See you not that she is just fainting?

Indeed, madam, said the vile seducer, my dearest love must not be moved in this point against her will. I beg it may not be insisted upon.

Fiddle-faddle, foolish man! What a pother is here! I guess how it is: you are ashamed to let us see, what sort of people you carried your lady among—but do you go out, and speak to your friend, and take your letters.

He stepped out; but shut the coach door after him, to oblige me.

The coach may go on, madam, said I.

The coach *shall* go on, my dear life, said he—but he gave not, nor intended to give, orders that it should.

Let the coach go on! said I. Mr. Lovelace may come after us.

Indeed, my dear, you are ill! Indeed you must alight—alight but for one quarter of an hour—alight but to give orders yourself about your things. Whom can you be afraid of, in my company and my niece's? These people must have behaved shockingly to you! Please the Lord, I'll inquire into it! I'll see what sort of people they are!

Immediately came the old creature to the door. A thousand pardons, dear madam, stepping to the coach-side, if we have any way offended you. Be pleased, ladies [to the other two], to alight.

Well, my dear, whispered *the* Lady Betty, I now find that a hideous description of a person we never saw, is an advantage to them. I thought the woman was a monster—but, really, she seems tolerable.

I was afraid I should have fallen into fits: but still refused to go out. Man!—Man!—Man! cried I, gaspingly, my head out of the coach and in, by turns, half a dozen times running, drive on! —Let us go!

My heart misgave me beyond the power of my own accounting for it; for still I did not suspect these women. But the antipathy I had taken to the vile house, and to find myself so near it, when I expected no such matter, with the sight of the old creature, made me behave like a distracted person.

The hartshorn and water was brought. The pretended Lady

Betty made me drink it.   Heaven knows if there were anything else in it!

Besides, said she, whisperingly, I must see what sort of creatures the *nieces* are.   Want of delicacy cannot be hid from me.   You could not surely, my dear, have this aversion to re-enter a house, for a few minutes, in our company, in which you lodged and boarded several weeks, unless these women could be so presumptuously vile, as my nephew ought not to know.

Out stepped the pretended lady; the servant, at her command, having opened the door.

Dearest madam, said the other to me, let me follow you (for I was next the door).   Fear nothing: I will not stir from your presence.

Come, my dear, said the pretended lady: give me your hand; holding out hers.   Oblige me this once.

I will bless your footsteps, said the old creature, if once more you honour my house with your presence.

A crowd by this time was gathered about us; but I was too much affected to mind that.

Again the pretended Miss Montague urged me; standing up as ready to go out if I would give her room.   Lord, my dear, said she, who can bear this crowd?   What will people think?

The pretended lady again pressed me, with both her hands held out—Only, my dear, to give orders about your things.

And thus pressed, and gazed at (for then I looked about me), the women so richly dressed, people whispering; in an evil moment, out stepped I, trembling, forced to lean with both my hands (frightened too much for ceremony) on the pretended Lady Betty's arm—O that I had dropped down dead upon the guilty threshold!

We shall stay but a few minutes, my dear!—but a few minutes! said the same specious jilt—out of breath with her joy, as I have since thought, that they had thus triumphed over the unhappy victim!

Come, Mrs. Sinclair, I think your name is, show us the way—following her, and leading me.   I am very thirsty.   You have frighted me, my dear, with your strange fears.   I must have tea made, if it can be done in a moment.   We have further to go, Mrs. Sinclair, and must return to Hampstead this night.

It shall be ready in a moment, cried the wretch.   We have water boiling.

Hasten, then.   Come, my dear, to me, as she led me through the passage to the fatal inner house.   Lean upon me—how you tremble! how you falter in your steps! Dearest Niece Lovelace (the old wretch being in hearing), why these hurries upon your spirits? We 'll be gone in a minute.

And thus she led the poor sacrifice into the old wretch's too well-known parlour.

Never was anybody so gentle, so meek, so low-voiced, as the odious woman; drawling out, in a puling accent, all the obliging things she could say: awed, I then thought, by the conscious dignity of a woman of quality; glittering with jewels.

The called-for tea was ready presently.

There was no Mr. Belton, I believe: for the wretch went not to anybody, unless it were while we were parleying in the coach. No such person, however, appeared at the tea-table.

I was made to drink two dishes, with milk, complaisantly urged by the pretended ladies helping me each to one. I was stupid to their hands; and, when I took the tea, almost choked with vapours; and could hardly swallow.

I thought, *transiently* thought, that the tea, the last dish particularly, had an odd taste. They, on my palating it, observed that the milk was *London milk*; far short in goodness of what they were accustomed to from their own dairies.

I have no doubt that my two dishes, and perhaps my harts-horn, were prepared for me; in which case it was more proper for their purpose, that *they* should help me, than that I should help *myself*. Ill before, I found myself still more and more disordered in my head; a heavy torpid pain increasing fast upon me. But I imputed it to my terror.

Nevertheless, at the pretended lady's motion, I went upstairs, attended by Dorcas; who affected to weep for joy that once more she saw my *blessed* face, that was the vile creature's word; and immediately I set about taking out some of my clothes, ordering what should be put up, and what sent after me.

While I was thus employed, up came the pretended Lady Betty, in a hurrying way. My dear, you won't be long before you are ready. My nephew is very busy in writing answers to his letters: so, I 'll just whip away, and change my dress, and call upon you in an instant.

O madam! I *am* ready! I am *now* ready! You must not leave me here: and down I sunk, affrighted, into a chair.

This instant, this instant, I will return—before you can be ready—before you can have packed up your things—we would not be late—the robbers we have heard of may be out—don't let us be late.

And away she hurried before I could say another word. Her pretended niece went with her, without taking notice to me of her going.

I had no suspicion yet that these women were not indeed the ladies they personated; and I blamed myself for my weak fears. It cannot *be*, thought I, that *such* ladies will abet treachery against a poor creature they are so fond of. They must undoubtedly *be* the persons they *appear* to be—what folly to doubt it! The air, the dress, the dignity of women of quality. How unworthy of them, and of my charity, concluded I, is this ungenerous shadow of suspicion!

So, recovering my stupefied spirits, as well as they could be recovered (for I was heavier and heavier; and wondered to Dorcas what ailed me; rubbing my eyes, and taking some of her snuff, pinch after pinch, to very little purpose), I pursued my employment: but when that was over, all packed up that I designed to be packed up; and I had nothing to do but to *think*; and found them tarry so long; I thought I should have gone distracted. I shut myself into the chamber that had been mine; I kneeled; I prayed; yet knew not what I prayed for: then ran out again: It was almost dark night, I said: where, where was Mr. Lovelace?

He came to me, taking no notice at first of my consternation and wildness [what they had given me made me incoherent and wild]: All goes well, said he, my dear! A line from Captain Tomlinson!

All indeed did go well for the villainous project of the most cruel and most villainous of men!

I *demanded* his aunt! I *demanded* his cousin! The evening, I said, was closing! My head was very, *very* bad, I remember I said—and it grew worse and worse.

Terror, however, as yet kept up my spirits; and I insisted upon his going himself to hasten them.

He called his servant. He raved at the *sex* for *their* delay: 'twas well that business of consequence seldom depended upon such parading, unpunctual triflers!

His servant came.

He ordered him to fly to his Cousin Leeson's, and to let Lady Betty and his cousin know how uneasy we both were at their delay: adding, of his own accord, Desire them, if they don't come instantly, to send their coach, and we will go without them. Tell them I wonder they 'll serve me so!

I thought this was considerately and fairly put. But now,

indifferent as my head was, I had a little time to consider the man and his behaviour. He terrified me with his looks, and with his violent emotions, as he gazed upon me. Evident *joy-suppressed* emotions, as I have since recollected. His sentences short, and pronounced as if his breath were touched. Never saw I his abominable eyes look as then they looked—triumph in them!—fiierce and wild; and more disagreeable than the women's at the vile house appeared to me when I first saw them: and at times, such a leering, mischief-boding cast! I would have given the world to have been a hundred miles from him. Yet his behaviour was decent—a decency, however, that I might have seen to be struggled for—for he snatched my hand two or three times, with a vehemence in his grasp that hurt me; speaking words of tenderness through his shut teeth, as it seemed; and let it go with a beggar-voiced humble accent, like the vile woman's just before; half-inward; yet his words and manner carrying the appearance of strong and almost convulsed passion! O my dear! What mischiefs was he not then meditating!

I complained once or twice of thirst. My mouth seemed parched. At the time, I supposed that it was my terror (gasping often as I did for breath) that parched up the roof of my mouth. I called for water: some table-beer was brought me: beer, I suppose, was a better vehicle (if I were not dosed enough before) for their potions. I told the maid that she knew I seldom tasted malt-liquor: yet, suspecting nothing of this nature, being extremely thirsty, I drank it, as what came next: and instantly, as it were, found myself much worse than before; as if inebriated, I should fancy: I know not how.

His servant was gone twice as long as he needed: and just before his return, came one of the pretended Lady Betty's with a letter for Mr. Lovelace.

He sent it up to me. I read it: and then it was that I thought myself a lost creature; it being to put off her going to Hampstead that night, on account of violent fits which Miss Montague was pretended to be seized with; for then immediately came into my head his vile attempt upon me in this house; the revenge that my flight might too probably inspire him with on that occasion, and because of the difficulty I made to forgive him, and to be reconciled to him; his very looks wild and dreadful to me; and the women of the house such as I had more reason than ever, even from the pretended Lady Betty's hint, to be afraid of: all these crowding together in my apprehensive mind, I fell into a kind of frenzy.

I have not remembrance how I was for the time it lasted: but
I know that, in my first agitations, I pulled off my head-dress,
and tore my ruffles in twenty tatters, and ran to find him out.

When a little recovered, I insisted upon the hint he had given
of their coach.   But the messenger, he said, had told him that
it was sent to fetch a physician, lest his chariot should be put
up, or not ready.

I then insisted upon going directly to Lady Betty's lodgings.
Mrs. Leeson's was now a crowded house, he said: and as my
earnestness could be owing to nothing but groundless apprehension [and O what vows, what protestations of his honour did
he then make!], he hoped I would not add to their present concern.   Charlotte, indeed, was used to fits, he said, upon any
great surprises, whether of joy or grief; and they would hold her
for a week together, if not got off in a few hours.

You are an *observer of eyes,* my dear, said the villain; perhaps
in secret insult: saw you not in Miss Montague's now and then,
at Hampstead, something wildish?   I was afraid for her then.
Silence and quiet only do her good: your concern for *her,* and her
love for *you,* will but augment the poor girl's disorder, if you
should go.

All impatient with grief and apprehension, I still declared
myself resolved not to stay in that house till morning.   All I
had in the world, my rings, my watch, my little money, for a
coach; or, if one were not to be got, I would go on foot to
Hampstead that night, though I walked it by myself.

A coach was hereupon sent for, or pretended to be sent for.
Any price, he said, he would give to oblige me, late as it was; and
he would attend me with all his soul.   But no coach was to be got.

Let me cut short the rest.   I grew worse and worse in my
head; now stupid, now raving, now senseless.   The vilest of
vile women was brought to frighten me.   Never was there so
horrible a creature as she appeared to me at the time.

I remember I pleaded for mercy.   I remember that I said
I would be his—indeed I would be his—to obtain his mercy.   But
no mercy found I!   My strength, my intellects, failed me—and
then such scenes followed—O my dear, such dreadful scenes!—
fits upon fits (faintly indeed and imperfectly remembered)
procuring me no compassion—but death was withheld from me.
That would have been too great a mercy!

. . . . . .

Thus was I tricked and deluded back by blacker hearts of my

own sex than I thought there were in the world; who appeared to me to be persons of honour: and, when in his power, thus barbarously was I treated by this villainous man!

I was so senseless, that I dare not aver that the horrid creatures of the house were personally aiding and abetting: but some visionary remembrances I have of female figures, flitting, as I may say, before my sight; the wretched woman's particularly. But as these confused ideas might be owing to the terror I had conceived of the worse than masculine violence she had been permitted to assume to me, for expressing my abhorrence of her house; and as what I suffered from his barbarity wants not that aggravation; I will say no more on a subject so shocking as this must ever be to my remembrance.

I never saw the personating wretches afterwards. He persisted to the last (dreadfully invoking Heaven as a witness to the truth of his assertion) that they were really and truly the ladies they pretended to be; declaring that they could not take leave of me when they left town, because of the state of senselessness and frenzy I was in. For their intoxicating, or rather stupefying potions, had almost deleterious effects upon my intellects, as I have hinted; insomuch that, for several days together, I was under a strange delirium; now moping, now dozing, now weeping, now raving, now scribbling, tearing what I scribbled as fast as I wrote it: *most* miserable when now and then a ray of reason brought confusedly to my remembrance what I had suffered.

Letter LXXXVII—Miss Clarissa Harlowe. [*In continuation*]

The lady next gives an account

Of her recovery from her delirium and sleepy disorder:

Of her attempt to get away in his absence:

Of the conversations that followed, at his return, between them:

Of the guilty figure he made:

Of her resolution not to have him:

Of her several efforts to escape:

Of her treaty with Dorcas to assist her in it:

Of Dorcas's dropping the promissory note, undoubtedly, as she says, on purpose to betray her:

Of her triumph over all the creatures of the house, assembled to terrify her; and perhaps to commit fresh outrages upon her:

Of his setting out for M. Hall:

Of his repeated letters to induce her to meet him at the altar, on her uncle's anniversary:

Of her determined silence to them all:

Of her second escape, effected, *as she says*, contrary to her own expectation: that attempt being at first but the intended prelude to a more promising one which she had formed in her mind:

And of other particulars ; which being to be found in Mr. Lovelace's letters preceding, and that of his friend Belford, are omitted. She then proceeds :

The very hour that I found myself in a place of safety, I took pen to write to you. When I began, I designed only to write six or eight lines, to inquire after your health: for, having heard nothing from you, I feared *indeed* that you *had been*, and *still were*, too ill to write. But no sooner did my pen begin to blot the paper, but my sad heart hurried it into length. The apprehensions I had lain under, that I should not be able to get away; the fatigue I had in effecting my escape; the difficulty of procuring a lodging for myself; having disliked the people of two houses, and those of a third disliking me; for you must think I made a frighted appearance—these, together with the recollection of what I had suffered from him, and my farther apprehensions of my insecurity, and my desolate circumstances, had so disordered me, that I remember I rambled strangely in that letter.

In short, I thought it, on reperusal, a half-distracted one: but I then despaired (were I to begin again) of writing better: so I let it go: and can have no excuse for directing as I did, if the cause of the incoherence in it will not furnish me with a very pitiable one.

The letter I received from your mother was a dreadful blow to me. But nevertheless it had the good effect upon me (labouring, as I did just then, under a violent fit of vapourish despondency, and almost yielding to it) which profuse bleeding and blisterings have in paralytical or apoplectical strokes; reviving my attention, and restoring me to spirits to combat the evils I was surrounded by—sluicing off, and diverting into a new channel (if I may be allowed another metaphor) the overcharging woes which threatened once more to overwhelm my intellects.

But yet I most sincerely lamented (and still lament), in your mother's words, *That I cannot be unhappy by myself*: and was grieved, not only for the trouble I had given you before; but for the new one I had brought upon you by my inattention.

She then gives the substance of the letters she wrote to Mrs.

Norton, to Lady Betty Lawrance, and to Mrs. Hodges; as also of
their answers; whereby she detected all Mr. Lovelace's impostures
She proceeds as follows:

I cannot, however, forbear to wonder how the vile Tomlinson
could come at the knowledge of several of the things he told me
of, and which contributed to give me confidence in him.[1]

I doubt not that the stories of Mrs. Fretchville, and her house,
would be found as vile impostures as any of the rest, were I to
inquire; and had I not enough, and too much, already against
the perjured man.

How have I been led on! What will be the end of such a false
and perjured creature! Heaven not less profaned and defied by
him, than myself deceived and abused! This, however, against
myself I must say, That if what I have suffered be the natural
consequence of my first error, I never can forgive *myself*, although
you are so partial in my favour, as to say, that I was not censurable for what passed before my first escape.

And now, honoured madam, and my dearest Miss Howe, who
are to sit in judgment upon my case, permit me to lay down my
pen with one request, which, with the greatest earnestness, I
make to you both: and that is, That you will neither of you
open your lips in relation to the potions and the violences I have
hinted at. Not that I am solicitous that my disgrace should be
hidden from the world, or that it should not be generally known
that the man has proved a villain to me: for this, it seems,
everybody but myself expected from his character. But
suppose, as his actions by me are really of a *capital nature*,
it were insisted upon that I should appear to prosecute him
and his accomplices in a court of justice, how do you think I
could bear that?

But since my character, *before* the capital enormity, was lost
in the eye of the world; and that from the very hour I left my
father's house; and since all my own hopes of worldly happiness
are entirely over; let me slide quietly into my grave; and let it
not be remembered, except by one friendly tear, and no more,
dropped from your gentle eye, mine own dear Anna Howe, on
the happy day that shall shut up all my sorrows, that there was
such a creature as   CLARISSA HARLOWE.

Saturday, July 8.

[1] The attentive reader need not be referred back for what the lady
nevertheless could not account for, as she knew not that Mr. Lovelace had
come at Miss Howe's letters; particularly that in vol. ii, pp. 291 et seq.,
which he comments upon pp. 367–9 of the same volume.

Letter LXXXVIII—Miss Howe to Miss Clarissa Harlowe

Sunday, July 9.

MAY Heaven signalize its vengeance, in the face of all the world, upon the most abandoned and profligate of men! And in its own time, I doubt not but it will. And we must look to a WORLD BEYOND THIS for the reward of your sufferings!

Another shocking detection, my dear! How have you been deluded! Very watchful I have thought you; very sagacious: but, alas! not watchful, not sagacious enough, for the horrid villain you have had to deal with!

The letter you sent me enclosed as mine, of the 7th of June, is a villainous forgery.[1] The hand, indeed, is astonishingly like mine; and the cover, I see, is actually my cover: but yet the letter is not so exactly imitated, but that (had you had any suspicions about his vileness at the time) you, who so well know my hand, might have detected it.

In short, this vile forged letter, though a long one, contains but a few extracts from mine. Mine was a *very* long one. He has omitted everything, I see, in it that could have shown you what a detestable house the house is; and given you suspicions of the vile Tomlinson. You will see this, and how he has turned Miss Lardner's information, and my advices to you [execrable villain!], to his own horrid ends, by the rough draft of the genuine letter, which I shall enclose.[2]

Apprehensive for *both* our safeties from the villainy of such a daring and profligate contriver, I must call upon you, my dear, to resolve upon taking legal vengeance of the infernal wretch. And this not only for our own sakes, but for the sakes of innocents who otherwise may yet be deluded and outraged by him.

She then gives the particulars of the report made by the young fellow whom she sent to Hampstead with her letter; and who supposed he had delivered it into her own hand[3]; and then proceeds:

I am astonished that the vile wretch, who could know nothing of the time my messenger (whose honesty I can vouch for) would come, could have a creature ready to personate you! Strange, that the man should happen to arrive just as you were gone to church (as I find was the fact, on comparing what he says with your hint that you were at church twice that day), when he might have got to Mrs. Moore's two hours before! But

---

[1] See pp. 94 et seq. of this volume.   [2] See pp. 1 et seq., ibid.
[3] See pp. 158 et seq., ibid.

had you told me, my dear, that the villain had found you out, and was about you! You should have done that—yet I blame you upon a judgment founded on the *event* only!

I never had any faith in the stories that go current among country girls, of spectres, familiars, and demons; yet I see not any other way to account for this wretch's successful villainy, and for his means of working up his specious delusions, but by supposing (if he be not the devil himself) that he has a familiar constantly at his elbow. Sometimes it seems to me that this familiar assumes the shape of that solemn villain Tomlinson: sometimes that of the execrable Sinclair, as he calls her: sometimes it is permitted to take that of Lady Betty Lawrance—but, when it would assume the angelic shape and mien of my beloved friend, see what a bloated figure it made!

'Tis my opinion, my dear, that you will be no longer safe where you are, than while the V. is in the country. Words are poor! or how could I execrate him! I have hardly any doubt that he has sold himself for a time. Oh, may the time be short! Or may his infernal prompter no more keep covenant with him than he does with others!

I enclose not only the rough draft of my long letter mentioned above; but the heads of that which the young fellow thought he delivered into your own hands at Hampstead. And when you have perused them, I will leave you to judge how much reason I had to be surprised that you wrote me not an answer to either of those letters; one of which you owned you had received (though it proved to be his forged one); the other delivered into your own hands, as I was assured; and both of them of so much concern to your honour; and still how much more surprised I must be, when I received a letter from Mrs. Townsend, dated June 15, from Hampstead, importing, "That Mr. Lovelace, who had been with you several days, had, on the Monday before, brought Lady Betty and his cousin, richly dressed, and in a coach and four, to visit you: who, with your own consent, had carried you to town with them—to your former lodgings; where you still were: that the Hampstead women believed you to be married; and reflected upon me as a fomenter of differences between man and wife: that he himself was at Hampstead the day before; viz. Wednesday the 14th; and boasted of his happiness with you; inviting Mrs. Moore, Mrs. Bevis, and Miss Rawlins, to go to town to visit his spouse; which they promised to do: that he declared that you were entirely reconciled to your former lodgings: and that, finally, the women at Hampstead told Mrs. Townsend, that he had very handsomely discharged theirs."

I own to you, my dear, that I was so much surprised and disgusted at these appearances against a conduct till then unexceptionable, that I was resolved to make myself as easy as I could, and wait till you should think fit to write to me. But I could rein in my impatience but for a few days; and on the 20th of June I wrote a sharp letter to you; which I find you did not receive.

What a fatality, my dear, has appeared in your case, from the very beginning till this hour! Had my mother permitted——

But can I blame *her*; when you have a *father* and *mother* living, who have so much to answer for? So much! as no father and mother, considering the child they have driven, persecuted, exposed, renounced, ever had to answer for!

But again I must execrate the abandoned villain—yet, as I said before, *all* words are poor, and beneath the occasion.

But see we not, in the horrid perjuries and treachery of this man, what rakes and libertines will do when they get a young creature into their power? It is probable that he might have the intolerable presumption to hope an easier conquest: but, when your unexampled vigilance and exalted virtue made potions, and rapes, and the utmost violences, necessary to the attainment of his detestable end, we see that he never boggled at them. I have no doubt that the same or equal wickedness would be *oftener* committed by men of his villainous cast, if the folly and credulity of the poor inconsiderates who throw themselves into their hands, did not give them an easier triumph.

With what comfort must those parents reflect upon these things, who have happily disposed of their daughters in marriage to a virtuous man! And how happy the young women who find themselves safe in a worthy protection! If such a person as Miss Clarissa Harlowe could not escape, who can be secure? Since, though every rake is not a LOVELACE, neither is every woman a CLARISSA: and his attempts were but proportioned to your resistance and vigilance.

My mother has commanded me to let you know her thoughts upon the whole of your sad story. I will do it in another letter; and send it to you with this, by a special messenger.

But, for the future, if you approve of it, I will send my letters by the usual hand (Collins's), to be left at the Saracen's Head on Snow Hill: whither you may send yours (as we both used to do, to Wilson's), except such as we shall think fit to transmit by the post: which I am afraid, after my next, must be directed to Mr. Hickman, as before: since my mother is for fixing a condition to our correspondence, which, I doubt, you will not comply with, though I wish you would. This condition I shall acquaint you with by and by.

Meantime, begging excuse for all the harsh things in my last, of which your sweet meekness and superior greatness of soul have now made me most heartily ashamed, I beseech you, my dearest creature, to believe me to be

Your truly sympathizing and unalterable friend,
ANNA HOWE.

Letter LXXXIX—Miss Howe to Miss Clarissa Harlowe

Monday, July 10.

I NOW, my dearest friend, resume my pen, to obey my mother, in giving you her opinion upon your unhappy story.

She still harps upon the old string, and will have it that all your calamities are owing to your first fatal step; for she believes (what I cannot) that your relations had intended, after one general trial more, to comply with your aversion, if they had found it as riveted a one, as, let me say, it was a folly to suppose it would not be found to be, after so many *ridiculously* repeated experiments.

As to your latter sufferings from that vilest of miscreants, she is unalterably of opinion, that if all be as you have related (which she doubts not) with regard to the potions, and to the violences you have sustained, you ought, by all means, to set on foot a prosecution against him, and against his devilish accomplices.

She asks, What murderers, what ravishers, would be brought to justice, if *modesty* were to be a general plea, and allowable, against appearing in a court to prosecute?

She says that the good of society requires that such a beast of prey should be hunted out of it: and, if you do not prosecute him, she thinks you will be answerable for all the mischiefs he may do in the course of his future villainous life.

Will it be thought, Nancy, said she, that Miss Clarissa Harlowe can be in earnest, when she says she is not solicitous to have her disgraces concealed from the world, if she be afraid or ashamed to appear in court, to do justice to herself and her sex against him? Will it not be rather surmised that she may be apprehensive that some weakness, or lurking love, will appear upon the trial of the strange cause? If, inferred she, such complicated villainy as this (where perjury, potions, forgery, subornation, are all combined to effect the ruin of an innocent creature, and to dishonour a family of eminence, and where those very crimes, as may be supposed, are proofs of her innocence) is to go off with impunity, what case will deserve to be brought into judgment; or what malefactor ought to be hanged?

Then she thinks, and so do I, that the vile creatures, his accomplices, ought by all means to be brought to condign punishment, as they must and will be, upon bringing him to his trial: and this may be a means to blow up and root out a whole nest of vipers, and save many innocent creatures.

She added that if Miss Clarissa Harlowe could be so indifferent about having this public justice done upon such a wretch for her *own* sake, she ought to overcome her scruples out of regard to her family, her acquaintance, and her sex, which are all highly injured and scandalized by his villainy to her.

For her own part, she declares that were *she* your mother she would forgive you upon no other terms: and, upon your compliance with these, she herself will undertake to reconcile all your family to you.

These, my dear, are my mother's sentiments upon your sad story.

I cannot say but there are reason and justice in them: and it is my opinion that it would be very right for the law to *oblige* an injured woman to prosecute, and to make seduction on the man's part capital, where *his* studied baseness, and no fault in *her will*, appeared.

To this purpose the custom in the Isle of Man is a very good one.

"If a single woman there prosecutes a single man for a rape, the ecclesiastical judges empanel a jury; and, if this jury find him guilty, he is returned *guilty* to the temporal courts: where, if he be convicted, the deemster, or judge, delivers to the woman a rope, a sword, and a ring; and she has it in her choice to have him hanged, beheaded, or to marry him."

One of the two former, I think, should always be her option.

I long for the full particulars of your story. You must have but too much time upon your hands for a mind so active as yours, if tolerable health and spirits be afforded you.

The villainy of the worst of men, and the virtue of the most excellent of women, I expect will be exemplified in it, were it to be written in the same connected and particular manner in which you used to write to me.

Try for it, my dearest friend; and since you cannot give the *example* without the *warning*, give *both*, for the sakes of all those who shall hear of your unhappy fate; beginning from yours of June 5, your prospects then not disagreeable. I pity you for the task; though I cannot willingly exempt you from it.

.   .   .   .   .

My mother will have me add that she must *insist* upon your prosecuting the villain. She repeats that she makes that a condition on which she permits our future correspondence. Let me, therefore, know your thoughts upon it. I asked her if she would be willing that I should appear to support you in court if you complied? By all means, she said, if that would induce you to begin with him, and with the horrid women. I think I could attend you, I am *sure* I could, were there but a probability of bringing the monster to his deserved end.

Once more your thoughts of it, supposing it were to meet with the approbation of your relations.

But whatever be your determination on this head, it shall be my constant prayer that God will give you patience to bear your heavy afflictions, as a person ought to do who has not brought them upon herself by a faulty will; that He will speak peace and comfort to your wounded mind; and give you many happy years. I am, and ever will be,

Your affectionate and faithful

ANNA HOWE.

The two preceding letters were sent by a special messenger: in the cover were written the following lines:

Monday, July 10.

I CANNOT, my dearest friend, suffer the enclosed to go un-accompanied by a few lines, to signify to you that they are both less tender in some places than I would have written, had they not been to pass my mother's inspection. The principal reason, however, of my writing thus separately is, to beg of you to permit me to send you money and necessaries; which you must needs want: and that you will let me know if either I, or *anybody I can influence*, can be of service to you. I am excessively apprehensive that you are not enough out of the villain's reach where you are. Yet London, I am persuaded, is the place of all others, to be private in.

I could tear my hair for vexation, that I have it not in my power to afford you *personal* protection!   I am

Your ever devoted

ANNA HOWE.

Once more forgive me, my dearest creature, for my barbarous tauntings in mine of the 5th!   Yet I can hardly forgive myself. I to be so cruel, yet to know you so well!   Whence, whence, had I this vile impatience of spirit!

Letter XC—*Miss Clarissa Harlowe to Miss Howe*

Tuesday, July 11.

"*Forgive you*, my dear!   Most cordially do I forgive you.   Will you forgive me for some sharp things I wrote in return to yours of the 5th?   You could not have loved me as you do, nor had the concern you have always shown for my honour, if you had not been utterly displeased with me, on the appearance which my conduct wore to you when you wrote that letter.   I most heartily thank you, my best and only love, for the opportunity you gave me of clearing it up; and for being generously ready to acquit me of intentional blame, the moment you had read my melancholy narrative.

As you are so earnest to have all the particulars of my sad story before you, I will, if life and spirits be lent me, give you an ample account of all that has befallen me, from the time you mention. But this, it is very probable, you will not see, till after the close of my last scene: and as I shall write with a view to that, I hope no other voucher will be wanted for the veracity of the writer, be who will the reader.

I am far from thinking myself out of the reach of this man's further violence.   But what can I do?   Whither can I fly? Perhaps my bad state of health (which must grow worse, as recollection of the past evils, and reflections upon them, grow heavier and heavier upon me) may be my protection.   Once, indeed, I thought of going abroad; and had I the prospect of many years before me, I would go.   But, my dear, the blow is given.   Nor have you reason now, circumstanced as I am, to be concerned that it is.   What a heart must I have, if it be not broken!   And indeed, my *dear* friend, I do so earnestly wish for the last closing scene, and with so much comfort find myself in a declining way, that I even sometimes ungratefully regret that naturally healthy constitution, which used to double upon me all my enjoyments.

As to the earnestly recommended prosecution, I may possibly touch upon it more largely hereafter, if ever I shall have better spirits; for they are at present extremely sunk and low.   But, just now, I will only say that I would sooner suffer every evil (the repetition of the capital one excepted) than appear publicly in a court to do myself justice.[1]   And I am heartily grieved that your mother prescribes such a measure as the condition of our future correspondence: for the continuance of your friendship, my dear, and the desire I had to correspond with you to my life's end, were all my remaining hopes and consolation.   Nevertheless, as that friendship is in the power of the *heart*, not of the *hand* only, I hope I shall not forfeit that.

O my dear! what would I give to obtain a revocation of my father's malediction!   A reconciliation is not to be hoped for. You, who never loved my father, may think my solicitude on this head a weakness: but the *motive* for it, sunk as my spirits *at times* are, is not *always* weak.

.   .   .   .   .   .

I approve of the method you prescribe for the conveyance of our letters; and have already caused the porter of the inn to be engaged to bring to me yours, the moment that Collins arrives with them.   And the servant of the house where I am will be permitted to carry mine to Collins for you.

I have written a letter to Miss Rawlins of Hampstead; the answer to which, just now received, has helped me to the knowledge of the vile contrivance by which this wicked man got your letter of June the 10th.   I will give you the contents of both.

In mine to her I briefly acquaint her "with what had befallen me, through the vileness of the women who had been passed upon me as the aunt and cousin of the wickedest of men; and own that I never was married to him.   I desire her to make particular inquiry, and to let me know who it was at Mrs. Moore's on Sunday afternoon, June 11, while I was at church, received a letter from Miss Howe, pretending to be me, and lying on a couch: which letter, had it come to my hands, would have saved me from ruin.   I excuse myself (on the score

---

[1] Dr. Lewen, as will be seen hereafter, presses her to this public prosecution, by arguments worthy of his character; which she answers in a manner worthy of hers.

of the delirium, which the horrid usage I had received threw me into, and from a confinement as barbarous and illegal) that I had not before applied to Mrs. Moore for an account of what I was indebted to her: which account I now desired.   And, for fear of being traced by Mr. Lovelace, I directed her to superscribe her answer, To Mrs. Mary Atkins; to be left till called for, at the Belle Savage Inn, on Ludgate Hill."

In her answer she tells me "that the vile wretch prevailed upon Mrs. Bevis to personate me [a sudden motion of his, it seems, on the appearance of your messenger], and persuaded her to lie along on a couch: a handkerchief over her neck and face; pretending to be ill; the credulous woman drawn in by false notions of your ill offices to keep up a variance between a man and his wife—and so taking the letter from your messenger as me.

"Miss Rawlins takes pains to excuse Mrs. Bevis's intention. She expresses their astonishment and concern at what I communicate: but is glad, however, and so they are all, that they know in time the vileness of the base man; the two widows and herself having, at his earnest invitation, designed me a visit at Mrs. Sinclair's; supposing all to be happy between him and me; as he assured them was the case.   Mr. Lovelace, she informs me, had handsomely satisfied Mrs. Moore.   And Miss Rawlins concludes with wishing to be favoured with the particulars of so extraordinary a story, as these particulars may be of use, to let her see what wicked creatures (women as well as men) there are in the world."

I thank you, my dear, for the drafts of your two letters which were intercepted by this horrid man.   I see the great advantage they were of to him, in the prosecution of his villainous designs against the poor wretch whom he has so long made the sport of his abhorred inventions.

Let me repeat that I am quite sick of life; and of an earth in which *innocent* and *benevolent* spirits are sure to be considered as *aliens*, and to be made sufferers by the *genuine sons* and *daughters* of *that earth*.

How unhappy that those letters only which could have acquainted me with his horrid views, and armed me against them, and against the vileness of the base women, should fall into his hands!   Unhappier still, in that my very escape to Hampstead gave him the opportunity of receiving them!

Nevertheless, I cannot but still wonder how it was possible for that Tomlinson to know what passed between Mr. Hickman and my Uncle Harlowe [1]: a circumstance which gave that vile impostor most of his credit with me.

How the wicked wretch himself could find me out at Hampstead, must also remain wholly a mystery to me. He *may* glory in his contrivances—he, who has more wickedness than wit, *may* glory in his contrivances!—but, after all, I shall, I humbly presume to hope, be happy when he, poor wretch, will be—alas!—who can say what!

Adieu, my dearest friend! May *you* be happy! And then your Clarissa cannot be wholly miserable!

Letter XCI—*Miss Howe to Miss Clarissa Harlowe*

Wedn. Night, July 12.

I WRITE, my dearest creature, I cannot *but* write, to express my concern on your dejection. Let me beseech you, my charming excellence, let me beseech you, not to give way to it.

Comfort yourself, on the contrary, in the triumphs of a virtue unsullied; a will wholly faultless. Who could have withstood the trials that you have surmounted? Your Cousin Morden will soon come. He will see justice done you, I make no doubt, as well with regard to what concerns your person as your estate. And many happy days may you yet see; and much good may you still do, if you will not heighten unavoidable accidents into guilty despondency.

But why, my dear, this pining solicitude continued after a reconciliation with relations as unworthy as implacable; whose wills are governed by an all-grasping brother, who finds his account in keeping the breach open? On this over-solicitude it is now plain to me that the vilest of men built all his schemes. He saw that you thirsted after it beyond all reason for hope. The view, the hope, I own, extremely desirable, had your family been Christians; or even had they been pagans who had bowels.

I shall send this short letter [I am obliged to make it a short one] by *young* Rogers, as we call him; the fellow I sent to you to Hampstead; an innocent, though pragmatical rustic. Admit him, I pray you, into your presence, that he may report to me how you look, and how you are.

Mr. Hickman should attend you; but I apprehend that all his motions, and mine own too, are watched by the execrable wretch: as indeed his are by an agent of mine; for I own that I am so apprehensive of his plots and revenge, now I know that

[1] See the note at the bottom of p. 374.

he has intercepted my vehement letters against him, that he is the subject of my dreams, as well as of my waking fears.

.　　　.　　　.　　　.　　　.　　　.

My mother, at my earnest importunity, has just given me leave to write, and to receive your letters—but fastened this condition upon the concession, that yours must be under cover to Mr. Hickman [this with a view, I suppose, to give him consideration with me]; and upon this further condition, that she is to see all we write. "When girls are set upon a point," she told one who told me again, "it is better for a mother, if possible, to make herself of their party, than to oppose them; since there will be then hopes that she will still hold the reins in her own hands."

Pray let me know what the people are with whom you lodge? Shall I send Mrs. Townsend to direct you to lodgings either more safe or more convenient for you?

Be pleased to write to me by Rogers; who will wait on you for your answer at your own time.

Adieu, my dearest creature. Comfort *yourself*, as you would in the like unhappy circumstances comfort

Your own

Anna Howe.

Letter XCII—*Miss Clarissa Harlowe to Miss Howe*

Thursday, July 13.

I am extremely concerned, my dear Miss Howe, for being primarily the occasion of the apprehensions you have of this wicked man's vindictive attempts. What a wide-spreading error is mine!

If I find that he sets on foot any machination against you, or against Mr. Hickman, I do assure you I will consent to prosecute him, although I were sure I should not survive my first appearance at the bar he should be arraigned at.

I own the justice of your mother's arguments on that subject; but must say that I think there are circumstances in my particular case which will excuse me, although on a slighter occasion than that you are apprehensive of I should decline to appear against him. I have said that I may one day enter more particularly into this argument.

Your messenger has now *indeed* seen me. I talked with him on the cheat put upon him at Hampstead: and am sorry to have reason to say, that had not the poor young man been very *simple*, and very *self-sufficient*, he had not been so grossly deluded. Mrs. Bevis has the same plea to make for herself. A good-natured, thoughtless woman; not used to converse with so vile and so specious a deceiver as him who made his advantage of both these shallow creatures.

I think I cannot be more private than where I am. I hope I am safe. All the risk I run, is in going out and returning from morning prayers; which I have two or three times ventured to do; once at Lincoln's Inn Chapel, at eleven; once at St. Dunstan's, Fleet Street, at seven in the morning,[1] in a chair both times; and twice, at six in the morning, at the neighbouring church in Covent Garden. The wicked wretches I have escaped from will not, I hope, come to church to look for me; especially at so early prayers; and I have fixed upon the privatest pew in the latter *church* to hide myself in; and perhaps I may lay out a little matter in an ordinary gown, by way of disguise; my face half hid by my mob. I am very careless, my dear, of my appearance now. Neat and clean takes up the whole of my attention.

The man's name at whose house I lodge is Smith—a glove-*maker*, as well as *seller*. His wife is the shopkeeper. A dealer also in stockings, ribbands, snuff, and perfumes. A matron-like woman, plain-hearted, and prudent. The husband an honest, industrious man. And they live in good understanding with each other: a proof with me that their hearts are right; for where a married couple live together upon ill terms, it is a sign, I think, that each knows something amiss of the other, either with regard to temper or morals, which if the world knew as well as themselves, it would perhaps as little like them as such people like each other. Happy the marriage where neither man nor wife has any wilful or premeditated evil in their general conduct to reproach the other with! For even persons who have bad hearts will have a veneration for those who have good ones.

Two neat rooms, with plain, but clean furniture, on the first floor, are mine; one they call the dining-room.

There is, up another pair of stairs, a very worthy widow lodger, Mrs. Lovick by name; who, although of low fortunes, is much respected, as Mrs. Smith assures me, by people of condition of her acquaintance, for her piety, prudence, and understanding. With her I propose to be well acquainted.

I thank you, my dear, for your kind, your seasonable advice

---

[1] The seven o'clock prayers at St. Dunstan's have been since discontinued.

and consolation. I hope I shall have more grace given me than to despond, in the *religious* sense of the word: especially as I can apply to myself the comfort you give me, that neither my will, nor my inconsiderateness, has contributed to my calamity. But, nevertheless, the irreconcilableness of my relations, whom I love with an unabated reverence; my apprehensions of fresh violences [this wicked man, I doubt, will not yet let me rest]; my being destitute of protection; my youth, my sex, my unacquaintedness with the world, subjecting me to insults; my reflections on the scandal I have given, added to the sense of the indignities I have received from a man of whom I deserved not ill; all together will undoubtedly bring on the effect that cannot be undesirable to me. The slower, however, perhaps from my natural good constitution; and, as I presume to imagine, from principles which I hope will, in due time, and by due reflection, set me *above the sense of all worldly disappointments*.

At present my head is much disordered. I have not indeed enjoyed it with any degree of clearness since the violence done to that, and to my heart too, by the wicked arts of the abandoned creatures I was cast among.

I must have more conflicts. At times I find myself not subdued enough to my condition. I will welcome those conflicts as they come, as *probationary* ones. But yet my father's malediction—the temporary part so strangely and so literally completed!—I cannot, however, think when my mind is *strongest* —but what is the story of Isaac, and Jacob, and Esau, and of Rebekah's cheating the latter of the blessing designed for him (in favour of Jacob), given us for in the 27th chapter of Genesis? My father used, I remember, to enforce the doctrine deducible from it, on his children, by many arguments. At least, therefore, *he* must believe there is great weight in the curse he has announced; and shall I not be solicitous to get it revoked, that he may not hereafter be grieved, for my sake, that he did *not* revoke it?

All I will at present add, are my thanks to your mother for her indulgence to us; due compliments to Mr. Hickman; and my request that you will believe me to be, to my last hour, and beyond it, if possible, my beloved friend, and my *dearer* self (for what is now my self?)

Your obliged and affectionate

CLARISSA HARLOWE.

Letter XCIII—Mr. Lovelace to John Belford, Esq.

Friday, July 7.

I HAVE three of thy letters at once before me to answer; in each of which thou complainest of my silence; and in one of them tellest me that thou canst not live without I scribble to thee every day, or every other day at least.

Why, then, die, Jack, if thou wilt. What heart, thinkest thou, can I have to write, when I have lost the only subject worth writing upon?

Help me again to my angel, to my CLARISSA; and thou shalt have a letter from me, or writing at least, part of a letter, every hour. All that the charmer of my heart shall say, that will I put down: every motion, every air of her beloved person, every look, will I try to describe; and when she is silent I will endeavour to tell thee her thoughts, either what they are, or what I would have them to be—so that, having *her*, I shall never want a subject. Having lost her, my whole soul is a blank: the whole creation round me, the elements above, beneath, and everything I *behold* (for nothing can *I enjoy*), are a blank without her!

Oh, return, return, thou only charmer of my soul! Return to thy adoring Lovelace! What is the light, what the air, what the town, what the country, what's anything, without thee? Light, air, joy, harmony, in my notion, are but parts of thee; and could they be all expressed in one word, that word would be CLARISSA.

O my beloved CLARISSA, return thou then; once more return to bless thy LOVELACE, who now, by the loss of thee, knows the value of the jewel he has slighted; and rises every morning but to curse the sun that shines upon everybody but him!

. . . . . .

Well, but, Jack, 'tis a surprising thing to me that the dear fugitive cannot be met with; cannot be heard of. She is so poor a plotter (for plotting is not her talent) that I am confident, had I been at liberty, I should have found her out before now; although the different emissaries I have employed about town, round the adjacent villages, and in Miss Howe's vicinage, have hitherto failed of success. But my lord continues so weak and low-spirited, that there is no getting from him. I would not disoblige a man whom I think in danger still: for would his gout, now it has got him down, but give him, like a fair boxer, the rising blow, all would be over with him. And here [pox of his fondness for me! it happens at a very bad time] he makes me sit hours together entertaining him with my rogueries (a pretty amusement for a sick man!): and yet, whenever he has the gout, he prays night and morning with his chaplain. But what must *his* notions of religion be, who, after he has nosed and mumbled over his responses, can give a sigh or groan of satisfaction, as if he thought he had made up with Heaven; and return with a new appetite to my stories?—encouraging them, by shaking his sides with laughing at them, and calling me a sad fellow, in such an accent as shows he takes no small delight in his kinsman.

The old peer has been a sinner in his day, and suffers for it now: a sneaking sinner, *sliding*, rather than *rushing*, into vices, for fear of his reputation: or, rather, for fear of detection, and positive proof; for these sort of fellows, Jack, have no real regard for reputation. Paying for what he never had, and never daring to rise to the joy of an enterprise at first hand, which could bring him within view of a tilting, or of the honour of being considered as the principal man in a court of justice.

To see such an old Trojan as this, just dropping into the grave, which I hoped ere this would have been dug, and filled up with him; crying out with pain, and grunting with weakness; yet in the same moment crack his leathern face into an horrible laugh, and call a young sinner charming varlet, encoring him, as formerly he used to do the Italian eunuchs; what a preposterous, what an unnatural adherence to old habits!

My two cousins are generally present when I *entertain*, as the old peer calls it. Those stories must drag horribly, that have not more hearers and applauders than relaters.

Applauders!

Ay, Belford, *applauders*, repeat I; for although these girls pretend to blame me sometimes for the *facts*, they praise my manner, my invention, my intrepidity. Besides, what other people call *blame*, that call I *praise*: I ever did; and so I very early discharged *shame*, that cold-water damper to an enterprising spirit.

These are smart girls; they have life and wit; and yesterday, upon Charlotte's raving against me upon a related enterprise, I told her that I had had it in debate several times, whether she were or were not too near of kin to me: and that it was once a moot point with me, whether I could not love her dearly for a month or so: and perhaps it was well for her that another pretty little puss started up and diverted me just as I was entering the course.

They all three held up their hands and eyes at once. But I observed, that though the girls exclaimed against me, they were not so angry at this plain speaking, as I have found my beloved upon hints so dark that I have wondered at her quick apprehension.

I told Charlotte that, grave as she pretended to be in her *smiling* resentments on this declaration, I was sure I should not have been put to the expense of above two or three stratagems (for nobody admired a good invention more than she), could I but have disentangled her conscience from the embarrasses of consanguinity.

She pretended to be highly displeased: so did her sister for her. I told her that she seemed as much in earnest as if she had thought *me* so; and *dared* the trial. Plain words, I said, in these cases, were more shocking to their sex than *gradatim* actions And I bid Patty not be displeased at my distinguishing her sister; since I had a great respect for *her* likewise.

An Italian air, in my usual careless way, a half-struggled-for kiss from me, and a shrug of the shoulder, by way of admiration, from each pretty cousin, and Sad, sad fellow, from the old peer, attended with a side-shaking laugh, made us all friends.

There, Jack! wilt thou, or wilt thou not, take this for a letter? There's quantity, I am sure. How have I filled a sheet (not a shorthand one indeed) without a subject! My fellow shall take this; for he is going to town. And if thou canst think tolerably of such execrable stuff, I will soon send thee another.

Letter XCIV—Mr. Lovelace to John Belford, Esq.

Six Saturday Morning, July 8.

HAVE I nothing new, nothing diverting, in my whimsical way, thou askest, in one of thy three letters before me, to entertain thee with? And thou tellest me that, when I have least to *narrate*, to speak in the Scottish phrase, I am most diverting. A pretty compliment, either to thyself, or to me. To *both* indeed! A sign that thou hast as frothy a heart as I a head. But canst thou suppose that this admirable woman is not all, is not everything with me? Yet I dread to think of her too; for detection of all my contrivances, I doubt, must come next.

The old peer is also full of Miss Harlowe: and so are my cousins. He hopes I will not be such a dog [there's a specimen of his peer-like dialect] as to think of doing dishonourably by a woman of so much merit, beauty, and fortune; and *he* says of so good a family. But I tell him that this is a string he must not touch: that it is a very tender point: in short, is my sore place; and that I am afraid he would handle it too roughly, were I to put myself in the power of so ungentle an operator.

He shakes his crazy head. He thinks all is not as it should be between us; longs to have me present her to him as my wife; and often tells me what great things he will do, additional to his former proposals; and what presents he will make on the birth of the first child. But I hope the whole of his estate will be in my hands before such an event take place. No harm in *hoping*, Jack! Lord M. says, *Were it not for hope, the heart would break.*

.   .   .   .   .   .

Eight o'clock at midsummer, and these lazy varletesses (in full health) not come down yet to breakfast! What a confounded indecency in young ladies, to let a rake know that they love their beds so dearly, and, at the same time, *where to have them!* But I'll punish them. They shall breakfast with their old uncle, and yawn at one another as if for a wager; while I drive my phaeton to Colonel Ambrose's, who yesterday gave me invitation both to breakfast and dine, on account of two Yorkshire nieces, celebrated toasts, who have been with him this fortnight past; and who, he says, want to see *me*. So, Jack, all women do not run away from me, thank Heaven! I wish I could have leave of my heart, since the dear fugitive is so ungrateful, to drive her out of it with another beauty. But who can supplant her? Who can be admitted to a place in it after Miss Clarissa Harlowe?

At my return, if I can find a subject, I will scribble on, to oblige thee.

My phaeton's ready. My cousins send me word they are just coming down: so in spite I'll be gone.

Saturday Afternoon.

I did stay to dine with the colonel, and his lady and nieces: but I could not pass the afternoon with them for the heart of me. There was enough in the persons and faces of the two young ladies to set me upon comparisons. Particular features held my attention for a few moments: but those served but to whet my impatience to find the charmer of my soul; who, for person, for air, for mind, had never any equal. My heart recoiled and sickened upon comparing minds and conversation. Pert wit, a too studied desire to please; each in high good humour with herself; an open-mouth affectation in both, to show white teeth, as if the principal excellence; and to invite amorous familiarity, by the promise of a sweet breath; at the same time reflecting tacitly upon breaths arrogantly implied to be less pure.

Once I could have borne them.

They seemed to be disappointed that I was so soon able to leave them. Yet have I not at present so much vanity [my Clarissa has cured me of my vanity] as to attribute their disappointment so much to particular liking of me, as to their own self-admiration. They looked upon me as a connoisseur in beauty. They would have been proud of engaging my attention, as such: but so affected, so flimsy-witted, mere skin-deep beauties! They had looked no further into themselves than what their glasses had enabled them to see: and their glasses were flattering glasses too; for I thought them passive-faced, and spiritless; with eyes, however, upon the hunt for conquests, and bespeaking the attention of others, in order to countenance their own. I believe I could, with a little pains, have given them life and soul, and to every feature of their faces sparkling information—but my Clarissa!—O Belford, my Clarissa has made me eyeless and senseless to every other beauty! Do thou find her for me, as a subject worthy of my pen, or this shall be the last from

Thy LOVELACE.

Letter XCV—Mr. Lovelace to John Belford, Esq.

Sunday Night, July 9.

NOW, Jack, have I a subject with a vengeance. I am in the very height of my trial for all my sins to my beloved fugitive. For here, to-day, at about five o'clock, arrived Lady Sarah Sadleir and Lady Betty Lawrance, each in her chariot and six. Dowagers love equipage; and these cannot travel ten miles without a set, and half a dozen horsemen.

My time had hung heavy upon my hands; and so I went to church after dinner. Why may not handsome fellows, thought I, like to be looked at, as well as handsome wenches? I fell in, when service was over, with Major Warneton; and so came not home till after six; and was surprised, at entering the courtyard here, to find it littered with equipages and servants. I was sure the owners of them came for no good to me.

Lady Sarah, I soon found, was raised to this visit by Lady Betty; who has health enough to allow her to look out of herself, and out of her own affairs, for business. Yet congratulation to

Lord M. on his amendment [spiteful devils on both accounts!]
was the avowed errand.   But coming in my absence, I was their
principal subject: and they had opportunity to set each other's
heart against me.

Simon Parsons hinted this to me as I passed by the steward's
office; for it seems they talked loud; and he was making up some
accounts with old Pritchard.

However, I hastened to pay my duty to them.   Other people
not performing theirs, is no excuse for the neglect of our own,
you know.

And now I enter upon my TRIAL

With horrible grave faces was I received.   The two antiques
only bowed their tabby heads; making longer faces than
ordinary; and all the old lines appearing strong in their furrowed
foreheads and fallen cheeks.   How do you, cousin? and, How
do you, Mr. Lovelace? looking all round at one another, as who
should say, Do you speak first; and, Do you: for they seemed
resolved to lose no time.

I had nothing for it but an air as manly as theirs was womanly.
Your servant, madam, to Lady Betty; and, Your servant,
madam, I am glad to see you abroad, to Lady Sarah.

I took my seat.   Lord M. looked horribly glum; his fingers
clasped, and turning round and round, under and over, his but
just disgouted thumbs; his sallow face, and goggling eyes, cast
upon the floor, on the fireplace, on his two sisters, on his two
kinswomen, by turns; but not once deigning to look upon me.

Then I began to think of the laudanum and wet cloth I told
thee of long ago; and to call myself in question for a tenderness
of heart that will never do me good.

At last, Mr. Lovelace!—Cousin Lovelace!—Hem!—Hem!—
I am sorry, very sorry, hesitated Lady Sarah, that there is no
hope of your ever taking up——

What's the matter *now*, madam?

The matter now!—Why, Lady Betty has two letters from Miss
Harlowe which have told us what's the matter.   Are all women
alike with you?

Yes; I could have answered; 'bating the difference which
pride makes.

Then they all chorused upon me.   Such a character as Miss
Harlowe's! cried one—A lady of so much generosity and good
sense! Another: How charmingly she writes! the two maiden
monkeys, looking at her fine handwriting: her perfections **my**

crimes. What can you expect will be the end of these things?
cried Lady Sarah. Damned, damned doings! vociferated the
peer, shaking his loose-fleshed wabbling chaps, which hung on
his shoulders like an old cow's dew-lap.

For my part I hardly knew whether to sing or say what I had
to reply to these all-at-once attacks upon me! Fair and softly,
ladies. One at a time, I beseech you. I am not to be hunted
down without being heard, I hope. Pray let me see these letters.
I beg you will let me see them.

There they are: that's the first. Read it out, if you can.

I opened a letter from my charmer, dated *Thursday, June* 29,
our wedding-day, that was to be, and written to Lady Betty
Lawrance. By the contents, to my great joy, I find the dear
creature is alive and well, and in charming spirits. But the
direction where to send an answer was so scratched out that I
could not read it; which afflicted me much.

She puts three questions in it to Lady Betty.

1st, About a letter of hers, dated *June* 7, congratulating me
on my nuptials, and which I was so good as to save Lady Betty
the trouble of writing—a very civil thing of me, I think.

Again: "Whether she and one of her nieces Montague were to
go to town, on an old Chancery suit?" And, "Whether they
actually did go to town accordingly, and to Hampstead afterwards?" and, "Whether they brought to town from thence the
young creature whom they visited?" was the subject of the
second and third questions.

A little inquisitive, dear rogue! and what did she expect to be
the better for these questions? But curiosity, damned curiosity,
is the itch of the sex—yet when didst thou know it turned to
their benefit? For they seldom inquire, but when they fear—
and the proverb, as my lord has it, says, *It comes with a fear*.
That is, I suppose, what they fear generally happens, because
there is generally occasion for the fear.

Curiosity, indeed, she avows to be her only motive for these
interrogatories: for though she says her ladyship may suppose
the questions are not asked for good to *me*, yet the answer can
do me no harm, nor her good, only to give her to understand—
whether I have told her a parcel of damned lies; that's the plain
English of her inquiry.

Well, madam, said I, with as much philosophy as I could
assume; and may I ask—Pray, what was your ladyship's answer?

There's a copy of it, tossing it to me, very disrespectfully.

This answer was dated *July* 1. A very kind and complaisant

one to the lady, but very so-so to her poor kinsman—that people can give up their own flesh and blood with so much ease! She tells her "how proud all our family would be of an alliance with such an excellence." She does me justice in saying how much I adore her, as an angel of a woman; and begs of her, for I know not how many sakes, besides my soul's sake, "that she will be so good as to have me for a husband:" and answers —thou wilt guess how—to the lady's questions.

Well, madam; and, pray, may I be favoured with the lady's other letter? I presume it is in reply to yours.

It is, said the peer: but, sir, let me ask you a few questions before you read it. Give *me* the letter, Lady Betty.

There it is, my lord.

Then on went the spectacles, and his head moved to the lines: A charming pretty hand! I have often heard that this lady is a *genius*.

And so, Jack, repeating my lord's wise comments and questions will let thee into the contents of this merciless letter.

"*Monday, July 3*" [reads my lord].—Let me see! That was last *Monday*; no longer ago! "*Monday, July the third.* Madam —I cannot excuse myself"—um, um, um, um, um, um [humming inarticulately, and skipping],—"I must own to you, madam, that the honour of being related——"

Off went the spectacles. Now, tell me, sir-r, has not this lady lost all the friends she had in the world for your sake?

She has very implacable friends, my lord: we all know that.

But has she not lost them all for your sake? Tell me that.

I believe so, my lord.

Well then! I am glad thou art not so graceless as to deny that.

On went the spectacles again. "I must own to you, madam, that the honour of being related to ladies as eminent for their virtue as for their descent"—*Very pretty, truly!* said my lord, repeating, "*as eminent for their virtue as for their descent*, was, at first, no small inducement with me to lend an ear to Mr Lovelace's address."

There is dignity, born dignity, in this lady, cried my lord.

Lady Sarah. She would have been a grace to our family.

Lady Betty. Indeed she would.

Lovel. To a *royal* family, I will venture to say.

Lord M. Then what a devil——

Lovel. Please to read on, my lord. It cannot be *her* letter, if it does not make you admire her more and more as you read.

Cousin Charlotte, Cousin Patty, pray attend. Read on, my lord.

Miss Charlotte. Amazing fortitude!

Miss Patty only lifted up her dove's eyes.

Lord M. [reading]. "And the rather, as I was determined, had it come to effect, to do everything in my power to deserve your favourable opinion."

Then again they chorused upon me!

A blessed time of it, poor I! I had nothing for it but impudence!

Lovel. Pray read on, my lord—I told you how you would all admire her—or, shall I read?

Lord M. Damned assurance! [Then reading.] "I had another motive, which I knew would of itself give me merit with your whole family [*they were all ear*]; a presumptuous one; a punishably presumptuous one, as it has proved: in the hope that I might be an humble means in the hands of Providence to reclaim a man who had, as I thought, good sense enough at bottom to be reclaimed; or at least gratitude enough to acknowledge the intended obligation, whether the generous hope were to succeed or not."—Excellent young creature!

Excellent young creature! echoed the ladies, with their handkerchiefs at their eyes, attended with nose-music.

Lovel. By my soul, Miss Patty, you weep in the wrong place: you shall never go with me to a tragedy.

Lady Betty. Hardened wretch!

His lordship had pulled off his spectacles to wipe them. His eyes were misty; and he thought the fault in his spectacles.

I saw they were all cocked and primed. To be sure that is a very pretty sentence, said I—that is the excellency of this lady, that in every line, as she writes on, she improves upon herself. Pray, my lord, proceed. I know her style; the next sentence will still rise upon us.

Lord M. Damned fellow! [Again saddling and reading.] "But I have been most egregiously mistaken in Mr. Lovelace!" [Then they all clamoured again.] "The *only* man, I persuade myself——"

Lovel. Ladies may persuade themselves to anything: but how can she answer for what *other* men would or would not have done in the same circumstances?

I was forced to say anything to stifle their outcries. Pox take ye all together, thought I; as if I had not vexation enough in losing her!

Lord M. [reading]. "The only man, I persuade myself, pretending to be a gentleman, in whom I could have been so much mistaken."

They were all beginning again. Pray, my lord, proceed! Hear, hear—pray, ladies, hear! Now, my lord, be pleased to proceed. The ladies are silent.

So they were; lost in admiration of me, hands and eyes uplifted.

Lord M. I will, to thy confusion; for he had looked over the next sentence.

What wretches, Belford, what spiteful wretches, are poor mortals! So rejoiced to sting one another! to see each other stung!

Lord M. [reading]. "For while I was endeavouring to save a drowning wretch, I have been, not accidentally, but premeditatedly, and of set purpose, drawn in after him." What say you to this, sir-r?

Lady S. and Lady B. Ay, sir, what say you to this?

Lovel. Say! Why I say it is a very pretty metaphor, if it would but hold. But if you please, my lord, read on. Let me hear what is further said, and I will speak to it all together.

Lord M. I will. "And he has had the glory to add to the list of those he has ruined, a name that, I will be bold to say, would not have disparaged his own."

They all looked at me, as expecting me to speak.

Lovel. Be pleased to proceed, my lord: I will speak to this by and by. How came she to know I *kept a list*? I will speak to this by and by.

Lord M. [reading on]. "And this, madam, by means that would shock humanity to be made acquainted with."

Then again, in a hurry, off went the spectacles.

This was a plaguy stroke upon me. I thought myself an oak in impudence; but, by my troth, this had almost felled me.

Lord M. What say you to this, SIR-R!

Remember, Jack, to read all their *sirs* in this dialogue with a double *rr, sir-r!* denoting indignation rather than respect.

They all looked at me as if to see if I could blush.

Lovel. Eyes off, my lord! Eyes off, ladies! [looking bashfully, I believe]. What say I to this, my lord! Why, I say that this lady has a strong manner of expressing herself! That's all. There are many things that pass among lovers which a man cannot explain himself upon before grave people.

Lady Betty. Among lovers, sir-r! But, Mr. Lovelace, can you say that this lady behaved either like a weak or a credulous person? Can you say——

Lovel. I am ready to do the lady all manner of justice. But, pray now, ladies, if I am to be thus interrogated, let me know the contents of the rest of the letter, that I may be prepared for my defence, as you are all for my arraignment. For, to be required to answer piecemeal thus, without knowing what is to follow, is a cursed ensnaring way of proceeding.

They gave me the letter: I read it through to myself: and by the repetition of what I said, thou wilt guess at the remaining contents.

You shall find, ladies, you shall find, my lord, that I will not spare myself. Then holding the letter in my hand, and looking upon it as a lawyer upon his brief:

Miss Harlowe says, "That when your ladyship" [turning to Lady Betty] "shall know, that in the progress to her ruin, wilful falsehoods, repeated forgeries, and numberless perjuries, were not the least of my crimes, you will judge that she can have no principles that will make her worthy of an alliance with ladies of yours and your noble sister's character, if she could not, from her soul, declare that such an alliance can never now take place."

Surely, ladies, this is passion! This is not reason. If our family would not think themselves dishonoured by my marrying a person whom I had so treated; but, on the contrary, would rejoice that I did her this justice; and if she has come out pure gold from the assay; and has nothing to reproach herself with; why should it be an impeachment of her principles, to consent that such an alliance should take place?

She cannot think herself the worse, *justly* she cannot, for what was done against her will.

Their countenances menaced a general uproar. But I proceeded.

Your lordship read to us that she had a *hope*, a *presumptuous* one; nay, a *punishably presumptuous* one, she calls it; "that she might be a means in the hands of Providence to reclaim me; and that this, she knew, if effected, would give her a merit with you all." But from *what* would she reclaim me? She had *heard*, you'll say (but she had *only* heard, at the time she entertained *that hope*), that, to express myself in the women's dialect, I was *a very wicked fellow!* Well, and what then? Why, truly, the very moment she was *convinced*, by her own experience, that the charge against me was *more* than *hearsay*; and that, of consequence, I was a fit subject for her *generous endeavours* to work upon; she would needs give me up. Accordingly she flies out, and declares that the ceremony which would repair all shall never take place! Can this be from any other motive than *female resentment*?

This brought them all upon me, as I intended it should: it was as a tub to a whale; and after I had let them play with it awhile I claimed their attention, and knowing that they always loved to hear me prate, went on.

The lady, it is plain, thought that the reclaiming of a man from bad habits was a much *easier task* than, in the *nature of things*, it *can* be.

She writes, as your lordship has read, "That in endeavouring to save a drowning wretch, she had been, not accidentally, but premeditatedly, and of set purpose, drawn in after him." But how is this, ladies? You see by her own words that I am still far from being out of danger myself. Had she found me, in a quagmire suppose, and I had got out of it by her means, and left her to perish in it; that would have been a crime indeed. But is not the fact quite otherwise? Has she not, if her allegory prove what she would have it prove, got out herself, and left me floundering still deeper and deeper in? What she should have done, had she been in earnest to save me, was to join her hand with mine, that so we might by our united strength help one another out. I held out my hand to her, and besought her to give me hers: but no, truly! she was determined to get out herself as fast as she could, let me *sink* or *swim*: refusing her assistance (against her own principles) because she saw I wanted it. You see, ladies, you see, my lord, how pretty tinkling words run away with ears inclined to be musical.

They were all ready to exclaim again: but I went on, *proleptically*, as a rhetorician would say, before their voices could break out into words.

But my fair accuser says that "I have added to the list of those I have ruined, a name that would not have disparaged my own." It is true I have been gay and enterprising. It is in my constitution to be so. I know not how I came by such a constitution; but I was never accustomed to check or control; that you all know. When a man finds himself hurried by passion into a slight offence, which, however slight, will not be forgiven, he may be made desperate: as a thief, who only intends a robbery, is often by resistance, and for self-preservation, drawn in to commit a murder.

I was a strange, a horrid wretch with every one. But he must be a silly fellow who has not something to say for himself, when every cause has its black and its white side. Westminster Hall, Jack, affords every day as confident defences as mine.

But what right, proceeded I, has this lady to complain of me, when she as good as says—Here, Lovelace, you have acted the part of a villain by me. You would *repair your fault:* but I won't let you, that I may have the satisfaction of exposing you; and the pride of refusing you.

But was that the case? Was that the case? Would I pretend to say I would *now* marry the lady, if she would have me?

Lovel. You find she renounces Lady Betty's mediation.

Lord M. [interrupting me]. *Words are wind; but deeds are mind:* what signifies your cursed quibbling, Bob? Say plainly, if she will have you, will you have her? Answer me, yes or no; and lead us not *a wild-goose chase* after your meaning.

Lovel. She knows I would. But here, my lord, if she thus goes on to expose herself and me, she will make it a dishonour to us both to marry.

Charl. But how must she have been treated——

Lovel. [interrupting her]. Why now, Cousin Charlotte, chucking her under the chin, would you have me tell you all that has passed between the lady and me? Would *you* care, had you a bold and enterprising lover, that proclamation should be made of every little piece of amorous roguery that he offered to you?

Charlotte reddened. They all began to exclaim. But I proceeded.

The lady says, "She has been dishonoured" (devil take me if I spare myself!) "by means that would shock humanity to be made acquainted with them." She is a very innocent lady, and may not be a *judge* of the means she hints at. *Over-niceness may be under-niceness:* have you not such a proverb, my lord? —tantamount to, *One extreme produces another!* Such a lady as this may possibly think her case more extraordinary than it is. This I will take upon me to say, that if she has met with the only man in the world who would have treated her, as she says I have treated her, I have met in her with the *only woman in the world* who would have made such a rout about a case that is uncommon only from the circumstances that attend it.

This brought them all upon me; hands, eyes, voices, all lifted up at once. But my Lord M., who has in his *head* (the last seat of retreating lewdness) as much wickedness as I have in my *heart*, was forced (upon the air I spoke this with, and Charlotte's and all the rest reddening) to make a mouth that was big enough to swallow up the other half of his face; crying out, to avoid laughing, Oh! oh! as if under the power of a gouty twinge.

Hadst thou seen how the two tabbies and the young grimalkins looked at one another, at my lord, and at me, by turns, thou too wouldst have been ready to split thy ugly face just in the middle. Thy mouth has already done half the work. And, after all, I found not seldom in this conversation, that my humorous undaunted way forced a smile into my service from the prim mouths of the young ladies. They, perhaps, had they met with such another intrepid fellow as myself, who had first gained upon their affections, would not have made such a rout as my beloved has done, about such an affair as that we were assembled upon. Young ladies, as I have observed on a hundred occasions, fear not half so much for *themselves* as their mothers do for them. But here the girls were forced to put on grave airs, and to seem angry, because the antiques made the matter of such high importance. Yet so lightly sat anger and fellow-feeling at their hearts, that they were forced to purse in their mouths, to suppress the smiles I now and then laid out for: while the elders having had roses (that is to say, daughters) of their own, and knowing how fond men are of a trifle, would have been very loath to have had them nipped in the bud without saying, By your leave, Mrs. Rose-bush, to the mother of it.

The next article of my indictment was for forgery; and for personating of Lady Betty and my Cousin Charlotte. Two shocking charges, thou 'lt say: and so they were! The peer was outrageous upon the *forgery* charge. The ladies vowed never to forgive the *personating* part. Not a peacemaker among them. So we all turned women, and scolded.

My lord told me that he believed in his conscience there was not a viler fellow upon *God's earth* than me. What signifies mincing the matter? said he. And that it was not the first time I had forged his hand.

To this I answered, that I supposed, when the statute of *Scandalum Magnatum* was framed, there were a good many in the peerage who knew they deserved hard names; and that that law therefore was rather made to privilege their qualities than to whiten their characters.

He called upon me to explain myself, with a *sir-r*, so pronounced, as to show that one of the most ignominious words in our language was in his head.

People, I said, that were fenced in by their quality, and by their years, should not take freedoms that a man of spirit could not put up with, unless he were able heartily to despise the insulter.

This set him in a violent passion. He would send for Pritchard instantly. Let Pritchard be called. He would alter his will; and all he *could* leave from me, he *would*.

Do, do, my lord, said I: I always valued my own pleasure above your estate. But I'll let Pritchard know that if he draws, he shall sign and seal.

Why, what would I do to Pritchard? Shaking his crazy head at me.

Only what he, or any man else, writes with his pen, to despoil me of what I think my right, he shall seal with his ears; that's all, my lord.

Then the two ladies interposed.

Lady Sarah told me that I carried things a great way; and that neither Lord M. nor any of them deserved the treatment I gave them.

I said I could not bear to be used ill by my lord, for two reasons; first, because I respected his lordship above any man living; and next, because it looked as if I were induced by selfish considerations to take that from him which nobody else would offer to me.

And what, returned he, shall be my inducement to take what I do at your hands? Hey, sir?

Indeed, Cousin Lovelace, said Lady Betty, with great gravity, we do not any of us, as Lady Sarah says, deserve at your hands the treatment you give us: and let me tell you that I don't think my character, and your Cousin Charlotte's, ought to be prostituted, in order to ruin an innocent lady. She must have known early the good opinion we all have of her, and how much we wished her to be your wife. This good opinion of ours has been an inducement to her (you see she says so) to listen to your address. And this, with her friends' folly, has helped to throw her into your power. How you have requited her is too apparent. It becomes the character we all bear, to disclaim your actions by her. And let me tell you, that to have her abused by wicked people raised up to personate us, or any of us, makes a double call upon us to disclaim them.

Lovel. Why this is talking somewhat like. I would have you all disclaim my actions. I own I have done very vilely by this lady. One step led to another. I am cursed with an enterprising spirit. I hate to be foiled——

Foiled! interrupted Lady Sarah. What a shame to talk at this rate! Did the lady set up a contention with you? All nobly sincere and plain-hearted, have I heard Miss Clarissa Harlowe is: above art, above disguise; neither the coquette, nor the prude! Poor lady! She deserved a better fate from the man for whom she took the step which she so freely blames!

This above half affected me. Had this dispute been so handled by every one, I had been ashamed to look up. I began to be bashful.

Charlotte asked if I did not still seem inclinable to do the lady justice, if she would accept of *me*? It would be, she dared to say, the greatest felicity the family could know (she would answer for one) that this fine lady were of it.

They all declared to the same effect; and Lady Sarah put the matter home to me.

But my Lord *Marplot* would have it that I could not be serious for six minutes together.

I told his lordship that he was mistaken; light as he thought I made of this subject, I never knew any that went so near my heart.

Miss Patty said she was glad to hear *that*: indeed she was glad to hear *that*: and her soft eyes glistened with pleasure.

Lord M. called her sweet soul, and was ready to cry.

Not from humanity neither, Jack. The peer has no bowels; as thou mayest observe by his treatment of *me*. But when people's minds are weakened by a sense of their own infirmities, and when they are drawing on to their latter ends, they will be moved on the slightest occasions, whether those offer from *within* or *without* them. And this, frequently, the unpenetrating world calls *humanity*, when all the time, in compassionating the miseries of human nature, they are but pitying themselves; and were they in strong health and spirits, would care as little for anybody else as thou or I do.

Here broke they off my trial for this sitting. Lady Sarah was much fatigued. It was agreed to pursue the subject in the morning. They all, however, retired together, and went into private conference.

Letter XCVI—Mr. Lovelace. [*In continuation*]

THE ladies, instead of taking up the subject where we had laid it down, must needs touch upon passages in my fair accuser's letter which I was in hopes they would have let rest, as we were in a tolerable way. But, truly, they must hear all they could hear of our story, and what I had to say to those passages, that they might be better enabled to mediate between us, if I were really and indeed inclined to do her the hoped-for justice.

These passages were, 1st, "That after I had compulsatorily tricked her into the act of going off with me, I carried her to one of the worst houses in London."

2ndly, "That I had made a wicked attempt upon her; in resentment of which she fled to Hampstead privately.

3rdly, Came the forgery, and personating charges again; and we were upon the point of renewing our quarrel, before we could get to the next charge: which was still worse.

For that (4thly) was, "That having betrayed her back to the vile house, I first robbed her of her senses, and then of her honour; detaining her afterwards a prisoner there."

Were I to tell thee the glosses I put upon these heavy charges, what would it be, but to repeat many of the extenuating arguments I have used in my letters to thee? Suffice it, therefore, to say that I insisted much, by way of palliation, on the lady's extreme niceness: on her diffidence in my honour: on Miss Howe's contriving spirit; plots on their parts begetting plots on mine: on the high passions of the sex. I asserted that my whole view, in gently restraining her, was to oblige her to forgive me, and to marry me; and this for the honour of both families. I boasted of my own good qualities; some of which none that know me deny; and to which few libertines can lay claim.

They then fell into warm admirations and praises of the lady; all of them preparatory, as I knew, to the grand question: and thus it was introduced by Lady Sarah.

We have said as much as I think we can say upon these letters of the poor lady. To dwell upon the mischiefs that may ensue from the abuse of a person of her rank, if all the reparation be not made that now can be made, would perhaps be to little purpose. But you seem, sir, still to have a just opinion of her, as well as affection for her. Her virtue is not in the least questionable. She could not resent as she does, had she anything to reproach herself with. She is, by everybody's account, a fine woman; has a good estate in her own right; is of no contemptible family; though I think, with regard to her, they have acted as imprudently as unworthily. For the excellency of her mind, for good economy, the common speech of her, as the worthy Dr. Lewen once told me, is, *That her prudence would enrich a poor man, and her piety reclaim a licentious one.* I, who have not been abroad twice this twelvemonth, came hither purposely, so did Lady Betty, to see if justice may not be done her; and also whether we, and my Lord M. (your nearest relations, sir) have, or have not, any influence over you. And, for my own part, as your determination shall be in this article, such shall be mine, with regard to the disposition of all that is within my power

Lady Betty. And mine.

And mine, said my lord: and valiantly he swore to it.

Lovel. Far be it from me to think slightly of favours you may any of you be glad I would deserve! But as far be it from me to enter into conditions against my own liking, with sordid views! As to future mischiefs, let them come. I have not done with the Harlowes yet. They were the aggressors; and I should be glad they would let me hear from them, in the way they should hear from me, in the like case. Perhaps I should not be sorry to be *found*, rather than be obliged to *seek*, on this occasion.

Miss Charlotte [reddening]. Spoke like a man of violence, rather than a man of reason! I hope you 'll allow that, cousin.

Lady Sarah. Well, but since what is done, *is* done, and cannot be undone, let us think of the next best. Have you any objection against marrying Miss Harlowe, if she will have you?

Lovel. There can possibly be but one: that she is to everybody, no doubt, as well as to Lady Betty, pursuing that maxim peculiar to herself (*and let me tell you, so it ought to be*); that what she cannot conceal from herself, she will publish to all the world.

Miss Patty. The lady, to be sure, writes this in the bitterness of her grief, and in despair.

Lovel. And so, when her grief is allayed; when her despairing fit is over—and this from *you*, Cousin Patty! *Sweet girl!* And would *you*, my dear, in the like case [whispering her], have yielded to entreaty—would you have meant no more by the like exclamations?

I had a rap with her fan, and a blush; and from Lord M. a reflection, that I turned into jest everything they said.

I asked if they thought the Harlowes deserved any consideration from me; and whether that family would not exult over me, were I to marry their daughter, as if I *dared* not to do otherwise?

Lady Sarah. Once I was angry with that family, as we all were. But now I pity them; and think that you have but too well justified the worst treatment they gave you.

Lord M. Their family is of standing. All gentlemen of it, and rich, and reputable. Let me tell you, that many of our coronets would be glad they could derive their descents from no worse a stem than theirs.

Lovel. The Harlowes are a narrow-souled and implacable family. I hate them: and though I revere the lady, scorn all relation to them.

Lady Betty. I wish no worse could be said of *him*, who is such a scorner of common failings in *others*.

Lord M. How would my sister Lovelace have reproached herself for all her indulgent folly to this favourite boy of hers, had she lived till now, and been present on this occasion!

Lady Sarah. Well, but, begging your lordship's pardon, let us see if anything can be done for this poor lady.

Miss Ch. If Mr. Lovelace has nothing to object against the lady's character (and I presume to think he is not *ashamed* to do her justice, though it may make against himself), I cannot see but honour and generosity will compel from him all that we expect. If there be any levities, any weaknesses, to be charged upon the lady, I should not open my lips in her favour; though in private I would pity her, and deplore her hard hap. And yet, even then, there might not want arguments, from honour and gratitude, in so particular a case, to engage you, sir, to make good the vows it is plain you have broken.

Lady Betty. My Niece Charlotte has called upon you so justly, and has put the question to you so properly, that I cannot but wish you would speak to it directly, and without evasion.

All in a breath then bespoke my seriousness, and my justice: and in this manner I delivered myself, assuming an air sincerely solemn.

"I am very sensible that the performance of the task you have put me upon, will leave me without excuse: but I will not have recourse either to evasion or palliation.

"As my Cousin Charlotte has severely observed, I am not *ashamed* to do justice to Miss Harlowe's merit.

"I own to you all, and, what is more, with high regret (if not with *shame*, Cousin Charlotte), that I have a great deal to answer for in my usage of this lady. The sex has not a nobler mind, nor a lovelier person of it. And, for *virtue*, I could not have believed (excuse me, ladies) that there ever was a woman who *gave*, or *could* have given, such illustrious, such uniform proofs of it: for, in her whole conduct, she has shown herself to be equally above temptation and art; and, I had almost said, human frailty.

"The step she so freely blames herself for taking, was truly what she calls *compulsatory*: for though she was provoked to *think* of going off with me, she intended it not, nor was provided to do so: neither would she ever have had the *thought* of it, had her relations left her free, upon her offered composition to renounce the man she did *not* hate, in order to avoid the man she *did*.

"It piqued my pride, I own, that I could so little depend upon the force of those impressions which I had the vanity to hope I had made in a heart so delicate; and in my worst devices against her, I encouraged myself that I abused no confidence; for none had she in my honour.

"The evils she has suffered, it would have been more than a miracle had she avoided. Her watchfulness rendered more plots abortive than those which contributed to her fall; and they were many and various. And all her greater trials and hardships were owing to her noble resistance and just resentment.

"I know, proceeded I, how much I condemn myself in the justice I am doing to this excellent creature. But yet I *will* do her justice, and cannot help it if I would. And I hope this shows that I am not so totally abandoned as I have been thought to be.

"Indeed, with me, she has done more honour to the sex in her fall, if it be to be called a fall (in truth it ought not), than ever any other could do in her standing.

"When, at length, I had given her watchful virtue cause of suspicion, I was then indeed obliged to make use of power and art to prevent her escaping from me. She then formed contrivances to elude mine; but all *hers* were such as strict truth and punctilious honour would justify. She could not stoop to deceit and falsehood, no, not to save herself. More than once justly did she tell me, fired by conscious worthiness, that her soul was my soul's superior! Forgive me, ladies, for saying that till I knew *her*, I questioned a soul in a sex, created, as I was willing to suppose, only for temporary purposes. It is not to be imagined into what absurdities men of free principles run, in order to justify to themselves their free practices; and to make a religion to their minds: and yet, in this respect, I have not been so faulty as some others.

"No wonder that such a noble creature as this looked upon every studied artifice as a degree of baseness not to be forgiven: no wonder that she could so easily become averse to the man (though once she beheld him with an eye not wholly indifferent) whom she thought capable of premeditated guilt. Nor, give me leave, on the other hand, to say, is it to be wondered at, that the man who found it so difficult to be forgiven for the *slighter* offences, and who had not the grace to recede or repent (made desperate), should be hurried on to the commission of the *greater*.

"In short, ladies, in a word, my lord, Miss Clarissa Harlowe is an angel; if ever there was or could be one in human nature: and is, and ever was, as pure as an angel in her will: and this justice I must do her, although the question, I see by every glistening eye, is ready to be asked, What, then, Lovelace, are you?"

Lord M. A devil! A damned devil! I must answer. And may the curse of God follow you in all you undertake, if you do not make her the best amends now in your power to make her!

Lovel. From you, my lord, I could expect no other: but from the ladies I hope for less violence from the ingenuousness of my confession.

The ladies, elder and younger, had their handkerchiefs to their eyes, at the just testimony which I bore to the merits of this exalted creature; and which I would make no scruple to bear at the bar of a court of justice, were I to be called to it.

Lady Betty. Well, sir, this is a noble character. If you think as you speak, surely you cannot refuse to do the lady all the justice now in your power to do her.

They all joined in this demand.

I pleaded that I was sure she would not have me: that, when she had taken a resolution, she was not to be moved: unpersuadableness was a Harlowe sin: that, and her name, I told them, were all she had of theirs.

All were of opinion that she might, in her present desolate circumstances, be brought to forgive me. Lady Sarah said that Lady Betty and she would endeavour to find out the *noble sufferer*, as they justly called her; and would take her into their protection, and be guarantees of the justice that I would do her; as well after marriage as before.

It was some pleasure to me, to observe the placability of these ladies of my own family, had they, any or either of them, met with a LOVELACE. But 'twould be hard upon us honest fellows, Jack, if all women were CLARISSAS.

Here I am obliged to break off.

Letter XCVII—Mr. Lovelace. [*In continuation*]

IT is much better, Jack, to tell your own story, when it *must* be known, than to have an adversary tell it for you. Conscious of this, I gave them a particular account how urgent I had been

with her to fix upon the Thursday after I left her (it being her
Uncle Harlowe's anniversary birthday, and named to oblige her)
for the private celebration; having some days before actually
procured a licence, which still remained with her.

That, not being able to prevail upon her to promise anything
while under a supposed restraint; I offered to leave her at full
liberty, if she would give me the least hope for that day.   But
neither did this offer avail me.

That this inflexibleness making me desperate, I resolved to
add to my former fault, by giving directions that she should
not either go or correspond out of the house, till I returned from
M. Hall; well knowing that if she were at full liberty, I must
for ever lose her.

That this constraint had so much incensed her, that although
I wrote no less than four different letters, I could not procure a
single word in answer; though I pressed her but for four words
to signify the day and the church.

I referred to my two cousins to vouch for me the extraordinary
methods I took to send messengers to town, though they knew
not the occasion: which now I told them was *this*.

I acquainted them that I even had wrote to you, Jack, and to
another gentleman, of whom I thought she had a good opinion,
to attend her, in order to press for her compliance; holding
myself in readiness the last day, at Salt Hill, to meet the
messenger they should send, and proceed to London, if his
message were favourable: but that, before they could attend her,
she had found means to fly away once more: and is now, said I,
perched perhaps somewhere under Lady Betty's window at
Glenham Hall; and there, like the sweet Philomela, a thorn in
her breast, warbles forth her melancholy complaints against her
barbarous Tereus.

Lady Betty declared that she was not with *her*; nor did she
know where she was.   She should be, she added, the most
welcome guest to her that she ever received.

In truth, I had a suspicion that she was already in their
knowledge, and taken into their protection; for Lady Sarah I
imagined incapable of being roused to this spirit by a letter only
from Miss Harlowe, and that not directed to herself; she being a
very indolent and melancholy woman.   But her sister, I find,
had wrought her up to it: for Lady Betty is as officious and
managing a woman as Mrs. Howe; but of a much more generous
and noble disposition—she is *my aunt*, Jack.

I supposed, I said, that her ladyship might have a private

direction where to send to her. I spoke as I wished: I would have given the world to have heard that she was inclined to cultivate the interest of any of my family.

Lady Betty answered that she had no direction but what was in the letter; which she had scratched out, and which, it was probable, was only a temporary one, in order to avoid me: otherwise she would hardly have directed an answer to be left at an inn. And she was of opinion that to apply to Miss Howe would be the only certain way to succeed in any application for forgiveness, would I enable that young lady to interest herself in procuring it.

Miss Charlotte. Permit me to make a proposal. Since we are all of one mind in relation to the justice due to Miss Harlowe, if Mr. Lovelace will oblige himself to marry her, I will make Miss Howe a visit, little as I am acquainted with her; and endeavour to engage her interest to forward the desired reconciliation. And if this can be done, I make no question but all may be happily accommodated; for everybody knows the love there is between Miss Harlowe and Miss Howe.

MARRIAGE, *with these women, thou seest, Jack, is an atonement for all we can do to them. A true dramatic recompense!*

This motion was highly approved of; and I gave my honour, as desired, in the fullest manner they could wish.

Lady Sarah. Well then, Cousin Charlotte, begin your treaty with Miss Howe, out of hand.

Lady Betty. Pray do. And let Miss Harlowe be told, that I am ready to receive her as the most welcome of guests: and I will not have her out of my sight till the knot is tied.

Lady Sarah. Tell her from me, that she shall be my daughter, instead of my poor Betsey! And shed a tear in remembrance of her lost daughter.

Lord M. What say you, sir, to this?

Lovel. CONTENT, my lord. I speak in the language of your house.

Lord M. We are not to be fooled, nephew. No quibbling. We will have no slur put upon us.

Lovel. You shall not. And yet, I did not intend to marry, if she exceeded the appointed Thursday. But I think (according to her own notions) that I have injured her beyond reparation, although I were to make her the best of husbands; as I am resolved to be, if she will *condescend*, as I will call it, to have me. And be this, Cousin Charlotte, *my* part of your commission to say.

This pleased them all.

Lord M. Give me thy hand, Bob! Thou talkest like a man of honour at last. I hope we may depend upon what thou sayest?

The ladies' eyes put the same question to me.

Lovel. You may, my lord. You may, ladies. Absolutely you may.

Then was the personal character of the lady, as well as her more extraordinary talents and endowments, again expatiated upon: and Miss Patty, who had once seen her, launched out more than all the rest in her praise. These were followed by such inquiries as are never forgotten to be made in marriage treaties, and which generally are the *principal motives* with the *sages* of a family, though the *least to be mentioned* by the *parties* themselves, and yet even by *them*, perhaps, the *first* thought of: that is to say, inquisition into the lady's fortune; into the particulars of the grandfather's estate; and what her father, and her single-souled uncles, will probably do for her, if a reconciliation be effected; as, by *their* means, they make no doubt but it will, between both families, if it be not my fault. The two venerables [no longer tabbies with me now] hinted at rich presents on their own parts; and my lord declared that he would make such overtures in my behalf, as should render my marriage with Miss Harlowe the best day's work I ever made; and what, he doubted not, would be as agreeable to that family as to myself.

Thus, at present, by a single hair, hangs over my head the matrimonial sword. And thus ended my trial. And thus are we all friends; and cousin and cousin, and nephew and nephew, at every word.

Did ever comedy end more happily than this long trial?

Letter XCVIII—*Mr. Lovelace to John Belford, Esq.*

Wedn. July 12.

So, Jack, they think they have gained a mighty point. But, *were* I to change my mind, *were* I to repent, I fancy I am safe. And yet this very moment it rises to my mind, that 'tis hard trusting too; for surely there must be some embers, where there was fire so lately, that may be stirred up to give a blaze to combustibles strewed lightly upon them. Love (like some self-propagating plants or roots which have taken strong hold in the earth), when once got deep into the heart, is hardly ever totally extirpated, except by matrimony indeed, which is the grave of love, because it allows of the end of love. Then these ladies, all advocates *for* herself, *with* herself, Miss Howe at their head, perhaps—not in favour to me—I don't expect that from Miss Howe—but perhaps in favour to *herself*: for Miss Howe has reason to apprehend vengeance from me, I ween. Her Hickman will be safe too, as she may think, if I marry her beloved friend: for he has been a busy fellow, and I have long wished to have a slap at him! The lady's case desperate with her friends too; and likely to be so, while single, and her character exposed to censure.

A husband is a charming cloak, a fig-leafed apron, for a wife: and for a lady to be protected in liberties, in diversions, which her heart pants after—and all her faults, even the most criminal, were she to be detected, to be thrown upon the husband, and the ridicule too; a charming privilege for a wife!

But I shall have one comfort, if I marry, which pleases me not a little. If a man's wife has a dear friend of her sex, a hundred liberties may be taken with that friend, which could *not* be taken, if the *single lady* (knowing what a title to freedoms marriage has given him with her *friend*) was not less scrupulous with him than she ought to be as to *herself*. Then there are *broad* freedoms (shall I call them?) that may be taken by the husband with his wife, that may not be *quite* shocking, which if the wife *bears before her friend*, will serve for a lesson to *that friend*; and if that friend *bears* to be present at them without check or bashfulness, will show a sagacious fellow that she can bear as much herself, at *proper time* and *place*. *Chastity*, Jack, like *piety*, is a uniform thing. If in *look*, if in *speech*, a girl give way to undue levity, depend upon it, the devil has got one of his cloven feet in her heart already.—So, Hickman, take care of thyself, I advise thee, whether I marry or not.

Thus, Jack, have I at once reconciled myself to all my relations —and, if the lady refuses me, thrown the fault upon her. This, I knew, would be in my power to do at any time: and I was the more arrogant to them, in order to heighten the merit of my compliance.

But, after all, it would be very whimsical, would it not, if all my plots and contrivances should end in wedlock? What a punishment would this come out to be, upon myself too, that all this while I have been plundering my own treasury?

And then, can there be so much harm done, if it can be so easily repaired by a few magical words; as *I, Robert,* take thee, Clarissa; and I, Clarissa, take thee, Robert, with the rest of the for-better and for-worse legerdemain, which will hocus-pocus all the wrongs, the crying wrongs, that I have done to Miss Harlowe, into acts of kindness and benevolence to Mrs. Lovelace?

But, Jack, two things I must insist upon with thee, if this is to be the case. Having put secrets of so high a nature between me and my spouse into thy power, I must, for my own honour, and for the honour of my wife and my illustrious progeny, first oblige thee to give up the letters I have so profusely scribbled to thee; and, in the next place, do by thee, as I have heard whispered in France was done by the *true* father of a certain monarque; that is to say, cut thy throat, to prevent thy telling of tales.

I have found means to heighten the kind opinion my friends here have begun to have of me, by communicating to them the contents of the four last letters which I wrote to press my elected spouse to solemnize. My lord has repeated one of his phrases in my favour, that he hopes it will come out, *that the devil is not quite so black as he is painted*.

Now prithee, dear Jack, since so many good consequences are to flow from these our nuptials (one of which to *thyself*; since the sooner thou diest, the less thou wilt have to answer for); and that I now and then am apt to believe there may be something in the old fellow's notion, who once told us that he who kills a man, has all that man's sins to answer for, as well as his own, because he gave him not the time to repent of them that Heaven designed to allow him [a fine thing for thee, if thou consentest to be knocked of the head; but a cursed one for the manslayer!]; and since there may be room to fear that Miss Howe will not give us her help; I prithee now exert thyself to find out my Clarissa Harlowe, that I may make a LOVELACE of her. Set all the city bellmen, and the county criers, for ten miles round the metropolis, at work, with their "Oyez's! and if any man, woman or child can give tale or tidings." Advertise her in all the newspapers; and let her know, "That if she will repair to Lady Betty Lawrance, or to Miss Charlotte Montague, she may hear of something greatly to her advantage."

.   .   .   .   .   .

My two Cousins Montague are actually to set out to-morrow to Mrs. Howe's, to engage her vixen daughter's interest with her friend. They will flaunt it away in a chariot and six, for the greater state and significance.

Confounded mortification to be reduced thus low! My pride hardly knows how to brook it.

Lord M. has engaged the two venerables to stay here to attend the issue: and I, standing very high at present in their good graces, am to gallant them to Oxford, to Blenheim, and several other places.

Letter XCIX—Miss Howe to Miss Clarissa Harlowe

Thursday Night, July 13.

COLLINS sets not out to-morrow. Some domestic occasion hinders him. Rogers is but now returned from you, and cannot well be spared. Mr. Hickman is gone upon an affair of my mother's, and has taken both his servants with him, to do credit to his employer: so I am forced to venture this by the post, directed by your assumed name.

I am to acquaint you, that I have been favoured with a visit from Miss Montague and her sister, in Lord M.'s chariot and six. My lord's gentleman rode here yesterday, with a request that I would receive a visit from the two young ladies, on a *very particular occasion*; the greater favour if it might be the next day.

As I had so little personal knowledge of either, I doubted not but it must be in relation to the interests of my dear friend; and so consulting with my mother, I sent them an invitation to favour me (because of the distance) with their company at dinner; which they kindly accepted.

I hope, my dear, since things have been so *very* bad, that their errand to me will be as agreeable to you, as anything that can now happen. They came in the name of Lord M. and Lady Sarah and Lady Betty, his two sisters, to desire my interest to engage you to put yourself into the protection of Lady Betty; who will not part with you till she sees all the justice done you that now can be done.

Lady Sarah had not stirred out for a twelvemonth before; never since she lost her agreeable daughter whom you and I saw at Mrs. Benson's: but was induced to take this journey by Lady Betty, purely to procure you reparation, if possible. And their joint strength, united with Lord M.'s, has so far succeeded, that the wretch has bound himself to them, and to these young ladies, in the solemnest manner, to wed you in their presence, if they can prevail upon you to give him your hand.

This consolation you may take to yourself, that all this honourable family have a *due* (that is, the *highest*) sense of your merit, and greatly admire you. The horrid creature has not spared himself in doing justice to your virtue; and the young ladies gave us such an account of his confessions, and self-condemnation, that my mother was quite charmed with you; and we all four shed tears of joy, that there is one of our sex [I, that that one is my dearest friend] who has done so much honour to it, as to deserve the exalted praises given you by a wretch so self-conceited; though pity for the excellent creature mixed with our joy.

He promises by them to make the best of husbands; and my lord, and Lady Sarah, and Lady Betty, are all three to be guarantees that he will be so. Noble settlements, noble presents, they talked of: they say they left Lord M. and his two sisters talking of nothing else but of those presents and settlements, how most to do you honour, the greater in proportion for the indignities you have suffered; and of changing of names by Act of Parliament, preparative to the interest they will all join to make, to get the titles to go where the bulk of the estate must go, at my lord's death, which they apprehend to be nearer than they wish. Nor doubt they of a thorough reformation in his morals, from your example and influence over him.

I made a great many objections for you—all, I believe, that you could have made yourself had you been present. But I have no doubt to advise you, my dear (and so does my mother), instantly to put yourself into Lady Betty's protection, with a resolution to take the wretch for your husband. All his future grandeur [he wants not pride] depends upon his sincerity to you; and the young ladies vouch for the depth of his concern for the wrongs he has done you.

All his apprehension is, in your readiness to communicate to every one, as he fears, the evils you have suffered; which he thinks will expose you both. But had you not revealed them to Lady Betty, you had not had so warm a friend; since it is owing to two letters you wrote to her, that all this good, as I hope it will prove, was brought about. But I advise you to be more sparing in exposing what is past, whether you have thoughts of accepting him or not: for what, my dear, can that avail now, but to give a handle to vile wretches to triumph over your friends; since every one will not know how much to your honour your very sufferings have been?

Your melancholy letter brought by Rogers,[1] with his account of your indifferent health, confirmed to him by the woman of the house, as well as by your looks, and by your faintness while you talked with him, would have given me inexpressible affliction, had I not been cheered by this agreeable visit from the young

[1] See p. 385.

ladies. I hope you will be equally so on my imparting the subject of it to you.

Indeed, my dear, you must not hesitate. You *must* oblige them. The alliance is splendid and honourable. Very few will know anything of his brutal baseness to you. All must end, in a little while, in a general reconciliation; and you will be able to resume your course of doing the good to every deserving object, which procured you blessings wherever you set your foot.

I am concerned to find that your father's inhuman curse affects you so much as it does. Yet you are a noble creature to put it as you put it—I hope you are indeed more solicitous to get it revoked for their sakes than for your own. It is for *them* to be penitent, who hurried you into evils you could not well avoid. You are apt to judge by the unhappy event rather than upon the true merits of your case. Upon my honour, I think you faultless in almost every step you have taken. What has not that vilely insolent and ambitious, yet stupid, brother of yours to answer for?—that spiteful thing your sister too!

But come, since what is past cannot be helped, let us look forward. You have now happy prospects opening to you: a family, *already noble*, prepared to receive and embrace you with open arms and joyful hearts; and who, by their love to you, will teach another family (who know not what an excellence they have confederated to persecute) how to value you. Your prudence, your piety, will crown all. You will reclaim a wretch that, for a hundred sakes more than for his own, one would wish to be reclaimed.

Like a traveller who has been put out of his way by the overflowing of some rapid stream, you have only had the fore-right path you were in overwhelmed. A few miles about, a day or two only lost, as I may say, and you are in a way to recover it; and, by quickening your speed, will get up the lost time. The hurry upon your spirits, meantime, will be all your inconvenience; for it was not your fault you were stopped in your progress.

Think of this, my dear; and improve upon the allegory, as you know how. If you can, without impeding your progress, be the means of assuaging the inundation, of bounding the waters within their natural channel, and thereby of recovering the overwhelmed path for the sake of future passengers who travel the same way, what a merit will yours be!

I shall impatiently expect your next letter. The young ladies proposed that you should put yourself, if in town, or near it, into the Reading stage-coach, which inns somewhere in

Fleet Street: and if you give notice of the day, you will be met on the road, and that pretty early in your journey, by some of both sexes; one of whom you won't be sorry to see.

Mr. Hickman shall attend you at Slough; and Lady Betty herself, and one of the Miss Montagues, with proper equipages, will be at Reading to receive you; and carry you directly to the seat of the former: for I have expressly stipulated that the wretch himself shall not come into your presence till your nuptials are to be solemnized, unless you give leave.

Adieu, my dearest friend.   Be happy: and hundreds will then be happy of consequence.   Inexpressibly so, I am sure, will then be

Your ever affectionate
Anna Howe.

Letter C—Miss Howe to Miss Clarissa Harlowe

Sunday Night, July 16.

My dearest Friend,—Why should you permit a mind so much devoted to your service to labour under such an impatience as you must know it *would* labour under, for want of an answer to a letter of such consequence to *you,* and therefore to *me,* as was mine of Thursday night?   Rogers told me on Thursday you were *so* ill; your letter sent by him was *so* melancholy!   Yet you must be ill indeed if you could not write something to such a letter; were it but a line, to say you would write as soon as you could.   Sure you have received it.   The master of our nearest post office will pawn his reputation that it went safe: I gave him particular charge of it.

God send me good news of your health, of your ability to write; and then I will chide you—indeed I will—as I never yet did chide you.

I suppose your excuse will be that the subject required consideration.   Lord! my dear, so it might: but you have so right a mind, and the matter in question is so obvious, that you could not want half an hour to determine.   Then you intended, probably, to wait Collins's call for your letter as on to-morrow!   Suppose—miss!—(indeed I am angry with you!—suppose) something were to happen, as it did on Friday, that he should not be able to go to town to-morrow?   How, child, could you serve me so?   I know not how to leave off scolding you!

Dear, honest Collins, make haste: he will: he will.   He sets out, and travels all night: for I have told him that the dearest friend I have in the world has it in her own choice to be happy, and to make me so; and that the letter he will bring from her will assure it to me.

I have ordered him to go directly (without stopping at the Saracen's Head Inn) to you at your lodgings. Matters are now in so good a way that he safely may.

Your expected letter is ready written, I hope: if it be not, he will call for it at your hour.

You can't be so happy as you deserve to be: but I doubt not that you will be as happy as you *can*; that is, that you will choose to put yourself instantly into Lady Betty's protection. If you would not have the wretch for *your own* sake; have him you must, for *mine*, for your *family's*, for your *honour's* sake! Dear, honest Collins, make haste! make haste! and relieve the impatient heart of my beloved's

Ever faithful, ever affectionate,

ANNA HOWE.

Letter CI—*Miss Howe to Miss Charlotte Montague*

Tuesday Morning, July 18.

MADAM,—I take the liberty to write to you by this special messenger. In the frenzy of my soul I write to you, to demand of you, and of any of your family who can tell, news of my beloved friend; who, I doubt, has been spirited away by the base arts of one of the blackest—oh, help me to a name bad enough to call him by! Her piety is proof against self-attempts. It must, it must be he, the only wretch who could injure such an innocent; and now—who knows what he has done with her!

If I have patience I will give you the occasion of this distracted vehemence.

I wrote to her the very moment you and your sister left me. But being unable to procure a special messenger, as I intended, was forced to send by the post. I urged her [you know I promised that I would: I urged her], with earnestness, to comply with the desires of all your family. Having no answer I wrote again on Sunday night; and sent it by a particular hand, who travelled all night; chiding her for keeping a heart so impatient as mine in such cruel suspense, upon a matter of so much importance to her; and therefore to me. And very angry I was with her in my mind.

But, judge my astonishment, my distraction, when last night the messenger, returning post-haste, brought me word that she had not been heard of since Friday morning! And that a letter lay for her at her lodgings which came by the post; and must be mine!

She went out about six that morning; only intending, as they believe, to go to morning prayers at Covent Garden Church, just by her lodgings, as she had done divers times before. Went on foot! Left word she should be back in an hour. Very poorly in health!

Lord, have mercy upon me! What shall I do! I was a distracted creature all last night!

O madam! you know not how I love her! My own soul is not dearer to me than my Clarissa Harlowe! Nay, she *is* my soul—for I now have none—only a miserable one, however —for she was the joy, the stay, the prop of my life. Never woman loved woman as we love one another. It is impossible to tell you half her excellences. It was my glory and my pride, that I was capable of so fervent a love of so pure and matchless a creature. But now—who knows, whether the dear injured has not all her woes, her undeserved woes, completed in death; or is not reserved for a worse fate! This I leave to your inquiry— for—your—[shall I call the man—your?] relation I understand is still with you.

Surely, my good ladies, you were well authorized in the proposals you made in presence of my mother! Surely he dare not abuse your confidence, and the confidence of your noble relations! I make no apology for giving you this trouble, nor for desiring you to favour with a line by this messenger,

Your almost distracted

ANNA HOWE.

Letter CII—Mr. Lovelace to John Belford, Esq.

M. Hall, Sat. Night, July 15.

ALL undone, undone, by Jupiter! Zounds, Jack, what shall I do now! A curse upon all my plots and contrivances! But I have it—in the very heart and soul of me, I have it!

Thou toldest me that my punishments were but beginning. Canst thou, O fatal prognosticator! canst thou tell me where they will end?

Thy assistance I bespeak. The moment thou receivest this, I bespeak thy assistance. This messenger rides for life and death—and I hope he 'll find you at your town lodgings; if he meet not with you at Edgware; where, being Sunday, he will call first.

This cursed, cursed woman, on Friday dispatched man and horse with the joyful news (as she thought it would be to me) in an exulting letter from Sally Martin, that she had found out my angel as on Wednesday last; and on Friday morning, after she had been at prayers at Covent Garden Church—praying for my reformation perhaps—got her arrested by two sheriff's officers, as she was returning to her lodgings, who (villains!) put her into a chair they had in readiness, and carried her to one of the cursed fellow's houses.

She has arrested her for £150, pretendedly due for board and lodgings: a sum (besides the low villainy of the proceeding) which the dear soul could not possibly raise; all her clothes and effects, except what she had on and with her when she went away, being at the old devil's.

And here, for an aggravation, has the dear creature lain already two days; for I must be gallanting my two aunts and my two cousins, and giving Lord M. an airing after his lying-in—pox upon the whole family of us!—and returned not till within this hour: and now returned to my distraction, on receiving the cursed tidings and the exulting letter.

Hasten, hasten, dear Jack; for the love of God, hasten to the injured charmer! My heart bleeds for her. She deserved not this! I dare not stir. It will be thought done by my contrivance—and if I am absent from this place, that will confirm the suspicion.

Damnation seize quick this accursed woman! Yet she thinks she has made no small merit with me. Unhappy, thrice unhappy circumstance! At a time, too, when better prospects were opening for the sweet creature!

Hasten to her! Clear me of this cursed job. Most sincerely, by all that 's sacred, I swear you may! Yet have I been such a villainous plotter, that the charming sufferer will hardly believe it; although the proceeding be so dirtily low.

Set her free the moment you see her: without conditioning, free! On your knees, for me, beg her pardon: and assure her that, wherever she goes, I will not molest her: no, nor come near her, without her leave: and be sure allow not any of the damned crew to go near her. Only let her permit *you* to receive her commands from time to time. You have always been her friend and advocate. What would I now give had I permitted you to have been a successful one!

Let her have all her clothes and effects sent her instantly, as a small proof of my sincerity. And force upon the dear creature, who must be moneyless, what sums you can get her to take. Let me know how she has been treated. If roughly, woe be to the guilty!

Take thy watch in thy hand, after thou hast freed her, and damn the whole brood, dragon and serpents, by the hour, till thou 'rt tired; and tell them, I bid thee do so for their cursed officiousness.

They had nothing to do, when they had found her, but to wait my orders how to proceed.

The great devil fly away with them all, one by one, through the roof of their own cursed house, and dash them to pieces against the tops of chimneys as he flies; and let the lesser devils collect their scattered scraps, and bag them up, in order to put them together again in their allotted place, in the element of fire, with cements of molten lead.

A line! a line! a kingdom for a line! with tolerable news, the first moment thou canst write! This fellow waits to bring it.

Letter CIII—*Miss Charlotte Montague to Miss Howe*

M. Hall, Tuesday Afternoon.

DEAR MISS HOWE,—Your letter has infinitely disturbed us all.

This wretched man has been half distracted ever since Saturday night.

We knew not what ailed him till your letter was brought.

Vile wretch as he is, he is, however, innocent of this new evil. Indeed he is, he *must* be; as I shall more at large acquaint you. But will not now detain your messenger.

Only to satisfy your just impatience, by telling you that the dear young lady is safe, and, we hope, well.

A horrid mistake of his general orders has subjected her to the terror and disgrace of an arrest.

Poor dear Miss Harlowe! Her sufferings have endeared her to us, almost as much as her excellences can have endeared her to you.

But she must be now quite at liberty.

He has been a distracted man ever since the news was brought him; and we knew not what ailed him.

But that I said before.

My Lord M., my Lady Sarah Sadleir, and my Lady Betty Lawrance, will all write to you this very afternoon.

And so will the wretch himself.

And send it by a servant of their own, not to detain yours.

I know not what I write.

But you shall have all the particulars, just, and true, and fair, from,

Dear madam,

Your most faithful and obedient servant,

CH. MONTAGUE.

Letter CIV—*Miss Montague to Miss Howe*

M. Hall, July 18.

DEAR MADAM,—In pursuance of my promise, I will minutely inform you of everything we know relating to this shocking transaction.

When we returned from you on Thursday night, and made our report of the kind reception both we and our message met with, in that you had been so good as to promise to use your interest with your dear friend; it put us all into such good humour with one another, and with my Cousin Lovelace, that we resolved upon a little tour of two days, the Friday and Saturday, in order to give an airing to my lord and Lady Sarah; both having been long confined, one by illness, the other by melancholy. My lord, Lady Sarah, Lady Betty, and myself, were in the coach; and all our talk was of dear Miss Harlowe, and of our future happiness with her. Mr. Lovelace and my sister (who is his favourite, as he is hers) were in his phaeton: and whenever we joined company that was still the subject.

As to him, never man praised woman as he did her: never man gave greater hopes, and made better resolutions. He is none of those that are governed by interest. He is too proud for that. But most sincerely delighted was he in talking of her; and of his hopes of her returning favour. He said, however, more than once, that he feared she would not forgive him; for, from his heart, he must say he deserved not her forgiveness: and often and often, that there was not such a woman in the world.

This I mention to show you, madam, that he could not at this very time be privy to such a barbarous and disgraceful treatment of her.

We returned not till Saturday night, all in as good humour with one another as we went out. We never had such pleasure in his company before. If he would be good, and as he ought to be, no man would be better beloved by relations than he.

But never was there a greater alteration in man when he came home, and received a letter from a messenger, who, it seems, had been flattering himself in hopes of a reward, and had been waiting for his return from the night before. In *such* a fury! The man fared but badly. He instantly shut himself up to write, and ordered man and horse to be ready to set out before daylight the next morning, to carry the letter to a friend in London.

He would not see us all that night; neither breakfast nor dine with us next day. He ought, he said, never to see the light; and bid my sister, whom he called an *innocent* (and who was very desirous to know the occasion of all this), shun him; saying, he was a wretch, and made so by his own inventions and the consequences of them.

None of us could get out of him what so disturbed him. We should too soon hear, he said, to the utter dissipation of all *his* hopes, and of all *ours*.

We could easily suppose that all was not right with regard to the worthy young lady and him.

He was out each day; and said he wanted to run away from himself.

Late on Monday night he received a letter from Mr. Belford, his most favoured friend, by his own messenger; who came back in a foam, man and horse. Whatever were the contents, he was not easier, but like a madman rather: but still would not let us know the occasion. But to my sister he said, Nobody, my dear Patsey, who can think but of half the plagues that pursue an intriguing spirit, would ever quit the right path.

He was out when your messenger came: but soon came in; and bad enough was his reception from us all. And he said that his own torments were greater than ours, than Miss Harlowe's, or yours, madam, all put together. He would see your letter. He always carries everything before him: and said, when he had read it, that he thanked God he was not such a villain as you, with too great an appearance of reason, thought him.

Thus then he owned the matter to be:

He had left general directions to the people of the lodgings the dear lady went from, to find out where she was gone to, if possible, that he might have an opportunity to importune her to be his, before their difference was public. The wicked people (*officious* at least, if not wicked) discovered where she was on Wednesday; and, for fear she should remove before they could have his orders, they put her under a *gentle restraint,* as they call it; and dispatched away a messenger to acquaint him with it; and to take his orders.

This messenger arrived on Friday afternoon; and stayed here till we returned on Saturday night: and when he read the letter he brought—I have told you, madam, what a fury he was in.

The letter he retired to write, and which he dispatched away so early on Sunday morning, was to conjure his friend Mr. Belford, on receipt of it, to fly to the lady, and set her free; and to order all her things to be sent her; and to clear him of so *black* and *villainous* a fact, as he justly called it.

And by this time he doubts not that all is happily over; and the beloved of his soul (as he calls her at every word) in an easier and happier way than she was before the horrid fact. And now he owns that the reason why Mr. Belford's letter set him into stronger ravings was, because of his keeping him wilfully (and on purpose to torment him) in suspense; and reflecting very heavily upon him (for Mr. Belford, he says, was ever the lady's friend and advocate); and only mentioning that he had waited upon her; referring to his next for further particulars; which Mr. Belford could have told him at the time.

He declares, and we can vouch for him, that he has been, ever since last Saturday night, the most miserable of men.

He forbore going up himself, that it might not be imagined he was guilty of so black a contrivance; and that he went up to complete any base views in consequence of it.

Believe us all, dear Miss Howe, under the deepest concern at this unhappy accident; which will, we fear, exasperate the charming sufferer; not too much for the occasion, but too much for our hopes.

Oh, what wretches are these free-living men, who love to tread in intricate paths; and, when once they err, know not how far out of the way their headstrong course may lead them!

My sister joins her thanks with mine to your good mother and self for the favours you heaped upon us last Thursday. We beseech your continued interest as to the subject of our visit. It shall be all our studies to oblige and recompense the dear lady to the utmost of our power, for what she has suffered from the unhappy man.

We are, dear madam,

Your obliged and faithful servants,

CHARLOTTE } MONTAGUE.
MARTHA

DEAR MISS HOWE,—We join in the above request of Miss Charlotte and Miss Patty Montague, for your favour and interest; being convinced that the accident was an accident; and no plot or contrivance of a wretch too full of them. We are, madam,

> Your most obedient humble servants,
> M.
> SARAH SADLEIR.
> ELIZ. LAWRANCE.

DEAR MISS HOWE,—After what is written above, by names and characters of such unquestionable honour, I might have been excused signing a name almost as hateful to myself, as I KNOW it is to you. But the *above* will have it so. Since, therefore, I *must* write, it shall be the truth; which is, that if I may be once more admitted to pay my duty to the most deserving and most injured of her sex, I will be content to do it with a halter about my neck; and attended by a parson on my right hand, and the hangman on my left, be doomed, at her will, either to the church or the gallows.

> Your most humble servant,
> ROBERT LOVELACE.

Tuesday, July 18.

Letter CV—Mr. Belford to Robert Lovelace, Esq.

Sunday Night, July 16.

WHAT a cursed piece of work hast thou made of it, with the most excellent of women! Thou mayest be in earnest, or in jest, as thou wilt; but the poor lady will not be long either thy sport, or the sport of fortune!

I will give thee an account of a scene that wants but her affecting pen to represent it justly; and it would wring all the black blood out of thy callous heart.

Thou only, who art the author of her calamities, shouldst have attended her in her prison. I am unequal to such a task: nor know I any other man but would.

This last act, however unintended by thee, yet a consequence of thy general orders, and too likely to be thought agreeable to thee, by those who know thy other villainies by her, has finished thy barbarous work. And I advise thee to trumpet forth everywhere, how much in earnest thou art to marry her, whether true or not.

Thou mayest *safely* do it. She will not live to put thee to the trial; and it will a little palliate for thy enormous usage of her, and be a means to make mankind, who know not what I know of the matter, herd a little longer with thee, and forbear to hunt thee to thy fellow-savages in the Libyan wilds and deserts.

Your messenger found me at Edgware, expecting to dinner with me several friends, whom I had invited three days before. I sent apologies to them, as in a case of life and death; and speeded to town to the wicked woman's: for how knew I but shocking attempts might be made upon her by the cursed wretches; perhaps by your connivance, in order to mortify her into your measures?

Little knows the public what villainies are committed in these abominable houses, upon innocent creatures drawn into their snares.

Finding the lady not there, I posted away to the officer's, although Sally told me that she had been just come from thence; and that she had refused to see her, or (as she sent down word) anybody else; being resolved to have the remainder of that Sunday to herself, as it might, perhaps, be the last she should ever see.

I had the same thing told me, when I got thither.

I sent up to let her know that I came with a commission to set her at liberty. I was afraid of sending up the name of a man known to be your friend. She absolutely refused to see *any man*, however, for that day, or to answer further to anything said from me.

Having, therefore, informed myself of all that the officer, and his wife, and servant, could acquaint me with, as well in relation to the horrid arrest, as to her behaviour, and the women's to her; and her ill state of health; I went back to Sinclair's, as I will still call her, and heard the three women's story: from all which I am enabled to give you the following shocking particulars; which may serve till I can see the unhappy lady herself to-morrow, if then I can gain admittance to her. You will find that I have been very minute in my inquiries.

Your villain it was that *set* the poor lady, and had the impudence to appear, and abet the sheriff's officers in the cursed transaction. He thought, no doubt, that he was doing the most acceptable service to his blessed master. They had got a chair; the head ready up, as soon as service was over. And as she came out of the church, at the door fronting Bedford Street, the officers, stepping to her, whispered that they had an action against her.

She was terrified, trembled, and turned pale.

Action! said she. What is that? I have committed *no bad action*! Lord bless me! Men, what mean you?

That you are our prisoner, madam.

Prisoner, sirs! What—How—Why—What have I done?

You must go with us. Be pleased, madam, to step into this chair.

With *you*! With *men*! Must go with *men*! I am not used to go with *strange men*! Indeed you must excuse me!

We can't excuse you: we are sheriff's officers. We have a writ against you. You *must* go with us, and you shall know at whose suit.

Suit! said the charming innocent; I don't know what you mean. Pray, men, don't lay hands upon me; they offering to put her into the chair. I am not used to be thus treated—I have done nothing to deserve it.

She then spied thy villain. O thou wretch, said she, where is thy vile master? Am I again to be *his prisoner*? Help, good people!

A crowd had before begun to gather.

My master is in the country, madam, many miles off. If you please to go with these men, they will treat you civilly.

The people were most of them struck with compassion. A fine young creature! A thousand pities! cried some. While some few threw out vile and shocking reflections! But a gentleman interposed, and demanded to see the fellows' authority.

They showed it. Is your name Clarissa Harlowe, madam? said he.

Yes, yes, indeed, ready to sink, my name *was* Clarissa Harlowe: but it is now *Wretchedness*! Lord, be merciful to me! what is to come next?

You *must* go with these men, madam, said the gentleman: they have authority for what they do.

He pitied her, and retired.

Indeed you must, said one chairman.

Indeed you must, said the other.

Can nobody, joined in another gentleman, be applied to, who will see that so fine a creature is not ill used?

Thy villain answered, Orders were given particularly for that. She had rich relations. She need but ask and have. She would only be carried to the officer's house, till matters could be made up. The people she had lodged with loved her: but she had left her lodgings privately.

Oh! had she those tricks already? cried one or two.

She heard not this, but said, Well, if I must go, I must—I cannot resist—but I will not be carried to the woman's! I will rather die at your feet than be carried to the woman's!

You won't be carried there, madam, cried thy fellow.

Only to *my* house, madam, said one of the officers.

Where is that?

In High Holborn, madam.

I know not where High Holborn is: but anywhere, except to the woman's.—But am I to go with *men* only?

Looking about her, and seeing the three passages, to wit, that leading to Henrietta Street, that to King Street, and the fore-right one, to Bedford Street, crowded, she started. Anywhere—anywhere, said she, but to the woman's! And stepping into the chair, threw herself on the seat, in the utmost distress and confusion. Carry me, carry me out of sight—cover me—cover me up—for ever! were her words.

Thy villain drew the curtains: she had not power; and they went away with her through a vast crowd of people.

Here I must rest. I can write no more at present. Only, Lovelace, remember, *all this was to a Clarissa ! ! !*

.   .   .   .   .   .

The unhappy lady fainted away when she was taken out of the chair at the officer's house.

Several people followed the chair to the very house, which is in a wretched court. Sally was there; and satisfied some of the inquirers that the young gentlewoman would be exceedingly well used: and they soon dispersed.

Dorcas was also there; but came not in her sight. Sally, as a favour, offered to carry her to her former lodgings: but she declared they should carry her thither a corpse, if they did.

Very gentle usage the women boast of: so would a vulture, could it speak, with the entrails of its prey upon its rapacious talons. Of this you 'll judge from what I have to recite.

She asked what was meant by this usage of her? People told me, said she, that I *must* go with the men: that they had authority to take me: so I submitted. But now, what is to be the end of this disgraceful violence?

The end, said the vile Sally Martin, is, for honest people to come at their own.

Bless me! have I taken away anything that belongs to those who have obtained this power over me? I have left very valuable things behind me; but have taken nothing away that is not my own.

And who do you think, *Miss Harlowe*, for I understand, said the cursed creature, you are not married; who do you think is to pay for your board and your lodgings; such handsome lodgings! for so long a time as you were at Mrs. Sinclair's?

Lord have mercy upon me! Miss Martin (I think you are Miss Martin!)—and is this the cause of such a disgraceful insult upon me in the open streets?

And cause enough, *Miss Harlowe* (fond of gratifying her jealous revenge, by calling her *Miss*)—one hundred and fifty guineas, or pounds, is no small sum to lose—and by a young creature who would have bilked her lodgings.

You amaze me, Miss Martin! What language do you talk in? —*Bilk my lodgings!* What is that?

She stood astonished and silent for a few moments.

But recovering herself, and turning from her to the window, she wrung her hands [the cursed Sally showed me how!]; and lifting them up—*Now*, Lovelace! Now indeed do I think I *ought* to forgive thee! But who shall forgive Clarissa Harlowe! —O my sister! O my brother! Tender mercies were your cruelties to *this*!

After a pause, her handkerchief drying up her falling tears, she turned to Sally: *Now*, have I nothing to do but acquiesce— only let me say, that if this aunt of yours, this Mrs. Sinclair; or this man, this Mr. Lovelace, come near me; or if I am carried to the horrid house (for that, I suppose, is the design of this new outrage); God be merciful to the poor Clarissa Harlowe!—Look to the consequence!—Look, I charge you, to the consequence!

The vile wretch told her it was not designed to carry her any-whither against her will: but, if it were, they should take care not to be frightened again by a *penknife*.

She cast up her eyes to Heaven, and was silent—and went to the farthest corner of the room, and, sitting down, threw her handkerchief over her face.

Sally asked her several questions; but not answering her, she told her she would wait upon her by and by, when she had found her speech.

She ordered the people to press her to eat and drink. She must be fasting—nothing but her prayers and tears, poor thing! were the merciless devil's words, as she owned to me. Dost think I did not curse her?

She went away; and, after her own dinner, returned.

The unhappy lady, by this devil's account of her, then seemed either mortified into meekness, or to have made a resolution not to be provoked by the insults of this cursed creature.

Sally inquired, in her presence, whether she had ate or drank anything; and being told by the woman that she could not prevail upon her to taste a morsel, or drink a drop, she said, This is wrong, *Miss Harlowe*! Very wrong! Your religion, I think, should teach you that starving yourself is self-murder.

She answered not.

The wretch owned she was resolved to make her speak.

She asked if Mabel should attend her, till it were seen what her friends would do for her in discharge of the debt? Mabel, said she, has not *yet* earned the clothes you were so good as to give her.

Am I not worth an answer, *Miss Harlowe?*

I would answer you (said the sweet sufferer, without any emotion) if I knew how.

I have ordered pen, ink, and paper to be brought you, *Miss Harlowe*. There they are. I know you love writing. You may write to whom you please. Your friend Miss Howe will expect to hear from you.

I have no friend, said she. I deserve none.

Rowland, for that is the officer's name, told her she had friends enough to pay the debt, if she would write.

She would trouble nobody; she had no friends; was all they could get from her, while Sally stayed: but yet spoken with a patience of spirit, as if she enjoyed her griefs.

The insolent creature went away, ordering them in the lady's hearing to be very civil to her, and to let her want for nothing. Now had she, she owned, the triumph of her heart over this haughty beauty, who kept them all at such distance in their own house!

What thinkest thou, Lovelace, of this! This wretch's triumph was over a Clarissa!

About six in the evening, Rowland's wife pressed her to drink tea. She said she had rather have a glass of water; for her tongue was ready to cleave to the roof of her mouth.

The woman brought her a glass, and some bread and butter. She tried to taste the latter; but could not swallow it: but eagerly drank the water; lifting up her eyes in thankfulness for that ! ! !

The divine Clarissa, Lovelace—reduced to rejoice for a cup of cold water ! By whom reduced !

About nine o'clock she asked if anybody were to be her bedfellow?

Their maid, if she pleased; or, as she was so weak and ill, the girl should sit up with her, if she chose she should.

She chose to be alone both night and day, she said. But might she not be trusted with the keys of the room where she was to lie down; for she should not put off her clothes?

That, they told her, could not be.

She was afraid not, she said. But indeed she would not get away, if she could.

They told me that they had but one bed, besides that they lay in themselves (which they would fain have had her accept of), and besides *that* their maid lay in, in a garret, which they called a hole of a garret: and that *that* one bed was the prisoner's bed; which they made several apologies to me about. I suppose it is shocking enough.

But the lady would not lie in theirs. Was she not a prisoner? she said. Let her have the prisoner's room.

Yet they owned that she started when she was conducted thither. But recovering herself, Very well, said she, why should not all be of a piece? Why should not my wretchedness be complete?

She found fault that all the fastenings were on the outside, and none within; and said she could not trust herself in a room where others could come in at their pleasure, and she not go out. She had not *been used* to it ! ! !

Dear, dear soul! My tears flow as I write. Indeed, Lovelace, she had not been used to such treatment !

They assured her that it was as much their duty to protect her from other persons' insults, as from escaping herself.

Then they were people of more honour, she said, than she had of late been used to.

She asked if they knew Mr. Lovelace?

No, was their answer.

Have you heard of him?

No.

Well, then, you may be good sort of folks in your way.

Pause here a moment, Lovelace ! and reflect—I must.

.   .   .   .   .   .

Again they asked her if they should send any word to her lodgings?

These are my lodgings now, are they not? was all her answer.

She sat up in a chair all night, the back against the door; having, it seems, thrust a broken piece of a poker through the staples where a bolt had been on the inside.

.   .   .   .   .   .

Next morning, Sally and Polly both went to visit her.

She had begged of Sally, the day before, that she might not see Mrs. Sinclair, nor Dorcas, nor the broken-toothed servant, called William.

Polly would have ingratiated herself with her; and pretended to be concerned for her misfortunes. But she took no more notice of her than of the other.

They asked if she had any commands? If she *had*, she only need to mention what they were, and she should be obeyed.

None at all, she said.

How did she like the people of the house? Were they civil to her?

Pretty well, considering she had no money to give them.

Would she accept of any money? They could put it to her account.

She would contract no debts.

Had she any money about her?

She meekly put her hand in her pocket, and pulled out half a guinea and a little silver. Yes, I have a little.—But here should be fees paid, I believe. Should there not? I have heard of entrance-money to compound for not being stripped. But these people are very civil people, I fancy; for they have not offered to take away my clothes.

They have *orders* to be civil to you.

It is very kind.

But we two will bail you, *Miss*, if you will go back with us to Mrs. Sinclair's.

Not for the world!

Hers are very handsome apartments.

The fitter for those who own them!

These are very sad ones.

The fitter for *me*!

You may be very happy yet, *Miss*, if you will.

I hope I shall.

If you refuse to eat or drink, we will give bail, and take you with us.

Then I will *try* to eat and drink. Anything but go with you.

Will you not send to your new lodgings? The people will be frighted.

So they will, if I send. So they will, if they know where I am

But have you no things to send for from thence?

There is what will pay for their lodgings and trouble: I shall not lessen their security.

But perhaps letters or messages may be left for you there.

I have very few friends; and to those I *have*, I will spare the mortification of knowing what has befallen me.

We are surprised at your indifference, *Miss* Harlowe. Will you not write to any of your friends?

No.

Why, you don't think of tarrying *here* always?

I shall not *live* always.

Do you think you are to stay here as long as you live?

That's as it shall please God, and those who have brought me hither.

Should you like to be at liberty?

I am miserable! What is liberty to the miserable, but to be *more* miserable!

How miserable, *Miss*? You may make yourself as happy as you please.

I hope *you* are both happy.

We are.

May you be more and more happy!

But we wish *you* to be so too.

I never shall be of your opinion, I believe, as to what happiness is.

What do you take our opinion of happiness to be?

To live at Mrs. Sinclair's.

Perhaps, said Sally, we were once as squeamish and narrow-minded as you.

How came it over with you?

Because we saw the ridiculousness of prudery.

Do you come hither to persuade me to hate prudery, as you call it, as much as you do?

We came to offer our service to you.

It is out of your power to serve me.

Perhaps not.

It is not in my inclination to trouble you.

You may be worse offered.

Perhaps I may.

You are mighty short, *Miss*.

As I wish your visit to be, ladies.

They owned to me that they cracked their fans, and laughed.

Adieu, perverse beauty!

Your servant, ladies.

Adieu, haughty-airs!

You see me humbled——

As you deserve, *Miss* Harlowe. Pride will have a fall.

Better fall, with what *you* call pride than stand with meanness. Who does?

I had once a *better* opinion of *you*, Miss Horton! Indeed, you should not insult the miserable.

Neither should the *miserable*, said Sally, insult people for their civility.

I should be sorry if I did.

Mrs. Sinclair shall attend you by and by, to know if you have any commands for *her*.

I have no wish for any liberty, but that of refusing to see her, and *one* more person.

What we came for, was to know if you had any proposals to make for your enlargement?

Then, it seems, the officer put in, you have very good friends, madam, I understand. Is it not better that you make it up? Charges will run high. A hundred and fifty guineas are easier paid than two hundred. Let these ladies bail you, and go along with them; or write to your friends to make it up.

Sally said, There is a gentleman who saw you taken, and was so much moved for you, *Miss Harlowe*, that he would gladly advance the money for you, and leave you to pay it when you can.

See, Lovelace, what cursed devils these are! This is the way, we know, that many an innocent heart is thrown upon keeping, and then upon the town. But for these wretches thus to go to work with such an angel as this! How glad would have been the devilish Sally to have had the least handle to report to thee a listening ear, or patient spirit, upon this hint!

Sir, said she, with high indignation, to the officer, did not you say last night that it was as much your business to protect me from the insults of others as from escaping? Cannot I be permitted to see whom I please; and to refuse admittance to those I like not?

Your creditors, madam, will expect to see you.

Not if I declare I will not treat with them.

Then, madam, you will be sent to prison.

Prison, friend! What dost thou call thy house?

Not a prison, madam.

Why these iron-barred windows, then? Why these double locks and bolts all on the outside, none on the in?

And down she dropped into her chair, and they could not get another word from her. She threw her handkerchief over her face, as once before, which was soon wet with tears; and grievously, they own, she sobbed.

Gentle treatment, Lovelace!—Perhaps thou, as well as these wretches, wilt think it so !

Sally then ordered a dinner, and said they would soon be back again, and see that she ate and drank, *as a good Christian should,* comporting herself to her condition, and making the best of it.

What has not this charming creature suffered; what has she not gone through, in these last three months, that I know of! Who would think such a delicately-framed person could have sustained what she has sustained? We sometimes talk of bravery, of courage, of fortitude! Here they are in perfection! Such bravoes as thou and I should never have been able to support ourselves under half the persecutions, the disappointments, and contumelies, that *she* has met with; but, like cowards, should have slid out of the world, basely, by some back door; that is to say, by a sword, by a pistol, by a halter, or knife! But here is a fine-principled woman who, by dint of this noble consideration, as I imagine [what else can support her?], that she has *not* deserved *the evils she contends with*; and that *this world is designed but as a transitory state of probation;* and that she is *travelling to another and better;* puts up with all the hardships of the *journey;* and is not to be diverted from her course by the attacks of *thieves* and *robbers,* or any other terrors and difficulties; *being assured of an ample reward at the end of it* !

If thou thinkest this reflection uncharacteristic from a companion and friend of thine, imaginest thou that I profited nothing by my long attendance on my uncle in his dying state; and from the pious reflections of the good clergyman, who, day by day, at the poor man's own request, visited and prayed by him? And could I have another such instance *as this,* to bring all these reflections home to me?

Then who can write of good persons, and of good subjects, and be capable of *admiring them,* and not be made serious for the *time,* if he write in character? And hence may we gather what a benefit to the morals of men the keeping of *good* company must be; while those who keep only *bad*, must necessarily more and more harden, and be hardened.

.   .   .   .   .   .

'Tis twelve of the clock, Sunday night. I can think of nothing but of this excellent creature. Her distresses fill my head and my heart. I was drowsy for a quarter of an hour; but the fit is gone off. And I will continue the melancholy subject from the information of these wretches. Enough, I dare say, will arise in the visit I shall make, if admitted to-morrow, to send by thy servant, as to the way I am likely to find her in.

After the women had left her, she complained of her head and her heart; and seemed terrified with apprehensions of being carried once more to Sinclair's.

Refusing anything for breakfast, Mrs. Rowland came up to her and told her (as these wretches owned they had ordered her, for fear she should starve herself) that she *must* and *should* have tea, and bread and butter: and that, as she had friends who could support her, if she wrote to them, it was a wrong thing, both for herself and *them*, to starve herself thus.

If it be for *your own sakes*, said she, that is another thing: let coffee, or tea, or chocolate, or what you will, be got: and put down a chicken to my account every day, if you please, and eat it yourselves. I will taste it, if I can. I would do nothing to hinder you. I have friends will pay you liberally, when they know I am gone.

They wondered, they told her, at her strange composure in such distresses.

They were *nothing*, she said, *to what she had suffered already* from the vilest of all men. The disgrace of seizing her in the street; multitudes of people about her; shocking imputations wounding her ears; had indeed been very affecting to her. But that was over. Everything soon would! And she should be still *more* composed, were it not for the apprehensions of seeing one man, and one woman; and being tricked or forced back to the vilest house in the world.

Then, were it not better to give way to the two gentlewomen's offer to bail her? They could tell her it was a very kind proffer; and what was not to be met with every day.

She believed so.

The ladies might possibly dispense with her going back to the house to which she had such an antipathy. Then the compassionate gentleman, who was inclined to make it up with her creditors on her own bond—it was strange to them she hearkened not to so generous a proposal.

Did the two ladies tell you who the gentleman was?—or did they say any more on that subject?

Yes, they did; and hinted to me, said the woman, that you had nothing to do but to receive a visit from the gentleman, and the money, they believed, would be laid down on your own bond or note.

She was startled.

I charge you, said she, as you will answer it one day to my friends, that you bring no gentleman into my company. I charge you don't. If you do, you know not what may be the consequence.

They apprehended no bad consequence, they said, in doing their duty: and if she knew not her own good, her friends would thank them for taking any innocent steps to serve her, though against her will.

Don't push me upon extremities, man! Don't make me desperate, woman! I have no small difficulty, notwithstanding the seeming composure you just now took notice of, to bear, as I ought to bear, the evils I suffer. But if you bring a man or men to me, be the pretence *what* it will——

She stopped there, and looked so earnestly, and so wildly, they said, that they did not know but she would do some harm to herself if they disobeyed her; and that would be a sad thing in *their* house, and might be their ruin. They therefore promised that no man should be brought to her but by her own consent.

Mrs. Rowland prevailed on her to drink a dish of tea, and taste some bread and butter, about eleven on Saturday morning: which she probably did to have an excuse not to dine with the women when they returned.

But she would not quit her *prison-room*, as she called it, to go into their parlour.

"Unbarred windows, and a lightsomer apartment, she said, had too cheerful an appearance for her mind."

A shower falling as she spoke, "What, said she, looking up, do the elements weep for me?"

At another time, "The light of the sun was irksome to her. The sun seemed to shine in to mock her woes.

"Methought, added she, the sun darting in, and gilding these iron bars, plays upon me, like the two women who came to insult my haggard looks by the word *beauty*; and my dejected heart, with the word *haughty-airs*!"

Sally came again at dinner-time *to see how she fared*, as she told her; and that she did not starve herself: and, as she wanted to have some talk with her, if she gave her leave, she would dine with her.

I cannot eat.

You must try, *Miss Harlowe*.

And, dinner being ready just then, she offered her hand, and desired her to walk down.

No; she would not stir out of her *prison-room*.

These sullen airs won't do, *Miss Harlowe*: indeed they won't.

She was silent.

You will have harder usage than any you have ever yet known, I can tell you, if you come not into some humour to make matters up.

She was still silent.

Come, *Miss*, walk down to dinner. Let me entreat you, do. Miss Horton is below: she was once your favourite.

She waited for an answer: but received none.

We came to make some proposals to you, for your good; though you affronted us so lately. And we would not let Mrs. Sinclair come in person, because we thought to oblige you.

That is indeed obliging.

Come, give me your hand, *Miss Harlowe*: you *are* obliged to me, I can tell you that: and let us go down to Miss Horton.

Excuse me: I will not stir out of this room.

Would you have me and Miss Horton dine in this filthy bedroom?

It is not a bedroom to me. I have not been in bed; nor will, while I am here.

And yet you care not, as I see, to leave the house. And so you won't go down, *Miss Harlowe*?

I won't, except I am forced to it.

Well, well, let it alone. I shan't ask Miss Horton to dine in this room, I assure you. I will send up a plate.

And away the little saucy toad fluttered down.

When they had dined, up they came together.

Well, Miss, you would not eat anything, it seems! Very pretty sullen airs these! No wonder *the honest gentleman had such a hand with you.*

She only held up her hands and eyes; the tears trickling down her cheeks.

Insolent devils! How much more cruel and insulting are bad women, even than bad men!

Methinks, *Miss*, said Sally, you are a little *soily*, to what we have seen you. Pity such a nice lady should not have changes of apparel. Why won't you send to your lodgings for linen, at least?

I am not nice now.

Miss looks well and clean in anything, said Polly. But, dear madam, why won't you send to your lodgings? Were it but in kindness to the *people*? They must have a concern about you. And your Miss Howe will wonder what's become of you; for, no doubt, you correspond.

She turned from them, and, to herself, said, *Too much! Too much!* She tossed her handkerchief, wet before with her tears, from her, and held her apron to her eyes.

Don't weep, Miss! said the vile Polly.

Yet *do*, cried the viler Sally, if it be a relief. Nothing, as Mr. Lovelace once told *me*, dries sooner than tears. For once I too wept mightily.

I could not bear the recital of this with patience. Yet I cursed them not so much as I should have done, had I not had a mind to get from them all the particulars of their *gentle* treatment; and this for two reasons; the one, that I might stab thee to the heart with the repetition; the other, that I might know upon what terms I am likely to see the unhappy lady to-morrow.

Well, but, *Miss Harlowe*, cried Sally, do you think these *forlorn airs* pretty? You are a good Christian, child. Mrs. Rowland tells me she has got you a Bible-book. Oh, there it lies! I make no doubt but you have doubled down the *useful places*, as honest Matt. Prior says.

Then rising, and taking it up—Ay, so you have. The *Book of Job!* One opens naturally here, I see. *My* mamma made me a fine Bible scholar. *Ecclesiasticus* too! That's Apocrypha, as they call it. You see, Miss Horton, I know something of the Book.

They proposed once more to bail her, and to go home with them. A motion which she received with the same indignation as before.

Sally told her that she had written in a very favourable manner in her behalf to you; and that she every hour expected an answer; and made no doubt that you would come up with the messenger, and generously pay the whole debt, and ask her pardon for neglecting it.

This disturbed her so much that they feared she would have fallen into fits. She could not bear your name, she said. She hoped she should never see you more: and were you to intrude yourself, dreadful consequences might follow.

Surely, they said, she would be glad to be released from her confinement.

Indeed she *should*, now they had begun to alarm her with *his* name, who was the author of all her woes: and who, she now saw plainly, gave way to this new outrage in order to bring her to his own infamous terms.

Why then, they asked, would she not write to her friends to pay Mrs. Sinclair's demand?

Because she hoped she should not long trouble anybody; and because she knew that the payment of the money, if she were able to pay it, was not what was aimed at.

Sally owned that she told her that, truly, she had thought herself as well descended, and as well educated, as herself, though not entitled to such considerable fortunes. And had the impudence to insist upon it to me to be truth.

She had the insolence to add to the lady, that she had as much reason as *she* to expect Mr. Lovelace would marry her; he having contracted to do so *before* he knew Miss Clarissa Harlowe: and that she had it under his hand and seal too—or else he had not obtained his end: therefore it was not likely she should be so officious as to do his work against herself, if she thought Mr. Lovelace had designs upon her, like what she *presumed* to hint at: that, for her part, her only view was to procure liberty to a young gentlewoman, who made those things grievous to her which would not be made such a rout about by anybody else —and to procure the payment of a just debt to her friend Mrs. Sinclair.

She besought them to leave her. She wanted not these instances, she said, to convince her of the company she was in: and told them that, to get rid of such visitors, and of the still worse she was apprehensive of, she would write to one friend to raise the money for her; though it would be death for her to do so; because that friend could not do it without her mother, in whose eye it would give a selfish appearance to a friendship that was above all sordid alloys.

They advised her to write out of hand.

But how much must I write for? What is the sum? Should I not have had a bill delivered me? God knows, I took not your lodgings. But he that could treat me as he has done could do this!

Don't speak against Mr. Lovelace, *Miss Harlowe*. He is a

man I greatly esteem [cursed toad!]. And, 'bating that he will take his advantage where he can, of *us* silly credulous women, he is a man of honour.

She lifted up her hands and eyes instead of speaking: and well she might! For any words she could have used could not have expressed the anguish she must feel on being comprehended in the us.

She must write for one hundred and fifty guineas, at least: two hundred, if she were short of money, might as well be written for.

Mrs. Sinclair, she said, had all her clothes. Let them be sold, *fairly* sold, and the money go as far as it would go. She had also a few other valuables; but no money (none at all) but the poor half-guinea, and the little silver they had seen. She would give bond to pay all that her apparel, and the other matters she had, would fall short of. She had great effects belonging to her of right. Her bond would, and must, be paid, were it for a thousand pounds. But her clothes she should never want. She believed, if not too much undervalued, those, and her few valuables, would answer everything. She wished for no surplus but to discharge the last expenses; and forty shillings would do as well for those as forty pounds. "Let my ruin, said she, lifting up her eyes, be LARGE! Let it be COMPLETE, *in this life*! For a *composition*, let it be COMPLETE." And there she stopped. No doubt alluding to her father's extensive curse!

The wretches could not help wishing to me for the opportunity of making such a purchase for their own wear. How I cursed *them*! and, in my heart, *thee*! But *too* probable, thought I, that this vile Sally Martin may hope [though thou art incapable of it] that *her* Lovelace, as she has the assurance, behind thy back, to call thee, may present her with some of the poor lady's spoils!

Will not Mrs. Sinclair, proceeded she, think my clothes a security till they can be sold? They are very good clothes. A suit or two but just put on, as it were; never worn. They cost much more than is demanded of me. *My father loved to see me fine*. All shall go. But let me have the particulars of her demand. I suppose I must pay for my *destroyer* [that was her well-adapted word!] and his servants, as well as for myself. I am content to do so. Indeed, I am content to do so—I am above wishing that anybody who could *thus* act should be so much as expostulated with, as to the justice and equity of this payment. If I have but enough to pay the demand, I shall be satisfied; and will leave the baseness of such an action as this, as an aggravation of a guilt which I thought could *not* be aggravated.

I own, Lovelace, I have malice in this particularity, in order to sting thee to the heart. And, let me ask thee, what now thou canst think of thy barbarity, thy unprecedented barbarity, in having reduced a person of her rank, fortune, talents, and virtue, so low?

The wretched women, it must be owned, act but in their profession; a profession thou hast been the principal means of reducing these two to act in. And they know what thy designs have been, and how far prosecuted. It is, in their opinions, using her *gently*, that they have forborne to bring to her the woman so justly odious to her; and that they have not threatened her with the introducing to her strange men: nor yet brought into her company their *spirit-breakers*, and *humbling-drones* (fellows not allowed to carry stings), to trace and force her back to their detested house; and, when there, into all their measures.

Till I came, they thought thou wouldst not be displeased at anything she suffered, that could help to mortify her into a state of shame and disgrace; and bring her to comply with thy views, when thou shouldst come to release her from these wretches, as from a greater evil than cohabiting with thee.

When thou considerest these things, thou wilt make no difficulty of believing that this their own account of their behaviour to this admirable woman has been far short of their insults: and the less, when I tell thee, that, all together, their usage had such effects upon her, that they left her in violent hysterics; ordering an apothecary to be sent for, if she should continue in them, and be worse; and particularly (as they had done from the first) that they kept out of her way any edged or pointed instrument; especially a penknife; which, pretending to mend a pen, they said, she might ask for.

At twelve, Saturday night, Rowland sent to tell them that she was so ill that he knew not what might be the issue; and wished her out of his house.

And this made them as heartily wish to hear from you. For their messenger, to their great surprise, was not then returned from M. Hall. And they were sure he must have reached that place by Friday night.

Early on Sunday morning both devils went to see how she did. They had such an account of her weakness, lowness, and anguish, that they forbore (out of compassion, they said, finding their visits so disagreeable to her) to see her. But their apprehension of what might be the issue was, no doubt, their principal consideration: nothing else could have softened such flinty bosoms.

They sent for the apothecary Rowland had had to her, and gave him, and Rowland, and his wife, and maid, strict orders, many times repeated, for the utmost care to be taken of her—no doubt, with an Old Bailey forecast. And they sent up to let her know what orders they had given: but that, understanding she had taken something to compose herself, they would not disturb her.

She had scrupled, it seems, to admit the apothecary's visit overnight, because he was a MAN. Nor could she be prevailed upon to see him till they pleaded *their own safety* to her.

They went again from church [Lord, Bob, these creatures go to church!], but she sent them down word that she must have all the remainder of the day to herself.

When I first came, and told them of thy execrations for what they had done, and joined my own to them, they were astonished. The mother said she had thought she had known Mr. Lovelace better; and expected thanks, and not curses.

While I was with them, came back halting and cursing, most horribly, their messenger; by reason of the ill-usage he had received from you, instead of the reward he had been taught to expect for the supposed good news that he carried down. A pretty fellow! art thou not, to abuse people for the consequences of thy own faults?

Dorcas, whose acquaintance this fellow is, and who recommended him for the journey, had conditioned with him, it seems, for a share in the expected bounty from you. Had she been to have had *her* share made good, I wish thou hadst broken every bone in his skin.

Under what shocking disadvantages, and with this addition to them, that I am thy friend and intimate, am I to make a visit to this unhappy lady to-morrow morning! In thy *name* too! Enough to be refused, that I am of a *sex* to which, for *thy* sake, she has so justifiable an aversion: nor, having such a tyrant of a father, and such an implacable brother, has she reason to make an exception in favour of *any* of it on *their* accounts.

It is three o'clock. I will close here; and take a little rest: what I have written will be a proper preparative for what shall offer by and by.

Thy servant is not to return without a letter, he tells me; and that thou expectest him back in the morning. Thou hast fellows enough where thou art at thy command. If I find any difficulty in seeing the lady, thy messenger shall post away with this. Let him look to broken bones, and other consequences, if what he carries answer not thy expectation. But, if I am admitted, thou shalt have *this* and the result of my audience both together. In the former case, thou mayest send another servant to wait the next advices from

J. BELFORD.

Letter CVI—Mr. Belford to Robert Lovelace, Esq.

Monday, July 17.

ABOUT six this morning I went to Rowland's. Mrs. Sinclair was to follow me, in order to dismiss the action; but not to come in sight.

Rowland, upon inquiry, told me that the lady was extremely ill; and that she had desired that no one but his wife or maid should come near her.

I said I *must* see her. I had told him my business overnight; and I *must* see her.

His wife went up: but returned presently, saying she could not get her to speak to her; yet that her eyelids moved; though she either would not, or could not, open them to look up at her.

Oons, woman, said I, the lady may be in a fit: the lady may be dying. Let me go up. Show me the way.

A horrid hole of a house, in an alley they call a court; stairs wretchedly narrow, even to the first-floor rooms: and into a den they led me, with broken walls, which had been papered, as I saw by a multitude of tacks, and some torn bits held on by the rusty heads.

The floor indeed was clean, but the ceiling was smoked with variety of figures, and initials of names, that had been the woeful employment of wretches who had no other way to amuse themselves.

A bed at one corner, with coarse curtains tacked up at the feet to the ceiling; because the curtain-rings were broken off; but a coverlid upon it with a cleanish look, though plaguily in tatters, and the corners tied up in tassels, that the rents in it might go no farther.

The windows dark and double-barred, the tops boarded up to save mending; and only a little four-paned eyelet-hole of a casement to let in air; more, however, coming in at broken panes than could come in at that.

Four old Turkey-worked chairs, bursten-bottomed, the stuffing staring out.

An old, tottering, worm-eaten table, that had more nails bestowed in mending it to make it stand than the table cost fifty years ago when new.

On the mantelpiece was an iron shove-up candlestick, with a lighted candle in it, twinkle, twinkle, twinkle, four of them, I suppose, for a penny.

Near that, on the same shelf, was an old looking-glass, cracked through the middle, breaking out into a thousand points; the crack given it, perhaps, in a rage, by some poor creature to whom it gave the representation of his heart's woes in his face.

The chimney had two half-tiles in it on one side, and one whole one on the other; which showed it had been in better plight; but now the very mortar had followed the rest of the tiles in every other place, and left the bricks bare.

An old half-barred stove-grate was in the chimney; and in that a large stone bottle without a neck, filled with baleful yew, as an evergreen, withered southernwood, dead sweet-brier, and sprigs of rue in flower.

To finish the shocking description, in a dark nook stood an old broken-bottomed cane couch, without a squab, or coverlid, sunk at one corner, and unmortised by the failing of one of its worm-eaten legs, which lay in two pieces under the wretched piece of furniture it could no longer support.

And this, thou horrid Lovelace, was the bedchamber of the divine Clarissa ! ! !

I had leisure to cast my eye on these things: for, going up softly, the poor lady turned not about at our entrance; nor, till I spoke, moved her head.

She was kneeling in a corner of the room, near the dismal window, against the table, on an old bolster (as it seemed to be) of the cane couch, half-covered with her handkerchief; her back to the door; which was only shut to [no need of fastenings!]; her arms crossed upon the table, the forefinger of her right hand in her Bible. She had perhaps been reading in it, and could read no longer. Paper, pens, ink, lay by her book on the table. Her dress was white damask, exceeding neat; but her stays seemed not tight-laced. I was told afterwards that her laces had been cut when she fainted away at her entrance into this cursed place; and she had not been solicitous enough about her dress to send for others. Her head-dress was a little discomposed; her charming hair, in natural ringlets, as you have heretofore described it, but a little tangled, as if not lately combed, irregularly shading one side of the loveliest neck in the world; as her disordered, rumpled handkerchief did the other. Her face [oh, how altered from what I had seen it! Yet lovely in spite of all her griefs and sufferings!] was reclined, when we entered, upon her crossed arms; but so as not more than one side of it to be hid.

When I surveyed the room around, and the kneeling lady, sunk with majesty too in her white flowing robes (for she had not on a hoop) spreading the dark, though not dirty, floor, and illuminating that horrid corner; her linen beyond imagination white, considering that she had not been undressed ever since she had been here; I thought my concern would have choked me. Something rose in my throat, I know not what, which made me, for a moment, guggle, as it were, for speech: which, at last, forcing its way, Con—con—confound you both, said I to the man and woman, is this an apartment for such a lady? And could the cursed devils of her own sex, who visited this suffering angel, see her, and leave her, in so damned a nook?

Sir, we would have had the lady to accept of our own bed-chamber; but she refused it. We are poor people—and we expect nobody will stay with us longer than they can help it.

You are people chosen purposely, I doubt not, by the damned woman who has employed you: and if your usage of this lady has been but half as bad as your house, you had better never to have seen the light.

Up then raised the charming sufferer her lovely face; but with such a significance of woe overspreading it that I could not, for the soul of me, help being visibly affected.

She waved her hand two or three times towards the door, as if commanding me to withdraw; and displeased at my intrusion; but did not speak.

Permit me, madam—I will not approach one step farther without your leave—permit me, for one moment, the favour of your ear!

No—no—go, go, MAN! with an emphasis—and would have said more; but, as if struggling in vain for words, she seemed to give up speech for lost, and dropped her head down once more, with a deep sigh, upon her left arm; her right, as if she had not the use of it (numbed, I suppose), self-moved, dropping down on her side.

Oh, that thou hadst been there! and in my place! But by what I then felt in myself, I am convinced that a capacity of being moved by the distresses of our fellow-creatures is far from being disgraceful to a manly heart. With what pleasure, at that moment, could I have given up my own life, could I but first have avenged this charming creature, and cut the throat of her *destroyer*, as she emphatically calls thee, though the friend that I best love! And yet, at the same time, my heart and my eyes gave way to a softness of which (though not so hardened a wretch as thou) it was never before so susceptible.

I dare not approach you, dearest lady, without your leave: but on my knees I beseech you to permit me to release you from this damned house, and out of the power of the accursed woman who was the occasion of your being here!

She lifted up her sweet face once more, and beheld me on my knees. Never knew I before what it was to pray so heartily.

Are you not—are you not Mr. Belford, sir? I think your name is Belford?

It is, madam, and I ever was a worshipper of your virtues, and an advocate for you; and I come to release you from the hands you are in.

And in whose to place me? Oh, leave me, leave me! Let me never rise from this spot! Let me never, never more believe in man!

This moment, dearest lady, this very moment, if you please, you may depart whithersoever you think fit. You are absolutely free, and your own mistress.

I had now as lief die here in this place as anywhere. I will owe no obligation to any friend of *him* in whose company you have seen me. So, pray, sir, withdraw.

Then turning to the officer, Mr. Rowland I think your name is? I am better reconciled to your house than I was at first. If you can but engage that I shall have nobody come near me but your wife (no *man !*), and neither of those women who have sported with my calamities, I will die with you, and in this very corner. And you shall be well satisfied for the trouble you have had with me. I have value enough for that—for, see, I have a diamond ring; taking it out of her bosom; and I have friends will redeem it at a high price, when I am gone.

But for *you*, sir, looking at me, I beg you to withdraw. If you mean me well, God, I hope, will reward you for your good meaning; but to the friend of my *destroyer* will I not owe an obligation.

You will owe no obligation to me, nor to anybody. You have been detained for a debt you do not owe. The action is dismissed; and you will only be so good as to give me your hand into the coach, which stands as near to this house as it could draw up. And I will either leave you at the coach door, or attend you whithersoever you please, till I see you safe where you would wish to be.

Will you then, sir, *compel* me to be beholden to you?

You will inexpressibly oblige me, madam, to command me to do you either service or pleasure.

Why then, sir [looking at me]—but why do you mock me in that humble posture! Rise, sir! I cannot speak to you else.

I arose.

Only, sir, take this ring. I have a sister, who will be glad to have it at the price it shall be valued at, for the *former* owner's sake! Out of the money she gives, let this man be paid; handsomely paid: and I have a few valuables more at my lodgings (Dorcas, or the MAN William, can tell where that is); let them, and my clothes at the wicked woman's, where you have seen me, be sold, for the payment of my lodging first, and next of your *friend's* debts, that I have been arrested for, as far as they will go; only reserving enough to put me into the ground, anywhere, or anyhow, no matter.—Tell your friend I wish it may be enough to satisfy the whole demand; but if it be not, he must make it up himself; or, if he think fit to draw for it on Miss Howe, she will repay it, *and with interest*, if he insist upon it.— And this, sir, if you promise to perform, you will do me, as you offer, both pleasure and service: and say you *will*, and take the ring and withdraw. If I want to say anything more to you (you seem to be a humane man), I will let you know—and so, sir, God bless you.

I approached her, and was going to speak——

Don't speak, sir: here's the ring.

I stood off.

And won't you take it? Won't you do this last office for me? I have no other person to ask it of; else, believe me, I would not request it of *you*. But take it or not, laying it upon the table —you must withdraw, sir: I am very ill. I would fain get a little rest, if I could. I find I am going to be bad again.

And offering to rise, she sunk down through excess of weakness and grief, in a fainting fit.

Why, Lovelace, wast thou not present thyself? Why dost thou commit such villainies, as even thou art afraid to appear in; and yet puttest a weaker heart and head upon encountering with them?

The maid coming in just then, the woman and she lifted her up on the decrepit couch; and I withdrew with this Rowland; who wept like a child, and said he never in his life was so moved.

Yet so hardened a wretch art thou, that I question whether thou wilt shed a tear at my relation.

They recovered her by hartshorn and water. I went down meanwhile; for the detestable woman had been below some time. Oh, how did I curse her! I never before was so fluent in curses.

She tried to wheedle me; but I renounced her; and, after she had dismissed the action, sent her away crying, or pretending to cry, because of my behaviour to her.

You will observe that I did not mention one word to the lady about *you*. I was afraid to do it. For 'twas plain that she could not bear your name: your *friend*, and the *company* you have seen me in, were the words nearest to naming you she could speak: and yet I wanted to clear your intention of this brutal, this sordid-looking villainy.

I sent up again, by Rowland's wife, when I heard that the lady was recovered, beseeching her to quit that devilish place; and the woman assured her that she was at full liberty to do so; for that the action was dismissed.

But she cared not to answer her: and was so weak and low that it was almost as much out of her power as inclination, the woman told me, to speak.

I would have hastened away for my friend Doctor H., but the house is such a den, and the room she was in such a hole, that I was ashamed to be seen in it by a man of his reputation, especially with a woman of such an appearance, and in such uncommon distress; and I found there was no prevailing on her to quit it for the people's bedroom, which was neat and lightsome.

The strong-room she was in, the wretches told me, should have been in better order, but that it was but the very morning that she was brought in, that an unhappy man had quitted it; for a more eligible prison, no doubt; since there could hardly be a worse.

Being told that she desired not to be disturbed, and seemed inclined to doze, I took this opportunity to go to her lodgings in Covent Garden; to which Dorcas (who first discovered her there, as Will was the setter from church) had before given me a direction.

The man's name is Smith, a dealer in gloves, snuff, and such petty merchandise: his wife the shopkeeper: he a maker of the gloves they sell. Honest people, it seems.

I thought to have got the woman with me to the lady; but she was not within.

I talked with the man, and told him what had befallen the lady; owing, as I said, to a mistake of orders; and gave her the character she deserved; and desired him to send his wife, the moment she came in, to the lady; directing him whither; not doubting that her attendance would be very welcome to her: which he promised.

He told me that a letter was left for her there on Saturday; and, about half an hour before I came, another, superscribed by the same hand; the first, by the post; the other, by a countryman; who, having been informed of her absence, and of all the circumstances they could tell him of it, posted away, full of concern, saying that the lady he was sent from would be ready to break her heart at the tidings.

I thought it right to take the two letters back with me; and, dismissing my coach, took a chair, as a more proper vehicle for the lady, if I (the friend of her *destroyer*) could prevail upon her to leave Rowland's.

And here, being obliged to give way to an indispensable avocation, I will make thee taste a little, in thy turn, of the plague of suspense; and break off, without giving thee the least hint of the issue of my further proceedings. I know that those least bear disappointment, who love most to give it. In twenty instances hast thou afforded me proof of the truth of this observation. And I matter not thy raving.

Another letter, however, shall be ready, send for it as soon as thou wilt. But, were it not, have I not written enough to convince thee that I am

Thy ready and obliging friend,

J. BELFORD?

Letter CVII—Mr. Lovelace to John Belford, Esq.

Monday, July 17, Eleven at Night.

CURSE upon thy hard heart, thou vile caitiff! How hast thou tortured me by thy designed *abruption*! 'Tis impossible that Miss Harlowe should have ever suffered as thou hast made me suffer, and as I now suffer!

That sex is made to bear pain. It is a curse that the first of it entailed upon all her succeeding daughters, when she brought the curse upon us all. And they love those best, whether man or child, who give them most. But to stretch upon thy damned tenterhooks such a spirit as mine—no rack, no torture, can equal my torture!

And must I still wait the return of another messenger? Confound thee for a malicious devil! I wish thou wert a post-horse, and I upon the back of thee! How would I whip and spur, and harrow up thy clumsy sides, till I made thee a ready-roasted, ready-flayed, mess of dog's meat; all the hounds in the county howling after thee as I drove thee, to wait my dismounting, in order to devour thee piecemeal; life still throbbing in each churned mouthful!

Give this fellow the sequel of thy tormenting scribble. Dispatch him away with it. Thou hast promised it shall be ready. Every cushion or chair I shall sit upon, the bed I shall lie down upon (if I go to bed) till he return, will be stuffed with bolt-upright awls, bodkins, corking-pins, and packing-needles: already I can fancy that, to pink my body like my mind, I need only to be put into a hogshead stuck full of steel-pointed spikes, and rolled down a hill three times as high as the Monument.

But I lose time; yet know not how to employ it till this fellow returns with the sequel of thy soul-harrowing intelligence!

Letter CVIII—Mr. Belford to Robert Lovelace, Esq.

Monday Night, July 17.

On my return to Rowland's, I found that the apothecary was just gone up. Mrs. Rowland being above with him, I made the less scruple to go up too, as it was probable that to ask for leave would be to ask to be denied; hoping also that the letters I had with me would be a good excuse.

She was sitting on the side of the broken couch, extremely weak and low; and, I observed, cared not to speak to the man; and no wonder; for I never saw a more shocking fellow, of a profession tolerably genteel, nor heard a more illiterate one prate—physician in ordinary to this house, and others like it, I suppose! He put me in mind of Otway's apothecary in his Caius Marius; as borrowed from the immortal Shakespeare.

> Meagre and very rueful were his looks:
> Sharp misery had worn him to the bones.
> ———Famine in his cheeks:
> Need and oppression staring in his eyes:
> Contempt and beggary hanging on his back:
> The world no friend of his, nor the world's law.

As I am in black, he took me, at my entrance, I believe, to be a doctor, and slunk behind me with his hat upon his two thumbs, and looked as if he expected the oracle to open, and give him orders.

The lady looked displeased, as well at me as at Rowland, who followed me, and at the apothecary. It was not, she said, the least of her present misfortunes, that she could not be left to her own sex; and to her option to see whom she pleased.

I besought her excuse; and, winking for the apothecary to withdraw [which he did], told her that I had been at her new lodgings, to order everything to be got ready for her reception, presuming she would choose to go thither: that I had a chair at the door: that Mr. Smith and his wife [I named their names, that she should not have room for the least fear of Sinclair's] had been full of apprehensions for her safety: that I had brought two letters, which were left there for her; one by the post, the other that very morning.

This took her attention. She held out her charming hand for them; took them, and, pressing them to her lips—From the only friend I have in the world! said she, kissing them again; and looking at the seals, as if to see whether they had been opened. I can't read them, said she, my eyes are too dim; and put them into her bosom.

I besought her to think of quitting that wretched hole.

Whither could she go, she asked, to be safe and uninterrupted for the short remainder of her life; and to avoid being again visited by the creatures who had insulted her before?

I gave her the solemnest assurances that she should not be invaded in her new lodgings by anybody; and said that I would particularly engage my honour, that *the person who had most offended her should not come near her without her own consent.*

Your honour, sir! Are you not that man's friend?

I am not a friend, madam, to his vile actions to the *most excellent of women.*

Do you flatter me, sir? Then are you a MAN. But oh, sir, your friend, holding her face forward with great earnestness, your *barbarous* friend, what has he not to answer for!

There she stopped: her heart full; and putting her hand over her eyes and forehead, the tears trickled through her fingers: resenting thy barbarity, it seemed, as Cæsar did the stab from his distinguished Brutus!

Though she was so very much disordered, I thought I would

not lose this opportunity to assert your innocence of this villainous arrest.

There is no defending the unhappy man in any of his vile actions by you, madam; but of this last outrage, by all that's good and sacred, he is innocent.

O wretches! what a sex is yours! Have you all one dialect? *Good and sacred !* If, sir, you can find an oath, or a vow, or an adjuration, that my ears have not been twenty times a day wounded with, then speak it, and I may again believe a MAN.

I was excessively touched at these words, knowing thy baseness, and the reason she had for them.

But say you, sir; for I would not, methinks, have the wretch capable of this sordid baseness!—Say you that he is innocent of this *last* wickedness? Can you *truly* say that he is?

By the great God of Heaven!——

Nay, sir, if you swear, I must doubt you! If you yourself think your WORD insufficient, what reliance can I have on your OATH! O that this my experience had not cost me so dear! But, were I to live a *thousand* years, I would always suspect the veracity of a swearer. Excuse me, sir; but is it likely that *he* who makes so free with his GOD will scruple anything that may serve his turn with his *fellow-creature?*

This was a most affecting reprimand!

Madam, said I, I have a regard, a regard a gentleman *ought* to have, to my word; and whenever I forfeit it to you——

Nay, sir, don't be angry with me. It is grievous to me to question a gentleman's veracity. But your friend calls himself a *gentleman.* You know not what I have suffered by a *gentleman!* And then again she wept.

I would give you, madam, demonstration, if your grief and your weakness would permit it, that he has no hand in this barbarous baseness: and that he resents it as it ought to be resented.

Well, well, sir [with quickness], he will have his account to make up somewhere else; not to me. I should not be sorry to find him able to acquit his intention on this occasion. Let him know, sir, only one thing, that when you heard me, in the bitterness of my spirit, most vehemently exclaim against the undeserved usage I have met with from him, that even *then*, in *that* passionate moment, I was able to say [and never did I see such an earnest and affecting exaltation of hands and eyes], "Give him, good God! repentance and amendment; that I may be the last poor creature who shall be ruined by him! And, in Thine own good time, receive to *Thy* mercy the poor wretch who had *none* on me!"

By my soul, I could not speak. She had not her Bible before her for nothing.

I was forced to turn my head away, and to take out my handkerchief.

What an angel is this! Even the gaoler, and his wife, and maid, wept.

Again I wish thou hadst been there, that thou mightest have sunk down at her feet, and begun that moment to reap the effect of her generous wishes for thee; undeserving, as thou art, of anything but perdition!

I represented to her that she would be less free where she was from visits she liked not, than at her own lodgings. I told her that it would probably bring her, in particular, *one visitor* who, otherwise, I would engage [but I durst not swear again, after the severe reprimand she had just given me] should not come near her, without her consent. And I expressed my surprise that she should be unwilling to quit such a place as this; when it was more than probable that some of her friends, when it was known how bad she was, would visit her.

She said the place, when she was first brought into it, was indeed very shocking to her: but that she had found herself so weak and ill, and her griefs had so sunk her, that she did not expect to have lived till now: that therefore all places had been alike to her; for to die in a prison *was* to die; and equally eligible as to die in a palace (palaces, she said, could have no attractions for a dying person): but that, since she feared she was not so soon to be released as she had hoped; since she was suffered to be so little mistress of herself *here*; and since she might, by removal, be in the way of her dear friend's letters; she would hope that she might depend upon the assurances I gave her of being at liberty to return to her last lodgings (otherwise she would provide herself with new ones, out of my knowledge as well as out of yours); and that I was too much of a gentleman to be concerned in carrying her back to the house she had so much reason to abhor; and to which she had been once before most vilely betrayed, to her ruin.

I assured her, in the strongest terms [*but swore not*], that you were resolved not to molest her: and, as a proof of the sincerity of my professions, besought her to give me directions (in pursuance of my friend's express desire) about sending all her apparel, and whatever belonged to her, to her new lodgings.

She seemed pleased; and gave me instantly out of her pocket her keys; asking me if Mrs. Smith, whom I had named, might not attend me; and she would give *her* further directions?   To which I cheerfully assented; and then she told me that she would accept of the chair I had offered her.

I withdrew; and took the opportunity to be civil to Rowland and his maid; for she found no fault with their behaviour, for what they *were*; and the fellow seems to be miserably poor.   I sent also for the apothecary, who is as poor as the officer (and still poorer, I dare say, as to the skill required in his business), and satisfied him beyond his hopes.

The lady, after I had withdrawn, attempted to read the letters I had brought her.   But she could read but a little way in one of them, and had great emotions upon it.

She told the woman she would take a speedy opportunity to acknowledge their civilities, and to satisfy the apothecary; who might send her his bill to her lodgings.

She gave the maid something; probably the only half-guinea she had: and then with difficulty, her limbs trembling under her, and supported by Mrs. Rowland, got downstairs.

I offered my arm: she was pleased to lean upon it.   I doubt, sir, said she, as she moved, I have behaved rudely to you: but, if you knew all, you would forgive me.

I know enough, madam, to convince me that there is not such purity and honour in any woman upon earth; nor any one that has been so barbarously treated.

She looked at me very earnestly.   What she thought, I cannot say; but, in general, I never saw so much soul in a woman's eyes as in hers.

I ordered my servant (whose mourning made him less observable as such, and who had not been in the lady's eye) to keep the chair in view; and to bring me word how she did when set down.   The fellow had the thought to step into the shop just before the chair entered it, under pretence of buying snuff; and so enabled himself to give me an account that she was received with great joy by the good woman of the house; who told her she was but just come in; and was preparing to attend her in High Holborn.   O Mrs. Smith, said she, as soon as she saw her, did you not think I was run away?   You don't know what I have suffered since I saw you.   I have been in a prison!—Arrested for debts I owe not!   But, thank God, I am here!   Will you permit your maid—I have forgot her name already——

Catharine, madam.

Will you let Catharine assist me to bed? I have not had my clothes off since Thursday night.

What she further said the fellow heard not, she leaning upon the maid, and going upstairs.

But dost thou not observe what a strange, what an uncommon openness of heart reigns in this lady? *She had been in a prison*, she said, before a stranger in the shop, and before the maid-servant: and so, probably, she would have said had there been twenty people in the shop.

The disgrace she cannot hide from *herself*, as she says in her letter to Lady Betty, she is not solicitous to conceal from the *world*!

But this makes it evident to me that she is resolved to keep no terms with thee. And yet to be able to put up such a prayer for thee, as she did in her prison [I will often mention the *prison-room*, to tease thee!]; does not this show that revenge has very little sway in her mind; though she can retain so much proper resentment?

And this is another excellence in this admirable woman's character: for whom, before her, have we met with in the whole sex, or in ours either, that know how, in *practice*, to distinguish between REVENGE and RESENTMENT, for base and ungrateful treatment?

'Tis a cursed thing, after all, that such a woman as this should be treated as she has been treated. Hadst thou been a king, and done as thou hast done by such a meritorious innocent, I believe, in my heart, it would have been adjudged to be a national sin, and the sword, the pestilence, or famine, must have atoned for it! But, as thou art a private man, thou wilt certainly meet with thy punishment (besides what thou mayest expect from the justice of thy country, and the vengeance of her friends), as she will her reward, HEREAFTER.

It must be so, if there be really such a thing as *future remuneration*; as now I am more and more convinced there must: else, what a hard fate is hers, whose punishment, to all appearance, has so much exceeded her fault? And, as to thine, how can *temporary* burnings, wert thou by some accident to be consumed in thy bed, expiate for thy abominable vileness to her, in breach of all obligations moral and divine?

I was resolved to lose no time in having everything which belonged to the lady at the cursed woman's sent her. Accordingly I took coach to Smith's, and procured the lady (to whom I sent up my compliments, and inquiries how she bore her removal), ill as she sent me down word she was, to give proper directions to Mrs. Smith: whom I took with me to Sinclair's; and who saw everything looked out, and put into the trunks and boxes they were first brought in, and carried away in two coaches.

Had I not been there, Sally and Polly would each of them have taken to herself something of the poor lady's spoils. This they declared: and I had some difficulty to get from Sally a fine Brussels lace head, which she had the confidence to say she would wear for *Miss Harlowe's* sake. Nor should either I or Mrs. Smith have known she had got it, had she not been in search after the ruffles belonging to it.

My resentment on this occasion, and the conversation which Mrs. Smith and I had (in which I not only expatiated on the merits of the lady, but expressed my concern for her sufferings; though I left her room to suppose her married, yet without averring it), gave me high credit with the good woman: so that we are perfectly well acquainted already: by which means I shall be enabled to give you accounts from time to time of all that passes; and which I will be very industrious to do, provided I may depend upon the solemn promises I have given the lady, in your name, as well as in my own, that she shall be free from all personal molestation from you. And thus shall I have it in my power to return *in kind* your writing favours; and preserve my shorthand besides: which, till this correspondence was opened, I had pretty much neglected.

I ordered the abandoned women to make out your account. They answered, *that* they would do with a *vengeance*. Indeed they breathe nothing but revenge. For now, they say, you will assuredly marry; and your example will be followed by all your friends and companions—as the old one says, to the utter ruin of her poor house.

Letter CIX—Mr. Belford to Robert Lovelace, Esq.

Tuesday Morn. (July 18), 6 o'clock.

HAVING sat up late to finish and seal in readiness my letter to the above period, I am disturbed before I wished to have risen, by the arrival of thy second fellow, man and horse in a foam.

While he baits, I will write a few lines, most heartily to congratulate thee on thy *expected* rage and impatience, and on thy recovery of *mental* feeling.

How much does the idea thou givest me of thy deserved torments, by thy upright awls, bodkins, pins, and packing-needles, by thy rolling hogshead with iron spikes, and by thy macerated sides, delight me!

I will, upon every occasion that offers, drive more spikes into thy hogshead, and roll thee downhill, and up, as thou recoverest to sense, or rather returnest back to *senselessness*. Thou knowest, therefore, the terms on which thou art to enjoy my correspondence. Am not I, who have all along, and *in time*, protested against thy barbarous and ungrateful perfidies to a woman so noble, entitled to drive remorse, if possible, into thy hitherto callous heart?

Only let me repeat one thing, which perhaps I mentioned too slightly before: that the lady was determined to remove to new lodgings, where neither you nor I should be able to find her, had I not solemnly assured her that she might depend upon being free from your visits.

These assurances I thought I might give her, not only because of your promise, but because it is necessary for you to know where she is in order to address yourself to her by your friends.

Enable me, therefore, to make good to her this my solemn engagement; or adieu to all friendship, at least to all correspondence, with thee, for ever.

J. BELFORD.

Letter CX—Mr. Belford to Robert Lovelace, Esq.

Tuesday, July 18.   *Afternoon.*

I RENEWED my inquiries after the lady's health, in the morning, by my servant: and, as soon as I had dined, I went myself.

I had but a poor account of it: yet sent up my compliments. She returned me thanks for all my good offices; and her excuses, that they could not be *personal* just then, being very low and faint: but if I gave myself the trouble of coming about six this evening, she should be able, she hoped, to drink a dish of tea with me, and would then thank me herself.

I am very proud of this condescension; and think it looks not amiss for you, as I am your *avowed* friend. Methinks I want fully to remove from her mind all doubts of you in this last villainous action: and who knows then what your noble relations may be able to do for you with her, if you hold your mind? For your servant acquainted me with their having actually engaged Miss Howe in their and your favour, before this cursed affair happened. And I desire the particulars of all from yourself, that I may the better know how to serve you.

She has two handsome apartments, a bedchamber and dining-room, with light closets in each. She has already a nurse (the people of the house having but one maid); a woman whose care, diligence, and honesty, Mrs. Smith highly commends. She has likewise the benefit of the voluntary attendance, and *love*, as it seems, of a widow gentlewoman, Mrs. Lovick her name, who lodges over her apartment, and of whom she seems very fond, having found something in her, she thinks, resembling the qualities of her worthy Mrs. Norton.

About seven o'clock this morning, it seems, the lady was so ill that she yielded to their desires to have an apothecary sent for. Not the fellow, thou mayest believe, she had had before at Rowland's; but one Mr. Goddard, a man of skill and eminence; and of conscience too; demonstrated as well by general character, as by his prescriptions to this lady: for, pronouncing her case to be grief, he ordered, for the present, only innocent juleps, by way of cordial; and, as soon as her stomach should be able to bear it, light kitchen diet; telling Mrs. Lovick that that, with air, moderate exercise, and cheerful company, would do her more good than all the medicines in his shop.

This has given me, as it seems it has the lady (who also praises his modest behaviour, paternal looks, and genteel address), a very good opinion of the man; and I design to make myself acquainted with him; and, if he advises to call in a doctor, to wish him, for the fair patient's sake, more than the physician's (who wants not practice), my worthy friend Dr. H., whose character is above all exception, as his humanity I am sure will distinguish him to the lady.

Mrs. Lovick gratified me with an account of a letter she had written from the lady's mouth to Miss Howe; she being unable to write herself with steadiness.

It was to this effect; in answer, it seems, to her two letters, whatever were the contents of them:

"That she had been involved in a dreadful calamity, which she was sure, when known, would exempt her from the effects of her friendly displeasure, for not answering her first; having been put under an arrest.—Could she have believed it?—That she was released but the day before: and was now so weak, and so low, that she was obliged to get a widow gentlewoman in the same house to account thus for her silence to her [Miss Howe's] two letters of the 13th and 16th: that she would, as soon as able, answer them—begged of her, meantime, not to be uneasy for her; since (only that this was a calamity which came upon her when she was far from being well; a load laid upon the shoulders of a poor wretch, ready before to sink under too heavy a burden) *it was nothing to the evil she had before suffered:* and one felicity seemed likely to issue from it; which was, that she should be at rest, in an honest house, with considerate and kind-hearted people; having assurance given her that she should not be molested by the wretch, whom it would be death for her to see: so that now she [Miss Howe] needed not to send to her by private and expensive conveyances: nor need Collins to take precautions for fear of being dogged to her lodgings; nor she to write by a fictitious name to her, but by her own."

You see I am in a way to oblige you: you see how much she depends upon my engaging for your forbearing to intrude yourself into her company: let not your flaming impatience destroy all; and make me look like a villain to a lady who has reason to suspect *every man she sees* to be so. Upon this condition, you may expect all the services that can flow from true friendship, and from

Your sincere well-wisher,
J. Belford.

Letter CXI—Mr. Belford to Robert Lovelace, Esq.

Tuesday Night, July 18.

I am just come from the lady. I was admitted into the dining-room, where she was sitting in an elbow-chair, in a very weak and low way. She made an effort to stand up when I entered; but was forced to keep her seat. You'll excuse me, Mr. Belford: I ought to rise, to thank you for all your kindness to me. I was to blame to be so loath to leave that sad place; for I am in Heaven here, to what I was there: and good people about me too! I have not had good people about me for a long, long time before; so that [with a half smile] I had begun to wonder whither they were all gone.

Her nurse and Mrs. Smith, who were present, took occasion to retire: and, when we were alone, You seem to be a person of humanity, sir, said she: you hinted, as I was leaving *my prison*, that you were not a stranger to my sad story. If you know it *truly*, you must know that I have been most barbarously treated; and have not deserved it at the man's hands by whom I have suffered.

I told her I knew enough to be convinced that she had the merit of a saint, and the purity of an angel: and was proceeding, when she said, No flighty compliments! No undue attributes, sir!

I offered to plead for my sincerity; and mentioned the word *politeness*; and would have distinguished between that and *flattery*. Nothing can be polite, said she, that is not just: whatever I *may* have had, I have *now* no vanity to gratify.

I disclaimed all intention of compliment: all I *had* said, and what I *should* say was, and should be, the effect of sincere veneration. My unhappy friend's account of her had entitled her to that.

I then mentioned your grief, your penitence, your resolutions of making her all the amends that were possible now to be made her: and, in the most earnest manner, I asserted your innocence as to the last villainous outrage.

Her answer was to this effect: It is painful to me to think of him. The amends you talk of cannot be made. This last violence you speak of *is nothing to what preceded it.* That *cannot* be atoned for; nor palliated: this *may*: and I shall not be sorry to be convinced that he cannot be guilty of so very low a wickedness. —Yet, after his vile forgeries of hands—after his baseness in imposing upon me the most infamous persons as ladies of honour of his own family—what are the iniquities he is not capable of?

I would then have given her an account of the trial you stood with your friends: your own previous resolutions of marriage, had she honoured you with the requested *four words*: all your family's earnestness to have the honour of her alliance: and the application of your two cousins to Miss Howe, by general consent, for that young lady's interest with her: but, having just touched upon these topics, she cut me short, saying, that was a cause before another tribunal: Miss Howe's letters to her were upon that subject; and she would write her thoughts to *her* as soon as she was able.

I then attempted more particularly to clear you of having any hand in the vile Sinclair's officious arrest; a point she had the generosity to *wish* you cleared of: and, having mentioned the outrageous letter you had written to me on this occasion, she asked if I had that letter about me?

I owned I had.

She wished to see it.

This puzzled me horribly: for you must needs think that most of the free things which, among us rakes, pass for wit and spirit, must be shocking stuff to the ears or eyes of persons of delicacy of that sex: and then such an air of levity runs through thy most serious letters; such a false bravery, endeavouring to carry off ludicrously the subjects that most affect thee; that those letters are generally the least fit to be seen, which ought to be most to thy credit.

Something like this I observed to her; and would fain have excused myself from showing it: but she was so earnest, that I undertook to read some parts of it, resolving to omit the most exceptionable.

I know thou 'lt curse me for that; but I thought it better to oblige her than to be suspected myself; and so not have it in my power to serve thee with her, when so good a foundation was laid for it; and when she knows as bad of thee as I can tell her.

Thou rememberest the contents, I suppose, of thy furious letter.[1] Her remarks upon the different parts of it which I read to her, were to the following effect:

Upon thy two first lines, *All undone! undone, by Jupiter! Zounds, Jack, what shall I do now! A curse upon all my plots and contrivances!* thus she expressed herself:

"Oh, how light, how unaffected with the sense of its own crimes, is the heart that could dictate to the pen this libertine froth!"

The paragraph which mentions the vile arrest affected her a good deal.

In the next I omitted thy curse upon thy relations, whom thou wert gallanting: and read on the seven subsequent paragraphs, down to thy execrable wish; which was too shocking to read to her. What I read produced the following reflections from her:

"The plots and contrivances which he curses, and the exultings of the wicked wretches on finding me out, show me that all his guilt was premeditated: nor doubt I that his dreadful perjuries, and inhuman arts, as he went along, were to pass for fine stratagems; for witty sport; and to demonstrate a superiority of inventive talents! O my cruel, cruel brother! had it not been for thee, I had not been thrown upon so pernicious and so despicable a plotter!—But proceed, sir; pray proceed."

At that part, *Canst thou, O fatal prognosticator! tell me where my punishments will end?*—she sighed: and when I came to that sentence, *praying for my reformation, perhaps*—Is that there? said she, sighing again. Wretched man!—and shed a tear for thee. By my faith, Lovelace, I believe she hates thee not! She has at least a concern, a generous concern, for thy future happiness! What a noble creature hast thou injured!

[1] See pp. 419–21.

She made a very severe reflection upon me, on reading ,these words—*On your knees, for me, beg her pardon.* "You had all your lessons, sir, said she, when you came to redeem me. You was so condescending as to kneel: I thought it was the effect of your own humanity, and good-natured earnestness to serve me— excuse me, sir, I knew not that it was in consequence of a prescribed lesson."

This concerned me not a little: I could not bear to be thought such a wretched puppet, such a Joseph Leman, such a Tomlinson. I endeavoured therefore, with some warmth, to clear myself of this reflection; and she again asked my excuse: "I was avowedly, she said, the friend of a man whose friendship, she had reason to be sorry to say, was no credit to anybody." And desired me to proceed.

I did; but fared not much better afterwards: for on that passage where you say, *I had always been her friend and advocate*, this was her unanswerable remark: "I find, sir, by this expression, that he had always designs against me; and that you all along *knew* that he had: would to Heaven you had had the goodness to have contrived some way, that might not have endangered your own safety, to give me notice of his baseness, since you approved not of it! But you gentlemen, I suppose, had rather see an innocent fellow-creature ruined, than be thought capable of an action which, however generous, might be likely to loosen the bands of a wicked friendship!"

After this severe but just reflection I would have avoided reading the following, although I had unawares begun the sentence (but she held me to it): *What would I now give, had I permitted you to have been a successful advocate!* And this was her remark upon it: "So, sir, you see, if you had been the happy means of preventing the evils designed me, you would have had your friend's thanks for it when he came to his consideration. This satisfaction, I am persuaded, every one, in the long run, will enjoy, who has the virtue to withstand, or prevent, a wicked purpose. I was obliged, *I see,* to your kind wishes. But it was a point of honour with you to keep his secret; the more indispensable with you, perhaps, the viler the secret. Yet permit me to wish, Mr. Belford, that you were capable of relishing the pleasures that arise to a benevolent mind from VIRTUOUS friendship! None *other* is worthy of the sacred name. You seem a humane man: I hope, for your own sake, you will one day experience the difference: and, when you do, think of Miss Howe and Clarissa Harlowe (I find you know much of my sad

story), who were the happiest creatures on earth in each other's
friendship till this friend of yours——" And there she stopped,
and turned from me.

Where thou callest thyself *a villainous plotter*; "To take crime
to himself, said she, without shame, oh, what a hardened wretch
is this man!"

On that passage where thou sayest, *Let me know how she has
been treated: if roughly, woe be to the guilty!* this was her remark,
with an air of indignation: "What a man is your friend, sir!
Is such a one as *he* to set himself up to punish the guilty? All
the *rough* usage I could receive from them was infinitely *less*—"
And there she stopped a moment or two: then proceeding—
"And who shall punish *him*? What an assuming wretch!
Nobody but *himself* is entitled to injure the innocent! He is,
I suppose, on earth, to act the part which the malignant fiend
is supposed to act below—dealing out punishments, at his
pleasure, to every inferior instrument of mischief!"

What, thought I, have I been doing! I shall have this
savage fellow think I have been playing him booty, in reading
part of his letter to this sagacious lady! Yet if thou art angry,
it can only, in reason, be at thyself; for who would think I might
not communicate to her some of the least exceptionable parts of
a letter (as a proof of thy sincerity in exculpating thyself from a
criminal charge) which thou wrotest to thy friend, to convince
him of thy innocence? But a bad heart, and a bad cause, are
confounding things: and so let us put it to its proper account.

I passed over thy charge to me, to curse them by the hour;
and thy names of *dragon* and *serpents*, though so applicable;
since, had I read them, thou must have been supposed to know
from the first, what creatures they were; vile fellow as thou
wert, for bringing so much purity among them! And I closed
with thy own concluding paragraph, *A line! a line! a kingdom
for a line!* etc. However, telling her (since she saw that I
omitted some sentences) that there were further vehemences in
it; but as they were better fitted to show to me the sincerity of
the writer than for so delicate an ear as hers to hear, I chose to
pass them over.

You have read enough, said she. He is a wicked, wicked man!
I see he intended to have me in his power at any rate; and I have
no doubt of what his purposes were, by what his actions have
been. You know his vile Tomlinson, I suppose. You know—
But what signifies talking? Never was there such a premedi-
tately false heart in man [*nothing can be truer, thought I!*]. What

has he not vowed! What has he not invented! And all for what?—Only to ruin a poor young creature, whom he ought to have protected; and whom he had first deprived of all other protection!

She arose, and turned from me, her handkerchief at her eyes: and, after a pause, came towards me again. "I hope, said she, I talk to a man who has a better heart: and I thank you, sir, for all your kind, though ineffectual, pleas in my favour formerly, whether the motives for them were compassion, or principle, or both. That they *were* ineffectual, might very probably be owing to your want of earnestness; and *that*, as *you* might think, to my want of merit. I might not, in your eye, *deserve* to be saved! I might appear to you a giddy creature, who had run away from her true and natural friends; and who therefore ought to take the consequence of the lot she had drawn."

I was afraid, for thy sake, to let her know how *very* earnest I had been: but assured her that I had been her zealous friend; and that my motives were founded upon a merit that, I believed, was never equalled; that, however indefensible Mr. Lovelace was, he had always done justice to her virtue: that to a full conviction of her untainted honour it was owing that he so earnestly desired to call so inestimable a jewel his—and was proceeding when she again cut me short——

Enough, and too much, of this subject, sir! If he will never more let me behold his face, that is all I have now to ask of him. Indeed, indeed, clasping her hands, *I never will*, if I can, by any means not criminally desperate, avoid it.

What could I say for thee? There was no room, however, *at that time*, to touch this string again, for fear of bringing upon myself a prohibition, not only of the subject, but of ever attending her again.

I gave some distant intimations of money matters. I should have told thee, that when I read to her that passage where thou biddest me force what sums upon her I can get her to take—she repeated, No, no, no, no! several times with great quickness; and I durst no more than just intimate it again—and that so darkly, as left her room to seem not to understand me.

Indeed, I know not the person, man or woman, I should be so much afraid of disobliging, or incurring a censure from, as from her. She has so much true dignity in her manner, without pride or arrogance (which, in those who have either, one is tempted to mortify), such a piercing eye, yet softened so sweetly with rays of benignity, that she commands all one's reverence.

Methinks I have a kind of holy love for this angel of a woman; and it is matter of astonishment to me that thou couldst converse with her a quarter of an hour together, and hold thy devilish purposes.

Guarded as she was by piety, prudence, virtue, dignity, family, fortune, and a purity of heart that never woman before her boasted, what a real devil must he be (yet I doubt I shall make thee proud!) who could resolve to break through so many fences!

For my own part, I am more and more sensible that I ought not to have contented myself with *representing against*, and *expostulating with thee upon*, thy base intentions: and indeed I had it in my head, more than once, to try to do something for her. But, wretch that I was! I was withheld by notions of false honour, as she justly reproached me, because of thy own *voluntary* communications to me of thy purposes: and then, as she was brought into such a cursed house, and was so watched by thyself, as well as by thy infernal agents, I thought (knowing my man!) that I should only accelerate the intended mischiefs. Moreover, finding thee so much overawed by her virtue, that thou hadst not, at thy *first* carrying her thither, the courage to attempt her; and that she had, more than once, without knowing thy base views, obliged thee to abandon them, and to resolve to do her justice, and thyself honour; I hardly doubted that her merit would be triumphant at last.

It is my opinion (if thou holdest thy purposes to marry) that thou canst not do better than to procure thy *real* aunts, and thy *real* cousins, to pay her a visit, and to be thy advocates: but, if they decline personal visits, letters from them, and from my Lord M., supported by Miss Howe's interest, may, perhaps, effect something in thy favour.

But these are only my hopes, founded on what I *wish* for thy sake. The lady, I really think, would choose death rather than thee: and the two women are of opinion, though they know not half of what she has suffered, that her heart is actually broken.

At taking my leave, I tendered my best services to her, and besought her to permit me frequently to inquire after her health.

She made me no answer, but by bowing her head.

Letter CXII—Mr. Belford to Robert Lovelace, Esq.

Wednesday, July 19.

THIS morning I took chair to Smith's; and, being told that the lady had a very bad night, but was up, I sent for her worthy apothecary; who, on his coming to me, approving of my proposal of calling in Dr. H.; I bid the women acquaint her with the designed visit.

It seems she was at first displeased; yet withdrew her objection: but, after a pause, asked them what she should do? She had effects of value, some of which she intended, as soon as she *could*, to turn into money; but, till then, had not a single guinea to give the doctor for his fee.

Mrs. Lovick said she had five guineas by her: they were at her service.

She would accept of three, she said, if she would take *that* (pulling a diamond ring from her finger) till she repaid her; but on no other terms.

Having been told I was below with Mr. Goddard, she desired to speak one word with me, before she saw the doctor.

She was sitting in an elbow-chair, leaning her head on a pillow; Mrs. Smith and the widow on each side her chair; her nurse, with a phial of hartshorn, behind her; in her own hand her salts.

Raising her head at my entrance, she inquired if the doctor knew Mr. Lovelace?

I told her no; and that I believed you never saw him in your life.

Was the doctor my friend?

He was; and a very worthy and skilful man. I named him for his eminence in his profession: and Mr. Goddard said he knew not a better physician.

I have but one condition to make before I see the gentleman; that he refuse not his fees from me. If I am poor, sir, I am proud. I will not be under obligation. You may *believe*, sir, I will not. I suffer this visit, because I would not appear ungrateful to the few friends I have left, nor obstinate to such of my relations as may some time hence, for their private satisfaction, inquire after my behaviour in my sick hours. So, sir, you know the condition. And don't let me be vexed: I am very ill; and cannot debate the matter.

Seeing her so determined, I told her, if it must be so, it should.

Then, sir, the gentleman may come. But I shall not be able to answer many questions. Nurse, you can tell him, at the window there, what a night I have had, and how I have been for two days past. And Mr. Goddard, if he be here, can let him know what I have taken. Pray let me be as little questioned as possible.

The doctor paid his respects to her with the gentlemanly address for which he is noted: and she cast up her sweet eyes to him with that benignity which accompanies her every graceful look.

I would have retired; but she forbid it.

He took her hand, the lily not of so beautiful a white; Indeed, madam, you are very low, said he: but, give me leave to say, that you can do more for yourself than all the faculty can do for you.

He then withdrew to the window. And, after a short conference with the women, he turned to me, and to Mr. Goddard, at the other window: We can do nothing here, speaking low, but by cordials and nourishment. What friends has the lady? She seems to be a person of condition; and, ill as she is, a very fine woman.—A single lady, I presume?

I whisperingly told him she was. That there were extraordinary circumstances in her case; as I would have apprised him, had I met with him yesterday. That her friends were very cruel to her; but that she could not hear them named without reproaching herself; though they were much more to blame than she.

I knew I was right, said the doctor. A love case, Mr. Goddard! A love case, Mr. Belford! There is one person in the world who can do her more service, than all the faculty.

Mr. Goddard said he had apprehended her disorder was in her mind; and had treated her accordingly: and then told the doctor what he had done: which he approving of, again taking her charming hand, said, My good young lady, you will require very little of our assistance. You must, in a great measure, be your own doctress. Come, *dear* madam [forgive me the familiar tenderness; your aspect commands love, as well as reverence; and a father of children, some of them older than yourself, may be excused for this familiar address], cheer up your spirits. Resolve to do all in your power to be well; and you 'll soon grow better.

You are very kind, sir, said she. I will take whatever you direct. My spirits have been hurried. I shall be better, I believe, before I am worse. The care of my good friends here, looking at the women, shall not meet with an ungrateful return.

The doctor wrote. He would fain have declined his fee. As her malady, he said, was rather to be relieved by the soothings of a friend, than by the prescriptions of a physician, he should think himself greatly honoured to be admitted rather to *advise* her in the *one* character, than to *prescribe* to her in the *other*.

She answered that she should be always glad to see so humane a man: that his visits would *keep her in charity with his sex*: but that, were she to *forget* that he was her *physician*, she might be apt to abate of the confidence in his skill, which might be necessary to effect the amendment that was the end of his visits.

And when he urged her still further, which he did in a very polite manner, and as passing by the door two or three times a day, she said she should always have pleasure in considering him in the kind light he *offered himself to her*: that *that* might be very generous in one person to offer, which would be as ungenerous in another to accept: that indeed she was not at present high in circumstance; and he saw by the tender (which he *must* accept of) that she had greater respect to *her own convenience* than to *his merit*, or than to the *pleasure* she should take in his visits.

We all withdrew together; and the doctor and Mr. Goddard having a great curiosity to know something more of her story, at the motion of the latter we went into a neighbouring coffee-house, and I gave them, in confidence, a brief relation of it; making all as light for you as I could; and yet you 'll suppose, that, in order to do but common justice to the lady's character, heavy must be that light.

Three o'clock, Afternoon.

I just now called again at Smith's; and am told she is somewhat better; which she attributed to the soothings of her doctor. She expressed herself highly pleased with both gentlemen; and said that their behaviour to her was perfectly *paternal*.

Paternal, poor lady!—Never having been, till very lately, from under her parents' wings, and now abandoned by all her friends, she is for finding out something *paternal* and *maternal* in every one (the latter qualities in Mrs. Lovick and Mrs. Smith) to supply to herself the father and mother her dutiful heart pants after.

Mrs. Smith told me that after we were gone, she gave the keys of her trunks and drawers to her and the widow Lovick, and desired them to take an inventory of them; which they did in her presence.

They also informed me that she had requested them to find her a purchaser for two rich dressed suits; one never worn, the other not above once or twice.

This shocked me exceedingly—*perhaps it may thee a little ! ! !* Her reason for so doing, she told them, was that she should never live to wear them: that her sister, and other relations, were above wearing them: that her mother would not endure in her sight anything that was hers: that she wanted the money: that she would not be obliged to anybody, when she had effects by her for which she had no occasion: and yet, said she, I expect not that they will fetch a price answerable to their value.

They were both very much concerned, as they owned; and asked my advice upon it: and the richness of her apparel having given them a still higher notion of her rank than they had before, they supposed she must be of quality; and again wanted to know her story.

I told them that she was indeed a woman of family and fortune: I still gave them room to suppose her married: but left it to her to tell them all in her own time and manner: all I would say was, that she had been very vilely treated; deserved it not; and was all innocence and purity.

You may suppose that they both expressed their astonishment, that there could be a man in the world who could ill-treat so fine a creature.

As to disposing of the two suits of apparel, I told Mrs. Smith, that she should pretend that, upon inquiry, she had found a friend who would purchase the richest of them; but (*that she might not mistrust*) would stand upon a good bargain. And having twenty guineas about me, I left them with her, in part of payment; and bid her *pretend* to get her to part with it for as little more as she could induce her to take.

I am setting out for Edgware with poor Belton—more of whom in my next. I shall return to-morrow; and leave this in readiness for your messenger, if he call in my absence.

Adieu.

Letter CXIII—Mr. Lovelace to John Belford, Esq.

[*In answer to Letter CXI*]

M. Hall, Wedn. Night, July 19.

You might well apprehend that I should think you were playing me booty in communicating my letter to the lady.

You ask, who would think you might not read to her the least exceptionable parts of a letter written in my own defence? *I'll tell you who*—the man who, in the same letter that he asks this question, tells the friend whom he exposes to her resentment, "That there is such an air of levity runs through his most serious letters, that those of his are *least fit to be seen*, which ought to be *most to his credit*." And now what thinkest thou of thy self-condemned folly? Be, however, I charge thee, more circumspect for the future, that so this clumsy error may stand singly by itself.

CXIII]   CLARISSA HARLOWE   471

"It is painful to her to think of me!" "Libertine froth!"
"So pernicious and so despicable a plotter!" "A man whose
friendship is no credit to anybody!" "Hardened wretch!" "The
devil's counterpart!" "A wicked, wicked man!"—But *did* she,
could she, *dared* she, to say or *imply* all this? And say it to a
man whom she praises for humanity, and prefers to myself
for that virtue; when all the humanity *he* shows, and *she knows
it too*, is by *my* direction—so robs me of the credit of my
own works? Admirably entitled, all this shows her, to thy
refinement upon the words *resentment* and *revenge*. But thou
wert always aiming and blundering at something thou never
couldst make out.

The praise thou givest to her *ingenuousness*, is another of thy
peculiars. I think not as *thou* dost, of her tell-tale recapitulations and exclamations: what end can they answer? Only that
thou hast an *holy* love for her [the devil fetch thee for thy oddity!],
or it is extremely provoking to suppose one sees such a charming
creature stand upright before a libertine, and talk of the sin
against her, that cannot be forgiven! I wish at my heart that
these chaste ladies would have a little modesty in their anger!
It would sound very strange, if I, Robert Lovelace, should
pretend to have more true delicacy, in a point that requires the
utmost, than Miss Clarissa Harlowe.

I think I will put it into the head of her Nurse Norton, and
her Miss Howe, by some one of my agents, to chide the dear
novice for her proclamations.

But to be serious; let me tell thee, that severe as she is, and
saucy, in asking so contemptuously, "What a man is your friend,
sir, to set himself to punish guilty people!" I will never forgive
the cursed woman who could commit this last horrid violence
on so excellent a creature.

The barbarous insults of the two nymphs, in their visits to her;
the choice of the most execrable den that could be found out, in
order, no doubt, to induce her to go back to theirs; and the still
more execrable attempt, to propose to her a man who would pay
the debt; a snare, I make no question, laid for her despairing and
resenting heart by that devilish Sally (thinking her, no doubt, a
woman), in order to ruin her with me; and to provoke me, in a
fury, to give her up to their remorseless cruelty; are outrages
that, to express myself in her style, I never *can*, never *will*
forgive.

But as to thy opinion, and the two women's at Smith's, that
her heart is broken; that is the true women's language: I wonder

how *thou* camest into it: thou who hast seen and heard of so many *female deaths* and *revivals*.

I 'll tell thee what makes *against* this notion of theirs.

Her time of life and charming constitution: the good she ever delighted to do, and fancied she was born to do; and which she may still continue to do, to as high a degree as ever; nay, higher; since I am no sordid varlet, thou knowest: her religious turn; a turn that will always teach her to bear *inevitable* evils with patience: the contemplation upon her last noble triumph over me, and over the whole crew; and upon her succeeding escape from us all: her will unviolated: and the inward pride of having *not deserved* the treatment she has met with.

How is it possible to imagine that a woman who has all these *consolations* to reflect upon, will die of a broken heart?

On the contrary, I make no doubt but that, as she recovers from the dejection into which this last scurvy villainy (which none but wretches of her own sex *could* have been guilty of) has thrown her, returning love will re-enter her *time-pacified* mind: her thoughts will then turn once more on the *conjugal pivot*: of course she will have livelier notions in her head; and these will make her perform all her circumvolutions with ease and pleasure; though not with so high a degree of either, as if the dear proud rogue could have exalted herself above the rest of her sex, as she turned round.

Thou askest, on reciting the bitter invectives that the lady made against thy poor friend (standing before her, I suppose, with thy fingers in thy mouth), *What couldst thou say* FOR *me?*

Have I not, in my former letters, suggested a hundred things which a friend, *in earnest* to vindicate or excuse a friend, might say on such an occasion?

But now to current topics, and the present state of matters here. It is true, as my servant told thee, that Miss Howe had engaged, before this cursed woman's officiousness, to use her interest with her friend in my behalf: and yet she told my cousins, in the visit they made her, that it was her opinion that she would never forgive me. I send to thee enclosed copies of all that passed on this occasion between my Cousins Montague, Miss Howe, myself, Lady Betty, Lady Sarah, and Lord M. I long to know what Miss Howe wrote to her friend, in order to induce her to marry the *despicable plotter*; the *man whose friendship is no credit to anybody*; the *wicked, wicked man.* Thou hadst the two letters in thy hand. Had they been in mine, the seal would have yielded to the touch of my warm finger [perhaps without the help of the post office bullet]; and the folds, *as other plications have done,* opened of themselves, to oblige my curiosity. A wicked omission, Jack, not to contrive to send them down to me by man and horse! It might have passed that the messenger who brought the second letter took them both back. I could have returned them by another, when copied, as from Miss Howe, and nobody but myself and thee the wiser.

That's a charming girl! Her spirit, her delightful spirit!—not to be married to it—how I wish to get that lively bird into my cage! How would I make her flutter and fly about!—till she left a feather upon every wire!

Had I begun there, I am confident, as I have heretofore said,[1] that I should not have had half the difficulty with her as I have had with her charming friend. For these passionate girls have high pulses, and a clever fellow may make what sport he pleases with their *unevennesses*—now too high, now too low, you need only to provoke and appease them by turns; to bear with them, and forbear; to tease, and ask pardon; and sometimes to give yourself the merit of a sufferer from them; then catching them in the moment of concession, conscious of their ill-usage of you, they are all your own.

But these sedate, contemplative girls, never out of temper but with reason; when that reason is given them, hardly ever pardon, or afford you another opportunity to offend.

It was in part the apprehension that this would be so with my dear Miss Harlowe, that made me carry her to a place where I believed she would be unable to escape me, although I were *not* to succeed in my first attempts. Else widow Sorlings's would have been as well for me as widow Sinclair's. For early I saw that there was no credulity in her to graft upon: no pretending to wind myself into her confidence. She was proof against amorous persuasion. She had *reason* in her love. Her penetration and good sense made her hate all compliments that had not truth and nature in them. What could I have done with her in any other place? And yet how long, even *there*, was I kept in awe, in spite of *natural incitement*, and *unnatural instigations* (as I now think them), by the mere force of that native dignity, and obvious purity of mind and manners, which fill every one with reverence, if not with *holy love*, as thou callest it,[2] the moment he sees her! Else, thinkest thou not, it was easy for me to be a *fine gentleman*, and a *delicate lover*, or, at least, a *specious* and *flattering* one?

[1] See p. 168.   [2] See p. 465.

Lady Sarah and Lady Betty, finding the treaty upon the success of which they have set their foolish hearts likely to run into length, are about departing to their own seats; having taken from me the best security the nature of the case will admit of, that is to say, *my word*, to marry the lady, if she will have me.

And, after all (methinks thou askest), art thou still resolved to repair, if reparation be put into thy power?

Why, Jack, I must needs own that my heart has now and then some retrograde motions, upon thinking seriously of the irrevocable ceremony. We do not easily give up the desire of our hearts, and what we imagine essential to our happiness, let the expectation or hope of compassing it be ever so unreasonable or absurd in the opinion of others. *Recurrings* there will be; hankerings that will, on every but remotely favourable incident (however before discouraged and beaten back by ill-success), pop up, and abate the satisfaction we should otherwise take in *contrariant* overtures.

'Tis ungentlemanly, Jack, *man to man*, to lie.—But matrimony I do not *heartily* love—although with a CLARISSA—yet I am in earnest to marry her.

But I am often thinking that, if now this dear creature, suffering time, and my penitence, my relations' prayers, and Miss Howe's mediation, to soften her *resentments* [her *revenge* thou hast prettily[1] distinguished away], and to recall repulsed inclination, should consent to meet me at the altar—how vain will she then make all thy eloquent periods of execration! How many charming interjections of her own will she spoil! And what a couple of old patriarchs shall we become, going on in the mill-horse round; getting sons and daughters; providing nurses for them first, governors and governesses next; teaching them lessons their father never practised, nor which their mother, as her parents will say, was much the better for! And at last, perhaps, when life shall be turned into the dully-sober stillness, and I become desirous to forget all my past rogueries, what comfortable reflections will it afford, to find them all revived, with *equal*, or probably *greater* trouble and expense, in the persons and manners of so many young Lovelaces of the boys; and to have the girls run away with varlets perhaps not half so ingenious as myself; clumsy fellows, as it might happen, who could not afford the baggages one excuse for their weakness, besides those disgraceful ones of *sex* and *nature*! O Belford!

[1] See p. 456.

CXIII]   CLARISSA HARLOWE   475

who can bear to think of these things!—Who, at my time of life especially, and with such a bias for mischief!

Of this I am absolutely convinced, that if a man ever intends to marry, and to enjoy in peace his own reflections; and not be afraid of retribution, or of the consequences of his own example; he should never be a rake.

This looks like conscience; don't it, Belford?

But, being in earnest still, as I have said, all I have to do, in my present uncertainty, is to brighten up my faculties, by filing off the rust they have contracted by the town smoke, a long imprisonment in my close attendance to so little purpose on my fair perverse; and to brace up, if I can, the relaxed fibres of my mind, which have been twitched and convulsed like the nerves of some tottering paralytic, by means of the tumults she has excited in it; that so I may be able to present to her a husband as worthy as I can be of her acceptance; or, if she reject me, be in a capacity to resume my usual gaiety of heart, and show others of the misleading sex, that I am not discouraged, by the difficulties I have met with from this sweet individual of it, from endeavouring to make myself as acceptable to them as before.

In this latter case, one tour to France and Italy, I dare say, will do the business. Miss Harlowe will by that time have forgotten all she has suffered from her ungrateful Lovelace: though it will be impossible that her Lovelace should ever forget a woman whose equal he despairs to meet with, were he to travel from one end of the world to the other.

If thou continuest paying off the heavy debts my long letters, for so many weeks together, have made thee groan under, I will endeavour to restrain myself in the desires I have (importunate as they are) of going to town to throw myself at the feet of my soul's beloved. *Policy*, and *honesty*, both join to strengthen the restraint my *own promise* and *thy engagement* have laid me under on this head. I would not afresh provoke: on the contrary, would give time for her resentments to subside, that so all that follows may be her own act and deed.

.   .   .   .

Hickman [I have a mortal aversion to that fellow!] has, by a line which I have just now received, requested an interview with me on Friday at Mr. Dormer's, as at a *common friend's*. Does the business he wants to meet me upon require that it should be at a *common friend's*? A challenge implied: is it not, Belford? I shall not be civil to him, I doubt. He has been an intermeddler! Then I envy him on Miss Howe's account: for if I have a right notion of this Hickman, it is impossible that that virago can ever love him.

Every one knows that the mother (saucy as the daughter sometimes is) crams him down her throat. Her mother is one of the most violent-spirited women in *England*, whose late husband could not stand in the matrimonial contention of *Who should?* but tipped off the perch in it, neither knowing how to yield, nor how to conquer.

A charming encouragement for a man of intrigue, when he has reason to believe that the woman he has a view upon has no love for her husband! What good principles must that wife have, who is kept in against temptation by a sense of her duty, and plighted faith, where affection has no hold of her!

Prithee let's know, very particularly, how it fares with poor Belton. 'Tis an honest fellow. Something more than his Thomasine seems to stick with him.

Thou hast not been preaching to him conscience and reformation, hast thou? Thou shouldst not take liberties with him of this sort, unless thou thoughtest him absolutely irrecoverable. A man in ill-health, and crop-sick, cannot play with these solemn things as thou canst, and be neither better nor worse for them. Repentance, Jack, I have a notion, should be set about while a man is in good health and spirits. What's a man fit for, when he is not himself, nor master of his faculties? Hence, as I apprehend, it is that a death-bed repentance is supposed to be such a precarious and ineffectual thing.

As to myself, I hope I have a great deal of time before me; since I intend *one day* to be a reformed man. I have very serious reflections now and then. Yet am I half afraid of the truth of what my charmer once told me, that *a man cannot repent when he will*. Not to hold it, I suppose she meant! By fits and starts I have repented a thousand times.

Casting my eye over the two preceding paragraphs, I fancy there is something like contradiction in them. But I will not reconsider them. The subject is a very serious one. I don't, at present, quite understand it. But now for one more airy.

Tourville, Mowbray, and myself, pass away our time as pleasantly as possibly we can without thee. I wish we don't add to Lord M.'s gouty days by the joy we give him.

This is one advantage, as I believe I have elsewhere observed, that we male delinquents in love matters have of the other sex: for while they, poor things! sit sighing in holes and corners, or run to woods and groves to bemoan themselves for their baffled hopes, we can rant and roar, hunt and hawk; and, by new loves, banish from our hearts all remembrance of the old ones.

Merrily, however, as we pass our time, my reflections upon the injuries done to this noble creature bring a qualm upon my heart very often. But I know she will permit me to make her amends, after she has plagued me heartily; and that 's my consolation.

An honest fellow still! Clap thy wings, and crow, Jack!

Letter CXIV—Miss Howe to Miss Clarissa Harlowe

Thursday Morn. July 20.

WHAT, my dearest creature, have been your sufferings! What must have been your anguish on so disgraceful an insult, committed in the open streets, and in the broad day!

No end, I think, of the undeserved calamities of a dear soul, who has been so unhappily driven and betrayed into the hands of a vile libertine! How was I shocked at the receiving of your letter written by another hand, and only dictated by you! You must be very ill. Nor is it to be wondered at. But I hope it is rather from hurry, and surprise, and lowness, which *may* be overcome, than from a grief given way to, which may be attended with effects I cannot bear to think of.

But whatever you do, my dear, you must not despond! Indeed you must not despond! Hitherto you have been in no fault: but despair would be all your own; and the worst fault you can be guilty of.

I cannot bear to look upon another hand instead of yours. My dear creature, send me a few lines, though *ever so few*, in your own hand, if possible. For they will revive my heart; especially if they can acquaint me of your amended health.

I expect your answer to my letter of the 13th. We *all* expect it with impatience.

His relations are persons of *so much* honour—they are so *very* earnest to rank you among them—the wretch is so *very* penitent: *every one* of *his* family says he is—*your own* are so implacable—your last distress, though the consequence of his former villainy, yet neither brought on by his direction, nor with his knowledge; and so much resented by him—that my mother is absolutely of opinion that *you should be his*—especially if, yielding to my wishes, as expressed in my letter, and those of all his friends, you *would* have complied, had it not been for this horrid arrest.

I will enclose the copy of the letter I wrote to Miss Montague last Tuesday, on hearing that nobody knew what was become of you; and the answer to it, underwritten and signed by Lord M., Lady Sarah Sadleir, and Lady Betty Lawrance, as well as by the young ladies; and also by the wretch himself.

I own that I like not the turn of what he has written to me; and before I will further interest myself in his favour, I have determined to inform myself, *by a friend*, from his own mouth, of his sincerity, and whether his *whole inclination* be, in his request to me, exclusive of the *wishes of his relations*. Yet my heart rises against him, on the supposition that there is the shadow of a reason for such a question, the woman Miss Clarissa Harlowe. But I think, with my mother, that marriage is now the only means left to make your future life tolerably easy—*happy* there is no saying. His disgraces, in *that* case, in the eye of the world itself, will be more than yours: and to those who know you, glorious will be your triumph.

I am obliged to accompany my mother soon to the Isle of Wight. My Aunt Harman is in a declining way, and insists upon seeing us both—and Mr. Hickman too, I think.

His sister, of whom we had heard so much, with her lord, were brought t'other day to visit us. She strangely likes me, or says she does.

I can't say but that I think she answers the excellent character we have heard of her.

It would be death to me to set out for the little island, and not see you first: and yet my mother (fond of exerting an authority that she herself, by that exertion, often brings into question) insists that my next visit to you *must* be a congratulatory one as Mrs. Lovelace.

When I know what will be the result of the questions to be put in my name to that wretch, and what is your mind on my letter of the 13th, I shall tell you more of mine.

The bearer promises to make so much dispatch as to attend you this very afternoon. May he return with good tidings to

Your ever affectionate

ANNA HOWE.

Letter CXV—Miss Clarissa Harlowe to Miss Howe

Thursday Afternoon.

YOU pain me, my dearest Miss Howe, by the ardour of your noble friendship. I will be very brief, because I am not well; yet a good deal better than I was; and because I am preparing an answer to yours of the 13th. But, beforehand, I must tell you, my dear, I will *not* have that man. Don't be angry with me. But indeed I won't. So let him be asked no questions about me, I beseech you.

I do *not* despond, my dear. I hope I may say, *I will not* despond. Is not my condition greatly mended? I thank Heaven it is!

I am no prisoner now in a vile house. I am not now in the power of that man's devices. I am not now obliged to hide myself in corners for fear of him. One of his intimate companions is become my warm friend, and engages to keep him from me, and that by his own consent. I am among honest people. I have all my clothes and effects restored to me. The wretch himself bears testimony to my honour.

Indeed, I am very weak and ill: but I have an excellent physician, Dr. H., and as worthy an apothecary, Mr. Goddard. Their treatment of me, my dea**r**, is perfectly *paternal!* My mind, too, I can find, begins to strengthen: and methinks, at times, I find myself superior to my calamities.

I shall have sinkings sometimes. I must expect such. And my father's maledict——But you will chide me for introducing that, now I am enumerating my comforts.

But I charge you, my dear, that you do not suffer my calamities to sit too heavy upon your own mind. If you do, that will be to new-point some of those arrows that have been blunted and lost their sharpness.

If you would contribute to *my* happiness, give way, my dear, to *your own*; and to the cheerful prospects before you!

You will think very meanly of your Clarissa, if you do not believe that the greatest pleasure she can receive in this life, is in your prosperity and welfare. Think not of me, my only friend, but as we were in times past: and suppose me gone a great, great way off! A long journey! How often are the dearest of friends, at their country's call, thus parted, with a *certainty* for years—with a *probability* for ever!

Love me still, however. But let it be with a weaning love. I am not what I was when we were *inseparable* lovers, as I may say. Our *views* must now be different. Resolve, my dear, to make a worthy man happy, because a worthy man must make *you* so. And so, my dearest love, for the present adieu! Adieu, my dearest love! But I shall soon write again, I hope!

Letter CXVI—Mr. Belford to Robert Lovelace, Esq.

[*In answer to Letter CXIII*]

Thursday, July 20.

I READ that part of your conclusion to poor Belton, where you inquire after him, and mention how merrily you, and the rest, pass your time at M. Hall. He fetched a deep sigh; *You are all very happy!* were his words. I am sorry they *were* his words; for, poor fellow, he is going very fast. Change of air, *he* hopes, will mend him, joined to the cheerful company I have left him in. But nothing, I dare say, will.

A consuming malady, and a consuming mistress, to an indulgent keeper, are dreadful things to struggle with both together: violence must be used to get rid of the latter; and yet he has not spirit left him to exert himself. His house is Thomasine's house; not his. He has not been within his doors for a fortnight past. *Vagabonding about* from inn to inn; entering each for a bait only; and staying two or three days without power to remove; and hardly knowing which to go to next. His malady is *within him*; and he cannot run away from it.

Her boys (once he thought them his) are sturdy enough to shoulder him in his own house as they pass by him. Siding with the mother, they in a manner expel him; and, in his absence, riot away on the remnant of his broken fortunes. As to their mother (who was once so tender, so submissive, so studious to oblige, that we all pronounced him happy, and his course of life the eligible), she is now so termagant, so insolent, that he cannot contend with her, without doing infinite prejudice to his health. A broken-spirited defensive, *hardly a defensive*, therefore, reduced to: and this to a heart, for so many years waging *offensive* war (nor valuing whom the opponent), what a reduction! now comparing himself to the superannuated lion in the fable, kicked in the jaws, and laid sprawling by the spurning heel of an ignoble ass!

I have undertaken his cause. He has given me leave, yet not without reluctance, to put him into possession of his own house; and to place in it for him his unhappy sister, whom he has hitherto slighted, *because* unhappy. It is hard, he told me (and wept, poor fellow, when he said it), that he cannot be permitted to die quietly in his own house!—The fruits of blessed keeping these!

Though but lately apprised of her infidelity, it now comes out to have been of so long continuance, that he has no room to believe the boys to be his: yet how fond did he use to be of them!

To what, Lovelace, shall we attribute the tenderness which a *reputed* father frequently shows to the children of another man? What is that, I pray thee, which we call *nature*, and *natural affection*? And what has man to boast of as to sagacity and penetration, when he is as easily brought to cover and rear, and even to love, and often to prefer, the product of another's guilt with his wife or mistress, as a hen or a goose the eggs, and even *young*, of others of their kind?

Nay, let me ask, if *instinct*, as it is called, in the animal creation, does not enable them to distinguish their own much more easily than we, with our boasted *reason* and sagacity, in this nice particular, can do?

If some men, who have wives but of doubtful virtue, considered this matter duly, I believe their inordinate ardour after gain would be a good deal cooled, when they could not be certain (though their *mates* could) for whose children they were elbowing, bustling, griping, and perhaps cheating, those with whom they have concerns, whether friends, neighbours, or *more* certain next-of-kin, by the mother's side however.

"But I will not push this notion so far as it might be carried; because, if propagated, it might be of *unsocial* or *unnatural* consequence; since women of virtue would perhaps be more liable to suffer by the mistrusts and caprices of *bad-hearted* and *foolish-headed* husbands, than those who can screen themselves from detection by arts and hypocrisy, to which a woman of virtue cannot have recourse. And yet, were this notion duly and generally considered, it might be attended with no bad effects; as good education, good inclinations, and established virtue, would be the principally sought-after qualities, and not money, when a man (not biassed by mere personal attractions) was looking round him for a partner in his fortunes, and for a mother of his future children, which are to be the heirs of his possessions, and to enjoy the fruits of his industry.

But to return to poor Belton.

If I have occasion for your assistance, and that of our compeers, in reinstating the poor fellow, I will give you notice. Meantime, I have just now been told that Thomasine declares she will not stir: for it seems she suspects that measures will be fallen upon to make her quit. She is Mrs. Belton, she says, and will prove her marriage.

If she give herself these airs in his lifetime, what would she attempt to do after his death?

Her boys threaten anybody who shall presume to insult their *mother*. Their *father* (as they *call* poor Belton) they speak of as an unnatural one. And their probably *true father* is for ever there, *hostilely* there, passing for her cousin, as usual: now her *protecting cousin*.

Hardly ever, I dare say, was there a keeper that did not make a keeperess; who lavished away on her kept-fellow what she obtained from the extravagant folly of him who kept her.

I will do without you if I can. The case will be only, as I conceive, like that of the ancient Sarmatians, returning, after many years' absence, to their homes, their wives then in possession of their slaves: so that they had to contend not only with those *wives*, conscious of their infidelity, and with their *slaves*, but with the *children* of those slaves, grown up to manhood, resolute to defend their mothers, and their long-manumitted fathers. But the noble Sarmatians, scorning to attack their slaves with equal weapons, only provided themselves with the same sort of whips with which they used formerly to chastise them. And, attacking them with them, the miscreants fled before them. In memory of which, to this day, the device on the coin in Novogrod in Russia, a city of the ancient Sarmatia, is a man on horseback, with a whip in his hand.

The poor fellow takes it ill that you did not press him more than you did to be of your party at M. Hall. It is owing to Mowbray, he is sure, that he had so very slight an invitation from one whose invitations used to be so warm.

Mowbray's speech to him, he says, he never will forgive: "Why, Tom," said the brutal fellow, with a curse, "thou droopest like a pip or roup-cloaking chicken. Thou shouldst grow perter, or submit to a solitary quarantine, if thou wouldst not infect the whole brood."

For my own part, only that this poor fellow is in distress, as well in his affairs as in his mind, or I should be sick of you all. Such is the relish I have of the conversation, and such my admiration of the deportment and sentiments of this divine lady, that I would forego a month, even of thy company, to be admitted into hers but for one hour: and I am highly in conceit with myself, greatly as I used to value *thine*, for being able, spontaneously as I may say, to make this preference.

It is, after all, a devilish life we have lived. And to consider how it all ends in a very few years—to see to what a state of ill-health this poor fellow is so soon reduced — and then to observe how every one of ye run away from the unhappy being, as rats from a falling house, is fine comfort to help a man to look back upon companions ill-chosen, and a life misspent!

It will be your turns by and by, every man of ye, if the justice of your country interpose not.

Thou art the only rake we have herded with, if thou wilt not except myself, who hast preserved entire thy health and thy fortunes.

Mowbray indeed is indebted to a robust constitution that he has not yet suffered in his health; but his estate is dwindling away year by year.

Three-fourths of Tourville's very considerable fortunes are already dissipated; and the other fourth will probably soon go after the other three.

Poor Belton! we see how it is with him! His only felicity is, that he will hardly *live* to want.

Thou art too proud, and too prudent, ever to be destitute; and, to do thee justice, hast a spirit to assist such of thy friends as may be reduced; and *wilt*, if thou shouldst then be living. But I think thou must, much sooner than thou imaginest, be called to thy account—knocked on the head perhaps by the friends of those whom thou hast injured; for if thou escapest this fate from the Harlowe family, thou wilt go on tempting danger and vengeance, till thou meetest with vengeance; and this, whether thou marriest or not: for the nuptial life will not, I doubt, till age join with it, cure thee of that spirit for intrigue, which is continually running away with thee, in spite of thy better sense and transitory resolutions.

Well, then, I will suppose *thee* laid down quietly among thy worthier ancestors.

And now let me look forward to the ends of Tourville and Mowbray [Belton will be crumbled into dust before thee, perhaps], supposing thy early exit has saved them from gallows' intervention.

Reduced, probably, by riotous waste to consequential want, behold them refuged in some obscene hole or garret; obliged to the careless care of some dirty old woman, whom nothing but her poverty prevails upon to attend to perform the last offices for men who have made such shocking ravage among the young ones.

Then how miserably will they whine through squeaking organs! Their big voices turned into puling pity-begging lamentations! Their now offensive paws, how helpless then! Their now erect necks then denying support to their aching heads; those globes of mischief dropping upon their quaking shoulders. Then what wry faces will they make! their hearts, and their heads, reproaching each other! Distended their parched mouths! Sunk their unmuscled cheeks! Dropped their under-jaws! Each grunting like the swine he had resembled in his life! Oh! what a vile wretch have I been! Oh! that I had my life to come over again! Confessing to the poor old woman, who cannot shrive them! Imaginary ghosts of deflowered virgins, and polluted matrons, flitting before their glassy eyes! And old Satan, to their apprehensions, grinning behind a looking-glass held up before them, to frighten them with the horror visible in their own countenances!

For my own part, if I can get some good family to credit me with a sister or a daughter, as I have now an increased fortune, which will enable me to propose handsome settlements, I will desert ye all; marry, and live a life of reason, rather than a life of a brute, for the time to come.

Letter CXVII—Mr. Belford to Robert Lovelace, Esq.

Thursday Night.

I was forced to take back my twenty guineas. How the women managed it, I can't tell (I suppose they too readily found a purchaser for the rich suit); but she mistrusted that I was the advancer of the money; and would not let the clothes go. But Mrs. Lovick has actually sold, for fifteen guineas, some rich lace worth three times the sum: out of which she repaid her the money she borrowed for fees to the doctor, in an illness occasioned by the barbarity of the most savage of men. *Thou knowest his name!*

The doctor called on her in the morning it seems, and had a short debate with her about fees. She insisted that he should take one every time he came, write or not write; mistrusting that he only gave verbal directions to Mrs. Lovick, or the nurse, to avoid taking any.

He said that it would have been impossible for him, had he *not* been a physician, to forbear inquiries after the health and welfare of so excellent a person. He had not the thought of paying her a compliment in declining the offered fee: but he knew her case could not so suddenly vary as to demand his daily visits. She must permit him, therefore, to inquire of the women below after her health; and he must not think of coming up if he were to be *pecuniarily* rewarded for the satisfaction he was so desirous to give himself.

It ended in a compromise for a fee each other time: which she unwillingly submitted to; telling him that though she was at present desolate and in disgrace, yet her circumstances were, of right, high; and no expenses could rise so as to be scrupled, whether she lived or died.   But she submitted, she added, to the compromise, in hopes to see him as often as he had opportunity; for she really looked upon him, and Mr. Goddard, from their kind and tender treatment of her, with a regard next to filial.

I hope thou wilt make thyself acquainted with this worthy doctor when thou comest to town; and give him thy thanks, for putting her into conceit with the sex that thou hast given her so much reason to execrate.

Farewell.

Letter CXVIII—*Mr. Lovelace to John Belford, Esq.*

M. Hall, Friday, July 21.

JUST returned from an interview with this Hickman: a precise fop of a fellow, as starched as his ruffles.

Thou knowest I love him not, Jack; and whom we love not, we cannot allow a merit to; *perhaps not the merit they should be granted.*   However, I am in earnest when I say that he seems to me to be so set, so prim, so affected, so mincing, yet so clouterly in his person, that I dare engage for thy opinion, if thou dost justice to him, and to thyself, that thou never beheldest such another, except in a pier-glass.

I 'll tell thee how I played him off.

He came in his own chariot to Dormer's; and we took a turn in the garden, at his request.   He was devilish ceremonious, and made a bushel of apologies for the freedom he was going to take; and, after half a hundred hums and haws, told me that he came —that he came—to wait on me—at the request of *dear Miss Howe*, on the account—on the account—of Miss Harlowe.

Well, sir, speak on, said I: but give me leave to say, that if your book be as long as your preface, it will take up a week to read it.

This was pretty rough, thou 'lt say: but there 's nothing like balking these formalists at first.   When they are put out of their road, they are filled with doubts of themselves, and can never get into it again: so that an honest fellow, impertinently attacked as I was, has all the game in his own hand quite through the conference.

He stroked his chin, and hardly knew what to say. At last, after parenthesis within parenthesis, apologizing for apologies, in imitation, I suppose, of Swift's digression in praise of digressions—I presume—I presume, sir, you were privy to the visit made to Miss Howe by the young ladies your cousins, in the name of Lord M., and Lady Sarah Sadleir, and Lady Betty Lawrance?

I *was*, sir: and Miss Howe had a letter afterwards, signed by his lordship and by those ladies, and underwritten by myself. Have you seen it, sir?

I can't say but I have. It is the principal cause of this visit: for Miss Howe thinks your part of it is written with such an air of levity—pardon me, sir—that she knows not whether you are in earnest or not in your address to *her* for her interest in her friend.[1]

Will Miss Howe permit me to explain myself in person to her, Mr. Hickman?

O sir, by no means. Miss Howe, I am sure, would not give you that trouble.

I should not think it a trouble. I will most readily attend you, sir, to Miss Howe, and satisfy her in all her scruples. Come, sir, I will wait upon you now. You have a chariot. Are alone. We can talk as we ride.

He hesitated, wriggled, winced, stroked his ruffles, set his wig, and pulled his neckcloth, which was long enough for a bib. I am not going directly back to Miss Howe, sir. It will be as well if you will be so good as to satisfy Miss Howe by me.

What is it she scruples, Mr. Hickman?

Why, sir, Miss Howe observes that in your part of the letter you say—but let me see, sir—I have a copy of what you wrote [pulling it out]. Will you give me leave, sir? Thus you begin —*Dear Miss Howe*——

No offence, I hope, Mr. Hickman?

None in the least, sir! None at all, sir!—Taking aim, as it were, to read.

Do you use spectacles, Mr. Hickman?

Spectacles, sir! His whole broad face lifted up at me. Spectacles! What makes you ask me such a question? Such a young man as I use spectacles, sir!——

---

[1] See Mr. Lovelace's billet to Miss Howe, at the end of Letter civ, in this volume.

They do in Spain, Mr. Hickman; young as well as old, to save their eyes. Have you ever read Prior's *Alma*, Mr. Hickman?

I have, sir—custom is everything in nations, as well as with individuals: I know the meaning of your question—but 'tis not the *English* custom.

Was you ever in Spain, Mr. Hickman?

No, sir: I have been in Holland.

In Holland, sir! Never in France or Italy? I was resolved to travel with him into the land of *Puzzledom*.

No, sir, I cannot say I have, as yet.

That's a wonder, sir, when on the Continent!

I went on a particular affair: I was obliged to return soon.

Well, sir; you was going to read. Pray be pleased to proceed.

Again he took aim, as if his eyes were older than the rest of him; and read, *After what is written above, and signed by names and characters of such unquestionable honour*—to be sure, taking off his eye, nobody questions the honour of Lord M. nor that of the good ladies who signed the letter.

I hope, Mr. Hickman, nobody questions mine neither?

If you please, sir, I will read on. *I might have been excused signing a name, almost as hateful to myself* [you are pleased to say] *as I KNOW it is to* YOU——

Well, Mr. Hickman, I must interrupt you at this place. In what I wrote to Miss Howe, I distinguished the word KNOW. I had a reason for it. Miss Howe has been very free with my character. I have never done her any harm. I take it very ill of her. And I hope, sir, you come in her name to make excuses for it.

Miss Howe, sir, is a very polite young lady. She is not accustomed to treat any man's character unbecomingly.

Then *I* have the more reason to take it amiss, Mr. Hickman.

Why, sir, you know the friendship——

No friendship should warrant such freedoms as Miss Howe has taken with my character.

I believe he began to wish he had not come near me. He seemed quite disconcerted.

Have you not heard Miss Howe treat my name with great——

Sir, I come not to offend or affront you: but you know what a love there is between Miss Howe and Miss Harlowe. I doubt, sir, you have not treated Miss Harlowe as so fine a young lady deserved to be treated: and if love for her friend has made Miss Howe take freedoms, as you call them, a mind not ungenerous, on such an occasion, will rather be sorry for having given the *cause*, than——

I know your consequence, sir! But I'd rather have this reproof from a lady than from a gentleman. I have a great desire to wait upon Miss Howe. I am persuaded we should soon come to a good understanding. Generous minds are always of kin. I know we should agree in everything. Pray, Mr. Hickman, be so kind as to introduce me to Miss Howe.

Sir—I can signify your desire, if you please, to Miss Howe.

Do so. Be pleased to read on, Mr. Hickman.

He did, very formally, as if I remembered not what I had written; and when he came to the passage about the halter, the parson, and the hangman, reading it, Why, sir, says he, does not this look like a jest? Miss Howe thinks it does. It is not in the lady's *power*, you know, sir, to doom you to the gallows.

Then, if it were, Mr. Hickman, you think she would?

You say here to Miss Howe, proceeded he, that Miss Harlowe is the *most injured of her sex*. I know from Miss Howe that she highly resents the injuries you own: insomuch that Miss Howe doubts that she shall never prevail upon her to overlook them: and as your family are all desirous you should repair her wrongs, and likewise desire Miss Howe's interposition with her friend; Miss Howe fears, from this part of your letter, that you are too much in jest; and that your offer to do her justice is rather in compliment to your friends' entreaties than proceeding from your own inclinations: and she desires to know your true sentiments on this occasion before she interposes further.

Do you think, Mr. Hickman, that, if I am capable of deceiving my own relations, I have so much obligation to Miss Howe, who has always treated me with great freedom, as to acknowledge to *her* what I don't to *them*?

Sir, I beg pardon: but Miss Howe thinks that, as you have written to her, she may ask you, by me, for an explanation of what you have written.

You see, Mr. Hickman, something of me. Do *you* think I am in jest, or in earnest?

I see, sir, you are a gay gentleman, of fine spirits, and all that. All I beg in Miss Howe's name is, to know if you really, and *bona fide*, join with your friends in desiring her to use her interest to reconcile you to Miss Harlowe?

I should be extremely glad to be reconciled to Miss Harlowe; and should owe great obligations to Miss Howe, if she could bring about so happy an event.

Well, sir, and you have no objections to marriage, I presume, as the condition of that reconciliation?

I never liked matrimony in my life. I must be plain with you, Mr. Hickman.

I am sorry for it: I think it a very happy state.

I hope you will find it so, Mr. Hickman.

I doubt not but I shall, sir. And I dare say, so would you, if you were to have Miss Harlowe.

If I could be happy in it with anybody, it would be with Miss Harlowe.

I am surprised, sir!—Then, after all, you don't think of marrying Miss Harlowe! After the hard usage——

What hard usage, Mr. Hickman? I don't doubt but a lady of her niceness has represented what would appear trifles to any other, in a very strong light.

If what I have had hinted to me, sir—excuse me—has been offered to the lady, she has more than trifles to complain of.

Let me know what you have heard, Mr. Hickman. I will very truly answer to the accusations.

Sir, you know best what you have done: you own the lady is the *most injured, as well as the most deserving, of her sex.*

I do, sir; and yet I would be glad to know what you have *heard*; for on that, perhaps, depends my answer to the questions Miss Howe puts to me by you.

Why then, sir, since you ask it, you cannot be displeased if I answer you: in the first place, sir, you will acknowledge, I suppose, that you promised Miss Harlowe marriage, and all that?

Well, sir, and I suppose what you have to charge me with is, that I was desirous to have *all that* without marriage.

Cot-so, sir, I know you are deemed to be a man of wit: but may I not ask if these things sit not too light upon you?

When a thing is done and cannot be helped, 'tis right to make the best of it. I wish the lady would think so too.

I think, sir, ladies should not be deceived. I think a promise to a lady should be as binding as to any other person, at the least.

I *believe* you think so, Mr. Hickman: and I believe you are a very honest good sort of a man.

I would always keep my word, sir, whether to man or woman.

You say well. And far be it from me to persuade you to do otherwise. But what have you farther heard?

(Thou wilt think, Jack, I must be very desirous to know in what light my elected spouse had represented things to Miss

Howe; and how far Miss Howe had communicated them to Mr. Hickman.)

Sir, this is no part of my present business.

But, Mr. Hickman, 'tis part of mine. I hope you would not expect that I should answer *your* questions, at the same time that you refuse to answer *mine*. What, pray, have you farther heard?

Why then, sir, if I must say, I am told that Miss Harlowe was carried to a very bad house.

Why, indeed, the people did not prove so good as they should be. What farther have you heard?

I have heard, sir, that the lady had strange advantages taken of her, very *unfair* ones; but what, I cannot say.

And *cannot* you say? Cannot you *guess*? Then I'll tell you, sir. Perhaps some liberty was taken with her when she was asleep. Do you think no lady ever was taken at such an advantage? You know, Mr. Hickman, that ladies are very shy of trusting themselves with the modestest of our sex, when they are disposed to sleep; and why so, if they did not *expect* that advantages would be taken of them at such times?

But, sir, had not the lady something given her to make her sleep?

Ay, Mr. Hickman, that's the question: I want to know if the lady says she had?

I have not seen all she has written; but by what I have heard, it is a very black affair—excuse me, sir.

I do excuse you, Mr. Hickman: but, supposing it were so, do you think a lady was never imposed upon by wine, or so? Do you think the most cautious woman in the world might not be cheated by a stronger liquor for a smaller, when she was thirsty, after a fatigue in this very warm weather? And do you think, if she was thus thrown into a profound sleep, that she is the only lady that was ever taken at such advantage?

Even as you make it, Mr. Lovelace, this matter is not a light one. But I fear it is a great deal heavier than as you put it.

What reasons have you to fear this, sir? What has the lady said? Pray let me know. I have *reason* to be so earnest.

Why, sir, Miss Howe herself knows not the whole. The lady promises to give her all the particulars at a proper time, if she lives; but has said enough to make it out to be a very bad affair.

I am glad Miss Harlowe has not yet given all the particulars. And, since she has not, you may tell Miss Howe from me that neither she nor any woman in the world can be more virtuous than Miss Harlowe is to this hour, as to her own mind. Tell her that I hope she never *will* know the particulars; but that she has been unworthily used: tell her that though I know not what she has said, yet I have such an opinion of her veracity, that I would blindly subscribe to the truth of every tittle of it, though it make me ever so black. Tell her that I have but *three* things to blame her for; *one*, that she won't give me an opportunity of repairing her wrongs: the *second*, that she is so ready to acquaint everybody with what she has suffered, that it will put it out of my power to redress those wrongs, with any tolerable reputation to either of us. Will this, Mr. Hickman, answer any part of the intention of this visit?

Why, sir, this is talking like a man of honour, I own. But you say there is a *third* thing you blame the lady for; may I ask what that is?

I don't know, sir, whether I ought to tell it you or not. Perhaps you won't believe it, if I do. But though the lady will tell the *truth*, and nothing *but* the truth, yet, perhaps, she will not tell you the *whole* truth.

Pray, sir—but it mayn't be proper—yet you give me great curiosity. Sure there is no misconduct in the lady. I hope there is not. I am sure, if Miss Howe did not believe her to be faultless in every particular, she would not interest herself so much in her favour as she does, dearly as she loves her.

I love Miss Harlowe too well, Mr. Hickman, to wish to lessen her in Miss Howe's opinion; especially as she is abandoned of every other friend. But perhaps it would hardly be credited if I should tell you.

I should be very sorry, sir, and so would Miss Howe, if this poor lady's conduct had laid her under obligation to you for this reserve. You have so much the appearance of a gentleman, as well as are so much distinguished in your family and fortunes, that I hope you are incapable of loading such a young lady as this, in order to lighten yourself—excuse me, sir.

I do, I do, Mr. Hickman. You say you came not with any intention to affront me. I take freedom, and I give it. I should be very loath, I repeat, to say anything that may weaken Miss Harlowe in the good opinion of the only friend she thinks she has left.

It may not be proper, said he, for me to know your *third* article against this unhappy lady: but I never heard of anybody, out of her own implacable family, that had the least doubt of her honour. *Mrs.* Howe, indeed, once said, after a conference with one of her uncles, that she feared all was not right of her side. But else, I never heard——

Oons, sir! in a fierce tone, and with an erect mien, stopping short upon him, which made him start back. 'Tis next to blasphemy to question this lady's honour. She is more pure than a vestal; for vestals have been often warmed by their own fires. No age, from the first to the present, ever produced, nor will the future, to the end of the world, I dare aver, ever produce, a young blooming lady, tried as she has been tried, who has stood all trials, as she has done. Let me tell you, sir, that you never saw, never knew, never heard of, such another woman as Miss Harlowe.

Sir, sir, I beg your pardon. Far be it from me to question the lady. You have not heard me say a word that could be so construed. I have the utmost honour for her. Miss Howe loves her as she loves her own soul; and that she would not do if she were not sure she were as virtuous as herself.

As herself, sir! I have a high opinion of Miss Howe, sir—but, I dare say——

What, sir, dare you say of Miss Howe? I hope, sir, you will not presume to say anything to the disparagement of Miss Howe!

Presume, Mr. Hickman! That is *presuming* language, let me tell you, Mr. Hickman!

The *occasion* for it, Mr. Lovelace, if designed, is *presuming*, if you please. I am not a man ready to take offence, sir—especially where I am employed as a mediator. But no man breathing shall say disparaging things of Miss Howe, in my hearing, without observation.

Well said, Mr. Hickman. I dislike not your spirit, on such a *supposed* occasion. But what I was going to say is this, that there is not, in my opinion, a woman in the world who ought to compare herself with Miss Clarissa Harlowe till she has stood *her* trials, and has behaved *under* them, and *after* them, as she has done. You see, sir, I speak against myself. You see I do. For, libertine as I am thought to be, I never will attempt to bring down the measures of right and wrong to the standard of my actions.

Why, sir, this is very right. It is very *noble*, I will say. But 'tis pity—excuse me, sir—'tis pity that the man who can pronounce so fine a sentence will not square his actions accordingly.

That, Mr. Hickman, is another point. We all err in some things. I wish not that Miss Howe should have Miss Harlowe's trials: and I rejoice that she is in no danger of any such from so good a man.

(Poor Hickman! He looked as if he knew not whether I meant a compliment or a reflection!)

But, proceeded I, since I find that I have excited your curiosity, that you may not go away with a doubt that may be injurious to the most admirable of women, I am inclined to hint to you what I have in the *third* place to blame her for.

Sir, as you please—it may not be proper——

It cannot be very *improper*, Mr. Hickman. So let me ask you, What would Miss Howe think if her friend is the *more* determined against me, because she thinks (in revenge to me, I verily believe that!) of encouraging another lover?

How, sir! Sure this cannot be the case! I can tell you, sir, if Miss Howe thought this, she would not approve of it at all: for, little as you think Miss Howe likes you, sir, and little as she approves of your actions by her friend, I know she is of opinion that she ought to have nobody living but you: and should continue single all her life if she be not yours.

Revenge and obstinacy, Mr. Hickman, will make women, the best of them, do very unaccountable things. Rather than not put out both eyes of the man they are offended with, they will give up one of their own.

I don't know what to say to this, sir: but, sure, she cannot encourage any other person's address! So soon too! Why, sir, she is, as we are told, so ill, and so *weak*——

Not in resentment weak, I'll assure you. I am well acquainted with all her movements—and I tell you, believe it or not, that she refuses *me* in view of *another* lover.

Can it be?

'Tis true, by my soul! Has she not hinted this to Miss Howe, do you think?

No, indeed, sir. If she had, I should not have troubled you at this time from Miss Howe.

Well then, you see I am right: that though she cannot be guilty of a falsehood, yet she has not told her friend the whole truth.

What shall a man say to these things!—looking most stupidly perplexed.

Say! say! Mr. Hickman! Who can account for the workings and ways of a passionate and offended woman? Endless would be the histories I could give you, within my own knowledge, of the dreadful effects of women's passionate resentments, and what that sex will do when disappointed.

There was Miss DORRINGTON [perhaps you know her not], who ran away with her father's groom, because he would not let her have a half-pay officer, with whom (her passions all up) she fell in love at first sight, as he accidentally passed under her window.

There was Miss SAVAGE; she married her mother's coachman because her mother refused her a journey to Wales, in apprehension, that miss intended to league herself with a remote cousin of unequal fortunes, of whom she was not a little fond when he was a visiting guest at their house for a week.

There was the young widow SANDERSON; who believing herself slighted by a younger brother of a noble family (Sarah Stout like), took it into her head to drown herself.

Miss SALLY ANDERSON [you have heard of her, no doubt] being checked by her uncle for encouraging an address beneath her, in spite, threw herself into the arms of an ugly dog, a shoemaker's apprentice; running away with him in a pair of shoes he had just fitted to her feet, though she never saw the fellow before, and hated him ever after: and at last took laudanum to make her forget for ever her own folly.

But can there be a stronger instance in point than what the unaccountable resentments of *such* a lady as Miss Clarissa Harlowe afford us? Who, at this very instant, ill as she is, not only encourages, but, in a manner, makes court to, one of the most odious dogs that ever was seen! I think Miss Howe should not be told this—and yet she ought too, in order to dissuade her from such a preposterous rashness.

O fie! O strange! Miss Howe knows nothing of this! To be sure she won't look upon her if this be true!

'Tis true, very true, Mr. Hickman! True as I am here to tell you so! And he is an ugly fellow too; uglier to look at than me.

Than *you*, sir! Why, to be sure, you are one of the handsomest men in England.

Well, but the wretch she so spitefully prefers to me is a misshapen, meagre varlet; more like a skeleton than a man! Then he dresses—you never saw a devil so bedizened! Hardly a coat to his back, nor a shoe to his foot: a bald-pated villain, yet grudges to buy a peruke to hide his baldness: for he is as covetous as hell, never satisfied, yet plaguy rich.

Why, sir, there is some joke in this, surely. A man of common parts knows not how to take such gentlemen as you. But, sir, if there be any truth in the story, what is he? Some Jew, or miserly citizen, I suppose, that may have presumed on the lady's distressful circumstances; and your lively wit points him out as it pleases.

Why, the rascal has estates in every county *in* England, and *out of* England too.

Some East India governor, I suppose, if there be anything in it: the lady once had thoughts of going abroad. But, I fancy, all this time you are in jest, sir. If not, we must surely have heard of him.

Heard of him! Ay, sir, we have all heard of him—but none of us care to be intimate with him—except this lady—and that, as I told you, in spite to me. His name, in short, is DEATH! DEATH! sir, stamping, and speaking loud, and full in his ear; which made him jump half a yard high.

(Thou never beheldest any man so disconcerted. He looked as if the frightful skeleton was before him, and he had not his accounts ready. When a little recovered, he fribbled with his waistcoat buttons, as if he had been telling his beads).

This, sir, proceeded I, is her wooer! Nay, she is so forward a girl that she *woos him*: but I hope it never will be a match.

He had before behaved, and now looked, with more spirit than I expected from him.

I came, sir, said he, as a mediator of differences. It behoves me to keep my temper. But, sir, and turned short upon me, as much as I love peace, and to promote it, I will not be ill-used.

As I had played so much upon him, it would have been wrong to take him at his *more* than half-menace: yet I think I owe him a grudge, for his presuming to address Miss Howe.

You mean no defiance, I presume, Mr. Hickman, any more than I do offence. On that presumption, I ask your excuse. But this is my way. I mean no harm. I cannot let sorrow touch my heart. I cannot be grave six minutes together, for the blood of me. I am a descendant of old Chancellor More, I believe; and should not forbear to cut a joke, were I upon the scaffold. But you may gather, from what I have *said*, that I prefer Miss Harlowe, and that upon the justest grounds, to all the women in the world: and I wonder that there should be any difficulty to believe, from what I have signed, and from what I have promised to my relations, and enabled them to promise for me, that I should be glad to marry that excellent creature upon her own terms. I acknowledge to you, Mr. Hickman, that I have basely injured her. If she will honour me with her hand, I declare that it is my intention to make her the best of husbands. But, nevertheless, I must say that if she goes on appealing her case, and exposing us both, as she does, it is impossible to think the knot can be knit with reputation to either. And although, Mr. Hickman, I have delivered my apprehensions under so ludicrous a figure, I am afraid that she will ruin her constitution; and, by seeking Death when she may shun him, will not be able to avoid him when she would be glad to do so.

This cool and honest speech let down his stiffened muscles into complacency. He was my very obedient and faithful humble servant several times over, as I waited on him to his chariot: and I was his almost as often.

And so *exit* Hickman.

Letter CXIX—Mr. Lovelace to John Belford, Esq.

[*In answer to Letters CXII, CXVI, CXVII*]

Friday Night, July 21.

I WILL throw away a few paragraphs upon the contents of thy last shocking letters, just brought me; and send what I shall write by the fellow who carries mine on the interview with Hickman.

Reformation, I see, is coming fast upon thee. Thy uncle's slow death, and thy attendance upon him through every stage towards it, prepared thee for it. But go thou on in thy own way, as I will in mine. Happiness consists in being pleased with what we do: and if thou canst find delight in being *sad*, it will be as well for thee as if thou wert *merry*, though no other person should join to keep thee in countenance.

I am, nevertheless, exceedingly disturbed at the lady's ill-health. It is entirely owing to the cursed arrest. She was absolutely triumphant over me and the whole crew *before*. Thou believest me guiltless of that: so, I hope, does she. The rest, as I have often said, is a common case; only a little uncommonly circumstanced; that's all: why, then, all these severe things from her and from thee?

As to selling her clothes, and her laces, and so forth, it has, I own, a shocking sound with it. What an implacable as well as unjust set of wretches are those of her unkindredly kin who have money of hers in their hands, as well as large arrears of her own estate; yet withhold both, *avowedly* to distress her! But may she not have money of that proud and saucy friend of hers, Miss Howe, more than she wants? And should I not be overjoyed, thinkest thou, to serve her? What then is there in the parting with her apparel but female perverseness? And I am not sure whether I ought not to be glad, if she does this out of *spite to me*. Some disappointed fair ones would have hanged, some drowned themselves. My beloved only revenges herself upon her clothes. Different ways of working has passion in different bosoms, as humours or complexion induce. Besides, dost think I shall grudge to replace, to three times the value, what she disposes of? So, Jack, there is no great matter in this.

Thou seest how sensible she is of the soothings of the polite doctor: this will enable thee to judge how dreadfully the horrid arrest, and her gloomy father's curse, must have hurt her. I have great hope, if she will but see me, that my behaviour, my contrition, my soothings, may have some happy effects upon her.

But thou art too ready to give up. Let me seriously tell thee that, all excellence as she is, I think the earnest inter-position of my relations; the implored mediation of that little fury, Miss Howe; and the commissions thou actest under from myself; are such instances of condescension and high value in *them*, and such contrition in *me*, that nothing farther can be done. So here let the matter rest for the present, till she considers better of it.

But now a few words upon poor Belton's case. I own I was at first a little startled at the disloyalty of his Thomasine: her hypocrisy to be for so many years undetected! I have very lately had some intimations given me of her vileness; and had intended to mention them to thee when I saw thee. To say the truth, I always suspected her *eye*: the *eye*, thou knowest, is the *casement* at which the *heart* generally looks out. Many a woman who will not show herself at the *door*, has tipped the sly, the intelligible *wink* from the *windows*.

But Tom had no management at all. A very careless fellow. Would never look into his own affairs. The estate his uncle left him was his ruin: wife, or mistress, whoever was, must have had his fortune to sport with.

I have often hinted his weaknesses of this sort to him; and the danger he was in of becoming the property of designing people. But he hated to take pains. He would ever run away from his accounts; as now, poor fellow! he would be glad to do from himself. Had he not had a *woman* to fleece him, his *coach-man*, or *valet*, would have been his *prime minister*, and done it as effectually.

But yet, for many years, I thought she was true to his bed. At least, I thought the boys were his own. For though they are muscular, and big-boned, yet I supposed the healthy mother might have furnished them with legs and shoulders: for she is not of a delicate frame; and then Tom, some years ago, looked up, and spoke more like a man than he has done of late; squeaking inwardly, poor fellow! for some time past, from contracted quail-pipes, and wheezing from lungs half spit away.

He complains, thou sayest, that we all run away from him. Why, after all, Belford, it is no pleasant thing to see a poor fellow one loves dying by inches, yet unable to do him good. There are friendships which are only *bottle-deep*: I should be loath to have it thought that mine for any of my vassals is such a one. Yet, with gay hearts, which *became intimate because they were gay*, the reason for their first intimacy ceasing, the friendship will fade: but may not this sort of friendship be more properly distinguished by the word *companionship*?

But mine, as I said, is deeper than this: I would still be as ready as ever I was in my life, to the utmost of my power, to do him service.

As one instance of this my readiness to extricate him from all his difficulties as to Thomasine, dost thou care to propose to him an expedient that is just come into my head?

It is this: I would engage Thomasine and her cubs (if Belton be convinced they are neither of them his) in a party of pleasure. She was always complaisant to me. It should be in a boat, hired for the purpose, to sail to Tilbury, to the Isle of Sheppey, or a pleasuring up the Medway; and 'tis but contriving to turn the boat bottom upward. I can swim like a fish. Another boat should be ready to take up whom I should direct, for fear of the worst: and then, if Tom has a mind to be decent, one suit of mourning will serve for all three: nay, the hostler-cousin may take his plunge from the steerage: and who knows but they may be thrown up on the beach, Thomasine and he, hand in hand?

This, thou 'lt say, is no *common* instance of friendship.

Meantime, do thou prevail upon him to come down to us: he never was more welcome in his life than he shall be now: if he will not, let him find me some other service; and I will clap a pair of wings to my shoulders, and he shall see me come flying in at his windows at the word of command.

Mowbray and Tourville each intend to give thee a letter; and I leave to those rough varlets to handle thee as thou deservest, for the shocking picture thou hast drawn of their last ends. Thy own past guilt has stared thee full in the face, one may see by it; and made thee, in consciousness of thy demerits, sketch out these cursed outlines. I am glad thou hast got the old fiend to hold the glass [1] before thy own face so soon. Thou must be in earnest surely, when thou wrotest it, and have severe convictions upon thee: for what a hardened varlet must he be who could draw such a picture as this in sport?

As for thy resolution of repenting and marrying; I would have thee consider which thou wilt set about first. If thou wilt follow my advice, thou shalt make short work of it: let matrimony take place of the other; for then thou wilt, very possibly, have repentance come tumbling in fast upon thee, as a consequence and so have both in one.

Letter CXX—Mr. Belford to Robert Lovelace, Esq.

Friday Noon, July 21.

THIS morning I was admitted, as soon as I sent up my name, into the presence of the divine lady. Such I may call her; as what I have to relate will fully prove.

She had had a tolerable night, and was much better in spirits; though weak in person; and visibly declining in looks.

Mrs. Lovick and Mrs. Smith were with her; and accused her, in a gentle manner, of having applied herself too assiduously to her pen for her strength, having been up ever since five. She said she had rested better than she had done for many nights: she had found her spirits free, and her mind tolerably easy: and having, as she had reason to think, but a short time, and much to do in it, she must be a good housewife of her hours.

She had been writing, she said, a letter to her sister: but had not pleased herself in it; though she had made two or three essays: but that the last must go.

By hints I had dropped from time to time, she had reason, she said, to think that I knew everything that concerned her and her family; and, if so, must be acquainted with the heavy curse her father had laid upon her; which had been dreadfully fulfilled in one part, as to her prospects in this life, and that in a very short time; which gave her great apprehensions of the other part. She had been applying herself to her sister, to obtain a revocation of it. I hope my father will revoke it, said she, or I shall be very miserable. Yet [and she gasped as she spoke, with apprehension] I am ready to tremble at what the answer may be; for my sister is hard-hearted.

I said something reflecting upon her friends; as to what they

[1] See Letter cxv.

would deserve to be thought of, if the unmerited imprecation were not withdrawn. Upon which she took me up, and talked in such a dutiful manner of her parents, as must doubly condemn them (if they remain implacable) for their inhuman treatment of such a daughter.

She said I must not blame her parents: it was her dear Miss Howe's fault to do so. But what an enormity was there in her crime, which could set the best of parents (as they had been to her, till she disobliged them) in a bad light, for resenting the rashness of a child from whose education they had reason to expect better fruits! There were some hard circumstances in her case, it was true: but my *friend* could tell me that not *one* person, throughout the whole fatal transaction, had acted out of character, but *herself*. She submitted therefore to the penalty she had incurred. If they had any fault, it was only that they would not inform themselves of some circumstances which would alleviate a little her misdeed; and that, supposing her a more guilty creature than she was, they punished her without a hearing.

Lord!—*I was going to curse thee, Lovelace! How every instance of excellence, in this all-excelling creature, condemns thee! Thou wilt have reason to think thyself of all men most accursed, if she die!*

I then besought her, while she was capable of such glorious instances of generosity and forgiveness, to extend her goodness to a man whose heart bled in every vein of it for the injuries he had done her; and who would make it the study of his whole life to repair them.

The women would have withdrawn when the subject became so particular. But she would not permit them to go. She told me, that if after this time I was for entering with so much earnestness into a subject so very disagreeable to *her*, my visits must not be repeated. Nor was there occasion, she said, for my friendly offices in your favour; since she had begun to write her whole mind upon that subject to Miss Howe, in answer to letters from her, in which Miss Howe urged the same arguments, in compliment to the wishes of your noble and worthy relations.

Meantime, you may let him know, said she, that I reject him with my whole heart—yet that, although I say this with such a determination as shall leave no room for doubt, I say it not however with passion. On the contrary, tell him that I am trying to bring my mind into such a frame, as to be able to *pity* him [poor perjured wretch! what has he not to answer for!]; and that I shall not think myself qualified for the state I am aspiring to, if, after a few struggles more, I cannot *forgive* him too: and I hope, clasping her hands together, uplifted, as were her eyes, my dear *earthly* father will set me the example my *heavenly* one has already set us all; and, by forgiving his fallen daughter, teach her to forgive the man, who then, I hope, will not have destroyed my eternal prospects, as he has my temporal!

Stop here, thou wretch! But I need not bid thee — for I can go no farther!

Letter CXXI—Mr. Belford. [*In continuation*]

You will imagine how affecting her noble speech and behaviour were to me at the time when the bare recollecting and transcribing them obliged me to drop my pen. The women had tears in their eyes. I was silent for a few moments. At last, Matchless excellence! Inimitable goodness! I called her, with a voice so accented, that I was half-ashamed of myself, as it was before the women. But who could stand such sublime generosity of soul in so young a creature, her loveliness giving grace to all she said? Methinks, said I [and I really, in a manner, involuntarily bent my knee], I have before me an angel indeed. I can hardly forbear prostration, and to beg your influence to draw me after you to the world you are aspiring to! Yet—but what shall I say? Only, dearest excellence, make me, in some small instances, serviceable to you, that I may (if I survive you) have the glory to think I was able to contribute to your satisfaction, while among us.

Here I stopped. She was silent. I proceeded: Have you no commission to employ me in; deserted as you are by all your friends; among strangers, though, I doubt not, worthy people? Cannot I be serviceable by message, by letter-writing, by attending personally, with either message or letter, your father, your uncles, your brother, your sister, Miss Howe, Lord M., or the ladies his sisters?—Any office to be employed in to serve you, absolutely *independent* of my *friend's* wishes, or of my own wishes to oblige him. Think, madam, if I cannot?

I thank you, sir: very heartily I thank you: but in nothing that I can at present think of, or at least resolve upon, can you do me service. I will see what return the letter I have written will bring me. Till then——

My life and my fortune, interrupted I, are devoted to your service. Permit me to observe, that here you are, without one natural friend; and (so much do I know of your unhappy case) that you must be in a manner destitute of the means to *make* friends.

She was going to interrupt me with a prohibitory kind of earnestness in her manner.

I beg leave to proceed, madam: I have cast about twenty ways how to mention this before, but never dared till now. Suffer me, now that I have broke the ice, to tender myself—as your *banker* only. I know you will not be obliged: you *need* not. You have sufficient of your own, if it were in your hands; and from *that*, whether you live or die, will I consent to be reimbursed. I do assure you that the unhappy man shall never know either *my* offer or *your* acceptance. Only permit me this small——

And down behind her chair I dropped a bank-note of £100 which I had brought with me, intending somehow or other to leave it behind me: nor shouldst thou ever have known it, had she favoured me with the acceptance of it; as I told her.

You give me great pain, Mr. Belford, said she, by these instances of your humanity. And yet, considering the company I have seen you in, I am not sorry to find you capable of such. Methinks I am glad, for the sake of human nature, that there could be but *one* such man in the world, as he you and I know. But as to your kind offer, whatever it be, if you take it not up you will greatly disturb me. I have no need of your kindness. I have effects enough, which I never can want, to supply my present occasions: and, if needful, can have recourse to Miss Howe. I have promised that I would. So, pray, sir, urge not upon me this favour. Take it up yourself. If you mean me peace and ease of mind, urge not this favour. And she spoke with impatience.

I beg, madam, but one word——

Not one, sir, till you have taken back what you have let fall. I doubt not either the *honour*, or the *kindness*, of your offer; but you must not say one word more on this subject. I cannot bear it.

She was stooping, but with pain. I therefore prevented her; and besought her to forgive me for a tender, which, I saw, had been more discomposing to her than I had hoped (from the purity of my intentions) it would be. But I could not bear to think that such a mind as hers should be distressed: since the want of the conveniences she was used to abound in, might affect and disturb her in the divine course she was in.

You are very kind to me, sir, said she, and very favourable in your opinion of me. But I hope that I cannot now be easily put out of my present course. My declining health will more and more confirm me in it. Those who arrested and confined me, no doubt, thought they had fallen upon the ready method to distress me so as to bring me into all their measures. But I presume to hope that I have a mind that cannot be debased, in *essential instances*, by *temporal calamities*. Little do those poor wretches know of the force of innate principles (forgive my own *implied* vanity, was her word), who imagine that a prison, or penury, can bring a right-turned mind to be guilty of a wilful baseness, in order to avoid such *short-lived evils*.

She then turned from me towards the window, with a dignity suitable to her words; and such as showed her to be more of soul than of body at that instant.

What magnanimity! No wonder a virtue so solidly founded could baffle all thy arts: and that it forced thee (in order to carry thy accursed point) to have recourse to those unnatural ones, which robbed her of her charming senses.

The women were extremely affected, Mrs. Lovick especially; who said whisperingly to Mrs. Smith, We have an angel, not a woman, with us, Mrs. Smith!

I repeated my offers to write to any of her friends; and told her that, having taken the liberty to acquaint Dr. H. with the cruel displeasure of her relations, as what I presumed lay nearest her heart, he had proposed to write himself, to acquaint her friends how ill she was, if she would not take it amiss.

It was kind in the *doctor*, she said: but begged that no step of that sort might be taken without her knowledge and consent. She would wait to see what effects her letter to her sister would have. All she had to hope for was, that her father would revoke his malediction, previous to the last blessing she should then implore: for the rest, her friends would think she could not suffer too much; and she was content to suffer: for now nothing could happen that could make her wish to live.

Mrs. Smith went down; and, soon returning, asked if the lady and I would not dine with her that day: for it was her wedding-day. She had engaged Mrs. Lovick, she said; and should have nobody else if we would do her that favour.

The charming creature sighed, and shook her head. *Wedding-day*, repeated she! I wish you, Mrs. Smith, many happy wedding-days! But you will excuse *me*.

Mr. Smith came up with the same request. They both applied to me.

On condition the *lady* would, I should make no scruple; and would suspend an engagement: which I actually had.

She then desired they would all sit down. You have several times, Mrs. Lovick and Mrs. Smith, hinted your wishes that I would give you some little history of myself: now, if you are at leisure, that this gentleman, who, I have reason to believe, knows it all, is present, and can tell you if I give it justly or not, I will oblige your curiosity.

They all eagerly, the man Smith too, sat down; and she began an account of herself, which I will endeavour to repeat, as nearly in her own words as I possibly can: for I know you will think it of importance to be apprised of her manner of relating your barbarity to her, as well as what her sentiments are of it; and what room there is for the hopes your friends have in your favour from her.

"At first when I took these lodgings, said she, I thought of staying but a short time in them; and so, Mrs. Smith, I told you: I therefore avoided giving any other account of myself than that I was a very unhappy young creature, seduced from good friends, and escaped from very vile wretches.

"This account I thought myself obliged to give, that you might the less wonder at seeing a young creature rushing through your shop, into your back apartment, all trembling and out of breath; an ordinary garb over my own; craving lodging and protection; only giving my bare word that you should be handsomely paid: all my effects contained in a pocket-handkerchief.

"My sudden absence, for three days and nights together, when arrested, must still further surprise you: and although this gentleman, who, perhaps, knows more of the darker part of my story than I do myself, has informed you (as you, Mrs. Lovick, tell me) that I am only an *unhappy*, not a *guilty* creature; yet I think it incumbent upon me not to suffer honest minds to be in doubt about my character.

"You must know, then, that I have been, in one instance (I had like to have said *but* in one instance; but that was a capital one), an undutiful child to the most indulgent of parents: for what some people call cruelty in them, is owing but to the excess of their love, and to their disappointment; having had reason to expect better from me.

"I was visited (at first, with my friends' connivance) by a man of birth and fortune, but of worse principles, as it proved, than I believed any man could have. My brother, a very headstrong young man, was absent at that time; and, when he returned (from an old grudge, and knowing the gentleman, it is plain, better than I knew him) entirely disapproved of his visits: and, having a great sway in our family, brought other gentlemen to address me: and at last (several having been rejected) he introduced one extremely disagreeable: in every *indifferent* person's eyes disagreeable. I could not love him. They all joined to compel me to have him; a rencounter between the gentleman my friends were set against, and my brother, having confirmed them all his enemies.

"To be short: I was confined, and treated so very hardly, that in a rash fit I appointed to go off with the man they hated. A wicked intention, you'll say: but I was greatly provoked. Nevertheless, I repented; and resolved not to go off with him: yet I did not mistrust his honour to me neither; nor his love; because nobody thought me unworthy of the latter, and my fortune was not to be despised. But foolishly (wickedly and contrivingly, as my friends *still* think, with a design, as they imagine, to abandon them) giving him a private meeting, I was tricked away: poorly enough tricked away, I must needs say; though others, who had been first guilty of so rash a step as the meeting of him was, might have been so deceived and surprised as well as I.

"After remaining some time at a farm-house in the country, and behaving to me all the time with honour, he brought me to handsome lodgings in town, till still better provision could be made for me. But they proved to be (as he indeed knew and designed) at a vile, a very vile creature's; though it was long before I found her to be so; for I knew nothing of the town, or its ways.

"There is no repeating what followed: such unprecedented vile arts! For I gave him no opportunity to take me at any disreputable advantage."

And here (half covering her sweet face, with her handkerchief put to her tearful eyes) she stopped.

Hastily, as if she would fly from the hateful remembrance, she resumed: "I made my escape afterwards from the abominable house in his absence, and came to yours: and this gentleman has almost prevailed on me to think that the ungrateful man did not connive at the vile arrest: which was made, no doubt, in order to get me once more to those wicked lodgings: for nothing do I owe them, except I were to pay them [she sighed, and again wiped her charming eyes—adding in a softer, lower voice]— *for being ruined.*"

Indeed, madam, said I, guilty, abominably guilty as he is in all the rest, he is innocent of this last wicked outrage.

"Well, and so I wish him to be. That evil, heavy as it was, is one of the slightest evils I have suffered. But hence you'll observe, Mrs. Lovick (for you seemed this morning curious to know if I were not a wife), that I *never was married*. You, Mr. Belford, no doubt, knew before that I am no wife: and now I never will be one. Yet, I bless God that I am not a guilty creature!

"As to my parentage, I am of no mean family: I have in my own right, by the intended favour of my grandfather, a fortune not contemptible: independent of my *father*, if I had pleased; but I never will please.

"My father is very rich. I went by another name when I came to you first: but that was to avoid being discovered to the perfidious man: who now engages, by this gentleman, not to molest me.

"My real name you now know to be Harlowe: *Clarissa* Harlowe. I am not yet twenty years of age.

"I have an excellent mother, as well as father; a woman of family, and fine sense—worthy of a better child! They both doted upon me.

"I have two good uncles: men of great fortune; jealous of the honour of their family; which I have wounded.

"I was the joy of their hearts; and, with theirs and my father's, I had three houses to call my own; for they used to have me with them by turns, and almost kindly to quarrel for me: so that I was two months in the year with the one; two months with the other: six months at my father's; and two at the houses of others of my dear friends, who thought themselves happy in me: and whenever I was at any one's, I was crowded upon with letters by all the rest, who longed for my return to them.

"In short, I was beloved by everybody. The poor—I used to make glad *their* hearts: I never shut my hand to any distress, wherever I was—but now I am poor myself!

"So, Mrs. Smith, so, Mrs. Lovick, I am *not* married. It is but just to tell you so. And I am now, as I ought to be, in a state of humiliation and penitence for the rash step which has been followed by so much evil. God, I hope, will forgive me, as I am endeavouring to bring my mind to forgive all the world, even the man who has ungratefully, and by dreadful perjuries [poor wretch! he thought all his wickedness to be *wit*!], reduced to this a young creature, who had *his* happiness in her *view*, and in her *wish,* even beyond this life; and who was believed to be of rank and fortune, and expectations considerable enough to make it the *interest* of any gentleman in England to be faithful to his vows to her. But I cannot expect that my parents will forgive me: my refuge must be death; the most painful kind of which I would suffer, rather than be the wife of one who could act by me as the man has acted, upon whose birth, education, and honour, I had so much reason to found better expectations.

"I see, continued she, that I, who once was every one's delight, am now the cause of grief to every one—you, that are strangers to me, are moved for me! 'Tis kind! But 'tis time to stop. Your compassionate hearts, Mrs. Smith, and Mrs. Lovick, are too much touched." [For the women sobbed, and the man was also affected.] "It is barbarous in me, with my woes, thus to sadden your wedding-day." Then turning to Mr. and Mrs. Smith: "May you see many happy ones, honest, good couple! How agreeable is it to see you both join so kindly to celebrate it, after many years are gone over you! I once—but no more! All my prospects of felicity, as to this life, are at an end. My hopes, like opening buds or blossoms in an over-forward spring, have been nipped by a severe frost! Blighted by an eastern wind! But I can but *once die*; and if life be spared me but till I am discharged from a heavy malediction, which my father in his wrath laid upon me, and which is fulfilled literally in every article relating to this world: that, and a last blessing, are all I have to wish for; and death will be welcomer to me than rest to the most wearied traveller that ever reached his journey's end."

And then she sunk her head against the back of her chair and, hiding her face with her handkerchief, endeavoured to conceal her tears from us.

Not a soul of us could speak a word. Thy presence, perhaps, thou hardened wretch, might have made us ashamed of a weakness, which perhaps thou wilt deride *me* in particular for, when thou readest this!

She retired to her chamber soon after, and was forced, it seems, to lie down. We all went down together; and, for an hour and half, dwelt upon her praises; Mrs. Smith and Mrs. Lovick repeatedly expressing their astonishment, that there could be a man in the world capable of offending, much more of wilfully injuring, such a lady; and repeating that they had an angel in their house. I thought they had; and that as assuredly as there is a devil under the roof of good Lord M.

I hate thee heartily! By my faith I do! Every hour I hate thee more than the former!

J. BELFORD.

Letter CXXII—Mr. Lovelace to John Belford, Esq.

Sat. July 22.

WHAT dost hate me for, Belford? And why more and more? Have I been guilty of any offence thou knewest not before? If *pathos* can move such a heart as thine, can it alter facts? Did I not always do this incomparable creature as much justice as thou canst do her for the heart of thee, or as she can do herself? What nonsense then thy hatred, thy *augmented* hatred, when I still persist to marry her, pursuant to word given to thee, and to faith plighted to all my relations? But hate, if thou wilt, so thou dost but write. Thou canst not hate me so much as I do myself: and yet I know, if thou really hatedst me, thou wouldst not venture to tell me so.

Well, but after all, what need of her history to these women? She will certainly repent, some time hence, that she has thus needlessly exposed us both.

Sickness palls every appetite, and makes us hate what we loved: but renewed health changes the scene; disposes us to be pleased with ourselves; and then we are in a way to be pleased with every one else. Every hope, then, rises upon us: every hour presents itself to us on dancing feet: and what Mr. Addison says of liberty, may, with still greater propriety, be said of *health* [*for what is liberty itself without health?*]:

> It makes the gloomy face of nature gay;
> Gives beauty to the sun, and pleasure to the day.

And I rejoice that she is already so much better, as to hold with strangers such a long and interesting conversation.

Strange, confoundedly strange, and as perverse [that is to say, as *womanly*] as strange, that she should refuse, and sooner choose to die [O the obscene word! and yet how free does thy pen make with it to me!] than be mine, who offended her by acting *in* character, while her parents acted shamefully *out of theirs*, and when I am now willing to act *out of my own* to oblige her: yet *I* not to be forgiven! *They* to be faultless with her! And marriage the only medium to repair all breaches, and to salve her own honour! Surely thou must see the inconsistence of her *forgiving* unforgivingness, as I may call it! Yet, heavy varlet as thou art, thou wantest to be drawn up after her! And what a figure dost thou make with thy speeches, stiff as Hickman's ruffles, with thy aspirations and prostrations!—unused, thy weak head, to bear the sublimities that fall, even in common conversation, from the lips of this ever-charming creature!

But the prettiest whim of all was to drop the bank-note behind her chair, instead of presenting it on thy knees to her hand! To make such a woman as this *doubly* stoop—by the acceptance, and to take it from the ground! What an ungraceful *benefit-conferrer* art thou! How awkward, to take it into thy head that the best way of making a present to a lady was to throw the present behind her chair!

I am very desirous to see what she has written to her sister; what she is about to write to Miss Howe; and what return she will have from the Harlowe-Arabella. Canst thou not form some scheme to come at the copies of these letters, or at the substance of them at least, and of that of her other correspondences? Mrs. Lovick, thou seemest to say, is a pious woman. The lady, having given such a particular history of herself, will acquaint her with everything. And art thou not about to reform? Won't this consent of minds between thee and the widow [what age is she, Jack? The devil never trumped up a friendship between a man and a woman, of anything like years, which did not end in matrimony, or in the ruin of their morals!—Won't it] strike out an intimacy between ye, that may enable thee to gratify me in this particular? A proselyte, I can tell thee, has great influence upon your good people: such a one is a saint of their own creation; and they will water, and cultivate, and cherish him, as a plant of their own raising; and this from a pride truly spiritual!

One of my loves in Paris was a devotee. She took great pains to convert me. I gave way to her kind endeavours for the good of my soul. She thought it a point gained to make me profess *some* religion. The Catholic has its conveniences. I permitted her to bring a *father* to me. My reformation went on swimmingly. The *father* had hopes of me: he applauded her zeal: so did I. And how dost think it ended? Not a girl in England, reading thus far, but would guess! In a word, very happily! For she not only *brought* me a father, but *made* me one: and then, being satisfied with each other's conversion, we took different routes: she into Navarre; I into Italy: both well inclined to propagate the good lessons in which we had so well instructed each other."

But to return. One consolation arises to me, from the pretty regrets which this admirable creature seems to have in indulging reflections on the people's wedding-day. *I* ONCE!—thou makest her break off with saying.

She once! What?—O Belford! why didst thou not urge her to explain what she *once* hoped?

What *once* a woman hopes, in love matters, she *always* hopes, while there is room for hope: and are we not both single? Can she be any man's but mine? Will I be any woman's but hers?

I never will! I never can! And I tell thee, that I am every day, every hour, more and more in love with her: and, at this instant, have a more vehement passion for her than ever I had in my life!—and that with views absolutely honourable, in *her own sense* of the word: nor have I varied, so much as in *wish*, for this week past; firmly fixed, and wrought into my very nature as the *life of honour*, or of generous confidence in me, was, in preference to the life of *doubt* and *distrust*. That must be a *life of doubt and distrust*, surely, where the woman confides nothing, and ties up a man for his good behaviour for life, taking Church and State sanctions in aid of the obligation she imposes upon him.

I shall go on Monday morning to a kind of ball, to which Colonel Ambrose has invited me. It is given on a family account. I care not on what: for all that delights me in the thing is, that Mrs. and Miss Howe are to be there; Hickman, of course; for the old lady will not stir abroad without him. The colonel is in hopes that Miss Arabella Harlowe will be there likewise; for all the men and women of fashion round him are invited.

I fell in by accident with the colonel, who, I believe, hardly thought I would accept of the invitation. But he knows me not, if he thinks I am ashamed to appear at any place where women dare show their faces. Yet he hinted to me that my name *was up*, on Miss Harlowe's account. But, to allude to one of Lord M.'s phrases, if it be, I will not *lie abed* when anything joyous is going forward.

As I shall go in my lord's chariot, I would have had one of my Cousins Montague to go with me: but they both refused: and I shall not choose to take either of thy brethren. It would look as if I thought I wanted a bodyguard: besides, one of them is too rough, the other too smooth, and too great a fop for some of the staid company that will be there; and for *me* in particular. Men are known by their companions; and a fop [as Tourville, for example] takes great pains to hang out a sign by his dress of what he has in his shop. Thou, indeed, art an exception; dressing like a coxcomb, yet a very clever fellow. Nevertheless so clumsy a beau, that thou seemest to me to owe thyself a double spite, making thy ungracefulness appear the *more* ungraceful, by thy remarkable tawdriness, when thou art out of mourning.

I remember, when I first saw thee, my mind laboured with a strong puzzle, whether I should put thee down for a great fool, or a smatterer in wit. Something I saw was wrong in thee, by thy *dress*. If this fellow, thought I, delights not so much in *ridicule* that he will not spare *himself*, he must be plaguy silly to take so much pains to make his ugliness more conspicuous than it would otherwise be.

Plain dress, for an ordinary man or woman, implies at least *modesty*, and always procures kind quarter from the censorious. Who will ridicule a personal imperfection in one that seems conscious that it *is* an imperfection? *Whoever said an anchoret was poor?* But who would spare so very absurd a wrong-head, as should bestow tinsel to make his deformity the more conspicuous?

But, although I put on these lively airs, I am sick at my soul! My whole heart is with my charmer! With what indifference shall I look upon all the assembly at the colonel's, my beloved in my ideal eye, and engrossing my whole heart?

Letter CXXIII—Miss Howe to Miss Arabella Harlowe

Thursday, July 20.

MISS HARLOWE,—I cannot help acquainting you (however it may be received, coming from *me*) that your poor sister is dangerously ill, at the house of one Smith, who keeps a glover's and perfume shop in King Street, Covent Garden. She knows not that I write. Some violent words, in the nature of an imprecation, from her father, afflict her greatly in her weak state. I presume not to direct you what to do in this case. You are her sister. I therefore could not help writing to you, not only for her sake, but for your own. I am, madam,

Your humble servant,

ANNA HOWE.

Letter CXXIV—Miss Arabella Harlowe. [*In answer*]

Thursday, July 20.

MISS HOWE,—I have yours of this morning. All that has happened to the unhappy body you mention is what we foretold and expected. Let *him*, for whose sake she abandoned us, be her comfort. We are told he has remorse, and would marry her. We don't believe it, indeed. She *may* be very ill. Her disappointment may make her so, or ought. Yet is she the only one I know who is disappointed.

I cannot say, miss, that the notification from you is the *more* welcome for the liberties you have been pleased to take with our whole family, for resenting a conduct that it is a shame any young lady should justify. Excuse this freedom, occasioned by greater. I am, miss,

Your humble servant,
ARABELLA HARLOWE.

Letter CXXV—Miss Howe. [In reply]

Friday, July 21.

MISS ARABELLA HARLOWE,—If you had half as much sense as you have ill-nature, you would (notwithstanding the exuberance of the latter) have been able to distinguish between a kind intention to you all (that you might have the less to reproach yourselves with, if a deplorable case should happen), and an officiousness I owed you not, by reason of freedoms at least reciprocal. I will not, for the *unhappy body's* sake, as you call a sister you have helped to make so, say all that I *could* say. If what I fear happen, you shall hear (whether desired or not) all the mind of   ANNA HOWE.

Letter CXXVI—Miss Arabella Harlowe to Miss Howe

Friday, July 21.

MISS ANN HOWE,—Your pert letter I have received. You, that spare nobody, I cannot expect should spare me. You are very happy in a prudent and watchful mother—but else mine cannot be exceeded in prudence: but we had all too good an opinion of somebody, to think watchfulness needful. There may possibly be some reason why *you* are so much attached to her in an error of this flagrant nature.

I help to make a sister unhappy! It is false, miss! It is all her own doings!—except, indeed, what she may owe to somebody's advice—you know who can best answer for that.

Let us *know your mind* as soon as you please: as we shall know it to be *your* mind, we shall judge what attention to give it. That's all, from, etc.   AR. H.

Letter CXXVII—Miss Howe to Miss Arabella Harlowe

Sat. July 22.

IT may be the *misfortune* of some people to engage everybody's notice: others may be the *happier*, though they may be the more *envious*, for nobody's thinking them worthy of any. But one would be glad people had the sense to be thankful for that want of consequence which subjected them not to hazards they would hardly have been able to manage under.

I own to you, that had it not been for the prudent advice of that admirable somebody (whose principal fault is the superiority of her talents, and whose misfortune to be brothered and sistered by a couple of creatures who are not able to comprehend her excellences), I might at one time have been plunged into difficulties. But, pert as the superlatively pert may think me, I thought not myself *wiser*, because I was *older*; nor for that *poor* reason qualified to prescribe to, much less to maltreat, a genius so superior.

I repeat it with gratitude, that the dear creature's advice was of very great service to me—and this before my mother's *watchfulness* became necessary. But how it would have fared with me, I cannot say, had I had a brother or sister who had deemed it their *interest*, as well as a gratification of their *sordid envy*, to misrepresent me.

Your admirable sister, in effect, saved *you*, miss, as well as *me*—with this difference: you, *against* your will—me, *with* mine: and but for *your* own brother, and *his* own sister, would not have been lost herself.

Would to Heaven both sisters had been obliged with their own wills! The most admirable of her sex would never then have been out of her father's house! *You*, miss—I don't know what had become of *you*. But, let what would have happened, you would have met with the humanity you have not shown, whether you had deserved it or not: nor, at worst, lost either a kind sister, or a pitying friend, in the most excellent of sisters.

But why run I into length to such a poor thing? Why push I so weak an adversary? whose first letter is all low malice, and whose next is made up of falsehood and inconsistence, as well as spite and ill-manners! Yet I was willing to give you a *part* of my mind. Call for more of it; it shall be at your service: from one who, though she thanks God she is not your sister, is not your *enemy*: but that she is *not* the latter, is withheld but by two considerations; one, that you bear, though unworthily, **a** relation to a sister so excellent; the other, that you are not of consequence enough to engage anything but the pity and contempt of

A. H.

Letter CXXVIII—Mrs. Harlowe to Mrs. Howe

Sat. July 22.

DEAR MADAM,—I send you, enclosed, copies of five letters that have passed between Miss Howe and my Arabella. You are a person of so much prudence and good sense, and (being a mother yourself) can so well enter into the distresses of all our family, upon the rashness and ingratitude of a child we once doted upon, that I dare say you will not countenance the strange freedoms your daughter has taken with us all. These are not the only ones we have to complain of; but we were silent on the others, as they did not, as these have done, spread themselves out upon paper. We only beg that we may not be reflected upon by a young lady who knows not what we have suffered, and do suffer, by the rashness of a naughty creature who has brought ruin upon herself, and disgrace upon a family which she has robbed of all comfort. I offer not to prescribe to your known wisdom in this case; but leave it to you to do as you think most proper. I am, madam,

Your most humble servant,
CHARL. HARLOWE.

Letter CXXIX—Mrs. Howe. [*In answer*]

Sat. July 22.

DEAR MADAM,—I am highly offended with my daughter's letters to Miss Harlowe. I knew nothing at all of her having taken such a liberty. These young creatures have such romantic notions, some of *love*, some of *friendship*, that there is no governing them in either. Nothing but time, and dear experience, will convince them of their absurdities in both. I have chidden Miss Howe very severely. I had before so just a notion of what your whole family's distress must be, that, as I told your brother, Mr. Antony Harlowe, I had often forbid her corresponding with the poor fallen angel—for surely never did young lady more resemble what we imagine of angels, both in person and mind. But, tired out with her headstrong ways [I am sorry to say this of my own child], I was forced to give way to it again. And, indeed, so sturdy was she in her will that I was afraid it would end in a fit of sickness, as too often it did in fits of sullens.

None but parents know the trouble that children give: they are happiest, I have often thought, who have none.   And these women-grown girls, bless my heart! how ungovernable!

I believe, however, you will have no more such letters from my Nancy.   I have been forced to use compulsion with her upon Miss Clary's illness [and it seems she is very bad], or she would have run away to London, to attend upon her: and this she calls doing the duty of a friend; forgetting that she sacrifices to her romantic friendship her duty to her fond indulgent mother.

There are a thousand excellences in the poor sufferer, not-withstanding her fault: and, if the hints she has given to my daughter be true, she has been most grievously abused.   But I think your forgiveness and her father's forgiveness of her ought to be all at your own choice; and nobody should intermeddle in that, for the sake of due authority in parents: and besides, as Miss Harlowe writes, it was what everybody expected, though Miss Clary would not believe it till she smarted for her credulity. And, for these reasons, I offer not to plead anything in alleviation of her fault, which is aggravated by her admirable sense, and a judgment above her years.

I am, madam, with compliments to good Mr. Harlowe, and all your afflicted family,

Your most humble servant,
ANNABELLA HOWE.

I shall set out for the Isle of Wight in a few days, with my daughter.   I will hasten our setting out, on purpose to break her mind from her friend's distresses; which afflict us as much, nearly, as Miss Clary's rashness has done you.

Letter CXXX—Miss Howe to Miss Clarissa Harlowe

Sat. *July* 22.

MY DEAREST FRIEND,—We are busy in preparing for our little journey and voyage: but I will be ill, I will be very ill, if I cannot hear you are better before I go.

Rogers greatly afflicted me by telling me the bad way you are in.   But now you have been able to hold a pen, and as your sense is strong and clear, I hope that the amusement you will receive from writing will make you better.

I dispatch this by an extraordinary way, that it may reach

you time enough to move you to *consider well* before you absolutely decide upon the contents of mine of the 13th, on the subject of the two Misses Montague's visit to me; since, according to what you write, must I answer them.

In your last you conclude very positively that you will not be his. To be sure, he rather deserves an infamous death than such a wife. But, as I really believe him innocent of the arrest, and as all his family are such earnest pleaders, and will be guarantees for him, I think the compliance with *their* entreaties, and *his own*, will be now the best step you can take; your own family remaining implacable, as I *can assure you they do*. He is a man of sense; and it is not impossible but he may make you a good husband, and in time may become no bad man.

My mother is entirely of my opinion: and on Friday, pursuant to a hint I gave you in my last, Mr. Hickman had a conference with the strange wretch: and though he liked not, by any means, his behaviour to himself; nor, indeed, had reason to do so; yet he is of opinion that he is sincerely determined to marry you if you will condescend to have him.

Perhaps Mr. Hickman may make you a private visit before we set out. If I may not attend you myself, I shall not be easy except he does. And he will then give you an account of the admirable character the surprising wretch gave of you, and of the justice he does to your virtue.

He was as acknowledging to his relations, though to his own condemnation, as his two cousins told me. All that he apprehends, as he said to Mr. Hickman, is that if you go on exposing *him*, wedlock itself will not wipe off the dishonour to both: and moreover, "that you would ruin your constitution by your immoderate sorrow; and, by seeking death when you might avoid it, would not be able to escape it when you would wish to do so."

So, my dearest friend, I charge you, if you *can*, to get over your aversion to this vile man. You may yet live to see many happy days, and be once more the delight of all your friends, neighbours, and acquaintance, as well as a stay, a comfort, and a blessing, to your Anna Howe.

I long to have your answer to mine of the 13th. Pray keep the messenger till it be ready. If he return on Monday night it will be time enough for his affairs, and to find me come back from Colonel Ambrose's; who gives a ball on the anniversary of Mrs. Ambrose's birth and marriage both in one. The gentry all round the neighbourhood are invited this time, on some good news they have received from Mrs. Ambrose's brother, the Governor.

My mother promised the colonel for me and herself, in my absence. I would fain have excused myself to her; and the rather, as I had exceptions on account of the day [1]: but she is almost as young as her daughter; and thinking it not so well to go without me, she told me, She could propose *nothing* that was agreeable to me. And having had a *few sparring blows* with each other very lately, I think I must comply. For I don't love jangling when I can help it; though I seldom make it my study to avoid the occasion, when it offers of itself. I don't know, if either were not a little afraid of the other, whether it would be possible that we could live together:—I, *all my father!* My mamma—What?—*All my mother*—What else should I say?

O my dear, how many things happen in this life to give us displeasure! How few to give us joy! I am sure I shall have none on this occasion; since the true partner of my heart, the principal half of the *one soul*, that, it used to be said, animated *the pair of friends*, as we were called; You, my dear [who used to irradiate every circle you set your foot into, and to give me *real* significance in a *second* place to yourself], cannot be there! One hour of your company, my ever-instructive friend [I thirst for it!], how infinitely preferable would it be to me to all the diversions and amusements with which our sex are generally most delighted! Adieu, my dear!   A. HOWE.

Letter CXXXI—*Miss Clarissa Harlowe to Miss Howe*

Sunday, July 23.

WHAT pain, my dearest friend, does your kind solicitude for my welfare give me! How much more binding and tender are the ties of pure friendship, and the union of like minds, than the ties of nature! Well might the sweet singer of Israel, when he was carrying to the utmost extent the praises of the friendship between him and his beloved friend, say that the love of Jonathan to him was wonderful; that it surpassed the *love of women!* What an exalted idea does it give of the soul of Jonathan, sweetly attempered for this sacred band, if we may suppose it but equal to that of my Anna Howe for her fallen Clarissa! But, although I can glory in your kind love for me, think, my dear, what concern must fill a mind, not ungenerous, when the obligation lies all *on one side*: and when, at the same time that your light is the

[1] The 24th of July, Miss Clarissa Harlowe's birthday.

brighter for my darkness, I must give pain to a dear friend, to whom I delighted to give pleasure; and not pain only, but discredit, for supporting my blighted fame against the busy tongues of uncharitable censurers!

This it is that makes me, in the words of my admired exclaimer, very little altered, often repeat: "O! that I were as in months past! as in the days when God preserved me! When His candle shined upon my head, and when by His light I walked through darkness! As I was in the days of my *childhood*—when the Almighty was yet with me; when *I was in my father's house*: when I washed my steps with butter, and the rock poured me out rivers of oil!"

You set before me your reasons, enforced by the opinion of your honoured mother, why I should think of Mr. Lovelace for a husband.[1]

And I have before me your letter of the 13th,[2] containing the account of the visit and proposals, and kind interposition of the two Misses Montague, in the names of the good ladies Sarah Sadleir and Betty Lawrance, and in that of Lord M.

Also yours of the 18th [3] *demanding* me, as I may say, of those ladies, and of that family, when I was so infamously and cruelly arrested, and you knew not what was become of me.

The answer likewise of those ladies, signed in so full and so generous a manner by themselves,[4] and by that nobleman, and those two venerable ladies; and, in his light way, by the wretch himself:

These, my dearest Miss Howe, and your letter of the 16th,[5] which came when I was under arrest, and which I received not till some days after:

Are all before me.

And I have as well weighed the whole matter, and your arguments in support of your advice, as at present my head and my heart will let me weigh them.

I am, moreover, willing to believe, not only from your own opinion, but from the assurances of one of Mr. Lovelace's friends, Mr. Belford, a good-natured and humane man, who spares not to censure the author of my calamities (*I think*, with undissembled and undesigning sincerity), that that man is innocent of the disgraceful arrest:

And even, if you please, in sincere compliment to your opinion, and to that of Mr. Hickman, that (over-persuaded by his friends,

---

[1] See the preceding letter.   [2] See Letter xcix.   [3] See Letter ci.
[4] See Letter civ.   [5] See Letter c.

and ashamed of his unmerited baseness to me) he would in earnest marry *me*, if I would have *him*.

"[1] Well, and now, what is the result of all? It is this: that I must abide by what I have already declared—and that is [don't be angry at me, my best friend], that I have much more pleasure in thinking of death than of such a husband. In short, as I declared in my last, that I cannot [forgive me, if I say, I *will* not] ever be his.

"But you will expect my reasons: I know you will: and if I give them not, will conclude me either obstinate, or implacable, or both: and those would be sad imputations, if just, to be laid to the charge of a person who thinks and talks of *dying*. And yet, to say that resentment and disappointment have no part in my determination, would be saying a thing hardly to be credited. For I own I *have* resentments, strong resentments, but not unreasonable ones, as you will be convinced, if already you are not so, when you know all my story—if ever you do know it. For I begin to fear (so many things more necessary to be thought of, than either this man, or my own vindication, have I to do) that I shall not have time to compass what I have intended, and, in a manner, promised you.[2]

"I have one reason to give in support of my resolution, that, I believe, yourself will allow of: but having owned that I have resentments, I will begin with those considerations in which anger and disappointment have too great a share; in hopes that, having once disburdened my mind upon paper, and to my Anna Howe, of those corroding, uneasy passions, I shall prevent them for ever from returning to my heart, and to have their place supplied by better, milder, and more agreeable ones.

"My pride, then, my dearest friend, although a great deal mortified, is not *sufficiently* mortified, if it be necessary for me to submit to make that man my choice, whose actions are, and ought to be, my abhorrence! What! shall I, who have been treated with such premeditated and perfidious barbarity, as is painful to be thought of, and cannot with modesty be described, think of taking the violator to my heart? Can I vow duty to one so wicked, and hazard my salvation by joining myself to so great a profligate, now I *know* him to be so? Do you think your Clarissa Harlowe so lost, so *sunk*, at least, as that she could, for

---

[1] Those parts of this letter which are marked with inverted commas [thus "] were transcribed afterwards by Miss Howe, in Letter xii of vol. iv, written to the ladies of Mr. Lovelace's family; and are thus distinguished to avoid the necessity of repeating them in that letter.

[2] See Letter xc of this volume.

the sake of patching up, in the world's eye, a broken reputation, meanly appear indebted to the generosity, or perhaps *compassion*, of a man who has, by means so inhuman, robbed her of it? Indeed, my dear, I should not think my penitence for the rash step I took, anything better than a specious delusion, if I had not got above the least wish to have Mr. Lovelace for my husband.

"Yes, I warrant, I must *creep* to the violator, and be thankful to him for doing me poor justice!

"Do you not already see me (pursuing the advice you give) with a downcast eye, appear before *his* friends, and before *my own* (supposing the latter would at last condescend to own me), divested of that *noble confidence* which arises from a mind unconscious of having deserved reproach?

"Do you not see me creep about mine own house, preferring all my honest maidens to myself—as if afraid, too, to open my lips, either by way of reproof or admonition, lest their bolder eyes should bid me look inward, and not expect perfection from *them*?

"And shall I entitle the wretch to upbraid me with his generosity, and his pity; and perhaps to reproach me for having been *capable* of forgiving crimes of *such* a nature?

"I once indeed hoped, little thinking him so *premeditatedly* vile a man, that I might have the happiness to reclaim him: I vainly believed that he loved me well enough to suffer my advice for his good, and the example I humbly presumed I should be enabled to set him, to have weight with him; and the rather, as he had no mean opinion of my morals and understanding: but now, what hope is there left for this my *prime* hope?   *Were* I to marry him, what a figure should I make, preaching virtue and morality to a man whom I had trusted with opportunities to seduce me from all my own duties?   And then, supposing I were to have children by such a husband, must it not, think you, cut a thoughtful person to the heart, to look round upon her little family, and think she had given them a father destined, without a miracle, to perdition; and whose immoralities, propagated among them by his vile example, might, too probably, bring down a curse upon them?   And, after all, who knows but that my own sinful compliances with a man, who would think himself entitled to my obedience, might taint my own morals, and make me, instead of a reformer, an imitator of him?   For who *can touch pitch, and not be defiled*?

"Let me then repeat, that I truly despise this man!   If I know my own heart, indeed I do!   I pity him!   *Beneath* my very pity as he is, I nevertheless pity him! But this I could not do, if I still loved him: for, my dear, one must be greatly sensible of the baseness and ingratitude of those we love. I love him not, therefore! My soul disdains communion with him.

"But although thus much is due to resentment, yet have I not been so far carried away by its angry effects, as to be rendered incapable of casting about what I *ought* to do, and what *could be done*, if the Almighty, in order to lengthen the time of my penitence, were to bid me to live.

"The single life, at such times, has offered to me, as the life, the *only* life, to be chosen. But in *that*, must I not *now* sit brooding over my past afflictions, and mourning my faults till the hour of my release? And would not every one be able to assign the reason why Clarissa Harlowe chose solitude, and to sequester herself from the world? Would not the look of every creature who beheld me, appear as a reproach to me? And would not my conscious eye confess my fault, whether the eyes of others accused me or not? One of my delights was, to enter the cots of my poor neighbours, to leave lessons to the boys, and cautions to the elder girls: and how should I be able, unconscious, and without pain, to say to the latter, fly the delusions of men, who had been supposed to have run away with one?

"What then, my dear and only friend, can I wish for but death? And what, after all, *is* death? 'Tis but a cessation from mortal life: 'tis but the finishing of an appointed course: the refreshing inn after a fatiguing journey: the end of a life of cares and troubles; and, if happy, the beginning of a life of immortal happiness.

"If I die not now, it may possibly happen that I may be taken when I am less prepared. Had I escaped the evils I labour under, it might have been in the midst of some gay promising hope; when my heart had beat high with the desire of life; and when the vanity of this earth had taken hold of me.

"But now, my dear, for *your* satisfaction let me say that, although I wish not for life, yet would I not, like a poor coward, desert my post when I *can* maintain it, and when it is my *duty* to maintain it.

"More than once, indeed, was I urged by thoughts so sinful: but then it was in the height of my distress: and once, particularly, I have reason to believe, I saved myself by my *desperation* from the most shocking personal insults; from a repetition, as far as I know, of his vileness; the base women (with so much reason dreaded by me) present, to intimidate *me*, if not to assist *him*!

O my dear, you know not what I suffered on that occasion! Nor do I what I *escaped* at the time, if the wicked man had approached me to execute the horrid purposes of his vile heart."

As I am of opinion, that it would have manifested more of revenge and despair than of principle, had I committed a violence upon myself, when the villainy was *perpetrated*; so I should think it equally criminal, were I now *wilfully* to neglect myself; were I *purposely* to run into the arms of death (*as that man supposes I shall do*), when I might avoid it.

Nor, my dear, whatever are the suppositions of such a short-sighted, such a low-souled man, must you impute to gloom, to melancholy, to despondency, nor yet to a spirit of faulty pride, or still *more* faulty revenge, the resolution I have taken never to marry *this*; and if not *this*, *any* man. So far from deserving this imputation, I do assure you (my dear and *only* love) that I will do everything I can to prolong my life, till God, in mercy to me, shall be pleased to call for it. I have reason to think my punishment is but the due consequence of my fault, and I will not run away from it; but beg of Heaven to sanctify it to me. When appetite serves, I will eat and drink what is sufficient to support nature. A very little, you know, will do for that. And whatever my physicians shall think fit to prescribe, I will take, though ever so disagreeable. In short, I will do everything I can do to convince all my friends, who hereafter may think it worth their while to inquire after my last behaviour, that I possessed my soul with tolerable patience; and endeavoured to bear with a lot of my own drawing: for thus, in humble imitation of the sublimest Exemplar, I often say: Lord, it is Thy will; and it shall be mine. Thou art just in all Thy dealings with the children of men; and I know Thou wilt not afflict me beyond what I can bear: and, if I *can* bear it, I *ought* to bear it; and (Thy grace assisting me) I *will* bear it.

"But here, my dear, is another reason; a reason that will convince you yourself that I ought not to think of wedlock; but of a preparation for a quite different event. I am persuaded, as much as that I am now alive, that I shall not long live. The strong sense I have ever had of my fault, the loss of my reputation, my disappointments, the determined resentment of my friends, *aiding* the barbarous usage I have met with where I least deserved it, have seized upon my heart: seized upon it, before it was so well fortified by *religious considerations* as I hope it now is. Don't be concerned, my dear. But I am sure, if I may say it with as little presumption as grief, That God will soon *dissolve my substance*; and *bring me to death, and to the house appointed for all living.*"

And now, my dearest friend, you know all my mind. And you will be pleased to write to the ladies of Mr. Lovelace's family that I think myself infinitely obliged to them for their good opinion of me; and that it has given me greater pleasure than I thought I had to come in this life, that, upon the little knowledge they have of me, and that not personal, I was thought worthy (after the ill-usage I have received) of an alliance with their honourable family: but that I can by no means think of their kinsman for a husband: and do you, my dear, extract from the above such reasons as you think have any weight in them.

I would write myself to acknowledge their favour, had I not more employment for my head, my heart, and my fingers, than I doubt they will be able to go through.

I should be glad to know when you set out on your journey; as also your little stages; and your time of stay at your Aunt Harman's; that my prayers may *locally* attend you whithersoever you go, and wherever you are.

CLARISSA HARLOWE.

Letter CXXXII—Miss Clarissa Harlowe to Miss Howe

Sunday, July 23.

THE letter accompanying this being upon a very particular subject, I would not embarrass it, as I may say, with any other. And yet having some further matters upon my mind, which will want your excuse for directing them to you, I hope the following lines will *have* that excuse.

My good Mrs. Norton, so long ago as in a letter dated the 3rd of this month,[1] hinted to me that my relations took amiss some severe things you were pleased, in love to me, to say of them. Mrs. Norton mentioned it with that respectful love which she bears to my dearest friend: but wished, for *my* sake, that you would rein in a vivacity which, on most other occasions, so charmingly becomes you. This was her sense. You know that *I* am warranted to speak and write freer to my Anna Howe than Mrs. Norton would do.

I durst not mention it to you at that time, because appearances were so strong against me, on Mr. Lovelace's getting me again into his power (after my escape to Hampstead), as made you very angry with me when you answered mine on my second escape.

<hr>

[1] See pp. 342-4.

And, soon afterwards, I was put under that barbarous arrest; so that I could not well touch upon that subject till now.

Now, therefore, my dearest Miss Howe, let me *repeat* my earnest request (for this is not the first time by several that I have been obliged to chide you on this occasion), that you will spare my parents, and other relations, in all your conversations about me. Indeed, I wish they had thought fit to take other measures with me: but who shall judge for them? The event has justified them, and condemned me. They expected nothing good of this vile man; *he* has not, therefore, deceived *them*: but they expected other things from *me*; and *I* have. And they have the more reason to be set against me, if (as my Aunt Hervey wrote [1] formerly) they intended not to force my inclinations in favour of Mr. Solmes; and if they believe that my going off was the effect of choice and premeditation.

I have no desire to be received to favour by them: for why should I sit down to wish for what I have no reason to expect? Besides, I could not look them in the face if they *would* receive me. Indeed, I could not. All I have to hope for is, first, that my father will absolve me from his heavy malediction: and next, for a last blessing. The obtaining of these favours are needful to my peace of mind.

I have written to my sister; but have only mentioned the absolution.

I am afraid I shall receive a very harsh answer from her: my fault, in the eyes of my family, is of so enormous a nature, that my *first* application will hardly be encouraged. Then they know not (nor perhaps will believe) that I am so very ill as I am. So that, were I actually to die before they could have time to take the necessary informations, you must not blame them too severely. You must call it a fatality. I know not what you must call it: for, alas! I have made them as miserable as I am myself. And yet sometimes I think that, were they cheerfully to pronounce me forgiven, I know not whether my concern for having offended them would not be augmented: since I imagine that nothing can be more wounding to a spirit not ungenerous than a *generous forgiveness*.

I hope your mother will permit our correspondence for *one* month more, although I do not take her advice as to having this man. Only for *one* month. I will not desire it longer. When catastrophes are winding-up, what changes (changes that make one's heart shudder to think of) may *one* short month produce!

[1] See vol. ii, p. 162.

But if she will not—why then, my dear, it becomes us both to acquiesce.

You can't think what my apprehensions would have been had I known Mr. Hickman was to have had a meeting (on such a questioning occasion as must have been his errand from you) with that haughty and uncontrollable man.

You give me hope of a visit from Mr. Hickman: let him *expect* to see me greatly altered. I know he loves me: for he loves every one whom you love. A painful interview, I doubt! But I shall be glad to see a man whom *you* will one day, and that on an *early* day, I hope, make happy; and whose gentle manners, and unbounded love for you, will make *you* so, if it be not your own fault.

I am, my dearest, kindest friend, the sweet companion of my happy hours, the friend ever dearest and nearest to my fond heart,

Your equally obliged and faithful
CLARISSA HARLOWE.

Letter CXXXIII—Mrs. Norton to Miss Clarissa Harlowe

Monday, July 24.

EXCUSE, my dearest young lady, my long silence. I have been extremely ill. My poor boy has also been at death's door; and, when I hoped that he was better, he has relapsed. Alas! my dear, he is very dangerously ill. Let us both have your prayers!

Very angry letters have passed between your sister and Miss Howe. Every one of your family is incensed against that young lady. I wish you would remonstrate against her warmth; since it can do no good; for they will not believe but that her interposition has your connivance; nor that you are so ill as Miss Howe assures them you are.

Before she wrote, they were going to send up young Mr. Brand, the clergyman, to make private inquiries of your health, and way of life. But now they are so exasperated that they have laid aside their intention.

We have flying reports here, and at Harlowe Place, of some fresh insults which you have undergone: and that you are about to put yourself into Lady Betty Lawrance's protection. I believe they would now be glad (as I should be) that you would do so; and this, perhaps, will make them suspend for the present any determination in your favour.

How unhappy am I, that the dangerous way my son is in

prevents my attendance on you! Let me beg of you to write me word how you are, both as to person and mind. A servant of Sir Robert Beachcroft, who rides post on his master's business to town, will present you with this; and, perhaps, will bring me the favour of a few lines in return. He will be obliged to stay in town several hours for an answer to his dispatches.

This is the anniversary that used to give joy to as many as had the pleasure and honour of knowing you. May the Almighty bless you, and grant that it may be the only unhappy one that may be ever known by you, my dearest young lady; and by

Your ever affectionate

JUDITH NORTON.

END OF VOLUME THREE.

CONTENTS OF VOLUME III

A letter from Miss Howe to Clarissa falls into Lovelace's hands; which, had it come to hers, would have laid open and detected all his designs. In it she acquits Clarissa of *prudery, coquetry,* and *undue reserve.* Admires, applauds, blesses her for the example she has set her sex, and for the credit she has done it, by her conduct in the most difficult situations.

This letter may be considered as a kind of summary of Clarissa's trials, persecutions, and exemplary conduct hitherto; and of Mr. Lovelace's intrigues, plots, and views, so far as Miss Howe could be supposed to know them, or to guess at them.

A letter from Lovelace, which further shows the fertility of his contriving genius.

Informs her of Lovelace's villainy, and of her escape. Her only concern, what. The course she intends to pursue.

Exults on hearing from his man Will that the lady has refuged herself at Hampstead. Observations in a style of levity on some passages in the letter she left behind her. Intimates that Tomlinson is arrived to aid his purposes. The chariot is come; and now, dressed like a bridegroom, attended by a footman she never saw, he is already, he says, at Hampstead.

Exults on his contrivances. By what means he gets into the lady's presence at Mrs. Moore's. Her terrors, fits, exclamations. His plausible tales to Mrs. Moore and Miss Rawlins. His intrepid behaviour to the lady. Copies of letters from Tomlinson, and of pretended ones from his own relations, calculated to pacify and delude her.

His further arts, inventions, and intrepidity. She puts home questions to him. "Ungenerous and ungrateful she calls him. He knows not the value of the heart he had insulted. *He had a plain path before him, after he had tricked her out of her father's house:* but that now her mind was raised above fortune and above him." His precautionary contrivances.

Character of widow Bevis. Prepossesses the women against Miss Howe. Leads them to think she is in love with him. Apt himself to think so: and why. Women like not novices: and why. Their vulgar aphorism animadverted on. Tomlinson arrives. Artful conversation between them. Miss Rawlins's prudery. His forged letter in imitation of Miss Howe's, No. i. Other contrivances to delude the lady, and attach the women to his party.

CONTENTS OF VOLUME III 533